Stones

from

the

River

■

Ursula Hegi

■

SCRIBNER PAPERBACK FICTION
Published by Simon & Schuster

NEW YORK

LONDON

TORONTO

SYDNEY

TOKYO

SINGAPORE

SCRIBNER PAPERBACK FICTION
Rockefeller Center
1230 Avenue of the Americas
New York, New York 10020

Designed by Songhee Kim
Manufactured in the United States of America

3 5 7 9 10 8 6 4
Hegi, Ursula.
Stones from the River / Ursula Hegi.
Library of Congress Cataloging-in-Publication Data
1. City and town life—Germany—History—20th Century—Fiction. 2. Women librarians—Germany—Fiction. I. Title.
PR911.9.H43S76   1994
823—dc20   93-33533
CIP
ISBN 0-671-78075-1
0-684-80035-7

An excerpt from *Stones from the River* entitled "Trudi" appeared in the Spring 1993 edition of *Story* magazine.

for Gordon

A c k n o w l e d g m e n t s

I'm deeply grateful for the generous help and support I received while writing this novel. My godmother, Käte Capelle, had the courage to answer questions I couldn't ask as a child while growing up in the silence of post–World War II Germany. In her late eighties, *Tante* Käte broke the silence by documenting her memories of the war years on tape for me. Author Ilse-Margret Vogel, who became active in the resistance before immigrating to the U.S., lent me photo albums of her childhood and offered valuable insights on what it was like to live in Germany between the two wars. Historian Rod Stackelberg trusted me with journals he wrote as a boy in Germany. Together with Germanist Sally Winkle, he guided me in my research and read the manuscript for historical accuracy. Author Sue Wheeler, whose wisdom and love for literature keep challenging me to reach further in my writing, has read drafts of nearly everything I've written since we met in graduate school. My agent, Gail Hochman, helped me with my research of Jewish traditions. Gordon Gagliano welcomed the essence of Trudi into our house and advised me in all matters Catholic and architectural. The women in my women's group have given me their loving support during eight years of sharing and celebrating our histories. The Northwest Institute for Advanced Study awarded me a faculty research grant during the summer of 1992. *Vielen herzlichen Dank.*

———————————————— ■ ————————————————

1 9 1 5 – 1 9 1 8

As a child Trudi Montag thought everyone knew what went on inside others. That was before she understood the power of being different. The agony of being different. And the sin of ranting against an ineffective God. But before that—for years and years before that— she prayed to grow.

Every night she would fall asleep with the prayer that, while she slept, her body would stretch itself, grow to the size of that of other girls her age in Burgdorf—not even the taller ones like Eva Rosen, who would become her best friend in school for a brief time—but into a body with normal-length arms and legs and with a small, well-shaped head. To help God along, Trudi would hang from door frames by her fingers until they were numb, convinced she could feel her bones lengthening; many nights she'd tie her mother's silk scarves around her head—one encircling her forehead, the other knotted beneath her chin—to keep her head from expanding.

How she prayed. And every morning, when her arms were still stubby and her legs wouldn't reach the floor as she'd swing them from her mattress, she'd tell herself that she hadn't prayed hard enough or that it wasn't the right time yet, and so she'd keep praying, wishing, believing that anything you prayed for this hard surely would be granted if only you were patient.

Patience and obedience—they were almost inseparable, and the training for them began with the first step you took: you learned about obedience to your parents and all other adults, then about obedience to your church, your teachers, your government. Acts of disobedience were punished efficiently, swiftly: a slap on your knuckles with a ruler; three rosaries; confinement.

As an adult Trudi would scorn the patient fools who knelt in church, waiting. But as a girl, she'd go to mass every Sunday and sing in the choir; during the week she'd sometimes slip into the church on her way home from school, taking comfort in the holy scent of incense as she whispered her prayers to the painted plaster saints that lined the sides of St. Martin's Church: St. Petrus next to the confessional, his eyebrows perpetually raised in an expression of shock as if he'd overheard every sin the people of Burgdorf had whispered to generations of weary priests; St. Agnes with her mournful eyes rolled up and her fingers clasped to her bosom as if rehearsing to withstand countless other attacks on her purity; St. Stefan with a pile of chocolate-colored rocks hiding his feet—except for one pasty toe—his bleeding arms extended as though inviting his enemies to hurl even larger stones at him and ensure his eternal salvation.

To all of them Trudi prayed, and her body grew, but—as though her prayers had been twisted in some horrible joke—her body did not stretch itself upward as she'd presumed it would, yet had failed to specify in every single prayer, but expanded into a solid width that would eventually make her forearms as massive as those of Herr Immers, who owned the butcher shop, and her jaw as formidable as that of Frau Weiler, who ran the grocery store next door.

By then Trudi had come up against that moment when she knew that praying for something did not make it happen, that this was it: that there was no God-magic; that she was as tall as she would ever be; that she would die some day; and that anything that would happen to her until that day of her death would be up to her to resolve. She knew all this with a stunning clarity that chilled her to the core that April Sunday in 1929 in the Braunmeiers' barn, when the circle of boys closed around her—those boys who spread her legs, who spread her soul until it felt as if that dried snot on her face would always be there, tightening her skin like spilled egg whites—and she saw herself as a very old woman and, simultaneously, as an infant, as if her past and future were at opposite ends of a taut rubber band that someone had let go of for just an instant, causing her entire life— every minute she had lived and would live—to coil in on itself and touch where she was that moment in the barn, and she knew that she'd be able to see that way again: she watched herself pull her mother from the earth nest beneath the house; dismantle a section of the stone wall in the cellar and dig a secret dirt tunnel to the Blaus' house; stroke her lover's back with both hands, and feel the fine oval of hairs at the base of his spine as the night sky swirled around them; recoil from the heat of the flames that spurted from the broken windows of the synagogue and showered the school and the Theresienheim with sparks the color of the fabric star, *Judenstern,* that her friend, Eva Rosen, would have to wear on her coat.

For months after Trudi Montag's birth, her mother wouldn't touch her at all. From snatches of gossip the girl would later conjecture that her mother had taken one glance at her and had covered her face as if to shut out the image of the infant's short limbs and slightly enlarged head. It didn't help that Frau Weiler, upon peering into the wicker carriage, had inquired: *"Hat das Kind denn einen Wasserkopf?"*— "Does the child have water on the brain?"

Trudi's eyes seemed older than those of other infants, as if they held the experiences of someone who'd already lived a long time. The women in the neighborhood took turns keeping her alive and clean. They were the ones who brushed her silver-blond hair into one wispy curl on top of her head and secured it with a dab of pine honey, who boiled goat's milk and fed it to her in a bottle, who whispered as they compared her shape to that of their own children, who sat next to the bed of Trudi's mother and guarded her restless sleep whenever she was carried home after running away from her house on Schreberstrasse.

It was the summer of 1915, and the town belonged to the women. With their husbands fighting on the Eastern front for the past year, they had relearned to open even the most difficult snaps on their salmon-colored corsets; they had become accustomed to making decisions—like which repairs to do themselves and which to leave until after the war; they continued to sweep their sidewalks and to remind their children to practice the piano; they persuaded Herr Pastor

Schüler to invite an old chess champion from Köln to give their children lessons for one entire week after school; they banned the trick images of their husbands' faces below the earth when they watered the plants on their families' graves. At times, when they forgot their hunger and their revulsion to turnips, which had become their major nourishment, it seemed odd that, all around them, a celebration of life persisted as if there were no war: the blossoms of the cherry and apple trees, the singing of the birds, the laughter of their children.

In this small town that was encumbered by centuries of tradition, women without husbands did not fit in: they were objects of pity or gossip. But the war changed all that. Without men, the barriers between the married and unmarried woman blurred: suddenly they were more alike than different. No longer did respect come to them because of their husbands' positions, but because of their own abilities.

It was something the old widows had figured out long ago. They were the ones who truly governed the town but were wise enough to keep this a secret. They defined the boundaries of the community with an invisible chain of their linked hands as they filtered their advice to their children and told ancient fairy tales to their grandchildren as if they'd never been told before.

They felt suspicious of the few men who had stayed in Burgdorf and they gossiped about them—like Emil Hesping, a skilled athlete, who managed the gymnasts' club and claimed to be unfit for military service because of weak lungs, and Herbert Braunmeier, who insisted that no one else could possibly take care of his dairy farm. Selfish, the old women said, but they coddled those men who'd been wounded in the war, like Leo Montag, the first soldier to return; they knitted woolen vests for him and brought him canned plums from their meager reserves to make up for his injury.

Two months after the battle of Tannenberg, in October 1914, Leo Montag had limped into Burgdorf, a steel disk in place of his left kneecap, wearing a long seal coat that used to belong to one of the Russian prisoners. It was on that silver-gray fur coat—spread on the floor between the shelves of the hastily closed pay-library—that Trudi Montag was conceived the afternoon of her father's arrival. He had only been away from home for a few months, but he clung to his wife as though he'd been gone for years. Gertrud's face, which often looked feverish when she got excited, was almost transparent in its loveliness, and she laughed and cried as she held him. People in Burgdorf said about her that she absorbed the joys and pains of others as if they were her own.

It wasn't like her, most agreed, to refuse her child. And it wasn't like her to run away from home. But a few would claim to have sensed that seed of craziness in Gertrud long before it flourished: they spoke of that summer when she was four and had stopped talking for an entire year, and they reminded each other of her first communion, when she'd refused to open her lips to receive the sacred host, making the other children wait at the altar railing until the pastor had finally agreed to absolve her from sins that had attached themselves to her in the hours since her last confession.

It was three days after Trudi's birth that Gertrud Montag fled from her bedroom and from the cries of the infant that caused her breasts to sting with unspilled milk. Blood from her hollowed womb had blossomed through the front of her batiste nightgown by the time Herr Pastor Schüler found her behind St. Martin's Church, her arms spread across the door of the sacristy as if to keep him from entering. Without thinking, he crossed himself as though compelled to imitate the contour of her body. While he tried to loosen her hands from the door and pull her into the sacristy to protect her shame, one of the altar boys ran to summon Trudi's father, who quickly hobbled the two blocks from the pay-library, where the people of Burgdorf continued to borrow those trashy romances and detective novels that Herr Pastor Schüler preached against in his Sunday sermons.

Leo Montag carried his wife home, wrapped in one of the altar cloths. Her blood seeped into the ancient lace, and although the pastor's housekeeper would soak the cloth in salt water, the stains would merely fade into rose-colored clouds. Soon Gertrud was back at the sacristy door—properly dressed—was the priest's first thought when he discovered her in her wool dress and her husband's gray cardigan, even though the air was moist and much hotter than he liked it. Already he felt the itch of his sweat on his chest and beneath his private parts, a sweat he detested yet was unable to restrain with anything except medicated foot powder that left bone-colored rings on his garments and a chalky trace of dust on the tops of his shoes.

The pastor—whose round face made you expect a heavy person when you initially met him—stood at a safe distance from Gertrud Montag, his slight body bent toward her. Pigeons picked at the ground around his feet and scattered when he reached into his pocket to disentangle his handkerchief from his rosary. He blotted his neck.

"Why are you here?" he inquired.

She raised her eyes to trace the path of a white stork that glided on lazy wings across the open market and headed for the roof of the *Rathaus*—town hall—its long amber legs trailing across the clay tiles before it landed next to the chimney. From the open windows of the bakery, a block away, drifted the yeast scent of warm bread. Two dachshunds yipped at the hooves of the ragman's horse.

"Why are you here?" the pastor asked again.

But she wouldn't reply, this tall woman with the blazing eyes that seared right through him, and because he didn't know what else to do and liked to consider himself a merciful man, the Herr Pastor blessed Gertrud Montag, much in the same way he would administer last rites. And when that didn't have any impact, he informed her that he absolved her from all her sins because, after all, that had appeased her once before, on the day of her first communion. While he kept peering over his shoulder, anxious for her kind and bewildered husband to appear, he even—without knowing—forgave her the one sin she would never forgive herself.

Long after her breasts had stopped leaking milk, Gertrud Montag kept running away from home, but she did not always hide behind the church. Sometimes she'd settle herself in the lilac hedge in back of the Eberhardts' house. Renate Eberhardt had the lushest garden in town: snapdragons, roses, geraniums, and daisies grew abundantly, huge splotches of color—not orderly as in most of the other gardens—and a magnificent pear tree produced golden-yellow fruits. She'd let Gertrud pick a bouquet of her flowers before leading her home, and she'd stay and settle her in bed, her cool fingers on Gertrud's flushed forehead. Renate's slender neck seemed too long to carry the heavy braids that she wore pinned around her head.

Gertrud's favorite hiding place was beneath the elevated section of her house which was set against a slight hill, level with the street in front where the entrance to the pay-library was, and raised in back on old pillars of wood and gray boulders. Near the opening hung the rack where Leo kept his bamboo rake and garden shovels. Beyond was a place where black bugs with hard-shelled bodies fused with the darkness, and lacy spider webs swung from rafters, rocked by a wind too distant for any human to feel. Leo would have to crawl in after his wife and drag her out, while she'd sing church hymns and dig her bare heels into the earth, leaving gouges in the ground. Afterwards, the muscles in her calves would be so tight that he'd have to massage them for her.

At times he wouldn't find her at all though he'd lock the library, where she used to work with him before Trudi's birth, and ride his bicycle—his right leg pedaling, the injured one extended—through the streets surrounding the church, and from there all over town, down Römerstrasse, around the fairgrounds, up Barbarossa Strasse and toward the Rhein where, in the broad meadow between the dike and river, he and Gertrud used to fly kites as schoolchildren.

Occasionally he'd come upon her, but usually she'd return on her own, her black hair snarled and smelling of the river, say, or of the wheat fields that surrounded their town. He'd take his comb from his shirt pocket and hold her gently with one arm, while pulling the teeth of the comb through the tangles. One Sunday he dug out a young chestnut tree from the woods near the flour mill and presented it to Gertrud as a gift, telling her—while he helped her plant it in front of the pay-library—that this tree would keep her home. But the following morning she was gone again, and two nuns brought her back.

To tire her, Leo decided to take her on longer walks than their daily *Spaziergänge* when he closed the pay-library at noon, but she'd rush ahead of him while he'd struggle with the double burden of his stiff leg and the baby carriage. He gathered clumps of camomile and, from the blossoms, brewed tea which he hoped would calm her—this woman he'd known since they both were children, this woman who was one day older than he. He'd always liked it that they were the same age, even if that was unusual for married couples. Most husbands he knew were quite a few years older than their wives, and he couldn't imagine being married to someone he hadn't grown up with.

At night, he'd try to wrap his limbs around Gertrud to keep her safe, but she'd laugh in his arms, an odd, wild laugh that made his groin numb with coldness, and though she'd fit the skin of her body against his length, his genitals shrank from her and he could only hold her like a sister.

Before their daughter's birth, Gertrud had gone about her work in the house and pay-library joyfully, but now she moved abruptly and loudly. She'd forget what she had come to buy when she did the marketing, and she'd spill ashes when she'd clean out the kitchen stove or the green tile stove that was set into the wall between the living room and dining room.

One early morning in September, when Leo woke before her and watched her tranquil face, she looked just as she used to, and he felt convinced that she would return to her old ways, that she was ready to be a mother to their child. Pulling back the weightless feather comforter, he got up and dressed in his good suit though it was a weekday. He fetched his daughter from Frau Abramowitz across the street where she'd stayed—the night before it had been with Frau Blau next door—but instead of settling her in the crib inside the nursery, out of her mother's sight as usual, he sat with her on Gertrud's edge of the bed.

Trudi was the first infant he'd held, and to him she didn't seem any different from the infants he'd glanced at over the years from a cautious distance. As he peered into her sage eyes, he marveled that, between him and his wife, two long and angular people, the child was like a pebble—round and solid. She had his light coloring, his strong chin and high forehead. Her tongue nudged at her upper lip as if trying to grasp some nourishment, forming a tiny, luminous bubble of spit. He let her suck on his little finger, amazed at the fierce tug of her tongue and gums. Lace curtains billowed in the open window, and in the morning light, the smooth brown woodwork glowed the color of honey. When he felt the high curve of Trudi's palate against his fingernail, he gently turned his finger sideways so as not to scratch her.

"Look at her, Gertrud," he said when his wife opened her eyes and sat up, startled. "Just look at her. Please."

But his wife, after whom he'd named the child as they had planned during her pregnancy, squeezed her eyes shut and twisted her face aside.

The pay-library was in its third generation of existence, providing an income for the Montag family even during the lean years of war because the people carried in coal and food and clothing in trade for the brightly colored books that brought a different kind of adventure into their bleak homes than the adventure they were living—the gray adventure of war, of poverty, of fear.

You could also buy tobacco in the pay-library. Wooden cigar boxes and glass bins that contained nine sorts of tobacco were set up on one end of the long counter, next to the ledger where Leo Montag recorded the books in the library, a separate page for each title. The length of each column below a title, listing the names of borrowers, would show how popular a book was.

The side walls of the Montags' house were less than an arm's length from the walls of the adjoining buildings—the Weilers' on the left, the Blaus' on the right. Herr Blau was a retired tailor, and Frau Weiler ran the grocery store. The façades of the three narrow houses were white stucco with a row of bricks set below the windows and above the high doors, and the foundations were built from great, smooth stones that had come from the bed of the Rhein. Most of the other shops and businesses in Burgdorf were also on the streets closest to the church square: Hansen's bakery and the beauty parlor, the hardware store and the milliner's shop, two taverns and the open market.

The Weilers had one son, Georg, who'd been conceived the night before his father had left for the Eastern front. Of an age to have grandchildren by the time she'd birthed Georg, Frau Weiler had a wide face with sad, protruding eyes, and often sounded frantic as if worried she wouldn't get all her work done. She'd never forgiven her son for not having been born a girl, and she was still trying to correct that error by dressing him in smocks and refusing to cut his hair.

The Blaus' children were already grown: Margret and her family rented an apartment near the chapel, and Stefan Blau, who'd run away to America as a young boy, had returned to Burgdorf only once, in 1911, to take Leo Montag's sister, Helene, with him as his third bride and mother to the children of his first two wives, who'd died in childbirth. Recently, Leo had been wishing that his sister still lived with him and Gertrud. She'd know how to get Gertrud to accept their child. But Helene was thousands of kilometers away and had three stepchildren and a child of her own now.

While the Montags' pay-library, kitchen, and living room with its piano took up the main floor of their house, the bedrooms were on the floor above. On the third floor was a sewing room with pansy wallpaper and a narrow window; it was there that Leo Montag would lock up his wife to keep her safe after she began to take off her clothes for the angels. The first time it had happened right at Sunday mass. Leo, who sat between two of the older men, was aware of the priest up in the pulpit, preaching, but he wasn't listening to the words be-cause he was noticing how the light—even though it was raining out-

side—blazed through the stained-glass windows in blue and purple
and gold stars as though the sun were shining. He hadn't even realized that Gertrud had her dress unbuttoned until the priest stopped in
the middle of a sentence, raising one scrawny arm toward the
women's side of the church, causing everyone to stare at Gertrud for
that interminable moment before Frau Eberhardt, who knelt in the
pew behind Gertrud, threw her coat across Gertrud's shoulders.

The next time Gertrud hadn't been caught that early: she'd slipped
out while the iceman was delivering a block of ice. After Leo had
paid, he'd watched the horse-drawn ice wagon pull away, and it was
only then that he'd seen Gertrud strolling toward the end of Schreberstrasse, naked, her head high. He'd grabbed the red-and-white-
checkered tablecloth from the kitchen table and had run after her.

From then on—every morning before he'd open the pay-library—
he'd squeeze a glass of the carrot juice Gertrud loved, slice an apple
for her, and struggle to get her upstairs to the sewing room, where
he'd lock her in. To please her, he hung up a small, gold-framed mirror that she'd admired in the Abramowitzs' living room. They had
brought it back from their trip to Venice, along with enough pho-
tographs to fill an entire album, as always when they traveled to
places as far away as China and Venezuela. In trade for this mirror,
Leo had offered Frau Abramowitz five years of all the books she
wanted to borrow.

"I'd rather just give it to you," she'd said. Her countless delicate
wrinkles, which had been there since she was a young woman, were
not visible until you looked closely—like the texture of a silky fabric
that has been crushed and then ironed out, leaving the surface
smooth except for the deeper, finer wrinkles.

"But I want you to have something in return."

"Two years of books are more than enough."

"Five. At least five."

"I guess I'll see more in those books than I'll ever see in that mirror," she had conceded.

Leo bought Gertrud a porcelain chamber pot with roses painted
along the rim and eight shiny cardboard sheets of paper dolls with
their lavish clothes. Reluctant to let her use the scissors, he cut out the
dolls and showed Gertrud how to fit the gowns, coats, and hats to
their wafer-thin bodies by bending paper tabs around their shoulders
and waists.

He brought her a blue velvet sofa that Emil Hesping had won in a chess game, but he didn't tell Gertrud where the sofa had come from. Though Emil had been his friend since first grade, Gertrud no longer tolerated him inside the house. She'd leave the pay-library if Emil came in to buy his tobacco.

"It's not your doing," Emil would assure Leo, who'd try to apologize for his wife's behavior. Emil was the brother of a bishop but did not go to church. Though only in his early thirties, he'd been bald for ten years; yet, he looked younger than other men his age because the pink skin of his face simply continued beyond his forehead and down the back of his head. He laughed a lot, and when he did, the only hair on his face—a nearly solid line of black eyebrows—would join above his nose.

Leo, who'd been a member of Emil's gymnasts' club until he'd been injured in the war, missed flying on the trapeze, swinging his body across double bars of smooth wood, and leaping across the solid leather body of the horse while his fingers barely touched the hide. And he missed the easy camaraderie of being near Emil. Earthbound with his aching knee, he felt in Emil the excitement of winning that he'd known as a member of the team. Emil Hesping could make you believe you still had it in you to win. He got you to smile, to laugh even. He got you to meet him at Die Traube for a beer or two when your wife no longer allowed him inside your house.

One afternoon Emil stopped by the pay-library with an old class picture of the fifth grade, Leo standing next to him, while Gertrud knelt in the front row with the other girls. "Look what I found," he said excitedly and pressed the photo into Gertrud's hands. "Do you recognize us?"

For a moment she stood holding the sepia picture, lips pulled back from her teeth as if she were about to snarl; then she dropped the photo at his feet and darted into the kitchen.

When Leo followed her, she was opening and slamming the white cabinet doors so hard that her great-grandmother's collection of flowered porcelain cups and saucers trembled on the shelf above the sink.

"Emil used to be your friend too," Leo reminded her.

"He thinks he can take whatever he wants."

"He was bringing you something. Besides, he pays for his tobacco."

She stared at him, her eyes savage, stared at the gentle face and stiff collar of the man she'd loved since they'd both been eight years old, the man who often stood for everything she disliked about this town, where life happened slower than in the city where she had spent her first years.

"We all pay, Leo." She listened to her words and had to laugh. "We all pay."

While his daughter lay in her wicker carriage between the wooden counter and the shelves, Leo would wait on his customers or study intricate chess moves on the carved board that was always set up on the counter in various stages of a game against an imaginary opponent. Occasionally, one of the old men would stop by to play a game against Leo, and they'd talk about the men at the front. They'd reminisce about the Burgdorf chess club and make plans to resume the Monday-night meetings once the war was over.

From time to time Leo would glance toward the ceiling to reassure himself that his wife was still in the sewing room. His eyes would narrow as if to penetrate the span of stone and lumber that lay between him and the third floor. He'd feel worried when he'd hear her agitated steps, but even more worried if he couldn't hear anything because—at least once a week—Gertrud managed to escape. He couldn't figure out how the only key to the locked door—a long key which he'd leave outside in the keyhole—ended up inside Gertrud's pocket when he finally caught her.

One day, when he saw her darting down the hallway past the open door of the library, he grabbed Trudi from her carriage and, holding her pressed against his chest, limped around the side of the house to the back.

"Gertrud?" He bent and peered into the dark gap. "Gertrud, are you there?"

It took a few moments before he could make her out, cowering among the weeds and boulders, her face half hidden by her hair. Leo didn't know why he did what he did next—didn't even know he was doing it until he found himself holding his daughter in front of him, much like a priest extending the sacrament. Suspended in the beams of pearl-gray light, he kept Trudi there though his arms began to quiver with her weight, held her there between him and his wife for what seemed the span of an entire lifetime, her round infant hands stirring the layers of air like tropical fish, until his wife scuttled to-

ward them with a sob and snatched the child from him with her
smudged hands, enveloping the three of them with the musty smell of
earth.

Leo's arms felt weightless—like wings almost—and as the lightness
moved into his chest and throat, he wanted to fold his arms around
his wife and child to keep himself anchored to the ground; yet, he
stepped back, not far enough to startle Gertrud, but enough to grant
her the seclusion to peel off their daughter's tiny socks and dress and
undershirt and diaper, to examine each part of the three-month-old
body—toes, navel, neck, buttocks, fingers, ears—the way a new
mother will when her child is handed to her at birth.

To Leo, that day would symbolize his daughter's birth, as though
all the moments leading up to this had merely been a preparation for
what he had expected a family to be, and he was struck by a boundless hope—even when Gertrud fumbled with her dress and pressed
the child's mouth to her dry breast. Although he would tell Trudi that
it was impossible to remember something that far back in your childhood, the girl would retain that moment when her mother first
touched her, and that sharp bliss she felt even though her belly remained hungry and her mother's hands were rough, as if accustomed
to moving aside great pockets of dirt.

From that day on, Trudi became the only one who could lure her
mother from her nest beneath the house without force—initially in
her father's arms, and as she learned to walk, by herself. It was there
that she'd start her search whenever her mother disappeared. A clean
pinafore over her dress, leather shoes laced up to her ankles, she'd set
out to find her mother, and what she discovered was an odd beauty in
that dark space which was lit by her mother's voice and airy movements, the kind of beauty that belongs to the underside of things and
rarely becomes obvious, the kind of beauty that—once you know of
it—will compel you to seek it out. You begin to recognize it where no
one else will—in the intricate pattern of creases around an old man's
lips; in the way the air grows dense with a potent egg smell moments
before lightning splits the sky; in the high-pitched scream of a small
child's rage.

And because she had begun to see like that, Trudi never thought to
shrink away that afternoon her mother caught a black bug, popped
its round body between her fingers, and sniffed it with an expression

of rapture. "It smells like strawberries," she said and thrust her fingertips beneath Trudi's nose. And it did. It smelled like fresh strawberries, and the specks of red on the white of her mother's fingers could easily have been sweet bits of fruit pulp.

Even at two, Trudi felt far older than her mother when she'd follow her beneath the house and sit with her, keeping her entertained by telling her of everyone who'd come to the pay-library that day. She'd make her visit so pleasant that her mother would want to follow her back into the light, and then she'd coax her, gently, until her mother would crawl toward her in sideways movements like a crab.

And it wasn't merely getting her out, but doing it without witnesses so that the neighbors wouldn't tell her father who'd only lock her mother up again. That's why it became Trudi's secret when her mother hid beneath the house—her earliest secret, a weighty secret for someone her age, especially since her mother had shown her the trick of escaping from the sewing room: you slipped a piece of paper below the door, jabbed at the keyhole with a hairpin, and when the key dropped outside the door on your piece of paper, you carefully pulled it into the room and unlocked the door.

To lead her mother by both hands from the dark—it was the one thing Trudi could do to offset her guilt that her mother had crossed the line to insanity because of her. She knew this not only from overhearing Frau Weiler and Frau Buttgereit in the grocery store, but also from staring into her mother's eyes and watching the swirl of images behind the blue irises, a web of images which confused her mother and which Trudi did not understand though she felt their terrifying force. And she saw something else: that her mother blamed herself, that there was a long-ago sin so loathsome that her mother believed it was the cause for giving birth to a child with a misshapen body.

To bring her mother from the dark and across that network of gouges from her heels that crisscrossed the dusty earth like the tiny pattern of tracks from the feet of the strawberry bugs . . . To rinse her mother's hands in the brook that ran from the end of Schreberstrasse behind the pay-library, where it forked on its way toward the fairgrounds . . . If only she could have brought her back to sanity like that, Trudi would have undone her birth and every breath she'd drawn since then. If only she could have returned this tall woman with the shadow hair to the way she'd looked in the old photos. But how could she, if even the priest and the doctor didn't know how?

• • •

It was the united decision of the old women in town that Gertrud Montag—discovered without clothes on the front steps of the Catholic school—should stay at the Grafenberg asylum for a while. The old women had been patient with her illness, but indecency was hazardous because it corrupted the young. They sent a delegation to Herr Pastor Schüler, who invited Leo Montag to the rectory where, over coffee and *Apfelstrudel* with raisins, he informed Leo of the town's concern.

"I wish I knew of an easier way," the pastor began, his voice filled with pity.

Leo listened, politely, as he had been taught as a boy; he praised the crust of the *Strudel,* accepted a second helping, but resisted the pastor's advice to send Gertrud to Grafenberg. Just as he accepted his daughter's difference and the aches in his leg—with occasional bursts of regret but an overriding hopefulness—he accepted his wife the way she had become. It was only after Gertrud broke her wrist during one of her escapes, and Frau Doktor Rosen, after setting Gertrud's wrist, suggested it might be best to have her examined in Grafenberg, that Leo gave in to the priest's urging—though not until he'd suggested the Theresienheim instead, the convent around the corner where the nuns cared for the old and the ill.

"She'd be close by," he told the doctor. "Trudi and I can visit her."

"The sisters—" Frau Doktor Rosen hesitated and rubbed the white, raised scar between her nose and upper lip, the trace of her cleft palate. "The sisters," she said gently, "mean well. . . . I'm sure they do a lot of good for the old people, but what your wife needs is a specialist, someone who knows about the human mind."

Gertrud was kept at the asylum for three weeks, and it was during her absence that the gift from the unknown benefactor arrived—a wooden phonograph and eight thick black records with music of Beethoven and Bach, which Leo discovered on the counter of the pay-library one morning when he opened the green shutters. The unknown benefactor had bestowed gifts upon the people of Burgdorf for nearly twelve years now—clothing and baskets of food and envelopes with money that would appear inside locked houses at times of turmoil without notes or anything to link them to their giver, whose identity mystified the entire town. The unknown benefactor had to be one of their own, the people agreed, because the gifts were always just right—like the gleaming bicycle Frau Simon had found in her bedroom two days after her old bike had been stolen, or the box with new coats for the entire Buttgereit family after storms had spoiled the crops.

Leo Montag set up the phonograph in the library, and Trudi nearly forgot about her mother when those first sounds filled the air with ecstasy and fury and passion. Standing completely still, she breathed in those reverberations and felt their force move through her, giving shape to emotions she hadn't yet experienced, but dimly perceived waiting for her.

When her mother was sent home with her dress buttoned to her neck and her wrist in a cast, her eyes were too dull to let through any images, and she moved as if wading through waist-high water. But the old women nodded their approval that Sunday when she knelt between Frau Blau and Trudi in church, wearing a blue hat fashioned by the town's milliner, Frau Simon, her only exposed skin that of her face and of her folded hands. When Frau Blau opened the pages of the black prayer book for her, she dutifully moved her lips with the words that swelled from the congregation.

With each day, her movements would become less restrained. Those were the best times for Trudi—after her mother's eyes unclouded and before she started her fast pacing through the house again—those times when her father would close the library, let her mother out of the sewing room, and take the two of them to the Rhein. There Trudi would untie her shoes, hike up her skirt and, in the shallow end of the bay, wade back and forth, or hop on one leg, showing off for her parents, who'd sit on the jetty and wave to her while silver ribbons from their cigarettes fastened the sky to the river.

"Promise you won't send me to Grafenberg again," Gertrud implored Leo one evening when he was frying white sausages and onions.

He took her into a gentle embrace. "If I can," he said. "If I can, *Liebchen.*"

Trudi climbed on top of the wooden icebox to be near her parents and squatted on her heels between the sugar bowl and the egg warmers. Her father's cardigan hung from the back of a kitchen chair as usual, and on the sill of the open window sat a fly, its wings iridescent, its front legs twitching and crossing like Frau Blau's knitting needles. In the grass behind the grocery store, Georg Weiler was doing somersaults, his dress flopping over his head as if he wanted people to notice by his underwear that he was not a girl.

Trudi's mother was as tall as Trudi's father. "Promise?" she said again, looking straight into his eyes.

He tilted his forehead against hers. She wore her favorite dress, white with colorful embroidery of flowers that bordered the ends of the sleeves and neckline and continued in one long vine that curved from her throat to her waist. It was a dress—so Trudi had been told—that her mother had made two years before Trudi's birth to wear to a costume ball. She'd gone as a princess with a crown and a scepter, while Trudi's father had disguised himself as a pirate with an eye patch and a cardboard saber.

"Promise?"

He nodded.

"You'll be glad," she said and laughed. Her hand—the one without the cast—darted between his legs.

He leapt back. "Gertrud!" he said, but stared at Trudi as if she'd caught him at something forbidden.

"Pope Leo . . ." Trudi's mother sang out. "How many popes named Leo did we have?" She swirled and grasped Trudi. "Holy man . . . Leo, Leo holy man. . . ."

Trudi clutched the fabric at her mother's shoulder as they spun around the kitchen.

". . . holy man. From now on we shall declare your father Pope Leo the Seventeenth who can't get—"

"Gertrud!" He caught her mother by the elbows to stop her from dancing and pulled Trudi from her arms. "Your mother needs her rest," he said.

Outside, Georg had stopped his somersaults and was peering toward their window, his head raised as if to hear better. Blond ringlets touched his round collar.

"Holier than any holy man . . ." Trudi's mother sang. "Blessed art thou among popes, and blessed be the fruit of—"

"The child," he said. "Don't— With the child here."

In the weeks to come, Gertrud's body took on a quicksilver swiftness that made her dash from room to room, chattering incessantly or singing hymns four times as fast as the organist at St. Martin's could play them. After the cast was removed from her wrist, she decided to redecorate the house. Though Leo didn't care for the wallpaper she chose for the living room—spidery white ferns against a brown background—he was so relieved by her interest in creating a special space *inside* the house, that he helped her to hang the wallpaper. He built her a wooden stand that held two clay pots with ferns and the stuffed squirrel his grandfather had shot as a boy, but before he was finished painting the woodwork white to make the living room look brighter, Gertrud took to hiding beneath the house again as if he had failed to duplicate the one place where she still felt safe.

Leo would find her, take her upstairs, and—as usual—lock the door of the sewing room from the outside; only now the key was tied with a frayed shoelace to the door handle so that, even if she managed to push it out, it could not drop to the floor.

If Trudi stayed with her inside this room, Gertrud would cease her agitated pacing between the door and the window, which was too small to let even a child squeeze through. Instead she'd show Trudi how to dress the paper dolls. Frau Simon had given her a satin hatbox, and she kept the dolls in there, always disrobing them before closing the lid as if getting them ready for bed. She sang *"Hänschen klein . . ."* for Trudi and *"Fuchs du hast die Gans gestohlen . . . ,"* and she taught her how to count to twenty on her fingers and toes, and how to clap her hands in rhythm with *"Backe backe Kuchen. . . ."* Often, she'd lift Trudi to the window, open it, and show her how far you could see—all the way across Schreberstrasse and past the church tower, toward the Braunmeiers' wheat fields and dairy farm, to the dike that kept the town safe if the Rhein spilled beyond its boundaries in the spring.

Trudi was never afraid of her mother, not even when she scratched words into the walls, always the same word: *Gefangene*—prisoner—as if leaving an urgent message for a mysterious rescuer. She'd use hairpins, the end of a spoon, her fingernails even. *Gefangene:* it tore through the pansy wallpaper into the plaster and caused pale dust to trickle down the wall. *Gefangene:* it was a word you could learn even if you were far too young to write, a word you felt in your heart by tracing the letters with your fingertips.

Trudi was three when the men of Burgdorf returned from the war. A few of them—like Herr Abramowitz, who had two rows of teeth and was too outspoken with his left-wing politics, people said—had come back wounded like her father. Many more—including Herr Sturm, who owned the toy factory and was one of the richest men in town—had been sent home in wooden boxes that brought the people of Burgdorf together at the cemetery, where carefully tended flowers on family graves were uprooted in order to break the earth for new coffins.

Most of the men reached the town in orderly formations, which quickly disbanded. It was a season of small revolutions: trucks would appear with rifles and pistols which were distributed among ordinary men, who carried those weapons even in the harsh light of day as though the war had caused extra limbs to sprout from their bodies.

Children, who had taken the absence of their fathers for granted, had to reacquaint themselves with their authority and tenderness, and women had to relinquish the responsibility they'd taken on during the war years—some with relief, many with reluctance. When they stood waiting in line to buy their daily food supplies at the bakery and the butcher shop and the grocery store, they no longer talked to one another about their accomplishments and fears, but about what their husbands or fathers liked for dinner.

With the men back home, the town felt as though its borders had been pulled in overnight; streets seemed narrower, rooms more cramped; boots, waiting to be polished by daughters or wives, took up space next to the kitchen stove; the two taverns—Potter's and Die Traube—were full again; voices sounded louder and even the church bells had a deeper ring to them.

Herr Abramowitz reopened his law office, dusted off his expensive camera equipment, and purchased a used 1908 Mercedes with a roof rack and white tires. On Sundays, he'd take his wife and two children on rides into the countryside, where he'd pose them against lakes and forests and hills for countless pictures.

When Anton Immers traded twenty pounds of sausage for the uniform of one of the returning officers—Kurt Heidenreich, a cheerful and generous man who was a taxidermist by trade—he asked Herr Abramowitz to photograph him in the uniform. Though the lawyer didn't care for the butcher's superior attitude, he never turned down a request for a photo because he took pride in seeing himself as the neighborhood photographer and chronicler. Holding his aching back as straight as he could, the butcher—who had felt disgraced ever since he'd been turned away when he'd tried to enlist—stared past the camera with an expression of triumph as if he could see battlefields too distant for anyone else to discern. Six years before the war, a cow had rolled over on him while he'd slaughtered her, breaking his back, and though he refused to speak of the accident, you could tell by the way he walked—slightly bent to his left—that he was in constant pain.

Herr Immers framed an enlargement of the photo, and whenever he looked at it in his shop, where it hung next to the patron saint of butchers—St. Adrian, the pagan soldier who'd become a Christian and had been tortured to death—he could imagine that, indeed, he had fought in the war, not as a common soldier, of course, but as a highly decorated officer. With the passage of years he would come to believe that fabrication, and it would be unwise for his wife and customers to remind him otherwise. Eventually, the entire town would pretend along with the butcher, even the taxidermist who'd traded him the uniform, and the next generation would be fed that illusion as history.

It was like that with many other events, and it took courage for the few, who would preserve the texture of the truth, not to let its fibers slip beneath the web of silence and collusion which people—often with the best of intentions—spun to sustain and protect one another.

Trudi's father, who had been back so much longer than the other men, was nudged into an informal leadership as the returning soldiers looked toward him to reintroduce them to the life they had left. His quiet acceptance drew them to the pay-library, where they'd buy portions of tobacco so small that they'd have an excuse to return the following day. Many of them couldn't fathom how Germany could have lost this war against the world, and they kept speculating about conspiracies and malicious forces that had brought about the shame of their defeat. Wearing stiff lines of exhaustion like masks, they walked with the tired sway of somnambulists because they'd forgotten how to sleep through an entire night without listening for the enemy. They didn't have to tell Leo about their dreams of splintered bones and empty eye sockets because he knew all about those dreams that hunt you out of your shallow pockets of sleep into foul memories, even if you've only been a soldier for a few months.

One of his hands floating above a chess piece as he contemplated the next move, Leo would listen to the men, and even when he wouldn't say much, the men would feel restored when they'd leave.

Leo revealed himself to very few people—not because he was shy or wished to hide, but because he didn't know the desire to have others understand him. Still, the men wanted to find out from him what had happened in Burgdorf after they'd been sent off with flowers and music in 1914—celebrated heroes before they'd ever encountered the enemy—as though the real story could only come to them from another man.

Hidden on the footstool behind the counter of the pay-library, enveloped in the lavish scent of tobaccos, Trudi would soak in the words that her father chose to tell the men about the town during their absence. His arc of vision was higher than hers, wider, and though he spoke of events that she, too, had witnessed, they took on a richer texture and became richer still if—afterwards, alone—she fused them with her own observations.

Although Leo Montag liked to eat, his body was extremely thin, and his skin so colorless that he usually looked as if he were recovering from a prolonged illness. The women in the neighborhood were always urging him to drink milk or eat meat. Yet, he was surprisingly strong and agile. As a gymnast, he'd won numerous trophies—gleaming statues of men whose muscles, unlike his, distended their bronze or silver plated skin, their bodies in various positions of flight that made them look as though, any moment, they might soar from the shelf in the pay-library where he kept them polished. People who borrowed books would find it more difficult with each year to connect those magnificent shapes to the man who limped behind the counter and bent over his ledger to sign out their books.

Early one morning in October, when Leo was frying apple pancakes, Gertrud swooped Trudi from her bed and carried her, propped on her hip, into the world of muted light and spider lace and strawberry bugs. Licks of frost had turned the grass blades silvery, but beneath the house the ground was still soft and molded itself to Gertrud's feet. There was a greater urgency to her touch, a tightness to her hands that almost pinched and, for the first time, made Trudi afraid of her.

"People die if you don't love them enough," her mother whispered to Trudi, her long body curved against the ground as if she'd already established her burying place.

"You won't die," Trudi said.

Her mother's eyes glistened in the dim light.

"I love you enough," Trudi said.

Her mother pushed her skirt aside and exposed her left knee. "Here," she said and guided Trudi's hand across her kneecap. "Feel this."

Trudi shook her head, confused. Her father was the one with the bad knee. Sometimes you could see the edges of the steel plate through the fabric of his trousers.

"Harder." Her mother pressed Trudi's hand against her knee.

Deep below the warm skin she did feel something—like uncooked kernels of rice—shifting under her fingers. She glanced up into her mother's eyes; they revealed such anguish that she thought she should look away, but she couldn't.

"It's gravel," her mother whispered. "From when I fell . . . Emil Hesping's motorcycle . . ."

Trudi's eyes stayed on her mother's face, taking in the story beneath the anguish, though her mother gave her only few words, but those words she said made the other words, which she would never bring herself to say aloud, leap into her eyes. One hand on her mother's knee, Trudi felt the secret shaping itself into images that passed through her skin, images filled with color and movement and wind—yes, wind. She saw her mother on the back of a motorcycle, her arms spanning the middle of Herr Hesping. Her mother was younger than Trudi had ever known her, and she wore a yellow summer dress with short sleeves. Dust billowed behind the motorcycle as it raced down Schlosserstrasse toward the Rhein, and her mother held on tighter as the front wheel disengaged from the ground for an instant and the motorcycle darted up the dike, then down the other side. Hair whipped her face, and when Emil Hesping stopped the motorcycle beneath a stand of poplars, the wide leather seat still held the warm imprint of her thighs. He let his palm rest on that imprint for a moment, and she felt a sudden heat between her thighs as though he were touching her skin. When he embraced her, she had to close her eyes against the sun and against the fear that had been with her since the day her husband had left for the Russian front—the fear that Leo would not return alive.

"We skidded . . . on the way back . . . the other side of the dike." Trudi saw Emil Hesping get up, awkwardly, from the rough road, brush the dust from his arms, and stagger past the fallen motorcycle to where her mother had been flung. Her face was scratched. Blood rose around the fragments of gravel embedded in her knee and streamed down her calf into her white sandal.

"The same knee." Her mother laughed that wild laugh. "The same knee as your father's. It happened to him, too. That day." She snatched Trudi into her arms and settled her in the curve of her waist and belly like a much younger child. "Because of me," she chanted and rocked her daughter as if to make up for all the days she hadn't rocked her as an infant, "because of me he got hurt. . . ."

"Gertrud?" Leo Montag's shadow sloped into the opening between the beams. Between his boots, sun glinted on the frozen grass. "Gertrud?" he called. "Trudi?"

Before Trudi could answer, her mother laid one finger against Trudi's lips. Her breath felt warm against Trudi's face. Carefully, the girl skimmed her fingers across her mother's knee. It was smooth; the skin had closed across the tiny wounds like the surface of the river after you toss stones into the waves. Only you knew they were there.

Unless you told.

———————————— ■ ————————————

1918 – 1919

THAT DAY TRUDI'S FATHER DID NOT OPEN THE PAY-LIBRARY. INSTEAD, HE borrowed the Abramowitzs' Mercedes. Its back had windows and looked so much like a coach that you almost expected to see horses harnessed to it, but the front of the car was open, with tufted seats and a steering wheel on a long, angled shaft. While Frau Abramowitz read Trudi the fairy tale of the devil with the three golden hairs and fed her *Brötchen* with Dutch cheese, Leo Montag settled his wife in the closed compartment of the car with a blanket and two pillows from their bed, which she would pluck apart, filling the compartment with feathers that would cling to her green coat and hat like snowflakes by the time they'd reach Grafenberg, where she was to stay for nearly seven weeks.

It was snowing real snow when Trudi was finally allowed to visit her mother. She'd been in the Grafenberg forest before—it was a popular hiking area—but she'd only seen the high walls of the asylum from a distance. This time, though, she and her father walked up to the wall, close enough to see the shards of glass in the mortar along the top edge. Sharp and pointed, they could tear up your hands if you tried to escape. Trudi dug her hands deeply into the fur muff that matched the rabbit trim around her bonnet and on the collar of her coat. She wondered if anyone had climbed across this wall. Maybe the Kaiser had climbed across a wall like this in his fancy uniform when he'd escaped from Germany. But what if countries had even higher walls around them?

A few days earlier her father had told her that the Kaiser had re-signed and fled the country. "He's in Holland," her father had said. "Now we'll have peace." Trudi had seen pictures of the Kaiser: his mouth looked vain beneath the fancy mustache, and he wore a shiny helmet with a stiff, glittering bird—the size of a pigeon—on top, its wings spread to keep from toppling off.

A guard dressed like a soldier opened the gate. His neck bulged, and his fingers were stained from tobacco. In his glance Trudi recognized that flash of curiosity she'd encountered before in strangers, but today it made her feel prickly, that curiosity, made her feel that she should be inside these walls where they locked up people who were different. In the eyes of the guard—she knew for certain—she was different, and it was a knowledge that would torment her from that day forward and fuel her longing to grow and take revenge on those who spurned her.

As the guard motioned toward the largest of the buildings, Trudi hesitated, but her father took her by the shoulders, and the guard shut the gate immediately behind them as if to keep them there. She had wanted to bring her mother's birthday presents—a thick bathrobe and fur boots—but her father hadn't let her though the birthday was only two days away.

"It's dangerous," he'd said. "We'll celebrate when she comes home."

His family had a history of disasters from celebrating special occasions too early: his Aunt Mechthild had drowned in the Rhein when her grandfather's birthday picnic was held one day early; a cousin, Willi, had been injured in a train crash after celebrating his parents' silver anniversary a week early; and his sister, Helene, had broken her arm when she opened a confirmation gift three days too soon.

In the lobby, which smelled of cinnamon and candles, Trudi's father wiped her nose and unbuttoned her coat. A friendly nurse with loud shoes led them down a corridor and through a smaller set of gates that also locked behind them. Trudi's mother stood waiting in a room with white chairs, all lined up along the walls. Her elbows angled as if she were carrying something fragile in her empty hands, she walked toward them, her eyes faded, and all at once Trudi no longer minded being inside these gates; she had missed her mother so fiercely that any place would be good, as long as she could be with both parents. Her mother smelled like the lobby. In front of Trudi she dropped to her knees and brought both palms against Trudi's cheeks as if to memorize the shape of her face.

A few other families were visiting patients, and Leo Montag led his wife and daughter into a corner, where he arranged three chairs in a triangle that separated them from the others in the room. Only then did he embrace his wife and touch her forehead with his lips. Her hair was braided in a way Trudi had not seen on her before—starting at her temples in tight coils that puckered her skin as though someone who didn't know her well had braided it for her.

Her mother wore those braids the following week when she was permitted to return home, and she smiled her weary hospital smile when Trudi untied the ribbons and brushed her hair until it crackled and floated on her shoulders like angels' hair. Though it wasn't silver like the angels' hair you drape over the branches of your Christmas tree, its dark mass took in strands of light with each brush stroke. At first, her mother slept much of each day as if gathering reservoirs of strength for any movement she might have to make, but by Christmas, when Leo lit the beeswax candles on the pine tree in the living room, she looked much more like the mother Trudi remembered.

They ate carp in beer sauce and the white veal sausage that the butcher made only from mid-December till Christmas. When Trudi sang two songs and recited one poem, her mother kept applauding until Trudi felt so flustered that she trapped her mother's hands between hers to make them stop.

They opened their gifts which were arranged on the round wicker table, beginning with the package from America: Aunt Helene had sent silver napkin rings with matching spoons and a *Hampelmann*—jumping jack. When Trudi opened her largest present from her parents—a porcelain baby doll with bright red lips—her mother pulled Trudi onto her knees.

"Wouldn't you like a real baby, a little brother or sister?" she asked, beaming as if she were already seeing a child who was perfect.

"No," Trudi said.

"A baby brother or sister who—"

"No!"

"Gertrud—" Trudi's father started.

"Storks adore sugar." Her mother's voice was joyful. "And they bring babies to houses where people leave sugar cubes for them on the windowsill. That's how the storks know where to take the babies."

Trudi dug her chin into her collarbone, wondering if storks ever made mistakes. Like with her. Slipping from her mother's knees, she ran past the stand with the potted ferns and the stuffed squirrel to the front door of the house. Her forehead against the cold glass panel, she stared into the fine whirls of snow. In the middle of the street stood the man-who-touches-his-heart. He raised his right index finger to his heart, his left index finger to his nose, and touched both at the same instant. Smiling as if satisfied that he'd accomplished that, he dropped his hands and raised them again, reversing the ritual: left to his nose, right to his heart. Before the war he used to be a biology teacher, but being a soldier had turned something within him. It was said that the man-who-touches-his-heart had seen his whole battalion die. Now he lived with various relatives, staying with one for a while before being sent on to the next.

But what if you had no relatives? Trudi shivered. Maybe the stork had been on his way to drop her off in a country where everyone had short arms and legs. Maybe she'd been brought by a cuckoo instead of a stork. Cuckoos left their eggs in the nests of other birds, letting them do all the work of sitting on the eggs. But when the young cuckoos broke through the shells, they were pushed from the nest. So far, her parents had kept her, even if she was the wrong baby. But what would happen if the stork brought them the right baby?

She felt her father's hand on her hair. "You haven't opened all your presents, Trudi."

When he carried her back into the living room, her mother was winding a red ribbon around and around her wrist. She laughed when she saw Trudi, and as she held out her arms for her, the ribbon sprang free and coiled at her feet like a blood-covered snake. That night, her mother did not talk about the baby again. She helped Trudi to fit together her new building-block puzzle. Each side of a block had a picture fragment of a fairy tale, and when you set them all on a flat surface and matched them, you could make six pictures, including *Hänsel und Gretel, Schneewittchen und die sieben Zwerge, Rumpelstilzchen,* and *Dornröschen,* who'd slept a hundred years.

Her mother played *"Stille Nacht"* on the upright piano and Trudi
sang along. Whenever her voice merged with her mother's in one of
the long notes, her body felt measureless and warm. But when her
parents kissed her good night in her room and settled a wrapped
warm water bottle by her feet, they laid the stiff baby doll next to her.
After the house became silent and dark, Trudi pushed the doll under
her bed, but she could sense the presence of its porcelain body
through her mattress. The following evening, her mother folded
Trudi's fingers around two sugar cubes and lifted her to the wide windowsill in the kitchen, where she made her lay the sugar on a saucer
for the stork.

As soon as she woke up the next morning, Trudi rushed to the window. Though it was closed, the saucer was empty. She pulled aside the
lace curtain, but the only animal outside was the baker's dog, who
kept barking at the clothesline behind the house, where the frost had
turned the laundry into stiff people shapes.

"The stork must have been here," her mother sang, a flush to her
cheeks.

Her father glanced up from his newspaper, his face grave.

Trudi could tell he didn't want the new baby either. But if they kept
leaving sugar on the windowsill, the stork would certainly bring her a
brother or sister who'd soon be taller than she. She took to climbing
from her bed whenever she'd wake up in the middle of the night. On
bare feet, she'd steal into the kitchen, push a chair against the wall below the window, and—if the sugar cubes which her mother had
handed her in the evening were still there—she'd cram them into her
mouth, scanning the night sky for the white shapes of storks while she
chewed, hard, to keep a sibling from arriving and pushing her out of
the house.

Storks. Though she hadn't seen any of the tall birds in months,
Trudi now looked for them everywhere: on chimneys, in trees, between clouds. She figured they couldn't hide babies beneath their
wings because, as soon as they'd spread their wings to fly, those babies would fall out. No, they'd carry the babies in slings attached to
their long beaks or riding on their backs.

Sometimes, while sitting on the front step, prepared to chase off
any stork with her mother's rattan carpet beater, she'd hear the melo-
dious voice of the Italian ragman. *"Lumpen, Eisen, Papier . . .
—Rags, iron, paper . . . ,"* sang the ragman as his wooden cart rum-

bled through the streets of Burgdorf. He rang his bell as he chanted, "*Lumpen, Eisen, Papier. . . .*" In back of his cart stood a scale where he weighed old clothes and metal and paper before counting out coins from the leather pouch at his waist. "*Lumpen, Eisen, Papier. . . .*" The ragman's name was Herr Benotti. He was from Italy and always wore a white shirt, even when he unloaded his day's gathering in the fenced yard behind his house on Lindenstrasse.

Every day Trudi's mother talked about the new baby, and Trudi increased her vigil for storks. The morning after Easter her father told her the baby had died. "Your brother," he said. Though Trudi hadn't seen the baby—how could a baby die before it was here?—there was a funeral. Frau Blau brought her best linen cloths to cover the tables in the dining room and kitchen, and the neighbor women spread out a funeral feast: sheets of plum cake and deep bowls of potato salad; tureens with pea soup and barley soup; platters with blood sausage and head cheese; loaves of black bread and baskets of crisp *Brötchen*; cheese from Holland and Switzerland; and delicious white asparagus from the Buttgereits' garden.

Frau Doktor Rosen urged Trudi's mother to rest, but she flitted through the rooms, rearranging the daffodils from Frau Abramowitz's flower beds, offering food to the guests, her beautiful eyes feverish, her skin nearly translucent. From whispered comments Trudi understood that her brother had arrived too early to be alive. Now she knew six dead people altogether. But the other five had died old, like Herr Talmeister, who used to spit on the sidewalk before he'd enter the pay-library.

She was sure her brother's death had to do with the sugar she'd stolen; because of it the stork had punished the baby. It would follow her, that guilt, even as an adult, making a sick-sweet bile rise in her throat whenever she tasted sugar; and yet, the craving for it would return, a craving for the forbidden delicious taste on her tongue, followed by the shame she'd felt that day of the funeral feast, when she'd eaten three pieces of plum cake and two chocolate eggs from her Easter basket and—with one unexpected hiccup—had spewed purple-brown vomit over the front of her dress.

Her mother took her out the backdoor. Their feet flattened the thin ribs of earth that Trudi's father had raked early that morning. He raked the yard once a week and had already finished it two days earlier, but this morning, when Trudi had woken up, he'd been out there again with his bamboo rake, snagging twigs and stones and pigeon droppings.

By the muddy edge of the brook, her mother squatted down, trapped the swift cold water in her fingers, and cleaned Trudi's face and dress. "Look," she said and peered into the brook as if trying to find something lost.

Slowly, beyond the surface of the current, another pattern emerged for Trudi—that of new leaves, their long reflections bobbing in one place while the water rushed through them, and amongst the leaves, the silver moon-shapes of two faces.

From that day on, her mother seemed distracted—even in her frantic behavior she seemed distracted, as if already drawn to something beyond the house and the town. No longer would she grasp Trudi to pull her against herself or lift her to the window; it was almost as if she were returning to that time after Trudi's birth when she hadn't wanted to touch her at all.

In May, Frau Doktor Rosen recommended another stay in Grafenberg, and Gertrud Montag went willingly, but Trudi was inconsolable. Leo found that he could soothe Trudi with music, and he'd lift her on the counter of the pay-library, where she'd sit quietly next to the phonograph, one finger tracing the swirls of the rich wood as she'd listen to the records. It made him uneasy when his customers would praise him for bearing up well under the burden of his wife and child. "They're no burden," he'd say.

When Gertrud returned home, she was even more bewildered than before. If Trudi reached for her, she'd smile and, perhaps, bend to adjust Trudi's collar or retie one of her shoelaces, though it was good and tight. She no longer had to be coaxed into the sewing room, but sought out that isolation and even took to sleeping on the velvet sofa, curled on only half of the space as though her body had shrunk.

Every morning, as soon as she was dressed, Trudi would dash up the stairs to be locked in with her mother: she'd pretend to make tea and place an imaginary cup into the slack hands; she'd dress the paper dolls and climb on the sofa to hold them up to the mirror so that each doll had a twin; she'd sit on her mother's lap and stroke her face. But beneath all that, she fought the shame that her mother's vision was forever tangled.

The last time Gertrud Montag went to the asylum, she hugged

Trudi by the open door of her wardrobe, holding her close for so long that it seemed she would never release her. It was the beginning of July, two weeks before Trudi's fourth birthday, and her mother was wearing a cotton dress printed with peach-colored roses. One of her travel bags was packed, but the suitcases and hatboxes were still stacked on top of the birch wardrobe—a sure sign that she wouldn't be gone for long.

"When I get back," she said, "things will be better between us."

And Trudi—her face against her mother's hip, breathing in the familiar clear scent of her skin and clothes—Trudi believed her.

That day, she stayed next door with Frau Blau, whose house always smelled of floor wax. While the old woman polished her keys and dusted her windowsills, Trudi followed her around. The tip of Frau Blau's right forefinger was bent to the side, and Trudi felt convinced it was that way from too much dusting. Frau Blau had soft, powdered cheeks and a broken heart. People said her heart had broken in 1894 when her son, Stefan, had run away to America. It was a sorrow that lapped into two centuries, a sorrow that already had lasted—so Trudi counted—twenty-five years.

Since the Blaus didn't throw anything away, their house was crammed full with ancient toys and furniture, doilies and flower pots, gifts that their son shipped from America, and clothes that had belonged to their children and long-dead ancestors. Of Dutch descent, Frau Blau cleaned her house every single day. If her Saviour came to her at night, she told Trudi, she wanted him to find her house in order.

"You can help," Frau Blau decided and showed Trudi how to dust the table legs, each ending in a lion's claws gripping a ball. A cloth around her crooked forefinger, she guided it into every little crevice.

"You can do the next leg," she said and extended the cloth.

Trudi hid her hands behind her back, terrified her finger would turn out like Frau Blau's. She didn't know if it would be worse to have a crooked finger or a thumb like that of Herr Blau who—during his many years at the sewing machine—had run a needle through his thumbnail, leaving a black crater-shaped puncture.

"Children have to obey," Frau Blau reminded her.

Trudi stared at Frau Blau's sturdy shoes. The cracks in the leather were magnified by layers of wax.

"Children have to obey!"

From the roof came the low, moaning call of pigeons. As Trudi felt

Frau Blau waiting, she was glad she didn't have a grandmother in her house, even if grandmothers baked and ironed and knitted and grew beautiful flowers. Most houses had grandmothers in them. Grandmothers made you finish what was on your plate and told you it was not polite to stare at grown-ups. Grandmothers made you say your prayers and wash behind your ears. Grandmothers could make you do whatever they wanted because they were old.

Frau Blau patted Trudi's hair. "Is it because you miss your mother?"

"Because I don't want my finger to look like yours," Trudi blurted.

"*Ach so.*" Frau Blau chuckled and held her crooked finger up between herself and Trudi. "Is that what you think? That it's from cleaning?"

Trudi nodded.

"Oh, but that finger was always like that. From when I was born. Just like you—" She stopped.

"It was always that way?"

"Always. You can tell a lot by a person's fingers. Let me look at yours." She crouched and brought her face close to Trudi's hands. Her gray hair was stiff and wavy from the beauty parlor. "See those white specks under your fingernails?"

Trudi looked at her fingernails. They were the color of her skin, only shiny, and some had tiny white spots.

"That's how you can tell how many mortal sins people have committed." Frau Blau ran one thumb across Trudi's fingernails. "Now with children . . . until they reach the age of reason, those specks are just a warning of mortal sins they might commit if they aren't careful. You have . . . let me see—five altogether. That means you have to choose five times against the devil. Come—" She straightened with a sigh and, still holding Trudi's wrist, headed for the kitchen. "Let me warm you a cup of milk."

Every morning Trudi would wake with the memory of what her mother had said—"*When I get back, things will be better between us*"—and she'd try to imagine their new lives: her father's eyes would lose that worry; she and her mother would sit by the river instead of in the sewing room or beneath the house; the three of them would stand in the church square after mass, talking with other families.

Except, her mother didn't make good on her promise.

She never came back.

And she didn't recognize Trudi the next time she saw her in Grafenberg. The rattle of her breath forced her neck into an arch on the hospital pillow. Above the metal bed hung a wooden crucifix. Jesus had his fingers spread as if to ward off the nails that held his palms to the cross. It was the only indication of a possible protest: the rest of his body had adapted itself to the shape of the cross as though made for it.

For over an hour Trudi listened to her mother's breath, standing frozen, her back to the window, enveloped by the asylum smell of candles and cinnamon. Her mother's features were distorted with the effort of straining for yet another breath that filled the room and made Trudi feel as though she herself were suffocating. She felt an urgency to know what would happen in her life from now on—every hour, every moment even, because if you knew ahead of time, you could stop bad things from happening.

When her mother's dreadful breathing finally stopped, Trudi was relieved at the silence until the nurse bent over the bed to close her mother's eyelids. The nurse had hairy wrists, and Trudi's father stopped her by grasping those wrists. Then Trudi ran.

From the room.

Down the corridor.

Past opened doors.

At the end of the corridor, the nurse caught her by the locked metal gate. Holding Trudi, she whispered words that the girl couldn't hear because her own breath had taken up the pattern that her mother had abandoned.

The nurse led her into a green room and made her swallow a bitter green liquid that looked as though it had bled through the green walls. After a while Trudi found herself sitting on a wooden slat seat in the streetcar next to her father, a heavy glow behind her eyes and in her legs. Her father stared straight ahead, his fingers tight on the rim of his black hat, which lay on his knees. When the *Schaffner*—conductor—came through to collect money for tickets, he had to click the silver change maker that hung on his chest by a leather strap before Trudi's father noticed him and fumbled for his wallet.

At some of the stops, people leapt off the streetcar before it came to a full stop. Frau Abramowitz had warned Trudi never to do that. It was dangerous, she said. Her daughter, Ruth, had chipped a front tooth when she jumped from the streetcar, and her son, Albert—who'd jumped that same moment—had fallen on top of her. Trudi rubbed her front teeth. They were smooth and even. "Trudi has good teeth," the dentist had told her mother. She didn't like Dr. Beck, who had kinky hair sprouting from his long nostrils.

At home her father wouldn't speak to anyone. He sat at the table in the dining room, his hands no longer tight but limp on the polished mahogany as if they contained no bones. Frau Weiler and Frau Abramowitz called the undertaker, chose a coffin and flowers, sent black-rimmed death announcements to relatives and friends.

When I get back, things will be better between us.

Trudi had believed her mother.

Her father took Trudi to the room in back of the cemetery chapel, where the coffin was propped up, but when Trudi looked into the coffin, she had to smile: the woman only resembled her mother a little. Her features were sharp and waxen. She wore a white dress and lay on a white pillow with a white cover to her waist. Like a bride, Trudi thought. The bride's wrists were crossed on her chest, and three candles in tall holders burned at the head end of the coffin.

Trudi lifted the cover from the bride's legs, but before she could touch the left knee and prove to herself that no fragments of stone were hidden beneath the skin, her father pulled her back and replaced the cover. How could he mistake the woman in the coffin for her mother? Didn't he see? What if her mother had only pretended to die to get out of the asylum and—by some elaborate scheme—had substituted the body of a black-haired bride already dead? Then, surely, she'd let Trudi know soon. All she had to do was wait and check for her mother in the gap below the house, and there she'd be—the scent of strawberry bugs on her fingers, singing *"Panis Angelicus"* or *"Agnus Dei."*

Early the next morning, before Herr Abramowitz left for his law office in Düsseldorf, Leo Montag asked him to bring his camera to the cemetery chapel, and the following day Frau Simon fastened a new black hat with a rubber band below Trudi's chin, while Herr Blau fussed with the buttons of Trudi's black coat, which he'd cut down to size from a jacket that his son, Stefan, had outgrown a quarter of a century ago.

Wreaths and bouquets of roses and lilies covered the earth around the oblong hole into which the coffin was lowered. Some of the war widows had brought their watering cans to sprinkle the flowers and keep them from wilting. Five nuns from the Theresienheim stood motionless, their heads bent while their fingers traveled the strands of their rosaries. From the maple trees, double-winged seeds the color of bones spun sluggishly in the sweltering air.

As the people of Burgdorf stepped forward—one by one, the women with hats or black scarves knotted beneath their chins, the men in black suits and hats—to drop handfuls of dirt into the grave, they kept glancing toward Trudi, prepared to comfort her if she cried, and when she didn't, they were baffled but told her that she was a brave little girl. They didn't know that the roots of her hair hurt, and that each breath clogged her chest.

Leo Montag stood rigid as if carved into the landscape. Next to him stood one of his comrades from the war, Judge Spiecker. Though the judge was only Leo's age, his body gave off an old smell that came from somewhere deep inside and traveled on his breath and sweat although he kept himself fanatically clean.

Swallows and pigeons swayed in the trees and hedges, and the scent of violets from Frau Simon's perfume muted the smell of the flowers. When Herr Pastor Schüler bent and reached beneath the cuffs of his trousers to scratch himself, Trudi noticed that the skin on his legs was taut and shiny as though the hairs had all been scratched away. Specks of white powder drifted from under his cassock to settle on the polished black tops of his shoes.

Trudi wondered where the grave with the hand was. Somewhere in the Catholic section of the cemetery, so she'd heard from several people, was the grave of a woman who'd hit her parents when she was a girl. As punishment and as a warning to other children—"Never ever raise your hand toward your parents,"—her hand had grown from her grave seventy years later when she'd died. Though Trudi had never found the grave, she was sure it was there, the hand curled between the shrubs like a blossom, ready to spread into a claw that would seize you if you came close.

A trick wind lifted the hem of Frau Doktor Rosen's skirt and shifted through the bouquets and wreaths so that—for an instant—they seemed to be sliding toward the hole. Eva Rosen and her two older brothers stood next to their mother, but Herr Rosen hadn't come with them. He was from a rich old family and seldom left his house. On days when the sun was out—even in winter—Trudi would see him resting on the canvas lounge chair on his veranda, a soft man with receding hair and pink skin, his body covered with a plaid blanket.

Some said he was quite ill; others insisted there was nothing wrong with him; yet, they all speculated why Frau Doktor Rosen wasn't able to cure her husband.

As the pastor sprinkled holy water into the grave, Trudi hooked one finger into the rubber band beneath her chin and let it snap, again and again, until all she felt was that sting.

"Don't hurt yourself," the taxidermist said and enveloped Trudi's hand with his warm fingers.

At the house, as if to make up for Leo Montag's silence, Frau Blau thanked the judge for coming. "We are honored," she said. It was her way of acknowledging that the judge was of a better class than most of the guests. She cut pieces of *Streuselkuchen* for Frau Doktor Rosen and her children, but she reminded Trudi, "Wash your hands before you eat." When she spit on her ironed handkerchief to clean Trudi's face, the girl squirmed away.

The tables were covered with an even larger display of delicacies than on the day of her brother's funeral, and Trudi took whatever she wanted: three stalks of juicy white asparagus, blood sausage, plum cake, a *Brötchen,* tomato salad, and two kinds of herring salad—one pink because of added beets. New amber fly strips hung curled above the tables, but already quite a few flies stuck to them. Trudi counted eleven. Two were still twirling their legs. At her brother's funeral feast, it had been too cold for flies.

All the guests wanted to talk to her or stroke her hair, and she felt more important than she ever had before. She even received a present—a stuffed white lamb made of real fur—from Alexander Sturm, who owned a toy factory. He had been only fourteen when his father had died as a soldier, and he'd left the *Gymnasium* to run his father's business for himself and his older sister.

Emil Hesping moved through the rooms as if reclaiming lost rights and, like a host, poured Mosel wine for everyone from green bottles he'd brought in a wooden case on the back of his motorcycle.

The taxidermist, Herr Heidenreich, helped Herr Hansen carry two *Schwarzwälder Kirschtorten* from his bakery. Propping his cigar against a plate, the taxidermist cut the first wedge of *Torte* for Trudi. Squatting on his heels, he handed her the plate. His eyes were brown and kind. "You're lucky to have such pretty hair, Trudi," he said.

"Such pretty hair," the baker agreed and stroked Trudi's head with the hand that had two fingers missing from the war.

Although Trudi felt wicked for liking all that attention, she couldn't stop herself from enjoying it. There was an excitement about all this, something new, unknown. And yet, whenever she recalled that closed coffin, she'd feel something cold rush throughout her body. As long as the coffin had been open, she'd been certain her mother was not the woman inside, but once the lid had been shut, it had been harder to stay convinced.

She walked past Herr Immers, but the butcher didn't even see her because he and Herr Braunmeier were busy complaining to each other about something called the Versailles *Friedensvertrag*—a *Schandvertrag*, they called it, a disgrace. Then they went on to protest about refugees who took food out of the mouths of decent people, like the Baum family, who had fled from Schlesien and opened a bicycle shop in Burgdorf.

"Those refugees have no manners, no values." Herr Braunmeier lit his cigarette. Though he was the wealthiest farmer in town, he stole words when he came into the pay-library. He'd buy his tobacco and linger among the back shelves, where the American Westerns were stacked, his eyes racing down the pages of recent arrivals, his haggard body turned toward the exit as if prepared for flight, his shoulder blades jutting out like clipped wings.

"They believe they can just move here and we'll start buying those bicycles like porkchops," Herr Immers said.

Since the town had its own complicated class system—fixed boundaries based on wealth, education, family history, and other intricate considerations—the people united against newcomers. Yet, their prejudices were often tested by their curiosity, and many of them had watched outside the shop's window as the burly Herr Baum arranged his display of four bicycles. Although the bikes already gleamed, he kept polishing them with an oily rag. Beyond the window, in the recesses of the store, stood his wife, frail and silent. On each hip she supported a child. "Twins," someone in the crowd mentioned, though the boy was larger than the girl. Both had runny noses and were almost Trudi's age, far too heavy to still be carried.

Trudi sauntered into the hallway where the coat tree was fat with black summer coats and jackets. She climbed beneath them, but as her fingers parted the layers of fabric, they came up against something that was far more solid—a sleeve that had an arm inside.

"What's that?" A man's voice.

A woman's hushed laugh and rose perfume.

Trudi came out behind the coat tree, where the baker's wife and Herr Buttgereit were kissing. They pulled apart so quickly that she felt an exhilarating sense of power because she was sure she'd seen something that they didn't want anyone to know.

Herr Buttgereit blinked at her. "You shouldn't sneak around like that, little girl."

"Don't get her all upset now," Frau Hansen said. "We were looking for my glasses, Trudi. Did you see my glasses?"

Trudi shook her head and backed away from them. By the kitchen door she stopped. The women were whispering about her mother: they agreed with one another that there had always been a little too much of everything about Gertrud Montag—not just that she laughed and cried too easily, but also that generosity. Frau Simon used the word "poise" for Trudi's mother. An exuberant woman with beautiful ankles, Frau Simon had red hair that she piled into restless curls on top of her head. If anyone knew about poise, it was Frau Simon—after all, she talked about it constantly and made the most elegant hats in the region. Even women from Oberkassel and Krefeld came to her shop, which was on the first floor of the apartment house on Barbarossa Strasse that she'd bought with her own profits. People gossiped about her because she was divorced and liked to argue like a man, but they agreed that she had a natural eye for fashion and that— even though everyone knew Jews could talk you into buying anything—she refused to sell you a hat if it didn't look right on you.

Trudi could tell that the women treated Frau Simon differently: they envied her outspokenness; they tried to get her to flatter them; but they kept her outside their circle. They were like that with Frau Doktor Rosen too, bringing her their respect and illnesses that the nuns could not cure in the Theresienheim, but not their friendship.

"Gertrud Montag always had poise," Frau Simon said.

Frau Buttgereit wondered aloud why, then, Gertrud had agreed to marry Leo Montag. Varicose veins bulged through her support stockings, and her belly was so big that she stood cradling it with her linked hands.

"It's his eyes." Frau Blau sighed and took a long drag from her cigarette. "Leo Montag looks at you with those exquisite eyes of his, and you follow him anywhere."

Frau Simon laughed. "At your age?"

"Any age."

"Leo is a saint for taking care of Gertrud those last five years," Frau Weiler declared. "A saint, and don't—"

"I know a joke about a saint," Trudi announced.

The women's faces spun toward her.

"A joke." Frau Weiler looked flustered. "This is not a proper occasion for telling jokes." Her black scarf was still knotted around her frizzy hair that was parted in the center. No one in town could remember having seen all of her head uncovered because she always wore scarves that exposed only the front of her hair.

"I'd like to hear the joke, *Kindchen*." Frau Abramowitz knelt next to Trudi and kissed her forehead. The collar of her black jacket was made of foxes—little claws and heads that came together in two pointed fox snouts between her breasts.

Trudi threw both arms around her neck and squeezed hard. The fox fur tickled her chin. She wished she could call Frau Abramowitz by her first name—Ilse, which was so much prettier than Abramowitz—but children had to call grown-ups by their last names and address them with *Sie*—the formal you. Only children were called by their first names and addressed with *Du*—the familiar you—by everyone. That was one good thing about being a child. Many grown-ups called each other by their last names all their lives, and if they agreed to switch to first names, they first had to link elbows while drinking beer or *Schnaps* to manifest the *Du*.

"Go ahead, Trudi," Frau Abramowitz said. "You tell us your joke."

"It's about St. Petrus." Trudi tried to remember the right sequence of the joke she'd overheard Emil Hesping tell her father last month when he'd come into the pay-library with the news that he'd been promoted to manage a second gymnasts' club in Düsseldorf. It was larger than the one in Burgdorf and belonged to the same owner who'd talked with Emil about having him open other clubs as far away as Köln and Hamburg.

"The joke starts with the Virgin Maria," Trudi said. "She wants to go to earth for three weeks. St. Petrus makes her promise to write every week. . . . The first week she writes that she saw three churches and two museums. She signs her letter 'Virgin Maria . . .' "

Frau Doktor Rosen, who'd just walked into the kitchen, raised one elegant eyebrow. Eva was holding on to her mother's belt, her dark eyes watchful. Trudi had seen her many times before—she looked like her mother, with those long wrists and black curls—but she'd never talked with her or stood this close to her. If she could have any wish right now, she'd want to be tall like Eva.

Trudi looked right at Eva. "The second letter," she told her, "says, 'Dear St. Petrus, I took a trip on a train and rode on a ferry boat.' She signs the letter again with 'Virgin Maria.' But the third letter—" She paused, hoping she'd get the joke just right so that Eva would laugh as her father and Emil Hesping had laughed. That's how she'd known it was a good joke, even though she hadn't understood what was so funny.

"The third letter says, 'Dear Petrus, I went to a tavern and danced with a sailor.' It's signed 'Maria.' " She waited for the laughter, but the only sound was an abrupt cough from Frau Weiler. It was quiet in the kitchen. Too quiet. Had she forgotten part of the joke? No—something was wrong. She had done something bad. It was hot in the house, hot and blue with tobacco smoke even though the windows were open.

Frau Immers chased a fly from the fruit compote. "I better check on that potato salad."

"Let me help you," Frau Blau offered.

"Herr Hesping—" one of the women said.

They all glanced toward the door, where Emil Hesping stood in a new suit, the kind of new that hasn't been worn before. The front creases of his black trousers were pressed knife sharp, and his pearl cufflinks shimmered. He looked like a groom at his own wedding—except that everyone knew he was the kind of man who made jokes about others getting married and sinned against the sixth commandment even though his brother was a bishop.

He lifted Trudi up. Though he kept his lips in a smile, she could tell he had cried because his eyes were red. "Let me tell you a joke that's proper for a little girl to tell. You too, Eva." He took Eva's hand. "You see, there's this teacher who has a dog, Schatzi, and he doesn't allow her to sleep on the sofa, but every day when he leaves for school, Schatzi jumps on the sofa and sleeps there all day. When the teacher comes home, she's lying on the floor, but he knows. Guess how?"

Most of the women were busying themselves with lighting fresh cigarettes or pushing pots around on the flat surface of the stove; yet, they kept their movements slow and soundless so as not to miss a word.

"I don't know how." Eva Rosen looked at Trudi and made a face by wrinkling her nose. When Trudi grinned and wrinkled her nose too, Eva laughed.

"Ah—but the teacher knows," Emil Hesping said, "because the sofa is still warm. And so he scolds Schatzi—teachers are very good at scolding, you'll find that out once you start school. The next day, when he comes home, the sofa is warm again. He spanks the dog, and the following evening, when he checks the sofa, it is not warm. He figures he has finally trained Schatzi. But one day he arrives home just a few minutes earlier than usual, and guess what he sees? There's Schatzi, standing on the sofa—" He pursed his mouth and made short puffs of breath that tickled Trudi's chin. "There's Schatzi, blowing air on the sofa to cool it down."

A few of the women laughed politely. Trudi thought it was a boring joke. She could tell it bored Emil Hesping too because he winked at her. It was their secret that he liked the Virgin Maria joke much better. But then he winked at Frau Simon too, and something odd happened: Frau Simon's neck grew longer, and her face turned as red as her hair.

When Eva slipped away, Trudi followed her. They wandered through the rooms where smoke shifted in hazy layers below the ceilings. People stopped talking as the girls came close to them; they stared at Trudi, told her again how brave she was. Her father leaned against the side of the piano, his face still, his eyes empty. Trudi remembered what Frau Blau had said about his eyes—exquisite—but they were ordinary, gray with blue specks, and they didn't see her, not even when she climbed on the piano stool. When she hit the first piano key, it sounded louder than ever before.

Herr Hesping walked up to her father with two shot glasses and a bottle of *Schnaps*. He filled both glasses, handed one to her father, and clicked his glass against her father's. They nodded to one another, their expressions grim, and—at the exact same moment—tossed the clear liquid down their throats.

Trudi's father shuddered as if awakening from a long dream.

"There, now," Emil Hesping said and clasped his shoulder. "There."

They stood in their half embrace like dancers, waiting, their trim gymnasts' bodies shrouded by their mourning suits, until Leo Montag held out his glass again.

Trudi struck all the raised black keys, then the white ones. Alexander Sturm stepped next to Eva and bent to listen when she said something to him. It was said that, when he'd taken over his father's toy factory, Alexander had changed from a boy into a man overnight: his voice had turned deep, and his mustache had filled out, causing some jealousy among other boys whose sparse mustache hairs looked like accidental smudges.

Spreading her arms as far as she could, Trudi drew her forefingers from opposite ends of the keyboard toward the middle, drowning the voices around her in an exhilarating crescendo that made her forget everything until Frau Abramowitz lifted her from the wooden stool and carried her to her house across the street. "It's important never to lose your dignity," Frau Abramowitz told her.

High in the air like that, Trudi managed to graze her hand across the narrow box that hung at the right post of the Abramowitzs' front door, just as she'd seen Herr Abramowitz do it. Carved into the wooden box were tiny flowers and symbols. From her father she knew that the box was called a *mezuzah* and that, inside, was a scroll with a prayer, called the *shema*. "It means God protects the house," he had said.

Frau Abramowitz opened the arched door and let Trudi down on the Persian carpet that covered the parquet floor in her entrance hall. The shutters of the living room stood open but the damask drapes were too heavy to sway in the breeze. Trudi could see the snapdragons and purple geraniums in the window boxes. Frau Abramowitz even kept a vegetable garden, though she could afford to buy whatever she wanted, and she was always giving red cabbage or beans or kohlrabi to the neighbors.

She had a piano too, a white baby grand. The lid was closed, and on top of it stood two silver candlesticks and rows of small silver frames with pictures of her children at various ages. On the piano bench lay a doctor-and-nurse novel, the most recent book Frau Abramowitz had borrowed from the pay-library against the trade of her Venetian mirror. From her locked glass cabinet, she brought out an album with her husband's photos of elephants and palaces. Trudi was allowed to turn the pages, and as Frau Abramowitz told her about all the exotic travels, her voice went so soft that Trudi had to stop swallowing in order to hear her.

When Trudi got sleepy, Frau Abramowitz spread a shawl over her and rocked her in her arms, feeling much closer to this girl with the short, thick body than to the children who had come from her own womb. Capable and self-sufficient and quick to debate any issue— "That's how we learn to think, by questioning," their father had told them—Ruth and Albert had acted embarrassed early on by their mother's affection. Though her body still screamed to embrace them, they had forgotten how much they'd loved to feel her arms around them when they were small. They had chosen to go to boarding schools in Bonn and Köln, and when they visited, they were more at ease with their father, who was preoccupied with his law office and radical politics. He considered himself a Communist and had joined the Independent Social Democrats. When he made his children sit still for yet another family photo to document the sequence of their development, they didn't object as they would to their mother's kisses, because they felt comfortable with his distance behind the camera.

Through half-closed lids Trudi watched the early-afternoon light flit across the roses in the crystal vase and Herr Abramowitz's pipe rack; it made the honey-colored wood on the lower halves of the walls gleam, and revealed the tiny creases in the dear face above her; it carried the shrill cry of a rooster and the voices of departing guests across the street.

Frau Abramowitz kept holding Trudi long after she had fallen asleep. She promised herself to teach Trudi proper manners now that the girl no longer had a mother. There wasn't even a grandmother in the house. It was too much to handle for a man alone. Not that Leo Montag wouldn't be the most tender of fathers. . . . Or husband, she thought. Or husband. And her face grew hot.

The week after the funeral it was Trudi's fourth birthday, and her father took her on the streetcar to Oberkassel, where, next to the Rhein bridge that led to Düsseldorf, fireworks drenched the sky and the river in every possible color. Music from trumpets and drums played fast and loud. Like thousands of others, Trudi's father spread a blanket on the grass. When the air grew cool, he took off his woolen vest and slipped it over Trudi's head so that it hung from her shoulders, longer than her dress, drowning her in the wonderful scent of tobacco and books as he lifted her toward the sky, toward those red and green and yellow showers of stars that shot up and spilled high above—miraculously without dropping on her—and even though her father had told her the fireworks were in celebration of the new Opernhaus, Trudi felt certain that all these people were celebrating her birthday with her, and she felt a slow sadness settling on her because no birthday could possibly be quite like this again.

The following day her father covered the walls of his bedroom with the photos of the stranger from the coffin. Someone had stuck the long stem of a lily beneath the bride's crossed wrists, and the white blossom lay against the curve of her chin. The flames of the three candles were milky—even whiter than the bride's face. Trudi began to pray for her mother's return. She didn't have to pray for it as something separate from her other prayers because it was all connected to the size of her own body. Once that stretched itself, her mother would be well again. She was only staying away until then—so that no one would confine her to the Grafenberg asylum again. One day, Trudi knew, she would hear her mother's familiar steps in the sewing room. She'd run up the stairs. The door would swing open, and her mother would stand by the window. She'd turn and look at her. "Well . . . Trudi, how tall you are," she would say.

But until then, Trudi had to pass through each new day without her mother, had to fight the habit that made her want to run upstairs the moment she woke up. Not being able to reach her mother—it filled her with a bottomless panic that prayers couldn't soothe, a panic that made her climb into her mother's wardrobe simply to stop the yearning. Standing motionless among the hangers, she'd feel the silky fabric of the dresses against her face, smell the clear scent of the Rhein meadows in early summer, and feel suffused with joyful certainty that her mother would soon be back. When she'd leave the wardrobe, she'd smile at the pictures of the dead bride, who was the only one to share her secret that her mother was still alive.

"Well . . . Trudi, how tall you are."

There had to be some kind of pill to make people grow faster. Frau Doktor Rosen would know. One morning, Trudi slipped from the house while her father was busy with a customer, crossed Schreberstrasse, and cut through the church square to the doctor's stone house. Unlike most buildings in Burgdorf, the house—which had been a cloister five hundred years ago—stood not close to neighboring buildings but lay surrounded by a sheltered garden and a low brick wall with a wrought-iron gate. On the second-floor veranda, the doctor's husband rested in his canvas chair, his round face tipped toward the sky. Orange flowers, shaped like Chinese paper lanterns, grew next to the front steps.

The door was locked, but when Trudi pressed the recessed doorbell and kept knocking, Frau Doktor Rosen opened it.

"I want a pill so I can grow."

The doctor's hand drifted to the ornate silver pin that fastened the collar of her white jacket. "I see. Does your father know you're here?"

Trudi shook her head.

"Why don't you come inside."

Trudi followed the doctor through the living room into her long office that faced the back of the garden where the goldfish pond and chicken coop were. Shelves with papers and cloudy bottles covered the walls all the way to the high ceiling.

"Sit over here." The doctor pointed toward a leather chair and walked around her desk, where she sat down and busied herself rolling a cigarette, her elegant fingers so clumsy at getting the tobacco shreds inside the thin paper, that Trudi could have done it much faster. From watching her father, she'd learned how to. Sometimes he let her roll a whole box of cigarettes for customers who liked to buy theirs ready to smoke.

"You see," the doctor started, "there is no pill for growing. . . ."

Eight pencils lay on her desk, and Trudi kept counting those pencils, over and over again, while the doctor's gentle voice explained about people who were *Zwerge*—dwarfs—and said Trudi was one of them. Trudi kept counting inside her head—*eins, zwei, drei, vier, fünf, sechs, sieben, acht. Eins, zwei, drei*—She laughed and shook her head. Dwarfs belonged in fairy tales, along with dragons and elves and enchanted forests. She knew the story of *Schneewittchen*. She even had a puzzle of the seven *Zwerge* who had rescued *Schneewittchen* from the evil witch—*eins, zwei, drei, vier, fünf, sechs, sieben.* Seven dwarfs. But eight pencils. *Eins, zwei, drei, vier*—She knew she didn't look like *Schneewittchen's* dwarfs. *Zwerge* were men, squat, little men with big bellies and funny, peaked hats like egg warmers.

"There is no girl *Zwerg* in *Schneewittchen und die sieben Zwerge*," she reminded Frau Doktor Rosen.

The doctor lit her cigarette and said that was quite true. She looked so sad that Trudi wanted to reassure her that whatever it was that had stopped growing inside her was just resting and would soon begin again, that it was just a matter of finding what would trigger it. But she didn't know how to say those words aloud to the Frau Doktor because the numbers of the pencils and the numbers of the *Zwerge* kept getting mixed up inside her head, and she knew if she said anything, it would be a jumble of numbers.

———————————■————————————

1 9 1 9 – 1 9 2 0

SHE DECIDED TO STRETCH HERSELF BY LOOPING HER LEGS OVER THE
iron carpet rod out back, where Frau Blau beat the dust out of her
rugs every Friday; but hanging upside down made her head so hot
and heavy that she had to stop. Instead, she dragged the kitchen table
into the open door frame to the living room, climbed up, and hung by
her fingers from the molding till her arms and shoulders ached. Gradually she was able to endure it for longer spells. Some nights she had
dreams in which she grew, and she'd feel an acute happiness in those
dreams that would evaporate within moments after waking to her un-
changed body.

One afternoon, when she was hanging from the door frame, her father walked from the pay-library into the kitchen to make himself a
cup of Russian tea. He didn't notice her until he'd poured a bit of the
strong essence that he brewed each morning, and had diluted it with
hot water to suit his taste. The cup in his hands, he turned to leave.

That's when he saw her. "What are you doing?" He set his cup on
the floor.

"Growing."

That sudden look of pain—like when his knee would buckle under him—settled around his mouth. "You don't need to do this." His voice sounded hoarse, and she suddenly knew the Frau Doktor had told him about her visit.

"I'll stop once I'm tall."

"Not everyone needs to be tall."

"I do."

He opened his lips as if to tell her to get back on the floor, but instead he stood watching her and stroked his face. "Be careful, Trudi."

She sensed that his warning didn't have anything to do with the kind of careful that keeps you from getting injured, but that it implied a far deeper danger. "I won't fall. See?" She swung her legs. "See what I can do?"

He caught her by the waist, lifted her down.

"No." She squirmed from his arms and stomped one foot on the floor. "No."

"Come," he said. "I need your help outside." He asked her to carry his teacup into the backyard, where he raked the dry dirt. As his long arms drew the rake toward his body, he kept stepping backward toward the grassy area that ran all the way down to the brook. His hair had been cropped at the barbershop the day before, and the tight, pale curls clung to his scalp like the fur of Trudi's toy lamb.

"It's not the falling," he said. "We all have to do some of that."

Her eyes followed the bamboo teeth of the rake as they caught clumps of debris and left fine, even ridges of earth.

"You are perfect the way you are," he said as if to convince himself.

She swallowed, hard, and clenched her fingers around her father's cup. He had never lied to her before.

From that day on, she made sure to hang from the door frame of her upstairs bedroom and to get down whenever she heard her father's steps. Already, her arms were getting stronger, and she took pride in carrying heavier stacks of books from the counter to the shelves when she helped her father arrange them back into place. Soon her legs would be long enough to pedal her own bicycle when she rode with her father to the cemetery or the river, instead of sitting between his outstretched arms on the leather seat—shaped exactly like his seat, only smaller—that he'd bolted to the front of his bicycle.

She liked to help him dry the dishes after he'd washed them in the two metal tubs: one filled with hot water that he'd heated on the kitchen stove, the other with cold water for rinsing off the soap. Afterwards he'd settle her on his knees and read to her from the special books that he didn't lend out to customers, books by Stefan Zweig and Heinrich Mann and Arthur Schnitzler, which he kept in the living room on shelves with glass fronts. Even if Trudi didn't understand much of what her father read to her, she listened closely and turned the pages for him.

Some of those books were bound in leather and felt precious to the touch. It bothered Trudi when her father took them into the bathroom. He'd always stay too long, smoking and reading, and if she had to use the toilet after he'd get out, she'd hold her pee because the air in there would be hazy with the stench of cigarettes and shit.

Every evening she tried to stay up as late as her father would let her, coaxing him into reading her another story after he told her it was time for bed, or climbing on his knees to snatch the comb he carried in his shirt pocket and press it into his fingers so he'd comb her hair. She was afraid of the empty sewing room on the floor above her bedroom because, with each night, it grew larger, its emptiness threatening to absorb the entire house. Only her mother's presence could have stopped that emptiness from expanding. Even as an old woman Trudi would be haunted by images of herself as a small girl returning to that door behind which her mother used to be confined, receiving no answer when she knocked. She'd see her father pull her away, gently, trying to console her with reasons that he didn't seem to believe himself: "Your mother has found a more peaceful place." And she'd see herself lift the Abramowitzs' mirror from its hook in the sewing room and carry it into the living room on the day she would finally understand that she would not see her mother again.

But when she was four, Trudi hadn't arrived at that recognition— not even when her father and Herr Hesping, who stopped by nearly every day for tobacco on his way to the gymnasts' club in Düsseldorf, carried the velvet sofa down two flights of stairs and positioned it by the back window in the living room; not even when Frau Blau helped her father empty her mother's wardrobe and gave everything to the church for the poor, except two silk scarves and one pair of suede gloves, which Trudi managed to hide beneath her skirt; not even when, after mass, she found a carved cross on her mother's grave that seemed to have grown from the rich earth since the previous Sunday.

Her father was looking at the cross, his eyes like the bottom of the brook that ran behind their house. The cross had a slender roof above Christ's crown of thorns, and beneath his feet were two panels with raised letters: one panel displayed her mother's name and two dates—her year of birth, 1885, and the year of the funeral, 1919—the other was for her brother, his death the same date as his birth. Her brother's name was Horst, and until she saw the cross, Trudi hadn't even known that her parents had named him.

She hoped her father had managed to christen her brother before he'd died. If not, her brother was a pagan baby. Next to the holy water basin in church stood a collection box where you could leave money for pagan babies. Painted on the front of the box was a picture of Jesus with children sitting on his lap. Trudi worried how the money could get to the babies if they were already in limbo.

Pagan babies, she knew, could live right in your town or in Africa or in China. As long as they weren't christened, the priest said, they were pagan babies. Protestant babies were pagan babies, even though their skin was white. Jewish babies were like Protestant babies, except that Jews prayed in a synagogue and didn't believe in Jesus. Protestants believed in Jesus but they didn't believe the right things. Ever since her brother's funeral, it seemed, she'd heard about other babies who'd died. Nearly every family had a dead baby. The Buttgereits had three dead babies. They were in heaven with the Baby Jesus now.

Only Catholics could go to heaven, Frau Buttgereit had told Trudi. But not if they had sinned. Sins took you into purgatory, which was half way between heaven and hell. Heaven was where angels in white gowns floated around the Baby Jesus, and hell was where Lucifer tortured pagans and Catholics who had died without confessing their mortal sins. Lucifer used to be an angel before he fell from the sky and became the devil. Purgatory was hot, but not as hot as hell. You had to stay in purgatory until you had suffered for your sins or until people on earth—Catholic people, that is—had prayed enough for your soul to release you from purgatory. Like Frau Weiler, who prayed eight Hail Marys every night to get her mother released from purgatory. In twelve more years her mother, who had died as a very old woman, would rise to heaven. Her stepfather, Frau Weiler said, was in hell anyhow—no reason to waste good prayers on him.

• • •

Two months after Gertrud Montag's funeral, Leo's sister, Helene, arrived from America with her son, Robert, who was Trudi's age. They had taken an ocean liner from New York to Bremen, and the afternoon they reached Burgdorf by train it was raining so hard that—with their drenched clothes and hair—they looked exactly as Trudi had imagined travelers who'd crossed vast bodies of water.

Though Robert was far taller and heavier than she, his features looked so much like hers that—within minutes of his arrival—she dragged him in front of her mother's mirror and made him sit on his heels so that his shoulders were at the same level with hers. Somberly, both children stared at their reflections: the solid Montag chins and foreheads, the silver-blond hair—though his was plastered to his temples—and for a moment Trudi actually believed that they were the same height. But then Robert straightened his body, and the buttons of his jacket appeared in the mirror.

Trudi stepped back. "Most of my growing is supposed to happen next winter," she announced, and when Robert nodded as if not one bit surprised, she added, "It's supposed to start the week after Christmas."

Robert had brought her gifts from America: a red wooden fish on wheels, a silver egg cup, china dishes for her dolls. He spoke English as well as German and taught her how to count to ten in English, while she taught him the words to her favorite song, *"Alle Vögel sind schon da. . . ."*—"All the birds are already here. . . ." He was quick to find any song on the piano, and she'd watch, mesmerized, as his round fingers bounced across the black and white keys, linking notes into melodies. In America, he told her, he had a piano teacher who came to his apartment every Tuesday and Friday.

"I want to have lessons too," Trudi informed her father.

"Maybe once I can afford them."

Where Robert was thoughtful and accommodating, Trudi was bold and quickly established herself as the leader. He followed her everywhere—beneath the house, where they caught strawberry bugs and played with the boxes in which the books were delivered; to the fairgrounds and the bakery; to the taxidermist's shop, where Herr Heidenreich was so glad to see them that he gave them each a glass eye and let them stroke the glossy fur of the cocker spaniel he was stuffing; to the post office, where they waited in line by the sliding window to buy stamps for the letters Robert's mother sent to America.

At forty, Helene Blau still blushed easily and walked with the awkward movements of the young girl who had grown too quickly and had never become accustomed to her height and the wide span of her shoulders; yet, oddly, it was just that awkwardness which now made her seem younger than other women her age. She was as brilliant and inquisitive as she had been as a girl, and since her brother, Leo, was one of the few people she didn't feel shy with, she sat with him in the library or the brown living room—which felt dark even in daylight—and the two of them talked for hours about their children and about those paths in their lives which they had to walk alone.

Leo was able to ask her the question that had tortured him ever since his wife's death—if Gertrud would have been happier living in the city, where she had been born.

"She would have told you," Helene said.

"Maybe I should have taken her back to the city anyhow."

"You were good for her."

"You think so?"

His sister nodded. "Gertrud was—unusual." She saw the tightening in his shoulders and continued gently, "I loved that in her—even when both of you were still children."

She persuaded him to take down the photos of his dead wife, and—for the duration of her visit—he placed them between the pages of the wildflower book that he kept by his bed. When she found him a washwoman, who came to the house one day a week and boiled laundry in the cellar, Trudi and Robert watched while the woman built a fire beneath the huge kettle, which was set into bricks, and stirred the soapy liquid with a wooden paddle.

Helene urged Leo to rejoin the chess club he'd belonged to ever since he'd been a boy but hadn't returned to since Gertrud's illness. The second Monday evening of her visit he dressed in his good suit and left for the Stosicks' house where, for four generations, the chess players of Burgdorf had met and collected hundreds of chess books that contained all the great moves of history. Though Leo was still one of the strongest players in town, the game didn't give him the same thrill of competition as gymnastics once had: in chess he was competing against himself, rather than an opponent.

The men would take the chess sets from the birch wardrobe, sit down at the long tables, and play, their silence punctuated only by

punched chess clocks and the clipped warning: *"Schach"*—"Check."
The white tablecloths would ripple, stirred by the rhythm of restless
knees. Gradually, as it got warmer in the room, they'd take off their
jackets and sit there in their suspenders.

Elated at having another child in the house, Trudi couldn't wait to get
up in the mornings. She showed Robert how to tie handkerchief diapers on the white toy lamb that Alexander Sturm had given her, and
they took turns nursing it by pressing its fleecy nose against their nipples. Down by the brook, they balanced on a plank across the water.
They picked the last daisies of summer and took them to the cemetery, where they set them into the pointed vase on the Montags' family grave. When they searched for the grave with the hand of the
woman sticking out, they couldn't find it, and Trudi led Robert instead to the other grave that intrigued her, that of Herr Höffenauer,
who'd been struck by lightning at his mother's gravesite.

It had happened long before Trudi was born, and she told Robert
the story she'd heard—along with a few embellishments that came to
her as she went along. This teacher, Herr Höffenauer, had lived with
his widowed mother long past the age when other men leave their
mothers' houses to start families of their own. He had taken care of
her until he was old enough to have grandchildren, and after she'd
died, he'd visited her grave each day after teaching school—standing
right where she and Robert stood that very moment—until, one
stormy afternoon, he'd been felled by lightning while peeling a fleck
of moss from the face of his mother's gravestone.

She took Robert to meet Frau Abramowitz, who served them pra-
lines and rosehip tea. While Frau Abramowitz practiced her English
with Robert, Trudi played with the silver spice box that used to belong
to Herr Abramowitz's grandmother, who'd been born in this house.
She could smell the aromatic spices inside the box, which was shaped
like a tower with filigreed balconies and a tiny silver banner on top.
When they looked at pictures of pyramids in the travel brochures that
lay on the table, Trudi pretended to herself that Frau Abramowitz
would take her along on her next trip. People on the train would think
she was her mother. All the children she knew had mothers. Lots of
children didn't have fathers, but that was because of the war.

"Let me see your handkerchief," Frau Abramowitz insisted when

Trudi and Robert were about to leave. She had embroidered ten hand-kerchiefs for Trudi, and she liked to make sure she always carried one folded inside her pocket. Clean handkerchiefs were part of good manners—Trudi knew that because Frau Abramowitz had informed her the week after her mother's funeral that she would teach her good manners from now on. "Children learn good manners from women," she'd said.

Good manners meant not poking your finger into your nose and not interrupting grown-ups when they talked. Good manners meant offer-ing your seat on the streetcar to grown-ups, bending to pick up things that grown-ups dropped, and opening doors for grown-ups. Already, Trudi had figured out that good manners could keep you real busy.

Good manners had a lot to do with grown-ups and with what chil-dren did or did not do around them. She'd been told all along by grown-ups that it wasn't polite to stare at them, but how could you see people if you didn't look at them? And about honesty . . . Grown-ups were always saying you had to be honest, but that only meant you could say good things about them and bad things about yourself. If you said bad things about them, you were rude, and if you said good things about yourself, you were bragging. She couldn't wait to be a grown-up because grown-ups were always right—except for grown-ups who were maids or cooks or servants: they had to be obedient like children.

"Come back soon," Frau Abramowitz called after them as they ran down her front steps.

In front of St. Martin's Church, Herr Neumaier, the pharmacist, was honoring the death of Christ as he did every Friday afternoon between three and four. Over the years, quite a few members of the congregation had complained to Herr Pastor Schüler that the phar-macist's ritual was excessive—a spectacle, they called it—and it had become a game for the children of Burgdorf to follow the thin-lipped pharmacist, whose fleshy cheeks grew even more distended as he staggered around the church square, cradling a bulky Jesus statue which he'd pried off a cross that had come from a demolished church in France.

"He lives all alone with that statue," Trudi told Robert as they trailed the pharmacist, who was chanting verses from the Bible. A tu-nic sewn from a potato sack flapped around his suit. "The statue sleeps on a cot. He covers it like a baby . . . up to the neck with a feather quilt."

"How do you know?"

"I saw it—once. . . . When my father was buying cough medicine. I sneaked into the storage room. You want me to take you there?"

"No," Robert said quickly, "no," his eyes on the statue which bobbed up and down in the pharmacist's trembling arms. Its skin was the color of vanilla pudding, while the crown of thorns and streaks of dried blood were the brown of beef liver.

"He doesn't speak to anyone in his family."

Robert looked down into Trudi's wide face, tilted toward him, the blue eyes filled with excitement as she waited for him to ask, *Why not?* "Why not?" he asked.

"Because . . ." she whispered, "his daughter, see, she married a Protestant. . . . They live on the same block with him. But he won't say a word to them. Not even to his grandchildren. Or to his wife. She moved in with the daughter."

"Is that why he goes around with the statue?"

Trudi didn't know the answer to his question, and Robert asked it again that evening when—as every evening since his arrival—they all went next door to the Blaus for dinner with his grandparents and his Aunt Margret.

"The pharmacist is a crazy man," his grandmother said.

His grandfather hushed her by saying, "Be careful what you say aloud. You wouldn't want him to hear." His teeth made a funny clicking sound.

His grandmother shook her head and ladled too many Brussels sprouts on Trudi's plate. "I'm not afraid to tell him right to his face."

"What Herr Neumaier does is like praying the rosary," Leo Montag told the boy. "Only more so. Some people think if you do a certain ritual—especially to do with suffering—your sins are forgiven."

Frau Blau leaned over and planted a kiss on top of Robert's head. Only a few months earlier Trudi had been glad that Frau Blau was not her grandmother, but she now felt so jealous that she pinched Robert's arm. Instantly, Frau Blau took her by the shoulders and marched her into the living room, where she set up a *Katzentisch*— cat table—a small separate table where children who misbehaved had to eat alone.

But on the way home, Robert played hide-and-seek with her in the dusk, and they found a bee squirming in a spider's web behind the Blaus' house. While Trudi sent Robert to fetch his grandfather's sewing scissors, she stood watch over the spider, which darted from a crevice in the wall and disappeared without touching the bee. When Robert returned with the scissors, he cautiously cut the bee free without destroying the net.

Saturday, while her father stoked the tall cylinder-shaped stove in the bathroom for the weekly bath, Trudi took her aunt into her room and showed her the funeral coat that had been made from Stefan's jacket.

Helene ran one finger down the sleeve and said she'd tell Stefan because he'd be glad to know. "Someday you'll have to visit us."

"When?"

"Any time your father wants to bring you. . . . You know what you can do before that? Talk to your uncle on the telephone."

"In America?"

Her aunt nodded. "Frau Abramowitz said she'd let me use her phone."

The Abramowitzs were one of the few families in Burgdorf who owned a phone. It had to do with being upper class. Usually the people who had phones also had maids and hired seamstresses who came to their houses several days each month to sew new clothes or make alterations. Employers competed with one another in feeding those seamstresses the most delicious meals—a practice that had little to do with generosity but rather with the expectation that the seamstresses would gossip to their other employers about how well they had been treated.

While some people with phones didn't let their neighbors use them, the Abramowitzs were always glad to take messages for you or invite you into their living room to make calls. Trudi had heard the phone ring when she'd been at their house, and she'd listened to Frau Abramowitz answer it, but she'd never used it herself.

"I don't know how," she told her aunt.

"I'll show you." Her aunt glanced around the room. "This used to be my room when I was a girl. Stefan's sister, Margret, was my best friend, and her bedroom was right across the way. We passed notes to each other from our windows. . . . You want the first bath?"

Trudi nodded.

"Raise your arms." Her aunt lifted the hem of Trudi's dress and pulled it over her head. Her fingers undid the button that fastened Trudi's undershirt to her billowy cotton pants.

In the bathroom, her aunt sat on the edge of the tub and made Trudi stand while she washed her hair and soaped her back with a sponge.

"Robert says in America children call grown-ups by their first names."

Her aunt nodded. "That's what my husband liked best when he first came to America." She smiled. "I rather missed the formality."

"Why?" Trudi sat down in the warm water and swished her legs back and forth.

"Maybe because I was older when I went to America and used to things being a certain way. Stefan was a boy when he immigrated." She asked Trudi to lean back so she could rinse the soap from her scalp. "He didn't come back for me until nearly twenty years later."

"My father says you were his third bride."

Again, her aunt smiled, but this time her smile looked sad. "They died young, his other wives. Stefan needed a mother for his children."

"Maybe they didn't die," Trudi offered.

Her aunt looked at her closely.

"Maybe they only pretended."

"Why would they do that?"

"So no one can lock them up."

Her aunt lifted Trudi from the tub and dried her, carefully. "She is gone—your mother," she said and carried Trudi into her bedroom. "You know that, don't you?"

Trudi didn't answer.

Her aunt combed the tangles from Trudi's hair and braided it for the night. "She really is gone," she said as she bent to kiss her good night.

When Trudi was allowed to speak on the phone to Uncle Stefan in America, his voice was thin and crackled into her ear.

Seized by a sudden longing for this uncle she'd never met, she shouted, "I'm coming to visit you."

"You don't have to yell," Frau Abramowitz whispered to her.

"That's good," her uncle was saying. "I'm glad. Bring your father too."

Aunt Helene and Robert stayed for five weeks, and before they left, Trudi gave Robert her white lamb and an egg-shaped rock she'd found in the brook. For days after their departure, she kept looking for Robert, expecting to hear his quiet laugh. She'd never known what it was like to have a friend. To be alone again felt as though a part of her had vanished along with him. It was different than with grown-ups leaving. You knew they were not like you.

"When can we visit Robert?" she asked her father.

"It's very far," he said. "And too expensive."

"But when?"

"Maybe once you're older. . . ."

She'd lie in her bed and stare through her window at the dark window across the alley. At least Aunt Helene used to have a friend close by when she'd lived here. But now Margret's old room was a storage space for bolts of cloth and dummies and sewing-machine parts. She felt impatient to start school, the place where, she believed, she would have friends like Robert. But school was still more than a year away, and the children in the neighborhood and those who came with their parents to borrow books or buy tobacco, shied away from Trudi as if afraid she'd touch them and make them look like her.

Except for Georg Weiler next door. But only because he was different from other children too. A boy who looked like a girl. Though he and Trudi had always been aware of each other, they didn't become friends until the day he asked her why her head was so big.

To stop the sting of his question, she shot right back at him, "It's smaller than yours."

They sat on the brick steps outside their buildings, she in front of the pay-library, he in front of his parents' grocery store. The low winter sun was in their eyes, and he was playing with his marbles, lining them up along the bottom step.

"It looks bigger," he insisted.

"It's regular size." Her neck began to itch. "It's the rest of me that's small. That's why it looks big. . . . But it isn't."

He had to think about that. His eyes pushed at her. They were the color of fine sand. "I bet you my best marble your head's bigger than mine."

"Let me see the marble."

"Georg. . . ." Frau Weiler stuck her head from the store. Her scarf had slipped back a little, and coils of gray trailed around her face as though she'd been out in the wind. The center part in her hair had been so long in the same place that it had widened, showing the scalp beneath. "Georg!"

Georg flinched.

"Get those marbles off the stairs. You don't want customers tripping over them and breaking their necks and being crippled for the rest of their lives."

Trudi took a deep breath. It was a lot to consider all at once, even though she was used to Frau Weiler's predictions of gloom: if you walked in the woods, you could get a rash from the *Brennesseln*; if you didn't chew your food properly, you'd end up with holes in your stomach before you were twenty; if you forgot to confess a mortal sin, you were sure to end up in hell. . . .

Georg scooped up his marbles.

His mother closed the door, but her voice stayed out there with the children: ". . . and then they'll sue us and we'll lose the store . . . everything I've worked for. . . ."

Georg held a red and yellow glass ball, the size of a cherry, toward the sun. It glinted. "What do I get if you lose?"

"I won't lose."

"Yes, you will."

"Then you can have all my marbles."

The door opened again, and Georg's mother appeared with two cups of steaming cocoa, her eyes as sorrowful as ever. "Don't drink it too fast. You'll burn your tongues."

"*Danke*, Frau Weiler."

"*Danke, Mutter.*"

"And don't you spill any on your clothes." She headed back into the store.

The cocoa was hot and sweet. A rash wind blew leaves across the sidewalk, their dry edges whispering against stone. Trudi caught a leaf from the chestnut tree, and as she tried to uncurl it, it crumbled in her hands. She wished Robert were here instead of Georg. With his mother's last letter, he'd enclosed a picture he'd drawn of himself playing the piano.

"Even your shoes don't look like boys' shoes," she told Georg.

"And you—you're just a girl."

"That's why *I* wear a dress."

He glared at her.

She glared right back. "And long hair," she said.

"Get a string," he ordered.

"What for?"

"To measure our heads."

"You get it."

"My mother won't let me out again." He tilted his head and directed a sudden smile at her. "Please, Trudi?"

She hesitated.

"Please please please, Trudi?"

She knew how to defend herself against his bullying, but not his charm. Dashing into the pay-library, she emerged with an end of string that had been tied around a recent delivery of romances.

"You first," he said.

Her head held high, she walked over to the entrance of the grocery store and climbed on the step above him. Still, her nose didn't even reach his shoulders. A dog barked from the direction of the market place. Wind slipped between her collar and her skin, cold and sudden, and rattled the wooden shutters outside the pay-library.

Bringing the string around her forehead, Georg measured carefully and marked it with a knot; when she wound the string around his head above his ears, it was a finger's width longer.

She laughed aloud when she showed him. "I knew it," she said, feeling that her head was at its perfect size.

"Yours," he said, handing her his marble.

"You're not mad?"

He beamed at her. "I'll win it back."

As he had predicted, Georg won back his glass marble; in addition, Trudi lost five of her clay marbles to him. From then on, they played nearly every day. Georg was lucky when it came to rolling the tiny balls into the hole he'd scooped into the damp soil between the two sets of steps, but he was just as generous in letting Trudi borrow marbles from him if she lost all of hers. To keep playing was far more important to him than winning. He could always win things. Trudi no longer teased him about his hair and his dainty smocks that buttoned in back. She was glad to see him when he stood outside her window and hollered for her to come out and play.

The morning after December 6, they shared sweets that St. Nikolaus had left for them in the shoes they'd set outside their bedroom
doors overnight, and the last week of December they licked fresh
snow from pine cones that looked as though they'd been dipped into
sugar icing. They built a snowman with a carrot nose and coal eyes
that smudged their mittens. Trudi's father gave them an old hat for the
snowman and let them borrow the kitchen broom, which they stuck
into his arm, bristles up.

They wore their boots and mittens to church on Epiphany, when
the priest and altar boys took down the manger that had been set up
on the side altar, Jesus as big as a real baby, Maria and Joseph as tall
as real parents. Both children liked church: the extravagant smell of
incense and the splendid garments of the priest, the stained-glass
windows and the mural of Christ's Last Supper above the altar, but
most of all the choir with its voices that drifted toward heaven. They
even enjoyed the moments of silence, which were far more meaningful than any other kind of silence when they knelt in a pew, half hidden by the blond wood, feeling the pulse of the community around
them.

You could tell a lot about people, they discovered, by the way they
occupied pews, how much space they took and how close they knelt
to the altar. There were those who liked to get to church early to
watch everyone arrive, and others who knelt with their faces buried
in their hands and never looked up. The proud and the humble—all
of them dressed in their best clothes. In church, you could tell quickly
how well people were doing: you'd notice new ailments as well as new
hats; you'd sense new friendships and new animosities.

The men's pews were on the left, the women's on the right. Until
you had your first communion, you could kneel on either side with a
parent. That meant Trudi and Georg could still kneel in the same
pew. The men's side of the church was always emptier than the
women's—not only because some had not returned from the war—
but because many of them spent the hour of mass in Die Traube, the
old tavern with wooden ceilings that had stood for over five centuries.
Die Traube—"this is where I pray," the men would joke—was the
closest bar to St. Martin's and in full view of the church, ideal for
those men who wanted to walk their wives and children to Sunday
mass; meet with their friends for a few quick beers at their
Stammtisch—their regular table; finish their final glass as the doors of

the church opened; and be there to pick up their families and walk home for the Sunday roast.

Of course, there'd always be a few husbands who'd have to order one more glass after the last, whose wives would stand in the church yard with expressions of brittle cheerfulness, pretending they liked nothing better than chatting with the priest after mass. Yet, as soon as their husbands arrived, they'd link their arms through theirs and drag the poor sinners home, hissing words of reproach through their church smiles.

That winter, the ice on the Rhein grew so thick that people would drive their cars across the river to Kaiserswerth and Düsseldorf. Herr Immers took his new truck on the ice despite predictions of disaster from his wife, and Herr Hesping borrowed his uncle's horse-drawn sled and brought his friends and their children on wild sleigh rides on the river. When the ice finally thinned, it tore in flat chunks that tried to mount each other like packs of wild dogs while the water hurled them downstream.

With each day the river rose, and as it left its bed, it washed across the winter matted meadows, freed the roots of young trees from the slack earth, and climbed the stone steps toward the crest of the dike that protected the town from the river. There, the people of Burgdorf would gather at dawn, shrouded by the smoke from their cigarettes and pipes as they'd stare at the shifting masses of gray waters and measure how far their river had risen during the night.

When Trudi's father carried her to the Rhein on his shoulders, the coat of the Russian soldier wrapped around both of them in such a way that, from a distance, they looked like one very tall man, she could smell the dank fields long before she saw the flood. Threads of cold rain stitched the earth to the gray sky. The lower trunks and branches of the half-submerged willows were darker than their crowns, up to a meter above the waves where the water had splashed. Last fall's dead leaves and debris had caught in the limbs, forming swampy pockets that bobbed in the waves like discarded hair nets. Some of the thinner branches were snagged by the currents and drawn beneath the surface before they whipped up again, completing a never ending circle. Ducks roosted in the V-shaped cores of trees as if holding court; whenever they braved the rapid waters, they were spun around madly or thrust in the opposite direction until, with great effort, they extricated themselves from the white crests and fluttered up again, seeking shelter in the willows.

Trudi counted twenty-three trees hurtling past her, two dead chickens, and four dead cats. She was good at remembering numbers. Though her mother had only taught her to count to twenty, she'd practiced counting the books in the pay-library, until she knew the names of the numbers all the way to one hundred. She counted eleven bushes that were carried by the waves, nineteen things she couldn't identify, and one dead goat, its belly the bluish-white tint of sour milk. Bloated, its stiff legs extended, it floated among the debris.

She didn't see the one human victim—Georg's father—because he hadn't been found. Two nights before, a group of men had straggled toward the river in the rain with a bottle of *Schnaps* after Potter's bar had closed, and Franz Weiler—always docile until he drank—had entertained everyone by doing handstands on top of the dike.

"We didn't even hear a splash," the taxidermist kept telling Frau Weiler. "Franz simply disappeared." When he tried to offer her his help, she sent him home.

Trudi heard several people tell her father that Frau Weiler insisted her husband must have slipped from the dike on his way to morning mass.

"Morning mass, my ass," Herr Immers said.

"He ordered the last round for us at Potter's," the pharmacist said.

Frau Blau pointed out that the church was only two blocks from the Weilers' and the river a good ten minutes' walk beyond the church.

"Must be some new detour," Herr Bilder said.

Yet, no one contradicted Frau Weiler but—as it had been the habit of generations—upheld the façade which, above all, preserved a family's respectability, no matter that beneath that façade all kinds of gossip festered. It was a complicity of silence that had served the town for centuries. Dressed in black and bearing proper words of condolence, the people assembled for the church service held in Franz Weiler's memory: the men from his *Stammtisch;* the families who had bought their groceries from him and his wife for many years; a group of nuns from the Theresienheim who had their own chapel yet rarely missed a funeral service at St. Martin's; and the bereaved wife, of course, with her possibly half-orphaned son, Georg, who wore a black smock that had been hastily fashioned from one of her blouses.

He knelt next to Trudi and whispered to her during communion—which the two children were too young to receive—that his father was just taking a long swim. If any of the men from Franz Weiler's *Stammtisch* had overheard the boy, they would have agreed with Georg: they already had speculated that, once in the river, Franz had kept on swimming to get away from his iron-haired wife.

When the people left the church, the man-who-touches-his-heart stood on the wet steps without a hat or umbrella. He was one of the few who always looked straight at Trudi. *See,* he seemed to say as his hands roamed up and down. *See what I can do.* Most grown-ups didn't look right at Trudi: they acted as if she were invisible and said things they would never say around other children. She found if she stayed very quiet they often kept talking, disclosing far more about themselves than they realized—even those who had trained their features to remain constant. The feelings they tried to hide sprang into their voices, and she could discern fear, joy, impatience, rage. When they got cautious, a certain flatness moved into their speech, and their sentences shrank; but when they became excited, their words grew colorful and rushed from them.

If she didn't remind people that she was there, she got to listen to all kinds of secrets. They fascinated her, those secrets, and she hoarded them, repeating them to herself before she went to sleep, feeling them stretch and grow into stories—like the one about Frau Buttgereit kneeling on lentils each morning when she prayed to St. Ottilia, the patroness of the blind, after whom she'd been named, imploring her to make sure her next child would not be another daughter. Trudi found it hard to believe that the gaunt woman, whose stomach always looked distended, had the reputation of once having been the most beautiful girl in Burgdorf.

Then there was the story about Herr Hesping, who'd bought a thousand blankets from one branch of the military and, within a week, had resold them to another branch for twice the price. He was often involved in some kind of deal that stretched the boundaries of the law without crossing them. If you asked him about a particular transaction, he'd overwhelm you with such a mass of facts and logic that you were glad once he stopped explaining. Some people said he had no values; others maintained that he did whatever he did out of contempt for the government.

•   •   •

The flood of 1920 that claimed Georg's father was not the worst the town had seen: it only seeped through a few small fissures in the dike and trickled into the Braunmeiers' pastures and peach orchard, as if to persuade the town that it was not only benign but also beneficial for the farmers; yet, instead it convinced the people to reinforce the mass of earth that protected them from the waters, which threatened the town nearly every spring.

The men talked about Franz Weiler as they labored on the dike in the nearly constant rain, and when the sun finally untangled itself from the clouds, they stopped their work and turned their faces toward the white light, which seemed more radiant after its long absence. Women left their stores and houses and came outside to sit in the sun on canvas chairs with their sewing. The teachers from the Protestant school and the nuns from the Catholic school brought the children outside for their lessons, instructing them how to identify leaves and insects even though the schedule might call for penmanship.

After the dike was rebuilt, it stood one meter higher and one meter wider than before, and if you looked at it from the direction of the town that summer after the flood, you'd notice the seam where the old part joined the new because the grass above it was the green of Easter candy.

Trudi would hold those pictures in her mind throughout the decades to come, and without even being near the river she would always know how it looked. She could close her eyes and picture the Rhein from the dike or close up from her favorite place on the jetty. She knew exactly how high the water could rise around the willows; knew the swift change of color—from moss green to molten black—and how the sun could shine on the surface so hard that it would blind you if you stared at the river; knew the pattern the current formed around the rocks in late summer, while early in spring they lay submerged.

It was like that with stories: she could see beneath their surface, know the undercurrents, the whirlpools that could take you down, the hidden clusters of rocks. Stories could blind you, rise around you in a myriad of colors. Every time Trudi took a story and let it stream through her mind from beginning to end, it grew fuller, richer, feeding on her visions of those people the story belonged to until it left its bed like the river she loved. And it was then that she'd have to tell the story to someone.

Georg was the ideal listener. Beneath the house, where Trudi's mother used to hide, the two children would sit on rocks, their knees nearly touching as they filled the dank space around them with words. Even in the dark there'd be a glint to Georg's hair as if he'd trapped the sun in his ringlets. If anyone could capture the sun, Trudi knew, it was Georg. As long as he felt lucky, treasures called out for him to pick them up—an empty snail house, a length of rope, the shiniest chestnut. He hoarded his collection in a box under his bed.

Once, he tried to teach Trudi how to make a bird out of mud. "The way Baby Jesus used to," he said. Squatting next to the front stoop of the pay-library, he shaped a ball of mud in his hands until it had wings and a head. He held it toward the sky. "First it'll open its wings," he told Trudi, "and then it'll fly into heaven."

"It looks like a lump of mud."

"That's because it isn't ready yet."

"Maybe you forgot to do something."

The bread wagon, which came once a week, rumbled past them, pulled by an old horse, and stopped at the end of the street. It was covered with heavy canvas. Several women with baskets over their arms crowded around it.

"Fly," Georg shouted, and threw the bird into the air. It dropped in front of his feet, wide and flat. "It didn't fly because we're sinners," he said.

"Maybe it's the wrong kind of mud."

"You think so?"

She nodded. "If we find the right kind of mud, we can do it."

"I bet the unknown benefactor could get us the right kind."

"The unknown benefactor can do anything."

They both were intrigued by the unknown benefactor, whose identity was still a mystery to the people of Burgdorf and who—despite the poverty—continued to steal into people's houses to leave his gifts like a thief who'd reversed the concept of thievery. The *Burgdorf Post* had published several articles about the unknown benefactor, each longer than the previous one, since the list of his contributions grew. A week after Georg's father had vanished, the unknown benefactor surprised Georg with the gift he wanted most in the world—*Lederhosen*—leather pants with leather suspenders and a leather strip across the middle of the chest, displaying a stag carved from the white core of an antler. Of course, his mother wouldn't let him wear the *Lederhosen*—"Once you're older," she said—but she conceded to let him keep them in his room, where he took them out at least once a day to touch the thick leather.

For Trudi's fifth birthday, Georg gave her a small cardboard box with needle holes pricked into its lid, and when she opened it, she found a black-and-orange butterfly on a bed of leaves.

"It won't fly away," he said proudly. "Ever."

"Why not?"

"It can't. I rubbed all the dust off the wings."

She touched the gauzy wings and felt limp with an odd sadness.

"You—you don't like it?"

"Will it live without the dust?"

"I'll catch you another one."

She wanted to tell him that she'd rather watch butterflies in the air, but his mother came out of the store and pulled something from the pocket of her apron. It was a silver medal engraved with an angel.

"Your guardian angel, Trudi. Make sure you don't lose it."

"I won't."

"It's blessed by the bishop."

Georg was fascinated with finding ways of courting luck, letting it envelop him instead of clutching it, and he told Trudi that the moment you started doubting your luck it vanished. You always had to assume it was there. Yet, she could see that it was hard for Georg to feel lucky when his mother was nearby—he even moved differently, docile and careful. It was as though he had something locked up inside him that he couldn't figure out.

Finding things was not the only kind of luck he taught her. Chimney sweeps also brought good luck, and he'd keep count of how many chimney sweeps he'd see in a week. Then there was the luck of not getting caught when you did something wrong. Trudi found out about that toward the end of summer, when the Eberhardts' pear tree was heavy with fruit that ripened the color of the sun and were so soft you could cut them like butter. Frau Eberhardt, whose husband had just died from pneumonia, had given Georg and Trudi two pears the morning after his funeral when they'd walked past her white stucco house, but when they returned the following day, hoping for more of the sweet fruits, whose juice had run down their necks and into their collars, Frau Eberhardt didn't come to the door.

Georg flipped a *Pfennig* to see who would have to knock. It was his turn. He rapped his knuckles against the glass pane of the door. They waited, knocked again, and then—without having to confer—ran toward the tree. Curls bouncing, Georg leapt up and grabbed one of the lower branches, yanking it down with his weight while Trudi's fingers closed around a pear. It snapped off in her hand as Georg let go of the branch, but instead of looking at her pear, he darted away from her, through a bed of geraniums, past the lilac hedge, and into the street, where he kept running.

Trudi's back felt as though the sun were searing through her dress. She didn't want to look behind her, but she knew she had to. Slowly, she turned her head, then her body.

Frau Eberhardt stood two steps away, her belly growing from her mourning dress like a half pear. Her eyes were sad, and her thick hair hung in two coils across her breasts as if she'd been interrupted before braiding and pinning them around her head.

Trudi tried to flee but couldn't lift her feet.

Slowly, Frau Eberhardt reached up into the branches of the tree and picked another pear. "Here." She gave it to Trudi. "You must like them a lot."

Trudi nodded, the pears so heavy that she thought her hands might snap from her wrists and topple into the grass with her fingers still curled around the fruit like those lion's claws on the legs of Frau Blau's table.

"I'll remember to save some for you from now on."

"I'm sorry."

"Oh—but I know that." Frau Eberhardt smiled at her.

Georg sat waiting for her behind their houses, where the brook forked. With a willow twig, he was drawing spirals in the muddy bank. Instead of telling Trudi that he was sorry for running off, he fixed an accusing stare on her. "You should have come with me."

"I didn't see her."

"What did she do to you?"

Trudi handed him both pears.

"Lucky you." There was real respect in his voice. He chose the smaller of the pears and gave the other one back to her. After twisting off the stem, he bit into the end of the pear and sucked hard to keep the juice from spilling. He was half finished before he noticed that Trudi wasn't eating. "You have to eat yours."

"I don't want it."

"You have to."

"Why?"

"Because if you don't—" he motioned toward her with his damp chin—"it means you think it's all my fault."

She didn't answer.

"You have to. So we're even. If you—" He stopped and his eyes flickered as though he'd just startled himself.

"If I what?"

He scrutinized her like an animal caught in a dark space too tight to turn around. "If you want to be my friend."

Something small and hard shifted low inside her belly.

"And you have to say that you're not angry at me."

"I am not angry at you."

"Prove it, then."

When she took a bite, her teeth ached as though any kind of coating between her nerves and the fruit had dissolved. She chewed, slowly, fighting a gagging sensation as she swallowed the sweet pulp to make room for the next bite.

Two weeks later Frau Eberhardt walked into the pay-library, carrying a new baby and a flawless pear for Trudi. When Trudi asked if she could hold the baby, who was sucking on the corner of a washcloth, Frau Eberhardt made her climb onto the counter and sit before she carefully positioned the baby in Trudi's arms, keeping her own arms around both children. The baby's name was Helmut, and as soon as Trudi touched his skin, she felt a chill that came from a place so deep within him that she no longer wanted to hold him; yet, she was unwilling to return him to Frau Eberhardt because, all at once, she knew that he had the power to destroy his mother. She would feel it again in the years to come whenever she'd get near Helmut—that danger—though he was one of the most beautiful children in town, with his wheat-colored hair and eyes of sky. That sense of dread would be with her even after he'd become an altar boy and would be considered more devout than any other boy his age in town, the most likely, people would say, to study for the priesthood.

"This is how you rock him," Frau Eberhardt said. Her black-sleeved arms holding Trudi and the infant, she swayed from side to side as if the three of them were connected.

Staring into Helmut's eyes, Trudi felt old, far older than any of the old people who lived in the Theresienheim, and she drew on all the courage she could find within herself. "If you want to," she offered gravely, "I will keep him."

Frau Eberhardt laughed and swung her son against herself. Tiny strands of hair sprang from the crown of her braids in a semicircle of light. "You'll have your own baby some day," she said.

f   o   u   r

———————————————■———————————————

1 9 2 0 – 1 9 2 1

W HILE TRUDI WAS LETTING GO OF THE IDEA THAT HER MOTHER WAS still alive, Georg—though without enthusiasm—kept expecting his father to swim back into Burgdorf or, perhaps, arrive on one of the barges that went up and down the Rhein. His parents had married late in life, and his mother had been forty-six when he was born. Franz Weiler had left the supervision of his store, his son, and his life to his wife, Hedwig.

Occasionally he'd given Georg an absent smile as though mildly surprised that this boy lived with him in the same apartment, which was overcrowded with heavy furniture. To Georg, it felt as though his father had shrunk into the shadow of his mother, and he rarely thought about him as a separate person.

Yet, late most nights, after the lights had been extinguished, Franz Weiler would get up, dress in the dark, and leave for Potter's tavern, excursions which no one in the family mentioned. His wife, who didn't permit alcohol in the house, had never seen Franz after he'd tipped down a few of the clear *Schnaps* that rose behind his eyes and coated the muscles in his arms, transforming him into a different man, the kind of man who'd swirl his partner across the dance floor.

But that was exactly what Hedwig was afraid of—the kind of passion that came from drink, the kind of passion that had sent her stepfather into her room many nights when she was a girl. To her, drink meant a rough hand clasped across her mouth and the weight of sin on her body, a weight that thousands of rosaries still hadn't negated.

Every morning she took her son to early mass and prayed for his soul because the souls of men—she had resolved long ago—were even darker than the souls of the women they contaminated. Though she tried to trade her prayers for happiness and absolution, she felt neither happy nor absolved, and even the coveted honor of cleaning St. Martin's on alternate Wednesdays left her feeling cheated by the world.

Convinced there was something lacking in him because his mother was not like other mothers, who smiled at their children, Georg tried to think of ways to make her smile too, but she'd only scold him for following her through the store in his attempts to help, or for talking too much. He'd never seen her embrace his father, and only rarely would she bend down and kiss Georg's forehead when she put him to bed at night.

Once, she called him to the window, lifted him onto the stuffed wine-red chair, and pointed down into the street, where the oldest Meier boy, Alfred, and the second Buttgereit daughter, Monika, walked together, his arm circling her shoulders, hers slung around his waist. "It's indecent," she said. "Don't you ever make a spectacle of yourself."

Sometimes strangers who shopped at the store mistook Georg for his mother's grandchild, and even as a man he would cringe when he'd recall her embarrassment and his wish to protect her when she explained that, no, this was her son. But it didn't seem to bother his mother that the neighborhood boys teased him about looking like a girl. While other boys ran and played, he'd watch them, feeling clumsy, hampered by the floppy smocks she sewed for him in styles that she might have worn as a girl. Still, there were moments when he'd forget about himself and—elated to be outside in the sun—throw his arms into the air, jumping and laughing. But his mother, who'd feel troubled whenever she'd sense a seed of passion in him, would stick her gray head from the store and remind him to play quietly.

Slowly, Georg learned to look back into her sorrowful eyes that peered into his, inspecting him for flaws. To avoid her gaze would have brought on questions. The first sin he became proficient in was lying. It became a necessity. But he would never tell a lie to Trudi. Not even after he'd grow up and marry Helga Stamm and lie to her. He'd never tell a lie to his first friend, the one who accepted his difference so much easier than her own, though he would come to betray her in other ways.

Leo Montag liked the playful, generous boy, whose movements became so much freer when he was away from his mother, and he encouraged Georg to visit Trudi whenever he wanted to. He brought the boy along when he taught Trudi how to build boats from birch bark and leaves. They set them to sail in the moat that encircled the Sternburg. It no longer was a castle with knights and a drawbridge, but the moat and baroque tower still made it seem like a castle—even if the dungeon had become a storage cellar for potatoes, and the armored horses had been replaced by sedate white cows that left steaming circles of dung all over the meadows. In back of the Sternburg, a felled oak trunk lay across the moat, and you could balance across it if you dared. But if you slipped, you'd drop into the murky water and come up shrieking, with green and yellow caterpillars in your hair—like Alexander Sturm, whose friends had challenged him to cross the moat blindfolded the night he'd turned seventeen.

Though Alexander hadn't been injured, the story of his mishap kept Trudi and Georg from trying to get across the moat, but some evenings, when she couldn't fall asleep right away, she'd see herself crossing it, her arms raised on either side of herself, her bare feet on the white bark.

Once, Leo took both children to a puppet show in Neuss; another time he borrowed the Abramowitzs' car to buy a sack of flour from the mill on the north end of town. With its brick arches and tall windows, the building looked more like a mansion than a mill, and when the children played tag in the surrounding woods, they ran not only from one another but also from a vague premonition of ruins and decay, a premonition which Georg would forget entirely and Trudi would not recall until one June evening, thirty-two years later, when she'd return to the flour mill long after it would have been destroyed by bombs and lie abandoned in a thickening tangle of forest and swamp, while the rest of Burgdorf had already been rebuilt. She'd walk through the roofless building, pick a dried thistle from a clump of camomile, and see herself and Georg that day her father had taken them to the mill, pulling thistles from the ground by their roots and taking their prickly bouquets back to the pay-library, where they'd brought a pot and two spoons down to the brook and had mixed the purple heads of the thistles with water and sand. Thistle soup, they'd called their concoction when they'd offered it to her father, who'd pretended to slurp it with sounds of delight.

In November, Trudi came along when Georg and his mother walked in the All Saints' Day procession. The procession started at St. Martin's Church, went all around the church square and the adjacent streets, and wound past the Catholic school and the synagogue to the cemetery where the people of Burgdorf laid wreaths on their families' graves and lit stubby white candles in glass lanterns.

Except for Trudi, Georg never invited any of his friends to come up-stairs to the third floor with him, and even her visits ended the day she let him talk her into cutting his hair with his mother's embroidery scissors. While he sat on a wooden stool in the kitchen, she perched on the edge of the table in the red wool dress and matching stockings that her aunt had sent her for Christmas, getting ready to guide the blades through Georg's fine curls.

But something kept her from making that initial cut—the fear that, once Georg was more like other boys, she would lose him as a friend—and yet, she wanted him to be liked by others, wanted him to be happy. She held the scissors in one hand, a lock of hair in the other.

"Do it," he said.

Four stuffed robins and one stuffed owl perched on top of the cup-board, their shiny, hard eyes watching her. It was cold in the kitchen, since Frau Weiler could only afford to heat the stove long enough to cook; yet, the skin on Georg's neck was hot against Trudi's fingers.

"Do it."

The scissors screeched as they claimed one curl.

"Let me see." He grasped it from her and stared at it, surprised to have this old enemy finally separate from his body. "Hurry up, Trudi."

Quickly she cut, filled with a sudden rage at him for endangering their friendship.

"Shorter," he said when he looked into his mother's hand mirror. His hair still covered his ears, and he kept urging Trudi, "Shorter," whenever she stopped, until he no longer looked like Georg, but like other boys who taunted her, and she readied herself to start pretending that she'd never liked him and kept snipping, snipping, till his ears and forehead were exposed and only a few pale tufts rose from his skull. He grasped her hands, jumping up and down with her on the polished floor, but she couldn't bring herself to laugh with him.

Leo Montag was about to close the pay-library when Hedwig Weiler dragged her son and Trudi in the door.

"Your daughter did this," she whispered. The lines in her cheeks looked deeper, and her lips trembled.

Quietly, Leo Montag inspected the boy, the sullen and fearful eyes, the proud tilt to the neck. "Like a little man," he said. "Georg, you look good."

"Your daughter had no permission—" Frau Weiler started.

But he shook his head. "Hedwig," he said gently, "Hedwig," turning his gaze on the angular woman in the black dress until—for an instant—she felt he understood everything that troubled her. It was a gaze a woman could rest herself in, a gaze that respected and sheltered her. And as he recognized that overwhelming sadness in her eyes, Leo thought of what people in town said about Frau Weiler— that she was a bitter woman who'd pulled down her husband and made her son resort to luck—but since he'd always seen deeper than most others, beyond façades to the many nuances of shade and light, Leo knew that Hedwig Weiler was not only terrified of God and of what the neighbors might say about her, but that she also yearned to be considered generous.

"Hedwig, it was time," he said, giving her that chance to be generous, as he recalled for her the day his father had taken him to the barber. "It's a big day in the life of a boy, Hedwig, an important day. Most remember it forever. I was three, and I can still feel that draft on my neck."

She looked down at her son's shorn head and raised one hand to touch it carefully.

"Doesn't he still have those *Lederhosen?*" Leo asked.

Georg's face shot up. His eyes leapt from his mother to Herr Montag to his mother.

"From the unknown benefactor." She nodded. "But they're probably too small by now."

"You'll be surprised, Hedwig, how much they adjust."

"He's grown a lot."

"One pair I had as a boy—I must have worn it for years. . . ."

Though Trudi was no longer allowed in the apartment above the grocery store, Georg became adept at sneaking out when his mother was busy with customers, and the two children would play between the shelves in the pay-library or sneak away from the neighborhood with chocolate cigarettes that Georg had stolen from his mother's store. They'd pretend to smoke, blowing imaginary puffs into the sky; chase pigeons across the church square and through the wheat and potato fields that surrounded the town; tease the geese behind the taxidermist's shop and run away when the huge birds waddled toward them, hissing through their hard bills. Georg was much faster on days he was allowed to wear his Lederhosen, but they never looked quite right because his smocks would be tucked inside.

In Trudi's room, they'd fit fairy-tale blocks into pictures or stack them on the windowsill until they toppled onto the painted floor boards. Georg was always trying to make bets with her—like how many birds would fly by her window, or how many worms they'd find by the brook.

Sometimes they climbed the circular stone steps to the tower of the Catholic church, where Trudi felt taller than anyone she knew, and when she watched her town from high above and imagined herself through the roofs and chimneys into the houses of the people, it no longer mattered that her body was stunted.

There, in the tower, Georg told her he wanted to die at age thirty-three. "The age Jesus was when he died on the cross."

"Thirty-three is very old."

"Maybe we can die together."

"All right."

Sometimes she'd try to scare Georg by telling him stories of skeletons and the ghosts of hanged people. If she succeeded so much that not only Georg but she, too, wanted to race down the circular stone steps, she switched to tales of water fairies that swam in the Rhein, of stars with bright tails that flared through the night, until she could actually see them, those stars and water fairies. It was something she would return to even as an adult—telling stories to keep fear away.

Georg was not allowed to play with Protestant children or with the Jewish children who went to the Catholic school since it stood across from the synagogue. The Protestant school and church were on Römerstrasse, far from the center of town, where the tower of St. Martin's Church pointed at the clouds. Georg and Trudi wondered what it looked like inside the Protestant church, which was lower and wider, without a bell tower and steeples—much more like a house than a church. But going inside a Protestant church was a sin. Georg said the devil could catch you if you opened the door, and even if you got away from the devil, Herr Pastor Schüler would know by simply looking at you.

Since Trudi was Georg's only friend, he was glad to help her with the errands she had taken over after her mother's death, making daily rounds to Anton Immers' butcher shop, to the open market where farmers sold fruits and vegetables, to Hansen's bakery for *Brötchen* or *Schwarzbrot,* to the Braunmeiers' farm for eggs and milk, which she'd carry home in a one-liter metal pail, and occasionally to the Buttgereits' house near the north end of town for white asparagus. The Buttgereits had nine daughters, and sold the most delicious asparagus in town. People would come from as far away as Düsseldorf to buy it. White and tender, it had a delicate taste that no one else in town who grew asparagus had been able to duplicate, and which the Buttgereits kept a family secret.

When Trudi was finally allowed to take piano lessons from the butcher's wife—a trade her father had worked out for library books— Georg came along and patiently sat in the Immers' kitchen, listening to the abrupt sounds and pauses that came from the next room as he watched the butcher's mother-in-law, a shrunken woman with bad hearing, who lived with the family and usually sat in her rocking chair by the stove, silent except when she slurped her saliva with great sighs.

It infuriated Trudi that the jarring sounds she produced on the ivory keys didn't match the music that had filled her with such awe ever since she was an infant. She couldn't reproduce it even when she practiced for hours, and she dreaded that pinched look that would come over Frau Immers whenever she'd hit a wrong key. But she was determined to be as good a player as Robert before she'd visit him in America. She knew it would be some time before she and her father would take their trip because the pay-library barely brought in enough earnings for food and wood.

Once, when Herr Abramowitz bought a new camera, he took a

photo of Trudi and Georg down by the brook. They had built a dam from stones, and their clothes and faces were smeared with mud. Though Trudi stood on a boulder with her chin held up, it was evident that she was much shorter than Georg. Her torso was wider than his, and her hips had already begun to spread as if some giant's hand hovered above her, trying to press her into the ground, causing that slow, deep buried pain in her hips and back that would afflict her throughout her life.

As a young woman, Trudi would come across that picture in an old praline box that held her other childhood photos, some of them of her as an infant, and she'd wonder how her mother had known right away that she was different. In the early photos, the differences were so slight—almost imperceptible. Perhaps her mother had seen something else in her—that wicked part Trudi hated and nurtured in order to survive.

Ever since the river had taken her husband, Georg's mother had kept the grocery store open by herself. Standing behind the U-shaped counter, which separated the line of waiting customers from the wide shelves that were stacked with boxes, cans, and bags, she fetched the items that people read to her from their grocery lists. On a piece of brown paper, she'd figure the sum of their purchases and wipe her fingers on her white apron, which would be smudged by the end of the day. When children brought their *Pfennige* to buy licorice or candy, she'd fix her protruding eyes on them and ask if they had their parents' permission. If they hadn't, but wanted the sweets, they had to buy the sin of lying along with the pleasure.

It was in church that the children of Burgdorf learned all about sin. Sin was lying or taking something that didn't belong to you. Sin was talking back to adults or refusing to obey. Sin was touching yourself between the legs or letting someone else touch you there. Even thinking about that was sin and so was rubbing the washcloth there for too long. Some people had sins attached to them like second skins, even the sins of their parents. Like Anton Immers, the butcher, who was older than many of their fathers, but everyone in town knew that he'd been born three months after his parents' wedding. A three-month baby. That meant sin. Or like Helga Stamm, who was Trudi's age but a bastard because her mother hadn't married at all. That skin of sin—the town wouldn't let the people take it off entirely even though everyone pretended it was not there. The town knew. Except for those sins that penetrated the skin and remained secrets—then the town didn't exactly know what had happened except that whatever had happened had changed that person. Like the bits of gravel under the skin of Gertrud Montag's left knee. They had stayed there, a reminder to her but to no one else unless she gripped your hand and guided your fingertips across the raised bumps below her skin, saying, "There, feel this?"

And then, of course, there were the sins that would take you straight to hell if you didn't confess before you died, sins that could get your picture in the paper, like murder or burglary. The most obvious distinction between sins was that some made you go straight to hell while others kept you waiting in purgatory. It made sense to go to confession as often as you could, even if you couldn't remember sinning.

"There are things," Trudi's father told her long before she was old enough for confession, "that the church calls sins, but they are part of being human. And those we need to embrace. The most important thing—" He paused. "—is to be kind."

In his eyes she saw a gentleness and wisdom that made her wrap her arms around his waist. "Promise you won't die?"

"I'll be here for a long time."

"How long?"

"Long enough for you to get tired listening to me."

Though Georg's hair was short now, and he wore his tunics tucked into his *Lederhosen,* other children still treated him as if he looked like a girl, but Trudi sensed that, gradually, their memories of him would be replaced by his new image. At times she hated him for being able to change. If only it were that easy for her—a haircut, a new way of moving. . . . The more he shed his difference, the further he seemed away from her. With an aching clarity she understood the nature of their friendship—it had worked only because each of them had found no other friends.

Georg felt confused when Trudi—to accustom herself to his loss—found excuses not to play with him. He pursued her, stole money from his mother's purse to win her back. One day he badgered his mother to invite Trudi to the blessing of the vehicles. Frau Weiler propped both children on her bicycle, Trudi on the metal seat above her rear wheel, Georg on the child's seat that was mounted on the handlebars, and pedaled to the fairgrounds to get her bicycle sprinkled with holy water.

While they waited for the Herr Pastor, two of Frau Weiler's customers arrived on their bicycles and lifted Trudi up, held her like a small child though she was far too old for that. No one lifted Georg up, and he was four weeks younger than she. Trudi felt poisonous: she wanted to spit, to scratch, and had to remember her good manners to keep herself from doing so.

"What pretty hair," the women said and laughed when she wriggled from their arms.

Georg stood with his elbow touching Trudi's shoulder while the pastor, surrounded by six altar boys with incense and silver buckets, scattered drops of holy water on bicycles, trucks, farm machines, and a few cars. Trudi had told Herr Abramowitz to bring his car in the hope that he would let her ride with him, but he'd laughed with his many teeth and said Catholic water rusted Jewish cars.

Georg brought Trudi a gold-veined rock he'd found at the fairgrounds, a speckled tail feather from a pigeon, chocolate beetles wrapped in shiny red paper with black dots from his mother's store. But his chocolate only evoked for her the sweet bile of loss from her brother's funeral. Once the other boys let Georg play, it felt to Trudi that everything he'd done with her had been just filling in days while he'd been waiting for them.

She'd watch him from behind the lace curtain of her room when he'd chase after a ball or play hide-and-seek with other boys. If her throat closed off, hot and sour, she'd run downstairs and ask her father to play one of the records the unknown benefactor had left, and as she'd listen to Beethoven's *Eroica* swell from the wooden phonograph—a miracle that it could be contained inside a place that small—she'd find it possible to swallow again.

One cloudy spring afternoon, she followed Georg to the Rhein, where he and Paul Weinhart, who walked funny, with his toes pointing sideways, tried to trap polliwogs inside canning jars. They squatted by the edge of the river beneath the hanging branches of an ancient willow, their backs to her, Paul's neck so thick that his shoulders seemed to slope right from his head.

Trudi crouched behind a tangle of blackberry bushes, fearing and yet wishing they'd call out her name and ask her to catch polliwogs with them. She knew how to. Her father had shown her. But the boys didn't call for her. She willed them to drop the canning jars, step into the shards, cut their feet. Her face felt hot as she saw their blood smeared across the pebbles, saw them getting scolded for taking canning jars. "Not something to waste," Georg's mother would say, and Paul Weinhart's mother would smack him, twice, across the jaw. Ah—she shivered with rage.

Georg and Paul didn't catch any polliwogs, and that was good. After they headed back toward town, Trudi stepped out from behind the blackberry bushes and dipped her arms into the cold river. A braided length of rope that some of the older boys had tied to the longest branch hung out over the shallow part of the water. Here, the Rhein bent, forming an elbow-shaped beach that was bypassed by the unruly waves. The long jetty that thrust itself into the stream upriver from the bay offered further protection from the current. On hot summer days, the people of Burgdorf liked to swim here: families with picnics would spread blankets on the sand, and the older children would climb into the tree, grab the rope by one of its many knots, swing themselves out over the water, and drop into the river.

Trudi propped her hands on her hips. Some day, she thought, she would try it, too, and she'd fly farther than any of them. But first she had to learn how to swim. Like a polliwog, she thought. No—a grown frog with four legs. She'd watched frogs dart through the water, had envied their light, rapid strokes. If she could imitate them, she'd be able to swim. Already she could see herself: she'd bring her legs together straight, pull them close to her body, then angle them out to the sides in a wide arc, and bring them together again. Hands folded as if praying, she would extend her arms in front of her, turn her palms outward, and push the water aside. Like Moses parting the Red Sea.

She looked around. The path winding along the river was empty. So was the meadow that led toward the dike. Quickly, she yanked off her pinafore and dress with the sailor collar, her stockings and shoes, the white cotton underpants that were buttoned to her undershirt. In the brisk water that still carried the memory of winter, she practiced her swimming as she had imagined. It was amazingly simple—as long as she held that picture of the frog inside her mind. Frogs were at home beneath the surface of the water, and that's where she swam, too, emerging only for deep gulps of air.

Early the following morning she left the house before her father was awake and walked to the river. All that spring she returned there nearly every morning when no one else was near. Staying close to the jetty, she'd streak through the shallow water like a frog, dive to the brown sediment of mud and let it billow around her, wishing her body matched its color so she could let it camouflage her. Here, the river belonged to her. In the water she felt graceful, weightless even, and when she moved her arms and legs, they felt long.

Her first day of school, Trudi brought a leather satchel, a *Schultüte*— that huge, glossy cardboard cone filled with crayons, erasers, sweets, pencils, oranges, and nuts that is given to all children when they start school. She also brought along years of longing to be like others. Overjoyed to finally be surrounded by other children, she also felt far more aware of her difference. It was not just the size of her body and the badly fitting clothes designed for three-year-olds that marked her an outsider but also her fierce wish to be included.

"Pushiness," the principal, Sister Josefine, called it when she talked about Trudi to the other teachers. "They don't want to include her, and she only tries harder."

"Pushiness," her teacher, Sister Mathilde, warned Trudi, "will make your life difficult." Her pretty, milk-white hands cupped Trudi's cheeks. "Look at the other girls. They don't barge right in with the answers. They wait until I call on them."

Trudi did look at the other girls, and what she saw made her uneasy—they kept silent even if they knew the answers, while the boys raised their hands, demanding to be heard. She felt as impatient with those girls as with women like Frau Buttgereit, even Frau Abramowitz, who were always suffering silently and saw it as a sign of virtue if you didn't complain. Once she'd heard Herr Abramowitz scold his wife, "You're like one of them, Ilse. Life is to live now."

The sister's desk stood below a large wooden crucifix, and the children sat in rows of double desks, their backs toward the one picture in the classroom, a painting of a praying Virgin Maria above the coat hooks.

One of the boys, Fritz Hansen from the bakery, whispered to Trudi that the nuns never slept.

"Why not?"

"They don't have to. They pray all night long."

Trudi began to watch Sister Mathilde's beautiful face for signs of tiredness, but all she saw in her eyes was the mystery of religious life. That's what Frau Blau had called it—the mystery of religious life. It came from being Christ's bride and living in a convent with his other brides.

Trudi loved quickly, rashly—Sister Mathilde, whose voice would tremble with emotion when she spoke of the martyrs; Eva Rosen, who sat next to Trudi in class, her spine so straight that she was always held up as an example for good posture; Herr Pastor Schüler, who would hear Trudi's first confession and tell her not to forget that she was God's child—loved quickly, rashly, as she had once loved Georg, as though there were no air between her and the other person.

There was always only one beloved—although that could change from one day to the next—and she would watch that person with her chaste, jealous love. It would devastate her when the Herr Pastor would visit her class and forget to smile especially at her, or when Sister Mathilde would frown at her for not sitting still, or when Eva Rosen would hold hands with Bettina Buttgereit on the way home from school.

Unlike most of the other girls who walked home with their best friends, Trudi had never held hands with another child. When school let out, she'd saunter home, usually on the opposite sidewalk from Georg, who was in her class but avoided looking at her directly. Inside her head, she'd repeat letters she'd learned that day, connecting the loops that formed them into words. She stopped wherever other kids played hopscotch or ball, wishing they'd understand that, inside, she was just like them. How she wanted to join in their games, but they didn't invite her—not even if she asked—and after a few months she ceased trying. She'd stand at a distance, watching the other children, keeping her wide face impassive as if she didn't care about any of this. She could feel their loathing. Could feel that they didn't want to touch her. But when they called her names—*Zwerg*—dwarf, and *Zwergenbein*—dwarf leg—names they knew would sting, she'd grab fistfuls of dirt to fling at their taunting faces. She'd fling names at them too—*Schweinesau*—pig sow, and *Arschloch*—asshole—vile names that earned her the reputation of having a dirty mouth and resulted in warnings from the nuns to control her temper, vile names that made her afraid that her soul was becoming as hideous as her body.

Even during recess the girls wouldn't let her play; they'd form circles, running and chanting: *"Ringel Ringel Rose . . ."* while she'd stand outside their circle, feeling a fury gather itself within her, a fury that would drive bright tears to her eyes and make her want to hurt those girls.

Usually, she could force down those tears, but one afternoon she came home crying. Her father met her by the door, his hands covered with white flecks from painting the cross on her mother's grave. With his gentle questions, Trudi's crying only became worse until she saw a reflection of her pain in his eyes, as certain as if he'd been the one to be excluded.

The next morning he braided her hair, pinned it into coils above her ears, and fastened her silver necklace with the cross. He put on his Sunday suit jacket over his knitted vest and limped next to her to school, where he talked with Sister Mathilde in the hallway next to the statue of St. Christopherus, the ugly giant who had carried the Christ Child across the river. The child was small, yet it carried the entire world. Turquoise plaster waves coiled around the bare feet of St. Christopherus, whose name meant Christ-bearer. Bowed under the immeasurable weight of the child, the giant looked about to collapse. According to the sisters, the child had become heavier and heavier though he was small, was always small, as if sentenced to an eternity as a *Zwerg*. And yet, in his eyes Trudi could already recognize the man, a crown of thorns tearing into his forehead as he staggered under the burden of the cross, as surely as the giant had staggered under his burden.

Sister Mathilde was late entering the classroom, a flutter of black skirts and sleeves. As she adjusted her starched linen wimple, her lips were set into a prim line that warned the children not to test her patience. At recess she took Trudi's hand into hers as if they were best friends and led her into the schoolyard, where she announced to the cluster of girls that Trudi had to be included in the games. Trudi wanted to shrink from the reluctant eyes, from that stiffness in the circle as it parted under the sister's watchful eyes. Obedient hands drew Trudi into their game. And she hated them. Hated them because they didn't want her. Hated them because she wanted them to like her. Hated them because she sensed that it would not get easier.

• • •

That Sunday her father pressed a basket covered with a towel into her arms. "Don't drop it," he cautioned her.

When she pulled the towel aside, a tiny dog peered right at her. He was black except for dark gray markings that covered his face like a mask. She lifted him out, held him against her cheek. His body felt lost inside folds of extra skin. His snout was damp, and he wiggled in her arms.

"You have to feed him twice a day till he's grown."

"What's his name?"

"You decide. He's your dog."

She set him down on the wooden floor and squatted next to him. After sniffing her feet—which made her laugh—he darted toward her father, turned back again, and explored the floor in widening loops that all led back to her.

"I don't know what to name him."

"It's good to wait. You'll know soon."

"How?"

"He'll let you know."

The dog was only black for several weeks—then his fur began to change to silver gray, diluting the black as if there were only a limited amount of pigment as his entire body stretched. Yet, the gray mask kept its deep color, even while the rest of him turned seal gray like the coat of the Russian soldier. That's why Trudi finally named him See-hund—seal. Sea dog. Herr Abramowitz took a photo of her and See-hund, surrounded by her dolls. Sometimes, when her father spread lard on a wedge of bread for her, she'd dip her finger into the lard and let Seehund lick it off.

While she was in school, the dog slept on an old pillow behind the counter of the pay-library, and when she came home, breathless from running because she couldn't wait to see him, he'd leap at her, throwing his puppy weight against her sturdy legs. She'd drop her leather satchel and pull him up into her arms. No one had ever loved her with such exuberance: her mother's love had been uneven, and her father's love, though constant, was tinged with a tender sadness. But Seehund hurled his love at her, his entire body. It was a love she recognized—she'd felt it within herself but had never been able to demonstrate it with such abandon. With Seehund she could. She could wrap her arms around him and feel his fur against her face, run through the tall weeds by the brook and know he'd follow her, feed him and watch him wag his entire rear end in appreciation. And if she felt gloomy, he'd take the flat edge of her hand into his mouth and pinch it gently until she'd stroke his head with her other hand.

When Seehund was four months old, she taught him to walk on a leash so that she could take him all over town. People would stop and admire him. They'd smile at her when they'd pet him. One Saturday, when she sat with her dog on the front steps, memorizing train schedules from the booklet of timetables that Frau Abramowitz had given her, Eva and her mother walked toward the pay-library. While Frau Doktor Rosen went inside to choose a new supply of American Westerns for her husband, Eva asked if she could play with the dog.

Trudi nodded. "He likes it when you stroke his back." She wished she had a green dress like Eva's, made of thin fabric that flutters around your legs when you walk.

Gently, Eva rubbed Seehund's fur, starting between his ears, all the way down to his tail. He shook himself like a duck and both girls laughed.

"Are you going on a trip?" Eva pointed to the timetables.

"I'm just reading where the trains go and where they stop."

"Why?"

"So I know."

"Can I walk your dog?"

Trudi hesitated, then handed Eva the leather strap, and the two girls walked to the end of Schreberstrasse and back, Eva more than a full head taller than Trudi, with long ankles and wrists. "I like dogs." She crouched to touch the ends of Seehund's whiskers. A golden heart hung from the thin gold chain around her neck. "But cats—" Her eyes grew alarmed and she looked around as if to make sure no cats were near. "Cats," she whispered, "they find your warm spot and choke you."

"What's a warm spot?" Trudi whispered back.

"They come into your room at night and lie on your throat because it's warm. And soft." Fine curls eluded Eva's braids and clung to her forehead as if painted to her skin with black ink. "My father says cats will choke you if they have a chance. One night he forgot to close his bedroom window and guess what happened?"

"A cat got in?" Trudi could see the cat, an amber cat with white paws.

"My father was dreaming. . . ." Eva nodded. "And in his dream, something heavy was pressing on him. When he could no longer breathe, he opened his eyes, and this cat, it was asleep, this cat, lying right across his throat—" She raised one hand and brushed across her throat as if to wipe away the shadow of that cat. "We always sleep with the windows closed."

"Even in summer?"

"Even in summer."

"How about during the day? When your father lies in his chair on the balcony?"

"He never sleeps during the day. He only looks that way. He's not very strong."

"My mother wasn't very strong."

"But my father is going to get better."

"My mother looks like a dead bride. Herr Abramowitz took pictures of her. In the coffin."

Eva shook herself. "Can I see?"

"I don't know. They hang in my father's bedroom."

"I saw a picture of a dead baby once. Someone gave it to my mother because she took care of the baby before it died."

"Was the baby killed by a cat?" Trudi could feel a story of a cat, a cat who'd killed a baby.

"Could be."

"What color was your father's cat?"

"No one told me."

"What happened to it?"

"It leapt out of the window when my father screamed."

Trudi closed her eyes. The cat—a sleek, amber cat—leapt from Herr Rosen's fleshy throat and through the bedroom window, landing on the grass below without a sound while Herr Rosen kept screaming. It darted behind the chicken coop and below the clotheslines, crossed the street in search of another open window, another throat. Trudi shivered though she liked cats and was fascinated by their agile movements, their unblinking stare that was much like her own.

As Eva stood up to leave, Trudi saw herself alone again, steeped in that familiar isolation. "My father almost got killed once," she said quickly to hold Eva there.

"By a cat?"

"No, a Russian bullet. It was aimed right for his heart." She paused deliberately, knowing that stories took on a new power once you gave them words. They had to start inside your soul, where you could keep them for a long time, but to make them soar, you had to choose words for them and watch the faces of others as they listened. "But the other soldier . . ." she said, drawing in the current of Eva's curiosity as she once had with Georg, longing for her to stay. Willing her to stay. "The other soldier tripped—they all were in a muddy field, see?—and the bullet went into my father's knee instead."

Eva leaned close. "What happened to the Russian soldier?"

"He was captured, and my father got to keep his coat." Grasping Eva's hand, she pulled her up the front steps and into the entrance hall, where the long seal coat hung from one of the wooden hooks. From the window at the end of the hall, light spilled across the Persian carpet runner and filtered through the intricate weave of the wicker chair.

"Touch the coat," Trudi urged. "It's made from the fur of seals." She had pieced together her own version of how her father had been injured in the war and come into the possession of the coat—to her those two had to be ultimately connected—but before she could captivate Eva with any of this, Eva's mother came out of the pay-library with several books.

That night, Trudi closed her window and lay awake till late, listening for cats and thinking of how she would tell the rest of the story to Eva. She smiled to herself, imagining Eva's face as she listened. *"The Russian soldier was the tallest man my father had ever seen, and they became friends. Well—not real friends like—"* She wanted to say, *"you and me,"* but even in her fantasy couldn't risk presuming that much. *"He tried to give my father his coat. As a gift. To make up for shooting him. But my father traded him some of his food rations. And one pair of boots. . . ."* Anticipating Eva's questions about size of feet, she decided to add, *"You see, my father's feet have always been large. They were the same size as the Russian's."*

But the next morning, when she ran to school, ready to tell her story, Eva turned away as soon as she saw her and started talking to

Helga Stamm, who was the plainest girl in class with those thick arms and colorless lips that made her look as though she were made of dough. Trudi, her heart beating madly, dashed past them into the classroom and pulled her slate from her satchel. Low in her back she felt an ache that stayed with her all that day.

On the way home, she heard children laughing behind her. Certain that they were making fun of her body, she walked faster, her face hot, hating her short legs and how they curved—outward at the knees, then tapering again at her ankles as though outlining the shape of a large cuckoo's egg. She pretended she wanted to be alone. Even if they asked her to play now, she wouldn't stop. Not for them.

She hadn't been home more than an hour when Eva appeared outside the pay-library, calling for her to come out and play.

"Bring Seehund," she shouted when Trudi stuck her head from the window of her room. "I have something for you."

Trudi wanted to duck back and hide beneath her bed, wanted to dump a bucket of dirty water on Eva's head, wanted to run downstairs and play with Eva. Slowly, she walked down the steps, counting them—*eins, zwei, drei, vier* . . . Her face grew hot. *Eins, zwei, drei, vier, fünf, sechs, sieben. Sieben Zwerge.* She stopped. The week before, she had asked the priest if there was a patron saint for *Zwerge,* and he'd peered at her with his kind eyes as if startled.

"I don't believe so, my child."

"But everyone has a patron saint."

The priest nodded, sadly. "Barbers, widows, epileptics, merchants . . ." He reached into his left sleeve and scratched his thin arm in long, even sweeps.

Trudi thought of Frau Simon, who wore a blessed medal of St. Antonius—the patron saint of everything that's been lost—along with a Jewish amulet on a fine silver necklace.

". . . beggars, dentists, orphans," the priest recited, "servants, librarians—"

"Even animals," Trudi said. She had a holy card of the patron saint of animals, St. Antonius. He was a hermit who'd lived inside a tomb in a cemetery. She waited for the priest to produce a patron saint especially for *Zwerge.* Surely, a saint like that would make her grow.

"Perhaps St. Giles . . ." The priest reached into his other sleeve.

She clapped her hands. "I knew you'd find one."

"He's the patron saint of cripples."

"I'm not a cripple," she cried.

"I know, dear child. . . ." He stroked her hair. "But St. Giles is the closest I can think of. He was fed the milk of a deer and—"

"Trudi . . ." Eva was shouting outside.

"I'm not a cripple," Trudi whispered and walked down the last steps. Seehund was already waiting for her to open the door.

"Just imagine—" Eva said as though it were still the day before and they hadn't stopped talking "—if that bullet had killed your father, you wouldn't have been born." She handed Trudi a lantern flower from her garden, its thin stem arching gracefully under the weight of the orange blossom.

"Then the stork would have brought me somewhere else."

"The stork?" Eva laughed. "Storks don't have anything to do with getting born."

"They do."

"My mother is a doctor and she knows. She says babies come out of mothers. They grow inside, and when they get too big, they crawl out."

Trudi shook her head.

"It's so," Eva insisted and lifted Seehund's ears, trying to make them stand up straight, but he flicked them the way he did when he chased away flies.

"He wants to go for a walk," Trudi said.

Eva held the leash and Trudi carried the flower as they walked the dog to the end of Schreberstrasse and back. When Trudi suggested taking Seehund to the river, Eva glanced down the street as if trying to make sure none of the other children saw her with Trudi. "Let's stay here today," she said.

When they returned to the pay-library, Trudi sat down on the front steps and Seehund laid his head on her knees. Eva stood in front of her as if waiting for her to say something, but Trudi plucked silently at the stem of the lantern flower.

"Mothers have a baby pouch inside their tummy," Eva blurted, "and fathers put seeds for babies there, and then the baby starts to grow."

It was the silliest thing Trudi had ever heard; and yet, she had a sudden image of her dead brother still inside her mother, buried with her, always to stay within her—a privileged place of residence—as both of them decomposed beneath the earth. She found herself wondering if the pebbles would last and saw herself opening the coffin and finding it empty except for a fistful of tiny gray stones.

"It's true," Eva said.

"Flowers and vegetables grow from seeds," Trudi explained to her, "not babies."

"After the man kisses the woman, he puts the seed inside her."

"Where?"

Eva shrugged and curled Seehund's ears around her fingers.

"See, you don't know." Trudi laughed at her. "It's just a story your mother is telling you because she thinks you're too little to understand."

"I'm not."

"I know what happens. I even know how to stop babies from coming."

Eva stared at her, sudden doubts at her own certainty in her eyes.

"I once stopped a baby from coming. It's a secret." Trudi stopped. Though she soaked up other people's secrets, she liked to guard her own because she knew how much power they could give to others.

Eva looped one arm around Trudi's shoulders. "I won't tell."

"Promise?" Trudi had heard whispers about women who had ways to keep babies from coming. Like Frau Simon, who'd never had a baby. Keeping babies from being born was a sin.

"I promise." Eva's mouth stood half open as though she'd forgotten to breathe.

"Not even your mother."

"Promise."

Trudi said it as quickly as she could: "I made the baby die before it could get here because I ate the stork's sugar and the baby came too soon to be alive and we had a funeral."

Eva let out a long breath. "Which baby?"

All at once Trudi couldn't speak.

"Which baby?"

"My—my brother."

"Did you get punished?"

"No one knows about it."

"I won't tell." Eva rubbed her knuckles up and down her high, narrow forehead. "Will you do it again?"

Trudi had to think hard. "I don't want to," she finally said.

"I know how you can tell if you're going to have a baby."

"How?"

Eva pressed one finger against Trudi's skirt where it covered the bone triangle. "Once you get hair there," she said, "you have to keep watching it. If it grows toward your belly button, you'll have a baby."

Though it stung Trudi to be ignored by Eva in school, she tried to understand. If Eva let on that she was her friend, the other children would exclude Eva too, as certainly as if her body had shrunk overnight. In her love, Trudi wanted to be like Eva—yet, she sensed that, in the eyes of the town, it would be the opposite: Eva would be treated like an outcast. It made her feel dangerous to the people she loved. Afraid of tainting Eva, she kept her love a secret, though sometimes it seemed to her that everyone had to notice because those feelings burned so strongly within her that they seared through her skin in fiery splotches.

And so, knowing the powers of contamination, she let Eva betray her, over and over again. If she were Eva, she probably would do the same. In a way she already did: ever since she'd started school, she'd turned from people who used to fascinate her, people whose otherness was even more evident than hers—like the third Heidenreich girl, Gerda, who drooled over herself and whose head ticked from side to side even though her father kept taking her to countless doctors as far away as Berlin; or Ulrich Hansen, the baker's oldest son, who'd been born without arms and had to be fed by his parents although he was twelve years old; and, of course, the-man-who-touches-his-heart. It made her ache to look at any of them, made her afraid of having to join their ranks if she dared to be kind to them, made her feel cruel as she shunned them.

She lured Eva back with the pictures of the dead woman on her father's walls. One afternoon, while her father had four customers in the pay-library, she sneaked Eva into her father's bedroom. Eva, who'd only seen the photo of one dead baby before, stood as far away from those pictures as she could, while the sun glinted through the tree pattern of the lace curtains and left lace shadows on the many faces of the dead bride.

She lured Eva back with her stories—stories about her father, who'd been a celebrated athlete and had won many trophies before his knee had been injured; stories about her cousin, who lived in a magnificent mansion in America; stories about the people in Burgdorf. Sometimes she even spied on Eva and her family and, through her stories, gave her back what she'd seen. Her stories grew and changed as she tested them to see how far they gave, how much Eva believed, what fit in and what didn't, but all of them started from a core of what she knew and sensed about people. And it was not even that she made up anything, but rather that she listened closely to herself.

SOMETIMES TRUDI AND EVA PLAYED WITH SEEHUND BY THE BROOK IN back of the pay-library, but he'd run from them, yelping, if they'd splash him with water. And whenever they dragged him into the brook to teach him how to swim, he escaped as soon as they let go of his collar. Soon he learned to stay at a safe distance from Trudi if she went near water.

"You should have named him something else," Eva said one fall afternoon after they'd given up on trying to submerge Seehund. "A seal is supposed to love water."

"We'll call him Earth Snail," Trudi suggested.

Eva laughed. "Turtle Breath."

Both arms stretched wide, Trudi whirled around. "Turtle Breath," she chanted. "Earth Snail. . . ." Her right foot banged into the end of the wooden planks that spanned the narrow arm of the brook soon after it forked. She cried out.

"Pinch your earlobe," Eva yelled.

Clutching her toe in one hand, Trudi hopped back and forth on the other foot.

"Just try it," Eva ordered. "It stops the pain."

When Trudi pinched her earlobe, it stung. Miraculously, her toe stopped hurting. "How come it works?" She plopped down on the grass next to Eva.

"It just does. I'll show you something else." Eva brought her face up against Trudi's. Her breath smelled of raspberry pudding as she opened her lips—so wide that Trudi could see deep inside her mouth. Its roof was curved like the ceiling in St. Martin's Church, and the dark gap in back was separated by a pink icicle. When Eva's tongue stretched up, it hid the gap but exposed bluish veins beneath her tongue and a taut membrane that connected it to the bottom of her mouth. "Try it." Eva's voice was muffled. The tip of her tongue danced against the roof of her mouth. "Move it so it tickles."

Trudi tried. "It feels silly."

Eva closed her mouth but right away yawned as if she needed to move her lips. "Remember to do this if you're ever hiding and have to sneeze and don't dare to because someone may capture you."

"Who would capture me?"

"You never know. It's an old Indian trick. Indians do it when they don't want their enemies to find them."

"How do you know?"

"My father. He read it in a book from your library. I know all kinds of other remedies."

"Can any of them—" Trudi felt her hands go sweaty. That morning, when she'd told Sister Mathilde she wanted to become a teacher, the sister had said it wasn't a good choice because children wouldn't have respect for a teacher who was shorter than they. She rubbed her palms against her skirt before she dared to ask Eva, "Can any of those remedies make you grow?"

Slowly, Eva pulled at a clump of grass until it came out by its roots. She tossed it into the brook, where it swirled in slow loops as it drifted away.

"I don't know of any remedies." Eva's voice was soft. "You'll grow on your own."

"Sister Mathilde—she says I can't be a teacher."

"My mother says people can be anything they want to be."

"What do you want to be?"

"A doctor. I'll be a doctor and you'll be a teacher."

"Teachers have to be tall."

"Teachers have to be smart. You're the smartest girl in class."

"I know," Trudi said without enthusiasm. She would gladly give up being smart if she could be tall. "I don't want to look different."

"Look." Eva unbuttoned her cardigan and blouse. "I'm different too." She pulled up her undershirt. A dark red birthmark, shaped like an irregular flower, spread across her thin chest. Its petals blossomed across her nipples and toward her waist in a paler shade of red than the center, as if they'd faded under a strong sun.

Air and sound and scent spun through Trudi as she raised one hand and brought it close to Eva's flower, spun through her, spun her, as though she were spinning in a world that would always and always spin through her. Her ears hummed and her arms tingled and it took impossible effort not to lay her palm against Eva's chest until Eva nodded, but when she finally did, the skin of the flower was the same warmth as her own hand and it felt as though she were touching herself.

Eva swallowed, twice, and Trudi felt her heart beating beneath the flower. With her free hand, she traced the outline of the petals, wishing she could trade her difference for Eva's.

"It's beautiful," she whispered.

Eva yanked down her undershirt so hard it dislodged Trudi's hands. Her long fingers jammed the buttons back through their holes. "You'll grow, but I'll always have this." She leapt up. "And when I have babies, they'll drink red milk from me." She dashed across the planks to the other side of the river and down the hill that led toward the fairgrounds.

When Trudi ran after her, Seehund raced toward the brook, barked, but recoiled a couple of times before he stalked across the planks like a very old dog. As soon as he was on the other side, he caught up with Trudi, then Eva, circling between the two girls like a sheepdog pulling in his flock.

Trudi wanted to keep running, wanted to keep hearing that conviction in Eva's voice: *You'll grow.* "You really mean it?" she shouted, her legs feeling long and light as if they'd already begun to stretch.

"What?" Eva stopped. One of her braids had come undone and hung in waves down one side of her face.

"About growing!"

"Yes," Eva shouted back and flung herself into the high grass. "Yes yes yes." Her head disappeared, and she stuck her feet high into the air—above the clover and daisies and cornflowers—her legs pumping the air as though she were riding a bicycle.

Trudi threw herself down next to Eva, her breath fast and dry, but Eva's legs kept flying through the air as if she were trying to get away from wherever she was. Trudi broke off a handful of purple clover and began to braid the stems.

"What are you doing?" Eva dropped her legs and lay motionless.

"Making a crown for you."

Seehund nudged Trudi's shoulder, then dashed off again. Careful not to snap any of the stems, she wove more of the purple flowers into a crown for Eva. The air was moist and still, very still. As Trudi set the crown into Eva's sweaty hair, she wished she could take Eva to the sewing room and keep her there, lock her up, her friend forever.

They stood up, and when Seehund ran toward them, a bird—a gray bird with a ruby chest—swerved from the grass near him. Like a lopsided top, it reeled and whirred, one wing spread, as it fluttered into the dog's path. Playfully, he stopped the mad flight with one paw and, before Trudi could come to the bird's aid, closed his jaws on it.

"Make him stop," Eva cried.

With both hands, Trudi pried Seehund's teeth apart. A startling trace of something ancient and rotting rose with his breath. As he let go of the bird, Eva scooped it up in her hands. Its chest was rising and falling rapidly, and one wing hung at a crooked angle.

Eva carried the bird home in the basket that Seehund had come in. Her mother would set the wing in her office, and Eva would keep the bird in the basket for two days and two nights before she'd find it dead. She would be inconsolable until her father would phone Herr Heidenreich. At his shop, the tall taxidermist would cradle the bird in his hands and promise Eva to give it a new soul. To convince her of his magic, he'd let her hold the lifelike bodies of other birds he'd preserved, inspiring in Eva a fascination with stuffed birds that would continue into her adult years.

But the night after Seehund hurt the bird which, quite likely, had already been injured, Trudi didn't let him into the house. Tied with a length of clothesline to one of the pillars of wood outside the earth nest where Trudi's mother used to hide, the dog spent the night outdoors. Alone in her room, Trudi kept seeing the flower on Eva's chest, kept seeing it through the layers of clothing, lit from within Eva's body.

In school, Trudi and Eva learned that the Jews had killed Jesus. That was true because the sisters said so; but Trudi didn't know if what

Fritz Hansen said was also true—that Jews killed Christians and drank their blood and offered them as sacrifices to the devil who was their God. Jews like that seemed far away and foreign—not at all like Eva and the Frau Doktor; or Frau Simon; or the Abramowitz family; or Fräulein Birnsteig, the concert pianist who, it was rumored, was a genius. The Jews in Burgdorf were different kinds of Jews, not the kind who killed Jesus—or anyone, for that matter.

They might beat you up, but not kill you. Trudi had already learned that belonging to one religion meant getting beaten up by kids of other religions. Mostly, though, the Catholic kids would be the ones to chase the Jewish or Protestant kids. There were lots of other reasons for getting beaten up: if you were a girl or if—in any way—you didn't look like others.

In school you also learned it was wrong to question anything that had to do with God and the saints. You had to believe. And for answers that demonstrated your belief you received holy cards—pictures of saints with rings of light around their raised heads. Questions were doubts. Doubts were sins. Even wondering why the Holy Ghost looked like a pigeon was a doubt. Or trying to figure out how that pigeon stayed up in the air between God and Jesus without having to flap its wings like other pigeons.

"There are things we do not ask. . . ."

"If God had wanted us to know, he would have sent us proof, but God wants us to believe. . . ."

But for Trudi, questions that weren't answered kept prodding at her. When she asked Sister Mathilde what God ate, the sister said, "God is nourished by his own eternal love," and when Trudi wanted to know how Jesus could change from being God to being that small, heavy boy on the shoulder of St. Christopherus, the sister told Trudi. "This is what faith is all about—believing what cannot be explained."

But it wasn't only during religion lessons that the sister talked about God. God and the saints had a way of appearing in every subject.

"If Saint Hedwig has ten plums and there are five lepers—how many plums will she give to each leper?"

"When God made the world, where did he put the North Sea?"

"It pleases the Virgin Mother when she sees tidy handwriting."

The prettiest statue of the Virgin Mother was kept in the church basement, but the last day of November it was dusted off and displayed on the side altar of St. Martin's, part of the nativity scene. Maria's gown was the color of heaven, and her mouth curved in a cryptic smile as she knelt next to the pile of straw where the Christ Child lay. St. Josef looked rather stodgy and old, like Herr Blau, the way he stood behind her, leaning on a stick. But all three had identical glittering halos and were surrounded by nearly a hundred clay pots, filled with lush violets, that belonged to the winner of the annual violet contest, an honor that the old women of Burgdorf dreamed about all year and competed for, fiercely.

That December Trudi became a member of the church choir. Sister Mathilde had selected her and Irmtraud Boden because they had the best voices in class and could memorize entire hymns. Trudi loved standing on the high balcony next to the organ, loved the way the other voices in the choir filled in around her voice, and as she belted out the hymns, she felt them vibrate in her chest, her toes, lifting her on the current of music.

"She has the voice of an angel," Herr Heidenreich, who also sang in the choir, told Trudi's father. That compliment meant a lot coming from the taxidermist, whose voice was so beautiful that the pastor always chose him for solos.

When, the first Sunday of Advent, Herr Pastor Schüler lit one of the four candles on the pine wreath that hung above the Holy Family, Trudi felt all sacred and still inside. The rich threads in the pastor's brocade chasuble glistened, and the scent of incense wove itself into her breath. If only she could become a priest. But only men could be priests. Women could be nuns, but she didn't want to be a nun. Nuns had to listen to priests and wear layers of black cloth and stiff wimples that made it hard to turn their heads. Still, if nuns went far far away and became missionaries, they were almost like priests. If she were a missionary, she could travel all over the world like St. Franziskus and baptize hundreds of thousands of pagans in India and China.

When it started to snow one afternoon, Trudi played mass in the sewing room. She covered an apple crate with a white pillow case, lit two candles, and chanted Latin words she recalled from mass as she lifted the sacrament—disks of rye bread that she'd cut with the rim of a cup—toward the ceiling. But then she crumbled them up quickly and hid them inside the pillow case because she remembered that girls who wanted to be priests could be locked up like the young nun in the Theresienheim, who, it was rumored, had been caught trying to celebrate mass.

"As if she were a man," the old women said. "A priest, imagine."

Her name was Sister Adelheid, and she came from a noble family. She had stolen the holy host—three communion wafers—from the convent chapel, and she kept them in her toothbrush glass on a low altar she'd set up in her cell. Ever since she'd been found out, the other nuns had kept her in solitude on the top floor of the convent.

"Banned and locked up," the old women said, shaking their heads.

But Trudi's communion wafers weren't real, just bread. Even God knew that. She had seen Sister Adelheid only twice, flanked by older nuns on her way to the cemetery, her heart-shaped face swiveling from side to side as if not to miss one minute outdoors, the range of her restless steps tempered by the pace of the other sisters. Trudi wondered if Sister Adelheid scratched messages into the walls of her cell. Although new wallpaper covered the letters that her mother had scratched into the walls of the sewing room—*Gefangene*—Trudi knew where the words were because if you pressed your fingers against the striped paper you could feel the gouges.

Some of the older girls in school whispered that Sister Adelheid was a saint because she bled every Friday from her palms. Like Jesus on the cross. Stigmata, those wounds were called. You were a saint if you had them. But how could you tell the difference between a locked-up saint and a locked-up crazy woman? How could anyone tell them apart?

High in the hazy sky, the snowflakes looked tiny and all alike, but as they drifted past the narrow window of the sewing room, all were unique—long or round or triangular—as if they'd borrowed their shapes from the clouds they'd come from. Random gusts of wind swept between them, molding them into wild hoops before letting them resume their solitary descent. Her face against the cold glass, Trudi tried to follow the course of one flake, but as soon as she had singled it out, it dropped past her and she lost it. Soon, a smooth, white layer capped the roofs and frozen ground.

Before dinner, Trudi's father oiled the runners of the wooden sled that had belonged to Trudi's mother when she was a girl. He tied a rope to it and pulled Trudi through the center of town and all the way to the Rhein, his shoulders arched into the wind. On top of the dike, he sat down on the sled behind her, his bad leg extended, and folded her into his arms. She laughed aloud as he raced with her down to the meadow while Seehund ran alongside, barking, the white powder flying around them. At the bottom, the dog stopped and rolled in the snow, wiggling his body like Herr Blau whenever he scratched his back against a door jamb. On the way home, when Seehund licked a frozen puddle, Trudi could hear the rasping of his tongue against the ice.

She described that sound to Frau Abramowitz, who drove her to Düsseldorf to buy a Christmas present for her father. She'd saved most of the birthday money her Aunt Helene had sent from America last July. Already she'd made him two small gifts—a crocheted pot holder and a felt bookmark—but since she'd never bought him anything, she wanted her big gift to be magnificent. The one extravagance he allowed himself was an occasional record for the phonograph. What he wanted more than anything, she thought, was a car of his own. Riding the bicycle hurt his stiff leg. Ever since the Talmeisters' bicycle had been stolen, he'd been keeping his inside the hallway. "It's the unemployment," he'd said to Herr Hesping when they'd talked about the increase in thefts, and they'd agreed that poverty was corrupting the young, who were growing up without ideals.

"Maybe I can buy a car for my father," she told Frau Abramowitz.

"Maybe you can . . . once you're grown-up. Cars are very expensive."

Frau Abramowitz took her through five stores, and it was not until Trudi saw the golden tie with silver stripes that shimmered when you moved the fabric that she knew she'd found the perfect present for her father—at least until she was grown-up—and even Frau Abramowitz's hint that a tie as festive as this might not be for everyday use couldn't sway Trudi from buying it.

In a restaurant that overlooked the *Hofgarten,* Frau Abramowitz ordered hot chocolate with whipped cream. Their table looked out over the frozen ponds, and Trudi wondered what had happened to the swans that were here in the summer. As Frau Abramowitz talked about her trip to Italy, the winter landscape outside their window was transformed: earth-colored houses of the Amalfi coast stacked up against the hillside above the sea; rows and rows of grapevines grew along the shore of Lago di Garda. . . . Trudi could even feel the bright sun that started the instant you stepped across the Italian border, where smiling guards presented you with rounded bottles of red wine.

When Frau Abramowitz buttoned Trudi's coat for the drive home, she kissed her forehead. She was far more affectionate than most grown-ups, who did not hug or kiss in public. Sometimes Trudi wished Frau Abramowitz lived with her and her father. She could tell that Frau Abramowitz liked her father—not just because she enjoyed bringing them things, like vegetables from her garden in summer or pies filled with her fruit preserves in winter—but because she confided in him.

"My children don't need me anymore," she'd told Trudi's father once, her smile brittle, her eyes blinking tears away.

Trudi hid the Christmas tie beneath her bed when they returned to the pay-library, and Frau Abramowitz borrowed two romance novels, insisting to Trudi's father, as she had for the past year, on paying for them. It was a conversation Trudi could predict, a conversation she knew would happen again.

"Please, let me pay for them."

"Absolutely not, Ilse."

"Our original trade was the mirror for five years of borrowing books. It's more than six now."

"But we're still enjoying the mirror."

That night Trudi left her shoes outside her bedroom door for St. Nikolaus, and in the morning they were filled with nuts and marzipan. St. Nikolaus arrived in school at recess in his crimson bishop's robe, carrying a scepter, accompanied by Knecht Ruprecht, all dressed in black and hunched over. While St. Nikolaus gave sweets to children who'd been good all year, Knecht Ruprecht chased the children who'd been bad and gave each a bundle of dried birch switches. Most received at least a few pieces of wrapped chocolate tied to the twigs, but Hans-Jürgen Braunmeier's switches were bare. A gangly boy with defiant lips, he came to school with dirt under his fingernails. He could whistle better than any of the other kids, but he lied to the nuns, stole coins and cookies from the girls, and bullied the boys in the schoolyard.

Hans-Jürgen hit Paul Weinhart with an ice ball outside the Theresienheim when Sister Mathilde took the first graders there to sing Christmas carols and recite poems to the old people. You lived in the

Theresienheim if you were old and didn't have anyone left to take you in—say, if you hadn't married or if your children had died before you. As long as you had even nieces or nephews, you lived with them. The Buttgereits had both grandmothers living with them; one of them had been blind since birth. "A house of women," Herr Buttgereit would mutter.

Most of the old people sat in the dining room, which was decorated with fresh boughs of pine and countless candles. Their movements were slow, and in their eyes Trudi saw a wonder and stillness that didn't need words and lent them a dignity despite their missing teeth and the age spots on their hands and faces. Some of the old people listened to the carols from their beds, their doors wide open as the lovely Sister Mathilde led the children through the long white corridors, and it was hard to tell if their tears sprang from gratitude or despair.

Trudi got to recite her favorite Christmas poem twice: *"Es weht der Wind im Winterwalde . . ."*—"The wind blows in the winter forest . . ."—letting the *w*'s in *weht* and *Wind* and *Winterwalde* hum from her lips like a swarm of bees. She remembered every word of the poem. Remembering things had always come easy to her, and she'd felt proud when she'd started to read complete words and sentences long before the other children; yet, she found it tedious to guide her hand in forming the perfect letters the sister expected from her. When she'd do her homework in the pay-library, her father would guide her right hand through the frustrating loops and lines of the letters, but he never had to help her with adding or subtracting numbers. That she could do inside her head.

Sister Mathilde praised her for being so good with numbers, but Trudi's favorite class was history. There she listened to stories about people who no longer lived, stories that gave her a new kind of satisfaction—that of knowing how something ended. History intensified her longing to find out ahead of time what would happen next in her own life, partly from curiosity, but mostly to protect herself against anything she didn't want to happen. And yet, she already sensed that, had she known her mother would die in the asylum, she could have done nothing to keep her safe.

History was unlike the fairy tales she loved: in fairy tales, there usually was a meaning to what happened and good people triumphed in the end even if they had to suffer; but in history the bullies often triumphed. History was also unlike the stories that continued to unfold around her every day without apparent endings—and yet, history began to influence how she saw those current stories: it taught her how people behaved and about the patterns between them. Like Napoleon—knowing how he'd kept invading new countries to protect his previous victories made her understand the bullies in the schoolyard. And the old Romans—finding out that only five of their many emperors had been good emperors helped her to grasp the disillusion in her father's voice when he discussed politics with Herr Abramowitz, who was often drafting letters on behalf of other Communists, many of them unskilled laborers without great prospects.

Politics were like history. Only they were happening now. But they were linked to history. Her father had told her about the feudal system, in which people used to get land from lords in return for total allegiance. Like fighting in battles. "We Germans have a history of sacrificing everything for one strong leader," her father had said. "It's our fear of chaos."

Fates, Trudi discovered in history class, had a way of repeating themselves, even if through someone else, and feelings that might seem unique to her—like that rage when other children taunted her— had probably been experienced by some girl hundreds of years ago. Because of the people in history, Trudi felt a far stronger link than ever before to the people in her town, and from all this grew new stories, which she told to Eva and her father, and to Frau Abramowitz who listened to every word and sighed, "Trudi, you and your splendid imagination."

But in school you couldn't tell stories.

In school you had to sit at your double desk and wait—the only child whose feet dangled high above the floor—and answer just those questions that Sister Mathilde asked. You had to raise your hand before you said anything, and if you forgot the rules and blurted out the answer, you had to stand in the corner to the left of the chalkboard. The dry scent of chalk tickling your nostrils, you'd wait there, your face to the wall, which was painted *kaka* brown on the bottom half and white above the stenciled trim. It happened to Trudi at least twice a week, but Hans-Jürgen Braunmeier, who fought in the schoolyard and always had bruises on him, spent more time in that corner than all the other students together. They became accustomed to the worn seat of his trousers, his frayed suspenders, his uneven heels.

You would have never guessed from the way Hans-Jürgen's parents dressed themselves and their four children in hand-me-downs, that they owned the biggest farm in Burgdorf. All Braunmeiers had bony faces and thin limbs, but while the parents and younger siblings slunk through town like shrinking ghosts, Hans-Jürgen stalked around with vengeful eyes, searching for fights as if seeking to get even for something too big to settle in one single battle. Lush brown curls, which even drastic haircuts couldn't tame, sprang from his head as if he were always walking into a formidable wind.

Since he occupied the corner several times a day, it was difficult for Sister Mathilde to punish other children for passing notes in class, say, or forgetting the line of a prayer, or throwing stones at the pesky ravens that hovered above the schoolyard during recess, screeching for bread crumbs. After conferring with the principal, Sister Mathilde assigned Hans-Jürgen his own corner—to the right of her desk behind the rubber plant that the bishop had given her. Whenever Trudi was sent to the corner, she'd glance over to Hans-Jürgen's corner, and he—without turning his head—would grin and stick his tongue out at the wall in front of him. In return she'd roll her eyes and make a fish mouth at the wall.

In second grade, Hans-Jürgen was the one student not allowed to come to the annual spring concert at the mansion, the only place where children from the Catholic and the Protestant schools came together peacefully. It was a concert that Fräulein Birnsteig, who was famous through all of Europe, gave for the children of Burgdorf every June. She hired farmers with hay wagons to bring them to her mansion, which was four kilometers from the center of town. They loved the concert, which began at dusk and lasted long past their bedtime.

She would play the piano in her music room, where flames from countless candles shimmered in the air, her beautifully shaped head thrown back, her lace-covered arms like the necks of swans as her hands descended on the keys. Although she'd never married, she had an adopted son who studied law in Heidelberg. As a young woman, she'd been disinherited by her parents because she'd chosen music over marriage, but she'd become so famous that her fortune now was far greater than her parents'.

She took on protégés—always just one at a time—and worked with them without charging. To be her student was a tremendous honor and meant acceptance to the best music programs in the country.

The double glass doors of her music room were flung wide open to the flagstone terrace, where canvas lawn chairs for the teachers had been set up. Sister Elisabeth, the second-grade teacher, was so big that she needed help lowering herself into her chair. Vines of ivy climbed up the stone walls of the white villa and cascaded from the red roof tiles. The rich scent of blooming lilac hedges suffused the air as the children spread blankets on the thick grass in the rose garden, where the pruned bushes were sending up new shoots.

Somehow—certainly not by intent, Trudi figured—Eva ended up sitting next to her, her skirt spread around her. Trudi adjusted her skirt to fall just like that. Two servants with starched aprons passed baskets with strawberries and vanilla wafers, and as the sounds of the piano drifted toward the children, they settled back into the fresh grass—even those who usually found it difficult to sit still—and let the magic of the piano fuse with the fragrant air and with that sense of festivity that comes with special occasions. They wore their Sunday clothes: the girls in smocked or embroidered dresses; the boys in suits with short pants and knee socks. The boys' hair had been combed wet, and you could see the straight parts and the ridges the combs had left; the girls' hair was in pigtails or braids that had been coiled above their ears or wound around their heads.

Georg Weiler was waving his hands like a conductor, and Helga Stamm began to wave her hands like that, too. Regular-size girls, Trudi was certain, had it easy, and she envied them, especially poor girls like Helga because the conspicuous line of her let-down hem announced to all of the world that this girl was growing.

The glow of the candles made it seem as if Fräulein Birnsteig were outside with her listeners. People said about her that she believed in her dreams, that she wrote them down and let them determine her decisions. Once, she had canceled a concert tour to America because she'd dreamed that the ship, which was to take her there, had sunk. Another time she had been in Hamburg and had brought a beggar woman home to live with her because she'd recognized the woman's features from a dream. In the dream, the beggar had been her sister. She still lived with the pianist and kept house for her, making sure Fräulein Birnsteig had absolute solitude during the long hours she practiced the piano.

As the music filled Trudi, it carried the crying of infants from some pocket of time far away; the high, swollen bellies of girls; the staccato of boots against marble floors. She didn't know what any of it meant, only that it was already there—waiting in its own time, moving through her in a gust of fear. Quickly, she pressed her eyes shut, then opened them again to look at the stars that were beginning to suck the dark from the sky.

A hand—Eva's hand—touched her hair, drew the fear from her heart. Fingers twirled the ends of Trudi's pigtails to form curls, combed through them as if no one else were there. Mute with sudden bliss, Trudi glanced at her friend, but Eva's eyes were on the pianist as though unaware of the gift she was bestowing, and Trudi understood that the love she felt meant far more to her than to Eva. Already she sensed that this was love at its purest. She tilted her head, glad that her hair was beautiful as its fine, thick texture grazed her neck and slid through Eva's fingers. The scent of fresh grass and ancient lilac bushes was overpowering, and she wanted to cry when Eva took her hand away, but it felt as though the music continued to touch her hair.

But the day after the concert, children began to shun Eva in school. Eyes red and averted, she stayed away from Trudi, who took out her mother's scarves again and tightened them around her head at night to keep it from growing even larger. In the mornings her temples would ache and her jaw would feel stiff.

She decided to stop taking piano lessons since she would never be good enough to be Fräulein Birnsteig's protégé. Maybe Robert could study with the pianist, who'd be sure to choose him if he lived in Burgdorf. Trudi wrote him a letter, telling him about the pianist, and her father promised to mail it the next day, together with two pictures she'd drawn: one of Robert sitting next to the pianist, the other of herself and her father and her dog on a big ship bound for America.

From the church library she borrowed eight picture books and read them in one day, all along thinking of Eva. Together with Frau Abramowitz, she brought *Streuselkuchen* to the butcher's mother-in-law, who'd broken her hip. Propped up on the living-room sofa, the old woman didn't complain about her pain, only about her inability to get up and do her housework. Behind her glasses, her eyes looked trapped as if she felt confined inside her body. She wore a pink cardigan above her nightgown, and was knitting another cardigan—brown, for her grandson, Anton.

When Eva resumed her visits to the pay-library two weeks after the concert, Trudi didn't show how glad she was to have her back. Eva seemed less cautious about being seen with her, and their walks through the neighborhood began to include other streets, even walks to the Rhein, where Seehund chased bees in the meadow. He had grown, and when he stood between the girls, his head reached Trudi's shoulder and Eva's waist.

In almost all families only the girls had to help with the housework, including shining their fathers' and brothers' shoes, but Eva's family distributed chores. Except for her father, everyone helped with the cleaning and cooking after the half-day maid had left, chores which—some of the old women said—were not suitable for boys.

Eva's seventh birthday was on a Monday, and her father arose from his invalid's bed in the afternoon. He surprised Trudi by opening the door for her when she arrived with her official present—a harmonica in a velvet case. Though she hadn't spoken to Herr Rosen before, he knew her name and told her that her father was a fine man. He worked hard for each breath, and his voice was as spongy as his body. When she followed his bulk into the dining room, he walked gingerly as if stepping on moss, making her feel that the floor beneath her feet was not nearly as steady as when she'd been in Eva's house before. She felt conspicuous in the yellow party dress her father had bought her from the little girls' rack at Mahler's department store in Düsseldorf.

Framed oil paintings of elegant women and somber men hung on the walls, and the chairs had carved armrests. Even though the leaded windows were closed—to keep cats out, Trudi figured—the rooms were saturated with light because the inside doors had panels of frosty glass, engraved with intricate flowers. The bird that Seehund had caught in the high grass nearly a year ago sat stuffed on a shelf in a nest, its beak tilted up, its ruby-red chest fluffed forever.

While Eva's mother drove to the Kaisershafen Gasthaus, Eva's father dozed in the passenger seat, his face and hands honey brown from the sun. But once they arrived, he was the one to request a table on the terrace and to order lemonade and *Erdbeertorte mit Sahne*—strawberry tart with whipped cream—for everyone. His legs were so bloated that he had to sit with them apart, and his stomach rested on his knees like a sleeping child. One of Eva's brothers had brought his guitar along, and they all sang the birthday song for her, *"Hoch soll sie leben, drei mal hoch. . . ."*—"High shall she live, three times high. . . ."

Eva's mother wore her pearls and a chic little cap. Below them the Rhein flowed in rich, green waves, and in the shimmering heat the trees across the river seemed to float above the ground. A stork flew past the terrace, heading in the direction of town, and a white excursion boat struggled against the current so slowly that it barely seemed to budge.

While Eva and Trudi took turns on her harmonica, her brothers rolled cardboard coasters across the tablecloth. Herr Rosen's face glowed with moisture, and when Frau Doktor Rosen looked at him, Trudi saw the same expression with which her father used to watch her mother—that look of concern and fear and pity—and she resolved to never let anyone look at her like that.

On the drive home, Eva's oldest brother got sick from drinking too much lemonade, and they stopped the car just in time for him to stagger out and vomit by the side of the road. In front of Eva's house, two Buttgereit girls stood waiting, and the Frau Doktor grabbed her black doctor's bag, turned the car around, and drove the girls to their farm.

The timing for Eva's second present couldn't have been better because Trudi's father had his chess club meeting that evening. As soon as it was dark, Trudi rolled two cigarettes in the pay-library and sneaked out to meet Eva behind the church. In the bushes outside the wall of the rectory, they took their first puffs, grimacing and coughing, and when they heard a door slam at a distance, they both tossed their cigarettes across the wall. All that night, Trudi lay awake, worried the rectory and church would burst into fire. She and Eva would burn in hell. But what if Catholics and Jews didn't go to the same hell? As she promised Jesus to go to church every day for an entire year—if only he prevented the fire—she already saw herself entering the church and crossing herself with cold holy water.

She was certain her prayers had been granted when the only light that came into her window was that of dawn. After breakfast she heard from Frau Blau that the Frau Doktor had stayed at the Buttgereits' house all night to deliver their tenth child. "A boy, imagine," Frau Blau said, and Trudi told her that—from the terrace of the Kaisershafen Gasthaus—she'd seen the stork who'd brought the baby.

Across town, Frau Buttgereit raised herself on her elbows and, cautiously, peered at the infant who slept in the cradle by her bed. After nine daughters, she had no longer hoped for a son, and when the child, still covered with her blood, had been handed to her, he'd seemed like some other woman's child—not only because his limbs were more delicate than those of her girls, but because she hadn't felt the resignation that had begun with the birth of her third daughter and had increased with each daughter since.

"An heir for the farm," her husband declared when he bought a box of cigars from Leo Montag.

"An heir for the farm," he announced when he distributed the cigars to the men at his *Stammtisch.*

Sometimes Trudi and Eva brought milk cans along on their walks to the river, swinging them by their handles as they walked past the wheat fields to fetch milk or eggs at the Braunmeiers' farm on their way home.

Frau Braunmeier would wait on them, the youngest child propped on her hip as her chapped hands counted their money. She'd come from a poor Protestant family in Krefeld, Trudi had heard, and she'd converted to Catholicism in order to marry into the Braunmeier money; yet, the irony was that her husband made her live with him in deeper poverty than she'd ever known. While the barn was huge and well maintained, the family lived in drafty rooms filled with shabby furniture, wore mended clothes, and subsisted on their farm products that were no longer fit for sale—milk about to curdle, bruised peaches, eggs that had lost their freshness.

One afternoon, when Trudi and Eva entered the gate of the Braunmeiers' farm, Hans-Jürgen jumped from behind the clotheslines where threadbare bed sheets were hung to dry. Wind rippled the sheets and flattened the leaves of the gooseberry bushes; it fanned Hans-Jürgen's curls from his forehead as he blocked the girls' way to the house.

"We have new kittens. You want to see?" His eyes glittered. "They're in the barn."

Eva reached for her throat. Trudi hesitated. Everyone knew that children were not allowed inside the barn, but she'd sneaked in once before while her father had bought eggs from Frau Braunmeier. Hans-Jürgen and two of his friends had crouched in the hay loft and hissed at her to go away, but she'd stayed, just to get back at them for not wanting her there.

"You can't make me leave," she'd said, her heart pulsing so hard in her ears that she could barely hear her own words, and the only thing that had kept her from running away had been the knowledge that— if she told on him—his mother would punish him for being inside the barn.

But this time Hans-Jürgen was asking her to stay. He even wanted to show her his kittens. "Come on," he urged her and rolled his eyes, imitating her fish mouth from school, until she had to laugh and walked with him to the arched barn door, Eva and Seehund close behind her.

"Your dog has to stay outside." Deftly, he tied Seehund to a stake next to the long trough. "Down, boy," he said and patted Seehund's rear. His eyes darted toward the house. "No one is allowed in the barn," he said in an important voice

"I want to go home," Eva said, her back and neck even straighter than usual.

"Goose." He opened the barn door.

It was almost like a church inside—as quiet and as hollow and as big. And since it was forbidden to be there, it was even more exciting. Trudi pulled Eva along by her hand as she followed Hans-Jürgen past the row of cow rumps toward the back of the barn. Behind a wooden partition lay a fat gray cat in a nest of clean straw, encircled by a litter of kittens.

Trudi squatted down and stroked the cat's back. Eva stepped closer, her expression a mix of curiosity and caution.

"You want to hold a kitten?" Hans-Jürgen offered.

Eva nodded.

"Here." He reached for a striped kitten, but the cat snarled. One rapid paw darted out and scratched his wrist. He cried out and turned his face from the girls. With one foot he pushed the cat aside and snatched something fuzzy from where she'd lain, before she could spread herself across the remaining small shapes again, her eyes like embers.

Trudi wanted to console the cat, but she was afraid of frightening her even more. "Put the kitten back," she said.

He hid it against the front of his faded shirt. "What kitten?"

"The kitten you took," Eva said.

"It's not even a kitten," he said. "It's a mole. A blind mole, see?" He held it toward Trudi, snatching it away before she could get it, and it was then that Trudi saw a rage in him that she recognized, a rage that she, too, had felt at times, the rage to destroy, and she shuddered.

"Put it back," she ordered though she knew it was too late.

He laughed. "And now—now it's a bird. See?"

Holding the kitten by its tail, he whirled. Eva wailed, a long keening sound that echoed through the barn, while Trudi tried to hang on his arm. But he kept whirling, faster, the striped kitten flapping at the end of his outstretched arm, faster even, his face oddly illuminated like the faces of saints while they're performing miracles. His fist opened and, while he kept whirling as though unable to stop himself, the kitten soared in a high arc toward the farthest wall, where its tiny body made an amazingly loud thud before it plummeted to the ground.

Eva stopped screaming and stood very still, both hands clasped across her mouth, but Trudi ran toward the kitten. Despite her horror, she already could feel the words she would use to describe to Sister Elisabeth and to her father how limp and sticky the kitten felt in her hands. She would tell them about the blood that seeped from its mouth, about its eyes that were dull as if covered by a bride's veil. And she would remember those eyes, just as she would remember the rapid shadow of panic that passed across Hans-Jürgen's face the following morning when he was called to the front of the class for twenty lashes with Sister Elisabeth's wooden ruler. His back to her, he stood in the corner for one hour, and she felt certain that, even if she were sent to the other corner, he would not acknowledge her.

That Sunday, Herr Pastor Schüler spoke with Herr Braunmeier after church, and Monday morning Hans-Jürgen arrived in school with new bruises on his face and arms. His eyes were sullen, but once, when Trudi caught him glancing at her, she saw the flicker of revenge in his pupils. Though her hair started hurting, she forced herself to keep her eyes steady on his until he was the one to look away.

"Keep your window open tonight," she hissed as she passed his desk on her way out of class.

He stood up, his shoulders and face above her, and she could see into the dark cavities of his nostrils. His hands rose along his sides as if to seize her and swing her around like that kitten.

"Hans-Jürgen!" Sister Elisabeth said sternly. Though she wasn't old, she walked with a cane.

Hans-Jürgen grabbed his satchel and ran from the room.

"What did you tell him?" Eva wanted to know when she appeared at the pay-library with a bone for Seehund.

"To keep his window open. So the mother cat can come into his room and lie on his throat."

Eva shivered. "And he will die a terrible death."

"He will fight for each breath."

"But the mother cat won't get off him."

"Not even when he screams."

Their eyes fused as if in a promise, and they each let out a deep breath.

"Not even then."

In preparation for first communion, Sister Elisabeth gave each child a rosary and demonstrated how you started the rosary by blessing yourself with the cross at the end of the little tail. Then you said the Apostles' Creed, one Our Father, three Hail Marys, one Our Father, and—at the very end—Hail Holy Queen.

"Your rosary has five decades with ten Hail Marys and one Our Father," Sister Elisabeth explained. "On these rosaries, each decade is a separate color so you can pray for the conversion of continents: black, of course, is for Africa; yellow for Asia; red for Russia; green for South America; and blue for Australia."

"Can blue be for the Arctic?" Hans-Jürgen Braunmeier asked.

"The Arctic doesn't count. Only penguins live there."

Hilde Sommer raised her hand. "Why can't we pray for penguins?" The strong, heavy girl was new in town and had fainted twice, so far, in church from the scent of incense.

The sister squeezed her lips shut, as usual when she got impatient, and when she opened them, she informed Hilde that, although there was nothing wrong with praying occasionally for animals, you only did so after you'd done all your praying for people. "Animals don't have souls. Except maybe the donkey and ox who were in little Jesus' manger."

"The sheep, too," Paul Weinhart reminded her. His parents had lots of sheep on their farm.

Sister Elisabeth nodded, a pained expression on her face as if already sorry she had ever mentioned animals at all. Her facial hair was colorless but thick above her upper lip.

Trudi raised her hand, and when the sister called on her, she said, "If the red is for a continent, it can't be for Russia."

The sister's expression of discontent deepened.

"My father was there in the war. It's on the same continent with Germany."

Sister Elisabeth talked about the apostle Thomas, who had doubted that Jesus had appeared to the other apostles until he could touch his wounds. "The mere act of doubting is sin," she said, emphasizing her words with a thump of her cane, and went on to tell the class how Thomas had redeemed himself by becoming a martyr in India.

To show the sister that she was sorry about doubting, Trudi stayed inside during recess to water the plants and clean the chalkboard. When Sister Elisabeth gave her a holy card of St. Agnes, the patron saint of girls, Trudi felt that sacred flutter inside that she sometimes got when she watched a procession or thought of Jesus dying for her sins. At home, she added the holy card to her collection of holy cards and practiced first communion in front of her mother's gold-framed mirror. As she opened her mouth as far as she could, she wished Eva could go to first communion with her. They'd both wear white dresses and wreaths of white satin roses in their hair. Too bad Eva was a Jew. Jews couldn't have communion. Trudi stuck out her tongue—keeping it flat and straight. If you didn't keep it flat, the communion wafer could fall off. You were not allowed to touch it with your teeth. And if you spit your communion wafer into your handkerchief, it turned to blood.

While Trudi dreaded confession—the relinquishing of her own secrets—many of her classmates came to crave the rewards of confession. Once they got beyond the fear of kneeling in the somber confessional, they looked forward to the Saturday absolutions that turned their souls white and glowing. Like actors trained to produce tears on stage, they learned to awaken remorse. But their new souls would lose some of the purity by Sunday afternoon, after having shimmered through nine-o'clock mass. Within the next days, those souls would become slightly worn, and by the end of the week they'd be stained. The children imagined their souls to be somewhere below their hearts, cloud-shaped, elongated forms inside the rib cage. The pressure of ribs left imprints on souls, that's how soft and pliable they were. And sins left long smudges like coal dust.

Sins and secrets—for Trudi they often were the same. Sins made the best secrets. They swelled and breathed until a priest slaughtered them with words of absolution. The blood of the lamb, blood of the sins, died for your sins. *Your mother's sins.*

Perhaps the Braunmeiers' cat never knew how dangerous she could be to Hans-Jürgen, because he kept returning to school every day, long after his bruises had healed and been replaced by signs of new schoolyard fights.

In spring, soon after the French occupied the Rheinland, he arrived in church with his right arm in a sling. His father had caught him with matches in the barn, and this—the danger to the building and live-stock—was far worse to his father than what Hans-Jürgen had used the matches for: to burn the fleshy pads on the paws of a tomcat. Per-haps some of the scratches on the boy's face and neck had been caused by the tomcat, who must have fought him, but the arm had been broken when his father had flung him to the ground and stamped out the flames from the match that had fallen from his son's hand. Yet, looking at Hans-Jürgen's rigid face, you'd swear that the fire had not died but had settled in his eyes instead, where it would continue to flare.

Trudi knew that fire only too well, knew it from inside herself. Sometimes she would love fiercely. Sometimes she'd feel a bolt of hate tear through her. She'd feel mean. Kind. Afraid. Like that Wednesday when the second graders were about to play *Völkerball*—nation ball—a game that had become increasingly popular since the French occupation.

Sister Elisabeth chose the team captains: for the French team Eva Rosen, and for the German team Hilde Sommer, whose fainting spells during mass had earned her the compassion of the nuns. The sister never let any of the boys be captains. Boys were unmanageable, she said, a quiver of dread in her voice, and made them sit at their desks with their hands on the wooden surface to keep them from dig-ging in their pants for a slingshot or something even more menacing. Girls, the sister believed, were not nearly as endangered by mysteri-ous urges.

Eva and Hilde stood in front of the other children, and whenever they called a name, a girl or boy would get in line behind them. Trudi willed Eva to pick her for her team, even though the French would start out in the middle of the field, dodging balls that were aimed at them from the German team until they'd all been hit. Then, the teams would switch positions, and you'd start all over again.

But Eva kept staring right past Trudi while the lines behind the captains were getting longer until everyone had been chosen. Except for Trudi.

"Your turn," Eva reminded Hilde.

"I don't want her on my team."

"But you have to."

"You take her."

"It's your turn to pick."

When Hilde said something to Georg Weiler behind her, he started to laugh. Georg was a fast runner and usually got picked right away. He was wearing his *Lederhosen* and a regular boy's shirt.

"We always lose if she's on our side," Fritz Hansen shouted.

"Children!" The heavy sister brought her palms together in two sharp raps. "Stop this. Right now."

"I don't want to play." Trudi pretended to tie her shoelaces so that the others couldn't see she was crying.

"You have to play, Trudi." The sister's voice was stern. She took Trudi's arm and led her to the end of Hilde's line.

Trudi's legs felt shorter than ever before, and as she followed the rules of the game—trying to pelt members of the French team, and running from the ball when the French team became the attacker—she felt the other children moving around her in one fluid mass, felt their oneness as though she belonged to a separate species. Inside her bones was a pulling as though her growing were struggling to come through. It often felt like that, especially in her back and legs; still, those aches were nothing compared to the shame she felt.

After school, she hid behind the gym until all the children were gone. From the Theresienheim came the smell of stale water, and a goat bleated from the direction of the bicycle shop. She reached into her pocket and counted the money her father had given her to buy a loaf of bread on the way home—fifteen banknotes, each for one million *Mark*. The bills used to be for one thousand *Mark* each, but the Reichsbank had printed the new amount diagonally across the original. She could still remember when bread used to cost a few *Pfennige*. But every day things were getting more expensive: in just a month, a pound of chicken had gone from six million to ten million *Mark*. To ride the streetcar you had to pay seven million *Mark*.

Herr Abramowitz, who'd become a member of the Communist Party, sometimes talked with Trudi's father about the poverty that spread with each devaluation of the money. People were afraid. Many had lost their jobs and were scrambling to do work they felt contempt for, like selling sewing machines from door to door or hiring on as day laborers. They felt humiliated when the court claimed their furniture against unpaid bills and the bailiff pasted the evidence of their failure, the *Kuckuck*—cuckoo, on the back of a cupboard or desk. And when they saw food behind the windows of stores and restaurants without being able to buy it, they became only more jealous of Jews like Herr Abramowitz and Fräulein Birnsteig, who were successful and could afford whatever they wanted. Some people had chosen suicide over the disgrace of being poor. Nearly all agreed that the Versailles *Friedensvertrag* was degrading and starving them all. They longed for the life they had known before the war, a life of order which—when they thought of it—seemed etched by sunlight.

Many people had lost their savings and pensions. And Trudi had heard Herr Hesping say that all of them would be giving up even more. As she walked toward Hansen's bakery, she pondered what she'd be willing to give up if she could be tall. Definitely an arm. Perhaps even a leg, since she would still have one long leg. An arm would be easier to do without. What if she had to give up both—an arm and a leg? It would be impossible to walk with crutches if you didn't have both arms. Unless—and she tried to picture this—unless the leg and the arm you gave up were on opposite sides.

She raised her right knee and hopped forward on her left leg, imagining herself with a crutch in her right hand. Though it was hard to keep her balance, she managed to propel herself toward the street corner on one leg until she stumbled. Still—as she sat on the ground, she knew she would give up both. If her guardian angel came up to her this moment and guaranteed that she'd be tall in exchange for one arm and one leg, she was ready to let her guardian angel saw both off right here.

She got up and hopped on her left foot, then the right, extending the opposite arm like a wing. Suddenly she had to smile. At least then Sister Elisabeth would no longer make her participate in stupid ball games. But maybe giving up a leg and an arm wasn't necessary. She stopped and stood still. Maybe it would be enough to give up two fingers like the baker, who'd lost them in Russia during the war. If you lost something that you'd once had—a limb, say, or one eye—people didn't treat you like a freak: they remembered you the way you had been. But if you were born without arms or sight, you were a freak. If your body didn't look like the bodies of others, you were a freak. And if you lived in a freak's body long enough, though you didn't feel like a freak inside—what could you do then to make sure your body wouldn't turn all of you into a freak?

That afternoon, Eva did not come to the pay-library, and the next morning in school she wouldn't look at Trudi once. The first person Trudi told about Eva's birthmark was Helga Stamm, who'd received the dreaded *Blaue Brief*—blue letter—from school, warning her that she might have to stay back.

"Like a red cabbage," Trudi whispered, "all over Eva's chest. Even her mother can't do anything about it, and she's a doctor."

She took Irmtraud Boden and Hilde Sommer aside and told them how the mark on Eva's chest had started out tinier than the pit of a cherry, and how it still kept growing although the Frau Doktor had rubbed every possible medicine on it.

"Soon," Trudi said to Fritz Hansen, "everyone will know because the red will creep up Eva's neck and down her arms. Once it covers her fingers, everyone she touches will turn red, too."

They bent close to her whispered words as if they were her friends, and though she couldn't hold them beyond the story, she understood that she could always lure them back with new secrets.

In the hallway, Paul Weinhart tried to pull up the front of Eva's sweater, but she ran back into the classroom; the following day, two of the girls asked if they could see her chest. Her face as crimson as the birthmark, Eva spun away from them, and when her eyes fastened on Trudi, they were dark and startled as if, finally, she knew what it was like to be betrayed by your best friend.

It was not until the end of the week, during recess, that several girls pinned Eva's arms against the school fence and unbuttoned her blouse to expose the birthmark. When they were summoned to the principal's office, where Frau Doktor Rosen, who had seen many of them through mumps and measles, met them, the girls mumbled that they'd only wanted to tickle Eva.

Eva stayed home from school the following Monday and Tuesday, and Trudi had a dream that Eva had turned into an invalid like her father. Eva lay next to him in a canvas chair. Both had their eyes closed. Except that Eva had no blanket covering her. The top of her dress was open, and the flower on her chest had sprouted vines that surrounded her like the hedge of thorns that grew around the sleeping princess, *Dornröschen,* on Trudi's fairy-tale puzzle blocks. Eva's expression was peaceful as if in a hundred year sleep, and the vines fastened her to the veranda, protecting her from the world beyond.

Yet, Wednesday afternoon Eva stood outside Trudi's window with a new leash for Seehund, hollering for her to come outside and play. Watching her from behind the lace curtains, Trudi felt the love and hate inside her fusing into something heavy and unyielding.

"Trudi," her father shouted from the hallway outside the pay-library, "Eva is here."

She couldn't answer.

"Trudi." His limp paused at the bottom of the stairs.

She felt nothing, except for that cold burden. A scant breeze shifted through the curtain and cooled her face. As she stepped from the window, she caught the white lace between her fingers, and all at once she felt a yearning to know someone shaped like her, someone whose torso would be solid, whose legs would be short and sturdy, whose arms would not span further than hers, someone who would look at her with recognition—not with curiosity or contempt.

■

IT WAS FROM FRAU SIMON THAT TRUDI HEARD ABOUT THE ZWERG MAN in Düsseldorf. Frau Simon had seen him in the audience at the Opernhaus, where she held a subscription. "About as tall as you, Trudi, and so—so elegant. You should have seen him. Wearing a night-blue tuxedo, almost black . . . and a beautiful top hat to match." Frau Simon's freckled hands whisked through the air to recreate the design of the top hat.

From that day on it became Trudi's goal to find that *Zwerg* man, and she begged her father to take her to Düsseldorf. She talked him into buying tickets for the opera and sat through *Der Bettelstudent*— *The Student Prince,* with the opera glasses that Frau Simon had lent her, scanning the audience. During the intermission, her father stood in line to buy her sugar-coated almonds while she pushed her way through groups of people—past hips and waists and bellies and hands—expecting to come face to face with the *Zwerg* man. But she did not find him, and when she ate those almonds during the second half of the performance, her stomach cramped with the sick-sweet memory of the stork's sugar.

When Trudi played with Seehund or walked to school, she'd embellish the few details she knew about the man—his size, his tuxedo, his top hat—into a story until she'd invented an entire life for him. It didn't come together all at once, but rather in fragments that kept knocking about inside her head and attached themselves to the roots of her story until it sprouted a trunk, branches, a skyful of leaves. The *Zwerg,* she decided, was a famous painter—no, a musician like Fräulein Birnsteig, a composer even. That's why he'd been at the opera.

The composer lived in a villa in Düsseldorf, on the other side of the Oberkassel bridge, and he had two children who were *Zwerge* too. One was seven, a year younger than Trudi, the other a year older than she. The composer would like nothing better than to find a friend for his children. One Sunday he'd drive through Burgdorf and spot Trudi in front of the pay-library. He'd invite her for a ride in a car like Herr Abramowitz's, ask her what her favorite food was, and—

"Don't ever take chocolate from strangers," the sisters had warned all the children. There were mass murderers, the sisters said, who did terrible things to children, like stuff them into sausages and feed those sausages to unsuspecting people. There was even a song about a convicted murderer, which the children were forbidden to sing: *"Warte, warte nur ein Weilchen . . ."*—"Wait, wait just a little while . . ." It went on to say how, soon, he would come to you too and, with his *"kleine Hackebeilchen"*—little hatchet—make ground meat of you. After her initial shock that the world was not safe, Trudi had chanted the words of the gruesome song along with the other children— *". . . aus den Augen macht er Sülze . . ."*—". . . from the eyes he makes head cheese"; *"aus dem Hintern macht er Speck . . ."*—"from the rear end he makes bacon . . ."; and she'd shuddered with delicious fear.

But certainly the *Zwerg* man was not anything like a mass murderer. He was rather like the unknown benefactor, anticipating what she would like before she could even tell him. Her father would meet him and talk with him about music and chess and politics. And then the *Zwerg* would take her and his children to the top of a mountain where snow lay year round, and they'd build a snowman with coal eyes and a carrot nose. They'd ride one long sled down the slope, and the *Zwerg* would tie the sled to the back of his car and pull them back up.

Yes, following a *Zwerg* would be different.

To not follow him would be unthinkable.

• • •

Trudi would not see another *Zwerg* until she turned thirteen, and that *Zwerg* was the new animal tamer of the carnival that came to the Burgdorf fairgrounds every July. Dressed in a glittering white dress with black lapels that sprang from her neckline like pointed leaves, the animal tamer led the elephants into the arena, and when her quick whip snapped around their massive feet without touching them, they bowed their knees as if to pay homage to her.

Her name was Pia. She had a mass of blue-black curls and a stocky body that moved with agility. While people laughed at the clowns and monkeys, they did not laugh at the *Zwerg* woman—they were awed by her skill and courage, and when she placed her head inside the lion's wide-open mouth, it became so quiet in the circus tent that even the youngest children hushed, and in that long moment before she extricated her head from the dangerous cavern—that moment when the scent of animals and sawdust and sweat thickened and soaked into the canvas of the huge tent—one single breath connected everyone in the audience. As Pia ran into the center of the arena and curtsied, sweeping one hand with a graceful flourish to the floor and then high into the air, the people stood up and applauded.

Trudi knew they didn't applaud because Pia was a *Zwerg,* and she clapped her hands until they stung, wishing that people would notice her, too, for the things she could do—like adding numbers in her head or remembering nearly every train connection in Germany—not for being a *Zwerg.* But even though she dreaded the attention she received, she'd become so accustomed to it that she craved and expected it.

As she sat back down in the first row, Trudi willed the animal tamer to look at her. She knew her braids looked pretty the way she had fastened them around the top of her head. Her new pink dress already felt tight again, but at least it was the right length. The washwoman, whom her father continued to employ despite rumors that she smuggled bleaching powders into people's houses, was good at opening side seams and setting in matching pieces of fabric. Her father still bought children's clothes for Trudi, frilly skirts and blouses and dresses, because adult clothes drowned her: waists were in the wrong place, and hems dragged. Men didn't know much about things like that.

If her mother still lived, Trudi was sure, she would have clothes that fit her just right—like that white glitter dress that looked as though it had been designed for Pia. Trudi wondered if Pia, too, had tried to force her body to stretch, but Pia was no taller than she. Despite everything Trudi had done, her limbs had stopped growing entirely by the time she was eleven. Pursuing the limits of her body with a magnificent hatred, she'd not only hung by her fingers from door frames but also from tree limbs, and occasionally she had fallen, causing bruises and scrapes. Often her arms and shoulders had ached for days, and she'd consoled herself with the promise that, once her body was fully grown, she'd move to a distant town where no one would know that she used to be a *Zwerg*. There, she'd imagine, it would be easier to confess to theft or murder than to having been a *Zwerg*.

A fat clown on a tiny bicycle wobbled into the arena, shrieking while a parrot with glorious tail feathers clung to his back like a vulture. After riding wildly around the animal tamer, who watched the spectacle with an amused frown, the clown threw himself into the sawdust at her feet as though begging her to rescue him.

Pia snapped her fingers, and the parrot fluttered up from the clown's back and settled on her wrist. "I need a volunteer from the audience," she announced with a confident smile.

Instead of raising her arm like others, Trudi slid from her seat and stepped forward, the ruffles of her dress scratching her elbows.

For a moment Pia looked startled, and her black eyes skipped past Trudi and back as if snared by her own reflection. But then she laughed with delight. "Come." She extended her free hand, and Trudi held herself straight as she walked toward Pia. "It looks like we have a volunteer. From the magic island which I call home. The island of the little people, where everyone is our height. . . ." She waved her hand from Trudi to herself. "Where figs and oranges and orchids fill every garden, where birds like Othello"—she whispered to the parrot, and it settled on Trudi's wrist—"are as common as your ducks."

Trudi held her wrist steady. The claws of the bird were cool like the rind of an orange.

The clown squealed, grabbed his bicycle under one arm, and left the ring with a sequence of cartwheels.

"It is an island very few people know of." The animal tamer fastened her gaze on Trudi. Her face was ageless—unlined, yet ancient—and beautiful with its painted mouth and broad cheekbones. "Do you remember our island?"

Trudi's neck felt stiff as she nodded.

"And what do you remember best, my lovely friend?"

Trudi was afraid to look past her at the familiar faces in the audience, faces that certainly had to be filled with ridicule, but when she did, they were watching her with admiration. She stroked one finger across the back of the parrot and took a long breath. "The waterfall," she said.

"She remembers the waterfall," Pia announced. "And a splendid waterfall it is on our island. Cool in the summer, warm in the winter." She whisked three golden loops from the empty air, and as she held them out, the parrot shrieked and flew through them as if they formed a tunnel, landing back on Trudi's wrist.

"And the tunnel," Trudi spoke up, drawn into the gaudy luster of the moment. "I remember a tunnel . . . made of jewels."

"It led from your house to mine, yes." In the eyes of the animal tamer was a mischievous glint that urged Trudi to go on.

Between them they wove the story of an island so glorious that everyone in the audience would have followed them there without questions, and all along the parrot flew between them like a weaver's shuttle, coming to linger on Trudi's wrist between its stunts. Once, as it shook its feathers, it tickled Trudi's face, and she stopped the urge to sneeze by touching the roof of her mouth with her tongue the way Eva had shown her. If only Eva could see her here with Pia. But Eva was now a student at the *Gymnasium* in Düsseldorf, and though she'd stop to greet Trudi if they saw each other on the street, it was not like being friends with her.

Before Pia led Trudi back to her seat, she reached into the empty air, extracted an immense wrinkled paper rose, and presented it to Trudi with a kiss on the cheek.

While the clowns and acrobats entertained the audience, Trudi barely looked at them. She kept waiting for the animal tamer to return, but Pia appeared only once more—at the end when all the performers ran into the arena and bowed to lengthy applause. Surrounded by others of normal size, she didn't look nearly as impressive.

When the tent had emptied, Trudi went looking for Pia, the paper rose in her hand. She didn't have any idea what she would say; yet, she had to speak with her. Pia would be able to look at her and see beyond her body. The people in town only saw her body and dismissed her as not being one of them.

One of the acrobats pointed Trudi past the merry-go-round and the fortune-teller's tent to a blue trailer that sat in a patch of clover and buttercups. A laundry line with lacy underwear and stockings hung between its side window and a birch tree. Glossy paint covered the wooden sides, even the stairs that led up to the door. For a moment Trudi was afraid to knock, but then she imagined her mother simply walking up those steps and raising her hand. The anniversary of her mother's death was only two days away. Strange how it took her time to remember the date of her mother's birth—somewhere the middle of March—yet, the day she had died, July 9, was engraved in her mind. She dreaded that date because not one year had passed when she hadn't relived that last hour of watching her mother die in the asylum, where they locked up people who took off their clothes for the angels. And it was unsettling to consider that the date of her own death already existed, that it passed each year without her knowing and—this was perhaps the worst—that it would never be as important to anyone as the death date of her mother was to her.

She pushed her shoulders back and knocked. Pia was in a silk embroidered dressing gown and didn't look surprised to see her.

"There must be others," Trudi blurted.

Pia stepped aside to let her enter. The inside of the trailer was the same cornflower blue as the outside: blue pillows, blue cabinets, a blue-fringed tablecloth.

"I have never met anyone like me." Trudi said it slowly. And then she said it again. "I have never met anyone like me."

"Oh, but they're everywhere." The *Zwerg* woman rolled a fat cigarette with nimble fingers and lit it. "In various places. All of them alone. In my travels, I never have to look for them. They find me." Her eyes were at the same level with Trudi's. "They want to know, just like you, about others."

"That island . . . ?"

"For all of us. Yours to dream your way to."

"Why can't we all be in one place?"

"We are. It's called earth."

"Not that. You know."

"Would it be any better?"

"I wouldn't be the only one then."

"You're not."

"In this town I am."

Pia nodded, gravely, and picked a shred of tobacco from her tongue. Her lavish hair fell to her shoulders. "When I get that feeling of being the only one, I imagine hundreds of people like me . . . all over the world, all feeling isolated, and then I feel linked to them." She pointed to a low stuffed chair. "Sit, if you like."

When Trudi sat down, her feet touched the floor instead of dangling high above it. She smiled to herself with the promise that in this world of high streetcar seats and store counters, of tall benches and chairs, she would from now on have furniture that was right for her inside her house. While other children had grown into their parents' furniture, things had remained too big for her; yet, she'd kept adjusting, scaling chairs, reaching up to the counter to prepare food, moving a wooden stool around to climb on whenever she needed to reach something. No more, she thought, no more.

"Tell me your name." Pia puffed on her cigarette.

"Trudi. It's short for Gertrud."

"A strong name. It suits you."

"Have you met a hundred like us?"

"One hundred and four."

"You count then."

"How can I not?"

"But there are even more."

"Oh yes. In Russia and Italy and France and Portugal . . ."

Dizzy with joy, Trudi could feel them—those one hundred and four—linked to her as if they were here in the trailer, and in that instant she understood that for Pia being a *Zwerg* was normal, beautiful even. To Pia, long arms were ugly, long legs unsteady. Tall people looked odd, too far from the ground with their wobbly gait. Trudi glanced at Pia who was watching her, silently, as if she knew what Trudi was thinking, and she felt herself connected to the earth, far more solidly than if she had long legs.

She thought of the book jackets of women and men looking into each other's eyes and wondered what it would be like to kiss and marry a *Zwerg* man. Part one of a kiss—so she'd been told by Hilde Sommer, who had heard it from Irmtraud Boden after she'd been kissed by the butcher's son—was lips against lips. Part two of a kiss was the man's tongue—regardless how disgusting that sounded—inside a woman's mouth.

Trudi swallowed hard. She had to ask Pia. Not that she expected to have a man ever love her or to have children, but—"Do any of them get married?"

"Some do."

"To each other?"

"Yes. Or to tall people."

"And their babies . . . ?"

"Some are *Zwerge*. Others not."

"Do you have a baby?"

"He's a grown-up." Pia laughed. "An odd word for us: grown-up. We become grown-ups even if we don't grow. . . . But my son—he's both, a grown grown-up." She stopped laughing. "Do I confuse you?"

"No." Trudi twirled the paper flower between her fingers. "Will you come back here?"

"Perhaps. I can't know those things in advance."

"What if I want to ask you questions?"

"Send them to the stars—they'll find me."

"Do you ever wish you could look straight into people's faces?"

"Instead of always looking up and seeing the underside of their chins or the hair in their noses?"

"And the boogers." Trudi giggled.

"Don't look up."

"But then I'll only see their bellies, their elbows, their belts—"

"Their fat bottoms. Girl . . ." Pia dabbed tears of laughter from her eyes. "But not for long. Tell me this—what do you do if someone has a very soft voice?"

"I lean closer."

"Right."

Trudi waited, but Pia watched her without saying another word, an amused expression on her face.

"You mean . . ."

"Try it."

"They'll bend down to me?"

"Not all of them. But many. As long as you remember not to look up."

"I'll try that. Thank you." Trudi looked around the trailer, which

was smaller than her bedroom. Still—she didn't need much space and
could always sleep on the sofa. "What if I came with you?" she asked,
her heartbeat high in her throat.

"But you don't want to."

"How can you say that?"

"This is where you belong, this town . . . where you matter."

"I want to come with you."

"You are still a child."

"I'll be fourteen next year."

"A child." Pia nodded. "And even if I welcomed you—it wouldn't
change that feeling of being the only one. No one but you can change
that. Like this." She wrapped her short arms around herself. Rocking
steadily, she smiled.

Trudi frowned at her.

"Some day you'll remember this," the *Zwerg* woman promised.

After the carnival left Burgdorf, Trudi began to sew her own clothes.
Up to then she had dreaded sewing lessons in school, but after seeing
how well that dress fit Pia, she thought of ways to change the patterns
and shorten them before she pinned them to fabric. Herr Blau showed
her how to use his old sewing machine: she had to stand to operate it,
but he was an eager teacher, giving her advice on darts and hems and
interfacing, and cautioning her to keep her fingers away from the
rapid needle so they wouldn't get punctured like his thumb.

In the upstairs room, from where the Blaus' daughter used to pass
notes to the young Helene Montag across the narrow alley, Trudi
stood at Herr Blau's sewing machine, one foot pumping, surrounded
by bolts of leftover fabrics and headless dummies—stained cotton-
covered torsos on poles—while Herr Blau, who was older than anyone she knew, kept rubbing his stiff hands and blowing on his
fingertips, as though impatient to do the sewing for her.

The first project she finished was a blouse the same shade of blue
as Pia's trailer. She sewed a skirt to match, a white jacket with blue
leaf-shaped lapels, a white coat. No longer for her the styles of children. She sewed slips that kept her skirts and dresses from clinging to
her legs, silky linings that made jackets lie smooth on her back, a
swimsuit which she wore only twice before autumn chilled the depths
of the river. Buttonholes were the most difficult part, and she was
grateful when Herr Blau volunteered to do them for her.

When Frau Simon complimented her on her appearance and told her how important self-improvement was, Trudi went after self-improvement with an obsession that depleted her savings and crowded her dreams with visions of shoulder pads and lapels, tailored waists and high-heeled shoes. Many women destroyed the style of a dress by wearing a cardigan above it, and Trudi swore to herself that she'd never take up that habit.

"You can tell so much by a woman's hands," Frau Simon said and wrote down the brand of her hand lotion for Trudi. "They only sell this in Düsseldorf."

When Trudi told her father about Pia's furniture, he was so apologetic that he hadn't thought of it himself, that she almost wished she hadn't said anything. But then he bought lumber and built her a birch chair with low legs. When he saw how pleased she was with the chair, he went into a fit of modifications. In the kitchen, he assembled a platform next to the cabinets and icebox, high enough for Trudi to stand on and reach counters and shelves, narrow enough not to get in his way when he worked in the kitchen. He agonized over whether he should build her a table to go with her chair, and when she assured him that she wanted to eat at the same table with him, he designed a chair higher than his with three wide steps leading up to the seat. He built several wide stools and placed them in the pay-library and all over the house. One evening, when Trudi went to bed, she was startled to discover that she no longer had to climb up on the mattress; after one delirious moment of believing that her body had suddenly sprung into its full height, she noticed traces of yellow dust on the floor, and when she crouched to check beneath her bed, she saw that her father had sawed off the bottom halves of the supports.

The day Hilde Sommer mentioned to her that eyelashes get longer and darker if you cut off the tips regularly, Trudi borrowed Frau Abramowitz's curved nail scissors and trimmed her blond eyelashes. She waited for them to come in, thick and dark, and when they didn't change at all, she asked Hilde, who, it turned out, hadn't tried cutting her own eyelashes—not yet, she said—but had heard about it from her cousin in Hamburg, who swore it worked.

"Maybe now I better wait until I see what happens with your eyelashes," she told Trudi.

Hilde, who wanted to be a midwife when she grew up, was friendlier to Trudi than most of her classmates. She liked to wear red, and even thinking about the smell of incense could make her faint. It was her ability to faint that made Hilde popular in school, where she taught the girls how to sway from side to side and buckle at the knees. They took turns competing over who could faint the fastest while others stood by to catch them by the elbows and carry them toward an imaginary church door. Even though Hilde was the heaviest of the girls, she was carried more often than anyone else.

When one of the girls in their class had to leave town and live with her aunt because she was getting big, Hilde told Trudi that the girl was pregnant. Though Trudi no longer believed in storks and had her doubts about Eva's theory that hair from down below grew toward your belly button when you were pregnant, she sometimes still checked the pale hairs that curled from the hard triangle between her thighs. Babies, she'd figured out, came from inside women. But she had no idea how they got inside. What she knew though was that plenty of babies came as a shock to the mothers; that some women died when babies were born; and that other women did mysterious things to keep babies from getting inside or from growing once they got in.

To improve herself, Trudi studied how others walked—not rotating from side to side like her, but straight forward—and she practiced that new stride, catching her reflection in every window she passed, monitoring her progress. Graceful hats from Frau Simon's shop added a few centimeters to her height. She felt delighted when she discovered she could make herself look even taller by wearing slightly longer skirts and keeping her jackets short. By now she could walk into any room and estimate anyone's height to the last centimeter by comparing it to her own.

She had her braids cut off so that her hair ended in a line with her shoulders, like Pia's, but the hairdresser talked her out of dyeing it blue-black and showed her instead how to pin the left side behind her ear to make her face look slimmer.

Whenever she'd imagine herself to be Pia, something would change in the way she'd touch her body. She found new pleasure in bathing herself in perfumed water—not just on Saturdays but also on Wednesdays—pleasure in washing and rinsing her hair. With her fingertips she'd rub scented lotion into her face and throat, relishing the contact with her own skin.

"You look perfect," her father would tell Trudi whenever she modeled her new clothes for him.

The people of Burgdorf commented to him that—almost overnight—his daughter had changed from a child into a young woman. It amazed Trudi how many of them would bend and bring their faces to the same level with hers if she remembered to keep her voice soft and avoided looking at them while she spoke.

Throughout the fall she daydreamed of being with Pia, feeling disloyal toward her father whenever she wished the *Zwerg* woman had taken her along. Her father was counting on her to start work full time in the pay-library in a few weeks, as soon as she'd finished the eighth school year of the *Volksschule*. She wondered if Stefan Blau had felt disloyal toward his parents when he'd run away to America. He'd been thirteen like her. Though she was certain that she, too, had the courage to leave Burgdorf, she knew that, wherever she went, she'd take her body with her—as it was now—while Stefan had grown, had changed to become a man.

She was sure most of the boys in Burgdorf would trade places with Stefan in a moment: there was a restlessness about them as if they were bored with their monotonous lives and had little to be proud of. But many of the girls had been trained to endure without complaining whatever boredom and discomfort encumbered their lives, to wait for someone else to make changes. When it came to making changes, Trudi felt much more like a boy and became impatient with the girls.

More than ever before, Stefan Blau came to engage her imagination as she pictured herself following Pia once she came back in the spring. There were lots of jobs she could do in the circus while Pia trained her to tame lions and elephants: sweep and cook, sew costumes, feed the animals. Stefan had chosen a new life, and his mother had survived—even with that sadness in her eyes. Trudi would come back and visit her father. Maybe she'd even get to America to see Stefan and her Aunt Helene, who still sent letters and gifts, though not as frequently as in the years after her visit, while Robert only scratched brief greetings at the end of his mother's letters.

In January Frau Abramowitz let Trudi copy the loden coat she'd just brought back from a trip to Austria. It had eight leather buttons, and

Trudi bought just as many buttons for her coat and simply reduced the distance between the buttonholes to get the same effect. She wore her new clothes to school and church and even dressed up for her walks with Seehund, whose movements had long since lost their early exuberance. Figuring seven dog years for each human year, he was over fifty, older than her father, who—although patient with her and everyone else—would get frustrated with himself when he was rushing to do something and his sore leg wouldn't carry him as fast as he wanted to go.

Sometimes, at night, he'd bolt up from a dream of a war more terrible than the war he'd fought. In this dream—and it always was the same dream—columns of clean bones held up the sky, and it was up to him to keep them from collapsing. Voices, too weak to scream, held forth in a trembling wail that cut his chest without drawing blood, and he'd surface to Trudi's face swimming above him.

"Wake up," she'd urge him. "You were crying in your sleep." She'd prop an extra pillow behind him and boil him a pot of camomile tea before she'd go back to her room.

He'd sit upright in his bed and keep his eyes wide open. On the wall across from him still hung the death photos of his wife. The wooden cross on her grave had long since fallen apart despite new coats of paint, and he'd replaced it with a marble stone. Her ashen stranger's face in the coffin had become so familiar to him in the years since her burial that he hadn't felt the desire to lie with any of the women in Burgdorf, whose vibrant complexions and smiles seemed unnatural in contrast.

Yet, with each year of celibacy, Leo's eyes stored more passion. They'd keep fastening themselves to a woman until she'd feel compelled to look at him. His gaze would be infused with tenderness, longing, admiration—with an undefined promise that could blind you. He'd feel alive, roused, when your eyes connected with his and kept returning to him as if a bond—far more significant than any touch could possibly be—had been established between the two of you. It happened in church, in stores, and of course in the pay-library, where the women asked his advice on books he thought they might like. They returned the books not only with praises of how well Leo understood their hearts, but also with delicacies from their kitchens: vanilla pudding with strawberry syrup; lentil soup with pigs' feet; egg cakes filled with fruit preserves or diced ham.

Occasionally, Leo's hand grazed a woman's arm, lightly, reverently almost. The women knew that his touch was not accidental, and they felt honored to be selected, but when they tried to feel out the promise of that touch, he spoke to them about Gertrud. Those who wanted more, he discouraged gently by confiding that he was still grieving his wife's loss.

"I haven't been able to become interested in another woman," he'd tell them, as though revealing a tragic illness which—each woman came to believe—only she could heal. "If things were different . . ." he'd say, letting each woman fill in her fantasies as his hand rose to stroke his own cheek.

Their eyes locked with his, the women encouraged him to talk about his wife. They found they could captivate him by sharing their memories about Gertrud: they reminded him how—as children—he and Gertrud had built kites of red silk paper and thin strips of wood, decorated with tails made of string and paper bows; they teased him about how nervous he'd been at fifteen when he'd asked Gertrud to go dancing with him; they described the day of his wedding and Gertrud's radiance as she walked on his arm from St. Martin's Church; they tempted him with fragments of half-forgotten incidents about Gertrud and fed his yearning by fabricating the rest.

It was from those overheard conversations that Trudi began to gather what her mother's life had been like before she had given birth to her, and she drank in those stories, relieved that no one spoke of the few mad years before her mother's death.

When the women were near Leo Montag, they felt coveted yet virtuous, and if they became uneasy with the yearning he evoked in them—a yearning that kept them from sleeping or praying because, say, they'd wonder what his hands would feel like if he were to loosen their hair and caress their faces in one long-drawn motion; or if that first time, that very first time, he would take them lying down or standing up against the wall of the locked pay-library—they could reassure themselves that nothing, really, had happened and that nothing was about to happen, a conviction that made it possible for them to extend their tongues to receive the blessed sacrament and return to their husbands with their honor intact.

And when they'd hear the translucent voice of Leo's *Zwerg* child in the church choir, floating from the high balcony, they'd touch their bellies through the fabric of their coats, reminding themselves of the fate of the one woman whose womb had given shelter to Leo's seed, and affirm their resolution to stay faithful to their husbands. Trudi's voice would shine during mass—high and strong and clear—soaring above the torrent of organ music. It was a voice that evoked your earliest longings—those ecstasies that had attached themselves safely to religion before you'd been given your family's approval to aim those passions at one particular Catholic boy. To name those feelings any sooner could have led you to sin. It was wiser to postpone, to harness that passion into singing in the choir or swooning at the communion bench, or feeling Christ's ultimate pain—at three o'clock each Good Friday—as the nails were pounded into his sacred palms.

As the women listened to Trudi's pure voice, they knew it was a voice you could never return to, a voice you could never reclaim as yours once your body had known the caresses of another body, once you understood what those old ecstasies had strained toward all along. Yet, some autumn at dawn, say, when you were the first to rise and light the kitchen fire, you might wonder if the passions of those women who had become nuns had surpassed your own passions, and you'd feel jealous of their power because they were the ones who taught your children and whose authority was held above yours.

Nuns shrouded their passions as well as their limbs. Nuns concealed their hands in their sleeves, baring only a fragment of their faces—eyes, nose, and mouth—scant evidence of womanhood. Though some of the nuns were bitter and petty women, the very best of them had eyes that contained a passion so pure that you could never look at them for long. Leo Montag had almost achieved that ecstasy in his eyes again—as if to validate that tasteless joke that his friend Emil Hesping kept circulating about people turning into virgins if they hadn't had *it*—and everyone knew what *it* was—for five years.

Though Emil Hesping still hadn't married, there was no danger of him turning into a virgin. People wondered what his brother, the bishop, would say if he knew about all those women—not just from Burgdorf but also from other towns—who'd been seen with Emil Hesping. Even walking on his arm across the church square was enough to taint your reputation. He had an ever-changing sequence of women except for one, Frau Simon, who had remained constant in his life. They'd flaunted their lust in public before she'd married her husband, and since her divorce he'd returned to her between his countless liaisons. With each year he seemed to look younger: his face had no lines, and his skull was still as smooth as ever.

All winter, Trudi kept waiting for the weather to become mild enough to swim again, and the first warm Sunday in April she got up at six, pulled on her swimsuit, a dress and jacket over it, and headed for the river with her dog.

Swallows rose from the willows when she ran down the far side of the dike, and for a moment the beat of their wings drowned the rush of the Rhein, which had been straining against its boundaries that spring without leaving its bed. Last fall's leaves covered the path, matted and brown, so unlike the airy shapes that had drifted from branches in showers of red and yellow. The grass—still dead and yellow-brown—lay flat against the earth, and the crowns of the trees looked tangled. A few bricks, half broken, were strewn among the pebbles. The sky was blue, but dark gray streaks ran across it, blocking the sun intermittently.

This early in the morning, no one else was on the path. The river looked moss green. Sometimes—even in the span of an hour—Trudi had seen it change from brown to gray and green, even silver, depending on how the light fell. Two ducks fluttered from the bare bushes as she neared the bank. She stepped across blackberry brambles that had grown over the path. In a few months she would come here to gather the purple-black berries and red currants, pour them into a deep soup plate with milk and sugar, and eat them with a slice of dark bread.

A fine column of mist rose near the river, thick enough to look like smoke from a fire, and for a moment she felt as if she were no longer alone, as if something were warning her to stay away. She called out to Seehund, just to hear the sound of her voice, but kept walking toward the mist. A branch tugged at her skirt. She froze. Her eyes skittered toward the dike. The entire hillside was moving, shifting each rotting leaf, each blade of grass, as if about to form an immense wave. The whole dike was whispering, whispering brown words, whispering, *"Come up here, now, now. . . ."* She felt those words, felt someone there, calling her. She cut through the bushes toward the river, away from the voices and the dike, and when she reached the willow with the braided length of rope, the gray mist was just that—mist—

and already the sun was diluting it, and the dike was just a solid ridge of earth built to protect the town from the river.

The bay was calm, and the choppy current surged past the tip of the jetty. She walked beyond the jetty toward the far end of the elbow-shaped embankment, where she took off her jacket and dress, hid them with her shoes between two bushes, and adjusted the straps of her swimsuit. Seehund was turning, sniffing the ground, before he settled on a patch of sand at the base of the bushes. As Trudi stepped into the water, it was far colder than the air, but she didn't let that stop her. Like a frog, she cut beneath the surface, brushed against some slimy rocks, and veered to swim into the deeper water. Here, the river belonged to her. Feathery strokes propelled her forward as she came up for air. From the bank, her dog watched her through sleepy eyes, his snout resting on his crossed paws. The rest of his body was hidden among the branches. She waved to him before submerging herself again. Eyes wide, she swam straight into the brown-green particles of mud that rose from the bottom. As the sun grazed them, they turned amber as if to encapsule her like that drop of amber Frau Blau wore around her neck on a silver chain; her Dutch great-grandfather had found it in the North Sea: in its center sat a tiny, bone-colored crab that looked as if—any moment—it could crawl out of that translucent drop of amber and up Frau Blau's neck.

Trudi kicked her feet, hard, heading for the shallow regions that were shaded by the willows. She shot up from the water and shook the river from her hair. In three months the circus would be back in town, and she'd bring Pia here to swim. As she tried to imagine the *Zwerg* woman in the water next to her, she couldn't see her in anything except that glittering dress. Drifting on her back, she kicked her feet and hands, making silvery loops. She'd look for fabric like that for Pia—something silvery and swirling—and sew a swimsuit for her. Smiling to herself, she glanced toward Seehund. He was sitting up, his head raised, his ears alert. From the other side of the jetty came voices.

Quickly, she lowered herself beneath the water and swam toward the end of the jetty. Holding on to the rocks to keep from being sucked into the current, she pulled herself out to where she could see: there were four of them—Georg, Hans-Jürgen, Fritz Hansen, and Paul Weinhart—absorbed in a competition of making water farts. Each artillery of bubbles was greeted with hoots and laughter. They were showing off for each other, taking loud gulps of air and holding their breaths as they tried to force the air through their intestines. When the bubbles broke through the surface, they leapt back in mock horror.

With an odd mix of fear and excitement, Trudi saw them the way they would never let any girl or adult see them, and she knew that by watching them without their knowledge she was taking something from them, something they'd never yield willingly to her. Those were the secrets she liked best—the ones that were stolen, the ones that made her tongue go light in her mouth at the thought of being caught, like that day in the bakery when Herr Hansen had sold *Brötchen* to Frau Buttgereit while hissing at her to keep her husband in her own bed; or that evening when she'd watched from the kitchen window as Frau Blau buried a small bundle next to her back steps; or that afternoon Frau Abramowitz had pressed her breasts against the arm of Trudi's father when she'd asked him to get a book for her from one of the upper shelves in the library.

Only Trudi's eyes and forehead were above water as she spied on the boys; she would raise her face long enough to take a deep breath, then submerge herself again. Seehund had settled down, and she was glad that the bushes protected him from being seen by the boys.

When Georg clambered into the willow, took off his swim trunk and draped it across a branch, she closed her eyes for a moment, not from embarrassment, but rather from compassion that—in his efforts to be like the other boys—he went further than they would have. The boys screamed with laughter and applauded. Georg grinned and waved both arms at them. Without his clothes he looked thin, defenseless, endangered even. His hair was trimmed so short you could see the bones of his skull.

Paul Weinhart cupped his hands around his mouth and shouted. "There's a naked boy here . . ."

Startled, Georg dropped his hands and covered his private parts.

Hans-Jürgen Braunmeier whistled.

". . . and his name is Georg Weiler," Paul continued.

"Shut your mouth!" Georg grabbed the braided rope and swung himself into the river. He dropped near Paul and started splashing him.

"A naked boy . . ." Fritz and Hans-Jürgen howled.

Georg tried to get out of the river and back to his swimsuit, which dangled high on that branch, but the other three blocked his way, their arms like wings of a windmill, flinging gauzy sheets of water at him.

"Let me out!"

As Trudi heard the tears behind his voice, those images of Georg leaping naked into the river tumbled into a story, and she felt a familiar power building in her—the power that came from her choice to tell or not to tell this story. And she felt something else that she knew well—a connection as potent as love or hate to everyone whose story entered her and began to ripen into something that belonged to her.

Georg retreated from the boys toward the open river. Kicking water with his feet, he swam on his back toward the end of the jetty, as though he'd decided to get out on the other side of it. As the three boys took up the chase, Trudi ducked between the rocks, hoping Georg would stop or that the others would catch him before he'd see her.

But he bumped right into her. Alarmed, he swung around, stared at her, and as she stared back into his sand-colored eyes, she was aware of his father who'd drowned in these waters that surrounded their bodies. Georg shivered as though he'd just had the same thought, and it seemed almost possible to her that they could both preserve the silence of their encounter and turn away from one another as if it had never happened.

But the other boys swam up behind him.

"That's why Georg took his pants off."

"Georg loves Trudi."

"Shut your trap!" Fists up, Georg threw himself against the other boys.

"Georg loves the *Zwerg.*"

She pushed herself from the rocks and beneath the water, darting away from them. A frog. She was a frog. But her legs were mere hindrances, and her arms felt too short to move the masses of water that pressed against her. A hand caught her right ankle and yanked her up. Hans-Jürgen.

She coughed and spit water. "Let go."

Seehund ran along the bank, barking, but as soon as his paws touched that damp line where the river darkened the sand, he leapt back, yelped, and advanced again as if fighting with himself to overcome his ancient fear of water.

Fritz Hansen grabbed Trudi by a strap of her swimsuit.

"Let go," she hissed, surprised when the boys dropped their hands from her. As she tried to touch bottom with her feet, the river was too deep, and she felt it again—that strange foreboding she'd ignored on her way to the river, that leaf-brown whisper of the dike, the column of mist. . . .

The back of his bottom chalk white, Georg was scrambling up the tree for his swimsuit while the other boys fanned around Trudi, their arms and legs stirring the water to keep themselves suspended. Their faces floated at the same level with hers, and it felt odd to see straight into their eyes instead of having to look up.

"What are you doing here?" Fritz demanded.

"Swimming. Like you."

"You were spying on us," Hans-Jürgen said.

"I was not." She felt furious at them. For finding her. For ruining her place. "I was here first."

Seehund's bark was at a high pitch. He was racing up and down the beach, his paws kicking up sand whenever he turned. Paul Weinhart dove and came up with a flat rock, which he flung at the dog. Seehund howled.

Trudi pushed Paul's shoulder. "Leave him alone."

"You make him shut up then."

"Down," she cried. "Down, Seehund."

The dog stopped. Body quivering, he lowered his hind legs halfway as if ready to leap up again.

"Down, Seehund."

He whimpered and lay down.

"Georg," Paul yelled. "Trudi says she wants you to take your pants off again."

"Liar," she cried.

His back to the river, Georg struggled into his shirt, his pants and shoes.

"She wants all of us to take our pants off," Hans-Jürgen declared.

Paul and Fritz laughed, high nervous laughs, as they grabbed Trudi's arms and dragged her toward the beach. Gathering gray and brown pebbles in the shallow water, Hans-Jürgen pelted Seehund as he charged toward them.

"Go home, Seehund," Trudi shouted. "Down— Home—"

But Seehund anchored his teeth in Fritz Hansen's calf. The boys let go of Trudi and fell upon the dog with fists and rocks.

"Stop it," she screamed, "stop," and heard Georg's voice too, "Don't hurt him."

Seehund kept fighting, but each time he was kicked or hit, his attempts became weaker.

"Go home," she shouted, tears in her mouth. She wished he'd run from those feet that kicked him away from her, but he kept yelping, coming back, until Paul hurled a sharp rock at him and Seehund fell over and lay still. When he tried to get up, his hind legs wouldn't straighten. Whimpering, he dragged himself toward Trudi, the whites of his eyes showing.

"Let her go." The skin around Georg's mouth was taut.

"So the *Zwerg* is all yours?" Fritz grinned.

"Don't be stupid." A slow, red burn stained Georg's neck and rose to his face.

Paul's hand shot out and pinched Trudi's breast.

She cried out.

"Your turn," he challenged Georg.

Georg's face stiffened. His eyes were right on Trudi, glassy and frightened, without seeing her. He tried to laugh. "Who wants her?"

Although he looked as though he were about to run, he stayed with his friends, even when they dragged Trudi across the meadow and the dike. She screamed, trying to wrest her arms—those useless arms that were solid but not strong—from the boys, and once she broke away, embarrassed that her legs, those *Zwerg* legs, were moving in the old sideways waddle that she'd tried to unlearn. Feeling the pulse of hate in her temples, she ran from them, faster than she'd known she could run, until Fritz tripped her. Seehund stayed further and further behind. Soon she could no longer see him. Her bare feet and legs got scratched, and she didn't know if she felt more horrified at the prospect of being rescued by others who'd see her body half naked in her swim suit, or at not being rescued before the boys got her to the Braunmeiers' barn—because that's where she realized they were heading. When she kept screaming, one of the hands—she couldn't even tell who it belonged to—clamped across her mouth while she was tugged and pushed around the back of the barn and into the side door that faced away from the farmhouse.

Slow patterns of muted light and shadows wove through the dust motes, and the highest rafters were hazy, enveloped by a viscous layer of air. Two metal pails were propped upside down on a table to dry.

She hadn't been in the barn since that day Hans-Jürgen had killed the kitten, and that vast, lofty space still reminded her of a church. At the same time there was the scent of the cows, a forever kind of warm scent that, somehow, made what happened so much worse, and what happened was warm and in some ways cold—the cold of the huge space, the warmth of cowering in one small space that was ablaze with the heat of her fear and the heat of their breaths and the heat of the cows, though nothing, nothing could touch that ice-cold space deep inside her, the space they couldn't reach, the space that could freeze them to death because she finally knew that praying would not make her grow, knew that the *Zwerg* had closed around who she really was, knew herself in a deep and distant way as she was and had been and would be, while a lifetime of images passed through her soul; and the worst thing was not that the boys tore off her swimsuit and fingered her breasts—that was terrible enough, but they would have done that to other girls too; no, the worst thing was their curiosity, those hands that explored her difference, those voices that laughed at the way her neck grew thick from her torso, at the short span of her legs as they pulled them apart—not to plant themselves in her, no—but to see how far her thighs could be spread, and what made all of this even worse was that, even here, she inspired their curiosity, not their desire, and yet, and yet, through her rage, she felt a dreadful longing to be liked by them, to have them see beyond her body inside her where she knew she was like every other girl.

Georg did not touch her. Hands jammed into his pockets like pieces of wood, he stood to the side, ready to flee, and once, when his eyes let themselves be trapped by Trudi's, they were wild with anger at her—for letting herself get caught.

"Frau Braunmeier . . ." A voice, so low-pitched it could only belong to Alexander Sturm, came from outside the front of the barn.

Hans-Jürgen dashed from the side door with Paul and Fritz close behind him.

"Ich möcht nur ein paar Eier kaufen. . . ."—"I just want to buy some eggs. . . ."

Georg grabbed a cattle blanket and threw it across Trudi before he ran out.

"Auch ein Pfund Butter"—"Also a pound of butter."

Trudi couldn't understand the muffled reply of Frau Braunmeier. She imagined herself shouting for help, imagined Alexander bending over her and helping her up, taking her home on the back of his bicycle, but then she thought of her father walking her to school in his Sunday suit to talk to the sisters, felt herself pushed into that closed circle of girls, and she knew she could never tell—not him, not anyone.

She waited until it was quiet outside again. Gripping the blanket around herself, she walked toward the door, feeling a curious absence of fear. It was over. She felt certain. They would not come back.

When she stepped from the barn, she felt as if she were standing on broken glass, though the ground was hard dirt, packed down by the hooves of cattle. It felt dangerous to step out of the space she had come to know as intensely as her room. Being inside that barn had made her even more separate from others, and the only kinship she could feel was to those boys, who had become far more like her than anyone else because they, too, had been part of what had happened to her. She felt the wind on her face, drying the cold snot against her cheeks and lips, stretching her skin taut the way egg whites will when you get them on your hands while baking.

Walking carefully as if crossing a desert of broken glass, Trudi thought of the shards that spiked the top edges of the walls which surrounded the Grafenberg asylum and understood why someone might wish to stay there. She saw herself within those walls with her mother, and she thought how comforting it would be to live there. Forever. Her legs ached, and her body felt monstrous beneath the blanket as she headed back toward the river, which now was a uniform leaden color that showed the pattern of ripples but no longer held those washes of light.

She wanted to crawl into the river with the shame of having been touched like that, singled out. As she bent and reached beneath the bushes to retrieve the clothes she'd sewn so carefully, it occurred to her that to girls of normal height it didn't mean a thing if a certain style made them look one or two centimeters taller. But she could change hemlines of skirts and jackets and, still, she would never be like other girls. Seehund grasped the side of her hand between his teeth, lightly, as if to console her, and she swung toward him and kicked him away—this witness to her shame. Beneath the cover of the blanket, she dressed herself hastily while Seehund limped around her, his seal-gray coat blotched with dry patches of blood.

Again, his damp snout nudged her hand.

Again, she kicked him away.

He followed her to the tip of the jetty, where she knelt in the cool pocket of sand and howled her rage. Frightened, the dog squirmed close, pushing his head at her, and though she blamed herself for his injury, she couldn't bear to touch him. She felt as hideous as Gerda Heidenreich, whose lips were always wet with saliva, as repulsive as the youngest Bilder boy, whose layers of fat nearly swallowed his eyes—the sum of all the freaks she had avoided.

Her hands found a heavy stone crusted with sand. Orange-red, the sun glowed through the hazy sky, and the air was soaked with the smell of her sweat as she raised the stone high above her head and hurled it into the Rhein. *Georg.* She reached for another stone. Holding it in both hands, she leapt up and flung it into the waves. *Paul.* Another stone. *Hans-Jürgen. Fritz.* The stones broke the skin of the river and sank to the bottom. *Georg. Fritz.* More stones, from the jetty now, some of them glistening with water that had splashed across them. Her eyes ached, and she squinted against the sun. Near the opposite bank of the river a dark cloud of swallows skimmed across the surface of the water. The rocks became weightier. *Hans-Jürgen. Paul.* Sharper. *Georg. Georg.*

■

SOME DAYS SHE COULDN'T EAT. HER MOUTH WOULD FEEL DRY, SWOLLEN, and if her father urged her to take at least one bite of the food she'd prepared for him, it would sit on her tongue, heavy and revolting. The only craving she had was for sweets, and she'd feel ill after eating them.

At night, she found it difficult to sleep, and she'd get up before dawn, sit in the living room with a blanket wrapped around herself, and read books from her father's personal collection. She rarely left the house. Her tailored clothes felt stiff, phony, and she hid her body behind the loose fabrics of housedresses, camouflaged herself with cardigans. When her father surprised her with a sewing machine for her fourteenth birthday, she set it up in her room but didn't use it.

She couldn't bear to touch her dog. His eyes would follow her with sad devotion, and occasionally he'd raise his head as if about to nudge her, but he'd learned it was wiser to wait for her to come to him than to startle her with his touch. Though she hadn't hurt him since that morning by the river, he dimly sensed that she was capable of a tremendous act of violence, punishing that part of herself that had been marred, punishing him for being her witness.

She wished she could travel like Frau Abramowitz and her husband, Michel—except she would never come back to Burgdorf. The Abramowitzs were always planning trips, the most recent of them to China, and their dining room table was usually covered with brochures and schedules. Frau Abramowitz had ordered an extra Chinese train schedule for Trudi; it was written in odd symbols that looked more like pictures than letters.

"If you ever go to China," Frau Abramowitz had said, "you'll be able to travel the trains for almost free. They don't go by age, but by height. If you're below one meter, you don't pay anything, but of course you're too tall for that."

Too tall. No one had ever told her that she was too tall for anything. "I'm one meter eighteen."

"Then you'll only pay one-quarter of the total fare. That's if you're between one meter and one meter twenty-nine."

What sustained Trudi was her work in the pay-library. There, wrapped in the impassioned music that spun from the gramophone, she could almost forget those boys while she bartered information, invading the lives of her customers with her questions, feeding them rations of gossip to lure them into sharing their secrets.

Yet she never bartered her own secrets. In the earth nest beneath the house, her mother had initiated her into the power of secrets. By taking Trudi's hand and pressing it against her knee, she'd transfused her with the addiction to the unspoken stories that lay beneath people's skins.

Trudi would reveal to Frau Simon what Judge Spiecker had told her the last time he'd come in to borrow mystery novels, while Frau Simon, in turn, would confide in Trudi what Herr Immers had said about Herr Buttgereit. She was discovering when to stay silent, when to let an interminable pause fill itself with the discomfort of the other person and hastily whispered information, while she—always the talker believing in words—listened, reeling in new material.

Yet, beneath the stories that poured through her and numbed her was her pain and the fear of her own rage. All that spring and summer she stayed inside the house, eating and sleeping very little, moving about the pay-library like an invalid, dodging her father's concerned questions—all through that fall and winter until the early spring when the flood loosened her rage.

The flood began with rain one April night. It rained the next day and the day after that, keeping most of the regulars away from the pay-library, even the wife of the taxidermist, who kept coming back for the same books. Both Trudi and her father had explained to Frau Heidenreich that it would be far less expensive for her to buy the books she reread, but she enjoyed leafing through the books on the shelves. She'd always bring her daughter, Gerda, and the big girl would sit on the floor and play with a fancy pocket watch that no longer had hands.

For weeks it kept raining, and the river kept rising. Although the people of Burgdorf filled potato sacks with sand and raised the dike with them, the water poured into the streets and gushed down cellar stairs. Trudi helped her father carry the books from the pay-library upstairs into the sewing room and stack them against the walls. The flood covered the two lowest shelves throughout the library, soaked the legs of the wicker table, and stained the underside of the sofa, even though Trudi's father, with the help of Herr Abramowitz, had lifted its legs onto bricks. They wound the ends of the long drapes around the curtain rods, creating an odd rococo effect that made the living room look far more elegant than before.

The third week of the flood the rain ceased, but the surface of the gray waters kept rising. It was a Sunday, and since the pews of St. Martin's Church were half under water, the people took boats to the chapel which stood on a hill near the Sternburg. It looked as if all the pigeons of Burgdorf had sought sanctuary on top of the bell tower, and it was impossible to see the slate roof tiles among the swarms of gray and iridescent birds.

As the Rhein kept rising in Burgdorf and other towns along its banks, Trudi felt as though the river were coming after her, urging her to take revenge on Georg, Hans-Jürgen, Fritz, and Paul—the only people in the entire world who shared with her the secret of what had happened. Gradually her movements took on her old energy, and she forced herself to leave the house at least once a day. She was amazed how the boys averted their eyes when they encountered her, how they flinched when she scorched them with the fury of her gaze. Their shame, she discovered, gave her power over them. And as the weight of what had happened kept gathering within her—dark and turbulent, threatening to obliterate her—she knew she had to release it.

Hans-Jürgen would be the first one, she decided.

She didn't know what she would do to him until she saw him hand in hand with a blond girl. From the way he looked at the girl, Trudi could tell he adored her. His first love, she thought, how sweet, how very sweet. She felt calmer than she had in many months as she settled into a patient wait for a chance to encounter him alone.

One morning in July, when Hans-Jürgen Braunmeier was getting ready to set up a stand in the open market with products from his family's farm, he saw it coming toward him, the short, rounded girl-shape that kept fastening itself to his dreams, evoking fear and that strange lust he despised in himself, unsettling him for hours after waking up. Quickly, he bent over an open crate, whistling as he pretended to busy himself.

When he was certain she'd passed his stand, he cautiously turned his head, but she stood right behind him, her moon face set into bitter lines, her skin the color of new frost as if to negate the heat it had sent to his fingers not too long ago. He wiped his hands against the sides of his trousers.

She stood there, not saying anything, forcing him to look at her as if taking pleasure in the discomfort he had with her body.

To his horror, he felt his flesh rise for her, and he hated her for that. "What *do* you want?" he blurted.

"I know something."

"So?"

"About you."

"I have work to do."

"Go ahead."

He slammed the supports of the wooden stand into position, lifted the crates to display fruits and cheese, marked slate markers with prices. And throughout all this she stood there, stubby arms crossed in front of her flowered housedress, simply stood there, making him want to bolt, even though it would mean the wrath of his father.

"So then—what is it you know?" he finally asked.

"That she does not love you."

His neck itched—hot and sudden. "Who?"

She lowered her eyes, murmured something he couldn't hear.

"Who?" As he crouched to bring his eyes down to hers, he thought she smiled, but it passed so quickly that he figured he'd imagined it.

"You know who."

"Go away."

"Don't you want to find out why?"

He shook his head, unable to pry his eyes from hers.

"I'll go then," she said and walked from him.

He told himself he'd be better off not to ask. Whatever she had to say to him would be worse than not knowing. "Why?" he shouted after her.

But she had reached the other side of the market and Barbarossa Strasse, where the constant shade from the canopy of oaks threatened to take her from him.

He ran, grasped her by the elbow.

She shook him off and whirled toward him.

"Why?" he hissed.

"Because," she said as if totally sure, "no girl, no woman will ever love you."

He laughed, a harsh laugh that hurt his throat. "You are crazy. Like your mother. Crazy *Zwerg.*"

The skin around her nostrils trembled but her voice remained even. "Crazy enough to know things. No woman will ever love you, Hans-Jürgen Braunmeier."

His face, his entire body was burning hot, and he found it hard to breathe. "You— You think you can put a stupid curse on me?"

"Sshh—" She raised one hand. "I'm not finished. No woman will ever love you back. And your love will make a woman turn to another man."

That night she slept—deeply and without remembering her dreams—and when she awoke, the sun was in her face and it was late morning and she understood that revenge did not always have to come through her directly.

Without mercy or haste, she began to spread stories about Fritz Hansen and Paul Weinhart, stories that were unlike her other stories and—she sensed—should have been left untold because they carried mere shards of truth, violating not only the core of the stories but also her own code of truth. Still—they gave her tremendous satisfaction as the position of those boys was weakened within the community. *But what about Georg?*—a voice within her persisted. *What about Georg?*

To the surprise of everyone, except Trudi, Paul Weinhart's uncle changed his mind about letting his nephew serve his apprenticeship in his jewelry store. Instead, after helping his father on the farm in the early hours of day, Paul worked for the potato man, delivering heavy sacks of potatoes all over town, including to the pay-library. And when Fritz Hansen took over his parents' bakery, many of the old customers began to buy their bread and pastries from the competition though it was owned by Protestants. Old Herr Hansen had to resort to buying a truck that wove through the streets and brought the bakery to the people's doors. Against a white background, large blue letters proclaimed: *Hansen Bäckerei*. The driver was Alfred Meier, who'd slow down whenever he'd pass the Buttgereits' house, pining for at least a glimpse of Monika Buttgereit, who was only allowed to speak to him in her mother's presence right after mass.

All of the books in the Montags' pay-library were covered with cellophane that grew dull and scratched over the years; yet, despite that protection, the books' paper jackets developed tears. You could tell if Trudi or her father had repaired them: Leo Montag's sections of tape were meticulously trimmed and ran along the insides of the book jackets, leaving no more than faint scars, while Trudi's tapes crisscrossed not only the titles and names of authors, but also the swooning heroines, brave soldiers, dedicated doctors, and American cowboys. Since the tape yellowed sooner than the covers, the faces of the characters often looked jaundiced, contradicting the titles which proclaimed blossoming love or triumphant victories.

As the people came to Trudi with their stories, she cherished the mystery of silence just before a secret was revealed. And the bigger the secret, the denser was the silence surrounding it. Timing was extremely important—to choose the best moment to tear the silence. If it happened too soon, the silence that nurtured the growth of a secret closed around it like a cocoon. And if she waited too long, most of the secret had already drained away.

Yet, some things, Trudi had to admit to herself, better remained secrets—like the identity of the unknown benefactor, whose presence still manifested itself in isolated bursts of generosity: there might not be anything for months, but then three or four gifts would be found inside people's houses within a single week. The secret of that identity gave the town of Burgdorf a fairy-tale quality, a shared and unspoken conviction that the unknown benefactor would shield the people from anything that could be worse than their daily troubles.

Behind the counter of the library stood one of the wide stools that Trudi's father had built for her and on which she'd stand to sell you tobacco, operate the cash register, or record the books you borrowed. Frequently only the top of her light blond hair would be visible above the counter. She was in the process of making a card file for the books, transferring the titles from her father's brittle ledger onto long beige cards, which she filed alphabetically in a wooden box. But she kept her father's system of entering a customer's name beneath the title of each borrowed book.

A ladder equipped with wheels allowed her to reach books on even the highest shelves, making her feel taller than anyone who wandered into the library. She liked the view of the tops of people's heads—a welcome change from having to stare up into their faces. It was for that same reason that she'd occasionally still climb into the tower of the church, high above the rest of the town. There she'd sit, watching miniature people dart between houses and through the open market.

If her father was in the pay-library while she was on the ladder, she'd stay up there if a customer entered, but if her father was resting or away at a chess tournament, she'd scramble down, her O-shaped legs finding the next tread with amazing surety.

Years of restricted movements had drained her father's body of its vitality, and he had settled into his limp as though it had been sculpted for him. Since he could rely on Trudi to open the pay-library, he slept longer most mornings; and at midday, when the bells from St. Martin's sounded across town and stores closed for two hours, he'd rest with one of the new books on the velvet sofa in the living room, a blanket across his legs, and read, the bony contours of his face transformed by an expression of bliss.

Seehund would lie on the floor next to the sofa, his nose on the worn leather of the shoes that Leo had taken off. It was as though he were aging along with Leo, both of them dozing more hours than they stayed awake. While Leo's hair was turning white, the dog's fur had blurred to a softer hue of seal gray. Often, Leo would pull his comb from his shirt pocket and untangle a fur ball from the dog's coat or, almost absentmindedly, run it through the thicker layers of hair around Seehund's neck. The dog had taken to sleeping at the foot of Leo's bed, though his blanket remained on the floor of Trudi's room. Sometimes he'd take one of his hind legs between his jaws and pinch it as if to allay a deep-seated ache.

Trudi still took him on her walks along the Rhein though she hadn't returned to the Braunmeiers' jetty, a place too terrible to even think about. Usually, she'd stay on the dike and hike south toward Düsseldorf for two kilometers. Her back felt better on the days she walked, more limber. If she stayed indoors for too long, the lower part of her back had a tendency to get stiff and heavy. Along the way, she'd slow down to wait for Seehund, until she'd reach a path that spilled at an odd angle through the meadow and down to the river. It slanted past a clump of four poplars and an immense flat rock that lay embedded in the earth just where the path met the trail that hugged the embankment. The rock's dark surface would get so warm that, even in the late fall, you could stretch out on it and feel your entire back warmed while the cool air moved across your face and body, as if you were held suspended between two seasons.

That meadow was so far from town that no one else was ever there. The river was rough and greedy—not ashamed to demand its rightful share: it strained against the embankment, swallowed rocks, and gushed through the tiniest crevices. Though it offered no sheltered bays, Trudi would ride its turbulent waves, dart beneath them in her frog-swim, her heart beating fast as she became the river, claiming what was hers. As the river, she washed through the houses of people without being seen, got into their beds, their souls, as she flushed out their stories and fed on their worries about what she knew and what she might tell. Whenever she became the river, the people matched her power only as a group. Because the river could take on the town, the entire country.

She thought of what people said behind her back—that she hadn't cried at her own mother's funeral—while to her face they said: "You're lucky to have such pretty hair." They didn't have any idea what she was like: they saw her body, used her size to warn their children, looked at her with disgust. But it was just that disgust of theirs which fused her to them with an odd sense of belonging. That disgust—it nourished her, horrified her. She would have done anything to be loved by them, and since she could not have their acceptance, she seized their secrets and bared them as she had bared Eva's birthmark.

• • •

She began to sew for herself again, taking pleasure in altering patterns to suit her. As her tolerance for food returned, she could see how
relieved her father was. When she'd call him into the kitchen where
she'd set the table for the hot midday meal, he'd tell her about the new
books and make a list of those customers he knew would like them.
His women customers would feel privileged when he'd pull a new
book from beneath the counter and whisper, "I've been saving this
one for you. It just came in." Their eyes rapt, they'd listen as he gave
them just enough of the plot to captivate them without revealing the
ending.

To Trudi, those books seemed as flat as her mother's paper dolls:
even though you could alter their appearance by folding the tabs of
elaborate gowns across their shoulders, they stayed flat, and their
smiles remained as constant as the happy endings in the books. She
was far more interested in the stories that unfolded around her in
Burgdorf, stories that breathed and grew and took on their own
shapes and momentum, like when the Buttgereits' second daughter,
Monika, was forbidden to become engaged to Alfred Meier until after her older sister had found a suitor; or when Frau Weiler, right
there in her store, saw the assistant pastor—that towering young man
who'd moved into the rectory and ate three times as much as the aging pastor and his housekeeper together—deposit a bar of chocolate
in the pocket of his cassock as if he had every right to do so; or when
Emil Hesping's cousin, a champion swimmer, made a bet that he
could swim across the Rhein six times and drowned in a whirlpool
during his final crossing; or when Alexander Sturm began the construction of an L-shaped apartment house, the largest building in
Burgdorf, with two entrances, three floors, four stores, and eighteen
apartments; or when Helmut Eberhardt and one of the other altar
boys were questioned, but not punished, by the sisters for trying to
push the fat boy, Rainer Bilder, in front of the ragman's wagon.

Some stories kept growing inside Trudi, finding their own passages, like moles tunneling through the earth. Others she tested and
pushed to see how far they'd give, what fit in and what didn't, and
what she brought to those stories was her curiosity and what she in-
tuitively knew about people. As she gleaned things about their lives,

she wove them into their stories. As an old woman she would see a magazine article about a cave; it had photos and a diagram of the many veins you could travel in exploring that cave. Some of those veins led into other veins; some ended; some sprouted a net of other paths. With the stories of people she'd known since her childhood it was like that: one incident in their lives might come to an ending, but others would lead into new veins, and what was fascinating was to look at the whole of it and discern a pattern, a way of being, that had shaped those passages.

In observing the world around her, Trudi would see one thing and deduce the rest. It was not only what happened to people, but what could have happened. She could encounter people on the street and then, in her head, follow them home and know what they would be doing and thinking—as with Georg Weiler who, by the time he was seventeen, had grown into one of the handsomest boys she'd ever seen, yet was frightened of pretty girls. Homely girls, he figured, were not as demanding. Easily dazzled by his smile, they were grateful that he paid attention to them. For them, he wouldn't have to change or improve himself. They gave him a feeling of accomplishment that he hadn't known before.

Helga Stamm was the fourth in a sequence of these girls. Her thick ankles and plain face made Georg feel certain that she had to be pleased with the way he was—superior to her in looks and intelligence. Trudi was sure he didn't know the quiet, deep-rooted strength below Helga's placid surface. It pleased Trudi, that strength, because she sensed that she wouldn't have to do anything herself to complete her own cycle of revenge. All she had to do was wait for the day when Georg would come up against Helga's strength.

His mother had wanted him to work in the store, but he'd moved to Düsseldorf and become an apprentice in a huge grocery store, where everything was already weighed and packaged, and where people took the items they wanted from shelves and carried them to one of the three cash registers. Most people in Burgdorf couldn't imagine that kind of grocery store. "It sounds like a train station," they said and watched Georg for signs of change when he returned to Burgdorf to visit Helga. His mother prayed for him every night—not just the regular prayers she'd allocated him since birth, but also the ten Hail Marys that she used to offer God for her mother's release from purgatory. According to her calculations, she'd prayed her mother into heaven the third week of May in 1932, and she had celebrated her mother's freedom by inviting both priests for Sunday dinner.

The books in the pay-library were predictable, alike, and Trudi was amazed that anyone would keep reading them, even after her father explained to her one afternoon, while shelving books, that people found assurance in the happy endings, in knowing ahead of time what would happen to their heroes and heroines.

"Their own lives are so uncertain," he said. "With the books, they can forget about themselves for a while . . . crawl between the pages."

"Like you?"

He smiled his slow, steady smile. "I could say that I have to study what I lend."

"You could say that."

"I wish you'd read them, too."

"I do. I read a few pages, skip to the middle, the last page, and then I know enough." She smiled back at him, delighted with this banter that was familiar, yet rare. "If I want to read happy endings, I'll go back to fairy tales. At least they have some meaning."

"About endings. . . . Unless we do them well, we have to keep repeating them."

Four gray-brown birds, a bit of red on their throats, landed in the chestnut tree outside the front window. One of them had an injury that protruded from the side of its head, a swollen mass of tissue that balanced the eye at its crest like a strange telescope. As Trudi wondered if the bird was in constant pain, it flew off, the other birds close behind. Almost immediately the door to the library swung open, letting in gusts of wind as Frau Eberhardt came in, wearing her new beige suit with the fitted skirt that revealed the round knobs of her garters. Trudi couldn't think of anyone in town who was as well liked as Frau Eberhardt.

"No, you're not," Frau Eberhardt was telling her son, Helmut, who followed her, his beautiful face sulky, a bandage on his left arm half covered by the sleeve of his doe-brown shirt. "Today you're staying right next to me."

"I'm not a baby." He closed the door.

"That's right. Babies have more sense than you." She tucked a few strands of hair beneath her hat, her movements as agitated as her voice.

The boy stalked to the end of the counter and leaned against it, staring at the floorboards as if he'd like nothing better than to hurt someone. In church he always looked so pure in his altar boy's smock, his eyes never wavering from the altar as he executed each step of the ritual without a single mistake.

"He's proud of this." Frau Eberhardt pointed to her son's arm and turned to Leo Montag. "Helmut is actually proud of this."

His eyes full of compassion, Leo took one slow step toward her, and though he didn't touch her, her features calmed. "What happened, Frau Eberhardt?" he asked.

With that old sense of uneasiness that was hers whenever Helmut was near, Trudi listened, interrupting with brief questions as Renate Eberhardt told how her son had initiated and won a test of courage that had left him and five other boys in his youth group with bleeding arms. They'd taken one of her good pillow cases and twisted the fabric into a stiff knot which they'd rubbed along their naked arms, hard, from the wrist to the shoulder, grating it up and down their skin until the raw flesh had been exposed.

". . . and the one who had the most terrible injury was the hero for the day." Frau Eberhardt glanced toward her son, who was pretending he hadn't heard a word.

"Hurting yourself like that . . ." Trudi shook her head. "Why would anyone do that?"

"It has nothing to do with courage," Leo said softly. "Right, Helmut? Just as what you did to Rainer Bilder has nothing to do with courage."

Helmut's perfect chin rose. "That fat pig," he said. Almost thirteen, he was nearly as tall as his mother, and quite likely—Trudi concluded—stronger and faster than any of them.

"I like Rainer." Leo's voice carried an edge of warning. "He is a kind, unfortunate boy who deserves—"

"He's got tits like a girl, that's how fat he is!"

"Stop it, Helmut," his mother said. "I say, stop it now and apologize to Herr Montag."

Helmut's face turned red, clashing with the brown shirt of the Hitler-Jugend. "I am sorry, Herr Montag," he mumbled and bowed in Leo's direction.

A few years from now he won't listen to her at all, Trudi thought. Or to any of us. Once he knows his strength, there's nothing his mother can do to make him obey. He won't listen to her out of respect—not that one. The only reason he's here right now is because he doesn't know his strength.

Trudi was glad her father had spoken out for Rainer Bilder. A shy boy with a body so immense that it embarrassed you to look at him, he was frequently taunted and beaten by the other boys in school, who unified against him. Some of the adults in town, who would have ordered other children to stop fighting, didn't interfere when Rainer was tormented, as if they justified that he brought on the beatings with his difference. His parents, who watched with bewilderment as their youngest son expanded in front of their eyes, felt so disgraced by him that they'd long since stopped complaining to the principal when Rainer lumbered home with bruises on his face and limbs.

Ironically, both parents were gaunt, despite a joint passion for food that had sustained their marriage through a quarter of a century. This passion gave them something to talk about to each other and to everyone they encountered. Where, say, a hypochondriac would welcome you with revelations of new ailments, or a traveler with descriptions of exotic places, Rainer's parents were sure to greet you with details of every single thing they'd consumed the day before. These accounts of elaborate meals would be accompanied by delicate clicks of the tongue and rapturous sighs. The family's six older children were lean-bodied like their parents, but Rainer was grotesquely fat, as though his parents' excesses had visited themselves upon him.

Trudi, too, felt uncomfortable with Rainer's freak body, but not nearly as much as with Helmut, who was a freak on the inside, yet— some of the old women claimed—looked like "an angel come back to earth." Now the angel was watching her from the end of the counter, his even features without expression, and she found herself thinking of Lucifer, the angel who'd been banished from heaven and—in the act of falling—had seized far greater control than any of the faithful angels.

She'd seen Helmut the week before, the day of the *Judenboykott*— Jew boycott—when he'd brought coffee to the SA men who were posted in front of Jewish stores, threatening customers who wanted to enter. The first time Trudi had come across Helmut in his uniform

had been during the *Fackelparade*—torch parade—that the Nationalsozialisten had held last January to celebrate their victory. In the dark,
ghosts of flames had pulsed across the strangely pious and enraptured
faces of uniformed girls and boys as they'd marched with their songs
amidst a sea of red, white, and black flags, swept forward by the current of music. *"Für die Fahne wollen wir sterben . . . ,"* they'd sung.
"For the flag we want to die." The only other place Trudi had seen
that beatific expression on Helmut's face was in church when he'd
been about to receive communion.

Frau Eberhardt took two romances from her handbag and laid
them on the counter. "These are overdue." She opened her wallet.
"By two days, I believe."

"Don't let it worry you." Leo waved aside her attempts to pay.
"You've brought others back early. It evens out."

His eyes followed her as she left with her son, and when the door
closed behind them, he limped to the window and stood watching the
two until he could no longer see them.

"A bad one," Trudi said.

Leo nodded. *"Aus Kindern werden Soldaten*—children become
soldiers. . . . He'll make a proper soldier. It's their kind of courage."

"What kind of a soldier were you?"

"A reluctant one. The kind they were glad to send home."

"Herr Immers would have liked to take your place."

"By now he believes he really fought the war."

The day before, when Trudi had been in the butcher shop, Herr Immers had told her, *"Wir leben in einer grossen Zeit"*—"We live in a
significant time." He liked to chat with customers while his son, Anton, and Irmtraud Boden—who'd gone to school with Trudi and was
sweet on Anton, weighed and wrapped meats and cold cuts. Behind
the marble counter, the traditional black, red, and gold flag had been
replaced by the new flag of the Nationalsozialisten. Ever since the
Fackelparade, more and more houses had been displaying that flag.

"Herr Immers will be glad when the next war comes along," Leo
said.

"What are you saying?"

He squinted at Trudi as if trying to gauge if she was strong enough
to hear his answer. "People have been whispering more. . . . You
know we're heading for a war when that kind of silence begins to

happen. The sound level of the town, the entire country, drops to a lower level . . . even the river, the birds. . . ."

"Maybe you're just losing your hearing." She tried to joke away the apprehension she'd felt the past few months and which her father was confirming with his words. When he didn't answer, she said, "I hope you're wrong."

"So do I," he said gravely. "But I worry about the German attraction for one strong leader, one father figure who makes you obey, who is strong enough to make you obey. . . . Who tells you: This is the right thing to do. I worry about the belief that our strength is a military strength." He walked to the first row of shelves and picked up books without looking at them. "Most people seem to think that life has been getting better: less unemployment, more excitement for our youth. . . . Those groups with their marches and songs and bonfires."

He didn't have to remind Trudi how monotonous things had been for the youth until the *Partei* had come into power. Now there were excursions, vigorous music, and uniforms. The people had been craving order, and many welcomed the Nationalsozialisten because they offered exactly that—order. Their goals sounded easy and promised to restore the pride that had been humiliated by the Versailles *Friedensvertrag*.

"Our young people—" Leo said, "they're easily swayed by all those speeches. . . . Their souls have been starved for so long that they're seduced by the promises, the instant camaraderie. Someone's constantly there to inspire them, to persuade them. . . ." He shook his head. "Little soldiers—the girls too—with their alarming pride in that vulgar flag. I'm so glad you're not part of all that."

"They wouldn't want me."

He flinched as though she'd cut herself intentionally in front of him.

"Besides, it's not for me."

"Because you know what you're about. You have courage and strength . . . intelligence . . . but most of them—they haven't developed stands of their own. That's why they take to the new ways. They'll only hear what they want to absorb. Bonfires—" He rubbed his chin. "Bonfires and new highways are not going to solve our problems. And they won't be enough for that fellow Hitler."

Trudi had seen Herr Hitler a few months ago. At a rally in Düsseldorf, soon after he'd become Reichskanzler—Chancellor. He was not nearly as tall as she'd expected from newspaper photos, and he looked straight at her when he talked, not excluding her like the assistant pastor, Friedrich Beier, who spoke above her head as if she were too insignificant to be included. Whenever she opened her lips and stuck out her tongue to receive the holy communion, she half expected him to bypass her. Herr Hitler's mouth moved independently of his eyes. There was something wrong with his face: the features didn't work together. But he looked directly at her—at everyone in the swollen crowd—like a magician performing some amazing trick of singling out everyone at once, and it was that gaze—filled with an immeasurable greed—that held all of them while his high-pitched voice spun silken ropes around them.

She fought the excitement of his gaze and voice because what he wanted from her was only too familiar—belief without doubts—something she'd resisted since first grade.

She fought him by reminding herself what her father had said to Emil Hesping—that they lived in a country where believing had taken the place of knowing.

She fought him until her entire body felt cold.

It was impossible to get out of the mob that cheered his words, and only after the speech could she push her way to the back. From the second-floor window of a nearly deserted store, she watched while the dark-haired man with the funny, postage-stamp square of a mustache—this man who didn't look anything like the Aryan ideal he had just spoken of—shook the hands of uniformed men and tilted his bashful smile at young women. When he lifted a little blond girl high into the air, Trudi had a sudden image of him, alone in his bedroom, attempting to read something he had written on lined paper, but his eyes kept skittering off the page as if—without the pitch of his own voice—his own message had no power to hold him. Yet, the greed she'd felt in him, that greed which had sucked all those people into his influence, was still in the room with him, and she was seized by a deep fear for the world.

Both Herr Heidenreich and Herr Neumaier had shaken Herr Hitler's hand that day. The hand was moist, the pharmacist had reported when he'd bought tobacco the following morning, and the eyes were a very light blue. At the chess club, he and the taxidermist had actually argued about the precise shade of blue. For days the pharmacist hadn't washed his right hand. "The sweat of our Führer," he'd sighed.

Trudi glanced at her father. "Maybe Herr Hitler won't be around very long."

"Maybe," he said without conviction.

For a while, they worked silently side by side, setting books back on the shelves.

Outside, the ragman's new used truck rumbled past, slowly, while Herr Benotti sang out: *"Eisen, Lumpen, Papier . . ."* He'd bought the truck from a florist in Düsseldorf and had painted it glossy white like an ambulance.

"Remember—" Leo touched Trudi's shoulder lightly with one of the romances Frau Eberhardt had returned. "People like recommendations . . . books they might like."

"They come to you for that."

"They won't always."

"Don't say that." She felt the panic in her voice.

"With you, all they get are questions. You probe at them instead of giving them plots."

"There are five basic plots in these books." She counted them off on her fingers, delighted when she got her father to laugh aloud, although she still felt chilled by their talk. "One, true love overcomes all obstacles and becomes eternal love; two, cowboys and Indians smoke peace pipes together after they've fought over territories; three, beautiful nurses and brilliant doctors save incurable patients and then get married; four, war heroes conquer their enemies in spectacular battles; and five, villains are always punished."

In real life, she knew, it was not that easy to tell who the villains were, and even if you could identity them, they were not total villains. No one was entirely all of one thing. Cowards could be courageous in some matters, and love was not always declared and might not be pure love, but mixed in with hate and fear and a powerful wish for revenge—like what she felt for Georg Weiler, who went to great efforts not to glance in her direction, even if both of them stood in front of their houses.

And Frau Abramowitz—Trudi was sure Frau Abramowitz had loved her father for nearly a decade now, just as sure as she was that her father had never noticed it and that Frau Abramowitz's love would stay submerged beneath her good manners. A woman could never declare her love first, and then, of course, there was the matter of sin. For a married woman to love a man other than her husband was a sin. To lust after anyone was a sin.

But in the books from the pay-library, men were always lusting after women, feeding the imagination of the people in Burgdorf as well as the feud between Leo Montag and the church, which had gone on for so long that it had become a tradition, manifesting itself in periodic sermons from the aging pastor, who had been getting thinner over the years as though—by scratching his scaly skin—he were wearing himself away, layer by itchy layer, until soon only his bones would be left. Already, he was coaching his assistant in carrying on this custom of admonishing his parishioners against passions of the flesh, which were described so tantalizingly in the pages of those books.

Without fail, each sermon enhanced the rental business and brought customers who had never entered the pay-library before: young mothers, widows, schoolchildren, and men who pretended to have stopped by only for tobacco would linger between the shelves and emerge with one or two novels, which they'd check out furtively and carry wrapped in a scarf at the bottom of their shopping nets, say, or clasped inside their coats. During their next visit to the library they wouldn't quite hurry so, and soon they'd forget to conceal the books before stepping outside.

It amazed Trudi that passions of violence didn't seem to bother the church. Novels about soldiers who killed their enemies in battle were never mentioned by Herr Pastor Schüler, and when he preached against nurse-and-doctor novels, it was not because of the gory operating-room scenes, but because of those moments of lust between the doctors and nurses.

She still attended mass every Sunday, though the assistant pastor's occasional prayers for the *Vaterland*—fatherland—felt uncomfortable. The hymns had become mere rituals for her, but she liked the way her voice fused with the voices of others when she sang in the choir. Besides—church was the best place to show off the stylish clothes she was sewing for herself. Whenever she completed a new outfit, she rotated one of her previous Sunday outfits to be worn during the week.

Once, to collect money for the missionaries, the assistant pastor brought an American Western from the Montags' pay-library to the pulpit—checked out by the pharmacist, Trudi soon figured out—and read the description of a Sioux Indian dancing for his gods. While the collection plate was passed from pew to pew, he spoke of pagans and the duty of missionaries to save them from certain hell by converting them to Catholicism.

It was that sermon which brought Ingrid Baum to the pay-library. She was a student at the Ursulinen *Gymnasium* in Düsseldorf. A year younger than Trudi, she'd moved to Burgdorf a few months before Trudi's mother had died. With her twin brother, Holger, and her parents, Ingrid had lived in the apartment above her father's bicycle shop for most of her life, and yet the town treated the Baums as if they'd just arrived. It was like that with all newcomers and could only be erased with a generation's span of residence.

Ingrid had come to the pay-library, she said, to borrow that book about the missionaries that the Herr Pastor had talked about, and as Trudi wheeled her ladder toward the shelves with the Westerns and climbed up, Ingrid announced, "I want to become a missionary." When she looked up at Trudi, planes of light lay on her even features as if she were someone in a religious painting who'd been told to stand just like that.

Trudi couldn't help herself. She felt wicked. "You probably have kept all the holy cards the nuns ever gave you."

But Ingrid didn't catch the sarcasm in her voice. "Yes," she said. "I have a whole collection."

"I'm not surprised." From the ladder, Trudi handed her the book. "There's not a single missionary in here," she warned and adjusted the waistband of the angora sweater her Aunt Helene had sent her.

Ingrid scrutinized the book jacket of a cowboy on a horse chasing an Indian on a horse. Actually, they were so close to each other that it was impossible to determine who was doing the chasing, except that in those books you knew it was always the cowboy in pursuit. The horses' flanks were nearly touching, and they were racing so fast that—the moment after the moment of that picture—they would have collided.

"Do you have other books about missionaries then?" Ingrid's brown hair was parted in the middle and hung down her back in one shining braid. Around her neck she wore a delicate gold cross.

"In here? Well—I do have one book about an actress whose sister is a nun. In Brazil. Or India, I think." In the romance section, Trudi showed Ingrid a book with the cover of a woman in a low-cut red gown raising her red lips toward the jaundiced face of a smug-looking man, while leaning into the curve of his arm.

Ingrid sighed. "The sister of the missionary?"

"Must be."

"Thank you. I'll take that with me."

When Ingrid brought the book back, she told Trudi the nun was only mentioned once. "The actress was crying out to be saved. . . . But I'm afraid it was too late for her."

"Have you ever considered that missionaries are arrogant?" Trudi challenged her.

"Why so?"

"Because they set about changing people whose own ways may be far better for them."

"Oh, but there is only one way to salvation." Ingrid took another look at the book jacket with the red-gowned woman. "This is the saddest book I've ever read," she said and borrowed two other romances.

That spring of 1933 more than two hundred authors were pronounced decadent, traitorous, Marxist, or corrupt. All over Germany, people were ordered, *"Reinigt Eure Büchereien"*—"Clean your libraries"—and incited to hunt down books by banned authors like Bertolt Brecht, Sigmund Freud, Irmgard Keun, Stefan Zweig, Franz Werfel, Lion Feuchtwanger, Heinrich Mann, and every writer on the blacklist. As bookstores, libraries, and private homes were raided, you risked arrest if you didn't relinquish those books. In school, children were encouraged to turn their parents in for owning forbidden literature.

Trudi and her father packed more than half of his personal collection into cardboard boxes and carried them upstairs to the sewing room.

"Remember how the old priest used to rant against the books in the pay-library?" Leo asked. "Ironic, isn't it?"

Trudi nodded. "Now the trashy books are safe. I would gladly give up every one of them instead."

They stacked the boxes against one wall, covered them with a plaid blanket and several pillows, and stood back to inspect the result.

"Not the best hiding place," her father said.

"Why not keep them in the open?"

He frowned at her.

"Let's do this—let's fill the top of each carton with rental books and keep the boxes right in the library."

"Of course." He smiled. "What better place to store boxes with books than in a library?"

The night of May 10 bonfires burned all over Germany, especially in university towns, where students were organized to burn the works of many authors they normally would have studied. In Berlin alone— so Herr Abramowitz would report later—a pile of twenty thousand books sent flames sky high, while the music corps of the SA played national marches. In some cities, trucks heaped with books paraded through the streets, gathering spectators for the ritualistic burnings that would wash across old and young faces in blond flickers.

Sometimes, when Ingrid returned library books, Trudi would invite her into the living room behind the pay-library and make lemonade or rosehip tea. While Trudi would set out her mother's flowered cups, saucers, and pastry plates on the freshly ironed tablecloth, Leo would walk to the bakery near the Protestant church—humoring Trudi's boycott of Hansen's bakery though she'd never told him her reasons—and buy *Bienenstich* or *Schnecken* for his daughter and her new friend.

As Trudi came to know Ingrid better, she became fascinated by the torment that Ingrid inflicted upon herself. Haunted by the possibility of sin, Ingrid went to confession at least twice a week and tried so hard to be virtuous that she moved through her days like a tightrope walker about to plummet. Though her sins were trivial—like falling asleep without her good night prayer, or envying Irmtraud Boden for her satin dress, or resenting that her brother constantly got the biggest piece of cake—they devastated her. She'd feel greedy for wanting the simplest things.

She had a way of fluttering her eyelashes—a habit that looked both helpless and controlled. A tortured soul with a beautiful body, Ingrid would have gladly traded places with Trudi because she felt ashamed of her body that tempted men. Just walking past them, she created sin

in them—all of them, she said, even her father—and to be this instrument of sin was the worst fate she could think of.

"You really would trade?" Trudi was incredulous.

"In a minute," Ingrid said without hesitation.

"You're crazy."

"And you are lucky."

"Should I thank you?" Trudi asked brusquely.

"Now I offended you."

"Look at me—" Trudi spread her arms. "Look at me and tell me
why I am lucky. Do you know what people say about me? That because I'm a *Zwerg,* my mother became crazy. They warn their children: don't eat butter with a spoon or you'll look like Trudi Montag."

Ingrid brought one hand to her mouth.

Trudi's words were coming so fast, her lips felt wet with spittle.
"Don't do this or that or you'll look like Trudi Montag. Don't kill
frogs, don't fall on your head, don't ride your bicycle in the middle of
the road. . . ."

Ingrid stepped closer and laid one hand on her shoulder, but Trudi
shook it off.

"Not to my face—they don't say anything like that to my face, but
I hear. I listen."

Ingrid's eyelids were like the wing beats of a frail bird. "I didn't
think you knew."

"I know lots more. And I'll tell you something else. I'm not like this
because something happened to me, but because it's the way I've
been—from the beginning." Both fists on her hips, Trudi demanded,
"Now tell me why I'm lucky."

"All I meant was that I admire you because you have more of a
chance to go to heaven than anyone I know."

"I don't understand you."

"It's because of original sin," Ingrid hurried to explain. "We're all
born with it. Doomed once we reach the age of reason." Her gray eyes
burned with conviction. "But you— Don't you see?"

Her voice rose, almost the way the voice of Trudi's mother used to
sound when she got too excited, and for an instant Trudi recalled her
mother touching her that very first time beneath the house, felt the
wiry arms seizing her, heard her mother's hoarse sob, breathed the
dank smell of the earth, and felt a total settling-in, a coming home
and belonging. It was the most sensuous experience she'd ever had, a

stilled yearning for something that had been given to her that one day and that she hadn't remembered since. Until that moment with Ingrid. And yet, at the same time she was overcome by an intense sadness because—if the embrace of her mother still was the most significant touch in her life—what had she missed?

"Your hardship here on earth is the biggest blessing," Ingrid said with awe.

Trudi blinked. "I could do without it."

"Don't say that. I used to pray that I'd die before I turned seven."

"But why?"

"Because seven is the age of reason. Before then, we don't know enough to choose sin. It's because the forbidden fruit was eaten."

"You really believe all that?"

"That's what the Pope says. And the Bible."

"I know, but—"

"If you'd died before you turned seven, you would have gone straight to heaven." Ingrid sighed deeply, and Trudi felt the breath pass above her. "You could be there by now. . . ."

"No, thank you."

But Ingrid went on to talk about the Virgin Maria who'd been free from original sin from the moment she was conceived. "Maria is the only human ever born that way."

Trudi felt tempted to tell her old Virgin Maria joke, but she didn't think Ingrid would appreciate it. "I don't know anyone as worried about sin as you. Not even the little priest."

Like many in town, Trudi referred to the priests according to their sizes: old Herr Pastor Schüler was the little priest, while the assistant pastor, Friedrich Beier, was the fat priest. Trudi liked the little priest much better, even if he had powder on his shoes and took forever to absolve you. Once, he had assigned her two rosaries for sins she hadn't committed, as though the transgressions of the previous sinner still crowded him in the stale chamber of the dark confessional. The fat priest would never make mistakes like that, but then he was not nearly as kind as the little priest. The fat priest got things done. The fat priest would not forget a sermon or your sins, and his raised eyes bored into whatever came into their path—except food: then those eyes would lose their focus and he'd sigh with contentment.

"Look." Ingrid pointed toward the Venetian mirror that used to belong to Trudi's mother. A spider was crawling along the top edge of the golden frame. "That's what's so hard about original sin," she said as the spider disappeared behind the mirror. "From now on, I'll see that spider whenever I look at the mirror. . . . Even when I just think of the mirror, I'll see the spider."

Trudi smiled. She would be good for Ingrid. She'd get her to shed some of this awful shame. Ingrid would be so glad that she was her friend. They'd pick raspberries and red currants by the river, go to a concert at Fräulein Birnsteig's mansion, take their sleds to the dike, sit in a movie theater in Düsseldorf, take a trip to the Mosel and stay in a youth hostel. . . .

But Ingrid was still staring at the mirror. "The spider will long be gone," she said, "and yet it will always be there. It's like that with original sin."

"But don't you see—" Trudi said. "You can choose another mirror." She motioned to the opposite wall, where a small, round mirror hung in an even more ornate frame. She'd bought it one afternoon in Düsseldorf when she'd been caught by a jagged longing for her mother, and when she'd hung it across from the Venetian mirror, she'd felt an odd peace as if two mirrors would be more effective at holding the reflection of her mother inside the house.

That night, Trudi awoke long before dawn and finally stopped trying to force herself back into sleep; instead, she let herself imagine trading places with Ingrid. She kept her own features, her own hair, but her body became tall and slender like Ingrid's, and her head narrowed. Her arms and legs lengthened, and she watched herself stride down Schreberstrasse, taking long steps, a white blouse tucked into the waistband of her slim skirt, a shiny leather belt around her waist. Wind cooled her forehead and blew through her hair, and she smiled to herself as she made a left turn on Barbarossa Strasse. She wandered past the rectory and the open market where farmers sold their vegetables and fruits, and wherever she went, people stared at her, but not the way they usually did; she saw the lust Ingrid had spoken of in the eyes of some men; envy in the eyes of some girls and women; and the joy of simply looking at her in the eyes of others.

I could live with this. I could learn.

But then she glanced over her shoulder and saw Ingrid following, close, her body solid and short and wide, wobbling from side to side on curved legs like some horrible windup toy, and she wanted to run from her, keep her from demanding that she trade back their bodies. Yet Ingrid's broad face was suffused with tranquillity, and the fear that used to thrive in her eyes had given way to a gentle fatigue as if she'd struggled for a long time to arrive at this.

e   i   g   h   t

———————————■———————————

1 9 3 3

With each instance that Trudi imagined herself into Ingrid's body, she became more aware of people's responses to Ingrid. It made her uneasy when Ingrid's father chuckled and tried to pinch his daughter's buttocks while telling her to put on a decent skirt, even though the one she wore was as modest as all her clothes. And it confused her to see how Klaus Malter, the young dentist with the shy eyes and red beard, who had set up his new practice half a block from the pay-library, looked at Ingrid. She could tell he liked Ingrid, and it startled her when she found herself returning his feelings as though, indeed, she had become Ingrid.

Since Ingrid barely nodded to Klaus when he greeted her, he began to ask her and Trudi out together. Trudi was the one who'd talk with him, who'd answer his questions about Ingrid, and he took to stopping at the pay-library to visit when he didn't have patients. Wearing his starched white jacket, he'd sit on the edge of the counter and peer through the window, ready to run across the street if a patient approached his door. His beard was full and curly, his hair cropped close to his head. Often, Leo Montag would set up one of his chessboards, and the two men would play a few slow moves before one of them would be interrupted. A game between them could easily span a week. Though Klaus had joined the local chess club, he still belonged to a club in Düsseldorf, where he'd grown up and where his mother taught philosophy at the university.

Leo had introduced Klaus to Herr Stosick, the principal of the Protestant school, at whose house the chess club met every Monday night. Herr Stosick was known for decisive, brilliant moves. "Don't let your hands betray your mind, Günther," his father had advised when he'd taught him to play chess at age three. To keep himself from rash moves, Günther Stosick had developed a habit that still served him well as an adult—that of rooting both hands in his thick brown hair when he sat at a chessboard, forcing himself to weigh each option beyond his instinct, though he usually returned to that first instinct.

The club had been founded in 1812 by a man who had left his family for chess. His name was Karl Tannenschneider, and the men in the club talked about him as though he were still a member.

"He left his wife and children for chess," they'd say with reverence and envy.

"He left everything for chess."

While Leo liked to ponder his moves in silence, Klaus enjoyed talking with Trudi while he played chess. "I don't have enough patients," he confided to her one afternoon. "People keep going to Dr. Beck."

"They're used to him—even if they come out hurting worse than when they went in."

"There's no need for that."

"I always dread going to him."

"With all the modern inventions in dentistry, it's almost painless now."

"I wish someone would tell Herr Doktor Beck. No one likes him much. He's not friendly like you."

Klaus grinned. "Maybe people don't want a friendly dentist. Maybe they want a dentist they can be afraid of." He raised his hands, curling them into claws, and the fine reddish hair on their backs and on the lower joints of his fingers gleamed like thin copper wires.

Trudi crossed her arms to keep herself from touching those beautiful hands. "I'll tell everyone you're real scary," she promised. "Just wait—soon your office will be full." She imagined herself asking Ingrid, *"Do you think Klaus Malter is handsome?"* Ingrid would frown and say something like, *"Just average looking,"* or—and this would be worse—*"He is awfully handsome."*

Klaus rolled a cigarette. "Can I offer you one?"

She shook her head. "I like the smell, but not the taste. Probably from almost burning the church down when I was seven."

"How did you do that?"

Her father glanced up from the chessboard.

"Eva Rosen and I, we smoked our first cigarettes behind the rectory and threw them across the wall when we heard a noise. I didn't sleep all night."

"That could have cost you fifty years of rosaries," Klaus said.

"At least."

"Or life in the convent," her father said. "I guess I'm lucky I don't know everything you've done."

The boys in the barn— The room tilted. "Lucky, yes." She pointed to the chessboard. "Whose move?"

"Mine." Klaus advanced his black knight. "Thank God for large families. The Buttgereits have been sending their daughters—two last week, two next Friday, three of them the week after. . . . How many of them are there?"

"Nine. But in that family daughters don't matter much. I remember when the boy was born. . . . I saw a stork that day."

"I used to believe in storks, too."

"The Buttgereits, see, they had given up on ever having a son after all those girls—I feel sorry for those daughters, I tell you—and when they finally had the boy, Herr Buttgereit kept parading him around as if he were their only child, talking about him inheriting the farm before he could even walk."

"I haven't met the boy yet."

"You won't. He lives away from home. A special school near Bonn. When he was three, he fell off the hay wagon and hurt his spine. After that, his back grew crooked. He can't walk straight."

Leo tapped against the chessboard. "Your turn."

"Thank you, Herr Montag." Klaus paused to assess his position, then castled on the king's side and turned back to Trudi, waiting for her to continue.

She made her voice go soft to bring him closer. "Frau Doktor

Rosen told his parents that he will never be strong enough to be a farmer, and that he won't live much beyond twenty."

"That's awful." Klaus Malter slid off the counter and crouched next to her. "How old is he now?"

She felt the warmth of his body, his breath. "Almost eleven. I think. Yes, that's right." Flustered, she took a step away from him. "Everyone says he's very intelligent. . . . That's why they sent him to this school. Paid for by the asparagus money, I guess."

He leaned toward her. "The what?"

Pia, she thought, some advice you've given me there. What do I do now? "The money the Buttgereits used to earn selling asparagus," she explained. "Until we found out, we all bought it from them. Now only the restaurant people from Düsseldorf come for it. It was the most delicious asparagus, tender and—"

"Found out what?"

"I thought you didn't like gossip?"

"I don't."

"This is gossip. Last week you told me the one thing you despise about small towns is gossip."

"Don't torture me. What did you find out about the Buttgereits?"

"They kept the asparagus in their bathtub after they cut it, and people would go to their house and buy it right out of that tub. Two years ago, Monika Buttgereit swore Helga Stamm to secrecy and told her how her family got the asparagus to taste so good. . . ." Trudi waited, letting her words settle, and just as Klaus opened his mouth to ask his next question, she whispered, "Pee."

"What?"

"Pee. Everyone in the Buttgereit family pees into that bathtub." Another meaningful pause. "That's why their asparagus tastes like no other asparagus in the whole world."

He shook himself like a wet dog. "I'm glad I've never eaten it."

"Oh, you may have." She smiled. "Some of the restaurants in Düsseldorf serve it. They still do."

"I don't want to know. Why doesn't someone tell the restaurant owners?"

"Helga told Georg Weiler, and his mother told Frau Abramowitz and the fat priest. . . ." She shrugged. "In Burgdorf, word moves around fast, but—" She moved her solid hands as if rotating a large ball. "—it usually stays right here, in town, as if held within some invisible borders."

When the carnival returned to Burgdorf that July, Klaus invited Ingrid and Trudi to go with him. While Ingrid wore sensible shoes and her gray Sunday dress, Trudi had sewn herself a chiffon dress that matched the embroidered bolero jacket Frau Abramowitz had brought her from Spain for her eighteenth birthday. Although the high heels of her sandals kept sinking into the ground, forcing her to walk on her toes, she didn't let that keep her from enjoying rides on the Ferris wheel and carousel, and when she and Klaus took turns at the shooting booth, she was the one to win a plush lion with a stiff mane, which she gave to Ingrid.

As each July since she'd met Pia, Trudi searched for the *Zwerg* woman's blue trailer, and though she didn't find it, she sat between Ingrid and Klaus in the circus tent, expecting Pia to lead the animals into the ring. Pia would know about her and Klaus the moment she'd look at her.

But the animal tamer was the same burly man with the same sure smile who'd come here for the past four summers, the same man who had stared at her when she'd asked him about Pia that summer after she'd met her.

"I don't know of anyone like her," he had said.

Trudi had raised one level hand to the top of her head. "About this tall."

"No."

"She was here . . . with the elephants and the lions and a parrot named Othello and—"

"It's not work for a woman." He straightened his shoulders, making his chest swell.

"Pia knew what to do."

He started to walk away.

"Pia was magnificent," Trudi shouted after him. "A lot better than you."

He turned and stared at Trudi as if to appraise her. "Listen, little girl—" His voice had lost some of its gruffness. "We circus people are an odd sort. We don't always stay with one outfit. Some of us find a place we like and—" He let out a surprising giggle and lifted his bulky arms as if to release something. "—we stop there for a while until we get restless, until a new circus with new dreams comes along."

Outside the circus tent Klaus picked a bouquet of clover blossoms and divided it equally between Ingrid and Trudi. In the crowded beer-garden tent, they ate crisp white sausages with spicy mustard and drank *Berliner Weisse*—beer mixed with a shot of raspberry syrup—while listening to the accordion band play waltzes and gaudy carnival music. Flies buzzed through the swirls of blue smoke and settled on forks and the rims of glasses. Where, the year before, the beer garden had been filled with balloons and streamers, it now was decorated with several huge, red flags displaying the black *Hakenkreuz*—swastika—inside a white circle. The same emblem was worn by quite a few customers on red armbands or on pins fastened to their collars.

When Klaus wanted to dance with Ingrid, she shook her head. "Ask Trudi," she said, and his moment of hesitation—before he asked Trudi and led her to the dance floor—was so brief that, even years afterwards, she would wonder if she had imagined it.

Her legs felt clumsy, and her arms uncomfortable from stretching them up. Though her neck got stiff from looking into Klaus Malter's face, she loved the dance, loved every moment of it. Klaus showed her how to move her feet, and between dances they returned to Ingrid, who looked heartbreakingly beautiful in her church dress and managed to discourage every man who wanted to dance with her. She had arranged the purple clover in an empty beer glass and set it next to her plush lion, but the waiter, who kept replenishing their *Berliner Weisse*, kept forgetting to bring the water she'd ordered for the flowers.

It was close to midnight when Eva Rosen and Alexander Sturm entered the beer-garden tent, arms linked, faces flushed with an excitement that didn't seem to have anything to do with drinking. Trudi had seen Eva excited, but Alexander, who'd been too serious even as a boy, had grown even more formal with his formidable Kaiser Wilhelm mustache. A man who chose his words carefully, he didn't allow himself time for frivolities. He took pride in his toy factory, his apartment building, and gave far too much significance to what others thought of him. Yet, as Trudi watched him dance with Eva, he seemed changed as if some closed chamber in him had finally opened. Already, wonderful silver strands had begun to soften the starkness of Eva's black hair, a contrast to her girl face that made her look both

young and sophisticated. Alexander's hair was a much lighter shade
than hers, sandy almost. Trudi felt something new between the two,
a connection, a secret that compelled her to watch them closely.

Trudi hadn't spoken with Eva for nearly a year, but when Eva
stopped at her table to say *"Guten Abend"*—"Good evening"—it felt
to Trudi as if they were continuing their last conversation. Eva talked
with such ease about Trudi's father and Seehund, about her classes at
the *Gymnasium* in Düsseldorf and her plans to enter medical school
that, for a moment, Trudi wanted to take her by the hand and lead her
outside beneath the stars.

"Do you think your father will ever get well again?" she would say
and: *"Is the red on your chest still like a flower?"* and, most impor-
tantly: *"I'm sorry I told."*

But Klaus was asking Alexander how the construction on his
apartment house was progressing, and when Alexander only said,
"Quite well, thank you," Eva explained that the building was nearly
completed, and that Alexander's widowed sister, who was moving
back into town, would live with her daughter, Jutta, on the third
floor. "She's had problems with her health and needs help bringing
up the girl, who's quite impetuous, from what I hear. I'm rather intrigued."

"Reckless," Alexander said.

"What?"

"More like reckless. You said: impetuous."

"A blond girl, tall?" Trudi asked.

Alexander nodded.

"Didn't she visit three summers ago?"

"Yes. When her father was still alive," Eva said. "Alexander says
even then the girl was always getting into accidents. The day she arrived with her parents, she broke her left arm, and still, she went on
to climb trees and managed to break the other arm."

"Only it was the right arm she broke first," Alexander said.

Eva shrugged. "Eventually both arms."

Alexander seemed about to correct her once more, but instead he
turned toward Klaus Malter and told him he already had several tenants signed up for the stores. "The butcher, the optician, and the
pharmacist for sure. Possibly the hardware store. We're still negotiat-
ing." But the cherry tree on the sidewalk across the street, he said,

was a problem because the carpenters kept dragging red pulp from
the fallen cherries into the house on the bottom of their shoes, stain-
ing the floors.

When Klaus suggested he'd keep water pails by the front door and
ask them to rinse their soles before entering, Alexander nodded
thoughtfully and thanked him for his advice before he took Eva to
their own table.

The waiter poured more of the red *Berliner Weisse,* and Ingrid
whispered to Trudi when the foam left a white stripe on Klaus Malter's beard. When he insisted on knowing what they were saying, Ingrid refused and Trudi reached up to wipe the foam from his face. His
beard was dense, yet soft, and she blushed and pulled her fingers
away; but he caught her hand, and all she could think of was how glad
she was that she'd been using lotion so faithfully.

"What were you whispering?"

"That Alexander is a stuffy man," she lied.

"Strange to think that he makes toys," Klaus said.

When the band played the last round, Trudi thought the tent was
whirling around her as the young dentist led her in a waltz. He laughed
aloud and she laughed with him, and it no longer mattered how hard it
was to keep her neck and arms at that angle, and his lips were wet as he
drew her closer and lowered his face toward hers, whirling her around
all along, and his tongue tasted of sweet berries and beer, and it was
only after they were back at the table and the accordionists were playing the national anthem, *"Deutschland, Deutschland über alles . . . ,"*
that she realized she had just received her first kiss.

"Stop," she wanted to shout at him, *"stop, we have to do this over.
I didn't even know what was happening,"* but the musicians were
packing up their instruments, and Klaus didn't look any different
than he had before, even though he had taken her across a border
she'd never expected to cross: she had joined the legion of women
who had been kissed.

Klaus Malter took both Trudi and Ingrid home as he had before,
walking between them, his arms linked through theirs, and he
dropped Trudi off first and said she was a fabulous dancer. Her house
was dark and silent, but the moon scattered enough light for her to
find her way into the living room, where she explored her face in the
gold-framed mirrors. Each reflection gave her a face that was leaner,

paler—as though she'd lived through uncountable experiences since she'd left the house earlier that day. It was the face Klaus had looked at when they'd danced, the face he'd bent toward and kissed.

She tilted her head, smiling with the assurance she'd seen in Pia's smile, and thought of Pia's magic island with its waterfall and jewels and orchids, the island she had helped to create—a place to go to in her thoughts, hers as long as she remembered it was there for her.

"Trudi Malter," she whispered to herself. "No, Gertrud Malter . . ." But the name Gertrud—the full version of her name, the adult version—carried that tinge of her mother's craziness.

"Trudi Malter," she practiced again. Klaus Malter was ten years older than she—a perfect age gap, since she was far more mature than other eighteen-year-olds.

"Frau Malter," she said aloud, trying to ignore Pia's voice deep inside her head: "*Some are Zwerge. Others not.*"

She shook her head, hard.

"*Some are Zwerge. Others not.*"

But Pia's baby was not a *Zwerg*.

"*A grown grown-up,*" Pia had called him.

Klaus was tall. Their babies would be tall like him. They would sleep in a wicker carriage in the pay-library while she'd work. She'd play records for them, rock them in her arms. Klaus would kiss her in the mornings before he'd walk across the street to open his office, and he'd come home for his noontime meals. All her customers would have their teeth fixed by him. He'd accompany her to church, and Sunday afternoons he'd walk with her everywhere in town, proud to be seen with her, his love for her so evident in his eyes that no one could help noticing. For their wedding—

She laughed aloud, reminding herself that the marriage would have to come before those babies. For their wedding she would sew a white satin gown with a train and wear the highest heels she could buy. "*Trudi must have grown,*" people would say when they'd see her sweep into church. After the wedding she'd dye the gown a deep blue to match her eyes and wear it for special occasions, to the Opernhaus in Düsseldorf, say, or to a fancy restaurant.

But when Klaus came to the pay-library two days later and played chess with Leo, he didn't mention the kiss, not even when Trudi walked him to the door. He crouched to stroke Seehund's back—as if to restrain his hands from touching her, Trudi thought as she looked down at the crown of his hair, where it grew in a cowlick.

"It's good to see you," she said.

"What have you and Ingrid been doing?" he asked without glancing up at her.

As the dog arched his neck, pushing himself closer against Klaus Malter's hands without any shame, Trudi felt envious.

"I haven't seen Ingrid since the carnival," she said, stressing the word *carnival* to jolt his memory.

He scanned the street as if waiting for a prospective patient and stood up. "I must get back to my office."

"What's wrong?" Leo asked when Trudi stormed past him and up the stairs.

But she didn't answer. In her bedroom, she pulled out the pattern and fabric for a new dress and began to pin and cut out the striped material, allowing for added centimeters on the side seams while shortening the bodice and skirt. Even if she was condemned to see the world from the angle of a child's height, the range of that vision was no longer enough for her desires. By the time she fed the second sleeve through the sewing machine, it was getting dark outside, but she kept standing by the machine, balanced on her left foot while her right foot pumped the wide pedal, and her reckless fingers rushed the fabric toward the rapid needle.

She felt afraid of her passions, afraid of her mother's passions revisiting themselves in her, afraid of losing her dignity by bursting into Klaus Malter's office and throwing her arms around him. She laughed bitterly. Throwing her arms around what? His waist? His belly? She'd have to get him to sit down before she could imagine the rest of that futile fantasy. Now, if she were tall like Ingrid, she could walk up to him and, lightly, raise one hand to his cheek. . . . An embrace from her own height would be obscene.

When—all that week—Ingrid didn't mention the kiss either, Trudi suddenly wondered if she had imagined it. By now, it felt as gaudy and unreal as the carnival. Perhaps Klaus had just bent down and touched her lips with his by accident. But no—his tongue in her mouth had definitely been part two of a kiss. Even if part one—the touching of the lips—had been accidental, she could think of no reason why his tongue could have filled her mouth, other than that he had intended to kiss her.

Although the beer garden had been crowded that night, none of the people in Burgdorf said anything about the kiss to her. She waited, but even without confirmation she knew that she was a woman who had been kissed and that—at least in that one moment prior to the kiss—she must have evoked lust in the young dentist.

The end of that summer one of Trudi's molars began to ache. She tried to keep her tongue from darting back because its left side was rubbing itself sore against the edges of the tooth. The more she decided to ignore the pain, the more she thought about it. Her tongue probed the surface of the molar until she no longer was sure if she imagined a small hollow or if it really was there. What if she had only talked herself into a toothache to find a reason to have Klaus touch her again? He would know it the moment he'd examine her.

His visits to the pay-library had become rare, but Trudi would find out about him from her father, who saw Klaus every Monday evening at the chess club. Though she wouldn't come right out and question him about Klaus, she might ask—in passing—who'd been at the club. At times she wondered if someone had told her father about that kiss at the carnival, because he'd look at her as if hesitant to stoke her feelings for Klaus with new information; and yet, he'd give her what she wanted, waiting however until she'd bring up the chess club as if he hoped that, somehow, she would forget about the young dentist.

From her father she learned that Klaus was thinking of hiring an assistant, and that he'd sprained his ankle when his bicycle had overturned in the ditch. If she saw him on the street or in church, they'd nod to one another or exchange a few polite words. Afterwards she'd go over those words in her mind, trying to find significance in his inflections and pauses, imagining what she could have said.

Perhaps he was even shyer than she.

Perhaps he'd been waiting for her to mention the kiss.

Perhaps he was devastated that she acted as though nothing had changed between them.

She daydreamed about him nearly all the time: his image had attached itself to her eyes, a silvery sheen through which she had to view everything else. He interfered with her days, fastened himself to her dreams. Sometimes she wished she could scrape him from her eyes. Too often she succumbed to the promise of his kiss and let herself imagine a continuation of that dance, spinning into marriage, his arms around her and a red-haired infant.

Once, she found herself free of her infatuation for nearly two hours after spotting him from the window as he headed toward his office where, just before he opened the door, he reached back to pull the fabric of his trousers from the crack between his buttocks. Delighted with the absence of those intense feelings, she thought they were gone for good, but as with anything you let go of abruptly, they left a void, and soon her infatuation rushed back into that void, familiar and heavy.

When her tooth continued to hurt, leaving a sweet, crumbling sensation deep inside her mouth—as much a taste as it was a smell—she briefly considered going to her old dentist, Dr. Beck. But if this toothache was real, it was too valuable to waste on Dr. Beck.

The raw side of her tongue chafed against her molar the Tuesday she saw Alexander and Eva in the open market with a long-limbed, blond girl, tall enough to pass for fifteen if it hadn't been for the scraped shins of a child. She turned out to be Alexander's eleven-year-old niece, Jutta, who had just moved into his apartment building with her widowed mother. Jutta's eyes were curious when she was introduced to Trudi—not the kind of curious that irritated Trudi—but rather a way of seeing, a total absorbing without judgment. When Jutta looked at you, it felt as though you were held and stored by the eye of a camera—except there was nothing impartial about her glance: she had a wildness about her, a passion that made Trudi want to pull her aside and find out everything about her.

Eva grasped Trudi's shoulder. "Alexander and I—we got engaged yesterday," she said, her thin face radiant.

"Congratulations. Both of you." Trudi managed to smile though she was annoyed—not only because she hadn't been invited—but because she hadn't found out about the engagement till now. Usually she knew about things before they happened and relished choosing the best time to tell others.

"It was a small family celebration," Alexander said as if to appease her.

"How about your studies, Eva?" Trudi mumbled without glancing up.

"My what?" Eva bent until her face was in front of Trudi's.

"Your studies. I was asking about your studies."

Alexander lowered himself too as if not to miss one word.

Only the girl stood tall, watching the three of them with almost the same amused expression as Pia's that day she'd taught Trudi this trick.

"I'll wait until after the wedding," Eva said.

"But you still want to be a doctor." It came out like a reminder, not a question.

"Some day. For now I'll do some office work for my mother."

After that meeting in the market, Trudi saw the girl Jutta nearly everywhere, as if she'd been there all along, roaming through Burgdorf with impatient strides, a dog-eared sketchbook under one arm. One blustery September evening Trudi followed her past the wheat and potato fields to the quarry hole at the south end of town. For the past months, cranes had scooped out the ground, loading gravel onto trucks that rumbled through the center of Burgdorf, but now all the equipment was gone. Trudi saw the girl on the opposite side of the wide hole, her dress blowing around her like a bell as she stood high in the branches of an unsteady birch that clung to the edge of the gouged earth by its roots. All at once—though her own feet were on solid ground—Trudi became the girl Jutta: she felt the tree swaying beneath her, felt a deep identification as their lives fused in an inexplicable way that would endure long beyond that day and shift itself to Jutta's unborn daughter, whose birth was still more than a decade away.

Beads of cold rain began to slant to the earth, and from a distance a low thunder reeled closer. The roots of the tree were half exposed, and it struck Trudi as an omen that Jutta would never be entirely safe in Burgdorf. As the egg smell of lightning suffused the air, Trudi raised one hand to warn the girl, but the young face was turned toward the sky—not in surrender, but rather in a fearless greeting of the elements, as if Jutta were welcoming her equals—and Trudi decided against disturbing her solitude and dropped the cool back of her hand against that side of her face which was swollen hot from her tooth.

When she reached home, the wind had plastered wet, long leaves from the chestnut tree against the door. Her clothes were molded to her body, and Seehund sniffed her drenched shoes without getting up as she stepped across him. Lately, it had become harder for him to raise himself onto his old legs, and she had to hoist him up most mornings, steady him as she led him to the backdoor. Her father liked to save morsels from his meal for the dog. Since Seehund could no longer climb the steps, they'd moved his blanket next to the kitchen stove, but he slept wherever the sun left a warm pool of light.

"You better get some dry clothes on," her father said and heated the bathroom stove for hot water even though it was not Saturday, and she didn't refuse the bath because she didn't know how to tell him that seeing the girl by the quarry already made her aglow with something wild and splendid deep within.

Far into the night she awoke with a start and saw Jutta standing in the tree, rain shrouding her like a second skin. In the morning she found out from Emil Hesping that water was spouting from the bottom of the quarry hole, and when he took her and Frau Simon there in his car, Trudi stood beneath Jutta's birch, watching the surface of the water rise and wishing the girl could see this with her. Yet, she had a feeling that Jutta already knew.

By the end of that week, the water had cleared, and some of the older children were swimming in it. The following Monday, at the chess club, Leo told Klaus Malter about Trudi's toothache. When the young dentist stopped by the pay-library the next morning to take her to his office, she protested.

"It will go away."

But he insisted with a warmth that bewildered her.

"I have to put these books back on the shelves and—"

"I can do that," her father said.

Klaus Malter smiled as he situated her in his tilting metal-and-leather chair. "Another patient. I might survive after all in Burgdorf. Open up now."

"It's already better." She was glad she was wearing her most recent Sunday dress, the green gabardine with the pointed lace collar that she'd rotated into weekday use only the month before when she'd finished sewing her newest outfit.

"At least let me take one look at your tooth."

As he leaned forward to peer into her mouth, she felt the starched sleeve of his white jacket against her shoulder. A medicine smell clung to his hands and to the metal tools that probed her molar and gums. She wanted to close her lips, wanted to keep him from thinking that she longed for him to fill her mouth once more with his tongue, wanted to get it over—that moment when he'd send her home because there was nothing wrong with her tooth. If only she'd gone to Herr Doktor Beck instead.

"You shouldn't have waited so long," he said. "This is pretty serious."

She tried to swallow.

"Keep it open," he reminded her as he started to drill. His hands were steady, his eyes alert. His beard was as dense and curly as the triangle of hair that grew low on her body where her thighs fused with her torso. His skin was fairer than hers—as if he hadn't been in the sun all summer—and a faint spray of freckles made his nose look darker than the rest of his dear face.

She barely felt the drill as she pictured herself telling her customers what a fine dentist Klaus was—words that would carry far more influence now that she'd become one of his patients. *"He has gentle hands,"* she would say. *"He doesn't have hairs sprouting from his nose like Dr. Beck."*

Glad that she'd come to his office after all, she watched his face, his frown of concentration; yet, at the same time, she felt sad knowing that, soon, she would no longer be with him. And all along he kept drilling deeper, a low rumbling that made her jaw, her head, her entire body vibrate.

If only that drilling would last so that she could stay here, free to look into his eyes and feel the skin of his hands on her face. If only she were beautiful. If only she'd attended the *Gymnasium* and gone on to study medicine or law—anything that would have spanned the gap between their classes and brought her the acceptance of his family. He had told her about his annual family reunions at the Kaisershafen Gasthaus, about his mother who was a brilliant professor, about his refined aunts and successful uncles, about relatives who traveled to those reunions from as far away as München and Bremen. . . . As Trudi imagined herself entering the restaurant with Klaus, wearing a pale gray silk suit with pearl buttons, she had to squeeze her eyes shut at the display of loathing in his relatives' faces.

Abruptly, the quiver of the drill ceased. "Trudi? Did I hurt you?"

She felt as though her body lay sprawled out on the chair, there for him to inspect, squat and ugly like a bug flattened by a magnifying glass. Her tongue found the hole he'd drilled into her molar—a hole big enough for one's entire world to disappear—and she swallowed the taste of copper and charred bone and wished she could swallow herself and vanish into that abyss.

"Trudi!" His hand shook her shoulder.

It would serve him right if she died right here in his chair. The scandal of it! Surely, he'd never have another patient after that. *"God knows how far he drilled into Trudi Montag,"* people would say at her funeral. Those who had been Klaus Malter's patients would cross themselves and light candles of gratitude to St. Appolonia, the patron saint of dentists, who'd leapt into a fire after her teeth had been yanked out during her torture. Klaus would have to leave town—no, the country, because newspapers as far away as Berlin and München would carry headlines: *Red-haired dentist kills patient. . . . Dentist does away with young woman after kissing her. . . .* But maybe St. Appolonia wasn't the right saint to pray to. She'd be the one to protect the dentist, not the patients. Who was the patron saint of patients? St. Margaret, who'd been tortured, imprisoned, swallowed by the devil disguised as a dragon? No, St. Margaret was only the patron saint of pregnant women—one saint Trudi would not need, judging from the way Klaus had evaded her ever since that kiss.

"Please, Trudi—"

It seemed ironic that her womb would shed blood every month, that she shared that experience with other young women when the rest of their lives were so unlike.

"Trudi!"

Reluctantly, she opened her eyes. He was bending over her, lips parted as though he'd forgotten to breathe. His teeth were exceptionally white and even. She found herself wondering who his dentist was.

"How are you feeling, Trudi?"

Already she could see the measured man he would settle into, a man who would look with amazement at his younger self. The older Klaus Malter would never kiss a *Zwerg* woman or whirl her around in an endless dance. The older Klaus Malter would find himself a wife who'd fit into his competent life.

"I was afraid you'd passed out on me."

"Maybe the women in *your* family pass out." She laughed to keep him from noticing her sudden anger. "Obviously, I am not refined enough for that." Stop it, she told herself, he doesn't even know you've been to his family reunion and back. Yet, her anger boiled, red hot. Even if he had said, *"Listen . . . that night when I kissed you—I don't quite know what happened there. I hope I didn't offend you,"* she would have tried to understand; but to say nothing made him like all the others who believed that, just because she was small, every-thing connected to her was smaller—smaller joys, smaller pains, smaller dreams—invalidating her, invalidating that kiss.

He handed her a glass of water. "Why don't you rinse your mouth."

She swished the water around her mouth, wishing she had the courage to spit it right up into his cowardly face.

"In here." He held a metal basin below her chin, catching the foamy liquid. With a white cloth, he carefully dried her chin. "Maybe you'd like to rest a minute before I finish your tooth?"

"It doesn't matter." She reclined her head and opened her mouth.

His face was puzzled but his hands were as capable as before when he scraped the last decay from her molar and packed the hole with something cold and metallic tasting.

"Let me know if it keeps bothering you." He walked her to the door, and as she crossed the street he stood outside his office, watch-ing her as though undecided if he should escort her home.

On the opposite sidewalk, Gerda Heidenreich wavered toward Trudi like a lost star spinning out of control. Her pocket watch with-out hands dangled on a shoelace around her neck, and the front of her pink dress was darkened by spit that seeped from the corners of her mouth. Her facial muscles were constantly in motion as if react-ing to a swiftly changing world that only she could see. When she rec-ognized Trudi, her lips pulled into a vast smile, and she gripped Trudi's arm, claiming her for the community of freaks.

Trudi felt Klaus Malter's eyes and curved her shoulders against his pity. "Go away." She shook herself free from the young woman. "Sshh—go!"

The face above her puckered.

"Stop it, you," Trudi warned. "Stop it. Now."

Silent tears spilled from Gerda's eyes, steadying her features so that—for an instant—there was the fleeting promise of a loveliness that could have been hers.

Feeling something hateful and cruel rise within herself, Trudi backed away. "I am not like you," she hissed, "you hear me?" She left Gerda standing on the sidewalk as she ran toward the pay-library.

Her father was dozing, his head resting on the counter next to the chessboard, the black bishop in his slack fist. She snatched the golden mirrors from the living-room walls and hauled them up the stairs to her room. Door locked, she stripped off her dress and slip and corset, positioning the mirrors against her pillows so that they reflected most of her body. Pale, solid flesh swelled from her arms and hips as if pushing away from her skeleton. The hooks of her corset had left crimson marks that ran down the front of her torso like a new scar, and the indentations of her garters branded her bulky thighs.

"Remember this," she whispered to herself, her jaw aching, "remember this the next time you want Klaus. This is what he would see."

Her breasts felt cold, and she covered them with her hands. Against her will, a tingling began in her nipples and, almost instantly, in her groin though she hadn't touched herself there. The very first time her fingers had evoked that forbidden bliss by coincidence while bathing, she'd felt stunned, overwhelmed by what she thought she surely must have invented. And what she had invented had to be a sin. Anything that felt this fabulous surely had to be a sin.

But it was not what she wanted now. Not now. And yet, she pushed the merciless faces of the mirrors aside and lay on her bed. "I don't need Klaus for that. . . . I don't need anyone." Her hands—they knew what to do, and she wished she could keep from crying the drooling woman's soundless tears while images of Klaus became one with the boys in the barn, invoking the familiar terror that she needed to feed her sin. That part she despised, but she didn't know how to get to the bliss without it, and so she sucked in that terror with each breath, sucked it in again and again, and fought the boys as they did to her— now, now—what they had not wanted to do to her in the barn, until the fat priest shouted from the pulpit and a large bird fell so high from the sky as if shot from a tower.

The Nazi time came upon Burgdorf like a *Dieb auf Schleichwegen*— a thief on sneaky paths—Herr Blau would say after the war. To him and many others in town, the men in the doe-brown shirts were *unsympathisch,* ridiculous even, but surely not dangerous. Who really paid much attention to the frequent speeches that were delivered—always in loud, slow voices—from podiums draped with *Hakenkreuz* flags? So what if their flags were in every public building?

Of course quite a few decent people, including Herr Heidenreich, were happy with Hitler. After all, the Führer was ending unemployment and improving the economy. He was helping the youth to find a new purpose and direction. Herr Heidenreich saw young people join-

ing in group activities instead of slouching about. The positive change
was obvious to him, even in the younger children of his customers, a
respect for themselves and their town that hadn't been there before.

Frau Weiler saw a fresh enthusiasm in her son, Georg, and his
friends. How much damage could the Nazis really do? she wondered.
Like many others, she stilled her misgivings by saying, "At least let's
wait and see what happens." Even those parents who felt a sense of
danger, like Frau Eberhardt and Herr Stosick, decided to wait.

When Emil Hesping warned about the Nazis, people thought he
was only sore because quite a few of the young men in his gymnasts'
club had joined the SA club instead, wooed by speeches and bigger
trophies.

"Some days," Trudi's father told her, "I feel I'm on a train that's
hurtling itself toward an unknown destination."

It was a comment both he and Trudi would recall years later when
their Jewish friends and customers would be taken away, but the day
Leo said it, none of this had begun to happen. The people of Burgdorf
were drawn in, gradually, almost imperceptibly. They didn't know the
destination; they only saw the beginning. Their days felt livelier. They
had work. Bowls of food on their tables. The Nazis assured them it
was far better to live under their regime; they reminded the people of
the unemployment they'd suffered until Hitler had promised to give
everyone work and they'd started building streets; they told the people that, had it not been for the Jews and their relentless drive for suc-
cess, their own positions would be far more stable; they promised
that German children would have better chances for advancement
without the competition of the Jews; they preached a purification of
the race, which would leave the German people stronger and more respected. Jews were described as a *politisches Problem*—a political
problem.

Many went along with Hitler's ideas of reclaiming territories that
rightfully belonged to them. Though they would have never voted to
kill the Jews, they felt justified in expressing their resentment against
Jews, in letting them know their place. They didn't know that they
were giving their power away, didn't know that—by the time the Nazi
regime would become bloated and monstrous with that power—it
would be too dangerous for the people to reclaim that power.

Frau Abramowitz was determined not to let herself be poisoned by the force of hate that stunned many Jews. "It's important to keep forgiving," she told her husband, Michel, when they received a typed, unsigned letter.

"*Verdammte Juden*"—"Damned Jews"—it started, and accused them of greed, sodomy, bestiality, mercilessness, incest, and adultery. It was filled with absurd references to the Bible. "Jews are children of the devil. Jews are responsible for Communism and conspiracies. Jesus and the prophets were killed by the Jews. Jews are not God's chosen people—the Christians are. Jews have always plotted against Christianity. Jews are born with the lust to murder in their hearts. Their persecution over the centuries only proves that they are justly being punished for what they did to Jesus. Jews have contaminated Germany. . . ." The letter ended by urging all Jews to leave the country.

Frau Abramowitz didn't want her husband to tell anyone about the letter and was mortified when he refused to let her burn it and decided to take it to the rabbi.

"The things they say about us. . . . You'll only call attention to us."

He refolded the page and stuck it into his vest pocket. "We can't just ignore the danger."

"All this will go away. If we just stick it out."

It turned out that several Jews in town had received identical letters, written on the same typewriter, giving Frau Abramowitz some consolation of not having been singled out, while it alarmed her husband to the magnitude of that animosity. As she tried to lead her life as normally as possible, forcing pleasure from her garden and books and travel brochures, he increased his secret meetings with people who'd belonged to the Communist party before it had been forbidden.

When one of his friends, who used to be in the party with him, had his passport confiscated, Michel decided to hide his family's passports, but they were no longer in back of his sock drawer where he'd kept them with the birth certificates.

He found his wife in the pay-library across the street, talking with Leo and Trudi Montag. "The passports—" he said. "Did you move them?"

She turned her face to the side.

"Where are they?"

"I knew you'd get angry."

"Ilse. When—?"

"Twelve days ago. The police—"

"They came to the house?"

She nodded, her face drawn.

"Michel—" Leo Montag tried.

But Herr Abramowitz raised his pipe to silence him. "What did they say?" he asked his wife.

She didn't look at him. "They didn't give me a reason."

"Why didn't you tell me?"

"I was afraid you'd go after them and that they'd keep you."

"Our passports." He slumped against the wooden counter, his lips half open so that Trudi could see the edges of his upper teeth, two rows crowded inside his mouth. "You handed them our passports."

"Michel— they took them."

Impulsively, Trudi reached for Frau Abramowitz's hand. Her gentle friend, who had traveled all over the world, now could no longer leave the country.

"Do you have any idea where this leaves us?" Herr Abramowitz asked.

"We'll get them back in time."

"In time for what?"

Ilse Abramowitz's eyes darted from Trudi to Leo as if apologizing for the argument.

"*Deine Anpassungsfähigkeit*—Your ability to adapt," her husband said, "is far more dangerous to you than any of them will ever be. You'll keep adapting and adapting until nothing is left."

Although Trudi agreed with him, she wished he would stop. *Anpassungsfähigkeit.* She remembered Frau Abramowitz whispering to her, "It's important never to lose your dignity." To Frau Abramowitz, it meant a loss of dignity if she rebelled against authority, while to Trudi just rage carried its own dignity. For her it came far more natural to rage against circumstances than to fit herself to them. Sometimes it harmed her, that willfulness, but she wouldn't have exchanged it for Frau Abramowitz's acceptance of oppression.

One Thursday in December, during recess, the fat boy, Rainer Bilder, who'd been tormented and ridiculed by other children for as long as anyone could recall, vanished from school as if to negate his body mass. Though he was only thirteen, no one made much of an effort to look for him, as though he were merely a repulsive growth that had attached itself to the community, whose youths were becoming trimmer and more organized with each day. Some of the boy's neighbors wondered if he'd been abducted. Most concluded that Rainer was happier wherever he'd chosen to live. Even his parents seemed relieved that he was gone. It made Trudi wonder if people would feel like that about her, too, if she disappeared.

Though she hadn't known Rainer well, she felt his absence everywhere in the weeks to come—huge gaps where his body had once displaced the air, gaps that had a sadness stored in them. Soon, it was like that for everyone in Burgdorf: if you walked into one of those gaps, sadness would pack itself around your body, invoking other long-forgotten sorrows—the death of a loved one, say, or the loss of something you'd dared believe was yours forever—making your body expand with that sorrow until it filled the gap that the fat boy had vacated. You tried to bypass those gaps as they sighed to you with the yearning of a restless ghost, but more often than not you'd be drawn in despite your caution.

That sadness spread throughout Burgdorf like a malady, exacerbating old ailments, tinging even the political speeches and parades with a grainy melancholy that settled upon everyone like sand, muffling the Horst Wessel song, *"Wenn das Judenblut vom Messer spritzt . . ."*— "When the Jew blood spurts from the knife"—slowing down the once so enthusiastic marchers, whose legs no longer kicked up as high as they used to in the practiced goosestep, but were slightly out of pace with one another as though the gears of a finely tuned mechanism had gone awry.

It was only then that the police distributed Rainer Bilder's picture and description to departments in other towns and cities. The boy's parents placed ads in the paper, offering rewards for information about their dear son's whereabouts. In church, Herr Pastor Beier shortened his prayers for the *Vaterland* and beseeched God and St. Antonius—patron saint of travelers and lost things—for Rainer's safe return. People would find themselves glancing from their windows, scanning the end of the street for the familiar bulk of the boy.

One afternoon a stiffness spread low in Trudi's back, making it impossible for her to bend or walk up the stairs. Her father called Frau Doktor Rosen, who recommended bed rest and warm applications. "Don't even use a pillow," she said. "Lie flat. Completely flat." She helped Leo to carry Trudi up the stairs and settled her in her bed, a rubber bottle filled with hot water beneath her back. There Trudi stayed while the women in the neighborhood brought her meals and gossip and advice. They told her about a cousin, say, or a grandfather who'd suffered from a sore back, and they clucked their tongues as they fluffed up her feather comforter and helped her with the bedpan. No one had heard from Rainer, they said.

Trudi read two of her father's hidden books, by Alfred Döblin and Lion Feuchtwanger. As long as she didn't move, she was without pain, but whenever she tried to sit up, her back tightened up on her. It made her feel old, older than her father, who limped up the stairs, the outline of the steel disk in his knee showing through the material of his trousers, older than Frau Blau, who came to her bedside, the scent of floor wax on her hands, carrying a tray with pigeon stew, potato soup, and Christmas *Stollen*.

Sitting on the edge of Trudi's bed, knitting egg warmers to match the tea warmer she was going to send to Stefan and Helene in America, she'd tell Trudi about those of her friends who were invalids and had to depend on their grown children for care. ". . . not that they aren't lucky to have family to live with, but it's difficult when you can't be useful. . . . Then you don't have the right to make your wishes known."

"I'm sure I'll be out of bed long before I'm an old woman."

"It's no joke, girl. And if you're having troubles like that already, who knows what it'll be like when you're my age. . . . Since it's not likely that you'll—" She stopped herself.

"That I'll what?"

"Nothing." Frau Blau dusted the top of the night table with a corner of her apron. "Nothing."

"Marry?" Trudi demanded. "Have children?"

"Now who would say anything like that?"

"Look at me—" Trudi raised herself on her elbows and stared at the old woman. "Look at me. I'm no longer a child. I— I've been kissed."

"You're always making up stories." Frau Blau began to pack up her knitting. "Better rest."

"It's not a story," Trudi called after her.

Just when she became afraid that she would always be stiff and immobile, the heaviness in her back vanished for one entire hour. The following day it lifted for nearly three hours, and by the end of a week, it was gone completely and she was able to resume her walks. She found that the pockets of sadness left by Rainer Bilder had begun to deflate during her illness, and even if she happened to step into one of them, her sorrow was only fleeting.

---■---

1 9 3 4

R<small>AINER</small> B<small>ILDER</small> <small>WAS QUICKLY FORGOTTEN WHEN</small> G<small>ÜNTHER</small> S<small>TOSICK'S</small> ten-year-old son took the lyrics *"Für die Fahne wollen wir sterben . . ."*—"For the flag we want to die . . ."—to a dreadful conclusion. A bookish and obedient boy, who had learned to play chess at the age of two—a year younger even than his father—Bruno Stosick had won his first trophy in a tournament before he'd been old enough to attend school. By the time he was eight, he'd already beaten every one of the men in the club.

No one questioned that the boy was destined to become one of Europe's great chess champions, and the town showed its pride by granting him the kind of respect reserved for adults. Yet, his parents treated him like the child he was, and when Bruno entered the Hitler-Jugend the week after his tenth birthday, he did so secretly, knowing his parents had nothing but contempt for the Nazis. He was called a *Pimpf* and had to prove himself by running sixty meters in twelve seconds, jumping 2.75 meters, and memorizing the promise of eternal duty, love, and loyalty to the *Führer* and the flag: *"Ich verspreche in der Hitler-Jugend allzeit meine Pflicht in Liebe und Treue zum Führer und unserer Fahne."*

For Bruno this meant an escape from the narrow life of his child-hood—from books and chessboards and polite family dinners—an initiation into something grown-up and significant. Infatuated with the mysterious force of the songs and drums and flags, the future chess champion of Europe would climb from his window at night to attend meetings and march in parades. Upon his return he—who'd never cleaned one single item of his clothing—would brush off his uniform, wrap it lovingly into a clean towel, and hide it behind the potato bin in the cellar.

While two of his classmates, who were reluctant to join the Hitler-Jugend, were assigned extra multiplication tables and an essay titled "Why I Love My *Vaterland*," Bruno learned how to build a magnifi-cent *Lagerfeuer*—bonfire—by the Rhein where, eyes blazing along with the flames, he recited the promise he had memorized alone in his room.

Bruno was in love—fervently and irreversibly—in love with Adolf Hitler and his youth group leaders and the other boys; and, like many great and tragic lovers in history, Bruno would not survive the sepa-ration from his love. When his parents found out that he'd joined, they not only pulled him out of the Hitler-Jugend despite threats from his leaders, but also supervised every moment of his day, walking him to school as though he were a little boy, picking him up, letting him leave the house only when one of them was with him.

When Bruno hanged himself in the birch wardrobe, where his fa-ther kept the club's chess sets and ledgers of games dating back four generations, he wore his uniform and, on his collar, a pin with the emblem of the red, white, and black flag to which he had sworn eter-nal love, as if to validate the song *"Für die Fahne wollen wir ster-ben...."*

The morning after his son's death, Herr Stosick felt an unfamiliar draft against his scalp when he awoke, and as he brought his hand to his head, he touched bare skin.

His wife stared at him. "Günther," she whispered and pointed to his pillow, which looked as though it had become a nest of brown caterpillars.

As Günther Stosick picked up a tuft of his thick hair, he let himself hope for one moment, one deranged moment, that he could strike a trade with God—his son for his hair—because, certainly, to lose both at once was too much for any man to bear.

• • •

At the boy's funeral, Ingrid leaned down to Trudi and whispered that, while she couldn't see dying for a flag, she could certainly imagine dying for her faith. "It would be a privilege," she sighed, her eyes taking on a faraway look of ecstasy as though she could see herself being tortured for Jesus.

"Maybe for Bruno that was his faith," Trudi said.

"You know there can only be one faith."

Trudi shook her head, impatient with her friend's intolerance. Hands folded, she stood between her father and Ingrid in the crowd of mourners—most of them Protestants—that encircled the narrow grave which had been hacked into the frozen ground. The cemetery felt more like the home of the dead in winter than any other time of the year: without the distraction of all the flowers and blooming shrubs, the headstones were stark and far more noticeable; it even smelled more like a cemetery, with that odor of damp earth and rotting leaves.

Trudi shivered. The waste of it, she thought, the waste of a country that would incite children to die for it. She thought of all the things Bruno Stosick would never do—ride a motorcycle or kiss a girl or learn a profession. . . . How she ached for the boy's parents, who stood alone as if the town held them responsible for their son's death. After the coffin had disappeared into the hole, she followed her father to where they stood. Frau Stosick's face was hidden behind the black veil that draped from her hat, and she kept her black gloves on, but Herr Stosick's hands were bare and feverish, and he held both of Trudi's hands until she felt his anguish seep through her skin.

When she left the cemetery with Ingrid, who tried to talk with her, she barely listened and gave brief, distracted answers.

"Klaus Malter . . ." Ingrid was saying, "he asked me to go dancing with him."

Trudi felt a sudden jolt of hate. How could Ingrid betray her like that? "I hope you'll enjoy yourself," she said, keeping her face impassive.

"But I'm not going."

Trudi stared up at her. "Why not?"

"Because— I liked it better when the three of us did things together."

"Is that what you told him?"

"Yes."

"And he—what did he say?"

"I—" Ingrid's eyelashes fluttered as if she were winking. "I don't remember."

"You have to remember."

"I don't. I really don't." Ingrid looked miserable, already burdened—Trudi saw—by this lie she'd have to carry to her next confession.

But Trudi felt light and warm. Reaching up, she looped one hand through Ingrid's angled arm. She hadn't thought she'd ever have a best friend again. Not after Eva. Or Georg. But Ingrid had proven herself because only a best friend would rather be with you than be half of a romantic couple. "Let's go to Düsseldorf," she said impulsively, "see a movie."

"Not after the funeral. It doesn't feel right."

"I know. Still—it'll be good to think of something else."

"I don't have enough money with me."

"I'll buy your ticket." Trudi knew she was being pushy, but she didn't want to go home, where she'd only be thinking about Bruno.

"I still have to do my midday prayers," Ingrid said.

How Trudi resented all those hours that Ingrid spent on her prayers each day—hundreds of Hail Marys and Our Fathers for the dead as well as those living their sins, one entire rosary for the conversion of one pagan baby of God's choice, another rosary for her family. In addition, Ingrid did three rosaries a day on the mysteries: the first, meditating on the joyful mysteries; the second, meditating on the sorrowful mysteries; and the third, meditating on the glorious mysteries of the life of Christ. The leather cover of her prayer book was so worn it felt like silk.

"Can't you do your prayers tonight when we get back?" Trudi suggested.

Ingrid hesitated.

"Or you could do them on the streetcar. I'll be real quiet."

As the blue-and-white streetcar rumbled toward the city, they sat so close on the wooden slat seats that Trudi could feel the stays of her friend's corset. Ingrid submerged both hands in her leather bag, where she kept her rosary. Her eyes were half closed, and her lips moved ever so slightly as her fingers slid across the beads.

From the empty seat across from them, Trudi picked up a leaflet with a caricature of Adolf Hitler—the open mouth and mustache taking up most of the face. Instead of pupils, he had *Hakenkreuze* in his eyes, and a procession of tiny uniformed people goose-stepped from his mouth and dribbled down the front of his jacket like vomit.

Trudi held the sketch out for Ingrid to see, but Ingrid was praying. Ever since she had started her studies at the university, she'd added an extra sorrowful rosary on Fridays to commemorate the day of Christ's death; even if she was in class, she'd pray at three in the afternoon—the hour the pharmacy was closed because Herr Neumaier hauled his French Jesus around the church square.

A hand snatched the sheet of paper from Trudi's hand. "Where did you get this?" The *Schaffner*—conductor—had lots of hair but hardly any chin. When Trudi pointed to the seat across from her, he grabbed the other leaflets. "Did you put them there?" His breath smelled of stale tobacco.

"No."

"Then who—"

"I didn't see." She curved her back, making herself look even smaller than she was.

"You didn't see anyone?"

"They were already there."

"Do you know you can get arrested for reading those?" His voice had the tone adults liked to use with small children.

Trudi's feet dangled high above the floor. "If I get arrested, I'll have to tell. . . . That I found them here. In your streetcar."

Grumbling something to himself, the *Schaffner* stuffed the pages into his uniform jacket. She handed him the money for the tickets, and even the clicking of the coin changer that hung on his chest didn't distract Ingrid from her prayers.

"Don't do that again," he said and walked away.

She leaned her head against the back of the seat, her face and neck sweaty. As the streetcar crossed the Oberkassel bridge, the sound of the wheels on the tracks grew tinny, singing *careful careful careful.* . . . On the other side of the bridge were far more cars than in the streets of Burgdorf, as if the wealth of the city began right there. Newspaper boys hawked their papers at the stop, yelling out headlines, and two women with fur coats got onto the streetcar.

Outside the movie theater, posters inside a wide glass frame an-

nounced coming attractions. Before the film started, the weekly news
show—*Wochenschau*—depicted rows of trim uniformed men, Hitler
giving a new speech, athletes achieving incredible feats. Ingrid's
brother, Holger, was a well-known athlete, who'd won dozens of trophies as a member of Emil Hesping's gymnasts' club, but a month
earlier he'd been summoned—"invited" was the word his proud father used when he'd told people about it in his bicycle shop—to join
the sports club of the SA.

"It's an honor for our entire family," he'd told Trudi when she'd arrived to pick Ingrid up for a visit to Frau Simon's millinery shop.

She dodged his wide, oil-stained hands as usual when he tried to
stroke her hair.

"Now our Holger can really pursue his athletic career," he called
after her as she ran up the stairs to the apartment above the bicycle
shop.

She was glad he was busy selling a tire pump to Herr Weskopp
when she left with Ingrid, but his eyes touched both of them, and his
voice stopped them by the door.

"What's that you're wearing, girl?"

Ingrid's hand smoothed down her skirt.

"I want my daughter to wear a decent skirt." His fingers rubbed the
fabric by her thigh.

"It is a decent skirt," she wailed.

He'd laughed and turned back to his customer while Trudi had
grasped Ingrid's wrist and pulled her from the bicycle shop.

On the big screen, a runner broke through the finishing line, face
naked with ecstasy, arms flying out as if he were about to leave the
earth. Then Adolf Hitler was shaking people's hands. You could tell
by their faces how proud and delighted they were to be near him.
Trudi couldn't look at Herr Hitler without remembering the leaflet
and all those people marching from his mouth. But here in the theater
his stern features were in the right proportion and ordered around the
square mustache—so unlike the stripped face of the runner. His hand
filled the entire screen, again and again, grasped by other hands.
Trudi thought of the pharmacist shaking the Führer's hand. *Der
Schweiss unseres Führers*—the sweat of our Führer.

The film was about to start: it was about the love between a blond
forest warden and the blond daughter of a doctor. They finally got
married despite the attempts of a Jewish banker to steal the young

woman's affection. Not that he ever had a chance—considering how all the others would pinch their nostrils to avoid his terrible smell.

Trudi found it unbearable to keep looking at the movie. It was frightening to see how people felt justified to discriminate, how that attitude of superiority was drilled into ten-year-old children like Bruno Stosick. More than once she'd overheard comments on street-cars or in restaurants about Jews smelling bad. Though not directed at specific Jews, who'd sit stiffly, their arms tight against their sides, the remarks were always loud enough for everyone to hear. Some people would laugh, but most would pretend not to hear. Including herself. It was terrible, that uninvolvement, and she wished she knew what to do about it without getting hurt. But she'd seen people shunned or beaten because they'd come to the defense of Jews. Once, she'd witnessed a group of schoolboys push a woman from a moving streetcar when she reprimanded them for taunting a gray-haired Jewish man. As they shoved her toward the door, they shouted that she was ignorant, that it was a scientific fact that Jews smelled, that they'd learned about it in school.

And they didn't even feel ashamed, Trudi thought, as the black and white of the screen flickered across Ingrid's face and hands, summoning images of Bruno Stosick bending over his father's chess-board, riding his bicycle past the pay-library, saluting the flag. . . . She shut her eyes, but it was impossible to dodge the final image, the persistent image that all the others pulled her toward—that of clumps of earth dropping on the small coffin.

Only a few of the people in Burgdorf had read *Mein Kampf,* and many thought that all this talk about *Rassenreinheit*—purity of the race—was ludicrous and impossible to enforce. Yet the long training in obedience to elders, government, and church made it difficult—even for those who considered the views of the Nazis dishonorable—to give voice to their misgivings. And so they kept hushed, yielding to each new indignity while they waited for the Nazis and their ideas to go away, but with every compliance they relinquished more of themselves, weakening the texture of the community while the power of the Nazis swelled.

But not everyone looked away when injustices happened to others. When little Fienchen Blomberg was stoned in front of the Weilers' grocery store by six older boys, Frau Weiler let out a howl, grabbed her broom, and whipped from the store. The boys were smashing Fienchen into the display window, smearing the glass with blood. Wielding the broom handle like a sword, Frau Weiler forced herself between the thin girl and the knot of boys.

"I'll tell your parents," she screamed, and pounded at whatever parts of the boys' bodies she could reach.

They covered their faces, their chests, as they backed away from her. "Witch," they howled, "crazy old witch."

"I'll tell your parents."

"Witch. . . . Witch. . . ."

"Enough, Hedwig." Leo Montag caught her in his arms. "It's enough. They're gone. Trudi is getting the Frau Doctor."

Frau Weiler's great jaw trembled, and in that moment when she let herself be braced by Leo's body, too weary to continue on her own, it occurred to her how foolish it was to live next door to this man, both of them without someone to warm them at night. A slow heat climbed into her cheeks. She freed herself from his arms and comforted the crying girl.

Klaus Malter came running across the street, the sides of his white jacket flapping. "It's an outrage," he said, "an outrage."

Leo Montag carried Fienchen into the storage room behind the grocery store. Several of the stones had cut her skin, leaving gashes on her arms and forehead. Blood from her nose was running into her mouth and down the front of her sailor collar. While Leo sat down on a wooden crate and held the girl on his knees, Klaus carefully washed off her blood.

"How about a nice piece of chocolate?" Frau Weiler offered, eyes glistening with sadness.

Fienchen nodded, parting her lips as though she could already taste the rare treat.

But Klaus advised, "Better wait until Frau Doktor Rosen has taken a look at her."

"Here." Frau Weiler slid a wrapped piece of chocolate into the girl's skirt pocket. "You can eat it later."

Fienchen sniffled and leaned her head against Leo's chest.

"It may be a good idea," Klaus told her, "to have a few friends with you when you walk around town."

The girl mumbled something.

"What is it?" Klaus bent closer.

"I don't have any."

"Friends, you mean?"

Fienchen squinted.

"You must have at least one," Klaus pressed.

"Don't—" Leo started.

"I used to have two." Fienchen's voice was monotonous as if reciting something she'd been told repeatedly. "They are not allowed to play with Jews."

"But that's—" Klaus Malter looked startled. "That's not right. You—you are a good girl, a sweet girl. You—" He would have kept talking if Frau Doktor Rosen hadn't rushed in, followed by Trudi, who was out of breath.

"You can stay right there, Fienchen, on Herr Montag's lap." The doctor knelt in front of the girl, and as Fienchen rested against Leo's knitted vest, the doctor's fingers moved across her face as if in a caress. Her dark eyes barely contained the anger, which did not spill from her until Trudi and Klaus walked her back out through the grocery store, where the display window was still smudged with Fienchen's blood.

"There has been more and more of this. The children who're brought to me, the adults too—as if some essential law had dissolved. . . . A free hunt, and we're the trophies."

"They can't get away with this," Klaus said.

"Oh, but don't you see? They are getting away with it."

"I'll call the police," Trudi decided.

"We've written letters, made complaints. . . . Nothing. They want to drive us out, and they're succeeding. I know at least five Jewish families who've left town." She walked away, shoulders drawn forward as if she were a much older woman, but then she stopped. "It wouldn't surprise me one bit," she said, "if Frau Weiler got into trouble for chasing those boys off."

Trudi glanced up at Klaus, who suddenly seemed embarrassed at finding himself alone with her on the sidewalk. He pulled an ironed handkerchief from the back pocket of his trousers. His face set in a grim frown, he wiped the window until the red smears were gone. Then he stared at his bloody handkerchief, confused as to what he could possibly do with it.

Not too long ago, she thought, I would have offered to wash it for him.

Awkwardly, he folded his handkerchief, trying to keep the soiled fabric on the inside. "I better get back to my patients."

"You do that." Trudi's voice sounded sharp and she headed toward the grocery store.

"Trudi—"

Her hand on the door, she turned.

He looked like a boy who'd been caught in the middle of a mistake. Raising both hands in a helpless shrug, he gave her an uneasy smile. He opened his lips to say something, and she could tell he was thinking of that kiss he'd never acknowledged—like our bastard child, she thought with surprise—but when he finally spoke, it was not what she knew he had intended to say. "I . . . I hope Fienchen won't have bad dreams."

She felt herself softening toward him. "Is that what happens to you, Klaus Malter? Does it all go into your dreams?"

His face stiffened.

"We'll look after Fienchen," she said.

He nodded, hard. "We all have to look out for one another," he said with a sudden urgency.

Frau Doktor Rosen was right because the following morning Hedwig Weiler was arrested for attacking six children. Although Leo followed her to the police station to verify that she'd come to the rescue of a girl far younger than those boys, Frau Weiler was jailed for a week. The oldest of those children was the eighteen-year-old son of the butcher, Anton Immers, who not only carried his father's name but also his enthusiasm for the Nazis; he walked through town with clean gauze bandages on one cheek and both wrists, claiming to have suffered serious injuries from the witch.

In the butcher shop, his father speculated to any customer who would listen that Hedwig Weiler quite likely had at least some Jew blood in her.

"I wish they'd make up their minds," Michel Abramowitz said to Leo when he bought his pipe tobacco. "Is Hedwig a witch or a Jew?"

"Why not both? The more labels they find for her, the more justified they can feel in what they're doing."

"Labels. . . . Well, she is a widow." Herr Abramowitz tried to laugh but his eyes were grim. "They might come up with a law against widows."

"Ah, but Hedwig is only a possible widow. Don't forget—Franz

Weiler may have gotten out of the river alive after all."

"A possible widow then. But that's even worse! There should be a law against possible widows. I might propose it myself."

Leo's voice was soft. "Jews, witches, and possible widows whose husbands may still be floating in the river." He rubbed one palm up and down his right cheek.

"At least Franz got away. Without a passport."

"Any news on getting yours back?"

"We got the passports back some time ago. Along with the encouragement to move out of the country and practically give my property away . . . to pure Germans, that is— No insult to you intended, Leo. And I'm not just talking about the house. They want my law practice, everything. . . ." His voice rose. "I'm fifty-three, Leo, too old to start all over again. I have worked all my life. For now, Ilse and I have agreed to stay—even though it's not for the same reasons: she's waiting for things to return to normal, while I refuse to be forced into giving up my legal practice." He was breathing heavily, and his collar was limp as he told Leo about colleagues who'd emigrated to France and America, where they'd found it impossible to practice law because of language barriers and extensive exams. "One of them works as a janitor. . . . We're told we can go to Palestine, that we'll be taken care of there and—"

"Herr Abramowitz?" Trudi pulled a chair over to where he stood. "Sit down. Please."

Leo laid both hands on his shoulder. "It's easier for the young to leave."

"My son—he's pulling at me to get out. He's ready to go to London, to Argentina . . . anyplace, as long as it's away from Germany. I'm losing my son, Leo." He turned his unlit pipe in his hands. "My daughter, she wants to be near her mother. Now that she's married, she's closer to Ilse than when she was a girl."

Trudi and her father had been invited to Ruth Abramowitz's wedding the year before. Her husband was a wealthy throat specialist with a clinic in Oberkassel, who treated singers and actors and teachers suffering the strain of using their vocal cords too much. According to Frau Abramowitz, he was an ambitious, but kind man. Ruth worked as a nurse in his office.

"Ilse thinks all this won't last long," Herr Abramowitz said, "that all we have to do is keep from being noticed. Be nice. Polite."

• • •

While Hedwig Weiler was in jail, her son, Georg, asked for time off from his job in the big city grocery store and moved back into his old room. His mother's customers told one another that Georg had a talent for building occasions out of fiascos: they were amused when he'd guess what they wanted before they read him their shopping lists; they enjoyed his easy laugh and pointed out to one another that he was like a different person when his mother wasn't around. He'd persuade them to make bets with him about the next day's weather, say, or the color of the fourth bicycle to pass by the store window, staking half a pound of store cheese or a pound of flour against a jar of Frau Eberhardt's pear jelly or two pieces of Frau Heidenreich's plum cake. Even those who did not care to gamble would go along, flattered that this handsome young man would try to extract from them the one specialty they prided themselves on.

Georg didn't seem to care if he won—to him the excitement lay in making the bet—and he'd part easily with what he'd wagered; yet, somehow, he always managed to come out ahead because his mother's customers would press upon him jars of preserves and wrapped pieces of fragrant cake. While he captivated the women with his charm, he won over the children of Burgdorf by giving them extra licorice and chocolate for the coins they counted out on the counter.

Trudi stayed away from the store while Georg worked there. To see him so content and well liked unsettled her, and she consoled herself with her premonition that she didn't have to do anything as she had with the others from that long-ago day in the barn, that he was moving toward his own destruction. It was a premonition that grew so strong while he lived next door that one morning she surprised herself by wanting to warn him—of what exactly she didn't know, only that it had to do with Helga Stamm.

Even those of Frau Weiler's customers who had waited for her return felt disappointed when, a week after her arrest, they walked into the store, the payoffs of their latest bets with Georg in their shopping nets, and found Hedwig Weiler behind the counter. The part in the center of her hair had widened, but the sadness in her eyes had been replaced by rage, as if—for the first time in her life—she had discovered a valid reason to vent decades of fury.

"A homecoming gift for you," her customers mumbled and handed her a jar of cherries, half a marble cake, a basket of fresh eggs.

"Look at this," she told Leo Montag, her voice shaking with emotion, "just look at all those presents. I had no idea people cared about me like that."

In the weeks to come, the town noticed a new vitality about Frau Weiler, a fighting energy that manifested itself even in the way she packed butter and weighed lentils. Without any regard for caution, she ranted against the Nazis to anyone who came into her store. Certain that Frau Weiler would soon be arrested again, some of her customers—including old Herr Blau who worried he might be implicated by being around her—began to buy their groceries across town, while Herr Heidenreich and others admonished her for not appreciating their government.

Leo finally had to take her aside. "You're taking unnecessary risks, Hedwig."

"We can't just be silent."

"No, but we don't have to put ourselves in danger."

"You share my views. I know you do."

"Yes, and I'll talk about them with people I can trust. Like you."

"My customers won't report me."

"Don't be so certain. Last week Herr Weskopp turned in one of his colleagues at the bank. His wife's in your store often enough."

"But she's not like him."

"Who knows what she tells him? Besides, you won't have any customers left if you keep talking like that. People are afraid, Hedwig."

"With good reason too."

"Listening to you is dangerous. Emil Hesping has two friends in the police who're always getting denunciations at the station. They have to follow up on all of them, even those they know are mean-spirited or vindictive."

She gave him an impatient laugh. "So what do we do, Leo? Just sit here, afraid of what anyone might say about us? Wait for it to get worse?"

"It will get worse. Much worse. Maybe all we can do is what you did with Fienchen—keep vigil right here. And if you're in jail, you won't do any good to anyone."

Occasionally the people who came to the pay-library brought Trudi bits of gossip about Klaus: he had spent four days on his uncle's estate in Bremen; he was about to buy a second chair so that one patient could recuperate while he tended to the next one; he'd had an ear infection, which Frau Doktor Rosen had treated with yellow pills big enough to get stuck in an elephant's throat; he'd gone dancing with a teacher from Oberkassel.

Strategically placed questions to Frau Simon and the pharmacist led Trudi to the information that the teacher's name was Brigitte Raudschuss, and that she was nearly twenty-nine, the same age as Klaus. The following week Klaus and the teacher were seen together on three separate occasions—one of them on the white excursion boat that floated between Burgdorf and Düsseldorf. Frau Weiler heard that Fräulein Raudschuss was from a good family, and Herr Immers confirmed that her father was a wealthy lawyer and her mother a baroness.

She sounded like the kind of woman Klaus would be proud to introduce to his family. *"She's perfect for my son,"* Klaus Malter's mother would tell her cousins on the phone, and at the family reunion they'd all be waiting impatiently to meet her. *"What lovely manners,"* they'd whisper to one another, while Fräulein Raudschuss would lift her elbow, just so, to bring dainty bites to her lips. . . . Still—if she was all that remarkable, why hadn't this Fräulein Raudschuss caught herself a husband by now?

The Sunday Trudi finally saw Brigitte Raudschuss, she felt as though all the guts in her body dropped down into her legs, leaving her head curiously light. She was standing with the choir on the church balcony, between Herr Heidenreich and the polished organ pipes that pulled her reflection sideways like a funhouse mirror, and she steadied herself with one hand against the cold metal when the teacher entered through the arched door below her, tall and slender, one gloved hand on the pin-striped cloth of Klaus Malter's suit jacket as if she owned him.

Trudi wished Fräulein Raudschuss would faint or, even better, start foaming at the mouth, embarrassing herself irreversibly, but the teacher kept walking at Klaus Malter's side, her moss-colored fall dress rustling with each deliberate step as if, already, she were practicing her wedding-day walk toward the altar. Ten rows from the front, she turned her face to smile at Klaus, lifted her gloved hand from his sleeve, and slid into a honey-colored pew on the women's

side of church, while he found a place on the men's side next to Judge
Spiecker.

A dainty ivory hat with moss-colored silk leaves hid most of her
hair, but Trudi could tell from above that her features had that sharp,
anxious look that settles on some women who long to get married
and worry about getting too old to attract a husband. The two older
Buttgereit daughters, Sabine and Monika, had that look, and even the
flamboyant hats that Monika Buttgereit ordered from Frau Simon—
hats so bright they hurt your eyes—did not conceal that look.

It gave Trudi a spiteful pleasure to think that Brigitte Raudschuss
was getting to the age where her father's status would no longer
matter. Soon, she would be too old to be anchored in her role as
daughter—like other women without husbands whose connection
to their fathers no longer carried the same value, isolating them
within their families and community. Old maids—strange, how
their otherness was not physical as with herself, or the crippled
Hansen boy, or even the Heidenreich daughter, who'd recently been
sent to live in an institution, but how it came upon them at a certain
age, turning them into outcasts even though, up to then, they had
belonged to the community.

It worried Trudi that life had become even more difficult for unmarried women since Hitler had come into power and had declared
that the family was the most essential unit of the nation. Only the interest of the nation was more important than that of the family. The
word *family* had worked its way into most political speeches. It had
become a sacred word, a powerful word. And of course you were not
a family if you were unmarried, because the individual was the least-
important unit of the nation. Trudi doubted that she and her father
were considered a family. You were only a family if you married,
preferably young, and were on your way to become *kinderreich*—
child rich. To strengthen your family and encourage you to reproduce, the government gave you incentives, interest-free loans of up to
one thousand marks—about what the pay-library brought in over five
months. For each child you set into Germany, your loan was to be reduced by one quarter, and after four children it would become a gift.
And there was an even greater reward: honor.

When the organ music began, Trudi's voice rose with the other
voices in the choir. As always, Herr Heidenreich sang with his head

tossed back, his chest heaving, and the pharmacist's fleshy cheeks trembled while the corners of his thin lips strained toward his chin. The priest and four altar boys, led by Helmut Eberhardt, had barely positioned themselves in front of the marble altar when Hilde Sommer brought one pudgy hand to her throat, swayed, and crashed into a faint that brought four men running from their side of the church to carry her outside. The priest had to nudge Helmut, who had spun around at the commotion and was staring at Hilde as if wanting to carry her off all by himself. Just the week before, Trudi had spotted him outside Hilde's house as if waiting to see her walk past the window.

Of course she'd told Hilde when she'd come into the library for one of the doctor-and-nurse novels she liked, expecting her to laugh and say something like, *"Such a little boy,"* but Hilde—who was five years older than Helmut and outweighed him by at least fifty pounds—had seemed pleased.

Soon after Hilde was carried from the church, the girl Jutta rushed in, hair tangled, shoulders rising and falling beneath her unbuttoned coat as though she'd run all the way from her Uncle Alexander's house. Hastily forming a lopsided sign of the cross, she pressed herself into the pew next to Fräulein Raudschuss, who pulled her arms against her body as if greatly inconvenienced and appraised the girl through a polite, sour smile.

Trudi could tell Fräulein Raudschuss was the kind of woman who gave great significance to what people wore to church: she'd time her own arrival late enough to be seen by those already there, yet early enough to size up everyone else; she'd dismiss a girl like Jutta as insignificant while being impressed by someone like the pharmacist, who was always formally dressed and wore a suit with a vest and hat even to picnics.

I know you, Fräulein Raudschuss, she thought, suddenly in awe of her own gift. *I know all about you.* She was glad she was ten years younger than the lawyer's daughter. Since she had been different from the beginning, no one in Burgdorf would scorn her for not getting married. Even if it turned out to be her choice to stay alone, it would be what everyone expected of her in this town, which judged harshly whenever a woman would not conform to its codes of behavior. In a strange way, she had more freedom than other women: the freedom to make her own decisions, to provide for herself with her work at the library, to listen to her own counsel.

Her difference was good for something after all.

It made her smile, made her sing louder. For most women, Trudi knew, it was not a preference to stay unmarried. Some did not find a suitor, while others didn't dare marry a man from another religion or a lower class. To marry into a class above yours was desirable but seldom possible. In some families the oldest daughter had to be married before the next one could encourage a suitor, resulting, as with the Buttgereit family, in nine unmarried daughters, whose gradual aging removed one after the other from the wedding market while the parents fretted over finding a husband for their oldest, Sabine, whose disposition and features were equally piercing.

Actually, if Klaus liked women with sharp features, he could marry Sabine Buttgereit and free Monika and the other daughters for marriage. Trudi grinned to herself. Now, that would be a good deed, something worthwhile. No need to go out of town for a sharp-featured old maid.

Ever since Klaus had kissed her, Trudi had been trying to figure out what men looked for in women. The marriage ads in the newspaper were the best place to start. She'd skim across the women's section to the briefer list of announcements from men who wanted to meet women for the purpose of possible matrimony. Many were searching for healthy Aryan women who were younger than they, women who possessed warm hearts or their own businesses, women who liked children and cooking and leisurely walks and opera. None of the men ever advertised for a *Zwerg* woman who knew people's secrets. They usually described themselves as cultured or successful—sometimes both—gave their height to the last centimeter, but left out any reference to hair color, making Trudi deduce that, quite likely, they were going bald. Herr Hesping was the only man she knew who looked good without hair—probably because he'd been like that since he was a young man.

To see how closely those men resembled the way they had advertised themselves, Trudi had answered two of those ads and had arranged a meeting with both men—who of course did not know about each other—one Sunday afternoon at four in the same restaurant in Düsseldorf. She arrived before they did. Both looked older and stodgier than she'd expected, and they ended up at tables next to one another, each with a maroon kerchief in the chest pocket of his suit jacket, the sign by which, according to her letter, she would recognize him. Although their eager, nervous eyes evaluated every woman in the restaurant, they didn't even consider that she might be the one they were waiting for.

At first it all felt like a hoax to Trudi: their impatience, their discomfort seemed funny to her, and she felt a peculiar satisfaction when they fussed with their maroon kerchiefs to make sure they were still in place; but what persisted in her long after that encounter was an overwhelming hate, a hate so ugly that she was afraid it would make her ugly inside, too.

As the priest raised the blessed sacrament toward the dark-eyed apostles in the "Last Supper" mural above the marble altar, Jutta blew her nose and Fräulein Raudschuss shrank further into herself. Klaus Malter bowed his head, and Judge Spiecker buried his face in his hands. As Trudi watched them pray, she felt impatient with them and all the others who found such easy solace in church; and yet, at the same time, she envied them because—until that day in the barn— she too had known that solace.

The members of the choir filed down the stairs and toward the altar to receive communion, and when Trudi raised her face and opened her lips to receive the round white wafer, a sudden longing for a child of her own cast her neck, her thighs in cool sweat. Though she told herself that she did not want children, all she could think of was what she did not have and would never have. She could no longer name anything worthwhile about her life and knew that the rich lawyer's daughter would get whatever she wanted.

That night, Trudi tried to evoke that old dream in which she grew. Though she had tried to temper her consuming wish to grow by reminding herself of how Pia accepted her size, she wanted that dream—just for now—wanted to feel her arms and legs stretching, her body growing agile, wanted that familiar bliss of the dream to blunt the edges of grief over her love for Klaus, which was turning into hate as other loves had before. But what she dreamed of instead was the jetty, the Braunmeiers' jetty—only it no longer jutted into the current but arched high across the Rhein in one mass of earth and stones. Klaus was shouting her name from the other side of the river, but she knew the arch would collapse if she stepped on it.

At daylight she awoke with the panic of Klaus being lost to her for-ever. She knew she had to return to the Braunmeiers' jetty, and she was afraid; yet, she slipped on her clothes as if acting out the final phases of her dream and walked through the cold, vacant streets, past windows that were still obscured by wooden shutters, and as the houses gradually fell back behind her as if wiped from the surface of the town, she smelled the river, that profuse scent of water and trees. Fallen leaves crunched beneath the soles of her black lace-up shoes, and when she reached the summit of the dike, two freighters with red smoke stacks struggled against the current. The jetty was the way it had always been—flat and solid and surrounded on three sides by wa-ter. It didn't look nearly as terrible as all those times she'd pictured it.

As she walked toward the jetty, it came to her that what Klaus had done was not all that different from what the boys had done. While they had violated her with their curiosity and contempt, Klaus' viola-tion lay in his silence, in his pretense that nothing had happened. Her feelings toward all of them were so jumbled and intertwined that it made sense to be here in this place she had avoided, and when she dropped to her knees in the circle of sand at the end of the jetty and raised a rock, she suddenly was thirteen again—only this time she did not hurl the rock into the river, but placed it in front of her knees like some offering to an unnamed power and murmured, "This one is for you, Klaus Malter."

She took that panic she felt at not being able to be with Klaus and added four stones—one stone for loving him, one for hating him, one for her longing, one for her rage. The rocks were cold to her touch, and she set a fifth one—for being ashamed of loving Klaus without him loving her back—on top of that formation, then other stones for feelings she couldn't understand, piling them up while those feelings welled up a hundredfold, making her jaw ache and filling her chest until she was nauseated. All at once she saw herself as a child stand-ing outside the sewing room where her tall, beautiful mother used to be locked up, felt the unyielding door against her raised fists while her father's arms drew her away. "Your mother has found a more peace-ful place." That awful darkness that filled her soul now—it must have felt like that until, finally, years later, the recognition had broken through that she would never see her mother again.

"People die if you don't love them enough." Her brother had died

before his birth, her mother the week before Trudi's fourth birthday. The last year before her mother had died, Trudi had sometimes felt embarrassed for her. And she had never wanted her brother to be born. The day of her brother's funeral, when her mother had washed Trudi's face by the brook, she'd pointed beneath the surface of the brook, where their faces bobbed silver among tongue-shaped leaves. That moment of clarity—of how things could be—what had happened to it? Had it been swirled away by the muddy flow of the brook? Or had her mother reached for her hand and taken her back to the house, surrendering their images, intact, to the water?

Teeth chattering, Trudi added stones for her mother, for her brother, stones for Georg, stones for Fritz and Hans-Jürgen and Paul and Eva and Brigitte Raudschuss, until her head was spinning. Bracing herself on her hands, she waited for the dizziness to subside. It felt like the end of something, the death of something—and yet, as her eyes followed the river, she could all at once see how the end of every motion became the beginning of the next, how the water that came up against a rock found a new pattern as it joined the rest of the stream, how the crest of every wave became the descent into the rocking hollow, where the movement of the water took on a momentary apple-green sheen.

Trudi sucked in a long breath, letting the power of the river flow through her. The pile of stones in front of her made her feel safe, made this place hers—more intimately hers than anything that had ever belonged to her before, more so even than Pia's island of the little people.

She saw Pia wrapping her arms around herself, rocking herself, giving her words, which—until now—Trudi had not understood: *"Some day you'll remember this."* Slowly Trudi raised her arms, hesitating before she brought them around herself as far as they could stretch. What else had Pia said? *"No one but you can change that."* They'd been talking about that dreadful loneliness that comes from believing there's no one else like you. Trudi felt the solid shape of her body, held herself—careful at first, then exuberant—as she rocked that body in her arms, claiming it as hers.

Prayers in church for the *Vaterland* became a custom, and frequently the assistant pastor—that's how some people still thought of the fat priest though he'd since become their pastor, while the little priest lived out his last frail years in the Theresienheim, pampered by the nuns, who shaved him and cooked the gravies he craved—would add a fervent prayer for the Führer, his hands raised toward the black marble altar, where five stocky candles burned evenly. When he christened newborns—his favorite ceremony since it always included an invitation to the celebration meal—his hands would draw the sign of the cross on their foreheads, lips, and hearts, and he'd rejoice if the infant was named Adolf, by far the most popular name for boys that year.

In school, a brisk *Heil Hitler* had replaced the morning prayer, and only a few teachers and students dared not to raise their arms in the prescribed greeting. Brown shirts and uniforms were everywhere— you saw them in stores, in restaurants, in train stations—trim and crisp, marking those who didn't wear them as outsiders, part of a mismatched crowd that shrank with each day.

For Trudi, it was amazing to discover how many reasons other than size could turn you into an outsider—your religion, your race, your opinions. Enemies could endanger you with rumors; friends might involuntarily destroy you by repeating something they'd heard you say.

She saw people arrested for their political beliefs, and she watched how Herr Stosick, who used to be one of the most respected men in Burgdorf, was made an outsider. The day after his son's funeral he'd been demoted from his position of principal at the Protestant school to that of a teacher. People shunned and harassed him as though he had caused his son's death. His salary was cut to less than half, and he could no longer afford payments on his new car. When he tried to sell it, he received such ridiculous offers that Leo Montag, who didn't really want a car, decided to buy it from him at a proper price.

The majority of the men in the chess club voted to move their meetings from his house to the narrow room in back of Potter's bar. Nearly half of them wanted Günther Stosick to resign from the club altogether, but when Leo Montag and five other members threatened to resign along with Herr Stosick, they agreed to let him stay, though certainly not as president.

Quite a few of the members were acting like soldiers even though they were civilians. When Leo Montag turned down the nomination for president, the chess club was without a leader for months until the pharmacist convinced several members that he was the best candidate. Two of the chess sets were stolen from Potter's bar, and Monday evenings took on a friction that went far beyond the challenge of the game.

Günther Stosick appeared at only three of the meetings, looking decades older with his hairless skull. His skin was puffy, unhealthy, and he'd hesitate before making even the simplest opening move, his rootless hands—no longer safely anchored in abundant hair—hovering above one chess piece, then another, as though he'd lost his old decisiveness.

At school he had been pressured to join the Nazis like others who were employed by the government, but he had managed to stay out, and he was relieved that the party was currently closed to new members. "To ban opportunists and ensure selectivity," the pharmacist had told Trudi and her father when he'd reminded them that it was a disgrace for any business owner in Burgdorf not to belong.

"Why would they want someone like me?" Trudi had asked him, her eyes challenging him with the knowledge of her otherness.

After that, the pharmacist left her alone, but whenever he came in to buy his cigars, he urged Leo to make sure he joined as soon as the membership opened again.

"I'm too old for all that," Leo objected.

"Nonsense, Leo." The pharmacist gripped his elbow. "You're a month younger than I."

"Then I must be too young."

"It's nothing to laugh about." The pharmacist's neck expanded. "I can put you on a waiting list right now. All you have to do is pay five *Mark*."

"It is not for me, Herr Neumaier."

"Someone might find all this highly suspicious."

"What I find suspicious is your five-*Mark* waiting list."

Herr Neumaier raised both hands as if to ward off an attack. "I wouldn't turn in another chess player. But you are being careless."

He was more successful with Frau Stosick. When she came to his pharmacy to buy ointment for a rash that had sprung up on her hands, he inquired, "Since when has your husband been a member?"

"He isn't," she mumbled and drew the black coat she'd sewn for her son's funeral closer around herself.

"Haven't you lost enough, Frau Stosick?"

She looked down at her hands and rubbed the raw knuckle of her thumb.

"Do you have any idea what danger your husband is in? He'll lose his job. You'll lose your house and end up on the street. Is that what you want?"

She shook her head.

"We have to change this. Immediately. You should be at least on my waiting list. I'll take care of it for you right now so there won't be any trouble for not having done it before. This is what you'll do. You pay five *Mark* for each of you, and once you're members, you'll get the papers in the mail."

"But then I won't have enough money for the medicine."

"What's more important? Your husband will be grateful to you."

But her husband was not grateful when she told him, and he swore he would tear up the papers once they arrived. In the meantime, the two of them waited, a silence between them which grew colder with each day that Herr Stosick had to face a classroom filled with children whose arms snapped upward from their bodies with an enthusiastic *Heil Hitler,* with each day he had to forfeit the words of warning that he yearned to howl at them.

Though Ingrid was at the university now, she still lived at home and took the streetcar to Düsseldorf. She was studying to be a teacher. Lately, several of her professors had either been fired, retired, or pushed into insignificant positions. Their replacements seemed eager to serve without critique of the new regime.

"None of them wants to call attention to himself," Ingrid told Trudi on Sunday afternoon when they were taking a walk. "I pray for them every day."

"Even with all your other prayers?"

"I had to add one more rosary."

"That means you'll have even less time for your friends." It sounded petty and jealous and slipped out before Trudi could stop herself.

Ingrid frowned. But then she smiled as though it had just occurred to her that martyrs had been in that position all along—defending their devotion to God. Not that she was in an arena about to face the lions. . . . Still, Trudi was good practice in case she ever had to face a real adversary. "It's what God wants me to do," she said firmly.

"I'm sorry."

Ingrid looked disappointed, as if she'd been denied the opportunity to sacrifice herself for her belief.

They were passing the Weinharts' meadow where, behind the fence, all the cows stood crowded in one clump as always, while the sheep were scattered all over the meadow, their black heads bobbing from pale woolly bodies as they grazed on the last blades of grass.

"It's not that I decided by myself to do one more rosary," Ingrid tried to explain. It's— I know I have to do it, but it doesn't come from me."

"Like hearing a voice?"

"It's not like hearing or seeing anything . . . more like knowing it." Trudi nodded.

"I have no idea how it gets inside me. It's just there. And then I have to obey."

"What if you don't?"

Ingrid looked startled.

"You've never tried?"

"I wouldn't dare."

"But what if you don't think it is right?"

Ingrid's face turned scarlet as if Trudi had reminded her of something she wanted to forget. "It's not mine to decide."

Trudi stared at her, hard, trying to pull from her what it was she had done that wasn't right. "You can tell me," she whispered and reached for her friend's hand. But the instant she felt Ingrid's skin against hers, she no longer wanted to know, because what she sensed had to do with Ingrid's father, with that discomfort she felt whenever she saw his eyes settle on his daughter with a look that no father should give his daughter. She heard him chuckle, heard him tell Ingrid to wear decent clothes. Swiftly, she dropped Ingrid's hand, but it was too late: she saw the shadow of Ingrid's father against the slanted ceiling of Ingrid's room, saw him lay one finger across Ingrid's lips as she sat up with a start in her bed.

"Sometimes I think I dream things. . . ." Ingrid's voice was far away.

Trudi felt ill. "You don't have to . . ."

Ingrid's expression was as blank and pious as that of saints about to be tortured.

"Nothing you don't want to—"

"But you don't understand."

"You'll come to America with me," Trudi said quickly. "When I visit Aunt Helene and Uncle Stefan."

"When are you going?"

"Oh—I don't know yet. Whenever I want. Their house, it's more like a palace, really, six stories high, with marble fireplaces and tapestries. Other people live there too, in apartments, but Uncle Stefan built the house." Words tumbled from her with details of her aunt's stories about America: the clear lake in which her cousins swam; the soft toilet paper—not harsh and gray like in Germany, her aunt had said; the elevator in the apartment house. . . . Already she could see herself with Ingrid on a ship bound for America, the land of tall buildings and cowboys, looking back at the receding shoreline of Germany and at this day, this conversation that had persuaded Ingrid to accompany her.

But it was Ingrid who went on a trip—and not with Trudi but with her family, to visit her uncle in München over Christmas. Trudi saw them off at the train station. While Ingrid's parents and brother got settled in the compartment, Ingrid leaned from the open window of the train.

"Here." Trudi gave her the present she had wrapped for her.

Ingrid looked embarrassed. "I don't have anything for you."

Trudi smiled hard to hide her disappointment. "I don't mind." She'd bought Ingrid's present four weeks earlier, taking pleasure in imagining her friend's surprise when she'd open it, as well as her own delight when Ingrid would hand her a beautifully wrapped gift.

"I'll buy your present in München," Ingrid called over the whistle of the train. "Can I open this now?"

"It's bad luck to celebrate anything early."

"Let the girl open it," Herr Baum called out from inside the train.

Trudi flinched.

"I won't celebrate Christmas until it's here," Ingrid promised. "I just want to look at your present." Carefully, she unwrapped the gold paper and ran one finger across the red leather of the jewelry box. "It's so pretty. Thank you, Trudi."

"You like it then?"

"Oh yes." She tried to wrap it again, but her father's hand reached out and took it from her.

"Let me see."

Don't go with him, Trudi wanted to say. *Stay here with me.*

"Fancy, fancy," he said.

"Your papers, please." A uniformed official opened the door to their compartment.

Ingrid's father tossed the jewelry box onto the shelf above his seat. The beads of Ingrid's rosary clicked inside her handbag as she dug for her *Personalausweis* and a small green folder.

A stout woman came running from the red phone booth near the entrance of the station, two heavy baskets swinging in her hands. She nearly stepped on her skirt as she climbed into the train. In the open window of the next compartment appeared a gray-haired man, and a young soldier handed him a shabby suitcase, tied with string.

"Remember to take your pills, Father," he shouted.

Two women with gray coats and flowered scarves knotted beneath their chins sat on a bench near the ticket office as if they'd been waiting a long time. The whistle blew again, and Ingrid waved through a cloud of steam as the train pulled forward and a late passenger leapt on.

Trudi stood waving until the train had left the station, swaying in its tracks before it gathered speed. Only then did she feel the cold of the winter air. She turned up her collar, tightened the wool scarf around her hair. When she was about to step out of the station, she saw—as if framed forever by the wide brick arch of the entrance—four boys playing ball. In the pure, cold light of the sun, they chased one another, laughing, shouting. Their cheeks were red, and if it hadn't been for their identical brown shirts, they could have been any group of boys, engaged in an ageless game. Trudi's heart ached as their carefree voices drifted toward her, and she wondered how long anything could possibly remain a game.

t e n

———————————————■———————————————

1 9 3 4 – 1 9 3 8

Trudi and her father were troubled by the recruiting sessions
in the schools that resulted in new members for the Hitler-Jugend.
Their customers who still had children in school came into the pay-
library with stories of how they'd been told by teachers it was a duty
of honor for all families to guide their sons toward the Hitler-Jugend
and their daughters toward the BDM—*Bund Deutscher Mädchen*—
Alliance of German Girls.

Trudi's interpretation of the letters BDM made Frau Abramowitz
worry for her safety. "Bund Deutscher Milchkühe—Alliance of German Milk Cows."

"Hush now, hush," Frau Abramowitz said, her hands flying about
her as if attempting to push the dangerous words down.

"But they are like cattle," Trudi insisted.

Already most of the other youth organizations had been absorbed
into the Hitler-Jugend according to Adolf Hitler's request, ending the
skirmishes between children from the HJ and other groups, while creating even more of a rift between the HJ and Jewish children. Emil
Hesping knew quite a few group members who originally had objected to the merger but attended the new meetings to preserve the

friendships they'd formed in their original groups. Some of the older boys, who still came to the gymnasts' club, complained to Emil that, where their previous group leaders had taught them to be true to their individuality, they now were ordered to be true to the Führer.

Teachers had to meet regularly with the new group leaders to ensure that their students registered, and employers were pressed to hire only apprentices who were members of the HJ or BDM. As a result, children were forced to think about their future much sooner than they used to: whatever work they wanted to do once they grew up, it was to their advantage to belong to the HJ or BDM now.

And how could the children not love the roaring bonfires and the magnificent folk songs—dark and melancholy and strangely victorious—as their voices united and soared toward the night sky beyond the blades of red-yellow flames, intoxicating them with the promise of equality, those children of shopkeepers and teachers, of farmers and lawyers and tailors? All around them, they felt a dwindling of the rigid class differences.

When Helmut Eberhardt had heard the Führer's promise that each worker would have bread, and that he would lead the *Vaterland* to greatness, happiness, and wealth, he'd felt consumed by the same holy feeling he'd first known as an altar boy. That feeling stayed with him and grew stronger with each month in the Hitler-Jugend, until he felt powerful in a way he'd never experienced with the priests. He trusted the Führer when he proclaimed that he would not rest until each and every German was an independent, free, and happy person in the *Vaterland*.

At home, that new power changed Helmut's days with his mother. No longer did he mind her words, and if she reproached him, he fixed his eyes on her until her words withered. Soon, he stopped asking for things and simply took them. While he felt the accumulation of his power in the lengthening of his body and his impact on the much older Hilde Sommer—who was far more enticing than girls his own age—he felt his mother growing weaker, paler.

Eva Rosen and Alexander Sturm married the month before the Nürnberg laws would deprive Jews of their German citizenship and forbid marriage, as well as *Geschlechtsverkehr*—copulation—between Jews and Germans. The day of their wedding, an August Sunday in 1935, Trudi felt her heart swell with love when she saw Eva, her rich dark

hair in a braided crown, the white strands at her temples swept back
from her young face like the wingtips of a tamed bird.

"I'm so glad you are here," Eva said and bent to embrace Trudi. She
wore a fitted wedding gown with a short open jacket that was decorated with a pearl-embroidered collar and matching cuffs.

I am sorry, Trudi wanted to say to her, but she didn't because Eva
would have only asked what she was sorry about, and Trudi didn't
know herself, except that it had something to do with having failed
her friend.

Though Eva had resisted Alexander's appeal to convert to Catholicism, she'd agreed to five sessions of marriage guidance with Herr
Pastor Beier, despite his attempts to talk Alexander out of marrying
her. She had even promised to have their children raised within the
Catholic church, something that deeply hurt her mother, who tried to
justify her daughter's decision to her Jewish friends.

"It's the only way Alexander can marry Eva and stay in the
Catholic church."

"Theirs is not the most generous church," Frau Simon reminded
her.

Fräulein Birnsteig said that nothing was irreversible.

"They might not even have children," Frau Abramowitz offered.

The Frau Doktor touched the ivory scar above her upper lip. "Is
that supposed to console me, Ilse?"

It was a small ceremony, celebrated in the white chapel near the
Sternburg. The reception was held in the garden behind the Rosens'
house. Eva's brothers had arrived from Switzerland, where they'd
both been studying for the past years. Her father had risen from his
invalid's bed for the occasion of his daughter's wedding; dressed in a
huge black tuxedo, a glass of champagne in his hand, he chatted with
the guests as though he'd only seen them the day before. His large
face was tanned as always, and had it not been for his lounge chair on
the balcony, the plaid blanket folded across the armrest as if awaiting
his return, you might have forgotten that this was the same man
who'd been resting up for decades. His appearance would only feed
the gossip that he was not really sick—even though by the following
day he would be reclining again in the sunshine, at most raising one
slack hand if you called out a greeting to him.

His new son-in-law, Alexander, who'd gone far too quickly from a
serious boy to a serious man, looked changed today, sultry and al-

most beautiful. It was as though with Eva he'd regained some of those
lost years, and he moved like a boy—not a businessman. A jaunty set
to his hips, his neck, he danced with Eva. When his niece, Jutta,
dropped an entire *Schwarzwälder Kirschtorte* on the lawn, he
laughed and helped her scrape bits of cherries and whipped cream
and chocolate cake from the grass.

"Let's blame it on your foot," he teased her.

"What's wrong with her foot?" Klaus Malter asked. "I thought she
was limping."

"Nothing." Jutta shrugged.

But her mother told Klaus that she had stepped on a rusty nail.
"Barefoot. She was swimming in that awful quarry hole again," she
said, and Trudi recalled the night she'd seen Jutta by the quarry, the
night before water had sprung from the bottom of the hole as if invoked by the girl.

Jutta's mother was telling the dentist how Jutta had hobbled over
to the Theresienheim, where Sister Agathe had pulled the nail from
her foot.

"When did that happen?" he asked.

"Yesterday." She sighed as if exhausted by her daughter. Her skin
was waxen, her voice limp. "I keep telling her to be more careful."

"Mother—"

"Make sure you keep your foot clean to avoid an infection," Klaus
Malter warned the girl.

"It doesn't even hurt."

"Infections can sneak up on you."

"Listen to the doctor," Jutta's mother murmured.

"He is just a dentist."

Instead of acting offended, Klaus surprised Trudi by smiling at the
girl. "You're right. Still—dentists know about infections."

Jutta spun away. "The sister gave me something to bathe my foot."

Klaus had brought Fräulein Raudschuss to the wedding. She stood
close to him, her arm touching his with such familiarity that Trudi
knew instantly they'd been sleeping together for some time. She tried
to feel amused: after all, it was a challenge to estimate the progress of
a romance by watching people's bodies, the casual touching of arms
or legs, how closely they sat together. She could tell—even with those
who sat stiffly, afraid to betray their lust by touching out of habit. Not
that Fräulein Raudschuss and Klaus Malter were trying to hide any-

thing: her hand stroked his cheek; he let his hand rest on the small of her back as they walked around; she fed him a piece of wedding cake from her fork. . . . And if that wasn't enough to make Trudi feel hot with spite, they announced their upcoming engagement.

"It's not fair." Startled, Trudi realized that she'd thought aloud. She glanced around. But the only person who'd heard her was Eva's father.

"What isn't fair, Fräulein Montag?"

"To— to upstage Eva like that. It's her wedding day."

He nodded, solemnly. "It's not fair," he agreed, looking at her with such compassion that she wondered how much he observed from his balcony.

Alexander had claimed the largest apartment in his building for his bride and himself, and Eva set upon decorating the spacious rooms with teak furniture imported from Denmark and her collection of stuffed birds of all sizes, including an owl which her new husband had bought for her as a wedding present from Herr Heidenreich. But her favorite was still the gray bird with the crimson chest that Trudi's dog had caught. It looked as animated as the day Herr Heidenreich had stuffed it and arranged it in a nest, far more animated than Seehund, who found it harder and harder to get up from the floor. His hind legs were covered with teethmarks, where he'd tried to chew out the ache, and when he stood up, you had to remember not to pat his back because he might collapse.

Often he moved with such difficulty that Trudi was afraid he might not survive the night. But he endured, all through that winter and into spring, which dragged on, a sodden extension of the long cold months, clustering around the old people's aching joints, even affecting their memories: they'd raise their hands to their foreheads, straining to retrieve thoughts that had just become lost to them. Even the insides of their heads had grown soggy, jumbling their yesterdays with what had happened to them decades ago. They walked slower and relied on canes to support themselves.

Eva and her new husband seemed to be the only ones who were celebrating—as if in defiance of the laws that shrank the world of the Jews, forbidding them to marry Germans or to employ German household help under the age of forty. "Never mind that we're German too," Eva told her mother, who'd lost the maid who'd worked for the family nearly ten years. So far, Frau Doktor Rosen hadn't been able to find a replacement. Her medical practice had dwindled in the past two years since health insurance no longer covered patients who chose to go to Jewish physicians. Though some of her Aryan patients still slipped into her office after dark for consultations, a few conveniently forgot to pay her.

Ever since the wedding, Trudi had become more a part of Eva's life again. Eva was no longer attending the university and would stop at the pay-library—not to get books but to talk with Trudi or coax her into letting her father take care of customers by himself while she'd take a walk with her. She'd tell Trudi about all the exciting things she and Alexander were doing—eating out and going to dances and giving parties—but not about her rage at the atrocities that happened all around her.

Trudi was invited to two of Eva's parties, a small dinner that included Eva's parents, who hardly said anything all evening, and a fabulous costume ball, where people arrived dressed as gypsies with gaudy jewelry and scarves, Chinamen with yellow jackets and pointed hats, Indians with feather headbands, and fairy godmothers with magic wands. Trudi disguised herself as a little Dutch girl with wooden clogs and a starched white kerchief that Frau Blau had arranged in a triangle on top of her head, and her father went as a gambler, wearing the old eye patch from his pirate costume and his golden tie with the silver stripes that Trudi had given him many years ago.

Somehow, Eva had gotten hold of a nun's habit, going too far, most of her guests—and especially people who had not been invited but heard about her brazenness—would agree afterwards, especially considering the way she danced with her husband, who was dressed as a sheik. For all the layers of cloth between the two—her black habit and the white sheet he'd wrapped around himself—they could have been naked, rubbing against one another like that. But then, people said, it was known that Jews had huge appetites when it came to pleasures of the flesh. Marriage had changed Alexander, the people agreed. But maybe that wasn't all that surprising, considering the influence. He used to be so dignified, a decent man, the kind of decent that's glad to help you out but wants everyone to know about the good deed. Not that he was no longer a decent man—although that quality did come under doubt that night of the costume ball. Even when he stopped dancing with his wife and opened another bottle of cognac at the opposite side of the room from her, it felt as though the two of them were still touching.

In April, Seehund began to lose control of his bowels. Trudi would feel his shame when she'd come downstairs in the mornings to light the kitchen stove and find him lying in his stench, dried feces crusting his fur. Pinching her nostrils to keep from gagging, she'd hoist the dog up and half carry him outside, where she'd settle him down while she'd return to the kitchen to clean the floor and warm a pail of water for cleansing him.

Some mornings, frost still laced the air and shimmered in the sun, tiny particles of ice, reminding her of how Seehund had enjoyed his first winter. She wished she could bring him a huge bowl of snow and let him lick it, but the snow had melted, and only membranes of ice shrouded the puddles. One day, while washing his haunches, she knew he wouldn't live another winter. She grasped his leather collar and tried to take him to one of the frozen puddles—a poor substitute for snow, but perhaps the closest he would come to it. When he hung back as if reluctant to trust her, that long-ago love for him broke through, and she cried and stroked his fur. He nuzzled against her neck.

"Come," she said, and he followed her to the puddle.

With her bare hands, she broke the flimsy ice and held out a long sliver to him, letting him lick it as if, somehow, it could replace what she hadn't been able to give him since that day by the river when he'd absorbed her humiliation. Each impaired step he'd taken since had reminded her that she, too, was damaged. He licked at the ice until the heat of his tongue had melted it, and then he kept licking her hands and wrists, his raspy tongue far more alive than the rest of his body.

That afternoon, he dragged himself away.

When he hadn't returned by dusk, Trudi grew restless. She dusted every piece of furniture in the living room, then took all the rugs to the low carpet rod behind the house and, with her long rattan paddle, beat them until they did not even have one puff of dust left in them. Her father was silent while they ate their dinner of potatoes with pickled herring and beets, but twice he stepped outside to call Seehund's name.

Trudi left the dishes in the sink and lit two lanterns. Throughout the evening, as they searched for the dog, she felt a revival of the sadness that the fat boy, Rainer Bilder, had made the town's legacy, and whenever she looked up at her father, she could tell that he, too, felt that sadness which was inflating to contain the loss of her mother.

It was after ten when they cleaned silver-white pigeon droppings from a bench in front of the chapel and sat down to rest. Pigeons, hundreds of pigeons, dozed on the slate roof, their whisper of talons like gravesite prayers, reminding Trudi of the pictures of the dead bride on her father's wall and of the rumors that she was the cause of her mother's craziness. For an instant she felt as though she were falling, falling, but her father spoke into the dark as if taking up her thoughts and pulled her into the safe and constant web of his acceptance.

He said, "She was not always like that."

Across the meadow, a half-moon illuminated the onion-shaped tower of the Sternburg, and a high moving wind bent the leafless crests of the poplars.

"She was not always like that," he said again, "and yet, it was always there . . . underneath somewhere. I don't know why."

From the Sternburg came a sound, and Trudi leapt up. "Seehund!" she shouted. "Here—Seehund." But it was just the water in the moat, rocking against the pilings of the drawbridge.

"Maybe he found his way home," her father said without conviction.

"Maybe." She wondered how her father would endure it if they never found the dog.

"She was fine in our marriage." He started walking back toward the center of town, and she kept up with him, their moon shadows side by side on the road, his nearly twice as long as hers.

"At first she was fine. And before that, too, when we were still in school. . . ." He shook his head and his shadow head on the road looked as though it were spinning. "I don't know why she was that way. At first I used to think it was my fault."

Trudi felt a deep sadness for her father and for the girl who had become her mother; yet it was a sadness that no longer carried blame for herself, a clear and separate sadness that swept through her body without residue.

"It's nobody's fault," she whispered, and her father stopped abruptly and drew her against his coat.

They did not find the dog that night. The following day they kept the pay-library closed and continued their search. Shortly before nightfall they came upon Seehund, lying beneath a clump of bushes on the far side of the fairgrounds, near where Pia's trailer had stood that one summer. His fur was soft, and he lay half curled, the way he had as a much younger dog when he'd slept and played with the same abandon. A fine membrane veiled his open eyes as if the frost had drawn him into a final embrace.

Although Trudi would help her father to bury Seehund near the brook behind their house, she'd keep hearing him in the weeks to come, slurping water or eating, and she'd find herself walking carefully when she'd enter the kitchen, prepared to step around him as he sprawled on the floor. She'd ache for her father when he'd pull his comb from his shirt pocket and look around for the dog, or when he'd set aside a morsel of food for him on his plate and then shake his head as if remembering that Seehund was dead.

They began to notice dogs everywhere: the Buttgereits' poodle, the taxidermist's dachshund, the black dog of uncertain heritage that belonged to the Stosicks, the Weskopps' German shepherd. . . . Those dogs had been there all along, but now they only emphasized the loss of Seehund.

To cheer her father up, Trudi decided to surprise him for his fifty-first birthday. She took money out of her savings account, told him to get all dressed up, and asked him to be ready to leave the house by one o'clock. She put on her best dress, blue velvet with a round neckline and half sleeves, and while she waited for her father, she printed a sign that the pay-library would be closed for the rest of the day. But what to give as a reason? Due to family matter? To illness? She finally decided to write *Herr Montag's birthday,* figuring it might distract him from missing the dog if people congratulated him or brought him presents.

She had to smile when he came down the stairs in his good suit and the glitter tie. A taxi drove them to a fancy restaurant in Düsseldorf, where a pianist in a sea-green gown played arias from Wagner's operas.

Trudi ordered champagne and her father's favorite dinner, *Wiener Schnitzel* with fresh peas and parsley potatoes. Their table stood in the heated glass enclosure that jutted into the sidewalk. It was set with a thick white linen cloth, long-stemmed glasses, and a crystal vase with fresh roses.

At the next table, three young SA men were drinking *Schnaps,* and one table away from them sat the parents of the fat boy, eating with serious and silent tenacity. Ever since Rainer's disappearance, their thin bodies had become bloated—not all at once, but bit by bit, as though they no longer had their son to absorb their indulgences.

Herr Bilder's brown uniform concealed the bulk better than his wife's flimsy dress. Trudi had heard that he'd tried to get into the SS, and while he was certainly fanatical and bureaucratic enough for them, his body had not met the elite qualifications. But the SA took anyone—especially those who liked to bash heads.

Long ago people had stopped asking the Bilders if they'd heard from their son. Since they never mentioned Rainer, his name had joined the informal list of those whose names—because of embarrassment to their families or church—were unspoken as if they'd never been born: the barber who'd been discovered at the zoo in Düsseldorf humping a wild boar; the woman who'd run off to Portugal with another woman and left her children with her husband; the man who'd been shot in the Opernhaus during the second act of *Die Zauberflöte* while robbing the ticket office; the nurse who'd been sentenced to thirteen years in prison for killing unborn babies, which was considered a *Sabotageakt*—act of sabotage—against Germany's racial future. You might think about those people, shudder at their indiscretions, but you would not speak their names unless, perhaps, in a whisper to someone you knew well.

A waiter in a white jacket brought the champagne, and Trudi raised her glass to her father. "To your birthday."

He smiled. "To my birthday— Oh, no."

"What is it?"

"The Bilders."

The two had hoisted their bodies into standing positions and were ambling toward them. Pinned to Frau Bilder's massive bosom was the silver *Ehrenkreuz der deutschen Mutter*—the cross of honor for the German mother. Every year on the birthday of Hitler's mother, August 12, *kinderreiche*—child-rich—mothers throughout Germany were celebrated with the *Ehrenkreuz*: the most cherished in gold for eight or more children, silver for six, and bronze for four. *Das Kind adelt die Mutter*—the child ennobles the mother—was the inscription.

"A special occasion?" Frau Bilder inquired.

"My father's birthday."

"Happy birthday, Herr Montag."

"They didn't bring your food yet." Her husband peered at Trudi's father.

"It'll be here soon enough."

"What did you order?"

"*Wiener Schnitzel*."

"I had the *Rouladen*."

"Exquisite," Frau Bilder sighed. "They were exquisite."

"A wonderful gravy." Her husband clicked his tongue.

"The best I've had."

"We almost ordered the *Sauerbraten*."

"Next time."

"Yes, next time, *Liebling*."

"Their potato pancakes are better this week than the dumplings."

"Nice and crisp."

"They serve a spectacular rainbow trout."

"With lemon and butter."

"On a bed of parsley."

"Fresh parsley."

"Always fresh here."

"Don't forget to order the *Käsekuchen* for dessert."

"They have a fantastic *Käsekuchen* here."

"Last time I had the *Bienenstich*."

"I hope you ordered soup?" Herr Bilder's eyes took on a glazed look.

"Their pea soup is like a stew." His wife sucked her teeth.

"That thick."

"But smooth. So smooth."

Trudi glanced at her father, who was listening with a pained expression to Herr and Frau Bilder as they blocked his view of the pianist, the front of their thighs bulging against the tablecloth as if waiting to taste his birthday dinner. Three layers of white flesh draped from their chins, and their nostrils were flared as if not to miss any of the culinary scents.

"Your son—" Trudi started. "Rainer. . . . Now I have been wondering if you've heard anything about him."

Frau Bilder took a long breath as though she'd suddenly come to life.

Her husband blinked and pulled out his pocket watch.

"We must go," she said.

"Yes, we're already late."

"Happy birthday, again, Herr Montag."

With amazing swiftness, they moved toward the door and, miraculously, squeezed through at the same moment without getting stuck.

"Why do I suddenly no longer feel hungry?" Trudi's father asked.

"Because those two have already eaten for us."

"That was cruel, you know."

"I know."

"Once in a while I do think about Rainer."

"He must be about sixteen now."

The waiter brought their food, and as they began to eat, they heard a thud. A blind man with a German shepherd had walked against the glass enclosure right next to them. A bewildered look on his face, he yanked the leash and took a few steps back. He was young, in his late twenties, with skin that looked chapped from the cold. His hands were bare.

"Come on, doggie doggie doggie," one of the SA men at the next table called. His pasty face was splotched with acne.

His friends were laughing.

Trudi felt her father go rigid.

The blind man said something to the dog and, tightening his fingers on the leash, let the dog move forward, following it—again—into the glass wall. His round face showed an embarrassment so acute that Trudi wanted to look away. As he backed up for the third time, the dog kept straining forward as though hypnotized by its reflection.

Trudi pushed her chair away from the table, making an ugly, scraping sound on the tiled floor.

Her father laid one hand on her wrist and shook his head. "He'd be even more embarrassed if he knew we were here."

"Here, doggie doggie. . . ."

"*Idioten*," Trudi muttered. "Thugs."

Her father looked alarmed.

"They couldn't hear me," she whispered.

". . . doggie, doggie."

Once more, the blind man walked into the enclosure, his free hand stretched out as though he were expecting it, and if he felt anger, he hid it well behind a resignation that must have come from years of finding himself against obstacles.

Trudi wondered if he sensed the faces on the other side of that fragile wall. Though she still wanted to rush outside and help him, she
knew it would mean alerting him to his audience.

"He must have borrowed someone else's dog," her father said.

She nodded. "His own dog probably died." Right away she wished
she hadn't said that. Even here, she thought, we can't get away from
thinking about Seehund. "Or maybe," she offered quickly, "it's his
dog but hasn't been properly trained yet."

Her father let out a deep breath when—with his fifth attempt—the
man finally cleared the glass wall and walked away, his back stiff, depending on the dog who had betrayed him.

The people of Burgdorf went to parades and speeches—some, like the
taxidermist, because they genuinely believed in their leaders; others,
like Herr Blau, because not to go would call attention to yourself.
Most practiced the silence they were familiar with, a silence nurtured
by fear and complicity that would grow beyond anything they could
imagine, mushrooming into the decades after the war which, some
began to fear, was about to happen.

To justify this silence, they tried to find the good in their government or fled into the mazes of their own lives, turning away from the
community. They knew how not to ask questions; they had been prepared for it by government and church. Over the years, they had forgotten that early urge to question. For some, their one act of
resistance was that—whenever they could avoid it—they didn't raise
their arm in the *Heil Hitler* greeting. But others, like Herr Immers and
Herr Weskopp, used that greeting whenever they could, often as a
challenge to test those they encountered.

At his son's engagement party to Irmtraud Boden that May of
1936, Anton Immers entertained his guests with stories of the First
World War, as though he'd really been a soldier, and by midnight—
when the beer kegs were empty and the butcher had opened five bottles of expensive wine—his few remaining guests, all members of his
Stammtisch—began to recall that they'd seen him in battle, performing incredible feats of courage.

"I'll show you the picture of me in uniform," he said.

"We've seen it, Anton," they assured him.

But he insisted on leading them to the butcher shop, and the unsteady procession staggered to Alexander Sturm's building. When the

butcher set down his briefcase and unlocked his shop, he pointed to the framed enlargement of the photo that Herr Abramowitz had taken of him in Kurt Heidenreich's uniform, and the men toasted him with an emotional *"Heil Hitler."*

Herr Immers bowed to them. "The one regret I have . . . that I didn't hire a real photographer."

"It's a good likeness, Anton," Herr Buttgereit consoled him.

"A good . . ." Herr Neumaier frowned as if trying to remember what he'd been about to say.

"Exactly like you, Anton," Herr Weskopp confirmed.

The photo hung between two other pictures—a close-up of Adolf Hitler, showing him from the shoulders up while giving a speech, and St. Adrian, the patron saint of butchers and soldiers. To show proper respect, of course, the Führer had been positioned several centimeters above the butcher and the saint.

"But it was taken by a Jew. . . . I'll always know that." Herr Immers turned and peered into the dark beyond the display window as if looking for new evidence to place in the leather briefcase that he'd started to carry with him wherever he went, even to chess club meetings. No one had seen the briefcase open, but people said that, inside, the butcher carried lists of people who'd said something against the Führer. Even his new daughter-in-law, Irmtraud, who'd resented the old man's abrupt manner ever since she'd come to work in his shop as a fourteen-year-old, didn't have a better explanation for what the butcher carried with him.

". . . good likeness," the pharmacist was saying.

"And that other Jew," the butcher said, "she'd kick me out of here if she could."

"What other Jew?" Herr Weskopp asked.

"The Frau Doktor's daughter. Acting like she belongs here. . . . Planting lilacs in the backyard. Airs. . . . But I got myself a ten-year lease. With her husband. Before he married her."

One Friday noon, when Trudi closed the pay-library and got herself on the way to the Buttgereits' house to find out more about some rumors concerning the fat priest, she passed the crazy nun, Sister Adelheid, raking the paths between the flower beds inside the fenced cloister garden of the Theresienheim. Trudi greeted her and walked on, trying to decide what gossip she would trade with Frau Buttgereit to obligate her to tell about the priest. According to the taxidermist's wife, the fat priest's housekeeper had complained about him to Frau Buttgereit.

"Wait, you," the nun called. Her heart-shaped face was smudged.

Trudi stopped, letting her hand rest on the lower bar of the locked gate. Two huge plum trees poured their shadows across the sidewalk, leaving her and the sister in one stream of sun that fell on them like light in holy pictures.

"What is your name?" the sister asked, one foot tapping the ground.

"Trudi Montag."

"I have seen you before. I am Sister Adelheid."

"I know."

"Do you also know that *der liebe Gott*—the dear God—has called you?" She pointed at Trudi, who tried to see if the sister really had the stigmata on her palms, but the nun's hands were covered with soil. *"Der liebe Gott* wants you to be one of us. He has asked me to tell you."

"I— I don't think so. But thank you."

On the clothes lines next to the building hung three rows of black habits, too wet to be stirred by the wind.

"Come. I want to show you something."

"Where?"

"In my cell."

Trudi had a vision of the sister kneeling in front of a wooden crate covered with white lace, raising circles of bread toward the ceiling. "I have to go," she said, though she didn't like leaving without at least some new information about the sister or about the convent wing that was closed to anyone except the nuns. She'd been inside the lobby and in the other wing of the Theresienheim, where the nuns took care of the ill and elderly, and where Sister Agathe had given her medicine for her cough last winter.

"When will you come back?"

Trudi hesitated. Maybe the gossip about the priest could wait. She asked what she would have never dared ask one of the other nuns. "What is it like inside the cloister?"

"Picky and petty and always the same." The sister laughed and clapped her hands. "No, no, no—that is disrespectful."

"But true?"

"True."

"Is it also true that even the priests are not allowed in there?"

Sister Adelheid nodded. "No priests. No death. Sisters who get ready to die have to leave."

"Where do they go?"

"Down the hall."

"To the hospital?"

"The priest brings them their death."

"You mean the last rites?"

"Yes, that. The priest can't come into the cloister. Only one priest—" From the schoolyard next door came the sounds of playing children, and the sister lowered her voice. "Only one priest can go everywhere."

"Who?"

Two widows pedaled their bicycles from the direction of the cemetery, black scarves tied around their hair, watering cans bobbing from the handlebars.

The sister beamed and straightened her back, adding to her substantial height. "I am a priest."

"I see."

"And it is my calling to tell you about your calling."

"It's not for me."

"You will understand once you have seen my cell."

"Do you still have communion wafers?"

"You'll see. Come."

"But I'm not a sister."

"I give you special consent."

"The gate is locked."

Sister Adelheid shook the latch and frowned. "Climb across then," she said impatiently.

"I— My legs . . . I'm not tall enough."

"Then come through the lobby. Tell them— tell them you are visiting one of the old people. I am an old person. Look at my wrinkles. You are visiting me. So it becomes true. Not a sin, not a lie, no hell. You see? Go inside, then walk out through the backdoor into the garden. The others—they are always spying on me so that I—" She peered around as if suddenly aware she might be watched.

"My mother used to be locked up."

"Did she escape?"

It was the most logical of questions. Trudi nodded. "Many times."

"Good." The sister smiled. "Good. You must learn from your mother."

"Sister!" From the backdoor of the Theresienheim sailed the imposing figure of Sister Ingeborg, the supervisor of nurses. "Sister Adelheid!"

The nun who was a priest knelt down. Her palms gripped the metal rods of the gate, and as she brought her face as close to Trudi's as possible, her breath was sweet like that of a small child. "As long as you keep escaping," she whispered, "they never get you. Even if they think they do."

By the time the German troops marched into Austria in March of 1938 and the Anschluss was celebrated by jubilant crowds in the streets of Vienna, Leo Montag had turned more of the pay-library over to Trudi. Confident that his daughter could deal with the customers, he'd reduced his work to his favorite part—choosing the books they would borrow.

He'd moved a stuffed armchair next to the counter, and there he'd sit, wearing one of the many vests that the women of Burgdorf knitted for him, surrounded by stacks of books, the wooden phonograph from the unknown benefactor, and his classical records. Whenever a woman customer approached him, he'd take off the reading glasses that obscured his eyes. Though he looked older than he was and his limp slowed him down, the power of his gaze had escalated. Even in church the women felt his eyes, causing a sweet, unsettling heat to rise from their loins to their necks, and they would try to regain their composure by formulating the words of chagrin they would trade to the priest in return for the bliss of absolution.

Distracted by the surge of confessions about impure thoughts that involved the proprietor of the pay-library, the fat priest had been watching Leo Montag for some time while he'd preached his Sunday sermon from the pulpit, flustered when he'd forgotten what he had been about to preach. He had started to write out his entire sermons and had waited for Leo Montag's confession, but Leo only entered through the purple drapes of the confessional three times a year and would emerge afterwards, shaking his head, baffled by the priest's repeated, "And are you sure, my son, there is nothing else you should ask God's forgiveness for?"

Herr Pastor Beier wished he could ask the old pastor about Leo Montag's confessions, but his predecessor had died in the Theresienheim the previous year, his poor, scaly shell so dried out that it had barely added any weight to the polished coffin. Besides, no priest should ever reveal what he'd learned in the confessional, even if—so the pastor had memorized as a seminarian—the sinner had committed murder. "It is one of the greatest burdens you may have to carry as a servant of God," the bishop had told him. Still, he would have liked to know, because Leo Montag's successes evoked his old, long-confessed fantasies of the flesh, driving him from his ironed sheets with prayers of shame that would bring him to his knees by his bedside. Often, he'd flee his bedroom and roam the dark halls of the rectory until he'd find himself at the kitchen table, blotting temptation with raspberry pudding and sardines, pigeon stew and marble pound cake, cheese *Brötchen* and ripe pears, white sausages and cold venison—causing the housekeeper he had inherited from the little priest to set her lips just so when, in the morning, she'd discover that the food she had prepared in advance had vanished again.

Her raincoat buttoned up, and a covered basket over one arm, Fräulein Teschner would depart for the stores and open market, stand in line—no easy feat with her varicose veins—and wait with grim satisfaction for Frau Weiler or one of the other merchants to comment, "He must be at it again."

Although the pastor's favorite foods were not always readily available, Fräulein Teschner knew enough parishioners who welcomed the chance to deprive themselves by giving her some delicacy for the priest—much in the way they'd add an extra rosary to their daily prayers—to balance out their sins and ensure their climb on the ladder of eternal salvation. She knew how to time her visits to their houses to coincide with entries from the pastor's diary and rumors of recent transgressions.

On days like this, when she served his midday meal late—through no fault of her own, of course—he would taste her resentment and triumph in the rich sauces and sweet puddings, and he'd rush to compliment her, profusely, on even the taste of boiled potatoes. He'd feel ashamed for not appreciating her enough, for all the times he'd let himself hope that she'd decide to work for some other pastor, far away. To fire her was unthinkable—not after everything she'd done for him.

• • •

"Do you think Leo Montag has any idea what he is doing to those women?" Frau Blau asked Frau Abramowitz one afternoon when they saw the optician's wife enter the pay-library with a radiant smile and half a plum cake.

Her face flushed, Frau Abramowitz shook her head. "I don't think so."

The old woman chuckled. "He is too good at it not to know what he's doing."

"They come to him because they find they can talk to him . . . about themselves, their husbands and children— in a way they can to no one else."

"That too." Frau Blau winked.

"Leo is considerate . . . a wonderful listener."

"That too. Have you ever noticed how he strokes his face?"

"Oh, stop it, Flora."

"No, really. His hands . . . he's always at it, caressing his own face. That's why he doesn't need a woman to do that for him."

"It's only a habit. It doesn't mean anything."

"He's a very sensuous man—our Herr Montag."

Once, when Trudi left the pay-library with the small metal pail to buy a liter of milk, she returned and found the oldest Buttgereit daughter trying to embrace Leo.

"But I want to," Sabine Buttgereit said, her thin arms straining to keep her hold on Leo. She wore her church dress with the pearl buttons though it was the middle of the week, and her smile was frightened, determined.

Leo held her as much as he pushed her away, his eyes gentle on her agitated face. "With Gertrud gone," he said, "I haven't been able to become interested in another woman."

"I'll let you go as soon as you kiss me. I've never—"

His voice reassuring, he loosened her arms and stepped out of her embrace. "If things were any different, Fräulein Buttgereit . . ." he said, letting her fill in the rest to suit her hopes as she smoothed her hair with both hands though not a single strand had come undone.

If things were any different . . . Trudi had heard her father say the same words to Frau Abramowitz years ago and to other women who came to the pay-library. The potential of this promise still quickened a yearning in all of them, drawing them far stronger than any plaster saint possibly could. His tragic attachment to his dead wife became the women's virtue. It was safe to long for Leo Montag, to cross borders you would never cross with another man, because Leo Montag would not take you up on your offer. With him you could feel safe to reveal your daydreams, your hopes—and you'd always be left pure.

He was not at all like that friend of his, Emil Hesping, who'd never married but had left two generations of women who distrusted him. Frau Simon would have been the first to agree that men like Emil took whatever they could. With them you had to stay guarded. Your smile could be misinterpreted. A casual word. And yet, although she didn't rely on him, Frau Simon always took him back when he returned to her, giving her new substance for the gossip she loved even more than him. Unlike Trudi, who guarded her own stories, Frau Simon could be counted on to circulate and embellish her own experiences because she enjoyed the notoriety. It amused her that people gossiped about her and Herr Hesping while refusing to acknowledge their relationship in public.

No, Leo Montag was not at all like his friend. Leo Montag would handle it with instinctive diplomacy if women quarreled over him. He might retreat to the living room behind the pay-library when two or three of his admirers were competing over him—not openly, of course, but rather in hidden and cutting comments against one another—but soon, Trudi would notice, he'd be looking for those women again, for that adoration, and the next time he'd see them, the intensity in his gaze would have increased. The longer his celibacy lasted, the stronger that passion lived in his eyes.

The women released their secrets to Leo because they longed to be understood, loved. They wanted excitement and purity all at once, something they could only get from him. When he turned his eyes onto you, you knew that—were it not for his tragic loyalty to his dead wife—you would be the most important woman in his life.

You brought your secrets to Leo but guarded them from Trudi. Yet, as soon as you thought—I hope Trudi Montag doesn't find out—she'd lure that secret from you as though you'd given off a scent, a signal that made her approach you like a hunter, the awareness of your secret in her eyes; and what she didn't already know or find out from you, she would guess—usually with amazing accuracy. Even what happened inside your house. Inside your soul.

You would recognize her from a distance—early evenings or during the midday break, her squat shape tilting from side to side as she propelled herself forward on those curved legs of hers. She moved with confidence and purpose, and though you'd long to find out the stories she carried, you'd often shy away from her—just in case those stories were about you. She was always curious about your life and gave you more attention than anyone you knew.

No one else looked at you with such interest, such compassion.

No one else knew how your secret burdened you.

No one but Trudi Montag understood your relief once you'd shared that weight with her.

Unlike other confessors, she would not assign prayers or punish you with disgust. She welcomed your sins, and it was tempting to tell her everything. But you had learned not to.

You had learned it from listening to the secrets she had seized from others and spread about town, like the one about the pharmacist having been adopted, something everyone talked about now, although—until recently—only one of the very old men in Burgdorf had recalled that fact. No one else of that generation had deemed it important enough to keep alive by retelling it. But Trudi Montag had brought the pharmacist's secret back. Trudi Montag had searched through dusty records in the Rathaus, where she'd found the dates of his parents' wedding and of his christening, yet no account of his birth.

"Not that it matters to me, but he could have come from anywhere," she would tell you, bent on shaking the superior attitude of the pharmacist who'd been instrumental in showing films at the school, which claimed that Jews were filthy and neglectful in personal habits. Every single student had to watch the films, even the Jewish children.

"He doesn't even know his parents," she would tell you.

Even if you were determined not to talk to Trudi Montag at all, you couldn't always guard your secret from her. You'd weaken: something in her generous eyes would make you want to tell her, and though you didn't want to give in, you already sensed that it was too late, that your secret was becoming hers, and that from then on you could only watch it grow as Trudi paraded it around town—much in the way a new mother takes pleasure in showing off her infant.

And yet, whatever the people gave Trudi was not enough, could never be enough. If she couldn't have their acceptance, at least she'd have their stories. That's what the people of Burgdorf owed her. Because she'd come into their middle. Because of her difference. Because they could not accept her—they owed her something. And she'd extract that payment, ruthlessly, banking on their pity, their guilt, their relief.

But to her own secrets she held on, accumulating power by keeping separate what was hers and what belonged to others. One day it struck her that it was almost like hoarding money for people who worshiped wealth. How much she had that was hers. What she took away from others. What she gave to others. What she hoarded. There was even interest because what she already owned grew as she added that which came from others. It gave her a sense of wealth, of pride; yet, sometimes the mass of secrets felt totally useless, a sharp-edged block that encumbered her. Those were the times when she would have liked to give up all the secrets if only she could have had what she craved most deeply—the connection to others.

e   l   e   v   e   n

---■---

1 9 3 8

THAT SPRING OF THE ANSCHLUSS, WHEN GERMAN TROOPS MARCHED
into Austria, came to be known in Burgdorf as the spring of the great
flood. After eight years of tolerating its boundaries, the Rhein spilled
its waters across a hundred towns, killing over four hundred people,
five of them in Burgdorf alone. The old women said the river had become accustomed to human flesh from the two recent suicides, both
of them Jews, who had chosen its chilly current for their grave, seeking out whirlpools and surrendering to their downward spin instead
of escaping through the root of the vortex the way that children who
live near the river are taught to by their elders.

The river—so the old women said—was like a wild animal which,
once it has sampled human blood, will always lust for that taste.

When the old women whispered that the river was hungry for
more, they crossed themselves and prayed for the flood—the most
terrible flood even the oldest among them could remember—to re-
cede from their kitchens and bedrooms. They longed for a day when
they could leave their slippers on the floor next to their beds again, for
a day when rowboats and kayaks would be used for family outings—

not to navigate the streets which lay blurred under shifting, muddy waters. Gifts from the unknown benefactor appeared in many houses as if they'd floated there on invisible rafts. Perhaps there wasn't just one benefactor, the old women speculated, but a whole group of benefactors. Because how could one person possibly collect and distribute all those gifts, each uniquely suited to its recipient?

As the river retreated, it left hollows in the cemetery, where the earth settled on the coffins beneath, the deepest of them on the grave where Herr Höffenauer and his mother lay buried. Near the bank at the north end of Burgdorf, the Rhein cleaved out a long basin, giving the town a second swimming hole, one gouged by men, the other by the flood. Throughout the region, the wet stench of rot lingered in walls and floorboards, in mattresses and drapes that had been touched by the river.

The first day the sidewalks were dry again, people dressed in the brightest clothes they owned as if to entice that brightness from the sky and back into their lives. What they wanted was a brightness far beyond the kind you can see with your eyes when the sun opens the sky, the kind of brightness that had been lacking from their lives since long before the flood, the kind of brightness that had been sucked out of each house, each town, and replaced with fear and suspicion.

Frau Simon had her busiest morning in years: she sold seven hats—none of them gray or brown, but all in vibrant colors: yellow and blue and red and green—the most elaborate of them to her best customer, Monika Buttgereit, whose thwarted passions for the driver of the bakery truck had funneled themselves into one obsession that her parents thought it wise not to object to though it embarrassed them: *hats*. Hats with fabulous feathers, with lace, with fancy clasps. Her newest acquisition was a two-tone purple satin turban with a pearl-studded veil, which—Frau Simon swore—suggested a definite hint of mystery.

Just before Frau Simon was about to close her store that noon, she walked out with her last customer, Trudi Montag, trying to persuade her, there on the front steps while the river-soaked wind blew heavily around their ankles, to let her set aside that second hat Trudi had liked, the red one with the speckled feather, which still perched on a wooden stand in the display window.

"For at least a few days," she implored. Her white blouse was tucked into the slim skirt of her elegant suit.

But Trudi was staring past her at a slow black car that approached from the direction of the church square.

"It suited you so, that red hat, Trudi. I'd hate to see it on anyone else." Frau Simon reached down to fluff Trudi's bangs and—with one practiced gesture—tilted the moss-green hat, which Trudi had just bought, slightly to the right. "There now." She sounded pleased.

On the opposite sidewalk, people walked faster, turning up the collars of their coats like half masks against the soggy, stinking wind, and in the street, women on bicycles pedaled harder, thighs straining against the fabric of their skirts, causing their shopping nets to swing from the handlebars like useless pendulums.

"Not that green isn't a flattering color for you, Trudi. Especially with that coat you sewed last month. It's only that I like both hats on you. With all the self-improvement you've done . . . It would be a pity to let that hat go to someone else. A pity. Maybe I'll mention it to your father when I return my books. Your birthday is only three months away, and it's never too early to—"

As the car came to a smooth stop in front of the milliner's shop, two Gestapo officers slipped out.

"Lotte Simon?" The shorter of the men stepped up to her.

Frau Simon backed into the entranceway and rubbed her arms through her sleeves as though suddenly cold.

"You have to come with us."

"But why?"

"An investigation."

"An investigation? Into what? I—"

"Only a routine."

"I haven't done anything."

Trudi felt numb, angry, afraid. And then numb again. She glanced around for help, but the street had emptied as if in anticipation of an even greater flood, and in a second-floor window next door a lace curtain moved.

"Let me call a lawyer—please!" Frau Simon's fingers grasped her silver necklace.

"Get into the car."

The short officer was giving all the orders while his partner stood next to him—more formidable because of his silence—as if prepared to back each word with force. Beneath his chin Trudi noticed an almost healed cut from shaving. His face was bony as though he delib-erately courted starvation.

Trudi found her voice. "Frau Simon hasn't done anything," she cried.

"You—" The man who hadn't spoken pointed at her, his voice kind, yet stern, like that of a teacher cautioning a willful child. "Go home, little girl."

"I am not a little girl." As she stared up into his eyes, she was stunned by their indifference. He doesn't care about any of this, she thought, not about us, not about the *Partei*, not about the Führer. And she knew that, to remain safe, he couldn't let anyone know that about him.

His eyes narrowed, fighting her invasion, barring her access to his secret, and she forced the knowledge of his indifference into her gaze. But he severed himself from her scrutiny by curving his arm between them like a scythe and let his fingers trace the side of her face.

"A little girl with pretty hair," he stated.

As she shrank from his touch, she would have given a lot not to be blond and blue-eyed, and it struck her as ironic that in the one area where she fit the ideal she didn't want to belong. How she yearned for dark hair—an even deeper shade of brown than that of Frau Simon, whose face had gone ashen, making her lipstick look like a smear of blood.

"Let her go. Please," Trudi pleaded.

The arrest was crisp, efficient, and Frau Simon vanished into the dark car as if swallowed by it. "Lock the store, Trudi," she screamed as they drove off with her. "And make sure to—"

Noon light blinded Trudi as she stood on the sidewalk, alone. She was overcome by a sense of having to be careful. Extremely careful. Only by chance had she been allowed to stay behind. She felt relieved and, instantly, guilty because of that relief. From a house across the street drifted the smell of boiling turnips; she couldn't understand how anyone could possibly bear to eat.

Inside Frau Simon's shop, dazzling, colorful hats were displayed on curved stands, always at angles that showed off their most intriguing features; yet, now their feather and lace decorations seemed frivolous. Trudi didn't know why she took off her new hat and reached into the display window for the red hat she'd admired earlier. As if watching herself from a place far away, she set it on her head and—ever so slowly—walked to the pyramid-shaped mirror that was set up on a table in the center of the long shop. But what her reflection gave her was the shame in her eyes. The roots of her hair began to ache, and she yanked off the red hat and replaced it on its stand, glancing around to make sure no one had watched her. But only the hats surrounded her, gaudy like carousel horses after the last ride of the summer, and she wouldn't have been surprised at all if, suddenly, they'd begun to swirl around her, propelled by the tinny wail of a barrel organ.

"You were foolish, Trudi," Frau Abramowitz scolded her that evening when a small group of neighbors gathered in the Abramowitz living room with the drapes closed.

Four standing lamps, their shades covered with flowered fabric that matched the sofa, cast amber rings of light against the wallpaper. The table was covered with a lace cloth, and Frau Abramowitz had made black tea and baked *Streuselkuchen.*

"So foolish . . . They could have taken you, too." The fine creases in her face had not deepened with the years—her skin still looked like expensive crushed silk, as though she'd barely aged after those early wrinkles had taken their tender hold.

"We can't just let them take Frau Simon like that," Trudi protested.

"There are other ways," her father said.

"They don't work, those other ways," Frau Weiler said. "You know they don't work, Leo."

"Hedwig is right." Herr Abramowitz picked up the cake knife, and his diamond cufflinks flashed in the light. "I've been saying this for years. And I'm prepared to tell this to our beloved Führer—that is, if he ever lets me get close enough to him."

Frau Weiler nodded excitedly, splotches of red blooming on her cheeks.

"We shouldn't be here," Herr Blau told his wife, who sat next to him on the deep sofa, hands folded on her starched apron.

"Michel," Frau Abramowitz pleaded. "You don't know what you are saying." Her fingers busied themselves, rearranging the bouquet of pussy willows on the table.

"I am not saying anything, Ilse. I am cutting the cake. Watch me."

"You're always doing it—discussing for the sake of discussion, shining with words, outdazzling."

Leo Montag limped to the drapes and made sure the windows were closed. He had brought Emil Hesping, who'd arrived at the pay-library soon after Trudi had rushed home with news of Frau Simon's arrest, and the three of them had returned to the milliner's building. With Emil's key, they'd opened her apartment and packed her jewelry, silver wine cups, and most of her clothes into boxes, which were now stored at the pay-library.

Except for greetings, Herr Hesping hadn't spoken since they'd arrived at the Abramowitzs' house. His lips set in a half-smile, he'd been leaning against the door frame, but now he loosened himself from the smooth wood and stepped next to Michel Abramowitz.

"If you manage to get close to our Führer, a cake knife won't do."

"It is not safe listening to this. Not safe." Herr Blau tried to raise himself from the sofa, his veined hands clawing the air as if reaching for some invisible hold. "For any of us. We better get home."

"Have some *Streuselkuchen,* Herr Blau." Emil Hesping pressed a flowered plate with a piece of cake into the old man's hands.

But the tailor shook his head and managed to stand up. "I did not hear a thing." His false teeth were clicking. "Don't worry. Good-bye Herr Abramowitz. Good-bye Frau Abramowitz. Thank you for a lovely—"

"Oh, sit down, Martin." His wife grasped the back of his suspenders and pulled him back.

He sank into the soft cushions, muttering to himself.

"That is a lovely necklace," Emil Hesping said to Frau Blau.

She smiled like a young girl as she touched the drop of amber that trapped a pale, tiny crab. "It's from the North Sea . . . nearly a century old."

"Remember, we're here to talk about Frau Simon," Leo said.

The others turned toward his calm voice. One hand on the damask drapes, he scanned the sidewalk through the gap. His curly hair was completely silver-white now, giving him the same coloring as Trudi. Her mother's hair had been black, and sometimes, when she searched in one of her mirrors for a trace of her mother in herself, she couldn't locate any evidence—as if her mother had vanished and Trudi had become entirely her father's daughter. It usually made her buy yet another mirror with a gold frame, the kind her mother would have chosen.

"We need to agree," her father said, "that whatever we talk about in here—even if it happens to be rash or thoughtless—" He raised one eyebrow and glanced at Herr Abramowitz, then at his friend, Emil, "—won't leave this room."

"Agreed," Michel Abramowitz said quickly.

Emil Hesping nodded.

Herr Blau adjusted his glasses and peered at the faces around him as if to make sure no one had taken offense and would turn all of them in. "As long as I don't have to listen to any inappropriate comments about Herr Hitler."

"You don't like him either," his wife reminded him.

"Flora!" He glared at her. "First of all that was a joke, and second it was told in the privacy of our—" he stammered, "—just before we went to sleep."

"You said the man isn't fit to hang wallpaper in this country and—"

"I did not."

"—and that the articles in the *Stürmer* are getting crazier. All that hate . . ."

"I don't even look at that paper."

She turned her eyes toward the ceiling as if to call upon the saints to witness his lies.

"The only comment I made about Herr Hitler referred to his—his background as—as an Austrian paperhanger. . . . It is a very respectable trade."

"That is one of the kindest things anyone could say about our Führer." Emil Hesping gave a funny little bow in Herr Blau's direction. "I am overwhelmed by your generosity."

Trudi remembered the last time Emil Hesping had talked with her and her father about the Führer. A devious man, he had called him. An evil man. A sentimental man.

Hitler ist ein Schwein—Hitler is a pig—someone had painted on the brick wall of the school, and the police had ordered two nuns to wash it off. "So they want to be heroes," one of the nuns had grumbled, "but what they forget is that someone has to clean up after them—usually the women."

Herr Hesping cleared his throat. "I heard that Frau Simon was taken to Düsseldorf. For questioning."

"Who told you?" Frau Weiler wanted to know.

"Someone in the SS who knows."

"And you won't tell us?"

"I can't, Hedwig."

"How can you have SS friends and be loyal to Frau Simon?"

"Some people don't understand the complexity of loyalty."

"The price of loyalty," she snapped. "When they held me in jail four years ago, I did not compromise one single belief."

"Times have changed since then."

"I refused to lie. Of course there were things I didn't volunteer. If they didn't ask me the right questions, that certainly was their problem."

"Wouldn't you lie to save someone's life?" Trudi asked.

"How could I?"

"How could you not?"

"Trudi." Herr Hesping touched her arm. "We're not even talking about a situation where that's needed."

"But we must know that about each other."

"It may never be necessary."

"I won't let anyone force me into lying." Frau Weiler's eyes glistened the way Ingrid's eyes did when she talked about martyrs. Ingrid was nearly finished with her studies to become a teacher, and during the past year Trudi had seen less of her.

"Let it rest, Hedwig—please," Leo Montag said.

"It seems Herr Heidenreich has been doing some quiet damage," Emil Hesping said. "Informing."

"Kurt Heidenreich?" Herr Blau shook his head. "But we always talk, and he never—" He clasped one veined hand across his mouth. "I hope I can remember everything I've told him."

"Let's rather hope that he forgot," Michel Abramowitz said.

"I heard that he refused to stuff Frau Kaminsky's parrot," Trudi said, "but he didn't tell her until she came to pick it up. It was rotting, too late to take to the taxidermist in Krefeld. She had to bury it."

"Let's talk about what we can do to to help Frau Simon," Leo Montag said.

"Any suggestions?" Frau Blau asked.

Michel Abramowitz hesitated. "I'll make some inquiries."

"That may not be good for her or for you." Leo Montag spoke slowly. "You know me, Michel, and this is hard to say, but—"

"She needs a good lawyer who's not a Jew, right?"

Leo flinched. "In this country—now . . . Yes. Unfortunately."

"Or a Communist," Herr Blau reminded him.

"That was so long ago," Frau Blau said.

Herr Abramowitz raised his chin and stared at the piano with the silver-framed photos of his children, dating from infancy to three years earlier when his son, Albert, had left for Argentina after many attempts to persuade his parents and sister to join him. We weren't ready then, Herr Abramowitz thought. We waited too long. And Ruth still wasn't ready to go without her husband. But he and Ilse had finally agreed to let Albert help. How he hated the waiting, the uncertainty. Nearly half of the Jewish community in Germany, which had numbered five hundred thousand in 1933, had already left the country. But for those who hadn't, it was becoming harder and harder to find a place that would take them. Even Palestine was no longer an option. Because of Arab objections, the British had restricted immigration into Palestine, hindering what had once looked like a workable agreement between the Palestinian Zionist Organization and the Nazis: to keep Jewish wealth in a fund in Germany, which was to be used for buying German exports to Palestine, while the Zionists were to take care of Jewish immigrants.

And other nations, including the United States, severely restricted Jewish immigration. Nobody wants impoverished Jews, Herr Abramowitz thought bitterly. There'd be no problem for us if we could take our money out of Germany. The real irony is that we're still here—not because the Nazis prevent us from leaving—but because we have no place to go.

"At least we have Albert," he said heavily.

"Michel—" Leo started.

Herr Abramowitz raised one hand to stop him. "I want all of you to know that our families—Ilse's and mine—have lived in *your* country for many generations. My great-grandfather built this house. . . . And about finding the right kind of lawyer—I agree with you. I have a colleague, Aryan head to toe, but human inside. He'll check into what's happening with Frau Simon."

"For now, just watch out, all of you," Emil Hesping warned. "You know how easy it is to get arrested."

Herr Blau nodded. "I know parents who won't discuss politics in front of their children. They're afraid they'll tell their teachers or Hitler-Jugend leaders—even if they don't mean to turn their parents in."

"Some of them mean to," Leo said.

Emil Hesping nodded. "That's what the pure German family is all about."

Suddenly, they all were very quiet. They knew only too well that those who were brave or foolish enough to speak out against the government were made examples of: they were beaten, had their belongings seized, or were sent away. To come to their defense was dangerous. You knew it was safer to pretend not to notice when the police came to your neighbor's house late at night, to keep your lights off even if you wanted to help, to walk away if one of your friends was pulled aside to be questioned.

"Last week they stuck a priest from Krefeld into the KZ," Emil Hesping said.

Trudi felt chilled at the mention of *Konzentrationslager,* those camps that were correction centers for so-called "asocials," for Communists and other political prisoners who didn't fit in.

She and her father were the last to leave the Abramowitzs' house, and as they stepped into the night, the stench that the flood had left seemed even harsher than during the day. The clouds—though it was too dark to see them—felt dense and close to the earth as if sheltering the town, infusing it with the deceptive promise of peace.

"If all the people who thought like us . . . ," Trudi said, "if we all got together—maybe we could stop this."

"Those points of connection—they're the weak spots. As soon as we build bridges to others, we're in danger. That's when they catch us."

"I don't think Herr Blau would tell."

"He's a good man, but he's frightened. You know that people only hear that part of a story they can handle."

What he said felt true because she'd seen it happen when she'd carried her stories around town. Some people didn't want to hear all the details. They would ask, but they'd distract themselves with interpretations that had little to do with her stories, yet gave her new material. Some would walk away or change her endings. But that was all right: a story stayed alive that way, shaped and reshaped in each telling, signifying something different to everyone who was affected by it.

"Most of what's happening we don't even know." Her father stopped in front of their door and fidgeted with his keys.

Trudi touched the bark of the chestnut tree. Above her, she felt the

span of its branches, still bare. Soon, buds would burst into leaves
and wobbly candle blossoms.

"The news we get in the paper is filtered." He unlocked the door
and turned on the light in the hallway. "Words have taken on new
meanings. We learn more from whispered rumors than from the
printed word. We live in a time when we all become messengers.
You—more than anyone I know—are prepared for that, Trudi."

She nodded. Ever since she had stood next to Frau Simon on the
sidewalk that morning, she had felt the language becoming even narrower. There was no space for disagreement. She had become suspect
just by being there with Frau Simon. Ineffective. At risk.

Her father was watching her. He was watching her with tired and
empathetic eyes, and Trudi wasn't even sure if he spoke or if she felt
his concern, because what she thought she heard was, *"Be careful, my
daughter."*

Every afternoon, Trudi checked Frau Simon's store and apartment on
Barbarossa Strasse, but the doors had been padlocked the day after
the arrest, and no one answered when she knocked. She thought
about Frau Simon every time she rubbed lotion into her hands, every
time she saw a woman with a hat designed by the red-haired milliner.
Some people thought she was still being held in Düsseldorf, while
others assumed she'd been released and was visiting her sister in Os-
nabrück. A month after her arrest, all hats disappeared from the display window, and the shop was turned into headquarters for the
Hitler-Jugend.

When Frau Simon was released after nearly four months and returned to Burgdorf, she looked as though she'd shrunk: her face
seemed smaller, and her once unruly curls lay flat on her head. Her vi-
vaciousness was gone, and she urged caution on her friends, saying
that if you kept quiet things would get better.

"You sound like Frau Abramowitz," Trudi objected.

"Don't—" her father said. "Unless you have shared Frau Simon's
experiences."

Though Frau Simon's clothes looked familiar, they no longer fit her
properly and looked as if they'd been made for someone else. Eva
Sturm furnished an apartment for her on the third floor of her husband's building. The rooms of Alexander's niece, Jutta, were right
next to Frau Simon's. At seventeen, the girl had lived there by herself

for nearly a year, ever since her mother, whose health had always been brittle, had died from pneumonia and Jutta had turned down her uncle's invitation to live with him and Eva on the first floor.

"But we have plenty of space," Alexander had insisted.

"I want to stay up here."

"You're too young to be by yourself."

"You were running a business when you were my age."

"She'll visit us every day," Eva had said. "Right, Jutta? And she'll eat with us."

When Jutta had agreed, her uncle had given in.

Frau Simon remained inside her apartment most of the time, and if she stepped outdoors, she'd avoid walking past her old building, where, in the center of the display window, her pyramid-shaped mirror reflected the somber smile of the Führer and the garish red of the flag. She would take a detour around the far side of the church square to get to the pay-library, where, every Tuesday, she'd check out two romances and two American Westerns.

"Have you gone to Frau Doktor Rosen about that headache?" Leo Montag asked her one mild afternoon, late that October of 1938, when she came in to return her weekly supply of books.

Frau Simon nodded. "She gave me some pills."

He handed the books to Trudi, who marked them as returned. "And did you take the pills?" he asked.

"I don't much believe in pills. But it's good of you to worry."

"Emil tells me you won't see him."

"Not the way I look. Not until I—"

"You are a very good-looking woman, Lotte."

One of her hands floated up to her hair.

"And that cardigan looks lovely on you."

"Emil gave it to me for my birthday. A few years ago." She told him to feel the white mohair sleeve. "Fifty percent mohair, fifty percent silk. I guess some people would say it's not proper to accept gifts from a man you're not married to."

"I wouldn't fret about that," Leo assured her.

She smiled, the first smile anyone had seen on her since she'd been released from prison. "My grandmother used to tell me that a gentleman is not supposed to give a lady any gift that lies next to her skin—except for gloves."

Trudi laughed. "Why gloves?"

Frau Simon had to think for a moment. "Only you would ask that. Maybe it has to do with shaking hands. I mean, when I shake a man's hand, his skin touches mine, right? Therefore, gloves would be all right because they cover a place that's . . . that's—"

"Available?" Trudi helped.

"Available, right. And any skin covered by this sweater should not be available to any man other than a husband."

"It's like saying the gift is like the man's hands. Just think of all the places that cardigan touches you."

Frau Simon did a little dance with her shoulders, and for a moment she looked as lively as she used to.

"Now you'll have to marry Herr Hesping," Trudi teased her.

"Stop it, Trudi."

"We'll have the wedding right here. I'll bake a cake and—"

"That man will never let a woman slip a ring on his finger. Maybe that's what I like best about him."

"Laughing becomes you," Leo said. "May I tell Emil that you're looking well?"

Frau Simon hesitated. "I'll bring the books back next Tuesday at three. That is—if he wants to see for himself."

The second Thursday of November, Trudi woke up early—tired and agitated as though she hadn't slept at all. She always felt more tired when winter set in as if her body needed time to adjust to the cold. Besides, her knees had been aching for nearly a week. Frau Doktor Rosen had told her the pain came from her hips.

"Then why do I feel it in my knees?" Trudi had asked.

The Frau Doktor, whose practice had diminished even more, had told her the joints in her hips were inflamed.

"But that happens to old people. I'm only twenty-three."

"Some *Zwerge* have those problems when they're quite young."

"But you don't have any other patients who're *Zwerge*."

"I've made it my business to read about them."

Trudi had stared at her."Because of me?"

"Because of you."

As Trudi shifted in her bed, trying to find a comfortable position to carry her into morning, she allowed herself to imagine the doctor surrounded by tall stacks of medical books, searching for information on *Zwerge* that would help her unlock Trudi's joints and lengthen her bones until her body would be of normal height and free of pain. Yet, deep inside, she had already accepted that there really wasn't anything that could be done. She thought of all the people who moaned about things they didn't like in their lives—their work, their houses, their friends—and she was envious because they could change all that.

When she opened the library, the bakery truck stopped outside, and Alfred Meier came running in to tell her that, during the night, windows of Jewish businesses and synagogues in Düsseldorf had been smashed. He'd been out making deliveries since dawn, and he'd heard that buildings had been set on fire, and that a whole block of apartments next to a Jewish jewelry store had burned down.

As the day progressed, other customers reported hearing from friends and family in Krefeld and Oberkassel and Köln. Trudi didn't even try to work in the library: she kept circling through Burgdorf, letting people know what she had found out, while picking up news of destruction in other cities and towns. In Burgdorf only two businesses had been damaged—a yarn shop and a restaurant, both owned by Jews. It looked as if someone had tried to set fire to the synagogue, because in back of the building the stucco beneath one window was blackened.

"Maybe it won't happen here," Frau Abramowitz told Leo Montag while her husband buttoned his camel hair coat and left for an emergency meeting at the synagogue.

But Leo recalled what his wife had said to him the year before their wedding—that things in Burgdorf happened slower and later than in most other places—and he kept troubled watch over his friends. That night, very few people in the neighborhood slept well, but when in the morning only a few broken windows were discovered in town—though the demolition was said to continue in Düsseldorf and Oberkassel—Leo hoped that Frau Abramowitz had been right.

Friday afternoon Trudi gift-wrapped a set of china cups that she and her father would take to Helmut Eberhardt's wedding the following day. His mother had come over to invite them in person, and they'd only accepted because they didn't want to disappoint her. Helmut was marrying Hilde Sommer, who had finished her training as a midwife and shared his passion for order. According to the pharmacist, she was pregnant, well on her way to a *kinderreiche Familie,* but Trudi found it impossible to confirm that rumor even when she got close to her, because Hilde was a heavy woman to begin with. Well, at least if she was pregnant, Helmut wouldn't be able to divorce her for *Unfruchtbarkeit*—barrenness—or *Nachwuchsverweigerung*—refusal to have offspring. Both were considered direct opposition to the government and had become valid causes for divorce.

Late Friday night, less than twelve hours before Helmut's wedding to the blond midwife at St. Martin's Church, he and two other SA men dragged Herr Abramowitz from his bedroom, and when the tall lawyer tried to protest, his pipe collection and cameras were trampled in front of him, and he was dragged across the fragments, screaming as they cut his feet and ankles.

Frau Abramowitz clung to Helmut Eberhardt's arm, begging him to leave her husband alone. And because she couldn't think of anything else, she cried out, "I know your mother well. You come from a fine family."

"Stay back," he warned her.

She heard them in the street—the smashing of glass, their heels on the sidewalk, car doors slamming. An engine started. Then silence. Tears clogging her breath, she tried to phone her daughter in Oberkassel, but she could no longer remember Ruth's number, though she dialed it nearly every day, and she had to look it up. Her hand shook so badly that her finger slipped from the dial, and she had to try several times before she reached her daughter.

When Ruth—against the advice of her husband—offered to drive to Burgdorf, Frau Abramowitz refused. "Don't come here. It's not safe."

"Then it's not safe for you either," Ruth argued.

"They didn't take me this time."

"Mother— Mother, I love you."

"I love you too, Ruthie."

"Let me send a taxi for you."

"I have to be here. For your father when he comes back."

There was a long pause on the phone.

"He will come back," Frau Abramowitz said.

"Of course he will."

"He is a lawyer, after all. He'll make them understand it's a mistake."

She hung up the phone after promising to call Ruth the moment she heard anything. Her beige sweater pulled over her nightgown, she dashed across the street, barely avoiding the broken glass on her side-walk, but before she could bang at the Montags' door, Trudi opened it.

"What happened?" She grasped Frau Abramowitz's hands.

"Michel . . ." The older woman began to cry. "They came for Michel—took him away."

"Come inside. Please . . ."

"I can't." She kept looking toward the door. "He may come back any moment."

Not right away, Trudi thought, but what she said was, "I'll watch for him from the window. Stay with us tonight."

"They made such a mess, breaking things . . . without any reason."

Trudi's father came hobbling down the stairs in his bathrobe. "Frau Abramowitz," he said, "Ilse," his voice helpless with grief, and opened his arms, embracing her as Frau Abramowitz must have imag-ined it many times, only under much different circumstances.

She briefly leaned into his embrace, then stepped away. "I must go home."

"You can stay here," Leo offered.

"Michel might phone."

"I'll go with you then."

"You will?"

"Of course. Let me get some clothes on." He started toward the stairs.

Though Trudi wanted to come along too, she sensed that her fa-ther, alone, would be able to comfort Frau Abramowitz far more than if she were with them. From the open door she watched the two, Frau Abramowitz in her thin nightgown, her father oddly formal in his Sunday suit as if the occasion deserved no less, their arms linked in such a way that they seemed to hold one another up—not unlike old couples who have decades of practice in adjusting their pace to one another. Carefully, they stepped across the shards. Trudi thought she heard the key turn after the Abramowitzs' front door closed behind them, as though they belonged inside that house together.

She wrapped the coat of the Russian soldier around herself and climbed onto the counter of the pay-library. From there, she could see through the window. The light in the Abramowitzs' living room was off, and Frau Abramowitz stood framed by the splinters that stuck from the window frame like translucent petals of an outlandish flower. The outline of her pale sweater filled the gap where the glass had been, unmoving, as if she had always been there, a guardian, until it became impossible for Trudi to remember a time when that window had not been filled with her shape.

The taller outline of Trudi's father saturated the space around Frau Abramowitz like a cloak. That entire night the two of them stood in the dark window above the littered street, waiting for Michel Abramowitz; and whenever Trudi dozed off on the counter, she was soon awakened by some faraway screams and shattering glass, and she'd see the contour of Frau Abramowitz in that window and, behind it, her father's as though the two of them had not moved at all, as though every word spoken had passed between them like this.

When the dense texture of night wore thin and cries of roosters swirled above the roofs, Trudi spotted something crawling across the intersection of Schreberstrasse and Barbarossa Strasse, an injured dog, perhaps, or some ancient beast dragging itself toward the dawn of mankind, the doom of mankind. It was a shape that embodied the ugliness of the night, and Trudi wondered how long it had been crawling toward them. Perhaps it had been there for a long time and only dawn had revealed it. But just then Frau Abramowitz loosened herself from the window and flew from the house—Trudi's father close behind her in his uneven gait—toward whatever it was that was crawling toward them.

Hoisting the seal coat to her knees, Trudi raced after them, and when she caught up, she saw Herr Abramowitz, his neck and face bloodied, his pajamas ripped. He could not stand, not even when Leo Montag tried to support him, and they had to spread the seal coat on the ground, roll him onto the rugged hide, and carry him—Frau Abramowitz and Trudi on one side, Leo on the other—up Schreberstrasse and through the arched door of his house. Trudi's arms were aching as they used to when she'd hung from the door frame, and her father's breath was coming in hard gasps. Only Frau Abramowitz's breath was even, because carrying her husband took far less strength than waiting for him.

When they laid Michel Abramowitz down on the sofa in his living room and washed him, careful not to touch his bruises, they found that his nose and several ribs had been broken. All along the inside of his left arm were cigarette burns, and his back was swollen with raw welts. He had lost quite a few teeth, all from the outer row, and his

wife could see the second row—a quirk of nature, she used to think—
as if he'd grown that extra set of teeth for this night.

His voice was hoarse, and they had to bend close to hear him when
he forbade them to take him to the Theresienheim or the hospital in
Düsseldorf. "I'm safer at home," he insisted in a murmur and asked
his wife to bring him the *Watte*—cotton—that she used for earaches
and taking off nail polish.

She looked confused but left the room to get it.

He gripped the lapels of Leo's Sunday suit. "I'll go into the river before I let those *Schweine* get me again."

"Michel—"

"I mean it, Leo. Promise you'll look after Ilse if that happens.
There's nothing that can make me go through this again if—" He let
go of Leo as his wife returned with the *Watte,* and he tore off two
pieces, rolled them into wads, and quickly inserted them in his nostrils. Tears ran down his mangled face.

Leo steadied him by the shoulders. "It's a promise."

"What is he doing?" Frau Abramowitz cried out.

"Trying to reshape his nose," Leo said.

"Let me get Frau Doktor Rosen," Trudi said.

Michel Abramowitz groaned. "I don't want to put her in danger."

"Let her decide."

"I have decided for her. She would come. You know her."

Frau Abramowitz dampened her handkerchief with spittle and
wiped the blood from his nostrils.

"Stop it, Ilse." He averted his face. "I'm not a child."

"What if it sets crooked?"

"Then you divorce me." He winced at his attempt at humor. "Get
yourself a husband with a nice straight nose."

"*And* a nice disposition." She slipped an embroidered pillow behind his head. "I'll start looking."

He circled her hip with one arm. "I bet you will."

Her face flushed, Frau Abramowitz looked at Leo and Trudi.
"Thank you for your help," she said, her voice oddly formal. "Michel
needs to rest now."

"Let us know what we can do," Trudi offered.

"Lock the door behind us," Leo reminded Frau Abramowitz.

Throughout the morning, Michel Abramowitz rested on the sofa,
dropping into brief, fitful periods of sleep from which he woke moan-

ing, while his wife sat on the floor next to him, her photo albums spread around herself, staring at the images that had emerged through the eyes of her husband's cameras. But now the cameras were broken: she knew because she had stepped across the shards, and it seemed like a trick that the photos were not broken. She remembered the endless arranging Michel had done, posing her and the children just so, telling them to smile as he prepared to fix their images for the future. But when all was added up, you could never do that: you could never take three or four people, say, and arrange them in such a way that they would remain like that forever. They were only like that for the moment of the photo, and it seemed a mockery that—all these years later—the pictures still held those images as if they could be true.

From the Catholic church came the ringing of the bells, celebrating the marriage of Helmut Eberhardt and Hilde Sommer. Frau Abramowitz stepped up to the broken window. The air was cold, laced with frost. She felt a deep compassion for Renate Eberhardt, whose body had carried Helmut toward the moment of his birth, Frau Eberhardt who—while Michel had crawled home with his wounds—must have already been up, preparing for her son's wedding reception, which was to be held at her house. Frau Abramowitz wondered if Helmut's mother knew what her son had done during the night, and she pitied the midwife, whose body would lie beneath Helmut's in the nights to come. A thought came to her that had insisted on settling with her for some time now, a thought that would anger Michel if she ever told him: given a choice, she would rather be the one who was persecuted than the one who did the persecuting. Both had a terrible price to pay, but she would rather endure humiliation and fear than grow numb to what it was to be human.

To Leo Montag's surprise, Trudi insisted on attending the Eberhardt wedding with him, and he understood why when he saw her step up to Helmut's mother before the ceremony and motion to her to bend down so that she could whisper into her ear. At least Trudi could have waited to tell her what her son had done until after the wedding, he thought as a look of desolation passed across Frau Eberhardt's face. It was a look that stayed on her face throughout the wedding mass and the reception, even though she tried to force a smile to her lips, a look that caused her new daughter-in-law to come up to her twice, asking if there was anything she could do. But Renate Eberhardt only looked at the young blond woman and shook her head.

Around noon, the Abramowitzs' daughter, Ruth, arrived on the streetcar despite her husband's misgivings, a large shawl around her head as if to disguise herself. She cried when she embraced her parents, and she cried again when she picked up the open albums and stacked them back on the shelves, assuming the SA had strewn them about the floor.

She told her father she was sure her brother would do whatever he could to help.

Her father nodded. "Albert is trying to get us out. He knows we're ready."

"And you, Ruth?" her mother asked. "What will you do?"

"If Fritz were Jewish too, we'd come with you, but he's so well respected—I don't think anyone would dare go after his wife."

"I hope you are right," her father said without conviction.

"We're careful." She touched the edge of her chipped front tooth, a habit that made her look like the girl she'd been when she'd jumped from the moving streetcar. "I— I keep out of sight. I mean, Fritz thinks it's better if I don't work in the office for a while."

"I see," her father said gravely.

"Only until things are back to normal," she said quickly.

Everyone in the neighborhood was shocked at what had happened to Michel Abramowitz. Frau Weiler prepared a basket of delicacies for them. "They are honorable, dear people," she said.

"Those who did it," Frau Blau said, "they'll find their own vengeance. They'll never have any luck."

"How could they do this to him?" Herr Meier asked when he parked the bakery truck in front of the Abramowitzs' house. "They shouldn't be allowed to," he said and insisted on leaving four glazed buns and a dozen *Brötchen*.

Herr Kaminsky, whose upholstery shop had been overlooked during that night of destruction, said he knew some people among the SA—their wives were customers of his—who were nice, who did not commit any crimes.

But Anton Immers and some of his friends said it was about time the Jews were shown reality, and when they heard that the mansion of the concert pianist, Fräulein Birnsteig, had not been damaged at all, Herr Immers figured it had to be because it was too far from the center of town.

The attack on Michel Abramowitz was only the beginning of the violence in Burgdorf, and during the following night—three nights after the first breaking of windows in the city—Burgdorf caught up with a fury. Surely, Trudi thought, the people could no longer pretend they didn't know what was happening as the stores of their Jewish neighbors were plundered and burned, as Jews were yanked from their beds at night and taken away. Windows that had been forgotten in the initial attack were broken by groups of roaming youths, who were lured by the fires and turbulence.

It became a show—"Look, they're getting another Jew"—a theater of the macabre that sucked the entire town onto its bloody stage that night, a night that never was allowed to replenish itself in the folds of its darkness because as soon as the sky reached its deepest hue, it immediately began to pale as if impatient for day. The light, Trudi realized, came from the north, blooming across the sky in an uneven arc. And with it came the smell of smoke.

She rushed into her clothes, and when she ran outside, smoke curled around her, filling her lungs, enveloping her in a heat that turned November into the hottest month of the year.

"Wait for me!" Her father was close behind her.

They cut through their backyard and waded through the icy brook, ran along the back of the Theresienheim and down the strip of grass between the Theresienheim and the school. There, across the street, the synagogue was burning—fast and hot as dried pine cones—spewing yellow sparks into the night. Limbs of fire reached from inside the broken windows, linked, and embraced the large building, crushing its structure.

Someone started the Horst Wessel song, and several others blared along: "Wenn das Judenblut vom Messer spritzt . . . "—"When the Jew blood spurts from the knife . . ." A woman carrying a small child pointed toward the high flames, her smile excited. Two Hitler Youths waved their flags. Trudi looked at the faces of the people around her: most of them she'd known all her life. Maybe now, she thought, now in the blaze of this fire, they surely will have to see. But it was as if they'd come to take the horrible for granted, mistaking it for the ordinary. It made her wonder what would have happened if all of them had gone along with Frau Weiler four years earlier, ranting against the government. Could that have prevented any of this?

As she listened to the voices of the people, she could hear that some were outraged, but what staggered her was what they were outraged by: the mess and the waste—not the injury to their Jewish neighbors. It shattered their *Ordnungsliebe*—their love for order—and in the days to come they would agree when Göhring and many other Germans expressed their indignation at the cost of the wreckage and demanded to know, *"Wer soll das bezahlen?"*—"Who shall pay for this?"

When the Jewish community was assessed a bill for the debt which arose from the devastation, and was forced to turn over valuables to the government, Leo Montag offered to hold things for his Jewish friends. He'd be glad to store them, he said, or sell them—whatever they needed most for him to do. While Frau Simon asked him to sell a ruby pin and her gold fountain pen, Frau Abramowitz insisted on obeying the law.

"At least my cameras were already broken," her husband railed when he found their solid gold candle holders and five sets of his cufflinks missing. "Otherwise you would have handed them over, too."

"I don't want to provoke them any more than necessary," she said.

That night, after Ilse was asleep, Michel took the mezuzah from his front door, lined a wooden crate with his old raincoat, and carefully packed the mezuzah along with the silver candlesticks that his parents had given Ilse on her wedding day for the Sabbath candles. After filling the box with other items he considered most precious, he carried it across the street. Outside, the air stank of smoke. Cold and heavy, it clung to his skin. Ever since that night of his arrest, he hadn't felt clean, not even after he bathed.

"I want to show you where I'm going to keep this," Leo Montag said. "In case something happens to us."

Trudi held the lantern as the two men followed her down the stairs into the cellar. The light spread the shadow of their collars against their chins.

Next to the shelves with the preserves, her father hid the box beneath old clothes in a wooden trunk. "You can always get it without asking me," he told Michel Abramowitz.

For weeks, the smoke hung above the town, getting into your lungs with each breath, making you cough; and after the rubble was cleaned up, you would still come across slivers of glass far from the areas of destruction as if they'd been carried there by the smoke. You wouldn't see them unless you'd step into one of them, say, or catch the reflection of a shard of sun in a bare tree limb while reaching up to hang out your laundry in the frosty winter air, making you feel as if you and your neighborhood, the world even, were held in the eye of a splintered mirror.

t w e l v e

———————————— ■ ————————————

1 9 3 9 – 1 9 4 1

IF THE RUMORS HAD BEEN ACCURATE AND THE MIDWIFE HAD, INDEED, been pregnant the day of her marriage to the eighteen-year-old Helmut Eberhardt, hers would have been the longest pregnancy in the history of Burgdorf—perhaps even the entire world, the old women would speculate—because Hilde would not give birth until the spring of 1941, nearly two and a half years after her wedding day. Of course, there would be gossip that she'd had a miscarriage and had become pregnant again before her young husband had left for the Russian front, after extracting from her the promise to christen their first child Adolf.

Helmut would not even consider that he might have fathered a daughter, and when Hilde would tell him that she'd like to name a girl after his mother, Renate, he would look at her as though she had insulted the Führer and God.

It was the same look that Helmut had given his mother whenever she had refused to write her house over to him, even though he'd explained to her it was the reasonable thing to do: she could stay in the upstairs rooms, where he and Hilde lived now, and they'd move into the five large rooms on the ground floor.

"After all, as a widow you don't need much space," he had told her the week after his wedding. "While Hilde and I will have a lot of children." He was determined to convert the government's marriage loan into a gift, and eager for Hilde to earn the *Ehrenkreuz der deutschen Mutter.* Already he pictured the bronze cross of honor on her dress, to be replaced, of course, by the silver cross and the gold cross as his family grew.

But his mother didn't understand. "You are welcome to live upstairs," she said.

He pointed to the gleaming parquet floor. "You have to admit that the entire house has been cared for much better ever since I married Hilde."

"I don't ask your wife to clean for me."

"She likes to clean. . . . Why are you so stubborn about the house?"

"I am too old to live like a guest."

In a few years, he would be the same age as his father had been when he'd died. His father had built this house. Surely, his father would want him to live here like a family man, not a son. He gave his mother a winning smile. "You're not old."

But she would not smile back.

Throughout that winter and early spring his mother resisted his efforts. The house should rightfully be his, he believed. But with him she was stingy, while her generosity toward others was known throughout town: not only did she give flowers to neighbors, coins to beggars, but she also was kind to Jews, even though it was plain enough for everyone to see that they were not wanted in Burgdorf, in the entire country. Couldn't she read the signs on the streets and in the windows of stores and restaurants? *Juden sind hier unerwünscht*—Jews are not wanted here. *Juden haben keinen Zutritt*—Jews are not allowed to enter. Maybe the Jews would finally leave if it became harder to make purchases. Unfortunately, they still could enter some stores, though it was impossible for them to buy rice, coffee, and certain fruits like oranges and lemons.

To deprive Jews only of the necessities of daily life—Helmut agreed with his friends—was far too kind. Besides, some of the store owners, he suspected, were smuggling groceries to Jewish families at night. It was a direct sabotage of the Führer. But Helmut was watching them. Already, he had turned in one of the farmers, who had promptly lost his vegetable stand in the market, and he was waiting for Frau Weiler to make a mistake.

Helmut would have liked to see more drastic measures to drive the Jews from the country, a repetition of those exhilarating nights of broken glass; but he had to recognize Göhring's wisdom that it had been a mess, a waste. Those resources belonged to the German people and would be theirs once the Jews were gone.

"You're impatient," the pharmacist told him, "and that's good. We need young men like you to remind us that patience can become a terrible habit."

Because of his increased political activities, the pharmacist—who still carried the French Jesus around the church square—had curtailed that ritual to the first Friday of every month. Distracted by visions of a different statue—one of his Führer, all in bronze—he enlisted Helmut Eberhardt's help, and the two went from house to house, cajoling and coercing funds for the monument from even the most reluctant donors. Yet, when the statue of Adolf Hitler was erected in front of the Rathaus, Helmut felt embarrassed. He had pictured it to be at least life size, but it stood no taller than an altar boy, and the pharmacist became very indignant when Helmut asked what had happened to all the money they'd collected. Immediately he tried to apologize for his question while the pharmacist shouted at him that, had he known this would be the thanks he'd get for letting Helmut take part in this glorious project, he would have asked someone more deserving.

Helmut tried his best to educate his mother to the obvious justice in driving the Jews out of the country and reminded her that the Führer had proclaimed Jews inferior to the German race, and that Jews were responsible for all the hardship because they grabbed power everywhere they could, earning better wages than decent Germans.

"The Jews in this country," she corrected him one Saturday afternoon when he followed her into the garden, lecturing her, "are Germans and far more decent than those—those friends of yours who terrorize them—"

He waved his hands, trying to cut off her words.

"—or those lunatics in uniforms who consider themselves superior."

Goose bumps sprang up on his chest and arms. It was God's will that the Führer was in power, and to him the two had almost become inseparable. "You could be arrested for saying this."

"But this is between you and me, Helmut." She crouched to pull weeds from around her Dutch tulips.

"You know it's my duty to inform on anyone who betrays the Führer."

"It is your duty—" His mother stood up and brought her face close to his. "—to be one of those decent Germans you like to talk about. And by decent I mean—"

"I know. I know. Jew-loving and old-fashioned and critical of the *Partei*. Don't you see that each crumb of bread swallowed by a Jew deprives a true German of nourishment?"

She watched him silently, a fine pulse beating in the hollow of her long neck.

A chimney sweep passed the garden door, and a knot of pigeons rose from the coop on the flat roof next door.

"It is a crime." Helmut made his voice sound forceful.

She had the expression of someone who'd just tasted spoiled meat, and he walked away from her, tired of cautioning her, of correcting her whenever she complained about the government. Once, when she'd joked about the Führer's mustache—"This thing on his face: it looks like a dirty toothbrush"—it had felt to him as though she'd spit on the holy sacrament. It had been a special day for him, the Führer's birthday, and he'd brought home a large portrait of his idol in celebration of the occasion.

Throughout the rest of that spring, Helmut became increasingly afraid that one of the neighbors would turn his mother in, and out of that fear grew the idea that it was his obligation to report her. Not that he thought about it constantly, but one evening, when she was doing her weekly mending in the kitchen and wouldn't even discuss the possibility of signing the house over to him, he realized that—although he couldn't turn her in for refusing him the house—he could certainly report her for spreading her dangerous ideas. He would be doing his country a service. After all, anyone who supported the Jews postponed the goal of a racially pure country.

He looked at her, bending across the elbow of his sweater. "If you don't—" He held his breath, frightened and exhilarated as he felt the power between them shift to his side. Deeply, he inhaled, feeling the brown uniform stretch across his chest. "If you don't give me the house, I'll turn you in for the things you've been saying." He heard his words and waited for her to acknowledge that something significant had changed between them, irreversibly, and he was prepared to console and uphold her through that transformation. He felt willing to forget every outrageous word she'd said—if only she crumbled.

But she kept pulling the needle though the knitted fabric, again and again, and when she finally spoke, she merely told him to go upstairs where he slept with his wife in the room of his childhood. "Go to sleep," she said as though he were not a family man but still a little boy.

Her obvious lack of fear and respect convinced Helmut that he should have reported her long ago. Just because she was his mother should not make her immune. What a risk he had taken, listening to her inflammatory comments about the Führer and the *Partei*. It would be good for her to contemplate her attitude while locked up. By the time she came back—

If she comes back . . . He pushed it away, that voice, after the first delirious pang of relief. To be free forever of her disappointment and her love, free of her concern and her carelessness.

If she comes back . . . No, they wouldn't hold her for long. But what if they did? He simply had to teach her a lesson. Once he and Hilde were established in his mother's rooms, she'd be grateful to live upstairs.

Renate Eberhardt did not believe her son would turn her in until that Tuesday in June of 1939 when Emil Hesping's car screeched to a stop in front of her house and he ran inside to warn her that she was about to be picked up. Within minutes after Renate refused his offer to take her to his uncle's apartment in Krefeld, Trudi heard the news, and when she reached the white stucco house, her heart beating high in her chest, two of the Eberhardts' neighbor women were already urging Renate to pack her things. They were watching the street, prepared to bolt from the backdoor as soon as the Gestapo drove up.

"Often people don't come back," one of them said, correcting herself quickly, "at least not for a while," and the other advised, "Better to have some belongings."

"You still have time to hide somewhere," Trudi implored Frau Eberhardt. "Herr Hesping, he wants to help."

"A bedroll." The other neighbor waved away the flies that buzzed through the kitchen. "She needs a bedroll."

"A change of clothing."

"Don't forget soap."

"And food."

"Yes, food. Something that will keep."

"A needle and thread."

"Slippers. Slippers are important."

"And a towel."

"Oh . . . I don't need anything." Renate Eberhardt spoke and moved slowly as though the air around her had thickened like pine honey. Her face had the serene look of the very old, who have forgotten much of their lives, except for a few childhood incidents, and are puzzled to discover all of a sudden that they no longer are young.

"You can bring everything home again."

"You can hide in my house," Trudi whispered to her.

Renate Eberhardt shook her head. She walked to the open back window and looked out into her abundant garden. Her thick braids were secured in a double rope in back of her slim neck—a style she'd worn on many occasions but which, now, seemed so ominous to Trudi that she wanted to loosen the graying hair, brush it for Renate, and make her wear it loose, perhaps, a curtain, a refuge.

"They'll find me," Renate said as though she had resigned herself.

"Don't say that."

"Yes, don't say that, Renate."

"It's important to keep up your hope."

"Be glad you're not Jewish."

"If you were Jewish, I'd be much more worried about you."

"You'll be grateful to have a change of underwear."

"And a cardigan."

"What I take won't matter." But she did not object when her neighbors packed for her.

They knew of people who'd been taken away, and they had given much consideration—though they assured themselves it would never happen to them—to what they would bring in case they were arrested. Those nights when sleep evaded them because they'd heard of yet another disappearance, they would recite their lists to themselves, revise them, make sure most items served at least two purposes, and fret over what to leave behind. Because that was by far the hardest part—to decide what to leave behind.

They had seen how the Nazis weakened the community by coming for people at all hours of the night, hauling them from their homes, punishing conspiracy, making examples out of those who tried to help others. Since laws no longer offered protection, they'd learned to look out for their own survival. And part of surviving was to remind themselves of the differences between themselves and those who had been taken away.

At least they were not Jewish.

At least they'd never said anything against the Führer—not openly, that is.

At least they hadn't refused to return Anton Immers' crisp *Heil Hitler* when they'd walked into his store to have an order of *Blut-wurst*—blood sausage—say, or *Sülze*—head cheese—weighed and packed in brown paper, and had found themselves face to face with the framed pictures of the Führer, the butcher, and the saint, the three sets of eyes boring through them and any other obstacle with the certainty of victory.

The neighbor women were grateful that their own children were not like Helmut Eberhardt, and they pitied his mother—not only for being betrayed by her son, but also for not having other children who'd certainly offset that guilt they were sure she must feel for having failed at motherhood.

They coaxed and hurried Renate Eberhardt into several layers of underwear and dresses, closing buttons and tying ribbons for her while she stood with her arms away from her body like an obedient child. Once, when they heard steps in the rooms above, they glanced at each other with alarm and then at her with pity.

"It's only his wife," Frau Eberhardt said as though she could not bring herself to speak her son's name.

I hope Helmut dies, Trudi thought. I hope he dies. "Come with me," she pleaded. "I'll get you out of town. There are others who'll be glad to help too."

Frau Eberhardt shook her head, and the neighbor women cleared the vase with wild flowers and the napkin rings from the table, arguing in whispers as they laid out on the wooden surface what she was to bring with her: flatware, a cup and bowl, slippers, a nightgown, five cakes of soap, stockings, two needles and thread, a toothbrush and toothpaste, a washcloth and a towel, a pencil and a notepad. They decided Renate's raincoat could double as a bathrobe, and they stitched money and small pieces of jewelry into its hem.

When they searched for a sleeping bag and couldn't find one, Trudi opened the sewing machine, tears of rage blurring her vision as she stood there, her right foot pumping while the needle raced through the two blankets that she stitched together, and with each jab of the needle she wished it would go straight through Helmut's heart. When the blanket bag was finished, the neighbor women rolled a pillow and the other items inside, securing everything with a leather belt that matched one of Renate's dresses while serving as a carrying handle.

"Let me make you some tea," Trudi offered.

But Renate Eberhardt walked away from her and out into her garden, her body oddly swollen in her extra skirts and dresses like that of a pregnant woman. Deep inside her was a bed for her son, a bed that had always been there, a bed that would always be there, but Helmut had made this bed with sheets of ice. Outside her body it was hot, humid, but inside that ice made her feel as though she would never be warm again. That immeasurable chill isolated her from the compassion of the three women who stood by her window; from the profuse scent of her lilac hedge and her lavish flowers; from the memory of her young husband's feverish touch the evening before he'd died; from that anguish when she'd stepped to his open grave with grains of earth in her hand.

All she felt was that cold and her love for her son, which would always be there, but frozen, and it was something she could do nothing about because it was of his making.

She walked through clusters of brilliant-blue forget-me-nots to the pear tree and raised one hand to its trunk as if to caress it in a gesture of farewell or, perhaps, to let it support her—she wasn't sure which— just that the bark felt rough against her palm, though not rough all over but only in angular patches that were flecked with gray and amber like rocks that have withstood the elements for several human lifetimes. Along the trunk, the stubs of pruned limbs thrust themselves outward—smooth wounds across which the bark had not healed but had merely raised itself like proud flesh.

Above her, the green canopy of branches, leaves, and unripe pears shut out the sky. She drew the rich scent of green into her lungs and smiled as she saw herself lifting her small son into that canopy. *He squeals with delight. When she tells him that this is the color green, Helmut rubs leaves across his face and neck. She kisses him. Tosses him into the air. He smells of those leaves and his skin is flushed, damp with warm child-sweat. For months he will point to grass and spinach and peas and pine needles and say they smell green. Though she tries to teach him that green is a color, not a smell, she soon agrees that, indeed, green is as much a scent as it is a color, and they both continue to think of green that way.*

Afterwards, the old women in town would be convinced it was that very day that the Eberhardts' pear tree withered—not died altogether, understand, but shrank into itself and stopped producing those lush yellow pears. They talked amongst themselves, describing what they'd heard from Trudi Montag: how Renate Eberhardt had stood beneath that tree, first touching the trunk, then raising both hands into the branches while smiling and moving her lips as if talking to someone sitting in the branches.

It was that smile the old women kept returning to, shaking their heads as they tried to puzzle out if the smile was a sign of impending sainthood or delirium, and they were not at all surprised when, at harvest time, brown spots marred the dull green peel of the pears. If you were to cut off the skin, the spots beneath would plug the white flesh like tiny corks. Though the tree would display its usual dazzle of fragrant blossoms the following spring, the pears would come in small and hard.

But that would happen later—after Renate Eberhardt was taken away; after her son and his wife moved into the front bedroom; after Helmut trimmed the bushes and trees, turned the flower beds into lawns, confined the forget-me-nots and geraniums in tidy window boxes, and pruned the lofty hedge of lilacs waist high so that people could see into his garden from every angle to admire the order and see that he had nothing to hide; after Germany opened its predawn attack against Poland that first day of September 1939, pressing from all sides in a tightening ring of decimation.

Wedged between two wars, the old women, who'd lost husbands and sons in the previous war, had seen those long-ago soldiers leave for battle in 1914 with music and laughter and flags. But no one flung blossoms at the new soldiers; it was as if the town had agreed to save the flowers for their burial rites. The old women crossed themselves as the men departed from Burgdorf in trains with their silent mask faces—many of them wearing helmets, some the medics' white armbands with the red cross, their hands stretched from the open windows as the train pulled forward, as if to attach themselves forever to the fingertips of their wives and mothers.

The old women were distressed by the tears of the young women, who did not remember the hope that had come with the last war, but they understood the terrible embarrassment in the eyes of some young women who could hardly bear to look at their men. At the train station, gloomy accordion players pulled and squeezed the creases of their instruments, reminding the old women how their town, too, was being compressed, shedding its men of fighting age. And as they thought of how it would expand again once the men came back—those who would, that is—they braced themselves to endure the accordion motion of ebbing and flowing, as well as the grieving over those men who would be killed.

When Alfred Meier, Fritz Hansen, and Hans-Jürgen Braunmeier were sent off to fight the war the same week in October, Monika Buttgereit wore a black hat to church—not nearly as beautiful as the hats she used to buy from Frau Simon. The bakery closed, and the delivery truck was parked on wooden blocks in the courtyard behind the Hansens' house. The retired baker and his wife, alone in the rooms above the shop, found it increasingly impossible to take care of themselves, much less of their remaining son, who had no arms. Ulrich had to be fed and washed, and they were relieved when their neighbor, who was in the SS, persuaded them to send Ulrich to a home for the crippled, where there were others like him, incapable of looking after themselves.

Three days before he was to leave for the war, Georg Weiler won a car in a daring game of *Skat* in a tavern, and he drove it from Düsseldorf to his old neighborhood in Burgdorf with the windows open though it rained. Laughing, he parked it in front of his mother's store and coaxed her into taking a ride with him. Both hands holding on to her scarf, she sat in the passenger seat, and whenever they approached an intersection, she prayed to her name saint, Hedwig, whose miracles and peacemaking had saved many lives.

The night before his departure, her son lost the car as well as a pair of new boots in another game of cards, and when she saw him off at the train station, his eyes were dulled with *Schnaps,* and he moved cautiously as if each step jolted him. Herr Weskopp, whose sons had already left for the war, was on the train with Georg, eager for battle and glory.

All over Germany, old women kept going to train stations because the men did not leave all at once: they kept flowing out of their towns like lifeblood, train after train after train, while reports of victories and defeats spread throughout the country; they kept departing after an attack on the Führer failed that November in München.

Trudi found out about the attack as she walked across the church square and Helmut Eberhardt came running toward her.

"The Führer—" he gasped, tears in his blue eyes, "an attempt on our Führer's life."

"Is he dead?" Trudi blurted.

He stared at her. His lips opened.

"Such terrible news," Trudi said quickly, afraid he could tell she wished the attempt had been successful. Ever since Helmut's mother had been taken away, Trudi hadn't felt safe in Burgdorf, and after her encounter with him, she half expected to be picked up that day.

When, within two weeks of the attack, the Führer proclaimed that Germany had only the choice between victory and defeat, Emil Hesping said that anything that was not a total victory was considered a defeat by Hitler.

Leo Montag nodded. "To win this war would be the worst possible fate for the Germans."

One of the pleasures in Trudi's life was to listen to the music of ten-year-old Matthias Berger—a boy rumored to like boys—who began to visit her to play her piano. Though she'd seen him in church and had heard the gossip about him, she'd hardly spoken to the boy before. His parents both worked in Düsseldorf, and his brothers were grown and lived away from home. That first winter of war, she'd found Matthias squatting by the brook behind her house, trying to rinse blood from a skinned elbow in the icy water. With the hem of her skirt, she washed his face and arms and hands, and it was only then that he started to sob.

"Who did this to you?"

"Some boys."

"Why?"

He sobbed only harder. "I just want to be their friend."

All at once she could smell the warm animal scent of the Braunmeiers' barn and felt herself reeling in the slow, hazy light that poured

through high rafters. Those boys—"Hush," she said and took Matthias
into her arms.

He shivered, and she felt his otherness as her own.

"Hush now," she said roughly.

She took him by the hand and led him inside the house, where she
positioned him next to the hot stove and warmed a cup of milk for
him. To take that sadness from his face, she brought him into the pay-
library and played the *Eroica* for him on the gramophone. He listened
to it with his eyes closed, and then asked if he could play her piano.
His head tilted as if hearing some inner imprint of that music, he
touched the keys almost reverently as if to map out a path through a
foreign country, and in the familiar sequence of notes Trudi heard her
own pain and rage.

Since then, Matthias had started to come to the pay-library at least
once a week, bringing his own sheet music, playing Chopin and
Beethoven. But sometimes his hands would fly up to his temples as his
eyes went dark with one of his fierce headaches. Leo Montag would
urge him to take a rest and sit him down by the chessboard. Patiently,
he'd teach Matthias the moves, and each visit he'd make him memorize a new opening sequence.

Trudi liked sharing delicacies from her Aunt Helene's packages
with the boy. Ever since the war had started, the parcels from America had arrived less frequently, with their cheeses, canned meats,
chocolate bars, and lengths of fabric with matching spools of sewing
thread. Quite a few had never been delivered. After two letters with
money supposedly were lost in the mail, Trudi's aunt began to roll the
bills up, tightly, insert them into the hollow centers of the spools, and
reaffix the round labels at the ends of the spools.

On Ash Wednesday Trudi gave Matthias a white shirt she'd sewn
for him from fabric her aunt had sent, and he played the piano for
her. All through Lent he played for her and her father, even on Passion Sunday, when each statue in the church was covered with faded
cloths that had been brought up from the church basement; he played
for them after the service on Good Friday, the one day of the year
when you could not receive communion and when the church was
stripped and left vacant like a tomb, symbolizing that Christ was
dead. On Easter Sunday, Fräulein Birnsteig visited the boy's parents
and told them she'd chosen Matthias as her student.

For a while, that honor caused the other children in school to leave him alone, but soon they were back to teasing and torturing him. Still, it no longer bothered Matthias as much as before. He thrived on the music lessons and on Trudi's stories of him becoming a famous concert pianist. She'd paint his future with stories of him traveling all over the world, adored by audiences.

The silence of the war was in direct contradiction to her story-telling. It was much closer to the silence of the church—fostering belief instead of knowledge, smothering mystery, muffling truth. Now that Trudi found herself dealing as much in silences as in incidents, she discovered new ways to tell her stories. You had to know your listeners before you decided what it was safe to let them know, or you could endanger others, yourself.

She recalled what her father had told her years ago about war— that the sound level of the entire country drops to a lower level. And in that stillness, the music became more important to her than ever before. She would listen to Matthias or play her father's records when she worked in the pay-library, letting herself be swirled into the fury, the passion, the tranquillity. Notes were to music what words were to her stories, and by linking the words, she could spin the power of the composer into that of the storyteller, make it hers.

In St. Martin's Church, the women prayed for their sons and nephews, and when they saw Helmut Eberhardt part his lips to receive communion, they added an extra prayer for his mother. They remembered him as an altar boy—that pious face, those perfectly folded hands—and they marveled how close virtue and evil could be.

After mass, Helmut Eberhardt would insist on lingering in front of the church with everyone, smiling through a grimace of anger when people returned his hearty greetings with curt nods. He'd keep one hand firmly on the plump arm of his wife, who looked as if she wanted to flee. Most of the time Hilde wouldn't even last through mass but would faint as she used to as a girl, only sooner now as if seeking oblivion, and she'd have to sit on the front steps of the church, her face in her hands, waiting for her husband.

When she went to the stores, she found it far easier to endure the food rationing than the contempt that many of the people had for her husband. It felt like walking into a constant, gritty wind, and she could barely raise her eyes. When she delivered children, the families of her patients were usually polite to her but seldom welcoming. She worried about those women who—lured by government incentives—endangered their lives by having pregnancies too close together. In addition to the coveted cross of honor, the reduction of the marriage loan, and tax advantages, families now received monthly allocations of *Kindergeld*—child money—starting with the third and fourth child, and doubling for each child after that.

Hilde didn't know how to explain to the people in town—not even to herself—why she continued to love her husband. Her love for him had been part of her since she was twelve and he, five years younger than she, still a child. Even then she had always imagined being with him once they both grew up. Although he'd betrayed his mother, she didn't know how to stop her love. Her body yearned as much for him as the first night he'd touched her, and she still felt pride at having been chosen by him.

At times, when Helmut Eberhardt used one of his mother's belongings—a favorite cup, say, or a tablecloth she had embroidered—he felt her thinking about him, loving him, even from a distance, wherever she was. He didn't want to think of her and her cumbersome love; yet, he had not found release from that love, and would not find it—not even when he would march east and crouch in the frozen dirt of regions he'd never seen before.

Her cumbersome love would always be with him, expanding more beneath his helmet with each war-soaked year, crushing his thoughts and infecting his dreams until he'd think his head would burst. And it would be with tremendous relief that he'd feel an enemy bullet enter his throat and rescue him from her love.

The night before her young husband left for the Russian front, the midwife's body told her that she was pregnant, but she waited to write the news to Helmut until she felt the movements of the child. She did not write him how often she remembered the dead child: it had been the second birth she'd assisted in, and what had happened horrified her so that she'd tried not to think about it at all but reminded herself that she should be grateful it had not been the first birth because that, surely, would have made her quit the profession before ever fully starting it.

But now she thought about the dead child all the time. The forty-year-old mother had sensed that her child had died within her, and her low, constant wail had shrouded Hilde Eberhardt as she labored to free the tiny corpse from the womb, forcing herself not to scream as the infant's hair and skin came off in her hands. After she'd wrapped the lifeless shape in a sheet to conceal the naked face from the mother's eyes, she'd scrubbed and scrubbed her hands, long after the dead skin had washed away.

That Christmas Eve, when Hilde Eberhardt's belly had risen far enough from the bulk of her body so that everyone could acknowledge her pregnancy, she laid four wrapped gifts beneath the decorated tree in her mother-in-law's house—that's how she still thought of the house: a shirt for her absent husband the color of his eyes, a bonnet she'd crocheted for her unborn child, the softest of all cashmere shawls for her mother-in-law, and, since no one had thought to remember her with a gift, a porcelain figurine for herself.

It was a few weeks after Christmas that Hilde saw the first yellow stars. They were made of cheap imitation silk and had to be worn by all Jews who were older than six on the left sides of their coats. The stars had the word *Jude* on them in oddly shaped letters, and the fabric was quick to unravel if not sewn to the coats in tiny, tight stitches.

The stars, Hilde noticed, gave a different texture to the town because they marked the Jews as obviously as the brown uniforms identified the SA. You knew right away where someone belonged. Except that the stars changed something about the eyes of many Jewish people: they no longer settled on you when they encountered you, but looked beyond you, beyond everyone and everything as if testing the perimeters of an invisible fence. They were like rocks, those eyes—unmoving and rigid—and whenever Hilde tried to say something kind to make up for that terrible humiliation of having to wear the star, or lower her fee for assisting the birth of a Jewish child, those eyes would cloud with shame and fear. Yet, there were some like Eva Sturm who walked with clear eyes, her chin raised as if prepared to challenge the sky.

In the bleak winter streets, those yellow stars often were the only color, and yet, many people pretended not to see them. Some, though, would try to show their compassion by carrying bags for elderly Jews or offering them their seats in the streetcars. A few merchants like Frau Weiler would slip something extra into a Jew's grocery order.

It stunned Hilde how many people were Jewish, people she'd never expected to be Jewish, people with blond hair and straight noses like hers. It was as though the Jewishness were something deep within, something that could be pulled out of anyone with a new law and made evident with a yellow star. She wondered what Helmut would do if she turned out to be a Jew. Of course it was silly to think that because, after all, she was not, but she couldn't keep from imagining the loathing in his face as she stood in front of him, the hastily sewn star yellow on her chest above her swollen belly. She couldn't allow herself to think of any of this before going to sleep because she'd keep crying and, even if she slept, her dreams would be of being banished from her house.

Though Helmut Eberhardt was far away when Hilde lay in the Theresienheim and stretched out both arms to receive her son from the hands of Sister Agathe, who had extricated the large infant from the pull of Hilde's womb, it would have pleased Helmut to know—so Hilde told Trudi Montag and Frau Weiler when they brought lentil soup and cherry preserves to her house—that the child was a boy just as he had assumed, and that she had honored his wish to name him Adolf. But it would have displeased him to find out that she called their son Adi. To Hilde, the child had nothing in common with the man who'd glared at her with his stern smile from the framed portrait until she'd stored it behind the dresser.

Trudi Montag sewed a batiste nightshirt for Adolf Eberhardt and attended his christening, but when one of the altar boys handed the holy-water basin to Herr Pastor Beier, who sprinkled drops over the screaming infant's head, a deviation of light in the stained-glass window made it appear that the fair-haired altar boy who stood next to the pastor in his long smock was Helmut Eberhardt. His even features taunted her. Trudi's back felt cold, rigid. She looked around, but no one else seemed to have noticed, and as the altar boy took one step back, his face became the boy's face once more and he was no longer Helmut.

Still, that incident spooked Trudi enough so that, after the ceremony, when the midwife extended the baby to her, she stepped back and shook her head.

"I'm sorry," Hilde said. "About your eyelashes."

Trudi squinted up at the blond woman.

"It's not that I tried to trick you. I— I really thought it would make them grow."

"Oh, that." Trudi saw herself with Frau Abramowitz's nail scissors, cutting the ends of her eyelashes. "It happened so long ago."

"If you hadn't cut yours so quickly, I would have cut mine. I've always wondered if that's why . . . you know, not liking me, I mean, and now, not wanting to hold Adi . . ."

"Oh no," Trudi said. "It's just that I don't feel well today." And it was not that she was lying. It was rather that Adolf, who smelled of powder and breast milk and who gurgled softly at her, resembled his father so much that by touching him, Trudi was afraid, she might summon that old dread that had come upon her at age five when she'd let Renate Eberhardt place her newborn in her arms and had offered to keep him because she'd known he would devastate his mother.

Trudi was fearful of that old dread revisiting itself in Helmut's son, and though she usually wanted to know everything, she believed that moment, outside St. Martin's Church, that it would be better not to know. And yet, she would catch herself watching the boy, Adi, whenever she'd see him from then on, half expecting that premonition of evil to manifest itself.

The month after Adi was born, when the blood of birth had dried up between the midwife's thighs, she pulled every piece of furniture away from the walls of the white stucco house and scrubbed all surfaces, up and down and sideways. She washed the ceilings, waxed the parquet floor to a harsh gloss, rinsed the windows with vinegar until you'd swear you could put your hand through them, and fertilized the pear tree with pigeon droppings; but the fruits would be forever lost to her and to Adolf, one of a whole generation of boys named after the Führer.

While her husband was in the war, Hilde lived with her son in the upstairs rooms, keeping the downstairs prepared for her mother-in-law's return. She stored the cashmere shawl inside the linen closet for Renate, and she would not take it out until after the war when—a widow for some years—she would find herself pregnant with a child she felt certain was a girl, and she would start wearing the shawl as if it were an embrace, planning to give it to her daughter, whom she would name Renate. "It belonged to your grandmother," she would say.

The one time Helmut visited home on leave, late in the spring of 1941, he was so moved when he took his son into his arms that he didn't protest his wife's foolishness. If Hilde had convinced herself that the downstairs was too big for her and little Adolf, Helmut had no objections to her living upstairs. Until he returned. Besides—he was a man now and had experienced enough to know that women without husbands acted in ways that were not rational. You saw it with widows. With spinsters. It only followed that the wives of soldiers would get to be that way too after living without their husbands for so long. In a way it was proof of their chastity.

He couldn't help thinking how pleased the Führer would be if he could see little Adolf, with his blond hair and sky-blue eyes, and when he tried to think of someone who could take the boy's picture, he wished he'd kept Herr Abramowitz's cameras instead of stepping on them. From what he'd heard, the Abramowitzs were still trying to leave the country. Helmut was all for that. "Let's get the Jews out of here," he'd told the taxidermist, and Herr Heidenreich had nodded and said, "All of them." Apparently the Abramowitzs had applied to get into Argentina where their son lived, and they'd been approved, had paid their fees and bribes, but the day before their departure, their permit had been canceled by the Argentineans. Now they were starting the whole process of application over again.

Hilde, who had restored Adolf Hitler's portrait to its old place of honor above the dresser for Helmut's visit, did not mention his mother in his presence and was careful not to call the child Adi. She felt bewildered by her contentment when her husband departed again. Her first night without him, she took down the Führer's portrait and stored it in its proper place behind the dresser, picturing herself living in the house with her mother-in-law and her son. That's what it was like in many houses—women of two generations looking after the children.

As Burgdorf was turning into a town without men, Emil Hesping, who still managed several gymnasts' clubs, was forced to close two of them, and he tried to keep the rest open by offering half-price memberships to women.

Gradually, Burgdorf also became a town without children. Ingrid Baum and Monika Buttgereit were two of the teachers who were sent to small villages with busloads of children whose parents had voluntarily registered them for the KLV—the Kinderlandverschickung—a program organized by the Hitler-Jugend to evacuate children who lived near cities that might be bombed.

It was Ingrid's first real teaching job. Ever since earning her degree, she had given private lessons to children who were hard of hearing. Teaching jobs were so scarce that others who had graduated with her worked in offices and stores, and she considered herself blessed to teach at all. After hearing rumors that teachers were being stationed in Poland, she had been relieved to be sent to the Black Forest instead. She would have preferred to teach at a regular school since the teachers in the KLV were treated like soldiers, but she knew she had to go wherever she was assigned.

The day Trudi helped Ingrid to get ready for her journey, the red jewelry box she'd given her stood no longer on the windowsill.

"Have you already packed it?"

Ingrid hesitated. "I traded it. For a rosary."

"But I bought it for *you*."

"The rosary was blessed by the Pope."

"The box was blessed by the Pope too."

Ingrid grew pale.

"It could have been," Trudi said.

"Was it?"

"By the Pope and five bishops."

"You're not telling the truth."

"And twenty-seven cardinals."

"Don't do that. Don't lie."

"Then it's your fault if I go to hell for sinning."

"I will pray for you."

"I don't want you to pray for me."

"I often pray for you."

"On the rosary you traded for my jewelry box?"

"When I pray, I sometimes can feel the presence of your guardian angel. She's pure and bright—"

"Oh, Ingrid."

"—much brighter than my own guardian angel. Often she goes away. Because I'm too sinful. And then everything goes dark."

"If I made up a list of people who are sinful, Ingrid, you wouldn't be on it."

"How can you know?"

"I know, believe me. What I don't know is who has my jewelry box."

"I didn't mean to make you angry."

Trudi waited.

"Klara Brocker."

"Klara Brocker?" Trudi felt a sudden dislike for the tidy Brocker girl, who wore cheap jewelry and had worked as a maid for the taxidermist's family ever since she'd finished school the year before. At least once a week, Klara slipped into the library to borrow the latest romances—for her mother, she said—as her eyes skimmed the jacket picture with polite greed.

Trudi could imagine her coveting the red leather box with that greed, scheming to offer Ingrid a worthless rosary in return. It felt as though the girl had stolen the red box directly from her to hoard her garish brooches and earrings, her flashy bracelets and rings, and Trudi found it difficult to be civil to her even after Ingrid left with the KLV to teach in the Black Forest.

After six years of polite engagement to the elegant and accomplished Fräulein Raudschuss, the dentist, Klaus Malter, fell in love one hot June afternoon of 1941—fell in love recklessly and irreversibly—shocking the town two months before his long-scheduled wedding day. His bride had her gown hanging in her closet, and every detail of the dinner had been planned, right up to the lemon and parsley fans that would decorate the cheese trays. Three years earlier, she had decided on the color of the damask napkins and tablecloth—a cool ivory—but only seven months before the scheduled ceremony she had followed an impulse that surprised her, and had ordered everything in a lavish pink that reminded her of sea roses—seen through a sheen of water when you lie beneath them. It was a color she'd never forgotten since that morning when she was two and had leaned forward to pick one of the perfectly round roses that floated in the pond behind the Swiss hotel where her family vacationed every August.

The water rocked her—smoother than her nursemaid's arms—and the stems of the sea roses reached far below the leaves. Above her swayed the leaves, their undersides the palest of greens, and above them danced the globes of roses, each a planet to itself. Brigitte wanted to laugh with delight, but her mouth filled with water, and she felt as though she had turned into her favorite doll who would lie—just like her—arms stretched up whenever you'd put her down, and then she felt even more like a doll because the sky broke the leaves and the roses tilted as white sleeves reached for her. The nursemaid's wail clogged the air, and Brigitte thought her heart would break if she could not lie beneath that shade of pink again.

She thought it was her nursemaid's wail she heard when Klaus asked her consent—with the proper regret in his voice as if regret could ever be proper when causing pain—to end their engagement, but she still felt the wail in her throat, rough and common like that of a market woman, and knew that she, too, was capable of that sound while her thoughts scraped for words that would make Klaus stay—words to assure him that love comes back if you're patient, and that many people learn to love after they are married. He listened—and that's what she would not forgive him afterwards—that he let her beg him, yes, beg him to stay with her before he told her about this . . . this child, this nineteen-year-old girl who was about half her age, unformed and awkward, with no family to speak of except her Uncle Alexander, no match at all for Klaus whose family—for years now—had treated Brigitte as one of its own.

She heard that wail again when she confessed her dishonor to her father, and again when her father returned from his meeting with Klaus Malter. But during those hours while she'd waited for her father, who had influenced people far more powerful than an ordinary dentist, Brigitte Raudschuss would have gladly lain at the bottom of any pond, submerged as long as she could endure, if this would have brought Klaus Malter back to her, but as she imagined their wedding taking place after all, she feasted on the terrible need to make him suffer too. And yet, during those hours of waiting, she felt more love for Klaus than she had ever before, more love than she knew herself capable of, because she sensed that—like sea roses seen from beneath—Klaus could never be entirely hers. She was seized by a powerful yearning for a gown that splendid shade of pink, and she sat down with a pen and ink to sketch the outline of a fitted gown which she would still wear to the Opernhaus as an old woman, where she would share a loge with two other unmarried women.

The rumors about Klaus and Jutta kept Trudi busy for weeks as she distributed each unfolding of their romance throughout Burgdorf. As long as she kept telling and retelling that story, she didn't have to let in her jealousy of Jutta that swallowed her when she was alone and silent, an ugly jealousy that found its only moments of reprieve when she could remind herself of her satisfaction that Brigitte had been ousted. Yet, Trudi had become so accustomed to seeing Klaus with the lawyer's daughter all those years that her initial resentment had been supplanted by the belief that the two suited one another.

But even the gossip about the dentist's reckless love made it impossible to forget that war kept spreading like ink on a linen cloth, and she gathered and distributed facts about the war along with gossip about Klaus. She read in the newspaper that the June attack on Russia had resulted in three hundred thousand Russian prisoners. It worried and infuriated her that the situation had worsened for the Jews: they were no longer encouraged to emigrate, but instead were ordered to vacate their homes on short notice. They were restricted to living in houses that had been declared Jewish houses, supposedly to monitor and hinder any interaction between Aryans and Jews. Closer and closer they had to live together, separated from the rest of the town by an invisible wall.

In some of the Jewish houses, the windows stayed covered with wooden shutters all day. Herr and Frau Kaminsky had been moved to one of the houses behind the cemetery, where they shared one small room; but some of the wealthier Jews lived in hotels or inns where their meals were included, freeing them from the humiliating and time-consuming shopping for decreasing food supplies. Though merchants like Frau Weiler helped as much as they could, others—including the butcher and pharmacist—took satisfaction in enforcing the laws that constricted the world of the Jews even further.

The number of Jews in Burgdorf had shrunk drastically. Two families had disappeared from the Catholic congregation, leading to speculations as to where they'd been taken. Even the priest hadn't known they were Jewish until the Gestapo had investigated their backgrounds. They'd attended St. Martin's for as far back as anyone could remember; their children had been christened there, had received their first communion.

Many others had fled, trying in vain to sell their pianos and large pieces of furniture, settling their neighbors with the nasty fear of the survivor and with a yearning for news that could distract them and engage their imagination—like which wedding the dentist would go through with.

From the window of her pay-library, Trudi had watched Brigitte Raudschuss' father arrive at Klaus Malter's office. He stayed one hour and twenty minutes. During that time, Trudi saw five patients enter. None of them departed. She imagined them cramped in the waiting room, which barely held four wooden chairs, hearing the voices of the lawyer and the dentist through the walls. If only she could be in that office. Perhaps the lawyer would challenge Klaus to a duel at sunrise to avenge his daughter's honor. He'd pull off one glove and—

No, it was summer. Too warm to wear a glove. Besides, duels happened only in those romances her customers kept borrowing. The lawyer would be more likely to offer Klaus money to rescue his daughter from everlasting spinsterhood. "An increase in dowry," he would call it.

Surprised by her compassion for Brigitte Raudschuss, Trudi wondered if Klaus was trying to pretend with her, too, that nothing had happened between them, although that would be much harder to accomplish after a six-year engagement than after one kiss. She thought of that morning in church when she'd seen Brigitte Raudschuss for the first time, and she asked her a silent forgiveness for the rage she'd sent her way. That rage should have been for Klaus—not for another woman.

She remembered Jutta running into the church, late, squeezing herself into the same pew with Brigitte Raudschuss, who yielded reluctant space to her. It would have never occurred to the lawyer's daughter then that the disheveled girl would dislodge her from the position she'd taken for granted.

"Did you hear anything? Anything at all?" Trudi would ask each of Klaus Malter's patients the day after he'd walked Brigitte's father out, their faces solemn as they parted with a polite handshake. But from what she could surmise, the voices of the two men had stayed muffled during their lengthy discussion.

"What was he like when he drilled on your tooth afterwards?" she would ask, nodding with satisfaction when she was told that Klaus Malter's eyes had looked sad and that his hand had not been as steady as usual.

Yet, the day of his wedding to Jutta, Klaus Malter's eyes were not sad. He arrived at St. Martin's too early and stood on the front steps with a dazed and exultant smile, the kind of smile you get when you amaze yourself by risking something you've never considered before. It was only a week after his meeting with the lawyer, sooner even than his wedding with the lawyer's daughter would have taken place, and when his relatives arrived in the expensive clothes they must have planned to wear to Brigitte's wedding, they looked disapproving, except for his mother, the professor, who took both of Klaus' hands into

hers and kissed his face before she let herself be escorted to her place
in the front pew. Her white hair, which—Klaus had told Trudi a long
time ago—used to be the same hue of red as his own, was braided in
a thick coil around her head.

When Jutta turned from the altar after the ceremony to walk up the
aisle on the arm of her new husband, there was something skittish
about the way she moved, and suddenly Trudi could see why the stable Klaus, who used to be so captivated by Ingrid, would also feel
drawn to Jutta, who would balance that settled side of himself.

But she still couldn't figure out why Jutta had chosen him. With a
tug of satisfaction and revenge, she whispered to Hilde Eberhardt,
who knelt next to her, "I finally understand why he fell in love with
her, but Jutta—she's so beautiful and young—she could have chosen
any man."

And Hilde agreed that Jutta could have chosen any man.

Most people in Burgdorf did not wonder at all why the wild young
woman was marrying the dentist, who already was thirty-six and so
different from her in temperament. He would make a reliable husband, they agreed. He'd quiet her down. Besides, it was not at all unusual for men to be substantially older than the women they married.

They regarded Jutta as odd, the people of Burgdorf. Not only did
she paint pictures in which the colors were all wrong and far too
bright, but she also, despite their warnings, swam in summer storms.
"She doesn't value her life," some would say. Lightning and thunder,
which made others seek shelter, would lure Jutta from the house.
Rain would drench her even before she'd arrive at the quarry hole or
river. "Crazy," some of the people would say.

But Trudi knew what crazy meant from her own mother, and Jutta
was not like that although she, too, had that high flicker, as Trudi
thought of it. Hers was not the kind of flicker that would burn itself
out but would only grow stronger, she believed, and even when Jutta
would die young in a fast-driving accident nearly two decades later,
Trudi would stay convinced that, without that one accident, Jutta
would have kept burning strong, her fire evident in her brilliant paintings of the town.

Trudi would see that same flame in the child who would ensue
from Jutta's body—the daughter, Hanna, who rightfully should have
been Trudi's daughter if the dentist had followed up on that one reckless kiss.

■

THE WEEK AFTER KLAUS MALTER'S WEDDING, TRUDI BEGAN TO READ the marriage advertisements in the paper again—not that she was looking for a husband, but they gave her something to laugh about. Because of the war, the list of men was shorter than ever before, and most of the ads had been written by retired men. Late one evening she decided to answer one of those ads, Box 241, in care of the newspaper: the man was younger than the others, a thirty-four-year-old schoolteacher who collected stamps, did watercolors, and described himself as curious. She gambled on that curiosity when she sent him a letter without a return address, asking him to meet her at Wasen's, an outdoor restaurant on the Königsallee in Düsseldorf, the following Saturday afternoon.

I will know you, she wrote to Box 241, *because you carry an umbrella and two white carnations.* She had thought about this for quite a while, rejecting the idea of having him wear a top hat because he might have to buy that, making it too expensive to meet this woman whose description—tall and slender with a mane of auburn hair— Trudi had taken from one of the colorful book jackets in the pay-library.

Actually, once she reread her letter, the woman sounded a lot like Ingrid, with her long hair and delicate hands, and when she looked at the book jacket again, the woman could have been Ingrid except that Ingrid would insist on martyrdom before letting herself be squeezed into a yellow dress that exposed not only her shoulders but also the high cleft of her breasts. The woman in Trudi's letter was warm hearted, loved to cook and dance, was in line to inherit the family business, and adored opera as well as children. Her name, Trudi decided, was Angelika, and she was the same age as Trudi, twenty-six. *I have been told that I am extraordinarily beautiful,* she wrote, chuckling to herself when she decided against adding that she was also exceedingly humble.

Not that she ever seriously intended to go to the restaurant and watch the man's discomfort as she had with the others years ago. . . . After all, with the suffering going on around her, games like that were too frivolous. Still, that Friday she traded books for an almost new lipstick; Saturday morning she found herself washing and setting her hair, just in case, and struggling with the choice of what to wear if she were to go. Ready to turn back, she arrived at the restaurant twenty minutes early in her gray suit with the fitted skirt. She hoisted herself onto a chair next to one of the flower pots that separated the tables from the sidewalk, her back to the sun so she could see everyone.

Although she was only planning to watch the man wait for this woman he would never meet, she was sweating under her breasts and arms when Box 241 arrived exactly at four, the umbrella hooked over his arm. By the door he hesitated. The skin around his eyes was lighter than the rest of his tan as though he usually wore glasses, giving him a startled look. Carrying the two white carnations like spears, Box 241 darted toward the last empty table without glancing at anyone, bumping into two chairs on his way, his lean shoulders curved forward as if he were accustomed to tolerating disillusion.

Only after he was sitting did Box 241 allow his eyes to roam— quickly though, as if hesitant to intrude on anyone—and then he pulled thick eyeglasses from his pocket and studied the menu with intense concentration as if it could provide him with clues to the woman who had summoned him here. His black hair touched the collar of his suit jacket, and he had a timid mustache.

Trudi was one of two women who sat by themselves—the other tables were occupied by couples or families—but the man's eyes kept shifting past her as if she were not there, returning to a heavy, dark-haired woman who was devouring a piece of *Bienenstich,* scooping out the custard filling and spreading it on top of the glazed almond topping. Box 241 ordered tea with lemon, checked his pocket watch, then took off his glasses, hastily, as if he'd only now recalled that he was wearing them. Unfolding a sheet of paper that looked like Trudi's letter from a distance, he frowned, and looked once more at the woman who was dissecting her cake.

I'm prettier than she, Trudi thought.

I'm much younger.

I don't eat like a pig.

But the man never even glanced at her, and all at once she was filled with an ancient rage at him and every man who simply dismissed her, a rage that uncoiled within her, fast and savage, making her want to inflict suffering on him—far beyond the humiliation of waiting for a woman who would never arrive. It always came back to feeling different. Always. Knowing there always would be that difference, that it would not get any better. And one way to get back at them was to express the nastiness many of them didn't dare to think. Though it was there, in their hearts, behind their smiles.

She wanted to get up and walk over to the man's table and tell him— Tell him what? She couldn't think of anything vehement enough to say to him. Besides, it wouldn't crush him if it came from her. She dug in her handbag for paper and a pen. *I have seen you,* she wrote, the notepad on her knees, *and I find you too—* She paused, thinking, and read what she'd written.

Box 241 lit a pipe, spilling some tobacco onto the tablecloth. His eyes fastened on every woman who passed the restaurant as if he hoped Angelika would still step up to his table, raise his two carnations to her lovely face, and murmur something like, *"I could feel you wait-ing for me."* The heroines in the romances would say something like that. The bolder ones might even ask: *"Is this how you imagined me?"*

Pitiful, Trudi thought. *Pitiful,* she wrote and finished her note. *I have seen you,* she read, *and I find you too pitiful to consider.* There. It was perfect. She signed it *Angelika* and paid her bill. Her heart a wild rhythm in her throat, she stood up. Her high heels felt wobbly as she neared the man's table.

"Excuse me," she said.

Box 241 squinted, his eyes moving from a space above her head to her face as if adjusting themselves to her height, shrinking her. "Yes?" he asked. His mustache was not skimpy as she'd thought but rather full and streaked with bleached hairs. Though his suit wasn't new, it was of good cloth and well cared for. But his shoes were dusty. "Yes?" he asked again and set his pipe into the ashtray.

She blushed, realizing he'd watched her inspect him. "This woman—" she said, the taste of lipstick on her teeth. "You see, this woman was walking by . . . there on the sidewalk next to my table." She pointed to where she'd sat, irritated with herself because she wasn't nearly as composed as she wanted to be. "And she asked me to—to give this to you." Before she could change her mind, she thrust the note at him.

"Thank you." His tanned hand reached for it. "When—"

"Oh . . . about ten minutes ago."

Hastily, Box 241 pushed the thick-lensed glasses back onto his nose and unfolded the lined paper. "Why did you wait this long?" He spoke in a rapid singsong, and she couldn't understand his words right away because they sounded outlandish and light as they floated from his lips and only came together for her after he'd stopped speaking. "Why didn't you come right over?"

"I'm— I'm somewhat shy."

For the first time he looked at her fully as though he knew what it was like to be shy, and it occurred to her that he seemed to be a man who was kind by nature. She wanted to retrieve the note, but his eyes fled down the words and then up again. He turned the paper as if hoping for a contradicting message, and then he gave a little cough that ended high in his throat. Carefully, he refolded the note.

The voices of the other people had receded as if a wide space had opened around his table. A cool draft moved up Trudi's legs, making her shiver. She no longer felt that rage—only deep shame. How could she have been so cruel?

"I'm sorry," she whispered.

Her words jolted him as though he'd forgotten she was still there. He worked his lips as if to reply and finally shocked her with a burst of laughter. "You—young lady—you—"

She took a step back.

"—you are very lucky." Still laughing, he pulled out a chair and motioned for her to sit down.

"I can't stay."

"In some countries they kill the messenger." He stopped laughing and regarded her so gravely that she was afraid he suspected the truth. "Fortunately, I don't engage in that custom. . . ." His peculiar singsong had slowed down, making it easier for Trudi to follow him. "What did she tell you, this woman?"

"Just to give the note to you."

"You know what it says?"

"Oh, no. It's private."

"Of course. Please . . . do sit down."

"I have to go."

"What did she look like?"

"The woman?"

"The woman."

"She—she was very beautiful . . . tall, with dark-brown hair pulled back. A yellow dress—she wore a yellow dress. With fabric-covered buttons."

"The poor woman."

"What?"

He smiled sadly and relit his pipe, drawing deeply. "That curse of beauty . . . Finding pleasure in trying to destroy others."

"Did she—?"

"Destroy me?" Box 241 rested his elbows on his knees and brought his face close to Trudi's. "Do you think she did?"

"I have to catch the streetcar and—"

"One cup of tea," he said. "Or one small glass of wine."

"I would. I really would, but my streetcar is leaving in ten min-utes."

"Where do you have to go?"

"Burgdorf," she said, wishing immediately she hadn't told him.

"That's where this woman lives."

"Really?"

"Her first letter was mailed from there."

"I haven't seen her before today." Liar, she thought as an image of the book jacket flashed before her.

"I'll drive you home."

"No," she said quickly, wishing she had mailed the letter from Oberkassel or Düsseldorf. "No."

"I'd be glad to. Thanks to your message, my plans for the afternoon have changed." He added as though he really meant it, "I would welcome your company." Extending his right hand, he introduced himself. "Max Rudnick."

She mumbled her name, making it impossible to understand as she shook his hand. Far too contrite to resist his invitation, she climbed on the chair across from him, her leather handbag on her knees, both hands clenching the curved handle. Two shimmering flies were knitting their legs on Max Rudnick's saucer. As the heavy woman who'd eaten the *Bienenstich* walked out of the restaurant, Trudi felt oddly abandoned.

"Tea?" Max Rudnick asked.

She nodded.

"Lemon?"

She nodded. Her feet swung high above the floor.

When the tea arrived, he squeezed the half-moon of lemon above her cup and stirred it. "Here," he said.

"Thank you." She burned her tongue as she gulped the tea, all of it, without looking at him. "It's very good."

"Not too hot?"

She sucked the tip of her tongue against her palate and shook her head.

"Were you thirsty?"

"I must have been." Before he could ask her anything else, she said, "Are you from another country?"

"Because of the way I talk?"

"It's not all that noticeable."

"The curse of being raised by my Russian grandmother, who played solitaire all day and refused to speak German. I stayed with her, talking Russian till I was old enough to go to school."

Now she was curious. "How about your parents?"

"Both worked. I was much closer to my grandmother."

"Where—"

"Köln. I lived there until recently when—when I was . . . let's say, transferred."

Is that why you wrote the ad? she almost asked, blushing hard as she realized how that would have given away her secret. "Why were you transferred?" she asked instead.

"It happens to teachers." Max Rudnick studied her carefully. "I don't know you well enough yet to tell you the reason. . . ."

The *yet* alarmed her, but she was not about to inquire what he meant. Besides, he was already paying the bill, and then his hand was guiding her shoulder as they walked toward the door.

"At least this time I can see where I'm going," he said and pointed to his thick glasses. "And to think that there are people who say that only women are vain."

"They don't look that bad."

"Bad enough. But without them I'm practically blind."

"At least that keeps you out of the war." She brought her hand to her mouth. How could she be so careless with someone whose politics she didn't know?

He glanced at her sharply. "That it does."

"I didn't mean anything."

"And I didn't hear anything." He led her toward a shabby blue car. "Would you like the window open?" he asked after they sat inside.

She nodded.

He reached for a screwdriver on the back seat, leaned across her, and rotated it inside the hole where the handle for the window used to be. The glass creaked as it moved down. When they crossed the bridge to Oberkassel, a cone of birds swirled from the high girders as the long blast of a barge rose from the river.

"I'd like to talk with you again," he said.

She stopped breathing. "Why?" she blurted, certain he was trying to prove she'd written the letters.

He looked at her from the side. "Will you say yes if I give you a good reason?"

She shook her head.

"Two good reasons?"

"I really can't."

"Three good—"

She had to laugh. "No," she said. "Not even with seventeen good reasons."

The curtain in the Blaus' living room moved when Max Rudnick parked his car in front of the pay-library, and Trudi climbed out before he could shut off the engine.

"I'll walk you to the door."

"You don't have to." Her burned tongue felt sore.

He pointed to the tobacco sign in the window. "I need to stock up."

"We're out of tobacco."

"Really now?"

"We've been waiting for a delivery."

"Who is we?"

"My father and I."

"I'll come back then. For tobacco."

And he did come back—the following week—but Trudi recognized his blue car in time to dart upstairs, leaving her father to deal with him. From behind the lace curtains of the second-floor hall window, she watched the sidewalk, and it took nearly fifteen minutes before Max Rudnick came out and drove off.

"What did he want?" she asked her father, who was taping the torn cover of a nurse-and-doctor novel.

He didn't look up. "Tobacco."

"Did he say anything?" She felt her ears go hot. "About me?"

Her father thought for a moment, then shook his head. Humming softly to himself, he fastened another piece of tape across a tear.

"Then what was he doing here all that time?"

"Looking at books. He borrowed a Western."

She groaned. "Why did you let him?"

"It's the kind of business we're in."

"Now he has a reason to come back."

Her father squinted at her. Smiled.

"Oh," she said. "It's nothing. Nothing."

In the days to come, she would keep checking the street, prepared to vanish again, and when Max Rudnick didn't return the following week and the week after that, she felt relieved; yet, when the due date of the book passed, her relief gave way to a peculiar disappointment that found its expression in periodic calculations of his mounting library fine.

I wish you could visit me, Ingrid wrote. *The mountains are spectacular, but I miss Burgdorf.* She lived with the schoolchildren, ate her meals with them, taught them everything from grammar to mathematics, gave them homework assignments, and made sure they washed properly before they went to bed. During her third night there, she'd been awakened by screams from the boys' dorm. They'd had a pillow fight, and one of the pillows had hit a lamp, causing a flame to surge up and set the pillow case on fire. *Thank God we put it out in time,* Ingrid wrote. *Most of the children are homesick. I've found out that boys get rough when they're afraid, while girls cry.*

Though Ingrid didn't complain directly in her letter about the Hitler-Jugend representative, Fräulein Wiedesprunt, who was in charge of the children's home, it was evident that she found it difficult to deal with the fault-finding woman, who told her she preferred male teachers and enjoyed setting curfews for everyone, including Ingrid. There were certain hours she was not allowed out, certain places she was not allowed to go.

The first weekend Ingrid was allowed to return to Burgdorf for a visit, she stopped at the pay-library before she saw her parents and told Trudi she dreaded her return to the home. "I thought I'd like teaching, but what's happening there has little to do with school. They've even removed all the crucifixes from the classrooms."

"Here too." Trudi took her into the living room, where they sat down on the velvet sofa. "I think it's like that everywhere."

"And the praying, even though we aren't allowed to pray in school, I used to say a short prayer before and after lessons." The skin on Ingrid's face looked red and dry. "The children—they really liked it, but once, when one of my classes was observed by Fräulein Wiedesprunt, a girl reminded me that we hadn't prayed yet."

Trudi winced.

"I said quickly, 'Oh, we'll catch up on that later.' But I was shaking . . . all that day I was shaking, Trudi." Ingrid leapt up, paced to the window and back. Her thin fingers straightened the lace tablecloth on the round wicker table, lifted the stuffed squirrel from the shelf. "I felt like a coward for not praying."

"But you couldn't pray. Not then."

Ingrid set the stuffed squirrel down again.

"You did the right thing."

"Fräulein Wiedesprunt, she didn't mention the praying, but she told me afterwards that when I raise my hand in the *Heil Hitler* it isn't vigorous enough."

"Vigorous. It's appalling that we have to do it at all."

"As a teacher you can't get away with not doing it. Students might tell on you. If they don't like you, they might even turn you in for something you didn't do."

"I know of a teacher in Oberkassel who was demoted. Two others in Krefeld were fired."

"The students . . ." Ingrid nodded. "It gives them too much power.

If they misunderstand something or are angry about their grades . . .
It's dangerous for teachers to be strict."

"But if you can't demand work from them, they learn less."

"At least I don't have to teach history. It's too easy to make mistakes
there."

"Like telling the truth?"

While Jutta Malter immersed herself in studies at the Art Academy in
Düsseldorf, the old women—who had been skeptical about the reasons for the hasty wedding—kept scanning her belly, but it did not
round out, though Jutta Malter seemed more grown-up, now that she
was married to an older man. Not that she lost the spring in her
step—it was rather a maturing of her entire body, an almost regal
bearing though, at times, she could still look like a girl.

"She is nearly half his age," Trudi would point out whenever she retold the story of how Jutta had arrived at the dentist's office late that
fated June afternoon to have him replace a filling and had ended up
replacing his fiancée. Sometimes it felt as if it had happened all in one
afternoon: the wedding, the visit of the jilted bride's father, and
Jutta—reclining in the dentist's chair, smelling the clean medicine
scent on Klaus Malter's hands, marveling at the tight curls of his red
beard and wishing the drilling would go on forever.

Early one morning, when Trudi returned from trading five books
for half a loaf of bread and two eggs, which she would smuggle to
Frau Simon, she saw Klaus and Jutta walk past the *Rathaus*, setting
out for their daily *Spaziergang*—stroll. Pigeons rose from the shoulders of the Hitler statue, whose early gloss had soon been dulled by a
greenish rust. If you looked closely, you could see that the Führer's
left ear was larger than the right one. A small child had noticed the
flaw at the dedication ceremony and had pointed it out aloud, causing the pharmacist additional embarrassment.

Arms linked, Jutta and Klaus were talking eagerly as if they hadn't
seen each other in weeks, and for a moment there—one generous moment—Trudi wished them well and released Klaus Malter.

That November—only months after Klaus had helped his bride
move her belongings down one flight of stairs in her Uncle Alexander's house and had settled with her in the large apartment that her
uncle had made available for the newlyweds on the second floor—his
mother was arrested while teaching her philosophy seminar. One of

her students called him, his voice muffled and urgent as if he were afraid of being apprehended any moment. He didn't know where the Frau Professor had been taken, he said, but he knew she'd been warned by the administration before to modify her views. "I admired her," he said as he hung up.

Klaus Malter's inquiries only brought him the information that his mother was in one of the prison camps; he demanded to see her, wrote letters and made phone calls to the police and the president of the university, and when he found out that there was nothing he could do, he became obsessed with the cold. It seeped into his veins as he kept thinking of his mother without warm clothes and blankets. He never worried about her starving or being tortured—only freezing to death, and he couldn't bear being inside heated rooms.

He'd roam the streets of Burgdorf, refusing to wear his coat or a knitted vest, blaming himself for not having resisted years ago. Like countless others, he'd simply grown more cautious—afraid to say the wrong thing, afraid to listen to forbidden radio stations that would tell you what was happening in the world. It was always possible that you might be picked up: at your place of work, in the streetcar, in a restaurant, in your own house. He had thought it was enough not to participate in the *Partei,* to stay away from marches and speeches. Now he wondered how much damage he'd done with his silence. Maybe if he'd officially protested when the boys had stoned little Fienchen Blomberg outside the Weiler's grocery store seven years before . . . Or if he'd fought the treatment that the Abramowitzs and his other Jewish patients had suffered . . .

Oh, he'd felt terrible for all of them, had slipped a couple of bank-notes to some of them—but what, really, had he done to prevent this avalanche of violence that had started small at one point, small enough to stop, surely, before it had become this frenzied mass that was still gathering momentum and, in its path, was sweeping his mother along?

He'd walk in his shirt even during sleet and rain, shivering hard, only stopping to stare at the naked branches, at the bleak sky. And his young wife let him—that's what the old woman clicked their tongues about. She'd even walk in the icy wind with him, not wearing a coat herself. It only proved that she was still a child. A proper wife would have coaxed her husband into warm layers of clothing, soothed his unrest with mulled wine.

Klaus was called to military duty a month after his mother's arrest, and when Jutta saw him off at the train, she promised to keep searching for his mother. As she left the station, she found Trudi Montag waiting for her outside the arched entrance, the collar of her wool coat turned up against the wind. Jutta raised one sleeve to dry her eyes, and Trudi handed her a folded handkerchief. Without saying a word, Trudi walked with her, and Jutta curbed her stride to match the *Zwerg* woman's pace.

When Herr Blau awoke to steady pounding against the door, his first thought was that the Gestapo had come for him. Fingers trembling, he reached for the water glass on his night table and fumbled his false teeth into his mouth. As he crept out of bed and down the dark stairs with a candle, he prepared what he would say if questioned—that he had never listened to anything anyone had said against the Führer and the *Partei,* that he was an old man and couldn't remember who had said what, and—

The pounding came from the back door. His hand on the railing, Herr Blau stopped. The police usually came to the front door, terrorizing not only the people they arrested but everyone else in the neighborhood. He peered from the kitchen window and saw a man standing on the stoop.

"Sshh." He opened the window a crack, and the pounding stopped. "Sshh. You're waking everyone up."

"Please—" The young man's eyes sat in hungry sockets. "Let me in, please." Two of the points on his yellow star were frayed.

Herr Blau trembled as if he were the one standing out there in the wintry night. "I don't even know you."

"They took my sister. They'll take me too if—"

"There must be people you can ask . . . family or friends. . . ."

"They're all gone."

"Go away. You—you must go away."

The man did not answer.

"I don't know you," Herr Blau said, his bowels twisting with sudden nausea.

The man blinked. His fingers closing around the straps of a rucksack, he turned and walked down the back slope toward the brook. With one stiff leap he reached the other bank and was blotted by the night.

When Herr Blau climbed back into bed, his feet felt frozen, and he took care not to press himself against his sleeping wife, though he longed to be wrapped into the warmth of her body. Lying near the edge of the bed, he closed his eyes and tried to return to sleep, but he kept seeing the man. He reminded himself that he'd never done anything against the Jews, even when others had humiliated them. He had not approved when Jews had lost their jobs and houses, and he'd always felt concerned about those who'd disappeared, hoping they'd found a better place to live. If he were Jewish, he had told his wife many times, he would have had the good sense to leave Germany long ago.

It wasn't good for his nerves to hear about arrests or transports to those camps where Jews were taken to work. That's what the camps were for, work, even if some people whispered about horrors that he couldn't allow himself to think about. . . . People like him had to suffer too: there wasn't enough food, not enough coal to heat even part of his house. People were afraid of freezing to death while they slept. They'd all heard rumors of old people who hadn't woken up.

It was always harder for the old. Always.

Toward dawn he finally slept, and when he awoke, he thought of the hunger in the man's eyes and saw himself reaching into the bread box to take out a wedge of rye bread for him. *"Take this,"* he could have said. He could have given him a blanket, an egg, his coat.

His wife no longer lay next to him, and he went downstairs in his bathrobe and squinted through the back window, but the frozen slope behind the house was empty, and no one stood by the brook.

"What are you looking for?" his wife asked and set a cup of *Zichorienkaffee*—chicory coffee—and a small bowl of hot oatmeal on the table for him.

"Nothing."

"Eat then."

"I can't."

"You're not feeling ill?" She laid one palm against his forehead.

He moved his head aside and walked out of the house. By the brook, he scanned the ground for footprints. There were quite a few, but all of them were old, frozen crusts of earth, impossible to discern whom they belonged to. Perhaps the man had already been captured. He was hardly a man yet, rather a boy. Seventeen perhaps? Maybe even younger. But taller than Stefan, who'd been small for his age, thirteen, when he'd left home one night, nearly half a century ago.

How many people had helped Stefan along the way before he'd reached America? And he hadn't even been hunted.

It would have been easy enough to hide the boy upstairs in Stefan's old room. And even if he had been discovered—whatever might have happened to all of them couldn't feel any worse than what Herr Blau was experiencing as the week wore on. He felt the loss of his son in a sharp and acute way—more so than ever before—as if somehow, by turning the young man from his door, he had jeopardized his son's safety. It didn't make sense because Stefan was a grown man who'd recently turned sixty, an old man, some would say. Again and again, he saw himself finding the note that Stefan had left behind, and felt that familiar despair at having failed his son.

Not that the note accused him of that—no, it had merely said that Stefan was on his way to America and not to worry about him. For an entire year before that, the boy had pleaded with his parents to let him go to America and make his fortune.

"Fortunes don't happen that way. Besides, you're too young," Herr Blau had kept telling him, hoping to stall him until he'd forgotten that dream and fastened on something else. Children were that way—all enthused about something one day and forgetting it the next. But Stefan had not forgotten, and the people of Burgdorf had tried to comfort his stunned parents by telling them there was nothing they could have done to hold their son.

Herr Blau took the brittle note from the box of family papers and unfolded it in his hands, remembering how inadequate he'd felt when his son had finally come home for a visit—twice a widower, but wealthy, as he'd dreamed. Stefan had only stayed one week and had taken Leo Montag's sister, Helene, with him as his third wife.

To deny help to someone in need, Herr Blau discovered, was far more devastating than to fear for his own safety. He wished there were someone he could talk to about what had happened, someone who wouldn't turn him in but could put those thoughts to rest. Maybe Leo Montag would understand. Herr Blau wasn't sure what he would say to Leo, but when he walked over to the pay-library one morning after he'd seen Trudi leave with her shopping net, he found the words.

"If you ever know of someone who needs help—" He leaned across the counter with a whisper. "Someone who maybe has to hide . . . I want to help too."

Leo studied him silently, then nodded. "That's good of you."

"Clothes, and food . . . and I'd keep quiet."

"It may not always be safe."

"That's what's wrong with everyone." The old man's voice burst from its cautious whisper. "Safe, safe. Is that all people can think of?"

"I'll remember that." Leo Montag laid one hand on the old man's wrist.

Herr Blau didn't cry until then, when he felt the warmth of the hand, and he started to tell Leo about the young man he'd sent away from his door.

"Not here." Leo walked around the counter to lock the door and led Herr Blau into the living room.

"I think about him." Herr Blau sat in the wicker chair, sobbing. "I think about him all the time." He rubbed his blackened thumbnail.

"You were afraid."

"A coward."

"Not anymore."

"Remember how small Stefan was when he ran off to America?"

"He seemed big to me then. I was only eight or nine."

The old tailor blew his nose and hiccuped.

"Fear," Leo said, "is a strange thing. It strips off masks. . . . In some people it brings out the lowest instincts, while others become more compassionate. Both have to do with survival. But the choice is ours."

"I made the wrong choice."

"But you didn't stay with it."

Herr Blau nodded, grateful for Leo's answer, but his tears came harder as he mumbled something that was impossible to understand.

The following week Frau Simon received an official notification from the SS that she was to be relocated. She was instructed to bring food for three days, one suitcase weighing no more than fifty kilos, one backpack or travel bag, and one roll of blankets. Twenty-eight other Jews received the same document and were removed from the community along with her. Ever since *Kristallnacht,* the SS had assumed control of Jewish policy, priding itself on rationality, efficiency, and order. To avoid public disturbances whenever possible, Jews were to be duped into thinking they were simply being moved to a new life in the East.

Frau Abramowitz, who had refused to leave her house ever since the yellow stars had to be worn, received the first letter from Frau Simon. They were being held in Poland. Their trip had taken three days and three nights. Five of the older people and one infant boy had died on the train. Several children were ill with coughs and fever. Their quarters were cold and cramped and shabby. They had never received their luggage.

They needed medicine.

They needed food.

They needed clothing.

It was that need which drove Frau Abramowitz from her house for the first time in a year. Her husband's attempts to get her to at least walk to the end of the street with him had resulted in tears of panic, and he'd finally stopped pressuring her to go out. But now she left her house as if she'd never retreated inside its walls and visited her friends to collect whatever they could spare. Trudi and Frau Weiler helped her to pack cartons with blankets and warm clothing, with food that would not spoil, with medicines from Frau Doktor Rosen, whose steps had slowed to a shuffle and whose hands trembled when she examined the few patients who still came to her.

As soon as the packages had been mailed, Frau Abramowitz made lists of other items that were needed, involving her daughter, Ruth, the women in her neighborhood, and women from her synagogue. Ruth had begun to spend occasional nights at her parents' house, and though Frau Abramowitz was always grateful to see her, it troubled her that her daughter avoided talking about her husband. In the beginning she'd asked why Fritz no longer visited them, and Ruth had said his throat practice had gotten so large that he hardly had time for himself. She didn't tell her mother that quite a few of her husband's patients were Nazi officials, who came to Fritz with the same concerns as his patients who were stage performers—to use their vocal cords to their fullest capacity without damaging them.

Herr Blau, who would always wonder if the young man he'd turned away from his house had been on the transport to Poland with Frau Simon, kept contributing coats and warm jackets, which he sewed from bolts of leftover fabric. When he learned from Frau Simon's next letter that fewer than half of the packages had arrived—only those with worn clothing—Herr Blau found ways to make new clothes look used: he removed occasional buttons and packed them inside balls of darned socks; he cut out labels and unraveled the edges of blankets;

he crumpled fabrics instead of folding them between layers of paper. That shipment arrived almost in its entirety.

By then, most of the Theresienheim has been appropriated for interrogations and detentions. While the sisters were confined to the cluster of cells adjacent to the chapel, most of the U-shaped building housed Jews and other "undesirables" while they waited to be transported or released. Many of them were old or ill. Usually four or five people were assigned to each small locked room.

But not only the Jews were in danger. Rumors were coming through that the weak and deformed and retarded were at risk. "Eaters," Anton Immers referred to them with contempt as though that had become their only function. He thought it only fitting that some were taken out of institutions and relocated to undisclosed places, while others were removed from their communities, like the man-who-touches-his-heart, who was arrested at the cemetery on All Saints' Day while placing a wreath on the grave of his nephew, who'd been shot down over England the year before.

In March of 1942 the parents of the Buttgereit boy received an urn, accompanied by a message that their nineteen-year-old son had died from an unnamed infection in the school outside Bonn where he'd lived for the past years. To avoid spreading the infection, the letter informed them, their son had been cremated immediately. The morning his ashes were placed into the chilly soil, his black-shrouded sisters encircled his open grave like obelisks. Two supported their father by his elbows. Their mother stood separate from them, her face rigid from stifling the silent scream: *But not like this. Not like this.* Ever since her son had fallen from the hay wagon as a small boy, damaging his spine, and Frau Doktor Rosen had predicted that he would not live beyond twenty, Frau Buttgereit had prepared herself for her son's death, anticipating a gradual weakening of his crippled body, an even stronger curving of his poor spine that would eventually reinstate him to the curled shape that had awaited birth within her—*when all was still well, oh God, when all was still possible*—but what she had not foreseen was an infection that would rip him from her—body and mind—in one swift, cruel gesture, without the long-rehearsed words of their final parting. No. That she could not accept.

Just one row away in the cemetery, Frau Weskopp waited for the priest to bless the coffin of her husband, whose body had been shipped back from Russia. He would lie next to her younger son, an

SS officer, who'd become a war casualty only the month before, not long enough for the worms to finish their task of scouring the skeleton. The family grave still revealed the seam of that burial: its earth had not had time to heal in the weeks between the two deaths. It was a wide grave, wide enough to cradle the remains of her parents and youngest son, while leaving space for this new coffin, as well as for herself and her oldest son, who was still serving the *Vaterland*.

When Trudi Montag and other parishioners followed the priest from the Buttgereits' gravesite to where the widow Weskopp knelt in her black coat and black hat, they passed the grave of Herr Höffenauer, who'd been buried next to his mother after lightning had struck him at her grave. One squat candle burned inside a glass lantern that was set in front of the granite marker.

Klaus Malter's mother was released a week after the two funerals. Trudi found out from the widow Blomberg when she came into the pay-library to borrow a mystery novel.

"I'm glad she's free," Trudi said. "Who told you?"

"The young Frau Malter."

"Jutta—she would know."

"They won't let the Frau Professor teach at the university anymore. I wonder what she's going to do for money."

"She comes from wealth," Trudi said. "I'm sure her family will help."

"You'd be surprised how many families drop away when you're in trouble."

"Not your family, though."

"Not my sister, anyway. I'm glad she got away to Holland in time. But my brother—I don't even know where he lives now." She shivered, and Trudi made her sit down on one of the boxes of banned books that were stored along the wall next to the counter. "If he lives, that is."

Trudi watched her silently—the grayish face marked by sorrow and hunger, the painfully thin hands. It hurt her eyes to look at the yellow star that was sewn with meticulous stitches to the front of Frau Blomberg's coat. No matter how many of those stars she saw, they hurt her eyes. She felt the loss of all the people who had left Burgdorf, those who had fled or been taken, those who were still fighting this dreadful war.

"I was thinking more of my husband's family. I'm only half Jewish, and they used to pretend that didn't count. But ever since my husband died, I'm no longer welcome there. Too dangerous, they said the last time I wanted to visit."

"You hear from Fienchen?"

"This is the second year I haven't been able to celebrate her birthday with her. She just turned fourteen." Frau Blomberg pulled out a folded handkerchief and blew her nose.

Trudi noticed a spot of blood, and her first thought was that Frau Blomberg must have spit a communion wafer into her handkerchief. Those old superstitions . . . She shook her head. Besides, Frau Blomberg wasn't even Catholic.

"I used to make plum cake for Fienchen on her birthdays, one sheet of cake for her, the other for my husband and me. Remember how she loved to eat hot plum cake, Trudi?"

Trudi nodded, but what she remembered was Fienchen as a six-year-old, her face bloodied from stones the boys had thrown at her.

"It's better for her, being with my sister in Amsterdam. They're after the Jews there too, but I don't think it's as bad as here."

The month after her husband had died from a burst appendix, Frau Blomberg and Fienchen had applied for visas to Holland, together with her sister's family, whose professional skills—she a nurse and he an accountant—turned out to be far more desirable to the Dutch than those of a widow whose secretarial training had been broken off when, at sixteen, she'd become a housewife and mother.

The night before their departure, Frau Blomberg's sister had offered to smuggle Fienchen out of the country as one of her own children. She had six, four of them girls, and they all pretended to be asleep in a tangle of arms and legs when they crossed the border. It was one of the stories Trudi knew she could never tell. She'd even cautioned Frau Blomberg when she'd first heard about the escape from her.

"I get so jealous of my sister, being a mother to Fienchen, watching her change," Frau Blomberg was saying. "I only had the one. . . ."

"You'll always be her mother." Trudi reached behind the counter and picked up two new mystery novels which hadn't been covered with cellophane yet. "These came in yesterday," she said. "How would you like to be the first one to read them?"

Frau Blomberg picked up both books, her eyes skimming across the gaudy jackets and down the summary on the inside flap. "I was only going to borrow one."

"I'd love to know what you think of them, so I'd be glad to let you have both for the price of one. You see," Trudi continued hurriedly as Frau Blomberg looked about to object, "usually my father likes to read books ahead of time, to recommend them to certain customers, you know, but he's been preparing for a chess tournament. I'm sure he'd appreciate it if you could do this for him."

She stood in the open door, watching Frau Blomberg walk away with both books, when Max Rudnick drove up. Before she could retreat, he leapt from his car, pointing at the sky. "Look," he shouted. "Look."

Above them, a huge formation of birds flew toward the river in one solid V-shape, but all at once its direction changed and—in that moment of change—became a dark cluster in the sky; yet, almost instantly, from that cluster the V-shape realigned itself as if imprinted on some ancient memory and headed toward the fairgrounds.

"How much do I owe?"

"For what?" She stared at Max Rudnick.

"In fines." He pulled the overdue book from the pocket of his raincoat.

"By now it would cost less to replace it." Trudi waved aside his offer to pay as he followed her inside. "Besides, you bought me that tea, remember?"

"But that was my pleasure." He said it with such sincerity that she wanted to bolt.

Her father came in from the hallway and greeted Max Rudnick.

"I have work to do." She grasped four books from the counter and retreated to the back of the library even though they didn't belong there. She heard his voice, then her father's, but not loud enough to understand their words. A fine business I'm running here, she thought, two books for the price of one, no overdue fines. . . . If people hear about this, they'll all want the same deals, and we may as well close up.

When she finally came to the front again, Herr Rudnick was paying for a pouch of tobacco.

He pushed his thumb against the bridge of his glasses. "How would you like to go for a walk with me?"

"I— there's too much I have to do here." She felt her father's eyes on her. He was watching her with an amused smile, and she resisted the temptation to make a face at him.

Without trying to persuade her to go on that walk, Max Rudnick left, and he didn't ask her again when he returned to buy tobacco the following week and the week after that. He no longer made an effort to draw her into talking with him, but instead spoke easily with her father.

"I no longer know my own daughter," Leo Montag said one afternoon after Max Rudnick had left.

"Why?"

"Because you don't ask this man any questions. You've never let anyone leave here without asking your questions."

"I'm not interested in his life."

Her father smiled. "Now that is the one answer I didn't figure on."

Her entire head felt hot. "What do you mean?"

"Oh— I'm not sure myself."

"I wish he wouldn't come in here."

"And why is that?"

"I— He is pushy. Nosy."

"He regards you highly."

"He just pretends." But she had to ask. "What makes you believe that?"

"It comes through."

"How so?"

"In the way he looks at you."

"You read too many of your trashy books."

"That's true."

"Has he said anything?"

"About what?"

"Me, of course."

"He must have."

"Like what?"

"Oh—" Her father gave her a deliberately vague smile. "What I know about him is that he rents a room in Kaiserswerth and that he supports himself by giving private lessons."

"What else did you find out?"

"And here you thought you had no interest in his life. . . ."

• • •

The next time Max Rudnick came to the pay-library, he followed Trudi between the stacks of shelves when she made her escape and watched her rearrange a shelf of war novels that didn't need any rearranging.

"Will you come for dinner with me on Sunday?"

"No," she said, angry at herself for feeling delighted at his invitation.

He was leaning above her, one arm stretched against a support bracket. "Why not?"

"You don't have to."

"Why would I even think I had to?"

"Because . . ." She lined up the spines of the books by running one thumb along them. "Because you're feeling sorry for me."

"Sorry for you? Why?"

"You want me to say it aloud?"

"I don't understand."

"All right then. Because I'm a *Zwerg*."

"What I see is a spirited young woman."

"Sure."

"A spirited and bright young woman who—"

"Who is a *Zwerg*."

"Who is a *Zwerg*," he said quietly.

It stung her, hearing the word from him. "See?" she demanded.

He crouched, bringing his face to the same level with hers. "It bothers you, not me."

"I don't believe you."

"Give me a chance to convince you then."

She shook her head.

"I'm asking you to have a meal with me—not to discuss the names of our grandchildren."

He grinned at her until she was grinning back at him. If only that secret of Angelika didn't exist between them. . . . Just eating dinner with him on Sunday wouldn't do any damage. But as she imagined sitting across the table from him, she felt the urge to confess how sorry she was to have played such an ugly game with him.

"I can't," she said abruptly, and when he nodded without trying to convince her, she felt she'd lost something she hadn't even begun to value.

After that discussion, she was sure Max Rudnick would buy his tobacco elsewhere, but he kept returning to the pay-library and talked with her father if she pretended to be busy, carrying stacks of books from one shelf unit to another. She thought of several other gentle ways to refuse his invitations, but he did not ask her again, not even when she began to join him and her father in their conversations.

One afternoon he told her father why he'd left his teaching job in Köln. He'd had a clash with one of the other teachers, who'd walked past his house one late afternoon when he was building a chicken coop in back of the garden.

"Can I take a look?" His colleague had studied the construction.

"Come on in."

"What are you building?"

Max Rudnick laid his hammer aside. "This will be a chicken coop. And that I build here is thanks to the Führer."

His colleague stared at him, horrified, and quickly walked away. Max Rudnick had intended his comment as a joke because it had become the custom that, wherever something was built, private or government, a sign would be attached to the building: *Dass ich hier baue verdanke ich dem Führer*—That I build here is thanks to the Führer.

The following day, the teacher did not speak to him in the faculty lunchroom, but in the afternoon he returned, opened the gate to the garden without asking, and stood by the chicken coop, watching while Max Rudnick continued the construction.

"Listen," the teacher finally said, "because of you I had a sleepless night."

"I'm sorry to hear that."

"You were ridiculing the Führer." He stood with his hands clasped in front of his stomach as if waiting for Max Rudnick to correct him, but when Max didn't speak up, he worked himself into a coughing fit. "I had to fight with myself," he sputtered, "and I'm still fighting with myself if I should notify the police. . . . They—they should know about you."

"You do what you need to do." Max resumed his hammering.

When he didn't hear anything for two weeks, he figured his colleague must have decided against informing on him. But one morning the principal blocked his way to his classroom and handed him a letter of introduction to an industrialist in Düsseldorf who wanted a tutor for his children.

"You were lucky. I'd suggest you practice greater caution in the future."

Max Rudnick was not allowed to say good-bye to his students or enter the classroom to collect his personal belongings from his desk. They'd already been packed into a paper bag, which felt ridiculously light as he carried it out of the brick building where he had taught for six years.

f o u r t e e n

———————————— ■ ————————————

1942

Trudi found the woman hiding in her mother's earth nest one chilly April afternoon when she carried the Persian hallway rug outside. She thought she must have imagined it—that flash of movement when she walked past the opening below the back of the house—and she kept walking and hoisted the rug across the metal rod and raised the rattan paddle. Her hair covered with an old scarf, she beat the rug, hard, while dust blossomed in thick plumes into the air. All at once she felt as though she were being watched. She turned toward the house, expecting to see her father's face in the kitchen window, but instead she noticed it again—that motion beneath the elevated part of the house—as though her mother had returned.

Trudi stood still, absolutely still. Her neck felt cold. Wielding the rattan paddle, she approached the boulders and aged timbers where her mother used to hide. She heard the breath before her eyes adjusted, not her own breath but one—no, more than one, much faster than hers.

She stopped next to the rack with the garden tools and gripped the handle of a shovel. "Who is there?" she called out, finding the sound of her voice reassuring. "Who is there?"

Silence. Then something shifted—like fabric being dragged across the ground. Her eyes made out two figures, one large, one small, crouched in the corner.

"He is just a child. Please." A high and urgent whisper as a child, a boy, was pushed toward Trudi. Behind him emerged a woman's face and graceful hands with red-lacquered nails, locked on the boy's shoulders as if in a death grip, holding him between herself and Trudi. "He is just a child."

For an instant there, standing within the half-dark and the smell of old earth, Trudi felt her own mother's hands on her shoulders, that taut grasp. *People die if you don't love them enough.* She saw the glitter in her mother's eyes, felt the secret kernels of sin beneath her mother's skin, heard that wild, wild laugh.

"Don't be afraid," Trudi said, as much to herself as to the boy.

The woman jerked him back against herself, locking both arms across his chest as if to dare Trudi to take him from her. Her red hat slipped down her blond hair and dangled on the back of her neck, held by a coated rubber band that cut across her throat like a badly healed scar.

The boy watched Trudi quietly, his eyes nearly at the same level with hers.

"Don't tell anyone we're here," the woman said.

"I won't."

"We'll leave. As soon as it's night."

"You can stay inside our house."

"It's not safe."

"Safer than out here."

"How do I know—" The woman stopped. She shuddered, and her arms tightened around the boy, whose eyes hadn't left Trudi's face once.

"I want to help." Trudi felt the woman's fear for her life, for the child's life, and when she reached forward and touched the boy's shoulder, her arms grew weak as though she'd been the one who'd carried his weight in her arms as they'd fled.

It was partly from the woman's jumbled words, but mostly from her anguished silences, that Trudi was able to assemble what had happened. They'd lost their house in Stuttgart eight months earlier when they'd been herded into one of the already crowded *jüdische Häuser*—Jewish houses—along with other families. During her first week there the woman had woken up each morning, thinking: This is as bad as it will ever get. But soon she realized that she was capable of withstanding far more than she'd ever imagined possible as long as she had her husband and child.

As others were shoved into the *jüdische Häuser,* the cold and hunger and constant bickering over the shrinking space grew worse. But even then she reminded herself that at least they were not taken away in cattle cars to unknown destinations, limited to bringing what they could fit into one suitcase. And she knew exactly why: There was a difference between her and those Jews who had been taken, a way of being in the world that did not allow for that kind of ultimate defeat. Not that she could escape the indignities altogether—that would have been unrealistic for someone like her who'd been trained as a biologist—but there were limits to the horrors she would let herself imagine, and that ability, she reasoned, kept her rational, that and her determination to survive, even if it meant taking a step away from whoever happened to be the next victim, and refusing to identify. The ones who suffered most, she'd observed, were those who panicked and saw no way out.

Her husband was like that. But she was able to keep him safe until one evening when he didn't return as usual with scavenged bits of coal. She waited for him through the night and all of the following day and the night after that until early morning. Then she woke her son, made him leave his cat in the cellar, and set out for the hotel where her husband's uncle had lived ever since he'd lost his villa. If only she had the money to stay in a hotel without worrying about food rations. She wanted to spit in the old man's face when he invited her and Konrad to have breakfast with him—"Before you go on your way," that's how he said it—but she stayed, though she couldn't bear to eat, and made her son finish his milk and eat her boiled egg too. Though convinced that she'd never see her husband again, she left a message for him with the uncle and accepted his gift of a leather suitcase before she returned to the *jüdische Haus.*

But the door stood open. One broken cup on the front steps was the only sign of struggle. All of the occupants had been taken away, validating the woman's beliefs about her survival as she scooped what she could use for herself and her son into the uncle's suitcase and a rucksack that used to belong to one of the other residents, a musician from Wildbad. With her nail scissors, she separated the cheap yellow

fabric of the *Judenstern* from her coat and burned it in the sink, together with her identification papers; but a faint outline of the star remained visible—much like the contour of a picture after it has been
taken from a wall—and she rubbed a pumice stone across the wide
lapel until it was no longer visible.

Her son's cat was still in the cellar, and he cried and refused to leave
the house until she allowed him to bring the cat along in his satchel.
The knowledge that they might be arrested any moment—on the
street, in the railroad station, on the train—set her face into a rigid
smile that would frighten her son into a silence so constant that she
wouldn't even have to remind him not to answer anyone's questions.

They took the train from Stuttgart to Frankfurt, where her
brother-in-law lived, but when they rang his doorbell, he was afraid
to take them in. She remembered a cousin, a distant cousin, who lived
near Düsseldorf in a small town called Burgdorf. On the train, she
was asked for her papers and travel orders, a question she had
dreaded, but the official accepted her fixed smile and explanation
that her papers had been stolen.

The cousin had disappeared from Burgdorf, and she found the hiding space beneath the pay-library when she got water from the brook
because the boy was thirsty. But she'd slipped on the muddy bank and
her hem was still dirty.

"See?" she said and raised the hem toward Trudi as if that one detail—the dirt-crusted fabric—proved that she had told the truth
about everything else.

"I saw white cows," the boy suddenly said. "I didn't know there
were white cows."

"Where did you see them?" Trudi asked softly.

"From the train. Many of them, all white. Have you ever seen
white cows?"

"Yes, at the Sternburg. It's a farm now, but hundreds of years ago
knights lived there. It still has a drawbridge."

"Like a castle?"

"With a beautiful round tower."

"And knights?"

"Not anymore. Just farmers."

"Will you take me there?"

Trudi hesitated. "If it ever becomes safe."

He nodded as though he'd anticipated her answer.

Trudi looked at his mother. "I'll come for you tonight and bring you into the house." She got the clean Persian carpet and spread it on the ground. "You can sit on this till then."

The woman's eyes probed into hers. "Promise you won't tell the police."

"I promise."

"If you do, I'll—"

"I promise."

"Who else lives with you?"

"Only my father. He'll want to help. Are you hungry?"

The woman nodded and let out a small sob as if humiliated by her hunger.

Trudi was back within minutes to bring them what was left of her meager rations of bread and of milk so thin it looked blue. *Blauer Heinrich*—blue Henry—people called the watered-down milk they'd come to associate with the war, and when the boy drank, he swallowed so hard that Trudi could hear him.

As soon as it was dark, she led the woman and the boy into the house, where she had closed the drapes and set the kitchen table with two soup plates and spoons. When her father took the woman's suitcase from her and welcomed her, that fighting stance left her body, and she slumped down in a chair as if, for the first time in months, she knew that others were looking out for her and that she no longer had to do it alone. Leo pressed one of his wife's flowered porcelain cups into the woman's hands. She drank the tea slowly and told them her name, Erna Neimann, and the boy's, Konrad.

Trudi heated the pea soup she'd made the day before, stretching it with water and a cubed potato to have enough for the four of them. "It's best if only two place settings are out at a time," she told Frau Neimann as she urged her and the boy to eat first. "In case the house is searched." She and her father waited to eat until they'd refilled the soup plates of their guests.

"I had a cat," Konrad said when he was finished. "She was on the train with us." His face took on an old look. "On the first train that is. I carried her in my satchel." He slid from his chair and opened the satchel for Trudi and her father to inspect. It was empty except for a folded dingy towel. "She slept in here," he explained, "until—"

"She kept making noise. Remember?" his mother said to him.

"She was drawing attention to us. How could we hide, having her with us?"

"She was a good cat."

His mother gripped her lower lip with her teeth. "She was, but the noise—"

"She was learning to be quiet."

"It takes a long time for animals to learn something. We didn't have that time."

But Konrad didn't look at his mother. His eyes were on Trudi. "My mother says she gave my cat away. In the railroad station. While I was in the bathroom." He closed his satchel. "I don't know if it is true."

His mother flinched and glanced at Trudi's father as if to enlist his help. "I gave the cat to a little girl. . . . A girl with a warm, expensive coat who has a good home for her."

He nodded, his face sad as though he not only accepted the loss of the cat but also his mother's lie.

Trudi felt the lie in the kitchen with them and knew that the mother was the kind of person who would twist the neck of a cat and drop it into a trash can, if that could protect her son and herself, and who would then lie about it. Trudi loved her for that. She would have done the same to protect the boy if he'd been hers. "Your mother is keeping you safe," she said.

"But I know that," the boy said as if surprised she needed to tell him.

Late in the evening, after Trudi and her father had settled their guests on a mattress in the sewing room, they went into the cellar to see if they could arrange a better hiding space. They moved the potato bin and the shelves, rigged up an old blanket to isolate one corner of the cellar from the rest, but whatever they did only made it look more conspicuous.

"Anyone could find them here," Trudi said.

"It's worthless without a second exit."

"A trap."

"We need to figure a way for them to escape if the police come into the house."

"The sewing room has to be enough for now."

"For now."

By midnight, they'd examined every nook of the cellar for possibil-ities and had relocated boxes and coals and the old laundry kettle without establishing a secure hiding place. Exhausted, Leo Montag dropped onto the wooden trunk that still contained the box Herr Abramowitz had hidden there more than three years earlier.

Trudi sat on the cellar stairs and rested her elbows on her knees. *"From your house to mine . . ."* Pia, she thought, feeling more of a connection to the animal tamer than she'd felt in a long time. She saw the two of them standing in the circus arena, their eyes at the same height, spinning the tale of the magical island. *". . . a tunnel made of jewels." "It led from your house to mine, yes."*

Yes. She leapt up. "What we need is a tunnel."

Her father stared at the stone walls and shook his head. "Too thick."

"Not if we get help."

Gradually, as it began to seem possible that, indeed, they could build a tunnel, their tiredness turned into fresh energy. Not only would they have a safe passage for the woman and the child, but for others who would come here after that. Without saying the words aloud to each other, they knew they were ready to take that risk. They considered both neighbors, the Weilers and the Blaus. Though Frau Weiler was younger than the Blaus and eager to help with food and other supplies, she couldn't be relied on because she'd never lie if questioned by the Gestapo.

Besides, Georg might come home on military leave and visit his mother. He'd been back once to marry Helga Stamm. After the wedding, he'd talked his mother into letting him take along his father's old skis since he was stationed near Zakopane, the Polish ski resort. "He'll probably gamble them away," Frau Weiler had told Frau Buttgereit; yet, she'd found herself comforted as she'd pictured her son skiing down snow-covered mountain peaks instead of aiming a rifle at another human being.

It would be best to have the tunnel lead into the Blaus' cellar, Trudi and her father agreed. Ever since he'd turned the young man away from his door, Herr Blau had changed. He would welcome the chance to help others. And his wife would keep quiet.

When Trudi finally went to sleep, she awoke soon after to a low, unfamiliar sound that came from above her ceiling, and for a moment she didn't dare move because she was certain the Gestapo had found out about the woman and the boy. She had an image of herself locked up inside a cell and felt furious at the woman for endangering her. But it was far too quiet for the Gestapo to be in the house—only that steady sound from the floor above. Ashamed for thinking only about herself, she wrapped herself in her bathrobe, lit a candle, and went up the stairs to the sewing room.

Listening hard, she laid the side of her face against the cool paint of the door. She could feel the boy's closeness. I'm not going to let them get you, she thought, I won't. Eyes half closed to hear better, she stood motionless. The sound was slow, grating. Carefully, she opened the door and stepped next to the mattress. She set down the candle holder. The woman and the boy were fast asleep, and he was grinding his teeth. His dark head rested on his mother's shoulder, and a deep frown made his features look far more grown-up than he was. Like a *Zwerg* man, Trudi thought, and clasped her hands in front of herself, her fingertips digging into the tender spots between the knuckles.

In the morning the water was frozen, and she had to break the ice in the porcelain basin on her dresser before she could wash. When she took breakfast upstairs to the sewing room, the boy was waiting for her on the other side of the door as if he'd stood there all night.

That first week, Erna Neimann slept much of the time, deeply, as though flinging herself into a bottomless lake. You'd find her asleep wherever you'd left her, while the boy would sit next to her, keeping vigil. Trudi took to spending more hours with him while her father did some of her duties in the pay-library, the connecting door to the hall locked to delay anyone who might try to enter that way. Trudi would tell fairy tales to the boy, comb his pale hair, build card towers for him, wash his face—always ready to rush him upstairs to the sewing room if someone came to the house.

When she found out that he didn't know how to swim, she taught him the movements in dry air. "Like a frog," she said. "Pretend you're a frog. That's how I learned to swim in the river." She made him lie with his belly on a stool and showed him how to move his arms and legs.

There was something invigorating about having Konrad in the house, something unsettling, too, because he made Trudi think of the times she'd imagined having a family of her own, a family as shown in magazines and movies, with a husband and children—even though her own body did not belong in any of those pictures; she would never look like those smiling young mothers, would never have what they had. And yet, sometimes she felt an unspoken communication with a small child she might see in church or on the street. She'd feel drawn, deeply, into the child's eyes, into a moment of recognition that choked her with love. *I know you,* something within her would chant, though her lips wouldn't make a sound. *I know you, and you will always remember me.* She'd feel a connection beyond that moment which—for a while at least—would lull the random longing for a child of her own. And when Konrad looked at her, it was with eyes that seemed to understand all that.

It pleased her that he, too, benefited from the narrow platform next to the kitchen cabinets which her father had built for her years ago. She let Konrad sit on her two special chairs, the birch chair with the short legs in the living room, and the eating chair with its three wide steps leading up to an elevated seat that made it possible for him to rest his elbows on the table.

Once, Trudi saw Erna Neimann enter the bathroom and back out immediately, fanning her face. Instantly she knew why. Her father's bad habit of lingering on the toilet with his cigarettes and newspaper had embarrassed her ever since she was a child, and she'd backed out of the bathroom many times just like that, waiting for the air to clear; yet, it made her feel defensive to see Frau Neimann do it. Still, the incident finally made her suggest to her father that, since others lived in the house now, it would be considerate to do his reading and smoking outside the bathroom. And when he said without hesitation, "Of course," she realized that she had asked for others what she would have liked for herself. No more, she thought. If he starts it again, I'll ask him to stop for me.

Nights she helped with the construction of a tunnel that would connect the two cellars. The wall of the Blaus' house was only a little over a meter away, but it took more than a week to dislodge the massive stones that had come from the river and dig a passage through the earth, deep enough so that it would not cause the ground above to collapse. Emil Hesping and Leo Montag did most of the digging, while Trudi and old Frau Blau carried the excess earth outside and distributed it in the brook. Even Konrad and his mother helped, though they did not leave the house: they carried pails of earth to the top of the cellar stairs, where Trudi and Frau Blau would pick them up.

Although the old tailor couldn't keep his hands from shaking, he insisted on doing his share of the digging. He was determined to make up for his failure of not sheltering the young man, but he was so slow that he got in the way.

"I bet Anton Immers would love to know what we're up to," he said one night in the cellar while trying to move an enormous stone, which Emil Hesping would take away in his car.

"No need to advertise it." Herr Hesping crouched and lifted the stone.

Frau Blau said she thought she'd heard years ago that Herr Immers' grandmother was Jewish. "If so," she said, "it would make sense why he's like that. . . . He'd be afraid of it, that part of himself. . . . Maybe that's why he can hate the Jews so."

"That man would deny his grandmother in a minute," her husband said.

"Even if his grandmother was Jewish," Trudi said, "he's probably convinced himself that she wasn't. You know how he is." Until now, she'd never thought of the butcher as afraid. She'd only seen his loathing for the Jews, his malice, but now she wondered if all of that was just fear and, perhaps, contempt for himself.

Recently, he'd hung up a flower shelf in the shop beneath the portraits of himself, the Führer, and the saint, and he was always fussing with the potted violets on that shelf, making you wait for your order and listen to his opinions while he watered the plants or snipped their dead stems and leaves. She pitied the prisoner from Cracow who had to help him in the shop. For some time now, prisoners of war had been arriving in town, some Greek and French, but mostly Eastern Europeans, who were assigned to farms and businesses for menial labor. Pressed into service, they had a place to stay, but no place they could run to without being hunted, and so they worked alongside the families. The Heidenreichs had a quiet, burly Frenchman from Avignon living with them who, the taxidermist suspected, understood German though he pretended not to. And Herr Buttgereit had warned the Polish prisoner who worked the fields with him to stay away from his daughters and reminded him that it was criminal for Poles to have sex relations with Germans.

"Herr Immers," Frau Blau said, "tells everyone who comes into his store that, if Germany loses the war, everyone's going to die . . . that there'll be no future."

Emil Hesping laughed, and his thick eyebrows touched above his nose. "There'll be even less of a future if the Nazis win the war," he said with absolute assurance, and shoveled harder.

There was something dangerous in his laugh, something that gave Trudi the feeling that, to him, building the tunnel was an adventure, a way of getting back at the Führer. It made her wish her father hadn't asked for his help. But Herr Hesping knew how to get fugitives out of the country; he was the one with connections, among them his brother, the bishop, who'd often disapproved of Emil's schemes and now found himself united with him in the same quest.

She watched him dig, his movements fast, his face and bald head smudged with earth.

"I've been wanting to ask you something for some time now," he whispered to her when he caught her looking at him.

She glanced around, startled. Her father was loosening mortar from an egg-shaped rock, and the others weren't close enough to hear. "What?"

"That day of your mother's funeral . . ."

She felt the gravel under her mother's skin, saw the motorcycle tilt—

"Why did you play the piano, Trudi?"

She didn't remember playing the piano, and when she told him, he said, "I wanted to make sure I remembered it correctly."

"Well, I didn't." She looked at him, puzzled, and when he said nothing else, she picked up a pail and filled it with dirt.

When Leo Montag and Emil Hesping tried to do the heavy lifting and digging for old Herr Blau, he objected, and the two put in a secret shift one night after the Blaus had gone to sleep. If Herr Blau noticed the progress on the tunnel the following night, he didn't mention it, perhaps because he was preoccupied with ideas for decorating his cellar. He talked about hanging up pictures to brighten the space for his Jewish visitors, as he called them, and he dragged bolts of fabric downstairs, intent on covering long pillows that would double as mattresses if laid side by side.

When Leo pointed out that the cellar had to look like a cellar, and that any touches of comfort like that would give it away as a hiding place, Herr Blau was disappointed.

"There's so much else you can do with the fabric," Emil Hesping comforted him. "They'll need clothes. Blankets."

Sometimes, while hauling pails of earth to the brook, Trudi would think of Max Rudnick and wonder where he was. She felt sure he'd want to help with the tunnel if she asked him. Not that she would—still, she had a feeling she could trust him. He hadn't come to the library in weeks, and she hoped nothing had happened to him. Not that she missed him, she reminded herself.

Working with the others on the tunnel—dirty, sweaty, and aching—she felt more of a sense of belonging to a community than she ever had before. When finished, the passage would allow people to escape from one house to the other in moments. The openings in the wall would be well hidden: on the Blaus' side, an old armoire was to be pushed in front of the gap, while the Montags had already emptied their potato bin to make it light enough for one person to pull in front of their entrance. If the police searched one house, the fugitives would enter the other house through the tunnel and pull the façade back into place. It would be a problem if both houses were searched at the same time: the tunnel was so short and low that, at most, two people could hide inside, and then only for a short while. But mostly the fugitives would live on the first floors of the houses, close enough to the cellar stairs to rush down if anyone knocked at the door.

The day after the tunnel was completed, Leo Montag was fixing sugar-and-margarine bread for the boy in the kitchen, when Frau Neimann pulled Trudi into the hall. Her pretty hands were rough, chapped, and only a few flecks of polish still clung to her fingernails.

"He hates me," she whispered urgently.

"Who?"

"Konrad. Because of the cat."

"Oh no. He just misses his cat."

"Has he said anything to you, Fräulein Montag?" Frau Neimann was watching her with such intensity that Trudi could only shake her head. "He's the only one I have left. I can't bear him hating me."

"Konrad doesn't hate you."

"Are you sure? He talks more with you than with me."

Trudi felt mortified by her sudden satisfaction that the boy preferred her to his mother. "I'm sure he can see that you feel terrible about the cat."

For a moment, the woman's eyes looked almost amused. Then she smiled. But beneath that smile lay something else, the possibility of an enormous coldness. "It's not the cat I care about," she murmured.

Trudi didn't know what to answer. "Your hands," she finally said, "we need to do something about your hands."

"My hands?"

"Wait here." She rushed up the stairs and into her room, grimacing to herself as she grasped her last bottle of hand lotion. *"You can tell so much by a woman's hands,"* Frau Simon had taught her. Sometimes Trudi had done without shampoo, using soap on her hair so that she could afford the lotion. If she applied it sparingly, this bottle would last her a few months.

Before she could change her mind, she took it downstairs. "For you," she said.

Frau Neimann eagerly accepted the gift, then hesitated. "Only if you have more for yourself." She extended the bottle halfway toward Trudi.

"You keep it."

"We could share it."

"While you're here. But then it's yours to take along."

Erna Neimann's face turned bone white, and she leaned against the wall.

"What is it?" Trudi took hold of her elbow.

"You're thinking of sending us away. That's why you're giving me this."

"No. No. You can stay. As long as we can keep you safe here. But that may change. You know that."

Frau Neimann nodded. "I know."

It confused Trudi that despite the suffering all around her, some parts of life were going on in a normal way and that she could enjoy them— like the scents from the new grass and the blossoms of the lilac bushes, the warmth of the spring sun on her arms, the playful dips of the swallows as they swooped down to the brook. Somehow, this spring was infusing her with new strength and hope, a deceptive hope, she reminded herself, and yet it soothed her, took her back to the river where, in the shallows below the weeping willows, the water had taken on a peculiar shade of opaque green as though it had soaked up the color of the new leaves, a green that suggested tranquillity, reverence almost. On the opposite bank, sheep grazed in the meadow.

She wished she could take Konrad to the river, but since that would have endangered him, she painted the Rhein for him with words that let him see how, beyond the sheltered bay, the river kept flowing, steady and clear, though there certainly were rocks in the riverbed that created some turbulence. With her stories, she took the boy to the meadows and the fairgrounds and the Sternhof, let him fill his chest with the spring air, and found that, in the telling, all those places became even more real for her. She relished the power of the stories to keep the outdoor world alive for the boy and, like a magician, replaced the sheep with white cows and positioned a parrot in the tower of the *Rathaus*, just for Konrad.

She didn't tell the boy about the caricatures of Jews in the newspaper; about the pastor in Neuss who'd been sent to the KZ for harboring Jews; about a bank clerk only four blocks away who'd been forced to take off her clothes and then had been beaten with rifle butts for giving two hard-boiled eggs to her Jewish neighbor who'd been about to be deported. She didn't tell the boy how often she woke up at night, paralyzed by what could happen to her and her father if they were caught, and how she'd get stuck trying to decide what would be the worst possible fate.

The boy would ask her about those white cows whenever she'd return from one of her walks, and she'd tell him there'd been eight on the other side of the river, the same number as the first day she'd mentioned them because to take any of them away might have terrified him.

Konrad had been told to stay away from the windows so that no one could see him from outside, but one morning Trudi found him behind the lace curtain of the dining room, his face pressed against the glass.

"What are you doing?" Quickly, she pulled him away and scanned the street. It was empty.

"Waiting. For my cat."

She took him into the living room and sat with him on the velvet sofa, wishing she could get a cat for him. But eventually Konrad would have to leave for another hiding place, and a cat would only mean one more loss.

"If you swear not to go near the window again, I'll tell you a story about a cat."

He nodded.

"A very special cat."

"I swear." He drew closer.

She laid one arm around his shoulders. Both their feet dangled about the same distance above the floor. She liked that. "It's about a cat and the father of my school friend Eva. . . . Her father, you see, he was ill. No one knew what was wrong with him, but he was too weak to get up, so weak he couldn't lift a teacup if it was half full. . . ." She pretended to pick up a cup and let her wrist go limp. "Her father also was deadly afraid. Of cats. He believed cats choke people by sleeping on their throats. That's why he kept his windows closed every single night."

"Even in summer?" Konrad asked, just as Trudi had asked Eva nearly twenty years before.

"Even in summer." She remembered how amazed she, too, had felt, and she smiled at the boy. "But Eva figured out that her father's illness was that terrible fear. She was only a little older than you and, like you, very smart. Eva figured if she could take her father's fear of cats away, he'd get well again. One night—after her parents were asleep—she sneaked into their bedroom and opened the window." She described the window for the boy, even the wind that billowed the fine lace curtains and two flies on the windowsill. "And before Eva could step back, a cat she'd never seen before—a sleek, amber cat with white paws—"

"My cat had white paws."

"She must have been a good-looking cat."

"She was." Konrad sounded pleased.

"Well, you see, that cat with paws like your cat's—it did exactly what Eva's father had been afraid of. It settled itself on his throat. . . ." Trudi raised one hand to the boy's throat. "And just when Eva was going to yank the cat from her father's throat, he opened his eyes. Like this." She widened her eyes. "Eva's father stared into the cat's eyes. They were like the lights of a faraway car that's coming closer—you've seen that, haven't you?"

Konrad nodded.

"Eva's father couldn't look away. But he kept breathing . . . breathing. . . ." Trudi stopped, trying to figure where the story was taking her, letting it unfurl within her till she could see Eva standing by her father's bed, wearing her thin green dress from first grade. And then she told Konrad what she saw. "Eva stood by her father's bed for a long time. . . . Her feet were freezing. But her father didn't notice her. He didn't look at anyone except that cat—the cat's eyes, that is—and neither of them blinked. Not even once. Toward morning the cat arched itself up from the throat of Eva's father, brushed its whiskers against the underside of his chin, and leapt through the bedroom window without touching the windowsill. It looked as if it were flying, and Eva didn't hear it touch the ground at all."

Konrad let out a deep breath. "I bet my cat could fly like that."

Trudi gave him a hug. "She must be a remarkable cat."

"When I find her, she can sleep on my throat."

"That may not be so good," Trudi said quickly.

"Do you think I'll find her?"

"Have you ever heard that cats have nine lives?"

He frowned.

She took his hands into hers and counted nine of his fingers. "Let's say your cat had her first life with you and her second life with the little girl from the railroad station. . . ." She folded two of his fingers toward his palm. "How many lives does she have left to find you?"

He looked at his fingers. "Seven," he said. "Did Eva see her cat again?"

"I don't believe so. But then it wasn't her cat to start out with."

"My cat was mine. Since she was a kitten. My father brought her home." He blinked as though he'd startled himself by talking about his father.

Maybe he can't let himself think about his father yet, Trudi thought. Maybe all he can let himself think of is that cat. She rubbed his hands between hers. "Eva went back to sleep after the cat was gone," she told him, "and when she woke up, she heard her father's voice downstairs. He was up and dressed—she'd never seen him up and dressed—and he lifted her up when she came running down the steps and—"

Konrad interrupted. "Before, he couldn't even lift a cup."

"That's right. Before that cat came to lie on his throat, he was very weak. You know what he told Eva when he set her back down on the ground? He told her he'd had a dream that night, a dream of a cat that had made him well."

"Did Eva tell him the truth?"

"No."

"Why not?"

"Because he was cured. Better to let him believe what he needed to believe."

"What if what you want to believe is a lie?"

Trudi waited.

"Like about my cat . . . Sometimes my mother lies to me."

"I can tell that your mother loves you a lot."

He nodded as though that had nothing to do with it.

"Running away and hiding . . . the way you and your mother have to—it's awfully hard, Konrad. Some people may do things they normally wouldn't do."

"I don't think there was a little girl."

Trudi stroked his hair.

"I think my cat still lives in that railroad station."

"Well—it wouldn't be such a bad place. Just think . . . it would be warm enough and people would feed the cat, even play with her."

"I'll go there. When the war is finished."

She felt dizzy with a longing for peace, a longing as powerful as the passion with which she used to will her body to grow, as consuming as the passion that had fueled her revenge on the boys who'd humiliated her. And what she wanted more than anything that moment was for all the differences between people to matter no more—differences in size and race and belief—differences that had become justification for destruction.

Nights, the woman and the boy slept in the kitchen. Leo Montag had rehearsed their escape with them so many times—a quick rap against the wall—that even the boy would automatically reach for his blankets and run down the stairs. One of the trunks in the cellar was left open for the bedding, and the two would throw everything in there, close the lid, climb into the damp tunnel, and pull the empty potato bin into place. On the Blaus' side, they'd push the armoire aside, replace it, and hide inside. Herr Blau kept a feather puff and pillows for them in the armoire, and Herr Hesping had drilled air holes into the top, which you could only see if you climbed on a chair.

To stay inside the tunnel for longer than a few minutes was even harder than they'd thought because water kept seeping through the ground. At first, Herr Blau had tried to line the tunnel with blankets, but they'd soaked through so quickly that they were useless. Finally, Trudi remembered that the Weskopps used to go camping, and she managed to trade two years of free library books for the huge tent, dodging the widow's question about what she was going to do with it. After Herr Blau cut the green canvas to fit the walls of the tunnel, the moisture still kept coming through, but at least the woman and the boy didn't get smeared by mud each time they fled to the tunnel.

So far, none of the visitors to the Montags' house had been a real danger to the fugitives, and if any of them noticed that Trudi and her father rushed them out of the front door soon after they arrived, they didn't say so.

"We'll stop over soon," Leo would say, or, "Come by the library tomorrow when it's open. I'll have time to talk then."

But it hurt Trudi, having to lie to Matthias Berger to keep him from coming back. And her father—he used to look forward to those visits too. Matthias had been playing chess with him about once a week and had ended each of his visits by playing the piano. His lessons with Fräulein Birnsteig had refined his technique without diminishing his intensity. He was accustomed to staying for hours at a time—an impossible risk now with Frau Neimann and Konrad in the house.

"The piano is broken," Trudi told him.

"Let me take a look. Maybe I can fix it."

"It needs major work. I— I'll let you know when it's ready."

"I could still play chess with your father."

"He hasn't been up to chess much lately. Better to wait for the piano. . . ."

Matthias left, confused she could tell, as she watched the slope of his shoulders. Even before he'd turned away from her, she'd already missed him. She worried about his headaches; though he never complained about them, she usually could see when he was about to get one because he'd press his palms against his temples as if to keep the pain out, and she'd make him camomile tea or urge him to lie down on the sofa until he felt better.

She would have liked to tell the truth to Matthias and Eva and the Abramowitzs, who'd been forced to vacate their house and now lived in one furnished room on Lindenstrasse, but Emil Hesping had impressed on her that each additional person who knew about the fugitives increased the risk of capture. "For all of us," he'd said.

He was against including Frau Weiler in any way, but since it was impossible to feed four on food rations that were barely enough for two, Leo managed to enlist Frau Weiler's support by asking her if she could spare some groceries for two people he knew were in need. "That's all I can tell you, Hedwig," he said when she wanted to know more.

"It's easy enough," she said, "with a grocery store. Setting aside a bit. Even the government can't always keep track, right? Things spoil, after all. . . ."

Though Ilse Abramowitz no longer received letters from Frau Simon, she kept mailing packages, depleting her own scant resources as if sending the supplies would keep her Jewish friends from vanishing.

"They'll be back," she insisted, refusing to listen to her husband's speculation that they might have already been killed in camps.

It was a Wednesday evening in May, and they were alone in their tiny room. He sat on the bed, which they'd covered with an embroidered tablecloth to make it look more like a sofa. The linen cloth was one of the few things they'd managed to bring from their house. He was reading the photography book that someone—no doubt, the unknown benefactor—had left outside his door early that morning. Despite his gratitude, he felt betrayed because what he really needed—protection for himself and his wife—not even the unknown benefactor could give him.

Ilse was darning socks at the scarred table, a silver thimble on her right forefinger. "They're for work, those camps," she said.

"That's what they tell us."

"You can't prove any of this," she cried.

He nodded, gravely, and told her she was right. "I can't prove any of this, Ilse." His hands itched. They'd been puffy and red for nearly three months, ever since he'd started forced labor in the soap factory. It took half an hour by streetcar and another half hour to walk there. Quite a few Russian prisoners worked alongside the Jews, and they weren't allowed to talk to each other.

"I'd rather be subjected to injustice," his wife said, "than to be the one who inflicts it on others."

"It doesn't have to be one or the other."

"But given a choice, Michel. If you had a choice . . . The price they pay is so much higher."

"Nonsense," he said. "If you—"

"They might survive, but they'll never recover."

He raised his hand to ward off the compassion in her voice—compassion not for their own people, but for the persecutors.

"And maybe the worst thing is that they won't know. . . ." Her voice grew soft. ". . . that they mistake what they are for being human."

"Don't ask me to feel sorry for them."

She pulled the wicker sewing basket closer and busied herself with the mending of his black socks, weaving the thread through the thinning material again and again and again—anything, her husband thought, to keep from thinking about what was happening to their people. As she finished mending the hole, she methodically pulled the thread through, twice, to make a knot, and then bit it off with her even teeth, although the scissors lay next to her. He used to remind her that she'd ruin her teeth doing that. But what difference did it make now?

As she rolled the sock with its matching partner into a tight, neat ball and picked up another sock, Michel Abramowitz turned the page in his book, though he couldn't remember a single word he'd read. There was so much he couldn't say to Ilse. He couldn't tell her about the rumors he'd heard of prisoners who'd had to undress in groups before they'd been shot in the neck. It was something he kept thinking about—especially at night when he lay awake. How could any country be this cruel, humiliating people before killing them with such gruesome efficiency? And what he kept coming back to was the question of the clothes. What had happened to the clothes after the people had been shot? It seemed like a petty question, considering the scope of devastation, and yet it was the one that tortured him. He'd find himself obsessed with visions of those clothes, being handed to new prisoners, who would wear them for a while until they, too, would be forced to strip for their deaths. And so on, and so on—until the one constant element was those clothes.

His wife had finished darning the next sock and was biting off the thread.

It's amazing, Michel thought, what people can get used to and still call life: we have lost most of our belongings; we have been crowded into small rooms; we're not allowed to leave our hometown; we can't use public transportation unless we work more than seven kilometers from home; we're no longer permitted to possess cameras or binoculars or opera glasses or electrical appliances; we've had to turn over our radios and jewelry; we're not allowed outside our rooms between eight at night and six in the morning; we've been kicked, beaten, and humiliated; we've had our families ripped from us . . . and yet, and yet, we go on living.

He thought of all the times he'd raged against his wife for accepting each new attack with dignity. "*Deine Anpassungsfähigkeit*—your ability to adapt—is far more dangerous to you than any of them will ever be. . . ." But how much better was he? He'd come to accept all that too—only out of fear.

"Don't work so hard, Ilse," he said gently.

Looking up, she smiled at him and threaded her needle.

It occurred to him how—all at once it seemed—she'd aged rapidly, the fine wrinkles in her face deepening, that stiffness in her shoulders and hands. Although still lovely, she had lost the essence, the spirit. . . . Still, she held on to that dignity of hers, keeping up her appearance and her hope even though—as of tomorrow—she too would have to work in the soap factory. At sixty, she was far too old for heavy work like that. But the new laws said that Jewish men up to seventy-five and Jewish women up to seventy had to do forced labor. That meant another thirteen years for him. Michel couldn't allow himself to think like that. Hitler's madness had to stop. Had to be stopped. Every night he prayed for Hitler's assassination.

At least his son had gotten out in time. And he and Ilse had come so close. At the Argentinean consulate in Düsseldorf, they'd received confirmation that they would get visas. But first, they'd been told, they had to get certificates of health and the necessary vaccinations. Four times they'd gone through the process, and each time a letter had arrived that their visas could not be issued since new directions from Argentina had arrived. Four times their son had sent the money for their journey, and four times they'd paid for that journey which, now, he doubted they would ever make.

And then there was his daughter, who had decided to divorce her husband because, she said, it would harm his practice if he stayed married to a Jewish woman. Noble, Michel Abramowitz thought; even here Ruth protects him. But he knew Fritz well enough to figure that he'd requested the divorce to cleanse himself from any Jewish connection. Ruth had found work in a small clinic in Dresden, and she'd written her parents not to worry about her, that her room had a sink and a view of the Zwinger.

A view of the Zwinger, Michel Abramowitz thought. As if that solved everything.

His wife rolled up the last socks. Gathering scissors and needles into the basket, she placed the tight balls of socks in the curve of her elbow and carried them to the dresser. "Ready to go to sleep?"

Michel closed his book. Together, they lifted the tablecloth from the bed, shook out its creases, and stepped toward each other to fold its length like so many decades of desire until the gap between them had waned to the thickness of the folded square of embroidered linen.

f i f t e e n

■

1 9 4 2

ALEXANDER STURM INSISTED ON BEING PRESENT WHEN HIS WIFE WAS
questioned about her parents. Stunned that his request had been
granted, he sat next to her; yet, his one act of assertion had drained
him so of his fighting spirit, that he could only listen silently as she denied any knowledge of her parents' plans to escape. He admired how
calmly she lied, how regally she held up her head. She hadn't looked
that composed the night her parents had left in a car they'd bought on
the black market. They'd been urging Eva to come with them, south,
and across the border into Switzerland, where Eva's brothers had settled after completing their studies.

"You know I'd go if Alexander came along. . . ." She was crying,
her eyes blurred behind her boyish glasses.

Alexander told her again it was a lot less safe—to drive through
Germany like that—than to wait out the war in Burgdorf. "It can't
last much longer," he said, and he listed all the laws her parents were
breaking. "Simply being out at night, not wearing the yellow star,
owning valuables . . ." He felt furious with Eva's father, who was
practically helpless, a burden, yet was prepared to risk his wife's and

daughter's lives with his impossible scheme for escape. "You can be stopped. Arrested. Shot."

And now Eva had to deal with the aftermath.

He was convinced the officer didn't believe her when she said she'd last seen her parents five days before. No, she had not noticed anything unusual. Her father had been resting in the living room—"he's an invalid, as you certainly must know"—while she and her mother had made potato pancakes in the kitchen. No, her husband had worked late that evening. No, her parents did not own a car. No . . .

Several times during the interrogation Alexander sensed Eva glancing at him as if for confirmation, but he felt paralyzed with fear. He'd always been able to count on himself to do the proper thing, to schedule and manage his life as well as his work, to follow the law. He couldn't believe his stupidity at having demanded to be here with Eva. If both of them were to be arrested, he wouldn't be able to do anything for her. Or myself, he thought, his palms wet.

He was shocked when he and Eva were allowed to leave. As he stepped out on the sidewalk, the sun on his forehead, he wanted to cry with gratitude. The sky was crisp and blue, and the wind carried the scent of the river meadows and the cooing of pigeons. Eva's arm locked into his, he hurried her home, all along checking over his shoulder, positive they were being followed. He didn't answer her until they were inside their locked apartment.

"What is it?" She grasped him by the hands. Behind her glasses her eyes looked magnified.

He slumped against the wall. "We have to hide you. We—"

"Wait. If I wanted to hide, I could have gone with my parents."

"There'll be other questions. They'll come for you again."

"And I'll answer them. As I did today."

"We were lucky today. You heard what they said, that they'll contact you if they need to know more."

"Your hands are ice cold."

He pulled them from her. "Your parents should have thought of this before they—"

"Maybe you should have thought of this before you refused to come with us."

"I didn't make you stay behind."

"Oh, but you did," she said softly. "I'm still here because of you."

He drew her close, his chest heaving. "I don't want to lose you, Eva." But her body felt stiff in his arms, and she turned her face away from him. "I'm sorry." He thought of the stories he and Eva had heard and retold to one another to keep up their courage, stories of courage—about the doctor who'd joined a group of his Jewish patients about to be transported to Poland, the young woman who'd accompanied her Jewish husband to the KZ. Until today Alexander had believed that he, too, would make that choice. But today he had tasted the danger, had felt the power of the enemy. He wished he had the courage of the doctor, of the woman, but what he couldn't stop thinking was, *fools. . . . Fools.*

"We have to hide you, Eva," he said.

"You need to hide," Trudi Montag told Eva that evening.

"Did Alexander talk with you?"

"No, I heard it from Jutta Malter. She told me about the interrogation this afternoon. I wanted to come right over, but I thought it would be better to wait until after dark."

"Alexander is after me to go into hiding. I don't want to."

"Of course not. No one wants to hide. But sometimes it's necessary. At least for a while." Trudi hoisted herself onto the Danish sofa with the teak armrests.

"I'm so afraid that something happened to my parents. I wouldn't even know. . . . And I can't imagine hiding in some strange place."

"It doesn't have to be a strange place."

Eva frowned.

"Think of it as . . . a visit. To a friend. An old school friend."

"Oh, no. I'm not putting you and your father in danger."

Trudi thought of Frau Neimann, who never once had shown concern for the risk taken by those who hid her. "That's all very admirable," she told Eva, "but not—"

"A few weeks from now they will have forgotten about my parents."

"Good. Maybe then it'll be all right for you to surface."

"In the meantime, they'll come to your house and find me and arrest you and your father in the process."

"Come here." Trudi motioned to the sofa. Her polished leather shoes dangled high above the parquet floor.

Eva sat down next to Trudi, her spine as straight as it had been in school—an example of good posture. The many tiny pleats of her skirt spread around her. She didn't look at Trudi but at her stuffed owls and sparrows and robins and swallows, preserved on the tops of the bookshelves in eternal poses of flight.

"They wouldn't find you," Trudi said.

"You have a potion that will make me invisible, right?"

"Let's say—" Trudi hesitated. "Let's say we're prepared."

"My cat lives in a railroad station."

"What?" Eva blinked, still half asleep. A boy's face was floating above her, blond hair swinging above his eyebrows. All at once she remembered Trudi bringing her here during the night, showing her a tunnel before she'd made up a bed for her on the kitchen floor near the cellar door.

"My cat lives in a railroad station."

Eva fumbled for her glasses. The boy was bending over her. Beyond him, a woman slept, curled on her side, her back toward them.

"People feed my cat. Every day."

"What a lucky cat."

He nodded. "She doesn't need much."

"What's your name?" Eva linked her arms beneath her neck.

"Konrad."

She almost said, "Eva Sturm," but figured it would be better for the boy not to know her last name if he ever were questioned. "You can call me Eva."

"Do you like to watch cats eat?"

"How do they eat?"

"Tidy. Not like dogs. Dogs slobber all over the place."

Trudi came into the kitchen with a bucket of coals and opened the front of the stove. "Did you sleep well?"

Eva yawned. "Better than I thought I would."

"My cat is waiting for me to come back to the railroad station," the boy said.

"That's good," Eva said.

"Do you think she will turn into a magical cat?"

The boy's mother mumbled something in her sleep and turned on her stomach, her face screened by her hair.

"A magical cat?" Eva whispered.

"Like your father's cat."

"The cat that slept on your father's throat," Trudi explained quickly. "I told Konrad about the cat you let into your father's bedroom so that she could cure him." Her voice implored Eva to go along with her story.

"Ah, that cat," Eva said, but in her eyes Trudi read the awareness of another cat—the kitten in Hans-Jürgen's outstretched arms, a living streak of fur—and for a moment they both were there again, girls in that barn, whirling, whirling within that immense church space and the smell of animals and straw, suspended in that ruthless sliver of time before the kitten was relinquished to its death.

"And then . . ." the boy said, "your father lifted you up."

"Yes . . . ?" Eva said slowly.

"He got strong enough to lift you up. Before the cat made him well, he couldn't even lift a cup."

". . . not even a cup."

"Did you see the cat again?"

She glanced past the boy at Trudi, who was shaking her head. "No," Eva said, "I never saw the cat again."

The boy looked disappointed.

"I read about her, though," Eva said.

Trudi stepped closer.

"I read about her in a magazine," Eva said. "She became very famous. A doctor—a Frau Doktor—wrote an article about the cat. The Frau Doktor used the cat to . . . to—"

"To cure those patients she couldn't help," Trudi said.

"Right. That's what she did."

"My cat has nine lives. Only two of them are used up."

"Eva knows a good trick for people who have to hide," Trudi said.

"I do?"

"Teach Konrad what to do if he has to sneeze."

Eva frowned and shook her head.

"The thing with your tongue. Remember?"

"I'd forgotten about that."

"I used to practice it."

"Then you show him."

"No, it came from you."

Eva sat up and pushed the blanket away. Her pleated skirt was wrinkled. "Watch this." Bringing her face close to the boy's, she opened her mouth wide, touched the tip of her tongue to the roof of her mouth, and wiggled it. "Now you do it."

The boy tried it and laughed. "It tickles."

"It's supposed to tickle, silly."

"An old Indian trick," Trudi said. "It keeps you from sneezing if you're hiding. But if you laugh, it doesn't do any good."

"That's right," Eva warned. "If you laugh, it—" She stopped and reached for Trudi. "Now I remember what you said that day when I showed you. God—"

Trudi knelt down by Eva's pillow. "What is it?"

"You said you didn't know who would want to capture us."

"Now we know." Trudi held her.

Eva's eyes clouded with defeat. "But Konrad won't let anything happen to us," she said resolutely. "Konrad will keep very, very quiet because he has things to do after all this is over. Konrad has a cat he needs to get from a railroad station."

The boy beamed at her.

Frau Neimann regarded Eva's arrival with alarm, and though Trudi tried to reassure her, she acted as though the new fugitive endangered all of them. But the boy was fascinated by Eva, who let him try on her dark-rimmed glasses; he liked to touch the intricate blue-and-silver pin that Eva's mother used to wear and had pinned to Eva's blouse the night they'd fled.

One evening, the third week of Eva's stay, Trudi braided her friend's hair in the living room while the others were still in the kitchen. The gathered collar of Eva's blouse lay below the delicate half ring of bones that linked her shoulder blades and the hollow at the base of her throat, and the fabric was the same shade of ivory as her skin. As Trudi stood behind Eva's chair and the dark strands of hair glided through her fingers, it was as though the two of them were back at the second-grade spring concert at Fräulein Birnsteig's mansion. She smelled the cut grass and the lilacs in the formal garden, saw the ivy winding up the white walls, heard the splendid piano music that poured from the open glass doors, and felt Eva's fingers move through her hair. . . .

"I miss him," Eva said.

Trudi recalled the sharp bliss of that concert evening, and her an-

guish when the other kids had spurned Eva the next day in school. For
an instant there, as she let her fingers weave the hair, she felt as if back
then she had tainted Eva with her difference, and that because of it
she was responsible for her persecution now; and even though she
knew it wasn't like that at all, it felt as though she personified the difference that made Eva an outcast.

"I wish I could sleep with him tonight. . . ."

Trudi's arms felt heavy and cold. She wanted to drop them, but
then the braid would come undone.

"People don't really know Alexander. He doesn't let them know
him—the way he really is. People see him as a hard-working man,
quite content with what he does . . . a bit formal."

Trudi had heard all that about Alexander, that and how much it
mattered to him what the town thought of him. Formal was too mild
a description for him. Stuffy was more like it. People like Alexander
made her impatient: they focused so much on their manners that they
missed the essence of what was going on.

"He took such a risk, coming with me to the police station," Eva
said. "Now I know that even if things get worse, if I get deported—"

"Don't even think about that."

"—he would come along. Don't you see how much comfort that
gives me—knowing he would?"

"I want you to take your comfort from knowing you won't get
caught. You hear me?"

Eva had never thought as much about her husband as during those
weeks she'd lived in Trudi's house. She'd only seen him once, when
he'd come without warning late one night, sending her and the boy
and his mother scurrying into the tunnel.

"I won't allow this." Leo Montag admonished Alexander, his voice
sterner than Trudi had ever heard it. "The Gestapo know by now that
your wife is hiding somewhere. All they need to do is follow you and
you'll lead them right here."

"No one was watching me."

"You can't be the judge of that. Not in the dark."

"I was careful."

"So are they."

"I—"

"This is not for discussion. I'm telling you not to come back.
You're jeopardizing all of us."

When Alexander embraced Eva before leaving, he moaned into her hair. "I wish you could come with me tonight. . . ." But immediately he said, "No, I'm selfish. Don't listen to me. I'm selfish. It's just that I want you so much."

"I want to be with you, too."

The rest of that night, Eva felt angry with Trudi and her father. How could they be so intolerant? How could they possibly understand a love like hers? Leo had been a widower for as long as Eva could recall, and Trudi—well, Trudi with her body the way it was would never experience the kind of passion that Eva knew.

As Trudi wound a thin ribbon around the end of the braid, Eva sighed. "I keep thinking about Alexander."

"Remember that time at the beer garden, about nine years ago? You and Alexander weren't engaged yet."

Eva smiled and nodded. They'd danced that night, and even when they'd stepped away from one another, she'd still felt it—that pull—as though they were caressing the air between them. She hadn't expected that pull to last this long, two years of courtship and seven of marriage, but if anything, it had become stronger with the years.

"You stopped at our table," Trudi said, her hands on Eva's shoulders as if to keep her from turning around and looking at her face.

Eva had to think for a moment. Across from her, the spidery pattern of ferns melted into the faded brown background of the wallpaper. When she and Trudi had been girls, those ferns had been white, but over the years they'd turned ashen, diminishing the contrast between them and what once had been a deep chocolate brown.

"At the beer garden," Trudi prompted her.

"You . . . you were with Ingrid Baum and Klaus Malter."

"Did you see me dance with him?"

"Yes."

"What did you see?"

"What do you mean?"

"Tell me what you saw."

"I saw you dance. . . ."

"And—"

"And Klaus kissed you."

Behind her, Trudi let out a breath—a single breath so deep that it felt to Eva it must have been held inside forever.

"What's wrong, Trudi?" She swiveled around and stared at her.

Trudi's eyes had gone pale and distant in her broad face.

"Trudi?"

"No one— No one ever said anything."

"What was there to say?" Eva asked, and then—catching herself—said softly, "Of course."

Trudi felt a cold swell of anger. "Of course what?"

"Nothing."

"Of course it has been the only kiss in poor Trudi's life. . . ." Now her eyes were tearing into Eva. "Is that what you're thinking, Eva Sturm?"

"I didn't mean anything like that."

"Then why did you say *of course?*"

"Because I didn't understand why you were asking me about that night. The *of course* had to do with Klaus. He said nothing about kissing you?"

"Not once."

"That— that swine. Until now, I had a much higher opinion of him."

"But you saw us."

"Yes, I saw you." Eva took Trudi's face between her hands. Her fingers lay warm against Trudi's wide jawbone and cheeks. "You looked beautiful that night."

"At times I've wondered if it really happened."

"It did." The crest of Eva's birthmark showed above the gathered collar of her blouse, and Trudi saw her as she had stood that long-ago day by the brook, her undershirt pulled up to reveal her own difference. She wondered if the mark had grown fainter as Eva's skin had stretched to accommodate her breasts and suddenly felt embarrassed because she would have liked to see if the birthmark still covered Eva's nipples. *"And when I'll have babies, they'll drink red milk from me."* Now Eva might never have babies. Not if she stays in this country, Trudi thought, wishing she could keep her friend sheltered within the fairy-tale vines she had once dreamed for her.

"I remember watching you as you danced," Eva said. "I remember feeling surprised because I didn't know you could dance so well."

"I didn't know how to dance."

"You must have some real talent then."

"What else? What else did you see?"

Eva smiled and released Trudi's face. "Klaus . . . very much taken with you, enjoying the dance and—"

"And what?" How greedy her voice sounded.

"Do you really want to hear this?"

Trudi swallowed.

"I saw him kiss you and loving every moment of it. Let's hope he rots in hell for this."

"Not for the kiss—only for pretending it never happened."

"He'll probably confess just before he dies so that he doesn't have to go to hell."

"Yes, five minutes before he stops breathing."

Eva laughed. "That's what I like about your religion: you can be an absolute swine, and if you time it right and confess before you croak, you're saved. Maybe I ought to convert. Your fat priest certainly tried to snag me."

"He's not *my* fat priest." Trudi grinned. "But you're right about timing. It all comes down to that . . . knowing when those last five minutes start so you won't miss them."

"Naturally, you'll have to have a priest handy by then."

"Naturally."

"Has there been anyone else?"

Trudi hesitated. "What do you mean?" she asked though she knew exactly what Eva was asking.

"Another man."

"No. . . . Except—" Trudi shrugged.

"Tell me."

"Oh, well, it doesn't really mean anything, but . . ."

"Tell me!"

"This—this man . . . who wants to have dinner with me."

"And?" Eva's eyes glistened.

"Well, I said no. But I sometimes wonder. . . . What if I'd said yes?"

"Anyone I know? What's his name?"

"Max. And you don't know him."

"What does he do?"

"He's a teacher, a tutor, actually."

"How did you meet him?"

Now Trudi wished she hadn't mentioned Max at all. Ashamed at how she'd deceived him with her letter, she walked over to the stand with the stuffed squirrel and flicked the dust from its fur.

But Eva was not about to let up. "How did you meet him? You can tell me."

"Oh . . . he sometimes comes to the library." It was part of the truth, not a real lie.

"Next time you see him, tell him you'll have dinner with him."

"I can't do that."

"Why not?"

"I don't know if I'll see him again."

Whenever Emil Hesping came over, Trudi and her father would listen with him to the forbidden British station on the radio that her father kept hidden in the back of his wardrobe. Herr Hesping understood enough English to translate the news for them. As the foreign words traveled to them on a crackling wave, they'd keep the volume low and press their ears against the curved wood of the radio that was the same shade of honey blond as the woodwork in Leo's bedroom. The station identification—*lalalala*—was so recognizable that, if you weren't careful, someone passing in the street might hear it and inform against you.

The information in newspapers and on the German stations was controlled, but from the British station you could at least find out how far the war had advanced. It felt essential to Trudi to get the correct news of what was happening, and to distribute it even if many of the people who used to wait for her stories were afraid to hear the truth about the war. They'd rather pretend that the British were *not* bombing the big German cities, or that the Germans had *not* killed every man in Lidice—the Czechoslovakian town that had harbored the assassins of Reinhard Heydrich, who'd been called the brain behind the persecution of the Jews.

"What do you think the Americans will do?" Trudi was asked frequently, as though her Aunt Helene in New Hampshire provided her with a direct link to the plans of the American military.

"The Americans won't let this go on for much longer," she'd declare with a certainty she wished she felt.

She was able to circulate her news faster with the bicycle that she'd bought with money her Aunt Helene had sent her the previous Christmas. It had been in the last package that had made it through from America. At first she'd hesitated to spend the money on herself, but half of the banknotes hidden inside the wooden cores of thread spools had been designated especially for her. In her letter Aunt Helene insisted she buy something for herself, and as soon as Trudi unrolled the bills, they sprang back into coils. After Trudi gave the thread to Herr Blau, who often sewed for the fugitives until late into the night, she bought a bicycle from Ingrid's father, a child's bicycle that made her a far more efficient messenger.

It was ironic—adult-size bicycles and tires were no longer available because the shortages of materials reached into every part of people's lives—but Herr Baum still had two children's bicycles, luxuries no one could afford, and he gave Trudi a good price on the one she liked best. He added a set of spare tires and an air pump without charging her—"Since it's for you," he said, bringing his smile close to her face—but she took care to step away from him, quickly, before he could pinch her bottom.

It was the first bicycle she'd owned. The tricycle she'd been given as a child had never been right for her: at first she hadn't been able to reach the pedals, and by the time she could, other children her age were racing around on two-wheelers and she felt ashamed to be riding a tricycle. But this new bicycle had the proportions of an adult's bicycle, except it was smaller altogether, built low, and there was nothing childish about its solid white frame and black seat.

Trudi learned how to ride it within a day. To make sure it wouldn't get stolen, she kept it indoors. Some evenings she taught Konrad, who hadn't learned to ride a two-wheeler yet, to ride it up and down the hallway, running behind him laughing as he wobbled along.

Now, if she had to, she could be ready to ride anywhere in minutes: not bothering with a corset or stockings, she'd throw on clothes without stopping to think if they matched. Once, when she saw her reflection on the bicycle in the window of the grocery store—her striped cardigan flapping around her flowered dress—she thought how horrified Frau Simon would be at her appearance.

Konrad was helping her to polish the bike with a chamois cloth the night they heard the shots nearby, but she didn't find out till morning what had happened. Two Jewish men had been discovered in the attic of the pharmacist's son-in-law, who was fighting in Russia. They'd both been shot immediately, in front of the pharmacist's daughter and her mother, who'd covered their faces with their aprons to keep from seeing the blood. When the women were taken to the Theresienheim for questioning, the pharmacist was brought in, too, still in the long gray underwear he'd been sleeping in when yanked from his bed.

He tried to convince the officer that he hadn't spoken to his daughter in over thirty years. "She married a Protestant," he said as if that would absolve him from any suspicion of complicity in hiding the Jews. His wife had divorced him the year after the daughter's wedding, he explained, and he hadn't said a single word to her since then. Or to his grandchildren, who were fully grown and lived elsewhere by now.

"When did you see your wife last?"

"Yesterday, but—" He pressed his narrow lips together, yet his fleshy cheeks kept working as if he were chewing the words. "It's not like that. I see her nearly every day. Because she lives around the corner and has to walk past the pharmacy on her way to the market." His eyes leapt to his ex-wife, then back to the officer, who looked totally unconvinced. "Tell him, Anneliese." His voice was shrill. "Tell him that we never talk."

She didn't answer.

"You are speaking to her now," the officer reminded him.

"But don't you see . . ." He offered the names of witnesses, Anton Immers and two other men from the chess club—good old friends, he called them—who turned out to be cautious about confirming any kind of close association with the pharmacist and could not make a definite statement as to the alleged silence between him and his former wife.

Despite his protest, he was held at the Theresienheim and, within a week, transported to a work camp on the same train with his wife and daughter.

"Those two women could have been shot, too," Emil Hesping told Trudi. He'd been urging her and Leo for nearly a month to send Frau Neimann and Konrad to a new hiding place. "It's dangerous to keep them too long. Not just for you. For them too."

Trudi gave him the same argument as she had before, "No one knows they're here." But what if Herr Hesping was right? She dreaded to have Konrad leave, and she couldn't bear the thought of not knowing what would happen to him. That uncertainty was much harder for her than the fear for her own safety.

Herr Hesping rubbed his thumb across a tiny spot on the lapel of his suit jacket and waited for her.

She felt pushed into agreeing with him. "All right," she said angrily. "All right then."

"I'll let you know the time. And, Leo, those banned books you still keep in the library—"

"I know. With people hiding here, I've been thinking I should get rid of the boxes."

"Burn them."

"That's what I was trying to avoid."

"I'm not going to cart them away in my car and get caught because of something like that."

"Burn them . . ." Leo said softly.

"I'm sorry." Trudi touched his arm. She turned to Emil Hesping. "Where will you take Konrad and his mother?"

"Someone else has already been lined up."

"And I can't ask."

He shook his head.

"I know," she said miserably.

"You're only good to us if we can keep this going."

"Us . . . Who is this us? Who else—?"

"You think it's a good idea for me to answer that?"

"Yes," she said. "No."

The following morning, Leo Montag issued calligraphy dinner invitations to Trudi, Eva, Frau Neimann, and Konrad. He banished everyone from the kitchen and refused to answer Trudi's questions about what was going on, except to request that they all dress formally. She felt impatient with his playfulness, his secrecy—it seemed trivial in view of sending Konrad away. Yet, because the boy was excited about the invitation, she pretended to look forward to the dinner.

All day she worked in the pay-library by herself. A few times, when she didn't have any customers, her father came in and removed an armful of books from the bottom of the boxes. "Actually," he told her, "these don't make bad cooking fuel."

"We'll replace them after the war," she said though she felt jumpy, without hope.

So far, she hadn't told Konrad and his mother that they would leave soon. Why worry them? It might be weeks. Or hours, she thought. Or hours. She had to force herself to listen to the gossip that her customers brought her. Reluctantly, she got ready for the evening. She dressed in the linen suit she'd sewn the year before the war, and she lent her good fringed shawl to Frau Neimann. Eva wore her pleated skirt and a green silk blouse, and the boy looked quite grown-up in a dark suit with knee-length pants that Herr Blau had tailored for him from ancient cloth.

When Trudi's father finally let them into the kitchen, he had changed into his Sunday suit and gaudy tie. Its stripes glittered and swirled in the light of six wax candles that he'd set on the table. There was a roast—an entire roast in a tureen of thick gravy. Trudi couldn't remember the last time she'd seen an entire roast. Somehow, her father had conjured up peas and asparagus and potato dumplings, even a strawberry pie and two bottles of champagne. A vase with red and yellow tulips sat in the middle of the table.

Konrad clapped his hands.

His mother took a step toward the table.

"Allow me." Leo Montag extended his right arm to her, his left to Eva, and led both to their chairs.

Trudi worried what he might have traded for all the food. Not the radio, she thought. Not that.

"Please, sit down," he said.

She climbed up the three steps of her dining chair, and when she looked at Eva—who had the same determined expression of gaiety on her face as that night of her costume ball, when she'd danced in her nun's habit with reckless abandon—Trudi decided to let herself get caught up in her father's celebration, a celebration that had also sprung from chaos.

And even if their laughter felt stolen from an unreliable future, the food warmed and filled their bellies, and the champagne flushed their faces. Her father was summarizing the silliest plots from the romance novels in the pay-library, and Trudi could see that Frau Neimann and Eva were dazzled by him. The feast he'd prepared and his tales of predictable love twists, which always resulted in sentimental reconciliations and sappy endings, were softening the terror that all of them had come to take into their beds at night and brace themselves against in the early hours of waking.

This is dangerous, Trudi wanted to tell them. Until now they'd been so careful, never having more than two place settings on the table, but as she glanced at the radiant faces around her, she knew that not to continue the celebration would be even more dangerous, a rotting of the spirit which, tonight, they were reclaiming.

Yet, as the evening wore on, Leo Montag became serious as though it took him effort to continue entertaining everyone.

"What is it?" Trudi finally asked.

He looked from her to Frau Neimann, who brought her hands to her mouth.

"No," Frau Neimann said.

The boy's head snapped up. His eyes were wild.

Leo nodded.

"Where?" Frau Neimann asked.

"I haven't been told. It's better that way. But I know you'll be secure there."

"When?"

"Tonight."

She jutted her chin toward Eva. "How about her?"

"Just you and your son."

"I see. . . . Who is taking us?"

"Herr Hesping. You can trust him completely."

Trudi climbed from her chair and brought her arms around the boy.

"Are you coming with us?" he asked.

"I can't."

"Why do people have to hide?"

Tears pressed into her nose, her eyes, and she held them back with one deep sob. "It wasn't always like that."

The wildness had left the boy's eyes. He was looking to her for an answer, not to his mother.

She began to shape her farewell story for him. "Let me tell you what it was like before people were hunted, Konrad. . . ." To stop all time, she closed her eyes and imagined Pia in the kitchen with her, imagined the parrot Othello flying between them as she and Pia wove the tapestry of the island for the boy, a tapestry so rich and enchanting that he could step right into it if he needed to. . . . "And on this island the sidewalks were built of white marble. Every night, a warm rain rinsed the streets and the thick leaves of the trees. During the day, the sun was always out, and you could swim in the bay."

"Even in winter."

"Even in winter. The trees, they were filled with tropical fruits and nuts, and no one knew what it meant to be hungry."

He sighed. "Why can't we go there?"

If only the island really existed. "Perhaps," she said, "it is time for me to return to the island."

"What is it called?"

"The island of the little people. Where I grew up." She felt her father's eyes on her, and when she glanced over, they were filled with almost unbearable anguish and love. "A magic island, Konrad, where no one is taller than you and me, where orchids and parrots and—"

"But why did you leave such a place?"

"Because . . ." She reached inside herself for the core of the story, and when she found it, it startled her because it would not sustain the boy as she had anticipated; and yet, she had to reel the story out for him, all along trying to understand its meaning for herself. "Because the waterfalls dried up. Birds dropped from the sky. Everything withered. Mountains caved in on themselves, burying beautifully arched tunnels. . . ."

"Why?"

God, she didn't want to let Konrad go. She'd never loved a child this way before, and she wanted to claim him as hers, shield him with her body against anyone who'd dare take him from her. *He's not mine. Not mine.* As she took a step away from him, it came to her that she hadn't even begun to comprehend the abrupt separations from family and friends that Jews suffered every day. She had lost her mother, had felt that grief, but that was one loss, not a sequence of losses encumbered with that constant fear of your own death.

Furious that she had to live in this time, with these laws, she fused her gaze to the boy's, imprinting herself on his soul. *You will always remember me. You will.*

"Why did everything wither?" he wanted to know.

"You see—regular-sized people wanted to live on the island. . . ." She found it difficult to talk, but she kept going. "They too wanted to dwell within the magic. But the little people were divided about what to do. Some of them said, 'Yes, let's all live on the island, regardless what size we are. . . . ' " Her chest ached. Her head ached. "But most of them wanted to keep the tall people out. They didn't know much about them—that's how prejudice starts, Konrad—and so they were afraid of their difference. They wanted their island all to themselves and began to hunt the tall people . . . hunt even those little people who were trying to protect the tall people."

She could feel the ending of the story curling around herself and the boy, drawing in the others at the table: they were listening closely—not with laughter as they had to her father's stories—but with a stunned sadness. "Everything on the island withered. The palm trees lost their big leaves. Peaches shriveled hard around their pits. Oranges turned brown. Even the biggest waterfall dwindled to one muddy trickle."

It was silent in the kitchen.

"Is that the end?" Konrad asked.

"For now." If only she'd found a story of hope to send with him on his way. If only she could get out of Germany with him the way Stefan Blau had nearly half a century before.

"It will change some day," Konrad surprised her by saying.

"It will have to," she agreed quickly.

Her father stood up. Everyone looked at him, but no one spoke.

Frau Neimann pushed her chair back. "I need to pack. It's—" Her voice skipped. "It's time. Isn't it? It must be time."

He nodded.

"I'll help you get ready," Eva offered.

Trudi dashed over to the sink and picked up the nearly empty bottle of lotion. "Don't forget this."

Frau Neimann's chin puckered. She shook her head.

Trudi pressed it into her hands. "Please. You and Konrad—you've brought so much into our lives."

By the middle of summer the canvas that lined the tunnel smelled of mildew, and when Leo Montag and Herr Blau peeled it off, patches of mold bloomed behind it, and a fine shower of dirt drifted down on them.

Their latest fugitive, a taxi driver from Bremen, who'd been hidden in nine other places so far, was concerned there might be some caving-in above. "If so, it could be seen from the street," he warned.

Herr Blau assured him, "No one walks between my house and the pay-library."

But when Leo checked the narrow strip of grass, he found a shallow puddle right above the area of the tunnel. That night, he and the taxi driver shored the tunnel up with posts and rafters that Herr Blau had kept stacked in his cellar. They debated about filling the puddle with dirt and decided against it, since dirt would be even more noticeable with all the grass around it.

Their next visitors, two elderly sisters from Köln, suggested laying boards across the floor of the tunnel to keep their skirts dry.

"Then the water could seep under the wood," the taller one said after Trudi had rehearsed the escape pattern with them.

"Yes," the other sister said. "We'd be able to crawl across the boards without getting muddy."

In some way each fugitive contributed to improving the tunnel. Eva stretched thin fabric from her nightgown beneath the ceiling to catch specks of earth that might sift into your eyes or settle between your neck and collar. She was the only one who'd been staying with Trudi and Leo since spring. The others came and departed quickly, bearing dreadful stories, far more dreadful than anything Trudi could have invented, as if some deity had gone mad while contriving demented plots; and each plot telescoped within itself the plots of others that the fugitives had encountered on their desperate journeys. As Trudi listened to them, she was overcome by a sense of the unbelievable, as if it all were transpiring in a world far more outlandish than Pia's island. Whatever had happened in her family and her town before Hitler and his brown gang had seized power—including the death of her mother and the disappearance of Georg Weiler's father and the wedding of Klaus Malter, even her rape in the Braunmeiers' barn—she could have imagined herself, spun forward into the texture of a much greater motif; but these new stories, carried to her by the people she harbored, she could have never invented: they stopped her, bludgeoned her with their finality, although their endings were obscure.

Twice, when the police searched the neighborhood while fugitives crouched in the tunnel, Trudi was shocked at how easy it was to lie to them: "No, we haven't had any visitors for days. . . . My father and I—we talk with customers who come into the library, but we lead rather private lives. . . . Eva Sturm?" She'd tilt her face toward them, sideways, draw her neck into her shoulders, make herself smaller, harmless, helpful. "Of course, I know Eva Sturm . . . have known her all my life. . . . I was invited to her wedding, you know. It was a beautiful wedding. You should have— No, no, I haven't seen her. Not in months. . . ." Her body would lean into a limp, slowing them for a few precious seconds as she'd offer to lead them through the house, and she'd hobble out of their way as they'd crush past her.

Her heart numb with a cold certainty that the tunnel was safe— had to be safe—she'd wait for them by the front door, her pulse steady, her expression polite as she'd hold the door for them on their way out. Only then, after she'd turn the key inside the lock, would she start shaking. Holding on to the banister, she'd tell herself that it had to be far worse for Eva and the others in the tunnel, that she should rush to let them know they could come out again, but she'd have to lower herself to the steps and sit there before she'd be able to walk.

Emil Hesping and the bishop were coordinating a constantly changing number of hiding places from Köln north to the Dutch border. Since Emil had always traveled between the branches of the gymnasts' club, people were used to his trips and didn't get suspicious if they didn't see him for days.

"It's crucial," he would remind Trudi, "not to have any of the groups know the identity of other groups. We also need to be careful what we say to the people we hide. Remember—they might be apprehended and forced to talk."

"You don't have to tell me again," she'd say.

"It's something I need to keep telling myself."

Already, her gossip had taken on a new pattern: she would select her stories, conscious of preserving the safety of the people who relied on her, even though she'd feel restrained because there was so much she couldn't tell—like about the woman crippled with arthritis whose husband had looked after her with such tenderness, unaware how amazed Trudi was by the kind of love that didn't flinch from physical differences; or the young nurse from Berlin who'd stolen two spoons from the Montags before she'd been taken to a new place; or the young priest who despised his name, Adolf, and had given her a new respect for the clergy, not only because he'd hidden Jews in his church in Dresden, but also through his stories of other priests and ministers—some of them fearful souls, he admitted—who had spoken out against the oppression of the Jews and had been arrested or even killed.

Those stories swelled inside Trudi, forming a reservoir that she couldn't draw on, though it deepened with each day of concern for everyone who'd left her house for an uncertain destination. She tried to tell herself that she'd be able to release those stories after the war, that she was only postponing them until then; and yet, part of her already sensed that those stories would never flourish, that—after the war—she would find very few who'd want to listen because the people of Burgdorf would be immersed in changing what had happened into a history they could sleep with, *eine heile Welt*—an intact world they could offer to the next generation. Ironically, Anton Immers—one of the few who would admit that he'd believed in the Führer—would make the good people of Burgdorf uncomfortable with his regret that the regime was over and with his dreams of its revival in even greater glory.

More and more, Trudi began to see herself as an underground messenger, safeguarding her stories while reporting details from the British radio station about the military situation, which usually contradicted what the German stations were broadcasting. She often thought of Konrad and fought the dread that, wherever he might be, he was in danger. With the priest Adolf, she'd known from the moment she'd met him that he would survive the war: it was in his eyes, that survival, in the way he moved his rugged body. Arrested during mass, he'd managed to escape into the dense forest just before the transport had reached the gates of the KZ Buchenwald outside Weimar.

The night before the priest was to leave the pay-library, Trudi watched him shave. She'd propped one of her gold-framed mirrors next to the kitchen sink for him. It was one of those hot, hot June evenings when the air is damp and your skin feels sleek with sweat. As Adolf lathered his face with her father's shaving soap, he showed her where one of the guards on the train had pushed a thumb into the soft spot behind his ear.

"For an instant there, I thought I'd die. That transport, it taught me about hunger. I didn't know hunger like that could exist. I felt ashamed of it." His voice was rapid, barely more than a whisper. "Beneath the hunger was a constant greed—like a wild dog that could be turned loose any moment. I was as afraid of that greed as of the guards, afraid of what it might make me do. . . ."

He stared into the mirror and raised the shaving blade. "That hunger—it brought out the worst in some of us, the best in others. On the train I saw a father grab food away from his daughter. . . . I saw an old man trampled as others fought over one raw potato. Not everyone was like that, of course. Many sacrificed and shared what little they had. I was dizzy and cold and weak with hunger—that was my entire focus. . . . I longed for my connection to God, tried to remember the joy I'd found in playing the organ in our church, but everything was reduced to my belly. It was my God, my one companion. . . .

"After I escaped—" He shook his head and started again, and what he told Trudi took away forever any doubts she might have still held on to, doubts that those rumors of people dying by the hundreds in camps were far too horrible to be true. She saw the priest crouched in the woods outside high loops of barbed wire, saw him stumble away from a vast grave—naked bodies shoved into the gouged earth, twisted in indecent embraces. He made his way through the woods to Weimar, where his favorite poets, Goethe and Schiller, had lived and written, and he hid between the tall monuments in the cemetery near the crypt where the two poets rested in splendid recognition.

"Those nights in the cemetery. . . ." The priest scraped the foam down his left cheek. "I thought I'd go insane. I could not understand how some people's graves could be marked while others were obliterated without evidence. It felt more horrible than any other injustice I'd ever known of. I couldn't fathom it. I tried to, and the trying was crazy making. . . ."

Gradually he'd moved west, aided by people he said he'd never forget. During his flight he'd met other fugitives but only one woman who'd actually escaped from inside a KZ, Dachau, smuggled out by a guard. The woman, who had shared a hiding place behind the false wall of a closet with the priest for eight days, had told him about the camp—the filth, the hunger, the open sores—but what had been the worst for her had been the washroom where, together with others, she'd had to strip, stand under the icy water, and get doused with disinfectants that made her eyes sting, while guards laughed or pushed them around.

All at once Trudi wanted to stop the information coming to her, wanted to block the remembering of what the priest had already told her, but knew that his words were carved into her soul as surely as any moment she had lived. "What happened to the woman?" she asked hoarsely, her forehead covered with sweat.

"They couldn't take away her spirit, though every day others went insane in the camp. Every day. For her, that washroom became her salvation because that's where the guard who would eventually help her to escape saw her. . . ." The priest winced as he cut his chin. "The guard didn't expect to fall in love with her." Blood ran down the white foam, spreading into a pink blotch.

Trudi ran into the bathroom and brought him a few pieces of toilet paper. "Here."

He pressed them against the cut. "She used him. Pretended."

"I would have done the same."

"The guard had it all figured out. False papers for her so that they could marry. Imagine that. . . . He'd keep doing his death work and she'd be at home, cooking his meals, keeping his uniforms clean, having his babies for the *Vaterland*."

"How did she get out?"

"She agreed to marry him, and he smuggled her out. Under layers of trash. He took her to this room he'd rented for the two of them above a bakery in München. At first he kept locking her in, but she made him believe that she would never want to go anywhere without him."

"And that's when he gave her a key."

"Yes."

"My father had to keep my mother locked up."

The priest looked at Trudi. He'd stopped the bleeding by sticking a small triangle of paper to his cut.

"He had to. She—she wasn't well. She died when I was four."

"How terrible for you."

"It happened a long time ago. Besides, compared to what you and many others have to suffer—"

"Ah, but we can't do that—compare our pain. It minimizes what happens to us, distorts it. We need to say, yes, this is what happened to me, and this is what I'll do with it." He rinsed his chin. "You know what I'm going to do as soon as I can?"

She shook her head.

"Change my name. Legally."

She felt disappointed by his answer. It seemed petty, considering all he could be doing. "You don't have to tell people that your name is Adolf. You didn't have to tell me. You could have made up another name."

"But don't you see?" He bent close to her. His face smelled of her father's soap. "Right now there isn't anything I can do legally without getting caught again, but that's what I tell myself when I get worn down, that I'll change my name. I despise that name. Of course there are things far more important that I want to do—like stop the transports, the camps—"

"The war," Trudi said.

"Yes, but I know I can't stop them, and so I need to fasten on one thing that's within my power to do." His eyes burned with conviction. "By saying that name aloud, I keep my rage, my determination. . . ."

She wished he would stay longer, but he'd only be there for a few more hours because Herr Hesping had already arranged a new place for him. She and her father were just one station on his way toward shedding his name.

When the oldest Weskopp son died on the Russian front that fall, the widow Weskopp, who had suffered silently, screamed and kept screaming. When the neighbor women came running, they found her standing in the room that her two sons used to share, staring at the framed butterfly collection—dusty shapes, once vibrantly colorful, impaled on stick pins—that hung on the wall between the two beds. You could hear her screams all over town. They couldn't have lasted very long, but they seemed to be there all day. And even during the night people would wake up and think they heard those screams, which gave voice to the pain that the town had endured—far more penetrating and unsettling than the sirens that warned when planes crossed Burgdorf on their way to drop bombs on Düsseldorf or Köln.

The widow Weskopp, who hadn't yet finished the year of wearing mourning clothes for her husband and youngest son, would stay in black from this day forward, the only color in her life except for the violets which she grew on every windowsill in her house as if to balance the harsh black of her garments.

When Trudi returned from the funeral of the Weskopp son, Eva stood waiting for her in the kitchen.

"I'm going home," she said, her voice clipped.

"You know it's not wise."

"I also know I can't go on like this. Sometimes I forget that you're my friend. . . . All I see is my jailer."

"Eva—"

"People can die. You've seen how quickly it happens. The Weskopp boy—"

"He was in the war."

"Alexander might be sent off to war any day."

"It's not his life I'm worried about."

"One short night, Trudi. One Goddamn beautiful night. Is that too much to want?"

"To want? Of course not, but—"

"If I can have one night with Alexander, I know I'll be able to deal with the hiding again."

"It's not worth it, Eva."

"How can you say that?"

"At least talk to my father."

"There's nothing he can say that will keep me here."

She left through the kitchen door after the streets were dark and empty, promising to return before dawn, and Trudi set her alarm clock. When she woke up, the sky was still black, and she felt that slow buried ache in her hips. She washed, dressed, and went downstairs into the kitchen. They'd had no fugitives for a week, and with Eva gone, the house felt like a shell, a useless prop that a strong wind might blow away. She pictured Eva embracing her husband good-bye, rushing from the apartment building, careful not to be seen, cutting through the market and past the church square. Any moment now her knock would come on the backdoor. Trudi would pull her inside, search her face for traces of that one Goddamn beautiful night.

But outside it was silent.

Now, if she had one Goddamn beautiful night in her lifetime coming to her, Trudi pondered, and the choice with whom to spend that night . . . She found an immediate certainty within her: Max Rudnick. Not even Klaus Malter? No, Max Rudnick. But probably Max Rudnick hadn't even considered a night with her. She wondered where he was, that night, that moment. It had been fifteen months since she'd met him, six months since she'd seen him.

"Stay out of danger," she whispered.

The sky was changing from black to a deep purple blue, then to a medium blue, and finally to the flat light blue of a cloudless morning. And when the knock on the kitchen door came, it was not Eva, but Frau Weiler, the scarf around her frizzy hair half undone.

Nearly incoherent with the news that she'd become a grandmother during the night, she dropped herself on the nearest chair. "Twin girls, Trudi. You have to see them. Oh—" She clasped her hands by her throat. "Eva Sturm—have you heard about Eva Sturm?"

"What happened?" Trudi gripped her arm.

"I was there when they were born." Frau Weiler sucked her false teeth into place. "Helga let me help. They're both—"

"Eva—what happened to her? How did it—"

"She was arrested. They searched the apartment, then the whole building, and found her in the attic."

"Where is she?"

"No one knows."

"Oh God, I was afraid of that. . . . Who told you?"

"Jutta Malter. She was there when they took Eva."

"And Alexander?"

"They didn't take him."

"He's still there?" Trudi started for the door.

"Locked inside his apartment, I hear."

s i x t e e n

1942

ALEXANDER DID NOT ANSWER THE DOOR THAT DAY OR THE DAYS AFTER.
Outside his windows hung the voices of women like souls of stuffed
birds. Some he identified by sound: Trudi Montag, his niece, the
butcher's daughter-in-law. Others blended into a chorus, faded out,
returned. He sat on the Danish sofa, and whenever he dozed off, he
made sure it was while sitting: at least he could do that for Eva—not
take comfort in lying down though his limbs yearned for rest. Stop it,
he'd admonish his body when it complained, this is not about you.
This is about Eva.

Sometimes he staggered to the bathroom.

Sometimes he ate and drank, disgusted that his body could force
him into those functions.

Trudi Montag came back.

Others.

Knocking.

Knocking and calling his name.

If the Gestapo returned, they would break his door down and he'd
welcome them. No reason to get up for anyone else. His mouth felt
dry and salty—not the fresh salt taste of the sweat beneath his wife's

breasts—but a nasty salt taste, old and used up. One evening he sat on the sofa when the sirens wailed, heard his tenants rush to the shelter he'd established in the cellar. Some banged on his door, shouted for him to follow them.

Except for a few stray bombs that planes had dropped on their way back from attacking much larger targets, Burgdorf had remained almost intact. Strange to think how afraid he'd been of bombs. He used to open his windows during bombing raids to keep them from vibrating until they broke, and then he'd dash down the stairs to his shelter. But now he remained sitting on his sofa and longed for the kind of sky he'd once seen in Köln during a bombing—a sky bright with shapes not unlike Christmas trees, sinking toward the city, casting their eerie glow over everything. He longed for his windows to shatter, letting in gusts of heat and smoke that would make it impossible to breathe. He longed for suffocation, for obliteration, for a sky brushed with fire. Without moving, he sat, praying to be buried in the rubble of his building. And then it was morning and his house stood around him and he sat on the sofa and his wife was gone. Normal.

She kept coming back, his wife's *Zwerg* friend, fists fluttering against his door, his caged heart. Soon it felt as though she were out there all the time, and he'd find himself listening for her wingbeat even in the void of night when all else was silent. The muscles in his thighs and buttocks felt flattened out. Against his skin, the clothes he'd worn when they'd taken Eva away were stiff and rank. He'd stumbled into them—trousers and a white shirt—when he'd heard the car stop outside the building.

Lucky I was awake, lucky, lucky. . . . He'd tossed Eva's clothes onto the bed. "Get dressed." Through the gap in the drapes he'd watched them get out of the car. Two of them, their suits blotted by the dark, balancing ghostly balloons of faces.

Before they reached the front door of the building, he had Eva by the wrist and was out of the apartment door with her—*lucky, lucky*—clicking it shut and up the stairs to the second floor, where he made her wait, each pulse of her wrist a shock through his entire body, until they'd broken into his apartment, giving him and Eva time to race up the rest of the stairs.

It was too new, the attic—not enough trunks and furniture and boxes stored yet to allow for shadows to grow into cluttered corners. It was an attic you could almost see all at once—not like his grandparents' attic, where each step had meant a discovery, a distraction. Quickly, he pulled Eva behind the crates of leftover building supplies: clay tiles for the roof; thin strips of wood for the parquet floors; rolls of wallpaper; cans of paint.

It took a lifetime for them to make their way to the attic—he heard them on the second floor in his niece Jutta's apartment, in the rooms on the third floor, their voices rising through the boards where he crouched with his wife, his wife—but then they were on the attic stairs.

He saw himself sitting in the police station, handcuffed in a cell, crowded into a train with Eva. If it weren't for her— Suddenly he hated her. "I love you," he whispered hoarsely. His fingers ached as they pressed into her arm.

"I love you, too." Her face was a painting, one-dimensional, still. She stood up. Slipped his fingers from her arm like a useless bracelet.

His back and neck felt drenched with sweat.

"Stay there." She was already walking toward the attic door as it flew open.

Afterwards, though not for long, Alexander would try to tell himself that his legs failed him when he tried to stand up as they took Eva away, stand up to join her as she must have believed he would—even during her last gesture of heroism—because that was what they had promised one another.

"I thought you'd like to be there," Matthias said as he handed Trudi two cream-colored envelopes, one addressed to her, the other to her father.

"What is it?"

"An invitation." He'd come to the pay-library but had waited between the stacks of books until Frau Bilder had checked out five war novels and maneuvered her bulk out of the door.

Trudi opened the envelope and read the announcement for his piano recital. "Oh, Matthias," she said. "I'm so pleased for you. Of course we'll be there. Thank you."

He flushed with pride. "I even have a tuxedo."

"You'll look all grown up then."

"The unknown benefactor left it in our kitchen."

"How about that? When?"

"Just this morning."

"And it fits?"

"The jacket. The pants are too long, but my grandmother is turning over the hem."

"He's been at it again, the unknown benefactor. I heard that Frau Immers—you know she gets that awful rash on her scalp—found two bottles of the medical shampoo she hasn't been able to buy. Right in her chicken coop. . . . Listen, can you stay and visit? My father is in the living room."

Matthias hesitated.

"I know he'd be glad to see you."

"Are you sure it's all right to go in?"

She thought of the times she'd sent him away from her door when she'd been hiding fugitives. "Just go on through." She motioned him toward the open door that led to the hallway. No need to keep that door locked any longer. Her house had been empty for two weeks since that night Eva hadn't returned.

Emil Hesping was refusing to bring them anyone else. "Let's wait a while," he'd said. "You have some recovering to do. And we don't know what she'll tell them."

"Not Eva," she'd said.

And he'd shaken his bald head but hadn't said anything that she hadn't already imagined about torture.

What Trudi knew of Eva's arrest had come from Jutta, who'd followed the Gestapo into the attic after they'd torn her rooms apart, searching for Eva. They'd found her standing in the middle of the attic, not even trying to hide.

"She walked toward them," Jutta had said when Trudi had come to see her.

"And Alexander?"

"They only took Eva."

Trudi looked at Jutta, hard. She felt Jutta was holding something back, but she couldn't tell what it was. "Did they search for him?"

"They came for Eva. They were satisfied."

"Tell your uncle I want to talk with him."

"He's not well."

"I need to find out what happened to Eva."

"He won't even speak to me."

Fräulein Birnsteig, though Jewish, had been protected so far because of her fame, but her mansion had been appropriated as a vacation villa for SS officers. She'd lost her housekeeper and her car, but had been allowed to keep her bedroom and the music room where, frequently, she was summoned to play the piano for officers and their guests. Even her practice sessions were no longer her own: officers would wander in, lean against the piano to watch her or, worse yet, continue conversations while she'd play.

It was to this music room that Trudi and her father came for Matthias Berger's recital. The audience was much smaller than at the spring concerts, and the windows were closed to the brisk October air. More than half of the guests wore uniforms, and next to the piano the red flag with the *Hakenkreuz* was prominently displayed. There were no candles as in the earlier years, but harsh light bulbs that made the pianist's once so elegant neck look pasty, wrinkled. When the concert began with *"Deutschland, Deutschland über Alles,"* Trudi couldn't bear to sing along, and as she glanced up at her father, he was moving his lips without sound.

She wondered how it made Fräulein Birnsteig feel, playing the national anthem. Did others, too, notice the hesitancy with which she sought out the keys? She no longer looked glamorous, but thin and ill—this woman who believed in her dreams, who had canceled tours because of dreams, who had hired a beggar woman because in a dream she was her sister. Where is the beggar woman now? Trudi wanted to ask Fräulein Birnsteig. And what have you done with your dreams? Did you dream this too—the flag and the uniforms and the camps? And if so, what did you do to adjust your life to this?

But then, mercifully, the anthem was over, and Matthias stalked to the piano, his face chalk white, his eyes on the ground. But as soon as he sat down on the piano bench, his shoulders filled out, and his back aligned into a lovely, strong curve. In his tuxedo he looked like the man he would become, not a thirteen-year-old boy. As he touched the keys, a wonderful confidence came over him. His head followed the motion of his hands. From where she sat, Trudi could see the transformation in his features, the green hue of his pupils, and she remembered that first time he'd come into her house. Music, even then, had been a way out of pain for him. She wished she had something like that, something that could sweep her away from the grieving that sat with her all too often. She'd grieved over Konrad, the priest Adolf, and now Eva, and each one tilted her right back to her oldest grief—the loss of her mother.

Trudi felt herself drawn into Matthias' music, but when she closed her eyes, the music became that of Fräulein Birnsteig and spun her through the images of that second-grade spring concert: the sound of boots on marble tiles; high white bellies of pregnant girls; babies crying— Trudi sat up straight, her eyes wide. The boots, they were here now. On these marble floors. And so was that fear she'd felt as a girl. The bellies, she thought as the music pumped through her, what about the bellies? She didn't want to know; yet, she felt the future sucking at her, trying to prove itself to her through those boots, vowing that the bellies and the babies, too, were waiting in that vortex of time.

Her father bent down, brought his face close to hers. "What is it, Trudi?" he whispered.

She shook her head, tried to reassure him with a smile. At intermission she was the first one out of the music room before the applause had stopped. But Frau Buttgereit caught up with her in the octagonal entrance hall, where a table with refreshments was set up, and pressed a glass of wine into Trudi's hand. The gold cross of honor for German mothers was pinned to her lapel.

"Are you enjoying the concert?" she asked and stepped closer to Trudi as others crowded around the table.

"I would enjoy it even more if we could do without the flag and the anthem."

"Sshh." Frau Buttgereit shifted her weight from one veined leg to the other and glanced around nervously. "Did you hear about all the teaching jobs in Düsseldorf? If Monika were still here, she could apply."

Trudi wanted to get away, but she was wedged between chests and backs and the table.

"They're pulling out more of the male teachers for the front."

Maybe that's where Max Rudnick was, at the front. Maybe already dead and buried. Stop it, Trudi told herself. He'd never be a soldier. His eyes were far too bad. Lately, just about anything made her think of Max: drinking tea, shelving books, weighing tobacco. . . .

"Not that I'm against Monika working with the KLV," Frau Buttgereit rushed to say. "It's just that she's so far away. We wish she lived closer to home. But at least she's doing the work she studied for."

When they returned to the music room, Matthias played a duet with his mentor. Trudi could see how proud Fräulein Birnsteig was of him. I bet he's the best student she ever had, Trudi thought, the very best. She was distracted by two SS officers who were walking along the side of the rows, talking. Why couldn't they wait until after the concert? One of them had the nerve to come down her row, his black uniform blocking people's view of the piano as he squeezed himself past their legs.

In front of Trudi he stopped and said something.

She couldn't understand. "What?"

"I said: Come with me."

Eva, she thought. They found out Eva stayed with us. In the rows ahead of her, no one turned around. People kept their eyes on the piano.

"Get up, you."

"What's this about?" Trudi's father asked.

Matthias stopped playing the piano. For an instant Fräulein Birnsteig continued the thin thread of her part, but then she, too, lifted her hands from the keys.

"Keep playing," the officer shouted. "And you—" He grabbed Trudi's shoulder. "Out. Now."

Eva Eva Eva—

"I'm coming along." Her father raised himself from his seat.

"You stay here." The officer shoved him down and pulled Trudi past him to the end of the row.

Matthias and Fräulein Birnsteig kept moving their fingers across the keys as if trying to pull some solace from the stark white and black. Trudi could still hear their music as she was taken outside to a car. Cold night air blew through the fabric of her wool dress. She shivered.

Her father came rushing from the building with her coat.

"Careful, old man." One of the officers raised his arm.

"At least let me give her this coat."

The coat wrapped around herself, she sat in the back of the car. Her father's white hair slid past the window, then the massive stone posts where the driveway dipped into the road, then trees, and the long, unlit stretch of road between the mansion and the cemetery, where some of the old graves had been leveled to make room for new coffins. Despite all the war dead, the old people in town kept dying as they had in times of peace. Death had taken on such a different meaning, it seemed to Trudi, that perhaps the old should have been given some postponement, some reprieve. Yet, their burials kept happening right along with the war funerals. It came in proper time, their dying, but what had changed was that they were encumbered by the bewilderment that their sons had died before them. Out of sequence. Or their daughters, Trudi thought, picturing her father alone.

The last time she'd been to the cemetery had been for the funeral of the priest-nun, Sister Adelheid. At the gravesite she felt spooked when she realized she was flanked by nuns, just as the sister had been whenever she'd left the convent. At least the sister with the heart-shaped face had done what she'd believed, even though it had meant punishment. But with that punishment had come an odd freedom, Trudi thought, not the resignation that suspended the lives of too many women.

The car passed the burned-out synagogue and pulled up in front of the Theresienheim. One officer on either side, Trudi passed the *Hakenkreuz* flag in the lobby. Above the bench, where the Jesus picture with the blue robe used to be, now hung a picture of the Führer, his mouth set as if about to erupt into one of the screaming speeches that Trudi had heard on the radio. His eyes were watching her, the kind of eyes, Herr Hesping had said, that lured people in.

"If they didn't see those eyes and only heard the shouting," he'd told her, "it would be easier to resist him."

It felt strange to be inside the Theresienheim without seeing a single nun. Trudi had heard that the sisters still had some rooms near the chapel, but she hadn't been here since the building had been confiscated. Maybe this was where Eva had been taken, waiting to be transported. If Eva had told them anything, it must have been under torture. As Trudi wondered how much torture she herself could withstand, she felt grateful that no one was hiding at her house who might be betrayed by her.

All night she was kept in a cell by herself. No one came to ask her questions. What kept the room from complete darkness were the moon outside the barred window and the slit of light beneath the locked door. She felt thirsty. At least I don't like to smoke, she thought. If I smoked, this would be a lot worse. I'd want it so badly. . . . She rubbed her arms, crossing back and forth from the window, which was less than a minute's run from her own backyard, to the only piece of furniture, a wardrobe. So this is what it must have been like for Frau

Simon. . . . She found some comfort in picturing Konrad safe, willing
him safe, out of the country, in Switzerland, perhaps, or England. He
wouldn't have to hide. He could go to school with other children, have
a cat again. And then she thought of the Abramowitzs who, twice, had
heard rumors that they were to be picked up; both times they'd readied themselves, though Trudi's father had offered to hide them or drive
them to a safe place. They'd refused to endanger him, and when he'd
asked Herr Abramowitz if he wanted his wooden crate, Herr
Abramowitz had said he'd rather leave it with him.

A few times Trudi sat down on the linoleum floor, squeezing her
thighs together to stop the urge to pee, but soon she'd be up again,
pacing. Although they'd let her keep her coat, she was cold. And hungry. The uncertainty of why she'd been arrested grew until it reeled
out of control like the walk of the Heidenreich daughter. The entire
war was like that, reeling out of control, and for all she knew, Gerda
Heidenreich might be dead, buried in a place where her watch without hands kept proper time.

Last summer, when a group of Jews had been rounded up outside
the taxidermist's shop, Gerda, who'd been sitting on the front stoop,
had been taken away in the truck along with them, despite her father's cry, "My daughter isn't Jewish." From what he'd been able to
find out, she'd been brought to a research clinic, supposedly to be
studied with other retarded people.

Herr Heidenreich—who went to every speech, every meeting,
every parade—tried to convince his wife that their daughter would be
returned to them, healed and more complete than she'd ever been before. His loyalty to the Führer was so absolute that he wouldn't allow
his wife to grieve. "They will find some treatment to help her, some
operation or medicine . . . ," he would tell the customers for whom
he'd preserve a favorite cat, say, or a wild fox, endowing lifeless bodies with a vitality far more real than in nature.

At dawn, when light from the single window turned Trudi's cell
deep blue and then gray, she found that the wardrobe was unlocked
and empty, except for a plaster statue dressed in white, a plaster thorn
embedded in her forehead—St. Rita, married against her will at
twelve. Twice a mother, once a widow, she'd kept trying to enter the
convent despite rules that only admitted virgins. She was the patron
saint of desperate causes. Trudi wondered what St. Rita would do if
she were confined in this cell.

"Forgive me," she whispered as she climbed into the wardrobe, "but this is a desperate cause." Pulling up her wool dress, she squatted in the corner opposite the saint and peed, feeling the last warm part of herself gushing from her. "Forgive me," she said again as she rocked herself on her heels to get rid of the last drip.

Several times that morning she heard steps in the hallway, voices, and by afternoon she had convinced herself that the officers who'd locked her up had forgotten to let anyone know she was here. She thought of Sister Adelheid. *As long as you keep escaping, they never get you. Even if they think they do.* Her stomach ached, and her mouth felt sore. What if her hunger became as terrible as the hunger the priest Adolf had described to her? What if she got to where—after everything else had been taken away, her dignity as well as her possessions—she'd be reduced to the tyranny of her belly?

She thought of knocking against her door but was afraid of what might happen to her once that door opened. When it finally did, she was glad that the guard was a young woman.

"Stand up!" Long keys hung on a ring from her belt.

Trudi scrambled up, her back against the wall.

"Name?" On her lapel, the woman wore a round button with the *Hakenkreuz*. Her close-fitting uniform and polished knee-high boots made her look both sexual and dangerous.

"Trudi Montag."

"Age?"

"Twenty-seven."

"Occupation?"

"Librarian."

As the woman screamed questions at her, Trudi flinched and tried to answer them, even those that didn't make sense.

"Why were you at the concert?"

"I like music."

"Were you meeting someone?"

"No."

"Was this meeting for the purpose of exchanging information?" The woman looked confident, the kind of confident that comes from wearing a uniform that gives you an authority you've never had before.

"I was there for the music."

Trudi kept waiting for Eva's name to come up, but the questions were all about the concert, where she'd sat, what she'd talked about, whom she'd talked with, and while the woman was shouting at her to answer, she imagined herself traveling through China for one-quarter fare, going four times as far with her money as a regular-size woman like this guard. Finally she realized her arrest had nothing to do with Eva or with hiding other fugitives. Someone had overheard her remark to Frau Buttgereit.

But the grim expression of the guard gave her no reason to celebrate her relief. "So you admit making that statement about the flag?"

"I—" Trudi sighed and lowered her eyes. If the guard sensed that she was not totally intimidated by her, she'd make things worse. "It was thoughtless of me to phrase it like that. It really was. You see— what I meant was that the flag was in the way, making it difficult for someone my size to see the piano."

"And our national anthem?"

"I have always preferred it at the end of a concert, rather than the beginning." When she leaned her head back and shot an appealing glance upward, she could tell the guard wasn't convinced. "I agree— it is unfortunate the way I expressed it."

"More than unfortunate." In the guard's eyes, Trudi recognized that old flash of curiosity she'd encountered from others all her life. "It undermines our country."

Late that evening, Trudi was given a bowl of pea soup and one slice of *Schwarzbrot*—black bread—and in the morning she was taken to the second floor and locked in a room with three other women, all much older than she. She'd only met one of them before, Frau Hecht, a Jewish seamstress whose husband had fought in Poland and become the town's first war casualty. The other two had been brought here from outlying towns.

Frau Hecht was ill. Her skin felt hot to the touch, and whenever she coughed, her entire body trembled. The others kept her covered up with their own blankets and saved some of their water ration for her. They begged the guard who brought the food and wasn't old enough to grow hair on his face to get one of the sisters to bring medicine for Frau Hecht.

But he shook his head as if afraid of listening to them. "Nuns are not allowed to talk to prisoners."

While Frau Hecht slept most of that day, mumbling fevered words, the other women were frantic, speculating where they might be sent. They worried about what had happened to their suitcases and lamented about what they'd had to leave behind. Upon their arrival at the Theresienheim, their luggage had been seized, and they were still waiting to have it returned.

That night, when the women slept in their clothes—two to each narrow bed—the young guard brought Sister Agathe. "Five minutes," he whispered and locked her inside the room with them.

The sister drew in her breath when she saw Trudi. "You— I didn't know you were here, Fräulein Montag."

"It's my third night."

"Where's the patient?"

Trudi motioned to Frau Hecht next to her in bed. "She's burning up."

After the nun unbuttoned Frau Hecht's blouse, soiled and reeking from having been worn too many days and nights, she inserted a thermometer beneath her left arm. Her fingers found the pulse. "This is not good," she said after a silence.

"Is she dying?" one woman asked from the next bed.

"Of course not," the other woman said.

"I didn't mean to—"

"Well, she might hear you."

From deep within the folds of her habit the nun produced a small bottle. She made Frau Hecht swallow two pills and pressed the bottle into Trudi's hand. "Give her two of these every four hours."

The door opened a gap. "Quick." The man-boy voice said, "Quick now."

"Please, tell my father—" Trudi whispered, but the nun rushed out without a glance back.

In the morning, when an older guard led them to the bathroom, Trudi was afraid the young man had been caught, but that evening he was back, carrying their food.

Trudi wondered what it was like for him, following orders, yet risking arrest for one act of kindness. "Thank you," she whispered to him.

His eyes skipped away from her with the beat of fear, and he set the lines of his mouth, hard. "No talking," he snapped.

She lowered her eyes. I'm sorry, she wanted to say, but even that would frighten him, implicate him. They both had to pretend nothing had happened that night.

During the brief periods away from the room, while waiting in line outside the bathroom door, Trudi found out about other prisoners. She'd stand close enough to whisper but not close enough to be reprimanded by a guard. She spoke with a young Jewish woman, a sales clerk, who'd been caught in a train station after she'd bought her ticket. A retired locksmith, whose spectacles were bent and had one lens missing, told her about the feather comforter he'd brought in his luggage; he was furious that it had been taken away from him, considering how he'd abandoned a lot of other belongings he could have brought instead.

"They would have taken those too," Trudi reminded him.

"It's not fair."

"Of course not."

Another man, a Jewish professor, had been arrested while stealing eggs. Two years earlier he'd left Heidelberg, and he'd been hiding ever since, sleeping in barns and forests, traveling on a bicycle though its tires had long since worn out and he'd had to tie rags around its metal rims.

"I won't be here for long," he assured Trudi. "It's not in my nature to stay anywhere more than a week."

She didn't point out to him that it was no longer his choice. "If you ever need help—" she started.

"That's kind of you, my dear. But you're hardly in a position to help."

She was glad for him when, the morning after their conversation, she heard he had managed to escape from the Theresienheim. Nearly everyone she saw that day whispered about him excitedly, even two of the guards, but the stories conflicted: the professor had climbed onto the roof and let himself down with a rope he'd made from bed sheets; the professor had walked right out of the front door, wearing a stolen uniform; the professor had bitten his way out. . . .

Trudi wasn't quite sure what it meant, biting your way out, but that was the version she liked best and circulated with her own stories because it embodied what she was beginning to feel herself capable of. But in the meantime she was not doing anything except wait. She worried about her father, hoped that he wasn't risking his safety for her.

Frau Hecht was still sick though her fever had come down. She told Trudi that Sister Agathe had visited her once before. "To bring me a boiled egg . . . Imagine. She's like that, the sister, taking things to prisoners when she can, even though it puts her in danger. One widow—she's gone now—lost her shoes when she was arrested, and the sister found her a pair, black leather, only a little too big. . . ."

When the two other women in their room were taken away within a day of each other, they offered no resistance. Eyes dazed, they retreated into decades of good manners, mumbling polite words of good-bye to Trudi and Frau Hecht.

One of Trudi's new roommates, a gypsy woman, had deep gashes down her back from crawling under barbed wire into a meadow, where she'd hidden for three weeks in a clump of bushes, drinking milk directly from the udders of cows until the farmer had spotted her one dawn.

Many of the prisoners were Jewish, but there were others like Trudi who'd said the wrong thing or, worse yet, had been caught hiding fugitives. The end of her third week in the Theresienheim, she was brought downstairs late one afternoon and led into the office that used to belong to the mother superior.

"The little girl from the hat shop." The man who sat behind the desk brought his bone fingers together as if in prayer—though without his palms touching—and drummed his fingertips against each other. "You didn't keep your mouth shut?"

Though she'd only seen him once, that day he'd arrested Frau Simon, she recognized him immediately. His face had lost more of its flesh, pushing his eyes further into their sockets, and he looked even more tired, more aloof.

She wanted to tell him again that she was not a little girl, but she remained silent because four years had passed and she understood more about things that could happen to you, understood hunger and fear and his authority to send her to her death. Her wool dress was matted beneath her arms, making her feel dirty.

He said: "The rules that used to temper curiosity no longer exist."

She waited, confused.

"Do you understand what I say?"

"No."

"You should. Don't you know what can happen to someone like you in our country?"

The Buttgereit boy . . . the man-who-touches-his-heart . . . the Heidenreich daughter . . . No, she was not like them.

"You become an experiment . . . a medical experiment for the almighty profession," he said, and told her of operations performed on twins, on people afflicted with otherness. "Because the rules that used to temper curiosity no longer exist . . . Some people might even tell you that a *Zwerg* has no right to live."

She felt her back seize up on her. Bracing herself against the familiar heaviness at the base of her spine, she asked, "And you? Is that what you believe?"

He looked at her, evenly, and she read in his eyes what she'd known four years before—that he didn't believe in anything or anyone.

She kept her expression impassive to match his. It still chafed at her—to hear the word *Zwerg* said aloud—but if she'd learned anything, it was how to be the *Zwerg*, to play the *Zwerg*. Funny almost, the way it gave you a strange power to let others look down on you, to let them bask in their illusion that they were better than you. That illusion was a gift—hers to grant, simply by being—a gift that turned some of them ugly and others defenseless and, therefore, useful.

A muscle jumped beneath his left eye, quivered, and jumped again. He raised one hand halfway but dropped it before it could reach his face. "What is it like, being a *Zwerg*?"

She knew it was a game for him, a distraction from his indifference, because it didn't matter to him what happened to her. For that to matter, she'd have to figure out exactly what it would take to yank him out of his apathy. The secret, she thought, the secret of not caring about anything, as she remembered her first impression of him years ago.

She lifted her face toward him. "Being a *Zwerg* means carrying your deepest secret inside out—there for everyone to see." She thought of an article she'd once read in the *Burgdorf Post* about an infant in Egypt who'd died hours after being born with her organs connected to the outside of her skin. "Like this man I knew who was born with his heart attached to the outside of his chest. People could see it pump. And because it was so obvious, they thought they knew all about him. He had to cover his heart with gauze to keep it from getting infected, to protect it from dust and heat and snow. . . ."

The Gestapo officer's eyes were on her, filled with a cold curiosity; his fingers had returned to their drumming.

She tried to feel out what would pull him into her story. She'd often sensed what people wanted to hear, but this was the first time it totally determined the story. And my life, she thought. "This man . . . you see, he had his suit jackets tailored in such a way that they were large in his shoulders and hung down his chest, but still, the swelling pushed out the fabric, moved it with each heartbeat. In his dreams, his chest was smooth, his heart safely anchored within his body. And when he prayed—"

"Praying is for fools."

"Praying is for fools," she agreed. "That's what he finally realized too."

"What does any of this have to do with being a *Zwerg?*"

"Everything." Her legs trembled, but she didn't dare sit down. "Everything," she said, forcing herself to expose what she hadn't yielded to anyone before: "You see, when I dream, I'm often tall. I—I used to try stretching my body by hanging from door frames. . . ."

The thin fingers stopped their drumming as she described how her arms had gone numb while she'd hung from the door frame, how she'd tightened scarves around her head to keep it from getting larger. From time to time her voice would clog, but she'd go on, even though it meant turning herself inside out like the infant with the organs fused to her surface, delivering herself, risking death, risking life.

Though he would look toward the door as if wishing he could dismiss her, his eyes were always drawn back to her. "Go on," he'd order whenever her voice faltered.

"I used to sew clothes that would make me look one or two centimeters taller. I used to believe praying would make me grow. . . ."

"Go on."

She felt a sudden rush of power, the power to stay alive. She'd kept others alive with her stories when they'd come close to being found. This time it was for herself. "The man whose heart beat outside his body, you see, when he was a boy, other children wouldn't let him play. They called him names, laughed at him. . . ." It was the right story. It had to be. She could see the boy standing outside the circle of other children, longing to be part of it, hating the others for not including him, and she let her words take the officer into that schoolyard when the boy's parents complained to the teachers and the other children were forced to let him play.

"Go on."

She felt drained, purged, as he followed her through the boy's school years and into a beer garden, where he danced for the first time, his arms extended to keep the girl he loved from colliding with his heart. "They felt stiff, his arms, they ached, but he didn't dare bring her any closer. . . ."

"Go on."

"People would not let this man forget about his heart. They'd look at him with pity, with interest. But that's where they made their mistake—by assuming that, just because they saw the swelling on his chest, they knew what it was like for him to live with his heart outside his body. And that . . . that is where the secret lies."

"He let them assume."

She nodded.

"He did not correct them."

She shook her head.

He watched her for several long minutes. "Of course," he said. "Of course."

Outside it was getting dusky, leveling the angles of the gaunt face, filling its hollows with the ghosts of perished flesh. Suddenly, and with absolute conviction, Trudi knew that, come spring, he would no longer be alive, and that his death would meet him through his own hands. She stared at those hands as they dipped a pen into ink and scribbled words on a sheet of paper.

"I don't want to see you back here."

Her eyes snapped from his hands to his face. "What?" she asked.

"I said I don't want to see you back here."

"You won't."

"Watch that mouth of yours. Salute the flag, sing when you must, and don't complain. About any of it."

As his huge signature crawled across the bottom of the page like a prehistoric insect, Trudi saw herself curled inside the narrow tunnel between the two cellars. Eva's mosquito netting swayed above her, and the earth held the damp, furtive scent of places that are only accessible to those willing to burrow down that far. *My mother would have loved that space,* she thought with a sense of wonder. *Another earth nest. Odd that I haven't thought of it till now.*

It was the coldest winter she would look back on even as an old woman. The river was frozen solid, a wide, empty surface without the familiar barges, mirroring the emptiness of the town. There was little to diminish the relentless cold. Trudi hadn't been able to get warm since that evening she'd been released from the Theresienheim and had dashed through backyards and across the brook to her house, flinging herself at the kitchen door and into her father's arms. Even when he stoked the tall stove in the bathroom for her and she lay in the steaming water, she still felt cold.

Fuel was scarce that winter, and for one hour each day she'd heat the green tile stove because it needed fewer coals than the kitchen stove. On its small surface she'd cook the scant midday meal in the living room. Even Matthias, who'd stop by to play the piano for her, could not warm her with his music.

She'd only been away a few weeks, but her father looked years older. It was as though he lived almost entirely through his eyes now. Though he'd rarely missed a chess club meeting in decades, he stopped going to the club the night several of the members—who cheered each new atrocity the Nazis committed—celebrated the arrest of Leo's friend, the judge Erwin Spiecker, who'd fought in the First World War with him.

From what the judge's wife told Leo, the arrest had happened half an hour after Erwin had walked out of his courtroom in Düsseldorf with two lawyers and had mentioned that, if things kept going like that with the military, Germany wouldn't win the war. He was taken to Berlin to be executed—treason, they said—and his wife, who was pregnant with their eighth child, kept waiting for permission to visit him in prison.

"I got out," Trudi tried to console her, "and his comment wasn't worse than mine."

"It's still a miracle to me how you managed that," Frau Spiecker said.

When she finally was allowed to see her husband, she rode on a train all night. In Berlin, she had to wait for hours in an unheated hallway before she was taken to see him. He reeked—his entire body reeked—and he wrenched himself immediately from her embrace. He, who'd always kept himself fanatically clean to combat the foul smell that emanated from his body, was so mortified that he insisted she stay at the opposite end of the room.

Four times Judge Spiecker's execution was postponed, and four times Frau Spiecker left her children with neighbors in Burgdorf and, carrying a package with soap and cigarettes and mystery novels that

Leo Montag sent along for Erwin, made the long journey to Berlin, prepared to—once again—say her final good-bye to her husband. But the last time he was no longer there when she arrived: he'd been transferred, she was told, to a prison camp south of Berlin, where no one could visit him.

"At least Erwin is alive," she told Leo Montag when he picked her up from the train station. "At least he's alive."

That Sunday he drove her and her children to church, where several men from the chess club knelt with pious faces as every Sunday, occupying the pews with an attitude of ownership, content with the familiar rituals: the opulent scent of the *Weihrauch*—incense—the angelic sounds from the choir, the flat communion wafers, the chalice with the blood of Christus.

Leo squinted at the faint pink clouds in the altar cloth with the lace edging, recognizing the markings of blood that had never washed out entirely after he'd carried his wife from the church. How long had Gertrud been dead? Twenty-three years, he thought, and the cloth is still there.

He glanced toward the women's side of the church, where the judge's wife knelt in prayer, her high belly pushing against the front of the honey-colored pew as if trying to prove that flesh was stronger than wood. Or stone, Leo thought. Or the knife of sorrow. Some day her husband would have been dead for years. And she would find that you survive what you never thought you could possibly survive.

When he brought Frau Spiecker to mass a month later, he carried her infant daughter, his godchild Heide, in his arms. By then, mass was held in the chapel. Since the war had continued to shrink the congregation, Herr Pastor Beier had decided to move the services there. Though the chapel was two kilometers from the rectory, it was small enough to heat, and after contemplating his choice of discomforts, the fat priest had selected travel over cold, figuring his housekeeper would manage to arrange rides for him—with the taxidermist, say, or the dentist's wife, who should feel honored at doing this for him. But it turned out that, frequently, he had to ride his bicycle after all, and he needed half the mass to settle his breath.

Those bicycle Sundays, as he came to think of them, his sermons were always shorter. He pointed this out to the bishop when he wrote him a letter, asking for a car that would make it possible for him to serve his parishioners more effectively. In his letter he emphasized his visits to the sick and elderly, but omitted the dinner invitations which he still managed to secure despite dwindling food supplies.

Leo never felt the division within the town as acutely as he did in the chapel. Once, the parish had felt like something whole, one body of people connected in one belief and many shared values—even if Leo had not always agreed—but now that belief had become tainted by those who used it to proclaim their superiority, who justified the crimes against the Jews by saying they deserved punishment because they'd killed Christus.

The blood of Christus. When the fat priest raised the chalice, Leo couldn't help but think of centuries of savagery that had been committed for the blood of Christus. Catholic voodoo, he thought as the priest brought the chalice to his lips to drink the sacred blood, as the good people of Burgdorf stuck out their tongues to consume the body of Christus.

Trudi was making *Bratkartoffeln*—fried potatoes—on the tile stove when her father mentioned that Max Rudnick would stop by that afternoon.

She turned her face away to hide her blush and jiggled the pan by its handle to keep the potatoes from burning. "Why?" she asked.

"He came by this morning when you were at the bakery, and I told him you'd be here this afternoon."

"Why would you do that?"

"Why not?"

She flipped over the crisp potato slices.

Her father stepped next to the stove and raised his hands above the pan to warm them. "He says he wants to talk with you."

When Max Rudnick entered the pay-library late that afternoon, Trudi was surprised how glad she was to see him; yet, she found it impossible to show that because all she could think of was the way she'd deceived him. That nasty note she'd brought to his table . . . She felt her shame as though it had happened the day before and knew she didn't want to hurt anyone again with that kind of deliberation.

With all that turmoil going on within her, she couldn't figure how to say *no* when he invited her to have dinner with him the following day.

"At six then," he called out to her when he left the pay-library. "I'll pick you up at six tomorrow."

As she got ready for bed, she agonized over ways to cancel their

plans. All at once she remembered the one Goddamn beautiful
night—as Eva had called it—that she'd dreamed up for herself and
Max. She cringed. Of course Max had never considered anything like
that with her. Their meal would end with him exposing her as Angelika and walking out, leaving her sitting right there with the unpaid
bill. She'd have to call her father to pick her up, ask him to bring
enough money. Some nerve Max Rudnick had. Tomorrow, when he
arrived, she'd come right out and tell him she wasn't interested in eating dinner with him. . . .

But in the morning she awoke tingling with anticipation. Only
eleven hours until she would see him. Was he thinking of her that moment? She felt silly, afraid, happy. Her energy was boundless as she
worked in the library. She pictured herself sitting across from Max at
the table, saw him bending over her in her bedroom, and she surfaced
to her customers' questions in a daze. Although she couldn't wait for
it to be six o'clock, she wanted to prolong this sweet suspense that
tinged her day and made her feel graceful on her feet, even somewhat
taller, as though, miraculously, her body had finally obeyed her old
prayers.

The first time Max Rudnick kissed her, Trudi felt the secret of Angelika between them, but she kissed him back, passionately, greedily because she felt she was stealing this kiss. Once he knew the truth about
the letters, he would no longer want to see her, much less kiss her.
And yet, she found herself smiling through that kiss because it occurred to her that it had been just about a decade since Klaus Malter
had kissed her and because she promised herself that it would not be
another decade before she'd kiss another man.

The second time Max Rudnick kissed her was right after the first
kiss, and then there were several other kisses that would make her
mouth feel fuller, delicately swollen. She became accustomed to his
melodic voice, though she couldn't always make out what he said
right away, but his hands would follow the swift words as if to preserve them in his palms until, all at once, she'd understand what he'd
said. And even if she didn't—Max Rudnick was a patient man who
didn't mind repeating his words.

When he held her in his arms, it felt as though he'd never been
away, though he told her he'd been back in Köln to nurse his Russian
grandmother through her last months of illness and to settle her es-

tate. There hadn't been much, but she'd left everything to him. It helped since the industrialist and his family had fled to Switzerland, and he had only found two new students to tutor.

He listened with compassion when she told him about her arrest. Before long, she began to find the ordinary in him beautiful: the curved shoulders now looked willowy, and the wave of black hair on his collar was not too long but rather followed the fine contour of his ears. She could not imagine why she would have thought of his mustache as timid when, in reality, its many hues of silken, bleached hairs only brought out the sensitive line of his upper lip. And as her love transformed what she saw—gradually, so that each encounter became a new discovery—she wondered if it was like that for him, too. Perhaps he only noticed her mass of silver-blond hair. Perhaps his eyesight was so bad that he barely saw her at all. She knew he liked the sound of her voice—he'd told her that—and she was certain he enjoyed their conversations. Ever since he'd said that she had spirited eyes, she'd found herself studying them in the mirror as though they belonged to another woman.

She didn't want to believe that he was only drawn to her because she was different, but their first disagreement was about just that. They were standing beneath the marquee of a movie theater in Düsseldorf, waiting for the cold rain to let up so they could run for his car. The film they'd seen had been romantic kitsch, a love story set in alpine meadows, complete with yodeling, *Lederhosen*, blond braids, and St. Bernards that carried casks of *Schnaps* around their furry necks and rescued blond heroes trapped on glaciers.

Peering into the rain, Max told her he admired her strength, her difference.

"Inside I'm just like others," she said.

"How can you possibly be like anyone else inside?"

"Why not?" she snapped back.

"Because your life has shaped you, has made you unique."

"Just because I'm different on the outside—"

"But that's not what I'm talking about."

"Yes, you are."

"What I'm saying is the opposite, really. Each one of us is different. Even those who are alike on the outside are totally unique on the inside." The dark street was deserted. "You take two old men, let's say, brothers, same height, same color hair—or no hair—who've lived in the same town all their lives. . . . As far as I'm concerned, they're not at all alike."

"Yes, but the two of them will look at me and use their sameness as a barrier to separate themselves from me. They'll believe I don't have anything in common with them."

"Then they're stupid old men."

"And there are thousands like them, men and women, who assume that with me everything is smaller—what I feel, what I think. . . ."

He brought his hand around the back of her head and bent down. In the light above the door of the theater, his glasses were fogged.

"You don't have to do this," she said as he kissed her, but then she saw the sadness and earth in his eyes, far too deep to be concerned about surfaces, and understood he wanted her as she was.

And yet, when he took her by the hand and ran with her across the wet pavement to the narrow hotel across the street, when he booked a room for them and dried her hair with a towel as soon as they got inside, she was terrified to take off her clothes and have him look at her with the same loathing she'd seen in her own eyes that day she'd run from Klaus Malter's office and her mirrors had thrown back her disjointed reflection, pale flesh swelling from the golden frames.

But Max was kissing her, gazing at her with affection. It was cold in the room. Rain drummed on the tile roof, against the window, and she closed her eyes, ready to let happen whatever would happen, because to dread it, to wait for it, was worse. Then his hands were on her breasts, and she got confused for a moment, thinking they belonged to Klaus Malter because they'd been his in those old fantasies, and she quickly opened her eyes and kept them open, reminding herself: *this is Max, this is Max*— And when he cried out under his rapid breath and ceased moving, poised above her like a comet the instant before its bright descent, she felt left behind. Her body felt warm and pliant, almost wonderful, but she was not moved by the tremors that she'd evoked for herself so many times.

He sighed, kissed her nose, her forehead, her left ear, settled against her side, one arm warm beneath her head, knees curved against her ankles. As she turned toward the length of his body, he murmured something. His arm twitched.

"Why me?" she whispered.

But he was already asleep.

She'd never slept in the same bed with anyone. It felt strange, crowded, exciting—as though her body had sprouted an extra torso and head, limbs of normal size that would disentangle from her in a few hours. But not yet. Not yet. It made her think how children who had siblings often slept in the same bed. She wondered if her parents would have had other children if she hadn't been a *Zwerg*. Just before she fell asleep, she remembered asking Frau Blau if her mother would have stayed sane if she hadn't given birth to a *Zwerg* child, and how important it had been to her what Frau Blau had told her: "Your mother was odd long before you were born. Don't misunderstand me, Trudi, I liked her. She was a dear, dear woman. But whatever was troubling her was there since she was a girl."

When Trudi did reach those tremors the next time she lay with Max Rudnick, she felt horrified because she'd used him to slip back to the barn and the boys and the old terror that brought her, brought her—

"Why are you crying?" he asked, stroking her hair.

She couldn't answer.

"Nothing you can say will be worse than this silence."

She shook her head.

"Did I hurt you?"

"Oh no," she said, ashamed of the fantasies that had claimed her, ashamed of the passion that needed fear. She'd often felt hollow afterwards, but now it was even worse because she was betraying Max.

He folded himself around her, rocked her.

It amazed her how, after such a short time together, his body could feel so familiar to her. She liked being with him in the room that he rented above a clock shop in Kaiserswerth, even though it was chilly as if the walls stored the winter's unrelenting cold. And what made it seem even colder was that the room was nearly empty: except for his bed, it held no soft surfaces, only the angles of two chairs and a table, a bookshelf and a wardrobe, a sink and a stove. Max had very few belongings, as though he were prepared to leave quickly, and the one surprise in these stark surroundings was his unframed watercolors, which he'd pinned to the walls, all of them of fabulous buildings that looked like exotic flowers as they swirled and opened toward the sky.

A few times she'd come close to letting her father know that something beautiful was happening between her and Max. Though he'd be asleep when she'd come home at dawn and wouldn't ask her where she'd been, she had a feeling he understood about them and was glad for her. But already so much had gone on between her and Max that to say anything to her father now would involve confessing about not telling him from the beginning.

Her instinctive secrecy when it came to herself made Trudi keep silent about Max to everyone else. They'd only shun him for choosing her, just as they'd shunned Eva after the concert. Besides, loving without marriage was sin. Though enough people did it, you couldn't admit it because then the town had to reject you.

"Some day," Max said, "if you feel ready to tell me, will you let me know why you cried? Even if I don't know the words to ask?"

She held his hand, lifted it to look at it closely. It wasn't just his hand that was tanned. His entire body was that soft brown shade. It would be so easy to forget all restraint and hurl her love at him the way Seehund used to with his puppy weight, his entire body and heart.

"Will you?" he asked.

"I like seeing your skin against mine. . . ."

"Why is that?"

"Because I always know where I end and where you begin. Look."

He reached behind himself for his glasses, and as he raised himself on his elbows, he, too, became intrigued by the contrast in their skin tones. "It's beautiful, the way your skin glows . . . as if lit from inside by a thousand candles."

Already she could see herself alone at home, looking at herself in her mother's mirrors, finding the glow he was talking about as a thousand candles warmed her from within. She was amazed at the sense of comfort she felt at being within her body—being whole, healthy, beautiful. Like Pia, she thought. Pia must have felt like that.

"My light spirit," Max murmured against her lips.

"My light spirit," she would murmur to herself in her bed at home, her smile turned into her pillow.

s e v e n t e e n

——————————————— ■ ———————————————

1 9 4 3

"Do you have any faults, Max?" she asked him one February night when she lay next to him in his narrow bed.

"What do you mean?" He ran one hand along the inside of her arm, lightly.

"You are too perfect, too kind. . . . It scares me. Makes me think I don't see you right."

"Well . . . If you promise not to tell—" He glanced around his room as if to make sure no one else would overhear his confession. Bringing his lips against Trudi's ear, he whispered, "I've stolen."

"What?"

"A pack of chocolate cigarettes. When I was eight."

"I'm impressed."

"You should be."

"Is that all?"

"Sometimes I get furious, break things."

"Like what?"

"Oh—toys, when I was a child. Once, I ripped my best friend's kite apart when he made fun of the one I'd built. . . . I broke a car window a few years ago."

"What happened?"

He hesitated.

"Tell me? Please?"

"I was traveling with—with a woman to Bremen. We were taking turns driving, and when I got out to walk around the car, you know, to the passenger side, she locked my door. We'd been joking around, and I guess she thought it was funny. She was sitting in there, laughing, and I warned her, I yelled, 'Open the door,' but she dangled the key behind the windshield, and I picked up a rock. At first she laughed, but as I raised the rock, her expression changed, and I could see she was afraid. Afraid to let me in. But I couldn't stop. Even though I knew something had gone too far and that I'd missed the moment when that had happened."

"Did you hurt her?"

"No. I broke the window on the passenger side."

"Did you see her again after that?"

"We—we were married."

Trudi sat up, pulled her arms close to herself, so that no part of her touched him any longer. On the floor by his wardrobe stood her black shoes, the ones with the highest heels, which she kept in his room so she could reach the table and sink easily.

"Look at me," he said. "I haven't seen her in years."

"You're divorced then?"

"Not legally. But I will be, if we ever agree enough to sign papers."

Her body felt stiff as if her heart had stopped beating.

"Come here." He opened his arms to her. "Please, Trudi?"

She shook her head. One of his hairs lay on her arm, dark and curled. She couldn't bear to touch it and blew it away.

"Ask whatever you need to know."

"You wouldn't have told me. . . ."

"I promise you the truth."

"You wouldn't have told me. . . ."

"I don't think of her, Trudi. I don't think of myself as married."

"But you are."

"People don't always tell each other everything right away."

Her face felt hot. "What do you mean?"

"Wouldn't you agree that it's better to wait to reveal some things until you know the other person is ready to hear them?"

"I— I'm not sure."

"Well, you wanted to know if I had faults."

"And you do."

"You said I was too perfect."

"I would have settled for something less dramatic than a wife."

The following day Ingrid Baum traveled to Burgdorf in the back of an open truck that had been used for transporting potatoes. The bed of the truck was covered with potato dirt, thick layers of gray dust that clung to her skin. With her were a shoemaker from Bonn and his large family on their way to an uncle's wedding in Oberhausen; they sang and laughed and fed her cake and insisted she share the bottle of *Schnaps* they passed around even to the children. Though Ingrid didn't like *Schnaps,* she took one sip, afraid to offend the shoemaker's wife who'd lean into her, whispering confidences about her husband's appetites and the thickening of her monthly flow.

As it began to rain, the family huddled closer, collecting around Ingrid as if she were one of them. The only part of her that was not freezing was her left ear: it burned into her skull, made half of her face sore. She tried to remember when it had started hurting, but she couldn't even remember packing the suitcase, which was getting soft from the rain. When its handle came off, she turned it between her fingers. The oldest son passed the *Schnaps* to her again, telling her it would warm her, but she shook her head. The potato dust soaked up the water until they all were sitting in thick mud. When the truck dropped her off in front of the pay-library, her hands and face were smudged, her clothes soggy.

Trudi, who'd been standing by the window, staring out into the rain while going over every word of last night's conversation with Max, didn't recognize the truck or the woman who stayed behind on the sidewalk when the truck drove off, holding a suitcase with both arms as though it were a sleeping child. But then the woman turned and became Ingrid. Trudi ran out, pulled her inside, made her take off her coat and wet shoes. After wrapping her in a blanket, she offered her soup and a bath though Ingrid was too exhausted to wash or eat.

"What happened to you?" Trudi asked after she'd heated the stove and settled Ingrid next to it in a deep chair, feet raised on a wooden stool.

Ingrid's eyes went blank. She reached up, pulled a strand of straight wet hair into her thin face.

"Why did you leave?"

"I . . . don't know."

But gradually Trudi was able to draw from her that she remembered running with her suitcase from the KLV school, where she'd taught for the past year and half. She remembered getting off a train, but she didn't recall the journey, not even buying a ticket. The truck? She'd been standing somewhere in the cold when the shoemaker had stopped for her.

"There is a man who wants to marry me," Ingrid said without enthusiasm.

"Who is he?"

"Ulrich."

"And . . . ?"

Ingrid leaned her head against the back of the chair and stared toward the ceiling. ". . . so well behaved."

"The man who wants to marry you?"

"No, no. One of the students, Suse." Ingrid's voice tapered to a murmur as though she were talking to herself. ". . . a face like an angel— But Fräulein Wiedesprunt kept taking her on drives, bringing her licorice, letting her sleep in her room. . . . I didn't know what to say to stop it. The girl— Maybe nothing happened. . . . Trudi?" She sat up straight. "Trudi."

"I'm here."

"I thought dirty about them. . . . The ink keeps running. Notebooks for school, they're always rationing them and—"

"Is that why you left there? Because of the girl?"

"The paper, it's so bad the ink runs. . . ." Ingrid's voice took on an official quality as though she were imitating someone: "We have to verify the necessity of each purchase."

"Why don't you tell me about this man who wants to marry you?"

"Ulrich Hebel."

"What's he like?"

"He's a soldier now."

"And before?"

"The railroad. He used to work for the railroad."

"Do you love him?"

"He says it's his, too."

"What?"

Ingrid peeled the blanket away and pointed to the slight mound of her belly. "The fruit of my sin," she said as if reciting from the Bible.

"Don't make it sound so ugly."

Ingrid covered her eyes.

"Oh, Ingrid—" Trudi embraced her and, gently, pulled her fingers from her face. "I know it must be difficult, but you'll get to love the baby. And I'll help. . . ." Already she could see herself taking Ingrid's baby for walks in a wicker carriage, sitting in the sun on the front step with the baby in her arms. She'd sew a gingham pillow cover, a matching—

"It belongs to the devil."

"Don't say that."

"Marrying doesn't undo the sin."

"It's not a sin."

"The church says."

"Forget the church."

Ingrid crossed herself and winced.

"What's wrong?"

"My ear—it hurts."

"I'll run over to the pharmacy and get some eardrops."

"It doesn't matter."

"Yes, it does. Do your parents know about the baby?"

"My father would kill me."

"He won't. Besides—" Trudi hesitated. If Ingrid stayed with her, she wouldn't be able to offer shelter to Jews. But ever since her arrest, the house had become too risky as a hiding place. Emil Hesping still hadn't brought any fugitives, but he accepted the food and clothing that Trudi collected for him. Most of the food she got from Frau Weiler, and Hilde Eberhardt was a good source for children's clothing, willing to part with whatever Trudi asked for without wanting explanations. It was well known in Burgdorf that the midwife often traded her services for shirts and pants and dresses that a family's last child had outgrown. She'd gathered quite an assortment, which she gave to people who couldn't afford clothes for their children. Sometimes—so it was told—she even brought clothes and diapers to poor families instead of letting them pay her.

"You could stay with us," Trudi told Ingrid. "For a while. . . . I'm sure my father would say it's all right."

"I have to face my just punishment, the laceration of my soul—"
Trudi groaned. "Don't do this to yourself."

"—the decline of my spirit—"

"Have you seen a midwife? A doctor?"

"—the deterioration of the flesh—"

"I could get Hilde Eberhardt . . . bring her here."

"No." Ingrid stopped her litany.

"How about this man? The one who wants to marry you."

"When he gets his leave."

"Then you'll marry him?"

"To save the child's name. It's too late for me. I'm forever damned.
I'll never be a missionary."

"You want me to get the priest?" Trudi asked without much confidence. Still, maybe even the fat priest was better than no priest at all.
"You could confess. Get rid of the sin."

"I am the sin."

"Ingrid—"

"I have always known that about myself."

"And what is it about you, then, that makes it impossible to get absolution? What makes you so special?"

But Ingrid shook her head. Her eyes glittered. "I am the sin."

While Leo Montag brewed strong Russian tea for Ingrid, Trudi ran to
Neumaier's pharmacy for eardrops. Though it had a new owner,
Fräulein Horten, people still called it Neumaier's pharmacy. In the
nine months since he'd been taken away with his daughter and former
wife, no one had heard from the pharmacist, and people suspected
that he'd not only kept some of the money he'd solicited for the Hitler
statue, but also most of the funds he'd collected from people for
membership in the *Partei*. The Stosicks hadn't been the only ones
who'd never received papers in the mail.

Trudi was about to pay for Ingrid's medicine when the sirens
sounded off. As she glanced toward the door, trying to decide if she
should race home, Fräulein Horten took her by the arm.

"My father—" Trudi said.

"Better stay here."

Fräulein Horten led her down into the huge cellar, where several
tenants from the apartment building already sat on apple crates and
suitcases, eyes turned toward the ceiling as if it were possible to see

the danger beyond. With all the bombings that could strike the major nearby cities any time during the day or night, you had to be prepared for stray bombs and rush to the nearest cellar with a ready-packed bag or suitcase, containing your most important belongings. Mothers would grab small children from their beds and fly down the stairs, while trying to calm their screams. Often the air raids wouldn't last very long, but you could sit in a cellar for hours, surrounded by others who handled their deadly fears by crying or praying or complaining.

The butcher and his daughter-in-law, still wearing their stiff aprons, were already in the cellar. The optician arrived soon after with his foreign worker from Greece, then the teacher who lived on the second floor with the Brocker girl, who'd recently started keeping house for her. Next came Jutta Malter and her husband's mother, the professor, who often stayed with her for a few days.

The last one to enter was Alexander Sturm, his face pasty, far thinner than it used to be. In the half year since Eva's arrest, Trudi had only seen him twice, and he hadn't spoken to her beyond a brief greeting. He no longer attended mass. The seriousness that had marked him during his boyhood had reclaimed him as though his passion and resulting handsomeness had only been inspired by Eva. Those shining years of marriage had fallen from him without a trace, and despite his dashing mustache he looked quite ordinary again, middle-aged already as if the passage from boy to stolid man had happened overnight.

During those years of his marriage to Eva, Trudi had come to like Alexander, and his house had been a place she'd enjoyed visiting. But ever since Eva's arrest, she—along with others—had speculated as to why he'd gone free, and since he didn't attempt to explain himself, he'd lost his reputation for being a decent man.

He sat on the bare floor, where the briquettes used to be stacked, his back against the wall that was black with coal dust, as if he didn't care about his clothes. High above him, the small windows had been covered with canvas to keep any light from seeping out. In the corner by the shelves leaned the cumbersome Jesus figure that Herr Neumaier used to carry around the church square, its knees angled and its arms linked above its head as if ready to resume its position on the cross. An immense wooden nail connected its palms, and liver-colored paint dripped from the crown. The new pharmacist had tried to donate the Jesus to the priest, who'd suggested she give it to the nuns, but she'd been afraid to enter the Theresienheim and had finally dragged the statue down to the cellar, where its lonely vigil was interrupted whenever the sirens sounded their warning.

Trudi thought of her father and Ingrid in the cellar of the pay-library. Every time she was afraid of what she might find after the bombing, and every time she was surprised that her town had been spared once again. It was different in Düsseldorf: there she'd seen children playing in the rubble of destroyed houses, women digging for lost possessions.

The Brocker girl whimpered and hid her face in her palms. Jutta Malter glanced at her from the side, then at the professor, as if waiting for her to do something. All at once Trudi felt sorry for Klara Brocker—even if she had traded that worthless rosary for Ingrid's jewelry box. Her father was fighting in the war, and her house had been one of the few crushed by stray bombs. She and her mother had moved into a small apartment on the fourth floor of the house that used to belong to Frau Simon.

"It won't be much longer." The professor reached across to stroke Klara Brocker's hair. "Not much longer."

In the half dark of the cellar, the girl shivered. "I'm fast on my bicycle. . . ."

The professor's eyes were tired as she stroked Klara's hair from her forehead and behind the small, pretty ears. Ever since her work had been taken from her, the professor had felt tired. She'd wake up tired, go to sleep tired.

"Real fast. . . ."

"I know."

From nearby came the sounds of a low-flying plane, then an explosion. The ground trembled.

"It's easy to lose your belief in humanity," the butcher was saying.

Trudi wheeled toward him. "It took you this long? Only now that you are in danger?"

"I'm not interested in an argument with you, Fräulein Montag." The butcher's breath carried more than half a century of tobacco smoke. "If the world would just leave Germany alone. All we're trying to do is restore the order in our own country."

The teeth of the Brocker girl were clicking against each other. "I bet if I got on my bicycle— I bet if I got on my bicycle and kept pedaling, I'd get away."

"You're not going anywhere," the butcher said.

"Please, leave her alone," the professor said.

They all fell silent, listening through the thick walls. Trudi felt Alexander watching her, but when she looked his way, he turned his eyes from her as if afraid to let her see into his mind. She felt him straining to shield the secret of Eva's capture from her. How does he bear it? she thought. She wanted to tell him that, ever since she'd been with Max, she'd understood Eva's longing for him and the risk she'd taken in returning to him for that one night.

"It wasn't just your doing," she whispered to him.

Alexander leaned his head against the black wall and shut his eyes.

Trudi wondered if Max had heard the explosion too and hoped he was safe. Last night, when they'd parted, she'd refused to kiss him. If we survive this, she thought, I won't even mention his wife again. Maybe he, too, was thinking about her right now. It had happened before: he'd tell her he'd been thinking about her, and when they'd compare times, it would turn out to have been at the very same moment.

"But I couldn't leave on my bicycle," the Brocker girl said, "I couldn't. Not with my mother the way she is." Her frantic eyes skipped from face to face as she told how, the last time they'd rushed to the nearest shelter, her mother had stumbled and fallen, bloodying her face and hands. "She's all alone," Klara cried and leapt up.

The optician blocked the door.

"I'm sure your mother feels better knowing that you're safe," the professor said.

"There's nothing we can do for our parents now," Trudi told Klara.

"Here." Klara's employer took her by the hands and pulled her down beside her. "It's always worse for the children."

"I'm not a child."

"I wasn't talking about you." She told Klara how, in school, her students no longer concentrated on her lessons because they lived with the fear that soon the bombs would start falling again. Often, in the middle of a class, they'd hear the sirens, grab their satchels, and run down into the school cellar. The teachers would try to soften the children's fear, but it was impossible to calm all of them. And when they came out again and the school stood intact, they were relieved. "The worst part," the teacher said, "is their worry about their parents."

"With good reason." Herr Immers took out a knife and a wedge of smoked ham and began to slice it. "People get buried under their own houses." He passed the slices of ham around. "Remember that time when the only damage in town was those blue bricks above the windows of the *Rathaus*? Knocked out on the sidewalk like bad teeth. . . . But the following week, they made up for it, right? Demolished the flour mill. We're lucky it's so far from the center of town."

"My father and I," Trudi said, "we drove out there. The roof is gone and the arches have caved in."

"We'll rebuild it after the war," the optician said.

"I don't think so," Trudi said softly.

"Why not?" Jutta Malter asked.

"I don't know. I just have a feeling we won't."

At the signal that it was safe to leave the cellar, Trudi got ready to rush up the stairs to make sure her father and Ingrid were all right.

"Wait."

She turned.

Alexander still sat by the coal wall, his forearms resting on his bent knees, palms turned upward like chalices.

She let the others pass her. "What is it?"

"What—" Alexander took a long breath. "What was it like for her, those last days with you?"

She stepped close to him and peered down into his face, waiting for him to tell her what had happened that night. And to find that out, she was willing to stay, to answer his questions first. "Eva missed you. That was the hardest part of hiding for her."

"What did she say about me?"

"That people didn't really know you. . . . She was afraid you might be sent off to war, and she said if she could have one Goddamn beautiful night with you—that's what she called it, Alexander, one Goddamn beautiful night—she'd be able to endure the hiding again."

He drew his legs closer to his body, rested his forehead on his knees. His shoulders trembled.

Trudi laid her hand on his sandy hair. "She was certain you'd go with her if she were caught. . . ."

"Every night I pray that I won't wake up in the morning." His voice was deep, urgent. "This morning I was praying that a bomb would hit the house."

"Let's hope your prayers won't get answered when you'll take all of us with you."

He looked up, startled. "Don't be so angry. I only thought of myself."

"Right."

"Of my death," he corrected her. "Maybe I ought to go into the army. . . . End it that way."

"Fight for them?"

"Fight anyone. Till I get killed."

"I want to know about Eva. What happened after she came to you?"

"I— I keep looking at those birds she collected. . . . Last week I bought her a stuffed nightingale."

"Last week?"

"For when she comes back. A present. Remember the owl I gave her?"

"For your wedding, yes."

"And that bird with the red chest that your dog killed."

"It lived for a few days. Eva's mother set its wing."

"We should have gone with Eva's parents. She wanted to. But she stayed because I didn't want to leave."

"After she came to you, Alexander—what happened that night?"

"Do you think someone tipped off the Gestapo?"

"I've wondered."

"She kept after me to get the butcher out of our building, but he has a ten-year lease. . . . I have to honor the contracts I sign."

"Ah yes, honor."

He drew up his shoulders. "I don't think the butcher turned her in. He didn't know Eva and I were arguing about his lease."

"They came to your house," Trudi prompted him, "and then you—?"

"We ran up the stairs. Into the attic. Hid there."

She could smell his fear of telling her too much. His eyes were guarded, and the words he gave her were insufficient by themselves. Yet it was his effort at shielding the truth that gave it away to her, evoking that night in the attic as if she'd been there herself. She inhaled the scent of the stored clay tiles and parquet wood as Alexander and Eva crouched behind the crates of building supplies. She heard steps approach on the stairs, felt the gush of air as the attic door burst open.

Sweat covered Alexander's temples. "We had enough time to say that we loved each other. . . ."

Trudi felt his confusion at the hate that had urged him into saying those words of love, understood his relief as Eva freed her arm from his hand and stepped forward.

"My legs—I couldn't move my legs. . . . Oh God."

"They didn't see you?"

"Oh God."

"They didn't look for you?"

He blinked, his eyes terror wide, and she heard the laughter as the Gestapo came around the crates and jabbed him with their feet.

"Some hero," one of them said.

"Some hero you got here." The other laughed as he turned toward Eva.

"You came for me. You found me," Eva said, her back as straight as ever.

Trudi grasped Alexander's hands. They were cold, damp. "What did you do then? Tell me!"

He snatched his hands from her and buried his face in them, trying to hide from her the spectacle of being forced to crawl around the attic on his hands and knees, two guns aimed at his head. But she could feel the rough wooden boards against his palms, could see Eva's ankles as he was forced to crawl past her.

"They left me there," he whispered. "On the floor." His voice had lost its tension, and his eyes looked spent as though he felt relieved at having told.

When they climbed from the cellar, the air smelled burned. In the heat, they could barely breathe. A yellow haze was lifting, revealing shapes of other buildings and roofs, and Alexander pointed across the street where the Talmeisters' house had been hit; yet, on the sidewalk the cherry tree stood intact, its leafless branches framing amber-gray clouds of smoke that rose from the heaps of stones and drifted across adjoining roofs.

Drawing the heat of war into her lungs, Trudi ran toward the pay-library, shouting her father's name. In her immediate neighborhood, the houses were still intact. Only three windows had been shattered in the library, and one section of roof above the grocery store had been torn off.

"All this can be repaired again," her father said.

"All this can be repaired again," Ingrid repeated after him, her body still wrapped in the blanket.

But Trudi shook her head, trying to combat the horror at all the lives that had been destroyed, including that of Alexander Sturm, who, though he walked and could point to a tree, had died as certainly as the Weskopp sons, who rotted beneath the earth.

Ever since Max had told her about his wife, she'd felt cautious around him. She wondered what he saw in her. Sometimes she was afraid that he only wanted to get even with her for humiliating him with the note, and that he would leave her once she loved him.

She finally found the courage to ask him. "Why me?" She came right out with it.

"What do you mean?" They were sitting at his table, and he was peeling an orange that one of his private students had given him.

"Why did you pick me, Max?"

Separating the cool sections, he arranged them on a white saucer. "Open your mouth," he said and fed one of them to her. "Because I like you."

After not eating an orange in years, the pleasure of tasting the sweet, juicy flesh brought tears to her eyes. "But how did it start for you?"

"I guess I was intrigued by you. . . ." He ate carefully, dabbing the juice from the corners of his mouth with one finger and sucking it as if not to lose one precious drop. "Here." He fed Trudi another slice. "I guess I was curious about you."

"Why?"

"Oh, that sense of mystery you have about you. I didn't know we'd become lovers the day we met. It happened gradually."

That evening he took her dancing for the first time, not to the Kaisershafen Gasthaus high above the Rhein, where she had imagined dancing with him, but in a cellar bar in Düsseldorf, where a saxophonist in a red vest played haunting variations of the same melody.

Max leaned his face close to hers. "I didn't know you were such a good dancer."

She smiled. "I've been told I have talent."

"I've been told that I am beautiful," he said, quoting what she'd written in the Angelika letter.

She stiffened.

"Keep moving your feet."

"When?" she asked, her voice high, dry. "When did you know?"

"The week after we met, when I came into the library and you weren't there. Your father was entering some books in the card file. . . ."

A frozen caricature of a dancing woman, she felt her feet shift to the left, to the right. Her hand was a wet stone in his palm. She stared straight ahead at the buttons of his suit jacket.

"I recognized your handwriting. I didn't even want to check out a book, but I did, just to get a look at another card."

"But then why did you come back?"

"I almost didn't, remember? I stayed away for eight months."

"Almost nine."

"That was a quite an overdue fine I'd accumulated. . . . I guess what brought me back was wanting to find out why you'd done it— brought that note to my table."

"Your ad said you were curious."

"Your letter said you were tall."

She flinched.

"I'm sorry, Trudi."

She wanted to run from him, slam the door of the bar, storm up the stairs to the street. "At least *you* told the truth."

"I said I'm sorry."

"I'm the one who needs to apologize."

"I didn't know how angry I still am."

She looked up. "I have felt terrible about hurting you. Ashamed. Many times— I wish I could undo that."

"Then we wouldn't have met."

"Why didn't you tell me right away?"

"You would have fled from me."

"And now?"

"Now you won't."

"How can you be so sure?"

"Because what we have now is strong enough to withstand that. . . . And it's not that I'm sure, rather that I'm hoping."

"We're still dancing."

"Would you rather sit down?"

"No." She shook her head. "That day in the restaurant—it all started as a hoax." She felt scared and relieved as she told him about reading the ads, about choosing his ad without any intent of meeting him, and then deciding to watch him. "I felt so furious. Humiliated."

"Why?" He stroked her hair, from the crown to where it ended in a thick line below her ears.

"Because you never saw me."

"Have you considered that you might have had something to do with that?"

"It was as if I didn't exist. That's when I decided to hurt you."

"I saw you," he said gently. "I saw a short, blond woman with extraordinary eyes. But I was waiting for a tall woman with auburn hair. And I kept looking for her. "

All at once she didn't know what to say.

"I'm glad it's out." He drew her closer. "It's hung between us."

"Like your wife," she said, and instantly remembered her vow not to bring up his wife again if they both survived the bombing.

"Like the woman I used to be married to. Maybe now you understand why I didn't tell you right away."

"You still are married to her."

"Not in my heart."

"But by law."

"It bothers you a lot?"

"Whenever I think of her."

"Don't think of her then."

"But I do."

"She doesn't want me back. I don't want her back. There's nothing to be afraid of."

"It's not that simple."

When they made love in his room, that night, it didn't take any effort to ban the savage fantasies that usually snared her. *This is Max,* her body sang to her, *this is now. . . .* And when she soared with him, it was as though she were leaving everything she knew behind—her country, language, customs. She'd heard women talk about giving birth like this—that flash of hesitation before you get to the moment when you can no longer reverse the process.

Now that he knew the secret of Angelika, she could tell him about her shame at returning to fantasies she didn't want. "But not tonight," she said. "Tonight I didn't need them."

He didn't ask what those fantasies were like. "And you may not need them again," he said. "But if you do, it's all right. Lots of people go away inside their heads when they make love."

"And where do you go, Max?"

"You already know." He motioned toward his walls.

"Are you telling me you climb the walls?"

He laughed. "My watercolors. I— I'll get embarrassed explaining this to you, but I think of them as orgasm pictures. That's what I see when . . . you know?"

She took in the lavish colors that spun into marvelous structures and soared toward the sky. "There's so much light and joy in those pictures. No darkness at all. . . . Can I ask you something?"

"If any of them are ours?"

She nodded.

He pointed to one above the table, another one by the window. "My best ones."

"Orgasms or paintings?" She smiled.

"I can't separate them."

"And the others?"

"Before you . . . Here, I want to show you something else." He climbed out of bed and returned with a charcoal sketch. "I did it this morning. It's my Russian grandmother, who brought me up."

"She has a wonderful face. . . . Those lines around her mouth— there's real kindness. Something childlike too."

"This is how I remember her. Ever since she died, I've tried drawing her from photos, but the sketches never looked right." He ran one thumb across the paper, softening the edge of his grandmother's chin. "But when I woke up today, I'd been dreaming about her, and I could still see her—just like this."

"How old was she when she died?"

"Almost eighty. She was born in 1863. In Smolensk. When she was two, she rode to the cemetery on top of her mother's coffin. It was her first memory. She talked about it more and more as an old woman."

Trudi saw her own mother's open coffin, her wrists crossed, and that lily—though it had not been there until her father had taken Herr Abramowitz to the cemetery chapel with his camera. "My mother died young," she whispered.

"How old were you?"

"Just before my fourth birthday."

"I'm sorry."

"She had a lover. Before I was born."

Max curved his arm around her.

"He had a motorcycle. My father was in the war then." She told him about the earth nest beneath the house and the asylum, about the stork's sugar and her brother's funeral.

And as he listened to her, totally absorbed, asking questions only when she paused, and then taking her further with those questions, she knew she'd found what she had been longing for—someone who wanted her stories, someone to whom she could tell everything, someone with whom she did not have to be selective about what to keep quiet. It was a link she'd had for brief intervals in her childhood, to Robert and Georg and then to Eva, and she hadn't realized how much she'd missed it until now.

That spring, Max's car was confiscated for the war effort, but the watchmaker from whom Max rented his room let him borrow his rowboat and bicycle. As the evenings grew warmer, Max would bring the bicycle in the boat across the Rhein and ride it to the Braun-meiers' jetty, where Trudi would meet him. Each time they made love on the jetty, Trudi felt herself reclaiming the place a little more.

"That cairn—" Max had asked when he'd first seen the pile of rocks at the end of the jetty, "Does it mean anything?"

She saw herself at thirteen, hurling stones into the river and coming back here, more than five years later, after seeing Klaus Malter with Brigitte Raudschuss—*one stone for loving him, one for hating him, one for her longing, one for her rage, one for her shame at loving him without him loving her back. . . .*

She felt a story stirring within herself, and she spun it for Max, for herself. "The cairn is hundreds of years old." She began her tale about a water fairy, a tale of betrayal and love and shame even though she didn't know the details yet. "Each stone means one life, and those long-ago people, who survived the revenge of the water fairy, swore to always remember her with this cairn.

"Those stones are restored after each flood, though no one knows who keeps up the ritual. Some say she's still there, in these waters, keeping vigil over the cairn, waiting to add other stones for other lives."

"What happened to her? Why was she so vengeful?"

"She wasn't always that way." Trudi spoke slowly, giving words to the images as they rose within her. "People used to watch her swim in the river, admiring her—uniqueness, her grace. You see, from the waist up, she was shaped like a woman, but instead of legs, she had the tail of a fish. It was silver and green and flashed when the sun touched it. Men fell in love with her beauty and wanted to possess her, and one morning four of them—" All at once she couldn't go on.

Max took her hands.

"They—they lured her to shore. Right here. With promises. Promises of being her friends. And then they carried her off . . . into a church, and tried to split her into being like a woman. But she escaped." Now the words were rushing from her. "She escaped from them and dragged herself back to the river, bleeding. It took her many months to heal, and after she was strong again, she brought the river into their houses and took her revenge. She drowned one of the men in his bed, another in his cellar.

"She killed every one of them," Trudi whispered, "every single one. And always—afterwards—she would bring a stone from the bottom of the river." She pointed to the cairn.

"To remember the dead," Max said.

"The living, too."

"There are more than four stones."

"Because when she was done, she came after their families too, after every person who had loved them." The story was frightening Trudi. She remembered hiding with Georg in the tower of the church, scaring him and herself with ghost stories, and then scattering their fear with stories of comets and water fairies. *Water fairies.* But now even her story about the water fairy was grim, and she couldn't think of a new story that would undo her fear.

"She went too far," Trudi said, "and with each stone she added she felt heavier inside. Colder." She glanced out over the river and thought how she'd undermined the boys who'd hurt her. Now the war had become her instrument of revenge—at least for two of them: Hans-Jürgen Braunmeier was reported missing in Russia, and Fritz Hansen had returned six months ago without a jaw. It had been shot off. Already, he'd had two surgeries and would need seven more, she'd heard from his mother, before his jaw would be restored as much as possible. He wore gauze from his neck up, and saliva ran down the front of it, making it look soiled even if it had just been changed.

"What if the water fairy were to toss those stones into the river?" Max asked.

"Why?"

"To release centuries of hate."

"But once the stones are gone, she might forget."

He looked at her steadily. "Right," he said. "She might forgive."

The identity of the unknown benefactor was discovered one night in May when—instead of following his pattern of leaving gifts—he attempted to take something away. What he stole was the Hitler monument in front of the *Rathaus*, the greenish statue with the flawed ear and crusts of pigeon droppings. The unknown benefactor was apprehended in the process of loading the short statue into a wheelbarrow, his open tool box next to him. From what the people of Burgdorf would hear afterwards, he was shot right there while trying to joke about taking the Führer for a stroll because it had to get boring standing in one place for so many years.

Not that the police figured out immediately that the thief was the unknown benefactor—that came when they searched his apartment and found a worn ledger, the kind a bookkeeper might have used decades ago, with detailed entries dating back over thirty years, listing people's shoe and clothing sizes, ages of children, illnesses, hobbies, needs, and secret wishes. Columns with check marks and dates documented all the gifts he'd mysteriously smuggled into houses—bicycles and baskets of food and books and toys and money and coats—including roller skates for a boy by the name of Andreas Beil, who had since grown up to become one of the policemen who'd shot the unknown benefactor.

"My God," Andreas Beil groaned when he discovered his name in the ledger. "All those years I've wanted to thank him."

"Why did Emil risk his life for such a useless stunt?" Leo Montag grieved.

Trudi shook her head, dazed.

The entire town was dazed. Where had Emil Hesping obtained the money for all those gifts? How had he found out about their secret wishes? Why hadn't they ever suspected him?

"Even I didn't know." Leo stroked the polished wood of the phonograph that the unknown benefactor had smuggled into the pay-library the first time Gertrud had been sent to the asylum. "You're too young to remember this . . . but Emil was rather fond of your mother."

The feeling of gravel beneath skin. A motorcycle tilting, tilting—
Trudi glanced up at her father. How much did he know?

"Some might say he adored her."

Gray spring light pressed against the front window, somber and ancient, challenging any bright color with its sameness. Trudi saw a chimney sweep pass by. Georg used to believe chimney sweeps brought you good luck. But Emil Hesping had not been lucky. Or perhaps he had been, living the mystery of the unknown benefactor for so long.

". . . but Gertrud, she didn't want him around those last years. Now they're both dead." Her father's voice carried a strange longing.

"I worry about that ledger," Trudi said. "What if he kept track of the hiding places, the people—"

"Not Emil. He wouldn't. Remember how he cautioned us against writing down any of the names or what we were doing? He wanted us to forget whatever it was we'd just done. There was no past, no future. That's why the gifts are different . . . something he could envision doing again. Those lists meant that there was a future he could believe in."

When Andreas Beil managed to get the body released, Emil's brother arrived for the burial and prayed over the grave. The bishop looked the way Emil would have with hair—same posture, same dense eyebrows, even the same laugh. Though it offended Pastor Beier, the bishop turned down the invitation to spend the night at the rectory and stayed with the Montags instead.

After Trudi had gone to sleep, Leo and the bishop sat at the kitchen table, between them a bottle of cognac, which the bishop had brought in his black suitcase.

"Emil valued his friendship with you," the bishop said.

"If only he'd spoken with me," Leo said. "We could have laughed about his plan, imagined carting that statue off together. It would have been as if we'd done it, and then I would have talked him out of it."

"Maybe something gave. . . . Maybe—" The bishop shook his head. "I was afraid it was getting too much for Emil. I just didn't know it would happen this soon."

"Are you saying he let himself get caught?"

"I don't believe he mapped it out like that. It's more like . . . even as a boy, when school got too much for him, Emil would take crazy risks."

In the alley between the library and the grocery store, two cats screeched, and as Leo stood up to close the window, a surge of lilac scent made him dizzy, and he steadied his hand on the windowsill.

"Like once," the bishop was saying, "Emil must have been ten, a year older than I, and afraid of getting the *Blaue Brief*—blue letter—and having to repeat fourth grade. Behind our house was this barn, and he climbed onto its roof and balanced along the top until he fell off. He broke his leg and two ribs. Another time he threw eggs at a church window. . . . I used to admire and fear Emil at the same time. Back then, we were not very alike at all. But now . . ." He turned his face aside.

Leo waited. Finally he said. "You have the same kind of courage."

"Really?" The bishop looked grateful. "I always thought of myself as rather timid. In comparison to Emil, that is."

"My daughter and I—" Leo sat back down. "We still want to help."

"It's too dangerous. Your connection to Emil . . . They'll be watching you. We need to be careful. I get so tired of being careful. . . . Sometimes I wish I could come out with what I think about the Nazis, use my influence—"

Leo shook his head.

"I know." The bishop refilled their glasses. "I've seen too many others pulled out of high positions. The only one I know of who's spoken up without harm to himself is the bishop from Münster. It's a mystery to me."

"You've done a lot of good, working in the background."

"In furious silence."

"The change in policy—" Leo said, "killing the Jews instead of trying to push them out of the country. . . . Emil used to argue that it did not arise from the war situation but was intended all along."

"And you?" the bishop asked. "What do you believe?"

"I'm not sure. I've never been as sure about things as your brother. But in my darkest moments I agree with him."

"So do I." The bishop hesitated. "There'll be rumors . . . so you better hear this from me."

"What is it?"

One of the flies that stuck to the amber fly strip above the table still twitched its legs.

"I had a phone call from the owner of the gymnasts' club. It turns out that, all those years Emil worked for him, he's been embezzling funds."

Leo's chin jerked up. "The gifts."

"What gifts?"

"The unknown benefactor."

The bishop frowned.

"That's how Emil must have bought the gifts." Leo told the bishop about the unknown benefactor, about three decades of gifts that had graced the lives of many people in Burgdorf. "Emil was the closest this town ever had to a hero. . . . And we didn't even know who he was."

"Ah yes," the bishop murmured and raised one hand as if in benediction, but halfway up he halted, a smile on his lips. "And we didn't even know. . . ."

Over the next weeks, Trudi and her father would marvel at long-ago incidents when, in Emil's company, they'd mentioned that the Braunmeiers had lost a calf to the storm, say, or that the Brocker girl had been looking at a rabbit muff in a store window, or that Herr Buttgereit couldn't afford coats for his family.

"We helped him."

"He knew how to listen."

Soon, they could no longer understand how they could possibly have missed all along that Emil Hesping had been the unknown benefactor. And so it was all over town.

"Remember when the pastor's housekeeper broke the handle of her shopping basket in the market? By the time she got back, a new basket with two cabbages was already on her doorstep."

"Remember when Frau Simon's bicycle was stolen and she found a new one right in her bedroom?"

"Remember when the Weiler boy got those *Lederhosen?*"

"Remember when the midwife—?"

"Remember when—?"

"Remember—?"

The people of Burgdorf liked to see themselves as accomplices of the unknown benefactor, and they cherished whatever small part they might have played in carrying information to him.

"I was the one who told him when Holger Baum lost his wallet."

"He heard about Frau Blomberg's broken ankle from me."

"If it hadn't been for me, he would have never found out about the Bilders' sick dog."

The people brought flowers to Emil's grave: tulips and forget-me-nots and lilacs; some whispered silent apologies about having ever considered him selfish or immoral. When they passed the Hitler statue, which had been bolted as well as chained to an iron base, they would cast sideways glances at the splatters of blood that had dried brown against the silver-white pigeon droppings on the Führer's chest. Even Herr Pastor Beier, who'd never shown much regard for Herr Hesping, now wished he'd reported his need for a car to him, rather than to the bishop, and based a long sermon on the words that it is better to give than to receive.

She arrived before Max and sat down on a rock wide enough for both of them. Within minutes the blue of the sky changed to gray, and a whitish mist began to roll in from the Rhein. It covered the end of the jetty, then whirled across the countryside as if summoned by a paint-brush, shrouding rocks, shrubs, and willows until Trudi, too, was sur-rounded. The quality of the mist—thick and white—made her eyes ache with its brightness, but as she adjusted to it, she felt invisible. She rather liked that sense of protection: she knew her surroundings well though she couldn't see them, but others wouldn't know where she was. It made her wish the mist had been there for the last decade, keeping all of them safe.

The mist had a dense texture—denser, it seemed, than her flesh. If only Max were already with her: they could make love in this mist. Low in her belly she felt the warm heaviness as if he'd already touched her. To hell with all the hiding . . . If it were up to her, she'd walk into the center of Burgdorf, right now, holding hands with Max, and make love in the church square with the mist shrouding them from curious and shocked eyes. She smiled to herself, but instantly felt frivolous, considering that there was a war and that people were so hungry and poor that someone had even stolen the collection box for pagan ba-bies from church. The last one of the geese behind the taxidermist's shop had disappeared—into someone's pot, no doubt—though everyone knew that Herr Heidenreich, who prayed for his daughter's return every day, was saving that goose for her homecoming meal. While Trudi and her father kept trading library books for food, nearly everyone she knew had sold some belongings in order not to starve.

In the deep silence of the mist, as Trudi longed to survive the war— even if just to know what would happen—she saw herself as an old woman, face lined, eyes tranquil yet knowing, and understood with absolute certainty that she would be alive for a long time to come. She wished she had that same certainty about her father and Max and Eva, or about Alexander Sturm who, after wavering between imagining Eva alive and dead, had convinced himself last month that she was dead. After making out a will that left everything to Jutta, he had enlisted in the army.

The mist gave a sameness to everything. Before, there'd been countless nuances in color and shape, but now everything was white-gray. Trudi could make out the shape of the bush right in front of her and then the shadows of birds flitting past her, but they only appeared for an instant before they were blotted by the mist. It was quite beautiful and eerie and made it possible to pretend there was no war and that—in some well-lit future—she might be able to remember whatever she chose.

She wondered how close Max was and if he too was discovering the beauty of the mist. Though she saw him once or twice a week, she thought about him when she was not with him. Sometimes too much, she worried. What if he turned away from her greed for his love? What if her love flipped into hate as it had before with others? The mist that separated her from him made her understand what it would be like not to have him in her life again, and she felt that old and absolute panic that, if you couldn't reach someone, that person had died or was lost to you. Only now there was no locked door to fling her child body against and bruise her fists, just that white barricade of mist that yielded to her movements, shaping itself to her body like new skin.

When the fog lifted, she realized she'd been sitting less than twenty meters from Max. At first neither of them moved. She felt a sharp bliss at having him in her life. All at once he laughed and sprang up, and she stood up too, amazed that the air offered no resistance to her body.

"What is it?" he asked. "What is it?" and brushed her hair from her cheek. "You weren't afraid, were you?"

She shook her head, and the air around her neck felt light and cool.

The first day Ingrid Hebel brought her newborn daughter to the pay-library, Frau Weiler came running over from next door, wiping her

hands on her starched apron. "Can I hold the baby?" she asked and
stretched out her arms before Trudi could even get a look at the newborn. Ever since Frau Weiler had become the grandmother of twin
girls, she'd blossomed. Now she fussed over every baby she saw, even
boy babies.

"If only she'd been that way with Georg," people would say, remembering the pathetic-looking boy in girl's clothing.

Frau Weiler's protruding eyes peered at the baby's face. "What's
her name?" She tickled her chin.

"Rita."

"She looks just like your husband."

Ingrid's face, which was already red from the sun, turned an even
deeper red. She had moved into the apartment above the bicycle shop
with her parents the day after she'd arrived in the potato truck, and
Trudi had heard Ingrid's father screaming three blocks away. From
the Heidenreichs Trudi had heard that Ingrid's father had met with
the pastor and that they'd made a number of phone calls from the rectory, including one to the army, requesting that a certain Ulrich
Hebel, who used to work for the railroad, be granted leave in time to
give his child a name.

The beginning of July, a week before the baby's birth, the soldier
Hebel arrived in Burgdorf for a hasty wedding. He didn't look at all
the way Trudi had imagined—a movie-star body and passionate eyes
that would have persuaded someone like Ingrid to part with her purity. Rather, he was shorter than Ingrid and quite a bit older, a considerate man, it was evident, who was easily flustered and adored his
new bride, even though his future father-in-law had boxed him in the
face upon meeting him, so that at the wedding ceremony as well as on
the day of his departure for Hamburg, where the British had attacked, the bridegroom's right cheek was the color of beef kidney past
its peak of freshness.

"Let me have the baby now," Trudi reminded Frau Weiler.

Leaning forward, Frau Weiler reluctantly positioned Rita in Trudi's
arms. "Careful now."

"You think I'm going to drop her? And that she'll turn out to be a
Zwerg too?"

"Oh, Trudi." Frau Weiler gave a quick, exasperated sigh. "You get
so . . . so—"

"What?"

"It's just they're fragile at that age. . . ." She turned for the door. "Bring her by soon, Ingrid."

"I will." Ingrid's voice was flat.

"Sit down," Trudi invited her.

But Ingrid stayed next to her, eyes trained on Rita as if waiting for her to sprout horns or make some horrible mistake. To Trudi, the baby looked beautiful with her dark halo of straight hair and tiny hands that curled into loose fists. She wore a smocked dress from the midwife's supply. Despite her mother's urging, Ingrid had refused to sew or knit for the baby during her pregnancy. She'd spent most of her days on her knees in church, asking God's forgiveness, while her body continued to swell until it looked as if a single pew could no longer hold her.

"She'll feel better after the wedding," her mother had told the neighbors, but Ingrid continued her empty-eyed pilgrimages to the church, even after she'd become Ulrich Hebel's wife.

"She'll feel better after the baby's born," her mother had told the neighbors to still her own worries about how Ingrid might be with her child; and she was relieved when Ingrid looked after her infant daughter properly, even though it seemed that only her body took over that function while her soul tangled with her sin.

"It takes longer for some women than others to feel like mothers," the old women would console Ingrid's mother while, amongst themselves, they'd whisper, "She's unnatural," and recount memories of that stunning blaze of love they'd felt as soon as their infants had been placed in their arms.

They were appalled that Ingrid hadn't even thanked the midwife, who'd arrived for the birthing with a flour sack full of tiny shirts and booties and dresses. Even the diapers had been ironed and folded and smelled as fresh as the air inside the midwife's house. Her floors were always spotless because the midwife not only cleaned every day but also took off her and her son's shoes inside the house. Before she'd let visitors enter, she'd inspect the soles of their shoes to make sure they hadn't stepped into pigeon droppings or dog shit.

But that August, a month after the midwife had delivered Ingrid's daughter, she did not check her visitors' shoes. Her face was swollen red from crying when they came into her house, wearing the summer grieving clothes they'd aired out overnight, bringing her generous cakes and meats and salads from their meager supplies to make up for the scant words of sympathy they managed to summon up for the man who'd turned in his own mother.

Late that evening, the midwife asked one of the old neighbor women to watch over Adi's sleep while she returned to the cemetery, where the wreaths and bouquets on her husband's new grave gleamed under a quarter moon. "I love you," she whispered, trying to evoke Helmut the last time she'd seen him, but instead she saw his mother the day she'd been taken away. "I love you," she tried again. Sometimes she had listened to Helmut's heart after he'd fallen asleep. Her cheek against his chest, she'd felt the slow, steady beat of his heart against her skin. *No more.*

"I'll miss you," she whispered, but already she knew that, in the few days since Helmut's body had been sent back to Burgdorf for his soldier's funeral of honor—including a mass for which the priest had decorated the altar with a steel helmet and *Hakenkreuz* flag—the people had begun to accept her far more than before.

She thought of her favorite red dress that she wouldn't be able to wear for an entire year. Maybe she should dye it black. *Widow's clothes.* At least the black would cover the stain from last Sunday, when she'd worn the red dress to mass. Just as she'd been about to faint again, she'd pressed Adi toward Frau Heidenreich, who'd knelt next to her, and when she'd come to on the church steps, her dress had been smudged and the *Zwerg* woman had been bending over her, fanning her with both hands. Trudi's face had looked so soft, dreamlike almost. Why, Hilde remembered thinking, Trudi looks like a woman who is loved. . . . But immediately she'd said to herself, No, this can't be, not the *Zwerg,* and she hadn't shared her observation with others because they would have laughed at her.

She shouldn't be thinking of clothes. Or other people. Only of Helmut, her husband. *Husband. Hus—band. Hus — band.* If you looked at it just as a word, it didn't mean anything. Strange to think she had ever been married.

"I miss you."

She said it again. "I miss you."

A shadow moved from a nearby grave as though she'd invoked a straying soul.

Hilde cried out.

"Sshh—it's only me." The shadow carried a tin watering can in one hand, and turned out to be the widow Weskopp, who came to the cemetery every day to tend the wide grave that held her husband and sons. Some people said she practically lived at the cemetery. "Hot days like this," the widow said, "it's better to water the flowers after the sun is down."

She pressed her watering can into the midwife's hand, grasped her by the elbow, and guided her to the nearest faucet, where she waited while Hilde filled it with cold water.

As Hilde tilted the can toward Helmut's grave, silver worms of water fused her hand to the dark earth. She dropped the handle. Leapt back as the tin clattered against the stone edging of the grave.

"Not like that." The widow hunched over to pick up her watering can. "It's important to water every day." There was something watchful about her. Everyone knew she prided herself on growing the best flowers, not just in her garden and house, but also at the cemetery.

As if those flowers could be a substitute, Hilde thought. At least *I* still have a son. Ashamed of her cruelty, she tried to come up with something kind she could say to the widow, who was walking along Helmut's grave, sweeping her arm in long practiced motions to douse every last flower petal.

Hilde tried not to look at the arc of silver worms.

"Don't forget the candles," the widow continued her instructions. "It's important to buy the right candles." She set the watering can down and took Hilde to her family grave. "Thick, short candles." She pointed to the flicker of light in the glass lantern that sat between two perfect rosebushes. "Some candles are too thin and tall and burn right out."

"I don't have a lantern."

"I'll bring you one. You also need a vase with a point at the end so it'll stay in the ground."

Now I'm one of them—a widow. For an instant the midwife felt a cloying sense of comfort, but then she saw herself, forever in black, riding her bicycle to the cemetery with her very own watering can, instantly aged as she stooped over the flowers and the earth that separated her from her husband's spoiled flesh—

"No," she said, "no," unable to move as the black shape of the widow Weskopp swayed toward her as if to absorb her.

■

1 9 4 3 – 1 9 4 5

"I WISHED FOR HELMUT'S DEATH THE DAY I STITCHED HIS MOTHER'S blankets into a sleeping bag and watched her touch the pear tree. . . ."

Trudi and Max lay in the sand pocket near the tip of the jetty, their hair wet from swimming in the river. Her head against his shoulder, she told him about the day Renate Eberhardt had been taken away. Beneath them, the sand was still warm from the sun though dusk had begun to blot the brightness from the sky, sharpening the contours of trees and rocks and freighters. Max was still naked, but Trudi had already slipped back into her dress, as always.

"I feel sorry for the midwife. Helmut's funeral is the only one I've been to where most people seemed glad to get someone beneath the ground—even people who're all for the brown gang. We stood by his grave, but I bet we all were thinking of his mother. I wish you could have met Renate Eberhardt. She was one of the best-liked women in town. . . ."

She raised her head toward the hollow wail from one of the Braunmeiers' cows and listened for a moment. "I once stole from her. Pears. When I was five. Georg Weiler and I, we sneaked into her garden, and when she came out of the house, Georg ran off and I was caught. She was pregnant with Helmut then."

Linking one hand through hers, Max rested the knot of their fingers on her stomach.

Trudi felt the warmth through her linen dress and shivered with pleasure. "You know what she did? She gave me two pears, and a few weeks later she came into the pay-library with her new baby and brought me another pear."

Warm wind carried the scent of camomile from the dike. Max raised himself on one arm and swung his body across Trudi's, keeping himself light above her on his elbows. He had taken off his glasses, and the pale skin around his eyes was in stark contrast to his tan. She pulled him close, let him block the first stars as she caressed his naked back. Her fingers circled the ring of hairs that grew low on his spine. She loved touching that ring of hairs—it was silky, and even though she couldn't see it now, she knew the exact pattern the hairs formed, an oval swirl like the crown of a small child's head. It filled her with wonder to know another person's body so completely—by touch and taste and smell and sound and sight—know it with a delight that had begun to carry over into an enjoyment of her own body.

"You . . ." Max sighed. "You're as vast as the night sky . . . as mysterious as a veiled moon. . . ."

She laughed in his arms, intrigued. "So that's how you see me?"

"Your energy . . ." he murmured, "it's so great that sometimes I feel it will suck me up right there into the sky with you."

"There could be worse fates."

"Oh, yes." He tickled her nose with his mustache, then kissed her fully. "Much worse. Like never having met you."

"Let me look at you." She made him move till she could see his features in the half-light. Sometimes she thought he was becoming more handsome in front of her eyes, but of course that was impossible. He must have been like this the day she'd met him, and she simply hadn't seen how extraordinary his face was. It looked extraordinary even when Max was troubled—as he had been for much of this last month, ever since he'd been drafted to work in the office of an ammunition factory. His bad eyesight had kept him out of the battle, but not out of working at a desk for the war industry, keeping records of inventories and of the foreign workers, who were heavily guarded to prevent acts of sabotage.

Long barges rode the current, some of them lit, others nearly dark. Intermittently, one of their whistles would slice the night, resonant and sad.

Max sat up. "Let's go away, you and I."

"On a vacation?"

"Leave for good. Where do you want to go?"

"China," she said without hesitation and knelt in the sand so that her face was at the same height as his.

He laughed. "For real."

"China. One: I can travel there for almost free—"

"So you've told me."

"And two: it's far away from Germany."

"A good reason." He wiped a few grains of sand from her temple. "But until we can afford China, we better think of a place that isn't quite that far. I wish we could live in France. There's a chapel I want to show you. In a village not far from Paris. Inside is a marble plate with an inscription that says the chapel was built during the First World War by French peasants, who promised God to build a chapel if the Germans didn't win. Being German, I felt odd, reading the inscription. Now I hope there'll be a second chapel for this war."

"I'd help them build it," Trudi said.

"You'd like Paris. When I was there in 1934, I saw a ballet dancer in front of Notre Dame. . . ." As he described her—the short red shift and black stockings—Trudi could see her, dancing as if she were on the most famous stage in the world. Hundreds of people stood watching her, and toward the end of her dance, she drew a man into the circle . . . a clown, who started off stumbling and awkward. But soon he was dancing with her as if she'd transformed him.

"Things like that can only happen in Paris," Max said.

Trudi smiled to herself. "Oh—I think they can happen everywhere."

"We'll live in Montmartre. I could paint there."

"And what will I do?"

"Tell stories . . . have babies . . . dance with me . . ."

She found herself reeling in the smell of the earth, the smell of the river. A child of her own . . . And yet, how could she risk bringing a child into life who might be inflicted with her size, her anguish? "About the babies? You mean that?"

Max rubbed his face with both hands, then linked his fingers behind his head.

"Do you?"

"I— I don't know why I said that."

She couldn't breathe. "It doesn't mean they'll have bodies like mine."

"Trudi—"

"A *Zwerg* can have regular-size babies."

"I don't doubt that. It's just that . . ."

"What? What?"

"I don't know if I want children."

"Then why say that about babies?"

"I don't know," he said miserably.

She sat back on her heels, stared past him.

"Please—don't be like that, Trudi."

"Like what?" She spread her short arms. "This is me. The way I was born—like that. A *Zwerg*. Do you have any idea how much I hate that word? *Zwerg* . . . There—take a good look, Max Rudnick."

"You know I didn't mean your body."

"Well, it is me."

"Part of you. And you use it well . . . as a shield, a weapon. It's your way of fighting. Your strength and your weakness."

She shook her head, furious at him for being right.

"You get angry when others dare to look at you. Yet, I've never known anyone who watches people as acutely as you." Words charged from him as though he'd restrained them too long: "You— you misunderstand things. You take everything so—so seriously. When people laugh, you're sure they must be laughing at you. . . ."

The air was still around her. As if the world had stopped moving. This is the end, she thought. Our last time together. I will never see him again. And that's good. If this is how he really feels about me—

"You make it awfully hard for others to be close to you."

"Then why— the hell— do you bother?" She felt the heat in her eyes that would surely turn into tears if she didn't get away from him.

"Because—" He caught her by the wrist as she scrambled up. "—I happen to love you."

She yanked her arm from him. "One moment you say you love me, and the next moment you tell me that I misunderstand things and that I won't let you be close. . . . Make up your mind. Which of them is it?"

"All of them." He crouched in front of her, naked, his eyes close to hers. "And not always at the same time. Trudi . . ." He laid his hands on her shoulders, shook her gently. "Trudi, what is it you want me to know? That you're not different from anyone else inside? You've taught me that already."

The heat sprang from her eyes, doused her face.

"Come here." He drew her close. "Do you believe that I love you?"

She sniffled. Nodded. Said, "Yes."

He tightened his arms around her. "How can we think about babies in the middle of death? Sometimes I get so afraid that I won't be alive by the end of the day. Working in that Goddamn factory—all I think of is running away."

She stroked his face.

"Maybe after the war, Trudi. If we survive . . ."

"We will," she said fiercely.

He rested his head on top of her hair. "Somehow I don't have much faith in getting out of this alive."

"We both will."

"If we do—maybe we can talk about babies then."

She didn't move.

He brought one hand under her chin and tilted her face up. "Look at you. You're all wet." With his hands, he wiped off her tears. "So then—you're glad you got me?"

She had to grin. "Sometimes."

"Even if I don't always know what I want?"

"Even if."

All at once the muscles in his chest twitched. "Sshh—" He raised one hand.

"What is it?"

"I hear something."

They listened, hard.

It was a voice, a man's voice, calling her name. Twice.

"My father." She smoothed her skirt.

Max grabbed his clothes, struggled into them, stepped into his shoes without tying the laces and was on the bicycle, pedaling away from her, before she heard her father's voice again.

"Trudi . . ."

She waited until she could no longer see Max. "Here," she called, and walked toward the voice.

Her father was halfway down the path from the dike to the river.

"A postcard." He was out of breath. "From Zürich. No words—just a drawing. Of a cat and a train."

"Thank God." She grabbed his hands. "Konrad— They're safe."

"Trudi!" Someone came running from the direction where Max's bicycle had disappeared.

Max, she thought, but the shape was shorter, wider.

"Trudi— Are you all right, Trudi?" It was the butcher's son, Anton, who was home on leave. "I tried to catch the man, but he got away on his bicycle. Was he bothering you?"

"No," Trudi said, "No. What man?"

"The one without clothes. I was fishing and heard someone call your name and then I saw him on the jetty with you and—"

"Oh, that man."

Anton stared at her.

"He was just asking me to watch his clothes. You see—" She felt her father's eyes on her face. "He wanted to take a swim and worried about someone stealing his clothes. So he asked me if I could watch them."

"And you believed him?"

She raised her face toward the butcher's son and nodded like an obedient child. "It's such a warm evening. I could see how someone might want to swim."

"He took his clothes off in front of you?"

"I wasn't looking."

"Don't you see what kind of danger you were in? We should call the police." He seemed ready to run into town and bring out a search party.

"Anton—" She reached up and laid her hand on his arm. "I'm sure he just wanted to swim."

"What else did he say?"

She glanced at her father, then back at the young Anton Immers. "Let me think," she said, stalling him. *Konrad is safe in Switzerland,* something within her sang, *Konrad is safe.*

"Did he ask you to take off your clothes?"

She made her voice go indignant. "I only swim when I have my bathing suit. All he asked me was if the river was dangerous, and I said it wasn't. Not if you stay close to shore."

"Are you sure he didn't touch you?"

"He was interested in swimming."

"Sometimes men will try to—"

"I told him to watch out for whirlpools and to stay away from the barges."

"That's not all he should stay away from."

"He was only here a few minutes. He didn't even have time to go into the water."

"Then why did he run off like that?"

"He didn't say." She wished she'd thought of a better answer.

Her father stepped between her and Anton Immers. "Thank you for your concern. I'll take care of this matter now. No need for you to—"

"But make your daughter understand the danger she was in."

Trudi felt furious. She wanted to shout at him that she had just made love, that she would move to Paris, where she'd never have to look at another Immers face again.

"Herr Montag, that man could have raped your daughter."

"I will speak with my daughter," her father assured Anton Immers. "Come now," he said to her, "time to get you home."

They didn't talk until they reached the dike. "Tomorrow everyone will be gossiping about this," she moaned.

"At least it's a pretty good story," her father said. "I'm sure Anton believed it. . . . You are all right?"

"Of course." She waited for him to ask her about Max, ready to answer with the truth.

"I'm so glad for Konrad and his mother," he said.

"It gives me hope. For all of us."

He glanced at her from the side. "And about your friend Herr Rudnick . . . Tell him he doesn't have to hide from me."

The coat of the Russian soldier still hung on the coat tree in the hallway that connected the pay-library and the Montags' living quarters, and Trudi would keep it there as if—the old women in Burgdorf became fond of saying—she expected a man to come home to her. There had been that one incident by the river, after all, which had caused all of them to reassess this *Zwerg* woman, who usually gossiped about *them*.

No doubt her inexperience with men had led her to be less than properly cautious with this stranger who'd presented himself to her late one August evening by the river and had asked her—so the rumor went—to watch his clothes for him while he swam.

"The nerve . . ." people said and agreed that the man's boldness was nothing compared to Trudi Montag's naïveté.

"When it comes to men, Trudi Montag is like a child," people said, shaking their heads.

The naked man was a foreigner, some of the people suspected, while others insisted he was one of the Jews hiding out. What they concluded was two things: that he was not one of them, and that Trudi Montag could have gotten herself raped or killed. Fortunately—so the story passed through town—Trudi's father and young Anton Immers had arrived at the river in time to chase the naked man away.

"He already had his clothes off," Frau Weiler said.

"And Trudi just stayed there." Herr Blau clicked his teeth.

"Any other woman would have run for her life," the oldest Buttgereit daughter said.

"It's because she had no idea what danger she was in," the pastor's housekeeper explained to Herr Pastor Beier.

"Like a child."

"Yes, like a child."

"My son got there in time," the butcher told his customers.

"A car for the parish would be helpful in preserving the honor of our young women," the pastor urged the bishop in a letter.

That version of what had happened that evening by the river was just what Trudi wanted the town to believe, and she was amused when she heard that her father, supposedly, was in the habit of looking for her whenever she wasn't home by nine.

"I'm usually asleep by nine," he said when she told him.

"I guess they like to believe that someone's looking after me."

Trudi massaged the rumors by pretending to let seemingly innocent comments slip from her, which—in return—compelled others to confide in her about near indiscretions within their families. And so she piloted her story. . . .

Let them think that she'd never been with a man.

Let them feel sorry for her.

Let them believe that, by chance, she'd come across that *one* man by the river that *one* night.

Had the people of Burgdorf known what had really happened to Trudi by the river, they would have been furious at her for deceiving them—not because of her words but because the truth would have mocked their expectations of her. Over the years, those expectations had solidified and engendered pity because she would never have a man and children, superiority because any one of them had to be better off than she, and fear because she knew too much about them.

They didn't have any idea that she'd known the naked man—as they came to speak of him—for over two years, and that she'd been his lover for ten months. They didn't have any idea how, with one fingertip, he would trace her entire body—hips and ears and knees and throat and breasts and chin and back and wrists and toes—and how she'd quiver under his slow touch and discover her body through the gentle pressure of his hands.

Had a young woman of normal size offered the kind of flimsy lie about watching a stranger's clothes on the jetty, no one would have believed her. At times it made Trudi furious that everyone in town was eager to embrace her fabrication, including Klaus Malter, who'd been sent home from the front with an infected shoulder wound and—after church one Sunday—asked her if she was all right as though she were marked from her encounter. His voice was concerned, and she came close to telling him that Max was a far better kisser than he.

In her anger, she let the story grow and found her vengeance in circulating it around town, keeping it alive, and it would become one of those stories that even people who hadn't been born yet—like the next generation of Immers and Baums and Malters—would grow up with and continue to tell about Trudi Montag once she was an old woman. So much more happened than she would disclose to anyone, even to Hanna Malter, the child of Klaus and Jutta, whose birth was still three years away and whom she would love as though she were her own daughter. Even Hanna would never know that Trudi kept seeing the naked man after that night on the jetty, that they would meet further south, where the river was turbulent and the shadows of the poplars couldn't touch the surface of the flat stone that was wide enough for both of them—far away from the eyes of the town where Trudi was the one who seized people's secrets.

One night in June of 1944, Herr Abramowitz died in his sleep. The week after his funeral, his wife was arrested when, in one unforeseen and magnificent act of rage, she demolished the office of the Hitler-Jugend in Frau Simon's former hat shop. The two uniformed youth leaders, who watched the slender old woman enter with her cane, were too stunned to move when she swung the cane around, scattering papers and files, smashing lamps and the pyramid-shaped mirror, which—at the instant of splintering—yielded to her images of everything that had ever happened in her marriage.

Her cane ripped through the membership maps with their tiny pin flags that covered the walls, knocked down framed photos of children singing around bonfires and marching in parades. Trying to dodge her cane, the youth leaders wrestled her to the floor and tied her wrists—but not before she'd broken one pair of eye glasses and left welts on their necks and faces.

In the days after Frau Abramowitz was sent away, the old women in town would tell each other stories of amazing strength that sometimes becomes available to women for brief periods of time: they would recall a mother who'd lifted a farm tractor from the chest of her trapped daughter; a wife who'd carried her wounded husband, twice her weight, two kilometers to the doctor.

In St. Martin's Church, Herr Pastor Beier continued to offer prayers for the soldiers who'd died in the war, but he never mentioned the Jews who'd been deported or killed. Standing on the blood-red carpet that led up the marble stairs to the black marble altar, he'd raise both fleshy arms and beseech Christus to embrace the soldiers who'd sacrificed their lives for the *Vaterland,* just as He had sacrificed His life on the cross.

Leo Montag walked around the pay-library, dazed, as though he'd become a widower all over again, and Trudi began to wonder how much Frau Abramowitz's unspoken love had braced him over the years. Late one evening he grew strangely restless: he rearranged his leftover books in the living room and sorted through old photos. Though she was tired, Trudi stayed up. Twice, she asked him if he wouldn't rather go to sleep. It was after midnight when he limped down the cellar stairs and brought up the crate that Michel Abramowitz had entrusted to him nearly six years earlier. Wrapped inside Michel's raincoat, they found linen napkins folded around the two silver candlesticks that used to stand on the Abramowitzs' piano; one ring with diamonds and another with an oval aquamarine; the necklace with rubies that Michel had given Ilse on their twentieth wedding anniversary; eight sets of cufflinks and three bracelets; a collection of antique gold coins; and the carved mezuzah that used to hang on the Abramowitzs' front-door post.

"We'll have to get these things to Ruth," Leo told Trudi.

"Don't you think it would be better to keep them until after the war?"

"I no longer know what that means: *after the war.*"

"It will end. It must."

"Ruth needs to know about her parents." He'd been with Frau Abramowitz when she'd tried to call Ruth from the dentist's phone to tell her about her father's death. But no one had answered the phone in the clinic where Ruth worked. "Ilse sent her a letter about her father. She should have written back by now."

"Maybe she's no longer in Dresden," Trudi said softly.

He closed the crate. "I'm taking this to her."

"What makes you think you'll find her? And where do you think you'll get gasoline for the trip?"

"Herr Blau has enough stashed away."

"He doesn't even have a car."

"You know how he is." Leo grabbed his keys. "Always saving things in case he'll need them. He'll understand that I'm not asking lightly."

"It's late. You're tired."

The crate under his arm, he headed toward the door.

"And it's way too far. You'll drive all night."

"Wouldn't you want to know if I were dead or deported?"

"At least let me come along."

"Someone has to be in the library."

"I'll put up a sign that we're closed because of illness." She made him set the crate down. "Let's wrap these in a less conspicuous way. In case we're stopped."

While her father went to speak with Herr Blau, Trudi packed a suitcase, hiding the jewelry and coins inside rolled-up socks, the mezuzah in the folds of a suit jacket. They stashed the candlesticks beneath the spare tire. Four canisters of gas in their trunk, they silently drove out of Burgdorf. The only light upon the landscape came from the beams of their car. As they lifted gutted buildings and torn fences from the dark, and flitted across broken arbors and bridges that had been blown up, Leo ached for the country he used to love.

For brief spans, Trudi kept falling asleep, and Leo felt like the only survivor in an unreal landscape. Each time she awoke—her back and knees stiff—it was from half dreams of being deported in a cattle car. She felt ashamed that she could sleep at all, ashamed that her body protested those minor discomforts; they were nothing compared to what Frau Abramowitz and Eva must have suffered. And yet, as she'd doze off and wake up and doze off again, her own aches gave her a small measure of understanding about how the Nazis took you and stripped you of everything that made you unique, stripped you of all that gave you identity, until they had created an awful equality: they took away your families, your right to practice your education, possessions you'd worked for, all that was important to you—your music, your books, your art. And when you thought there was nothing else they could possibly deprive you of, they came for the basics that you took for granted—your food and your clothes; your privacy to go to the bathroom or wash yourself. They herded you into KZs—a flour sack between you and the hard floor—robbed you of your dignity, made all of you alike in an awful way. And as you survived each torment and endured the discomforts, the excrement, the terrible lack of privacy, and the hunger that became your predominant feeling— stronger even than your fear—it proved the judgment they'd already formed about you: that you were all like animals.

Trudi shivered. To her left, her father's profile rode the night, framed by the dark window on the driver's side. His lips were closed, and he looked serious, determined. She thought of the priest Adolf, who used to live in Dresden, and she longed for the certainty that he was safe like Konrad. Maybe they'd drive past the church where he'd been arrested. Though she didn't remember the name of his church, she felt certain she'd know it once she saw it. Adolf had promised to write her after the war if he was still alive. *Don't you dare forget,* she beseeched him, willing him to read her thoughts. *Don't you dare or I'll think you're dead.*

It wasn't right that Adolf and other priests who'd spoken out against the Nazis were hunted or imprisoned or killed, while the fat priest was free—secure and well fed in his rectory—restricted only by the virtuous complaints of his housekeeper, Fräulein Teschner. Trudi's eyes closed. Far away, she felt the fat priest turning in his bed, dreaming of the car the bishop would surely give him after the war.

"It took us all of the following night to drive back," she would tell Max after she'd return from Dresden. They'd be in his room in Kaiserswerth. Outside, on the windowsill, a pigeon would land on the clay pot with its one dried-out geranium and peck at the dirt.

"We found the address of the clinic, but Ruth no longer worked there. She hadn't shown up for her shift two months earlier, and when her supervisor had stopped by her apartment, no one had answered. We went there, my father and I, knocked at the door of the owner, who lived on the first floor, but he kept telling us to go away, that Ruth had moved. He looked afraid."

"He probably was."

She would tell Max how they'd driven through Dresden all that day, just on the chance of seeing Ruth, how urgent it had felt all at once to let Ruth know how her mother had taught Trudi good manners—"*She was a kind and generous and loving woman, your mother*"—and how reluctant her father had been to leave there without bringing Ruth her family's possessions.

"If you want," Max would offer, "we can take a trip there after the war. See if we can find Ruth. I have an aunt not far from there, in Leipzig. We could visit her."

The day of his ninth wedding anniversary, Alexander Sturm returned to Burgdorf without leave. For more than a year he'd been fighting, flinging his body into battle with the fury of obliterating himself, but it was as though he'd been cursed: while soldiers all around him had died or been maimed, he hadn't even earned a simple scar.

In his uniform, he walked from the train station to his apartment building, asked Jutta for his keys, avoided her eyes that had witnessed his cowardice, and stalled her questions by promising to talk with her soon. When he unlocked the door to his apartment, his rooms were the way he'd left them: his niece had obviously hired someone to clean them regularly. He stripped off his uniform, bathed without hurry, washed his cropped hair, and dressed in his good blue suit, which felt as though it must have been tailored for a heavier man. The jacket was too spacious, and without his suspenders the trousers would not have stayed up. It was late afternoon when he mounted the stairs to the attic.

While, only a few blocks away, Trudi was checking out two romances to Klara Brocker—supposedly for Klara's mother again— Alexander Sturm stood in the middle of his attic.

"I should have come with you and your parents," he said aloud.

Only silence confronted him.

"I used to believe I'd go with you into exile, death even. . . . I'm ready for that now."

Through the closed window, he could see the cherry tree across the street and, behind it, the burned upper half of the Talmeisters' house and the first floor where the family still lived.

"Even if you are in the worst of places, I would rather be with you than here by myself. Even if you are dead, it would be better to be dead with you."

He stepped up to the window. The sun was plunging behind the tile roofs of his town. Pigeons and sparrows picked at the fallen cherries that stained the sidewalk, and for a moment, as Alexander stared at the mess of red pulp and white kernels, it became Eva's flesh, merging with a pile of flesh and bones. His body heaved, yearned to become part of that pile. Dry moans hiccuped from his throat. He crawled behind the crates.

"Don't you see?" he whispered. "I never meant to break my promise." He remembered Jutta pulling him to his feet after the Gestapo had left him behind, remembered her strong arms as she'd led him down the stairs to his apartment, where she'd wrapped blanket after blanket around him because his body wouldn't stop shaking.

"I was too late, Eva. A few minutes more—and I would have been able to get up. I wanted to come with you. You have to believe me."

The sky outside the attic window was streaked with mauve, and in that kindest of lights—where time can shift and restore itself—Alexander Sturm was given his moment of grace. Trembling with awe, he watched Eva walk toward him in a blue evening gown, her hair braided into a crown. *"You still mean it? About coming with me?"* she asked, and he leapt up, his legs obeying him, "Yes," he said, "yes," and she held out one hand and he felt it, felt it, no ghost hand this; it was real, warm as his own flesh. "You are not dead then," he said, and she laughed, *"No. No, of course not,"* and all the anguish and shame he'd suffered for so long spun away and, still, still, he was allowed to keep the wisdom that had come from his torment as he stepped into her arms. Her skin smelled of summer and was wonderfully soft under his hands, and it occurred to him that, certainly, this was as much happiness as one human could bear, almost too much for one single heart to contain without bursting. He embraced his wife tightly, his face against her hair, and when he held her away from himself—his hands on her shoulders so he could see her eyes—she looked at him without reproach. *"People will tell stories about how you followed me,"* she said and he could feel the approval of the town that he'd missed so bitterly flow toward him. She fastened a white carnation to his lapel. "Where did you get the flower?" he asked because he hadn't seen it until then, and she kissed him and said, *"They are waiting for us."* He meant to ask who was waiting for them, but already she was telling him to open the window, and he felt the exhilaration he'd known the day of his wedding, the certainty that he and Eva would always be together. "Always . . . Only I didn't know it would be like this," he told her, giddy with gratitude that he'd been granted this reprieve, this absolution. It made him feel chosen, confident that he must be quite extraordinary to be allowed to relive this most crucial event of his life. Never before had he felt so free of fear. It occurred to him that perhaps that other time in the attic—crawling around with the Gestapo men taunting him, *some hero some hero some hero you got here,* kicking him, *some hero some hero*—had only been a shadow-dream summoned by his fear of what might have happened. *"Come,"* Eva said, and as they both climbed out and stood up on the flat part of the roof outside the window, it struck him that they were dressed for a celebration, she in her evening gown, he in his good suit. *"But it is a celebration,"* Eva said as though she'd skimmed his thoughts, and he said, "A celebration, yes." Up here, the air was cooler than in the street, clearer. Laced with the scent of wildflowers from the meadows and carefully tended blossoms from nearby window boxes, it wove itself around his neck, through his Kaiser Wilhelm mustache. Eva spread her arms, and in that moment as he stepped into her embrace, Alexander was granted a glimpse of Jutta's daughter, who would be conceived in his house and grow up with stories about the love between her Great Uncle Alexander and his wife, Eva. He wanted to tell Eva about the girl, but the summer air rushed through his body, became his flesh, his voice—

It was not until the morning of Alexander's funeral, when the priest sprinkled holy water into the grave, that Trudi would recall Alexander's voice outside the Braunmeiers' barn. All those years, she thought, I'd almost forgotten that part of it.

"Your uncle," she told Jutta Malter at the apartment house where

Alexander's funeral feast was held, "once did something very important for me."

Jutta bent, bringing her face down to Trudi's. "He never told me." Her hair lay blond and loose on the shoulders of her black dress.

"That's because he didn't know."

"What was it?"

Trudi shook her head. "He— He rescued me."

Jutta waited but didn't press. "He would have been glad to know that."

"Now I wish I'd told him."

Deep circles smudged the crescents beneath Jutta's eyes. She had fought Herr Pastor Beier for two days over his refusal to allow her uncle to be buried in the Catholic section of the cemetery.

"But he is a suicide," the pastor had insisted.

"There's nothing to prove that."

"Frau Talmeister saw him jump."

"Maybe he was inspecting the roof. He'd been away for a long time."

"A deserter. You know, don't you, that two other soldiers, too cowardly to fight our war, were shot near the Sternburg while stealing vegetables."

"Maybe they were the heroes. They refused to be part of—"

"I won't listen to this." The priest took a step away from her. "Frau Talmeister watched your uncle from her window."

"If Frau Talmeister doesn't have anything better to do than hang in her window all day, it doesn't mean she knows what's going on."

"I wish I could help you—I truly do—but the rules of the church are clear when it comes to suicide."

"It matters nothing to me where my uncle is buried. The only reason I'm here is because I know it would have mattered to him."

They kept looping back through the same words, and when Jutta left, the pastor felt weak with hunger. It seemed that his hunger grew with each year, leaving him dissatisfied only minutes after a large meal. Yet, his body kept expanding, straining against the seams which his housekeeper grudgingly let out or reinforced with inserts.

All that night Jutta painted, unable to step back from the canvas that summoned from her the bright red shapes of two bodies whirling from a yellow sky like winged seeds.

Early the following morning, before mass and breakfast, she rang the doorbell of the rectory and walked right into the priest's study though Fräulein Teschner tried to stop her.

"Herr Pastor Beier is still asleep."

"Wake him then. Please."

"Once I do, he'll have to get ready for mass."

"This won't take long."

Jutta stood in the middle of the study when the priest came in, his hair combed only in front. Apparently he hadn't stopped to brush his teeth because his night breath preceded him.

"You keep my uncle out—you keep me out too."

"Now . . . now, Frau Malter." The priest laid one hand on her shoulder.

She dropped her shoulder, stepped back. "No. I won't be back in church."

It was the determination in her eyes—much more than her words—that convinced the priest she meant what she said. How could he let her soul slip from the graces of the church? Besides, his parish had shrunk and become so poor that he couldn't afford to lose someone prosperous like the dentist's wife, who, everyone knew, was her uncle's only heir.

"Tell me . . ." He looked at the polished tips of his shoes, the only part of them that wasn't obstructed by his belly. "So your uncle was in the habit of doing some of his own repairs?"

"Usually he hired people."

"But first, first he would check out himself what needed to be done?"

"Seldom."

"Still—" He peered into Jutta's eyes. "This is a unique situation, returning after a long absence. . . . Tell me," he prompted her, "were there problems with the roof?"

"No."

The priest kept his impatience from his voice. "But if there were problems . . ." he said, blotting out Frau Talmeister's description of Alexander Sturm standing on his roof for several minutes in his Sunday suit, arms spread—"Like the statue of an angel," Frau Talmeister had told him—"If there were problems," the priest said, "it could have been treacherous . . . that high up."

• • •

Ingrid lived with her daughter, Rita, above the bicycle shop in the room that used to be hers as a girl, and every night she prayed for Rita's salvation. Her new husband had returned to the war, and she felt guilty for not missing him.

At least once a week she'd bring Rita to the pay-library and let her crawl and play between the shelves where she and Trudi had held their very first conversation. They'd watch the little girl from the wooden counter where the glass bins stood empty. It had long since become impossible to get tobacco, and the customers who walked through the door came for books or gossip.

Since just about every able-bodied man between fifteen and sixty was being drafted, most teaching positions were filled by women. When Ingrid found work at a school in Düsseldorf, her mother offered to look after Rita. Ingrid's class was huge, more like a holding tank for hungry children than a place where they might learn anything. Nearly sixty students filled the benches, squatted along the walls when they got too tired to stand, and sat on the windowsills, eyes dull in their thin faces.

Repeated bombings of Düsseldorf made the teaching even more difficult. Ingrid would have to interrupt her lessons to hurry the children into the huge cellar. There, she'd make them pray with her till the end of the air attack, and whenever she worried about her daughter's safety, she'd remind herself that, if God chose to claim Rita this young, she'd go to heaven for sure.

Sometimes when she emerged from the cellar, Ingrid would be confronted by new horrors: mutilated people transported in hand carts to the hospital; dead goats or cats in the middle of the street; people buried beneath the ruins of their houses while others tried to dig them out. Some would be found alive, most dead. One of her students, eight-year-old Hermann Blaser, was missing after a bombing and not found until hours later, his body burned. On her way from the school to the streetcar, Ingrid encountered his mother who, demented with grief, carried a cardboard box that used to contain soap and in which she'd collected Hermann's bone remains.

The earth of the cemeteries was never at rest. It became confusing to Ingrid to figure out where the front was. Didn't the civilians suffer as badly as the soldiers? What kind of world was it where you could emerge from a cellar after a bombing, emerge into air that was opaque and dense, and feel relieved that you'd been spared?

In her neighborhood, Ingrid saw people become more sober about the government as they suffered destruction and witnessed each other's powerlessness and anguish. She'd never seen the people of Burgdorf this poor, this hungry, this afraid, and she envied Trudi's father, who was content even with *Steckrübensuppe*—turnip soup— and who had the gift to see the good in everyone, even in her who was always so hungry that she even craved the smell of boiling potatoes and sour milk. On the outside she knew she didn't show her greed and discontent, but within she railed against her hunger.

Many in town longed for the days of the unknown benefactor, when their distress would have summoned a gift from him. As winter began, the cold intensified the hunger. Refugees from Schlesien and other parts of the country settled in Burgdorf. Several old people and two infants froze to death in their houses.

Cellars were colder than any other place, and even prayers did little to alleviate the physical pain that came with extreme cold. In her parents' cellar it occurred to Ingrid that her concept of hell had to be all wrong because, surely, hell must be the coldest place you could imagine. During air raids, she'd try to keep her daughter warm by wrapping her in extra layers of her own clothes, which she kept in her broken suitcase by the stairs. The floor, where she and her parents spent many nights, was hard despite the blankets that her father spread out. Those blankets were the only comfort she would accept from him; whenever he'd offer her one of his jackets she'd decline, unable to tolerate anything he'd worn so close to his skin. Yet, even with several blankets and two coats, she'd feel cold. And something would always stick out—her legs, her arms, or her cold, cold neck. Though she never mentioned the cold, she felt selfish for noticing it, for crying inside about the misery it caused her.

Throughout that winter, Max talked more and more about finding Ruth Abramowitz and introducing Trudi to his aunt. By then, Leo's car had been seized for the war effort, and when Trudi asked Max how he planned to get to Dresden, he said they could go on the train. To get money for the tickets, he sold three of his paintings to a wealthy woman whose daughter he used to tutor. He pretended to be ill at the ammunition factory, collapsing several times at his desk, until he was told to stay home for a week. The second Sunday of February 1945, a day before his thirty-eighth birthday, he and Trudi were prepared to set out for Dresden and Leipzig on the train, when her father developed a sudden high fever and cough.

"Just go," Leo told Trudi. "I'll be all right without you."

But she seized the chance of staying with him. She had been nervous about meeting Max's aunt. How would she react if she saw her nephew walk up to the front door with a *Zwerg* woman?

"We could make the trip later," Max suggested.

"Why don't you go without me?"

"Because we've wanted to do this together."

"We'll make another trip. In the summer. Maybe you can . . . you know, get your aunt sort of ready for me? Besides, it would be good if Ruth knew about her parents."

"But I don't want to take the jewelry and things if I go by myself."

"Why not? I trust you. And she may need them."

When Max left, he told her, "I still wish you'd come, or that we'd go later, together."

Afterwards, she would go over these two options in her mind, again and again—picturing herself in Dresden with Max as the firebombs annihilated the city, then picturing herself postponing the trip. If only they had waited as he had suggested. Then they'd both still be alive. And they would have celebrated Max's birthday on its proper day. She should have known better than to let him talk her into wishing him happy birthday one day early, considering the misfortunes those early celebrations had brought upon her father's side of the family. But the morning of his departure Max had brought a cake made out of turnips to the pay-library and had teased her into letting him have his gifts, two shirts and a vest she'd sewn for him. Her misgivings had felt silly—after all, nothing terrible had happened in her lifetime—but then again, maybe that was only because she had honored the superstition she'd grown up with and had not celebrated anything before its time. When Max vanished in Dresden two days after his departure from Burgdorf—or perhaps on the way to Leipzig, Trudi would tell herself, hoping that he'd first visited his aunt or that even, against all reason, he'd absconded with the Abramowitzs' treasures though she knew he'd never steal from anyone—it was as though his disappearance proved the superstition.

• • •

She felt stunned by the magnitude of the destruction. Thousands and thousands of people had perished in Dresden that February Tuesday, many of them refugees who couldn't be accounted for. Canisters of phosphorus had been dropped on the city, turning people into live torches, driving hordes of burning, shrieking bodies toward the ponds that had been established for extinguishing fires and now became graves as many drowned, trampled or crowded by others into deeper water. And then the bombs began to rain on the city. For forty minutes. Everywhere. Without selection. On churches and hospitals and prisons and schools. Killing, maiming. A carpet of bombs.

With each horrible detail she'd find out, Trudi would despair more; and yet she'd try to picture Max alive—wounded and unable to let her know what had happened to him—but alive. She'd be patient. She'd wait. For as long as it would take. Nights, her fears presented her with every possible disaster that could have happened to him, and the worst was that he'd become one of the burned bodies buried in the mass graves that had been dug in an immense ditch around the center of Dresden.

Wavering between fear for his life and feeling rejected—maybe he'd wanted to get away from her; maybe he'd returned to his wife—she wandered through Burgdorf, searching for him though she was sure she wouldn't find him. She tried to imagine him close by, tried to evoke him by willing him to return to her.

Several times she took the streetcar to Kaiserswerth and talked to the watchmaker, who hadn't seen Max since he'd left for Dresden. "He said he'd be back in a week," he'd tell her and let her borrow the key to Max's room above the shop, where she'd sit for hours.

If an airplane passed low above his roof, she wouldn't even bother to look from the window. She remembered how impatient she'd become with Alexander for praying his house would be hit by bombs. I didn't understand then, she thought and sent him a silent apology.

Most of the time she'd be staring at the paintings, and she'd see herself in his arms, asking him, "What did you see this time?" And Max would tell her, first with words, then with colors. In his arms, she had tried to see what he saw—exotic buildings, entire cities—and once she'd managed to glimpse a yellow flower at the moment, the brink, a flower the warm shade of yellow-orange that blossomed behind her eyelids, blotting out everything else until all of her was yellow-orange warm.

She walked. She slept. Without regard for time. In the middle of the night she might find herself by the river or on the fairgrounds without recalling getting there. On her face, she'd feel the old tears and snot, and she'd move her arms to shake off invisible assailants. She stopped caring for her clothes, her hair. Since the town had not known about her love for Max, people did not come forward to comfort her, to share her grief, or tell her that she was not the only one who'd lost someone, that all of them had friends and family who'd vanished— dead perhaps, or living in foreign countries. The only one who understood was her father, who'd close the pay-library to look for her as he once had for her mother, who knew how to find her and bring her home, who'd sit her down and feed her something warm and soothing, who'd pull his comb from his shirt pocket and untangle her hair.

She kept returning to Kaiserswerth, and when the watchmaker told her, "I'll have to rent the room—that is, if your friend doesn't come back soon," she left her shoes with the high, high heels inside Max's wardrobe, but she took his paintings from the walls and carried them home, where she wrapped them and stored them in back of her closet.

A month after the firebombing of Dresden, the saddest of all trains passed through Burgdorf, a long train filled with people from a KZ, gray faces and striped suits behind the windows. Thin, hungry, and ill, they were transported to another camp because the Americans were getting close. When the train stopped at the Burgdorf platform for more than half an hour, none of the prisoners got off. Armed SS men stood along the platform, separating the train from the line of townspeople, who stood watching at a distance.

The air was damp and cool and still as if it were solid, poured around the three groups like those half globes of glass that fit into your hand and contain an entire town and which—unless picked up and shaken to distribute a shower of snowflakes—will remain immobile. Yet, all at once, something moved, a woman's shape in a beige raincoat, loosening itself from the line of watchers, setting in motion a sequence of other motions. It was the third-youngest Buttgereit daughter, Bettina, flying from the restraining hands of her sisters toward the train, thrusting the half loaf of bread that she'd just traded from Frau Bilder for an embroidered purse, toward one of the half-open windows of the train. Several gaunt hands tried to clutch the bread, but before any could seize it, four SS men closed around Bettina Buttgereit, their black uniforms one impenetrable knot that absorbed her pale coat and rendered her invisible until they disentangled. Gripping Bettina between them, they thrust her toward the train. Into the train.

Silently, the line of townspeople retreated, shrank. Just as the train pulled out of the station, the people noticed the face of an old man who looked strangely familiar, though no one could say who he was. Behind the passing window, he wrenched up his bony chin, pressed his fleshless lips together, and focused his sunken eyes on something above the people's heads.

After that train, it felt as though the Americans might arrive any day. It was the end of March when they approached Burgdorf, and what announced them from a distance was the rumbling of their tanks. When Trudi rose from her bed and looked from the upstairs hall window, people in the street were running for shelter as though they'd heard the air-raid sirens. As she grabbed a white sheet and hung it from the window, the front door flew open.

It was Frau Weiler, carrying a basin of holy water. "Quick now, Leo, Trudi—" she yelled. "To the church. We have to hide." She stared at Trudi as she came down the stairs, still in her nightgown, her hair disheveled. "At least put a coat on."

Not too long ago, Trudi would have welcomed the Americans as rescuers, but since the firebombing of Dresden that had changed. Besides, her aunt had warned her in a letter that a lot of Americans thought all Germans were Nazis. Trudi already knew what it was like to be considered an enemy within your own country because you were against the Nazis, and now she felt even more isolated because she might well be regarded an enemy by both sides.

Her father's hand on her elbow, she found herself in the street with him and Frau Weiler, whose scarf was slipping from her gray hair as she flung drops of holy water around them. They hurried across the church square and ducked into the cellar of St. Martin's Church, where the priest was trying to calm nearly two dozen people, most of them more terrified than during the air raids which—compared to this—had come to feel familiar.

Leo and Trudi sat next to Ingrid, who was there with her baby and parents.

"Nothing will happen to us." Frau Weiler was splashing her holy water on everyone.

The priest waved her away.

"Nothing will happen to us. . . ."

"Don't be so sure," the taxidermist said. "Those Americans have killed plenty of us with their bombs."

Fräulein Teschner clutched a long white cloth that she'd snatched right from the altar during a quick detour on her flight from the rectory.

"They come with bayonets," the taxidermist whispered. "And they stab anyone who resists them."

"Someone has to be our messenger," his wife decided.

"Someone who knows English," the priest said.

"My daughter has studied English," Herr Baum announced, and everyone looked at Ingrid, who sat there with Rita, rocking her stiffly.

Without speaking, she laid her daughter in Trudi's arms though her mother reached for her. Trudi blinked. The child was peering into her face with Ingrid's eyes. Curving her arms, she brought Rita closer. *Max. If only you'd waited. Seven weeks. That's all it's been since you left. Seven weeks.*

"To signal peace." Fräulein Teschner thrust the white cloth at Ingrid.

"You don't have to do this," Leo Montag told Ingrid as she stepped next to the door.

The taxidermist was saying, "They push their bayonets into straw and mattresses to see if anyone is hiding."

His wife nodded. Her hand trembled as she applied fresh lipstick.

But Ingrid was wearing the expression of a martyr who has finally found the tormentor who'll grant her eternal salvation.

"Remember now," the priest said, "you need to talk English with them when they come. . . . Tell them—tell them that we surrender. That we have suffered, too."

"That we are glad they're here," Ingrid's father said.

Leo Montag spoke up. "First tell them there are no soldiers here." His eyes skimmed across everyone in the cellar and returned to Herr Heidenreich. "That pin—" He motioned his chin toward the *Hakenkreuz* on Herr Heidenreich's lapel. "—today it could cost you your life."

The taxidermist, who'd once prided himself on having shaken the Führer's hand, fumbled with the clasp. "*Mein Gott*, I can't get it off. I—"

The pastor's housekeeper darted across the cellar, shoved his fingers aside, and yanked at the pin so hard that a piece of fabric came off with it. Her eyes wild, she scanned the cellar and ran to the corner where the life-size nativity set was stored. Without hesitating, she shoved the pin beneath Maria's long plaster skirt.

They all stared at the statue.

"Don't look at it," she hissed.

Ingrid began to flap her white cloth.

Her mother was reciting the Lord's Prayer: *"Vater unser, der Du bist im Himmel . . ."*

"They're here!"

Herr Baum whimpered.

". . . geheiligt werde Dein Name . . ."

"I don't hear any—"

"Sshh—"

". . . zu uns komme Dein Reich . . ."

The priest's chins trembled.

". . . Dein Wille geschehe . . ."

The altar cloth billowed in Ingrid's hands as four American soldiers charged in. "No German soldiers here," Ingrid cried. "No German soldiers . . ."

"No— German— soldiers," the priest echoed the foreign words.

The taxidermist joined in. "No— German— soldiers. No—"

". . . wie im Himmel so auf Erden . . ."

"We surrender," Ingrid cried, forgetting any aspirations of martyrdom.

"Surrender . . . surrender . . ." other voices echoed.

The people of Burgdorf told each other they were glad the Americans—Amis, they called them—were the ones who occupied their region, not the Russians. Although several civilians had been killed while resisting their occupiers, all that was in the past now, and the Americans were organizing *Schulspeisung*—meals in school. Children who arrived for class, some barefoot, all hungry, were each given a tin container and a spoon to keep. Between ten and eleven on school mornings, they'd line up and proceed toward the smell of the hot soup that simmered in tall kettles. The recipe changed frequently: pea soup, mixed vegetable soup, beef broth with rice, cream soup, lentil soup.

The children's favorite was *Kakaosuppe*—cocoa soup: sweet and brown, it filled more than their bellies, saturating them with memories of chocolate they'd tasted long ago. Some days, if they could no longer tolerate their hunger and soup time seemed too far away, the children would bang their spoons against their tin containers. One of them would start, a hesitant clang that immediately drew a chorus, steady and mounting until the voices of the teachers were drowned. Some teachers would take their soup portion home with them to share with their families, grateful for what the Amis were doing.

American soldiers were stationed in houses throughout Burgdorf. Despite warnings not to trust any German, some of them became friendly with the townspeople and showed them photos of their wives and children. The *Rathaus* and the former Hitler-Jugend quarters became offices for the American military, and the pianist's mansion— where Fräulein Birnsteig had committed suicide in January after learning that her adopted son had died in a KZ—was turned into an officers' club. *Hakenkreuz* flags and SS emblems disappeared from the graceful rooms, and on Saturday nights a dance band played American music.

Although the townspeople approved when some of the more industrious boys ran errands for the soldiers or shined their shoes, bringing home packs of chewing gum and narrow bars of American chocolate, they scorned the young girls who dared to go dancing with the soldiers or were seen taking drives with them.

Klara Brocker was one of those girls. At nineteen, she was the prettiest she would ever be—small and cheerful and neat—the kind of briefly held beauty that never fully flourishes but becomes contained, lacquered by its very tidiness. The Ami who was assigned to her house gave her a crate of peaches that annulled years of hunger in her flat belly. He brought her nylon stockings and paid for her new permanent. A blond man with a small birthmark on his temple, he was so much taller than Klara that she could fit her head below his chin when they danced.

One day Klara Brocker's American stopped by the pay-library because he'd heard that the Montags had relatives in America. While he and Leo talked, piecing together fragments of German and English, Trudi—who'd resumed her work in the library—stayed on the wooden ladder and busied herself by rearranging books on one of the top shelves. When the American said he'd like to come by with a young friend who'd grown up in New Hampshire, only an hour from Lake Winnipesaukee, where Stefan and Helene Blau lived, Trudi let herself imagine becoming friends with this young soldier and visiting him too once she went to America. He'd pick her up from the ocean liner, drive her to New Hampshire, where her Aunt Helene would welcome both of them to a big family dinner. . . .

The young soldier, who came to the pay-library a few days later, turned out to be not nearly as tall as Klara Brocker's Ami, and when he came back to the ladder to introduce himself to Trudi, she looked down into his lonely boy-face and shocked herself with the thought that it wouldn't be all that difficult to get him into bed. It would serve Max right.

Immediately, she felt unfaithful. The young soldier was saying something to her, but she couldn't answer because she was back in the mist—only this mist was not beautiful, but gray and thick and suffocating, and it had grown thicker with each day that Max hadn't returned to her. Once the mist lifted, she told herself, she'd be able to see Max. He would be much nearer than she'd expected.

That night, she felt so angry at Max for not coming back that she reached for herself, trying to bring herself to that warm yellow-orange blossom, but what she found herself spinning toward was the terror in the barn, and she stopped before she could trap herself in the old hate.

W HEN THE MEN OF BURGDORF CAME HOME, THEY WERE SILENT, BUR-
dened by secrets they couldn't let themselves think about. Many of
them had lice and diarrhea. Their faces were ashen and rough with
beard stubble. Eyes ashamed or defiant, they'd come into the pay-library with the excuse to ask when Leo Montag expected to get a tobacco shipment.

But Leo was no longer the leader he'd been for the soldiers who'd
returned from the previous war; he'd grown tired, old, and he lived
more and more in his books. Gradually, he'd begun to replenish his
own collection, trading library books for works by authors who used
to be banned. Trudi had taken over the raking of the yard, a task Leo
had always enjoyed. His limp had worsened, and his left leg kept
falling asleep. Already he'd slipped several times as he'd stood up on
it, and Trudi was afraid he might break something. Mornings, before
she'd open the green shutters of the pay-library, she'd settle him on
the sofa that Emil had won in a poker game, his aching leg elevated
on a pillow, a stack of books on a chair next to him.

Families welcomed their husbands and sons back without daring
to ask questions about what they'd done in the war. Since they didn't

want to believe that one of their own could have participated in the atrocities that the Americans claimed had happened, they focused on healing the wounds, finding crutches for the crippled, feeding the hungry. They cut SS and SA insignia from wartime photos, and when one of their men would wake from a nightmare, screaming so fiercely that even the neighbors would wake, there'd be a wife or a mother or a sister who'd bend over him, cradle his head, and murmur, "It's all over now."

But of course it was not all over.

For some, their own hell was just beginning. And Trudi was one of the few who made sure it did by prying at the words they'd buried beneath untold horrors. *And what did you do in the war?* she'd think when she'd look at them. *And you? And you?*

Yet, what she shared with the returning soldiers and everyone else in town was a sense of wonder that you could simply go to bed at night and sleep, that you could lie down without half listening for the enemy or wondering when you'd have to leap up again.

As during the First World War, boundaries between unmarried and married women had dissolved as they'd sustained one another and found strength in performing tasks they'd been taught to believe only men could do. But now that the battle had ended, Trudi noticed that women who'd never married were outcasts once again—less likely than ever to find husbands, since there were many more women than men in town.

Wives whose husbands had died instantly seemed aged, as if flipped into the previous generation, a new crop of old women though they were not old in years. To look at these war widows made the women whose husbands had come back even more grateful, and they turned from the widows and toward their men. Children had to share their mothers with those awkward men they were supposed to call father, though some had been born after their fathers had left for the war, or had been too young to remember them. Though most widows were raising their children alone, some children had to become used to uncles—men who slept in their mothers' beds.

Despite pleasant façades of togetherness, Trudi would notice the fracture within families, the numbing that many of the soldiers only found with alcohol, the shame in the eyes of some wives when they walked at the arms of their husbands. To her, the town had a smell of death—almost more so than during the war—and it didn't surprise her when three of the men killed themselves within a month after coming home, and when the wife of an SS officer started weeping one sunny morning at the breakfast table and didn't stop until three that afternoon, when she took her husband's razor to her wrists.

"Focus on the positive things in life," people would tell Trudi when she'd walk through town with those stories.

"It's not good to dwell on the things that were terrible."

"Let's never talk about that again."

"Nobody wants to relive those years."

"We have to go forward."

Even people who'd always followed a code of personal values would become upset when confronted with the war years and would protect one another. "Our men have gone through enough. . . ."

They did not understand why Trudi Montag wanted to dig in the dirt, as they called it, didn't understand that for her it had nothing to do with dirt but with the need to bring out the truth and never forget it. Not that she liked to remember any of it, but she understood that—whatever she knew about what had happened—would be with her from now on, and that no one could escape the responsibility of having lived in this time.

The people's silence made Trudi think of her mother's skin closing around her old sin, made her think of how the river, too, closed across everything in spring, even though, late in summer, it would reveal what it had hidden: the tips of the jetties, the rocks close to the bank, debris that had been tossed into the river. And she thought of how—even when the river ran high—she knew where the large stones lay and where the jetties ended because she had looked at the river for countless hours, just as she had looked at her community and knew its deepest currents.

It amazed her, the ability of people to forget their support of the Nazis, to deny what had gone on right here in their country, events which—ten years earlier—they would have never believed could happen. From Klara Brocker's American soldier she heard that even in the town of Dachau, where people had breathed the smoke from burned bodies, some still insisted the death camp had merely been a work camp.

The townspeople worried and speculated about everyone who was still missing—everyone except the Jews, of course. Very few people shared Trudi's excitement when she found out that Eva's parents were alive in Sweden. They'd sent her their address in case she ever heard from Eva.

As the prisoners of war drifted back into town, you could tell by their appearance where they'd been held: if they came from Russian prison camps, they were in rags and wore shoes stitched from wood and scraps of leather and fabric, while soldiers released from England had new uniforms—the rich brown of a Sunday roast—and proper-fitting shoes made of leather; those from Russia carried the shadow of famine beneath their eyes, while those from England looked well fed; those from Russia were timid, while those from England dared to talk of a future.

Georg Weiler arrived from a Russian prison camp, his fingernails chewed, his sun-colored hair without its luster. His laugh sounded flat, and when he spoke of the Russians, it was only to say that the prison camps had been their way of taking revenge for all the Russians who'd died in the war. Though Trudi felt compassion for him, she couldn't bear to show it because his betrayal of her still leapt up between them whenever she saw him. It was from his mother that she found out about his ordeals. The prisoners had slept in an open field. In the mud, his mother said. Without adequate shelter, food, and medical care, quite a few of the men had died.

"But I was lucky," Georg told his mother. "They didn't break me."

"I like seeing Georg with the twins," Frau Weiler said to Trudi. "He is a wonderful father to those girls. . . ." She glanced around to make sure no one overheard her. "Except when he drinks. He's always liked a *Schnaps* or two, but not like this. . . . I'm sure that'll stop. It's still close to the war. Once he gets all that behind him—"

"He'll never forget," Trudi said.

Georg found work at a farm near the cemetery, where he cleaned stables and cleared rocks from the fields. One day, when Trudi came out of the cemetery, where she'd watered the family grave, Georg was loading manure onto a wooden cart.

When he noticed her, a sudden shame came into his eyes. "Some day I'll drive a car again," he called out to her, his voice defiant as if he'd always owned a car.

She thought of the car he'd won and gambled away before going into the war. "You only had it for a few days."

Though he grinned at her and raised his pitchfork as if in a greeting, she still saw his shame: it connected him to her; it was better than nothing.

All of the Bilders' sons, except for the fat boy, of course, who'd vanished about twelve years ago, returned to Burgdorf, beaten down by the war, but not crippled like some—their mother would tell her friends—not killed like most of the boys they'd grown up with, including the Weskopp brothers next door. It was out of pity for the widow Weskopp that Frau Bilder restrained her joy at having her sons back: she did not hold the elaborate feast she'd dreamed of whenever she'd been paralyzed by uncertainty during the war years and had found comfort in imagining the homecoming dinner, from soup to the last sprig of parsley, even the tablecloth that her grandmother had embroidered with a border of blue roses.

At times, it felt suffocating to Trudi to have the four from the barn back in town. The war hadn't claimed a single one of them, though Hans-Jürgen had been presumed missing in Russia, and Fritz Hansen was almost like a dead man without his jaw. Despite five surgeries, Fritz still looked hideous. His parents had reopened the bakery with the help of Alfred Meier, who drove the bakery truck, but their own son worked only in the cellar, where the bread ovens were. Though Fritz wanted to wait on customers, his parents figured people wouldn't buy from them if they had to look at their son's mangled face and the gauze which, regardless how often Fritz replaced it, looked soggy and quivered with each breath like a small, white animal that had sucked itself to his throat.

Paul Weinhart had escaped miraculously when American tanks had advanced toward the trenches that he and nearly two hundred German soldiers had dug—rain-drenched ditches in which the men had squatted, dozing off from fatigue and hunger. Only Paul and four others managed to scramble up into trees and hide before the tanks pounded across the muddy ground and buried the Germans alive. And it was not an accident, because Paul watched as the tanks backed up and, beneath their heavy tracks, crushed all life below.

Hans-Jürgen Braunmeier had surfaced in an American prison camp. When his mother came to the grocery store, she told Frau Weiler that some of the Americans had taunted prisoners by withholding water even though the barracks were on a hill next to a clear brook. One twenty-year-old from Bavaria, crazed with thirst, had crawled under the wire fence and rolled himself down that slope toward the brook. As he immersed his face in the stream, he was shot. Her son, Frau Braunmeier said, was certain that, even though there'd been enough food in the camp, the Americans had kept their prisoners close to starvation, with only two bowls of soup per day. "Their idea of punishment," Hans-Jürgen told his parents. "They said it was only fair because the Jews got even less food in the KZs."

Comments like that evoked indignation throughout town. Hadn't they all been deprived of housing and food? They too had lost husbands and sons—not to the KZ, granted, but to the war and to prison. And for them it hadn't stopped with the end of the war. At least the Jews had been released from the KZs.

In the American camp where her son had stayed—so Frau Braunmeier reported to the taxidermist—prisoners had been forced into hard labor, restoring demolished streets. Every day, two or more of the underfed prisoners had collapsed. Quite a few died. For a while her son was allowed to work in the camp kitchen, but after he was caught eating potato peels from the trash heap, he was assigned to the latrine crew.

"The Amis acted like each one of our men was Hitler," Frau Braunmeier whispered to the priest's housekeeper. "My son says it brought out the worst in them. And to think they believe they're better than the Germans."

Those stories made the people of Burgdorf wary of the American soldiers who lived in their midst, those men who were kind to them on occasion, who let the small children ride on their shoulders. It was evident that the Amis were much tougher with the men, interrogating them and demanding proof that they had not participated in what the Amis called *Kriegsverbrechen*—war crimes.

Even men who had not fought were questioned, including Herr Pastor Beier, who was exhausted from trading absolution for dreadful war confessions. Irate at being summoned to the *Rathaus*—though it was only across the street from the rectory, where his housekeeper was complicating his life enough with glances that made him feel he'd failed her in some significant way—he had to wait nearly an hour before a young American officer, whose knees quite likely had never pressed the hard wood of a church pew, inquired what the priest's position had been during the war.

"I lived for my parish." Hands folded on his raised belly, Herr Pastor Beier recited the statement that he'd worked out more carefully than any sermon. He had written it the morning after the Americans had come to Burgdorf, and he'd since revised it daily. As he told the Ami officer about everything he'd done for his parishioners, his voice shook with conviction as it would in his very best sermons. "I know you people are attacking us because we stayed silent. What good would it have done? Look at all the priests who tried." He paused dramatically. "They were arrested. Killed in KZs. I chose to be silent because I knew I'd be of greater help to my parish if I could stay here."

Though the pastor worried that his reputation might have been sullied by the questioning, he consoled himself after dark by spreading three *Brötchen* with *Leberwurst* and starting in on the *Graupensuppe*—barley soup—that Fräulein Teschner had cooked for the following day. As he ate, he imagined the car the bishop would surely provide for him now that the war was over. A car . . . the priest thought as he finished the rabbit stew and opened the last jar of canned cherries, a nice car . . . with blue upholstery if he were given the choice. . . .

He dreamed about the car that night, and in his dream the car had soft blue upholstery, new, but the steering wheel was an egg, a huge egg still in its shell, and when he tapped it with the golden cross that his mother used to wear around her neck when he was a boy—carefully, of course, because he didn't mean to break the shell but simply test how strong it was—it stayed intact while from within its oval shape came the ringing of a single bell. Though the priest didn't know what to make of that dream, it seemed like a good omen, and he wasn't at all surprised when he received a letter in the morning, informing him that the bishop was considering his request for transportation.

Trudi had waited for Max Rudnick when the camps had emptied, thinking that surely now, if he had been imprisoned, he would return to her. And when he didn't, she tried to accept that he must be dead. But if he were, his flesh would be decaying somewhere beneath the earth, and she couldn't allow herself to envision him like that. It was less painful to think of him somewhere with Ruth Abramowitz, who had become his lover. He must have found her right away in Dresden, the night before the firebombing, and they'd taken one look at each

other and fallen in love, even though Ruth's front tooth was chipped
and Max was blind without his glasses. Maybe his lenses had been
broken, and he couldn't see her chipped tooth. Without his glasses, so
he'd told her, everything looked blurry, a merging of colors without
distinct outlines. But then a man who could love a *Zwerg* woman
could probably love any woman. . . .

With the Abramowitzs' treasures, which would afford them a
rather cozy life, the two had driven in Max's car to a small hotel in
South Germany, where Ruth had once stayed as a child with her parents. She'd always wanted to return there, and as soon as she saw
Max, she knew she'd go there with him. By now, the two of them
were talking about names for the children they would have.

Even though Trudi knew that the scenarios she imagined were as
predictable and foolish as the plots in the romance novels she lent to
her customers, she couldn't cast off her jealousy. She'd picture the two
in their hotel room, or in the apartment they'd found, always making
love, always. The windows would be open, wide open, and a warm
breeze would billow the lace curtains and nuzzle their nude bodies.
Stop it, she'd tell herself, stop it. But instead she'd simply place Max
and Ruth somewhere else, north of Dresden, say, in Hamburg or on
the island Rügen, where they'd stroll by the water, arm in arm.

She came to hate Ruth Abramowitz, felt herself capable of killing
Max for deceiving her with Ruth. And still, still—she would have forgiven him if he'd returned to her. Now. She kept extending the dead-
line by which she'd accept him back into her life: at first it was the end
of May, then it became the middle of June, and as she passed both
dates, as well as the anniversary of her mother's death, she granted
him till July 23, her thirtieth birthday. Even if Max arrived the evening
before her birthday, she promised herself, they would not celebrate it
one hour before its time. Even if he begged her.

"Look what happened when we celebrated your birthday early,"
she'd tell him, "look what happened to us then. You disappeared and
I was afraid you'd never come back."

"There's not a single day I didn't think about you, Trudi."

Her thirtieth birthday would be the glitziest birthday she'd ever
had—more spectacular than the fireworks her father had taken her to
on her fourth birthday, more dazzling than Pia's circus coming to
town, more festive than the dinner party her father had given for Kon-

rad and his mother the night of their departure. And for Eva, she thought, and for Eva, feeling guilty that she'd even let herself think of her birthday. She was selfish. Selfish and greedy. Eva would never have another birthday. Neither would Ruth's parents. Or the priest Adolf. If any of them were alive, they would have written or come home by now. And Ruth, she was probably dead too, burned and shattered in Dresden. Along with thousands of others, including Max who, more likely than not, had not found her in the brief time before the city had been decimated.

That first year after the war was the hardest for the people of Burgdorf. There was little food or coal. Some people froze. Milk still had a bluish sheen and was thinned down so much you could look through it. If you could no longer pay your debts, the *Gerichtsvollzieher*—bailiff— would enter your home to paste the cuckoo—a sticker indicating a lien—on the back of your furniture. You'd still have some time to pay your debts, but if you couldn't, the entire neighborhood would watch as your piano, say, or your chest of drawers was carried from your house.

The shame of it.

Though nearly everyone was struggling, it hurt your pride if your family went hungry. In the face of such poverty, it became even more important to keep things clean. Poverty like that made you think of the unknown benefactor, whose memory caused you—at your poorest ever—to take up the habit of leaving anonymous gifts on the front steps of those who were more in need than you.

Yet, even during the leanest of times, the people came to Trudi for her stories, stories she told them about others in their small town that was infected by silence. When they looked down at her, they could feel superior—an attitude most had been infused with since the day of their birth. They could glance at her stunted body, the broad features, and even the most hideous among them could feel superior. Next to Trudi Montag, they could reinvent themselves, could obliterate whatever doubts were theirs alone at night, and—with a trace of benevolence even—accept her stories as something due them.

Trudi's gift lay in knowing. Knowing the words that named the thoughts inside people's minds, the words that masked the fears and secrets inside their hearts. To force their secrets to the surface like water farts and let them rip through the silence. They called her a snoop, a meddler. But even though she was more inconvenient to them than ever before, they kept coming back—to borrow books, they liked to believe—yet, what they really came for, even those who feared Trudi Montag, were the stories she told them about their neighbors and relatives. What they brought Trudi in return were stories of their own lives, which they yielded to her questions or, unknowingly, to her ears as she overheard them talk to each other between the stacks; and they didn't even miss what she had taken from them until the words they'd bartered in return for her tales had ripened into new stories that disclosed far more about them than they knew themselves.

To flip his luck, Georg Weiler played cards two evenings a week. Although Helga protested that he drank too much, he was quick to charm her, asking her if she wasn't glad her husband was home from the war, unharmed. "What are two measly evenings," he'd ask, "compared to years of battle?" And he'd lean over the bed where his twin daughters slept side by side and kiss their hair.

How could Helga possibly stay angry with a man who was a tender father like that? Most fathers she knew, including her own, gave scant attention to their children, especially if they were girls. But Georg would bounce the twins on his knees or let them chase him through the apartment until they'd scream with delight; he'd sing to them so beautifully that Helga would open her windows for the entire town to hear how happy her husband was with his family.

When Georg lost his job at the farm for coming in late three mornings, Helga was pregnant again, but he managed to find employment within a month, just as he had promised. Though driving a taxi took him away from home more, Helga was glad for him because he looked so proud behind a steering wheel. Besides, the twins adored their father, as did every child in the neighborhood: he was never too tired to squat on the sidewalk and play with them, to show them how to win marbles or spin a top.

"I told you I'd be driving a car soon," he called out to Trudi when he dropped off a passenger at the train station, where she stood by the ticket counter with Matthias Berger.

"And there I thought you were talking about your own car," she snapped. Shaking her head, she turned to Matthias, who looked at her, startled. "That Georg Weiler . . ." she said. "When you take away the bragging, he's just a coward."

Matthias was on his way to enter the seminary in Kaiserslautern, even though Trudi had tried to persuade him to stay out and study music instead. Ever since Fräulein Birnsteig's suicide, he'd spent far more time in St. Martin's Church than in the pay-library, praying for the soul of the pianist. It was Leo who'd figured out that Matthias had found a new mentor, Herr Pastor Beier, who'd pounced on the boy's hesitant questions about what it was like to be a priest with such enthusiasm that Matthias had been propelled into applying to the seminary though he was only sixteen.

"Your talent . . ." Trudi urged him once again, "it'll be wasted there."

But playing the piano only made him sad. Somehow Trudi felt she'd failed him. If she hadn't kept him from entering her house during those years of hiding fugitives, he might have stronger ties to Burgdorf. Of his relatives, only a grandmother was left, too frail to see him off at the station. Trudi supposed that she and her father were probably the closest he had to a family. It hadn't been until after the Americans had arrived that she'd felt safe telling Matthias why she'd had to send him away from her door.

"One day I saw a boy inside your window," he'd said. "A small boy."

"That must have been Konrad. He and his mother were hiding with us."

"He ducked when he saw me. . . ." He laughed, an embarrassed laugh that made his green eyes go dark. "I remember thinking that you and your father must have found another boy to play the piano for you."

"Oh, Matthias."

"I was younger then."

"It would have endangered you, knowing about them."

The sound of the approaching train burst into the station, and the front line of waiting people slanted back from the edge of the platform as if singed by a hot wind.

Matthias reached for his suitcases.

"Promise to visit us."

"I will. And I'll write."

"You have your ticket?"

"In my pocket."

To keep herself from crying, she tried to make him laugh. "Did you know that I wanted to be a priest when I was a little girl?" She told him about the candles and the Latin chants, the apple crate which had become her altar, and the sacrament—circles of rye.

"I'm not surprised," he said. "I've always thought you're one of the most courageous people I know. You do exactly what you want."

"But that's just stubbornness."

"To me it's courage."

Although the green Hitler statue had long since been removed by the Americans, people would stare at the spot where it had stood whenever they'd pass the *Rathaus*, remembering the unknown benefactor who had lost his life there.

Inside the gates of the cemetery, the town erected a marble monument with three tall columns that listed the names of the soldiers who had died for the *Vaterland*. Still, on days when the light fell just so and memory offered a brief lull, you could almost convince yourself that the war had never happened. You'd grasp at the good moments and tell yourself all was well, and if you didn't look too closely for too long, you could deceive yourself, along with all the others who had been broken in some way, altered. And then just when it felt that your life was back to the way it had been, something would happen to remind you of your brokenness: a father might fracture his child's arm while punishing her; a dog might get run over by a tractor; a young man might choke on a fish bone; an American officer might come to your door.

As the Americans carried on their investigations, teachers who'd been members of the *Partei* lost their jobs. There were trials, convictions. Some were prosecuted unjustly, others went free even though they were guilty. Several teachers who feared upcoming interrogations fled overnight with their families, abandoning their homes. One threw himself in front of a train. Others swore they'd only joined the *Partei* out of fear for their lives or because they'd been forced to in order to enter their profession or be promoted. Their behavior during the war years had been exemplary, they insisted. Once they'd been in the *Partei,* of course, they'd been afraid not to comply because they would have been sent to a KZ.

"Undercover freedom fighters," Klara Brocker's American would say to her after another day of questioning. And he'd take her down to the cellar where he'd thrust into her on the blankets he'd spread across the cement floor by the potato bin. "Did you know— my German *Fräulein*—" His narrow face would move above hers, his hair much lighter than his eyebrows. "—that your entire country— was filled— with undercover— freedom fighters?"

Not only the teachers were investigated. People all over town were afraid of being turned in to the Americans by their neighbors or children, of hearing knocks at their doors and being picked up, of not finding work or losing the jobs they had. It struck Trudi as an ironic and just parallel to what the Jews had suffered for so many years, and she didn't feel any sympathy when people like Frau Heidenreich and her friends elaborated on their own suffering. Hadn't they become the real victims? Hadn't they endured separation within their families? Panic when the bombs had fallen? Many of them lamented the years without their children. While the Jews were treated like royalty, ordinary people like them were still persecuted, questioned about their political beliefs, although they'd had no idea what had really been going on in the KZs till after the war, and then they'd been shocked, no—horrified.

It became a scramble to get letters of recommendation from those who had not joined the *Partei,* people who had resisted the Nazis, though at the time it had seemed to everyone else like foolishness. But now it was good to know people like that, better yet if they owed you a favor.

The pay-library had never been so busy. People tugged at Trudi and her father, begging them to write letters that would testify to their impeccable character and prove they'd always opposed the *Partei.* And as they brought tales that proclaimed their innocence, tales they hoped Trudi would distribute, she felt used: as a storyteller, she knew the border between truth and lies, and she would circulate their tales with introductions like "This is what he would like people to believe. . . ." And then she'd speculate about what had really happened. If it was within her conscience, she wrote the letters, but she refused to back up versions of a fabricated truth, especially if they were connected to gifts. In those months after the war, she had more enemies and friends than ever before.

Frau Blau was less selective than Trudi about the letters she wrote.

"If we can help each other," she'd say, "we may as well. Times are difficult enough."

Two Protestant families in Burgdorf, who, it turned out, had also hidden Jews, felt more like Trudi and refused to whitewash anyone who had sympathized with the Nazis. One family lived next to the taxidermist. When he asked these neighbors to vouch for him in a letter, they turned him away.

"I can't," Trudi told him when he came to her.

"You hid Jews. I never turned you in."

"You didn't even know I had people here."

"I knew. I saw them . . . coming late at night. Leaving with Herr Hesping. But—I didn't want trouble for you and your father."

She stared at him, realizing he was speaking the truth. "That's not enough."

"I lost my daughter too, Fräulein Montag."

"About that I'm sorry. . . . But I can't help you."

He leaned across the counter, pushing two piles of books aside. His eyes were tortured. "Herr Hitler only wanted the best for us."

"And look what we got. Just look what we got, Herr Heidenreich."

"But he wanted the best. He did. If I can't believe that—" He stopped abruptly. Shivered. "You have to admit, in the beginning he wanted the best."

Though Herr Stosick, whose hair had never grown back after his son's death, did not ask for her support, Trudi went to his house one evening and volunteered to write a letter for him.

"That's kind of you, but I don't think I need to impose on you." He led her into the kitchen, where his wife was unraveling a moth-eaten cardigan, saving the intact yarn for socks she would knit.

Herr Stosick pulled out a chair for Trudi and urged her to sit down. "I have reason to be grateful to Herr Neumaier for keeping the membership money he took from my wife. Thanks to him, I can prove that I didn't join the *Partei*. So few teachers have been allowed back into the schools again . . . none of the ones who were in the *Partei*. Such a dilemma. I probably would have ended up having to join, but I kept saying that I'd already paid my membership fee."

It sounded as if he'd regained some of his self-respect. "It's my life, the teaching," he said. "But I worry about the children. They don't have the same kind of respect for their teachers as before the war. And we have no schoolbooks, no teaching materials. Most of us teach from memory."

One morning in October, when Trudi opened the library, Paul Weinhart's elderly mother stood waiting outside, eyes swollen, fingers plucking the front of her tweed coat. "Paul—he has been arrested. The Amis took him in while he was delivering potatoes. You've known him since you were children, Trudi. Please—just write that he's not the kind of person who'd harm anyone. . . ." She opened her handbag and thrust a pad of ivory stationery at Trudi. "Please?"

Trudi could see Paul's face as though he were standing in front of her. At thirty, he looked the way he had as a boy—only taller, broader—and his toes still pointed outward when he walked. "Did your son send you?"

The old woman shook her head. "I haven't seen him since they took him away . . . yesterday."

I don't want your son to know any happiness. No happiness at all. But what Trudi said was: "I'm not the right person to ask."

"You are in a position to help him. The Amis will listen to you."

"I'm not the right person to ask, Frau Weinhart."

"You were in school together."

Trudi was silent.

"Why can't you then?"

Trudi shook her head.

"What is it?"

"You are a good woman, Frau Weinhart. . . . I don't want to hurt you. But I can't write that letter," she said, choosing her words carefully, "because I know that your son is the kind of person who would harm someone."

The Buttgereits who, along with many others, had been *gehorsame Bürger*—obedient citizens—now claimed they had opposed the Nazis. As proof they offered the fate of their third-youngest daughter, Bettina. "A war heroine," they called her, and retold the story of how she'd run up to the saddest of all trains with the bread to help the starving and how she'd been captured, wrestled to the ground, taken away forever with the prisoners.

"My daughter stood for what our family believed in," her father would declare in Potter's tavern, pounding his hand on the table, the same hand he used to raise in the *Heil Hitler.* "Any member of my family would have done what Bettina did. And don't forget—" Here his eyes would grow moist. "—don't forget that my only son died, a victim of the Nazis because he was a cripple."

His wife would tell you she had tried to be good to Jews whenever she could. "I spoke out for the Jews," she'd inform you, "I did, as long as it didn't put me in danger." Yet, she still wore her golden *Ehrenkreuz der deutschen Mutter*—the cross of honor for the German mother—and didn't seem to understand that wearing it implied support of Hitler. "It's too valuable to throw out," she'd protest. "Besides, I earned it."

Trudi found it harder to tolerate cowards like Herr and Frau Buttgereit than fanatics like the butcher, who took pride in having supported the Führer. At least old Anton Immers was honest. Wrong, but honest. But she was getting fed up with all those who vowed that—although they'd been in the *Partei*—they had resisted in their hearts.

Hearts. "They either don't have hearts," she told Ingrid one Sunday when they took Rita to the playground, "or if they do, those hearts are hollow."

"My father's heart is black." Ingrid sat down on the bench, hands folded on her knees. "My father cuts up pictures. He keeps the faces, the bodies."

Rita pulled at her mother's black coat, but Ingrid's eyes stared past her.

"Come," Trudi said and lifted Rita onto the wooden swing. "Hold on tight. I'll push you."

"He cuts out *Hakenkreuz* pins from lapels. . . ." Ingrid's voice rose above the squeaking of the swing chains. "He cuts out hands that hold flags. He cuts out the insignia on my brother's and husband's uniforms. . . ."

Ingrid's husband, Ulrich, had arrived home from the war in May, found work with the railroad in August, impregnated Ingrid in September, and died in October, when a coal train derailed in Bonn. Ingrid was certain his death was her penance, that she'd been meant to be an illegitimate mother.

"But you're a widow," Trudi had pointed out to her the morning of his funeral.

Ingrid had shaken her head. "It's God's way of telling me he never accepted my marriage."

As far as Ingrid was concerned, she had two illegitimate children—one already born and another expanding within her—and she fretted that this tainted her children's status regarding original sin. "It has to be even worse for them than for children who come from blessed marriages."

"The priest blessed your marriage," Trudi reminded her.

"It was a coverup marriage. I already was with child. It would have been better for my daughter never to have been born."

"Don't say that."

"For the new child, too . . . The sin begins with the parents. It's passed down."

Ingrid even felt responsible for the sins and suffering of her brother, Holger, who'd been a member of the SA and was a prisoner in an American camp near Würzburg. Before Ingrid's husband had died, he'd taken her on the train to visit Holger. Though they couldn't enter the camp, they were allowed to talk with her brother through the links of the fence. At first Ingrid didn't recognize him—his face was gaunt, and his body was stooped like that of an old man.

Her brother looked worse than Judge Spiecker, who'd weighed less than ninety pounds when he'd come home after being in an American hospital in Berlin for months. The judge still seemed too weak to climb the front steps of the pay-library when he visited Leo, and he had aged a generation in the years he'd been away. The only reason he'd survived at all, he told Leo, was because he'd escaped three weeks before the end of the war, when he and all other prisoners were taken out of their KZ to be herded through woods and grassy areas toward an undisclosed destination, prodded by the rifles of camp guards. Those who got tired or were too ill to continue the gruesome march were shot.

One night in the forest, when he knew he could not walk another step, the judge threw himself behind a dense growth of blackberry bushes and crawled into their thorny center, certain he was about to be found and killed. But as he crouched there, oddly revived by the scratches and the thorns embedded in his skin, the wretched line of prisoners passed him by. Four days later, straying through the woods, incoherent, he was found by a black American soldier, who carried him to a truck and drove him to a hospital.

When the judge arrived in Burgdorf, he found out that the lawyer who'd denounced him had prospered during the war and was a partner in a law firm. Though his wife urged him to inform the Americans, Judge Spiecker didn't want to live with revenge.

"What about justice then?" his wife wanted to know.

"Not everything can be just."

"That's not what you used to believe."

The judge was offered his old position and accepted before he'd recovered his health, but he seemed far more interested in playing with his children, especially his eighth, the girl Heide, who'd been born after his arrest.

"It's as if he knew he'd die soon," his pregnant widow would tell Leo Montag after the judge would collapse on the sidewalk, and the old women would try to console her by reminding her it was a miracle the judge had come back at all, a miracle considering how much he'd suffered, and that at least he'd known happiness with his family in those brief months.

"He left you with a new life," they'd say, their fingertips reaching for the new widow's belly, yet pulling back as soon as they'd touch her, as if not quite trusting their words that, indeed, this was something to be thankful for.

After the judge's funeral, Herr Stosick stayed behind to light a candle on his son's grave. When he reached home, two Americans were waiting for him, and he was taken in for questioning. It turned out that a certain Günther Stosick had been responsible for the deaths of several hundred Jews in the KZ Buchenwald, and though Herr Stosick told the Americans that he'd fought on the Russian front and had never been near Buchenwald, he lost his teaching position and was imprisoned.

Like many other soldiers, he'd come home from the turmoil of war without having been properly dismissed from the military: he had no paperwork, nothing to prove where he'd served. When Leo Montag went to the prison to find out what was happening to Herr Stosick, the American officer who met with him spoke German and was kind to him.

"I can vouch for Herr Stosick," Leo offered. "I'll send you a letter. I know him well—as a friend and a chess player. It's not in his nature to attack." He told the American about Bruno, who'd killed himself after his parents had taken him out of the Hitler-Jugend. "He was opposed from the very beginning."

Although the officer listened with obvious sympathy, he said Herr

Stosick's background needed to be checked, and that it would take time.

"My friend never joined the *Partei*," Leo persisted, trying to draw on reserves of strength he no longer felt. "He didn't support the Nazis."

"Not exactly a common name," Günther Stosick told Leo when they were permitted to speak. "I can see where they'd have to make sure I wasn't the one."

When Leo reached home, Trudi had to help him from the car into the house. His hands shook as he sat down on the sofa and lifted his left leg so that she could push a pillow beneath it. Carefully, she helped him to roll up his pants leg. The steel disk that had replaced his kneecap over thirty years ago pushed against his skin, which was red and tender to the touch.

She rinsed a towel in cold water and folded it across her father's knee. "Is this better?"

He mumbled something, and though she bent closer, she couldn't understand him.

"What is it?"

"*Wenn man älter wird, stirbt einer nach dem anderen hin, bis man endlich ganz alleine ist. . . .*"—"When you get older, one after the other dies until you're finally all alone."

"You're not going to die." She wrapped his gray cardigan around him, covered him with a blanket. "How about some tea? I'll make you Russian tea."

"No."

"Something to eat then."

He shook his head.

"You're not going to die. And you're not alone. Don't forget that. You have me. And I know Herr Stosick will get out of prison."

They kept waiting for Günther Stosick all that winter, and one morning in March of 1946 he was released unexpectedly: the Americans had tracked down the other Günther Stosick, who'd been at Buchenwald. Herr Stosick did not stop to call home—he only wanted to get out. It was snowing when he ran from the prison to the train station, the bag with his few belongings thumping against his legs. Platforms were crowded, and as the train pulled in and mobs of people shoved and hollered to get on, he was afraid he'd never see his wife again. Behind him the lines pushed forward. He fell. Scraping his hands on the cement, he roared with his final strength, "I won't be trampled," and in that moment—when he took hold of his future and the people behind him hesitated—Herr Stosick scrambled onto his feet and climbed into the train.

The pregnant women that spring of 1946 made Trudi long for Max Rudnick more than she'd longed for him in months. Although the awareness of him had never left her, those high, swollen bellies that flaunted new life made it unbearable to be without her lover. She took his paintings from her closet, hung them up in her room, but looking at them only increased her sadness. *"My light spirit,"* he'd called her. People claimed sadness lessened with time, and perhaps that was so, but what Trudi found harder than sadness was the uncertainty. What had happened to Max? If she knew for sure that he was dead, she could at least grieve for him and trust that each single hour would move her further away from the moment of his death; even if she could be certain that he was alive and had no intent of returning to her, she could rage and cry and begin getting over him; but this not knowing—when she might learn of his death or, all at once, come face to face with him—was wearing her down.

Some days, when the longing pressed on her, she would try to escape it by thinking of people who were much worse off than she—like the many amputees who'd come back from the war. One of them, the barber's nephew Wolfgang, had lost both legs. Trudi had seen his widowed mother hoist him into the wheelchair with amazing strength: the old woman would bend toward him, and he'd link both arms around her neck while she'd lift him, cradle him like the infant he used to be, as if trying to undo all harm that had come to her son since she'd first held him like this.

Without his legs, Wolfgang was shorter than Trudi. Although she would never grow another centimeter, she had at least functional legs and could go wherever she wanted. Looking at him filled her with empathy and reminded her to focus on what she had, rather than on what she would never have. She told herself that, if she looked at her life—all thirty years of it—in one flash, one overall view, it had been good. Not that she had forgotten or dismissed every moment of despair or fury, but the total sum of her life was good. She thought of Max and how fortunate she was to have her memories of him.

Max— It always came back to him.

She might never have Max in her life again.

Sometimes she'd find refuge from her pain by picturing herself escaping from Germany altogether. Her Aunt Helene and Uncle Stefan would be glad to see her. After all, she'd had an invitation to visit since she was four. She'd see herself walking through the building that her aunt had described to her, speaking words of English that she'd practiced with the American soldiers. In the carpeted elevator she'd ride to the sixth floor and admire the view of the lake and mountains, sit in front of a marble fireplace with her aunt and uncle while Robert played the piano.

Packages from America had begun to arrive again since the end of the war: Aunt Helene had adopted Trudi's entire neighborhood, sending crates with dry milk, dry eggs, rice, and flour not only for her relatives but also for their friends. In her apartment house she'd organized people to help, filling the lists she'd asked Trudi to send to her, but as Trudi wrote those lists, which contained many basics— food, clothing, soap—they only reminded her of the lists people used to make for their final journeys to KZs. This past Christmas, eight packages had arrived from America, each of the gifts beautifully wrapped, including a huge red blouse for the midwife, who'd been in the pay-library the last time a package with staples had arrived and who'd sighed, "I wish I had family in America."

"But they don't even know me," the midwife exclaimed as she buttoned the red blouse. "It fits, and they don't even know me."

"Now they do," Trudi said, and stirred dry milk into a cup of water for Adi.

In spring, Robert, who was already the father of a one-year-old, Caleb, started to send his son's outgrown clothes. Some of them were hardly worn, and Trudi took them to Ingrid, who'd entered her seventh month of pregnancy, and to Jutta, who was a few weeks further along.

The day Jutta had found out about her pregnancy, she'd surprised Trudi by confiding that she'd been trying to have a child ever since her wedding and had come to believe that she was barren. There was a part of Trudi—the nasty, greedy part—that could have easily said, *Hey, you who have everything, the man I once wanted, the child I would have liked to give birth to. . . . It is easy for you to look down on me.* Only Jutta did not look down on her. And that's why Trudi decided to honor her confidence by not turning it into gossip. It felt good to deal with a secret mercifully, especially if it belonged to someone else who wasn't accepted by the town. People said Jutta set herself apart from them with her painting; and her husband's family—except for his mother—had never taken to her as they had to Brigitte Raud-schuss. Jutta was too tall, too young, too independent. She smoked too much, was not refined enough, didn't try to flatter the old aunts at the family reunions.

Of all the unborn children in Burgdorf, the child of Jutta Malter was the one whose progress fascinated Trudi the most. To follow the changes in Jutta's body, she often took walks past Alexander Sturm's apartment house, hoping to see Jutta. While Jutta walked with her belly out as if glorying in her pregnancy, Klara Brocker was ashamed to be seen by anyone. Though she concealed her body in loose coats and dresses, her belly pushed from her tidy frame with the life that her American soldier—who'd given her so many other gifts—had planted in her before he'd let himself be transferred from her reach. All Klara had left of him were eleven canning jars with peaches and the contempt of the townspeople, who used to shake their heads when they'd seen her in nylon stockings. And the child, of course; she had the child who was distorting her body and parading her sin.

The judge's widow was bigger than Jutta, Klara, or Ingrid, perhaps because her body had expanded so many times already. The midwife took care of the pregnant women, except for Jutta, who'd chosen to go to Sister Agathe, unaware that the sister was suffering a crisis of conscience. All Jutta remembered was how skillful and gentle the sis-ter used to be when she'd performed medical procedures, and how she'd never blamed her for not being careful enough.

But now the sister had become hesitant. She barely ate and de-clined the other nuns' advice to rest. Her body sweated easily, drench-ing her undergarments and habit. Throughout the winter and into spring, her flesh had grown nearly translucent as though she wanted to see into her own womb, which was no place for babies, like the dis-tended wombs of women all over Burgdorf.

When Herr Pastor Beier was brought in to speak with her, Sister Agathe asked to meet with him in the cloister garden, where she con-fessed that she'd helped the Nazis during the war.

"But that's impossible."

"Oh yes. By trying to bring comfort to the prisoners. I wanted to make their lives more bearable and took them medicine and food whenever I could. Now I wish I'd urged them to run instead, to escape."

"You did what you believed was right at the time."

"But it wasn't."

"You did the best you could."

"The best for myself . . . Don't you see? It made me feel better when I could ease their suffering."

"We couldn't know how it would all end." The priest stared down on his hands, plump white hands with square nails, hands that still looked the way they had when he'd entered the seminary. All at once he was choked with the loss of everything he'd believed in then. "I . . ." He raised one of those hands to his forehead. "I've questioned some of my decisions since."

"That's good," the nun murmured.

He raised his eyes, startled.

"I handed the prisoners over to the Nazis . . . that terrible obedience. I wanted to make their last days here as comfortable as possible, to have them leave with dignity. . . . Yet, looking at all that happened, I was only one more tool, an accomplice."

"Don't say that." The priest's round face looked distraught. "That would make all of us accomplices."

"But we are. Don't you see?"

To lay her hands on the taut belly of the dentist's wife troubled Sister Agathe, and she was terrified when, one morning in May, she felt no life. Convinced that her touch had brought on the unborn child's death, she called her supervisor, Sister Ingeborg, who confirmed that the child was dead. Sister Agathe tried to soothe Jutta and felt devastated when the young woman climbed from the white-shrouded table and stormed out of the Theresienheim. From that day on, the sister took to her bed; and even when she would find out the following day that Jutta Malter had ridden in back of the bakery truck to the midwife's house, where she'd given birth to a girl—alive and healthy—Sister Agathe would refuse to harm anyone else with her care.

The pastor had never held that many christenings in such a short time: there was the Malter girl, Hanna; Georg Weiler's son, Manfred; old Anton Immers' granddaughter, Sybille; the children of the two widows—a son, Heinz, for the judge's widow, a second daughter,

Karin, for Ingrid Hebel; and then, of course, Klara Brocker's illegiti-mate son, Rolf. The Klein family followed with a daughter, the Müller family with a son, and two other unmarried women with children whose fathers were American soldiers.

Then, as if by mystery, another child appeared. Afterwards the people would say that it all started when the midwife—after tending to the last of her pregnant patients and waxing her floors—left Burgdorf one Thursday with her son, Adi. When she returned to her stucco house the following afternoon, she carried an infant in her arms.

"Whose is it?" people asked.

"Where did you get it?"

But the midwife only said, "This is my daughter, Renate."

The townspeople approved that Hilde Eberhardt named the infant girl after her mother-in-law as if to make amends for her husband who, everyone knew, would have never let her use the name Renate. Though the girl was dark and foreign-looking—not at all like her blond mother and grandmother—she reminded the people anew of the gap that the older Renate Eberhardt's absence had left in their midst, and they welcomed the child as one of their own.

They were ready for this child and asked fewer questions than usual, though this didn't stop them from making guesses about Re-nate's parents. Some wondered if she'd been adopted from gypsies. Renate had that look, that intense darkness. Still—not too many gyp-sies had survived the KZs. Others figured that the midwife was her real mother and that the bulk of her body had made it possible for her to conceal her pregnancy. She could have birthed the child alone, propping her back against pillows and reaching between her massive thighs. When even Trudi Montag couldn't find out from where the midwife's child had come, the town resigned itself to this being one of the secrets it would never know.

Hilde Eberhardt liked to wrap the infant in the cashmere shawl she'd bought for her mother-in-law. "This shawl belongs to your grandmother," she would tell Renate while she'd rock her. Adi, who was already five, would watch her silently—his light features so much like his father's that sometimes she had to look away—and he'd stretch out one fair hand and touch Renate's face. At least he was un-like his father in nature, rather shy and kind, taking after her. If only she'd insisted on giving him a different name. Even though he'd been called Adi all his life, she could not forget that his full name was Adolf, a name that no one gave to newborn boys any longer.

Gradually, the pattern of days in Burgdorf returned to normal. People resumed their *Spaziergänge,* a habit many of them had discontinued during the war. An ailment like Frau Buttgereit's enormous kidney stones—which would have seemed trivial compared to the crises of war—now could evoke sympathy. Life was normal again, enough so that women could talk about a new pattern for a dress, say, or have their hair set once a week at the beauty parlor.

The outside walls of houses were scrubbed, and new *Gardinen*— lace curtains—were sewn, first for windows that faced the street, so that the façades of houses presented a good impression. In her daughter's room, the midwife hung wallpaper and *Gardinen* with the lacy pattern of dolls holding hands. Window boxes were lusher than ever before. Near the Burgdorf cemetery, people restored their *Schrebergärten,* those tidy vegetable and flower plots where they could cause something to grow. The chestnut tree in front of the pay-library flourished, and the shadows of its leaves became longer. Where some of the ruins had been, modern apartments were built, boxy brick structures with nearly flat roofs and large windows; the rubble was carried off to a dump, which was established along the road to the abandoned flour mill.

Normal meant that the white excursion boats floated again on a regular schedule—not the intermittent journeys of the past years. Weekend nights music would drift from the Rhein, and if Trudi stood on the dike, she'd see couples dancing on the boats while lanterns bobbed around them like red and blue moons. She'd battle that all too familiar yearning for Max that had become part of her as much as breathing. If he had returned, she could be dancing there with him.

Children stopped by the pharmacy and asked for *Pröbchen*—samples—of skin cream or lipstick or cough drops that the sales representatives left with Fräulein Horten. The ragman built an addition on his house. Chess-club meetings resumed at the house of Herr Stosick, whose reputation had been reinstated to such a degree that people now came to him for letters. Members of the club attended tournaments in Köln and Bielefeld and brought home a respectable number of trophies as well as stories of losing their way in those cities they'd known so well before the war. But now entire building blocks had been demolished, making every street seem unfamiliar.

When the priest was finally assigned transportation—a motor scooter the same shade of blue as the car upholstery he'd dreamed of—people would see him practice behind the rectory and around the church square, his lips pressed together in what might have been concentration or disappointment, his legs extended sideways to balance his massive body.

During Sunday mass, men would sit around their *Stammtisch* in Die Traube again and walk their families home from St. Martin's Church after the priest had blessed them with the final: *". . . in nomine patris et filii et spiritus sancti."*

"Back to normal," people would say.

"Back to normal," they would remind one another.

But Trudi knew that beneath that sheen of normalcy the town was a freak. She could see the ugliness, the twistedness, made even more evident by the tidiness, the surface beauty. All the town's energy went into this frenzy to rebuild, to restore order, to pretty itself up as if nothing had changed in the war.

Some people still claimed they couldn't comprehend how the KZs could have happened, and it was never clear to Trudi how many had known, and how many had been afraid to believe the horrors.

"Until my death . . . I won't be able to understand that."

"We weren't told what was going on."

"If I'd known, I wouldn't have wanted to continue living."

"Someone told me in '44, and I didn't believe it, but then I later found out it was the truth."

"Don't forget—Hitler was an Austrian, not a German."

Most didn't like to think back on Hitler, and if they spoke about him at all, it would be to tell you they hadn't liked what had gone on. Their allegiance to one powerful leader now became their excuse: since they had not made decisions but merely obeyed orders, they were not to blame. They took it as a challenge when the *Burgdorf Post* reported that other countries claimed Germany would never recover again, that it would always be in poverty. They agreed with one another that it wouldn't serve any of Germany's enemies to leave her sitting in the middle of Europe like a dead country. After all, they were industrious, and though they had few materials, they knew how to work. Hadn't they always known how to work? Certainly the world must know that about the Germans by now. And even if sometimes the damage they faced seemed so absolute that it seemed nothing could ever be fixed, they didn't consider giving up. As they felt the eyes of the world on their efforts, they strived even harder to gain respect, admiration.

All over Germany, women helped with the reconstruction. They carried stones and built walls; worked in dust and dirt without complaint; created miracles out of the faith that there would be better years ahead. Evenings, the women opened the seams of old clothing, turned them inside out, and sewed the fabric into something that almost felt new: short pants for boys, pleated skirts for girls, shirts with stiff collars for men, dresses with belts for themselves. No longer were they shabby as during the last years of war, but normal. Almost normal.

———————————◼————————————

Nᴏɴᴇ ᴏꜰ ᴛʜᴇ Bᴜᴛᴛɢᴇʀᴇɪᴛ ꜱɪꜱᴛᴇʀꜱ ʜᴀᴅ ᴍᴀʀʀɪᴇᴅ. Mᴏɴɪᴋᴀ, ᴛʜᴇ ꜱᴇᴄ-
ond oldest, was now the music teacher in the Catholic school; two
helped with the care of the children of their married cousins; one entered a convent in Koblenz; Bettina was never seen again after she'd
been taken away on that train; two found work in the wool factory in
Neuss; one became a court stenographer; and the oldest, Sabine,
stayed with her parents, determined to nurse them with grim obligation into old age.

Monika Buttgereit and the driver of the bakery truck, Alfred
Meier, had resumed their courtship as soon as he'd come home from
the front. Though he'd introduced Sabine to two of his friends, hoping she'd marry and clear the path for him and Monika, both men had
gone out with her only once. Herr Meier was about to forsake hope
that he and Monika could ever be man and wife, when Sabine began
to spit up blood. Her parents said her lungs were weak, and while the
entire town waited for her to die, speculating on the passion that
would erupt once the music teacher and the driver of the bakery truck
could get married, the chaste courtship continued. Smoldering fires
of what could have been manifested themselves in more extravagant

hats for Monika and a murderous look in Herr Meier's eyes whenever he'd glance at Monika's oldest sister.

Yet, when Sabine died late that summer, Alfred and Monika did not set a wedding date. Because it's too soon after the death, people would rationalize. But gradually they came to understand that the two were not about to alter the courtship they'd become familiar with. They still met once a week, and sometimes they included Monika's parents on their outings, tucking napkins into their collars as if they were small children.

Alfred was saving his money to open a small fish restaurant like the one he'd seen as a boy near the ocean, where crisp chunks of fish were served hot in greasy paper cones. He worked overtime at the bakery and took to playing cards with Georg Weiler, who'd moved with his wife and children into the smallest apartment in Alexander Sturm's building. Alfred wished he could laugh as easily as Georg, who would have never waited years for a woman, who was lucky more often than not because he believed in his luck, who'd buy pastries from him whenever he had money left and feed any child who happened to be playing on the sidewalk. And yet, he could feel something buried inside Georg, something terribly familiar, yet impossible to name that no soldier wanted to remember. He'd felt it within himself, had seen it in the eyes of other men. It made him feel dirty, made him spill himself inside whores instead of soiling a good woman like Monika. With Georg it burst through when he drank too much and his face turned into a bloated mask. He'd need Alfred's help to get home from Potter's bar. After hoisting Georg up the flights of stairs to the third floor, Alfred would leave quickly because good women with reproachful eyes made him uneasy.

It was no secret in town that Helga Weiler had every reason to be reproachful when her husband was drunk, because he'd rage at her and the children until—the baby in one arm, both girls clutching her free hand—she'd bolt down the steps, coats over their nightclothes, and across the backyard to the other wing of the L-shaped building, where she'd knock on the Malters' door. There it was safe, even if Jutta Malter would have to be persuaded not to charge up the stairs to confront Georg.

Freak lightning struck Burgdorf one Tuesday in October of 1946, killing twelve milk cows on the Weinharts' farm. It had rained for nearly a week, and the cows stood huddled in a vast puddle next to the oak tree when it was split by a lightning bolt. Immediately they were electrocuted.

To Trudi, the accident only mirrored the crippled state of her community. Though the war had ended a year and a half before, she could still feel its presence in the vengeance of nature, in the dreadful suffering of individuals, and in sudden acts of personal violence—all made worse by the silence that she tried to keep from folding around her town. She could see its presence in the painful limp of an amputee; in the living gauze on the throat of the baker's son; in the wail of the soldier who'd shot his wife ten months after coming home. . . .

People would assure one another that things were normal again, but you could feel great sorrows everywhere, left by those who'd died or were missing or had gone to prison, and what you'd need to do was let those sorrows surge across you, stun you; because if you didn't, those sorrows would hunt you, break through your skin, ugly and red like boils. If you fled from those sorrows, they could trip you, maim you.

Jutta Malter saw that brokenness as clearly as Trudi. What Trudi chronicled with words, Jutta chronicled with paint. Her obsession with painting had spiraled since the war as if she needed to recreate this town where her mother had brought her and had died, where her uncle had leapt from the attic window, and where her daughter anchored her in a way she'd never expected anyone to hold her. While Hanna would play on a soft blanket next to her easel, Jutta would paint bright, bright buildings that looked like paralyzed faces, yellow clouds that whipped across the red sky like flames, people without faces, whose bodies were angled gray lines against an overwhelmingly colorful background. And as she'd work, feverishly—honoring the covenant with her vision to show it all: the pain and the joy—her paintings would evoke that peculiar beauty that arises only from darkness.

Early afternoons, after she'd eat the midday meal with her husband and wait for him to return to his patients, she'd take Hanna out in the wicker baby carriage, pushing her with one paint-smudged hand while holding a cigarette in the other. Almost every time she'd pass the pay-library, Trudi Montag would come running out and ask if she could hold the baby. Ever since she was a girl, Jutta had been fascinated with the *Zwerg* woman. Once she'd painted her, but she hadn't shown Trudi the canvas because she was afraid to offend her. In the painting, part of the town showed through the gap between Trudi's O-shaped legs, while the rest of Burgdorf fit into her wide body.

Trudi would lift Hanna from the carriage and bounce her gently in her arms. "If you want to paint for a while without interruptions," she'd say, "Hanna will be fine here." The first few times Jutta had objected, but Trudi had sensed the restlessness in her, that struggle between being a painter and being a mother.

"Afternoons it gets so quiet here. I'd be glad for the company."

Soon Jutta came to look forward to those hours of solitary work. Without her daughter, she could roam the outskirts of town again, stride through the fields, prop her easel by the quarry hole or by the flour mill that still lay in ruins.

If you went to the pay-library for gossip, you'd discover that it was futile to expect any worthwhile rumors from Trudi Montag if she had Hanna with her. She'd check out your books, mark them in her card file, give you the correct change, but she'd be carrying the blond child around, cooing and murmuring to her without interest in what you might have to say. And Hanna would murmur right back to her, a sequence of bubble sounds that didn't have meaning to anyone but Trudi. Even questions about the health of Leo Montag—who walked with a cane now and seemed weaker all the time—would only bring brief answers, and if you were to leave a wedge of pound cake for him, say, or a jar of pickles, Trudi would merely thank you without reporting how her father had liked the last delicacy you'd given him.

Sometimes, when Jutta came to retrieve her daughter, she'd hold her tight and study her small face as if searching for something that might have been taken from her during her absence. Once, she didn't bring Hanna to the pay-library for ten days because she felt like an unnatural mother for cherishing her time alone; and since she didn't know how to explain this to Trudi, she avoided her by varying her walks with the child. But it was impossible to immerse herself in her work when her daughter was with her, and she finally convinced herself that Hanna enjoyed her time with Trudi.

Since Trudi refused to accept money for looking after Hanna, Jutta invited her over one afternoon, while her husband was pulling Frau Weskopp's infected wisdom tooth, and told Trudi to choose any one of her canvases. The painting of Trudi was safely hidden beneath her bed, and she'd leaned the rest of her work against the sofa, chairs, and table legs in her living room.

"I see you've kept Eva's sofa," Trudi said.

"It reminds me of her and my uncle. Most of the furniture stayed when we moved into their apartment."

"Eva would have wanted you to have them." Trudi looked around. "But you didn't keep the stuffed birds."

"I think of them as dead birds. There's been too much death already." Jutta pointed toward her painting of Schreberstrasse. "Recognize it?"

Trudi nodded. Jutta had painted her street at an odd angle, tilted toward the fiery sky, with the pay-library, the grocery store, and the Blaus' house blazing blue triangles.

Jutta had figured Trudi would choose that one, or the one she'd done of the quarry during a thunderstorm with slashes of light above the shadowy caldron of water, but Trudi walked past the paintings of the town, pausing in front of the canvas with two red figures floating from a yellow sky.

"Your uncle?"

Jutta nodded.

"And Eva?"

"I don't know."

Trudi nodded. "It has to be Eva."

Goose bumps rose along Jutta's arms. *Of course it's Eva, has been Eva all along. How could I have not known and yet painted her?*

Trudi headed toward the painting that Jutta had never considered giving away—her only one of Hanna so far—and stood silently in front of the square canvas that was filled with the shape of Jutta's child, a week after her birth, and with Jutta's hands in a deep hue of green, cradling the small, perfect body, which was the color of clay as though it had just been carved from the earth. And with this painting, features had emerged under her brush—unmistakably Hanna's.

"There are others," Jutta said, uneasy with the way Trudi stared at the picture.

"That one," Trudi said in a voice that did not allow discussion.

She hung the canvas in her bedroom along with Max's paintings. Sometimes those hands that held the child became her own, and she had to remind herself that Hanna had Jutta and Klaus as parents. Once again, she found herself aching with fantasies of a marriage and family, and she'd admonish herself: Who are you to believe you can have that? Yet, that old urge of needing, of wanting, would burst through her, fastening itself to this child, Hanna, whose parents had the power to keep her away—as they had on Hanna's first Christmas, when they'd taken her on a visit to one of Klaus' rich relatives, while all along Trudi had looked forward to Christmas Eve when she would give her the doll clothes she'd sewn so lovingly on long winter evenings.

She had bought the fabric in Düsseldorf, in Mahler's department store, and the saleswoman had asked her what she was making.

"A dress. For a doll."

"Your daughter's doll?"

Somehow, she'd nodded.

"What's your daughter's name?"

"Hanna."

"How old is she?"

"Six months."

"A lovely age."

"She's starting to sit up."

"Does she have your hair?"

"Very light, yes."

"And blue eyes?"

"Yes."

It didn't feel like lying. Especially since she'd started off with the truth. Yet, she felt uneasy about that conversation when she sewed the outfit for Hanna's doll, a pink dress with royal-blue trim and a royal-blue hat so stylish even Frau Simon would have admired it.

When Matthias Berger returned to Burgdorf to visit his grandmother, he stopped by the pay-library and confessed to Trudi that he was thinking of leaving the seminary. He'd been in for a year and a half, and with each day, he said, he felt more set apart from the other seminarians.

"You can live with us," she offered impulsively.

"I— I couldn't impose."

"You'd be renting a room. The whole third floor, actually. You know how scarce apartments are."

"Yes, but—"

"Have you been playing the piano?"

"Not since I entered the seminary."

"Such a waste . . . There's a piano waiting here for you." Her voice skipped with excitement. "Let's tell my father."

"Wait," he said, "wait."

"He'll be so glad. I haven't thought of renting to anyone until now. Imagine—having you live in the house with us." Already she could see her day-to-day life with him, meeting him in the hallway, eating meals together, watching him play chess with her father. Of course he'd take up the piano again.

"I haven't decided for sure. About leaving."

She knew she was being pushy but she couldn't stop. "It would be such a comfort to my father to have you here. He hasn't been well."

Matthias brought his hands to his face and pressed his fingers against his temples.

"You still get those headaches?"

He nodded, and then he was silent for so long that she thought he'd forgotten her.

"Something happened," she said. "Something happened in the seminary. I know it."

He looked startled.

She grasped his elbow, led him between the shelves, and climbed to the fourth rung of the ladder, where she sat, her face at the same level with his. "Tell me."

"I should go."

"Please."

"It's so ugly."

And it was ugly. A group of other seminarians had surrounded Matthias outside the chapel after night prayers, dragged him into the forest behind the buildings, and knotted a rope tightly through the belt loops of his trousers. After forcing castor oil down his throat, they hunted him through the woods with sticks, hissing "queer, filthy queer," while he struggled to get his pants down and crouch behind a tree away from them to relieve the terrible pressure in his bowels. But their sticks kept him from untying the rope, and soon he was sobbing with humiliation while feces ran down his legs.

"Those bastards." Trudi was furious.

"You know what I kept thinking while they were chasing me?" His face was strained. White. "That I deserved it. Even though I've never touched one of them."

"No one deserves to be treated like that. Those bastards. And they weren't even original. Mussolini's Fascists—they used to do that to people. You were just a boy then. . . . Did you report them?"

"No."

"Why not?"

"Because I've tried . . . For other things. Before. Nothing that bad. Only shoving around. Taunting. Our superiors don't take it that seriously. They have me figured as different anyhow."

"Our country has a history of that, justifying attacks on those who are different. Erasing them."

"You're making this into something bigger than it is."

"It's much bigger than anything I could make, believe me, Matthias. Don't you see—this war is still going on. And will be going on . . . Until we all accept everything that has happened, we won't have the peace that people believe we already have."

He was silent for a long time. Finally he looked into her face. "What do you do if you're called to the wrong thing?"

She was terribly afraid of saying words that would make him feel even worse. It was obvious to her that he was not talking about the church, but about battling that within him that called him to seek out his own gender. She wanted to lay her hand on his arm, yet he looked so brittle as he stood before her that she was certain he'd splinter if she touched him. "It must be awful," she said carefully, "to be called to something one does not want."

"And what does *one* do with that?" His voice was raw. Mocking.

"I don't know. Unless—"

"Unless what?"

"Unless there's some way one can learn to want what one is called for." You're a good one to preach, Trudi Montag, she told herself. How about you, how well have you learned to want what you're called to be? Body and soul and mind. All. Like Pia. Who wouldn't have wanted it any other way.

Pia would have never believed the traveling healer, an ancient Dutchman with youthful steps and mesmerizing eyes, who'd come through Burgdorf and into the pay-library only two months earlier with his magic potions. Of course Trudi hadn't believed either that this sweet-smelling liquid he'd tried to sell her would really make her grow. And yet, how could she pass up the chance that the healer might be telling the truth? And so she bought the potion, quickly, before a customer could enter or before she could talk herself out of it.

She was glad Max wasn't there because if she looked through his eyes at her decision it embarrassed her. Or through Pia's eyes. She didn't need their voices of reason. That evening, when she took the first dose of the thick, honey-flavored liquid—doubling it so it would work faster—she found herself believing with the same intensity that she'd brought to the God-magic as a girl. And of course she felt betrayed when the potion did not change her and furious at herself for that bottomless capacity to believe and let herself be swindled.

"What if that calling is a sin?" Matthias whispered.

Trudi shook her head, slowly. "My father—he has a theory about sin. . . . I'm sure the pastor wouldn't agree with him, but my father says much of what the church calls sin is simply being human."

"I wish I could agree with that."

"He says being kind is the most important thing."

"I've always liked your father. He—" Matthias stopped and looked at Trudi as if worried she'd ask him to leave. "Not like that, I mean, liking him. More like—like admiring . . ." His voice faltered. "I hold your father in the highest esteem," he said stiffly.

"And he would be honored to know that. He'd also be honored to hear you play our piano. There hasn't been enough music in this town for too long, Matthias. Don't forget—your gift with music is a calling too."

His eyes filled with tears.

"A calling more sacred than the priesthood," she whispered.

He watched her without speaking.

"Will you think about what I said?"

He nodded. "I have to go."

"But you haven't seen my father yet."

"I— I'll come again. I promise. Tomorrow."

But when he returned the following afternoon, it was only to say good-bye to her and her father. He was returning to the seminary early, he said, and she could tell it was to end the chaos of indecision.

Angry at him for betraying his talents, for seeking punishment, she demanded, "Why would you want to go back there?"

"Because . . ." His smile sad, he crouched next to her and took one of her hands into his. "If I stay on the outside, the temptation is stronger."

"But the seminary is not a safe place."

"Maybe not for my body. But at least for my soul."

• • •

One morning in April of 1947, Ingrid Hebel tried to save her children by giving them the greatest gift she could fathom: an eternity in heaven. Nights when she had knelt by their beds in prayer, God had reminded her that no one but she loved her children enough to do this for them. It would be their one chance at redemption. If they continued living, they would reach the age of reason and succumb to sin as she had. Now they were both still pure, although she'd seen their greed—even in the eyes of her younger daughter when she nursed her.

Though the age of reason was seven years of age, Ingrid didn't dare wait that long: she had to assure her children's safe passage into eternity. And fortunately God was calling her while they were still pure. Once she decided to obey, the turmoil that had been hers for as long as she could remember fell off her. She felt tranquil. Almost holy. The one thing that saddened her was that she would not be with her children; but since she was tainted already, leaving her life behind would be a mortal sin. No, her own redemption would come from relinquishing her daughters to heaven and then waiting until God called her to join them.

Rita was nearly four and the baby, Karin, was just learning to walk when Ingrid took the two in the streetcar to the Oberkassel bridge, a bottle of holy water in her purse. It was early in the morning, and her daughters wore the matching long-sleeved white dresses she'd knitted for them over the winter in preparation for this day. She carried the baby, and Rita held on to her hand as they climbed from the streetcar and walked toward the bridge that spanned the Rhein between Oberkassel and Düsseldorf.

The river was running high, and its sounds rushed across her children's voices. Halfway across the bridge, Ingrid stopped. Pale light was shrinking the edges of the gray clouds, breaking through to link heaven and river in translucent steps. Rita saw it too: she laughed and pointed to the gap in the clouds. Ingrid lowered the baby, Karin, to the sidewalk, and transferred the fine chain with the golden cross from her own neck to Rita's. Then she opened the holy water, blessed both children—*"Im Namen des Vaters und des Sohnes und des Heiligen Geistes"*—and lifted Rita toward the radiant steps. Suffused by such a warm and unfamiliar joy that she felt certain she was doing God's will, Ingrid kissed Rita, whose forehead was still damp from holy water.

"Yes," Ingrid told her, "yes, God is waiting for you . . . soon we'll all be together again . . . don't forget to prepare a place for me too . . ." and then Rita was weightless in her arms—an angel already, an angel—as she flew from her and up those steps, singing, singing high— and as Ingrid bent and reached for her baby girl—*This is what I was born to do. . . . Into your hands, your heart, O Heavenly Father . . .* whispering: "Oh, my sweet my sweet—" Karin's body was heavier than Rita's, far heavier; it resisted Ingrid's arms, stayed on the ground as if God were rejecting her even though Ingrid strained, strained to raise her arms against the weight that held them down, weight that became hands, then bodies, pinning her, snatching her daughter from the grasp of God—*So near, my Lord, so near*—offering God instead the arched body of a woman—*far too old for redemption*—leaping toward the light . . . blocking the light . . . extinguishing the light—

"She was too late," Ingrid's mother told Trudi when she met her outside the locked room where Ingrid was kept in the Theresienheim. "The woman who tried to save my granddaughter—" Frau Baum was crying. "She was too late."

The river had been so cold and fast that Rita had been dead by the time a barge had found her ten kilometers downstream. The woman and two men had been driving across the bridge to work when they'd seen Ingrid raise the older girl toward the railing, but they didn't get to her in time to stop Rita's fall into the Rhein. While the men held Ingrid and wrestled the baby from her arms, the woman climbed onto the railing and leapt.

"That woman—she could have died, too. She's still in the hospital." Frau Baum dried her eyes with a wadded handkerchief and rapped against the door till a tall, slender nun unlocked it. "Come." Frau Baum nudged Trudi forward. "Maybe Ingrid will speak to you."

Ingrid was lying on her back, eyes glazed, unseeing. Her features were flat, sunken, as if her flesh had disintegrated in the three days since she'd taken her daughters to the bridge. On a chair next to the bed, the nun was guiding the wooden beads of a rosary through her skilled fingers. Until the night before, Ingrid had been in jail, where she'd refused food and drink, and when the police had acknowledged that she was too ill to be kept there, the sisters had offered to guard her and nurse her back to health so that she could stand trial.

"Has she eaten?" Frau Baum asked the nun.

"Not yet. We've tried to feed her."

As Trudi reached for Ingrid's hands—those same hands that had brought death to Rita—they felt like wax that had melted into the white blanket. In contrast, the surviving child had been warm flesh and skin. Trudi had held Karin hours after Ingrid had been seized. When she'd arrived in the apartment above the bicycle shop, Karin had been sitting on her grandfather's lap, playing with his mustache, giggling, and it had seemed terrible and miraculous that she could giggle and play.

"I wonder how much she remembers," Trudi had said.

Herr Baum stroked his granddaughter's neck. "Very little . . . and she won't know what it means. Tomorrow she'll remember less. And soon she will have forgotten. Children are like that."

"Ingrid never forgot," Trudi whispered.

His broad hand moved down Karin's back. "Here now," he said, "here, girl."

That's when Trudi had reached out to lift Karin from his lap. How she wished she could have brought her along now, pressed her into Ingrid's arms, and said, "This is your daughter. You can't leave her like this."

Frau Baum was bending across Ingrid, crying again. "Say something to her, Trudi."

"Ingrid? It's me, Trudi. . . . Please, look at me?"

But Ingrid was suspended on the bridge of nothingness, arrested in that moment when God had stunned her by redeeming and denouncing her in one fiery breath of omnipotence, scorching her soul, forsaking her body a shell that would wither and, in less than a week, lie beneath the earth with her older daughter, whose funeral had been held only that morning.

The town would close around Karin's secret and protect her by letting her grow up with the lie that her mother's brother, Holger, and his wife were her real parents. They were decent people, Holger and Erna Baum, serious about the responsibility they had taken on, well trained in the long practice of silence, and determined to do well by this child who'd come so close to being murdered by her own mother. Responsible, though not very imaginative people, they would teach Karin right from wrong, take her to church, and never mention the name Ingrid as though she hadn't existed. They would destroy any family photos that showed Ingrid or, if she stood to the side of a picture, cut her away like incriminating evidence.

And yet, Holger and Erna Baum—along with the town—would keep waiting for Ingrid's flaw to manifest itself within Karin, an expectation they would see confirmed when, at thirteen, the girl would swell with her grandfather's sin as though her drowned sister had found a way to return to her family through Karin's womb and claim her right to grow up after all.

In the months after Ingrid's death, Trudi stayed away from Ingrid's surviving daughter. Still, it seemed, she saw Karin everywhere: being wheeled in her stroller by her grandmother; riding in a child's seat on Erna's bicycle; sitting in the display window and playing with shiny bicycle parts. . . . What kept her from approaching Karin was her struggle of wanting to tell the girl about her mother, whom she resembled more and more, and knowing that it would be harmful for Karin to find out that her mother had killed her sister and had tried to kill her, too.

At least she no longer had to be careful about endangering the lives of fugitives with her stories. The risk her stories posed to others—and to herself—was more subtle. When she was younger, she had used secrets as if they were currency, but she'd found out how secrets could use her instead by becoming stronger than she. It happened whenever she couldn't stay away from a secret—drawn to it the way Georg Weiler was drawn to the bottle—though she sensed it would be better for her not to know. Once she had the knowledge, it became difficult not to use it.

And yet, in an odd way, if she chose to keep secrets, those secrets would become her children: she'd feel them under the same roof with her, listen to their whispers at dawn, be certain that they'd always be there for her.

As long as she didn't misuse them.

When in 1948 everyone was allowed to exchange fifty *Marks* for a new currency, stores suddenly offered all kinds of things that hadn't been available—including chocolate and perishables—as though, somehow, they'd been there all along. As people celebrated, it seemed as if the town had finally recovered. By then, the heap of blackened stones where once the synagogue had stood had been removed, and two small restaurants had been built on one side of the lot: an Italian ice-cream parlor offered eleven flavors, including a purple-red rasp-berry that tasted sweet and sour all at once; and in Alfred Meier's fish restaurant you could buy hot golden fillets of breaded fish in paper cones, along with fried potato sticks, called *pommes frites,* which you'd dip into mayonnaise.

Trudi had never eaten *pommes frites,* and the first time she tasted them she felt such greed that she ordered two more portions and ended up sick all night. For weeks, just the thought of the crisp pota-toes made her gag, but eventually her greed won out and she went back, limiting herself, however, to one serving. Sometimes Monika Buttgereit would sit at a table with a book; between customers, Alfred Meier would join her, and as they talked, their voices would touch while their hands lay apart on the red-and-white checkered tablecloth.

The other side of the synagogue's land had been paved by the town as a parking lot for the Theresienheim, which had been restored to its use as a convent and hospital. Walls into which swastikas had been carved had long since been patched and painted. Though no one said anything openly against Jews, Trudi still sensed remnants of that old prejudice against the few who had survived and chosen to live in Burgdorf.

She knew the brokenness would manifest itself again, as it had in Ingrid, in the judge, in Fritz Hansen, in countless others. And it didn't take long. That November, Hans-Jürgen Braunmeier killed his fi-ancée. He found her half naked in the car of the man who had asked her to dance the previous Saturday at Die Traube, where she and Hans-Jürgen had been celebrating his thirty-third birthday. Without glancing at Hans-Jürgen, she'd stood up and followed the man to the dance floor. For five days and five nights Hans-Jürgen stalked his fi-ancée and the man as they acted out every last one of his jealous fan-tasies as if he were the one who'd put them up to their fornication.

After he shot both of them, he went home to the farm and sat at the kitchen table, quiet and immensely tired, the gun on the tablecloth between his limp hands. His parents called the police, and his trial drew more people than Easter mass. Lined up on the steps of the courthouse, they waited for the chance of a seat inside, where the judge listened to testimonies of Hans-Jürgen's classmates, neighbors, and an amazing number of people who had, in some way, come into the path of his rage.

One of his neighbors recalled that Hans-Jürgen's mother had told her his birth had been a difficult one, and that he'd rejected her breast for the first two days of his life.

His first-grade teacher, Sister Mathilde, was quoted as saying, "The murderer spent most of his school years in the corner, his back to the rest of the class."

"Hans-Jürgen Braunmeier was incorrigible from the day he came to us," his seventh-grade teacher confirmed.

For nine days the people of Burgdorf unburdened themselves of a litany of Hans-Jürgen's wrongdoings, while his mother hid in her bedroom with the curtains drawn, and his father sat in the front row of the courtroom, bony shoulderblades rising against the back of his shabby Sunday suit, face grim and satisfied as if he'd always known his son would come to this.

Hans-Jürgen was tried not only for the murder but for every offense he'd ever committed, going back to the day of his birth. It was a cold, damp winter, and people were afraid—less of him than of what they'd buried deep within themselves—but now they could let their fears rise and blame them on him; they could gasp at the crimes of the five- or seven-year-old Hans-Jürgen and disregard the slaughter of war. Though he was locked up in jail each night, children were kept indoors; young women were warned that even a stroll to the fairgrounds could lead to death; and young men took to carrying knives or guns when they courted.

When one of his classmates came forward to reveal how Hans-Jürgen had burned a cat's paws in second grade, Trudi considered testifying that Hans-Jürgen had killed a kitten one day when she'd been inside the barn with him and Eva. But she didn't dare speak out because she knew that—once she stood on the witness stand—she wouldn't be able to keep herself from telling the town about that other time in the Braunmeiers' barn because, ever since Hans-Jürgen's arrest, that secret had been swelling within her as if seeking a way into the open.

She told herself that the town didn't need her to convict Hans-Jürgen: there were enough others, eager to list their grievances against the man with the luxuriant beard and wrathful eyes, who refused to speak a single word in his defense but watched his accusers as if to memorize each face into eternity.

Though newspapers all over the country wrote about the murder, they soon dropped coverage, but the local paper fanned panic by running interviews with nearly everyone who'd testified against Hans-Jürgen Braunmeier. They printed childhood photos of his fiancée and of her grave. She'd been buried in Neuss, where her family lived, but Kalle Husen, who'd been shot with her—a married man, imagine—had grown up in Burgdorf on the same block with the Bilders and the Weskopps. Despite the disgrace he'd brought upon his family, his wife, children, parents, and siblings had mumbled words of prayer around his open grave, the edges of their bodies blurred as if they'd fused into one massive shape. In a wider circle that encompassed the family and the grave, the people of Burgdorf had stood in their funeral clothes and whispered how terrible it had to be for the parents, this loss. How much could one family bear? Wasn't it enough that two of the Husens' older sons had been killed in the war? But at least they'd died heroes, while Kalle, whose death had exposed his adultery, had brought shame and grief to the family.

Beyond the fringe of that larger circle, a lanky man had stood by himself, hands folded in front of his expensive coat. To those who noticed him he seemed oddly familiar, though they couldn't recall having met him before. Perhaps a distant relative who'd come for Kalle's funeral, they figured, and forgot about him till they saw him once more, approaching the front door of the Husens' house an hour after everyone else had arrived for the funeral feast.

It was Frau Bilder who called out his name, steadying herself with one hand on the door frame, and once she did, everyone, of course, knew who the man was.

"He's changed so much," people whispered.

"He's gotten so thin."

"It's a miracle."

"Why didn't he let his family know where he was all those years?"

The people crowded around Rainer Bilder and his parents, told him they'd missed him, and took the news of his arrival into their neighborhoods. In the days to come, quite a few would claim to have known all along that the man by the gravesite had been the fat boy who'd vanished fifteen years earlier.

"I had a feeling it was Rainer."

"It didn't surprise me at all."

"You see—people come back after all."

"A miracle. It's a miracle."

"I used to worry that someone had kidnapped him."

"Him? Who would want a boy that fat?"

"Now he's quite famous, I hear."

"And rich."

"Rich, yes."

"A journalist."

"All kinds of awards."

"He read about the murders in a newspaper."

"He works for a newspaper."

"No, no, a magazine."

"In Hamburg."

"Heidelberg."

"I hear he's married."

"To a rich woman."

"Children, too."

"Who would have thought . . ."

"You think he'll stay?"

But Rainer Bilder seemed far more interested in the murderer than in his own family. At least he spent more time with Hans-Jürgen Braunmeier than in the brick house where he'd grown up. He was the only journalist Hans-Jürgen allowed to interview him. In the visiting room of the jail, the two would sit across from each other at the gray table, hunched forward, talking rapidly and so low that Andreas Beil, the policeman who stood watch, could make out the pattern of their voices but not the words.

People who encountered Rainer Bilder on the street tried to help him with information he didn't need. One night, when his brother Werner pushed at him with questions about the murderer, Rainer felt a sudden, inexplicable dread as he explained how he couldn't reveal what he and Hans-Jürgen talked about; but he pacified his brother by promising to send him a copy of his article. That dread was still with Rainer when he fell asleep, but in the morning he had forgotten it, and he wouldn't recall it until ten years later, when his brother would become Hans-Jürgen's next victim.

Rainer would leave Burgdorf long before his interview was published, but he would keep his promise and mail a copy of the magazine to his brother, who would pass it along to the rest of his family and all through Burgdorf. "When Love Becomes Lethal" would be the title, and Hans-Jürgen would be portrayed as a lonely and troubled boy—barely tolerated by his town—who had grown into an even lonelier man. Nearly everyone would be incensed by Rainer's shameless sympathy for the murderer.

"He is blaming the town, not Hans-Jürgen."

"I wish he'd stayed away."

"The suffering he's causing his parents . . . all over again."

"As if the first time hadn't been enough."

"There are many ways of losing a son."

"And to think that we welcomed him back."

By then, the judge had committed Hans-Jürgen Braunmeier to the asylum in Grafenberg, which was already overcrowded, mostly with soldiers who'd come back from the war deranged, but also with some Jews who'd been left mute or incoherent after surviving the KZs. Though the people of Burgdorf complained that Hans-Jürgen's sentence was too lenient, most were relieved to have him locked up.

Months after the trial, Trudi woke up one night, unable to breathe, as if that old snot were clogging her nose and mouth, drying on her skin. *How many more times do I have to go back there?* Afraid to get sucked into the dream again, she threw off her covers and crouched on the edge of her bed.

"You are crazy. Like your mother. . . ." Hans-Jürgen's face swam above her, young as he'd looked that hot summer day when she'd told him no woman would ever love him and that his love would make a woman turn to another man. *"Crazy Zwerg,"* he'd called her, and now he was in the asylum with her mother, behind walls crowned with shards, inside green rooms that smelled of candles and cinnamon. Her mother was in danger with him there. Trudi strained for breath, and as she sucked it in long gulps, she knew Hans-Jürgen would escape from the asylum and kill others—always lovers, always in their cars. She saw grainy newspaper photos of blood-splattered cars; photos of victims shot in their chests and bellies and necks while embracing; photos of Hans-Jürgen, older, still wearing a beard; and photos of a balding man, identified as his psychiatrist, who said in an interview it was likely Hans-Jürgen Braunmeier was reenacting the murder of his fiancée.

"It was not a curse," Trudi whispered in the dark of her room.

But the face laughed—*"A stupid curse. Your stupid curse"*—as if she'd planted the jealousy in him, destroying not only him but also those he had killed.

"No. You were like that long before I ever said anything to you. Look what you did to me . . . to the cat. I was only getting back at you—" She turned on the light and the face dissolved, but what she couldn't dissolve was her remorse at having hurt Hans-Jürgen with such purpose. It terrified her to consider how something she'd said so many years ago might have swayed what he'd done to his fiancée. "No—" she cried, "you would have killed her anyhow. It has nothing to do with what I said." But if you thought about it, really thought about it, it might keep you from saying anything at all, except the kindest of words.

That winter, she noticed the bare trees against the landscape more than ever before. It seemed that, all at once, they'd taken on a beauty of their own, exposing their many intricate lines. Fine details in the color and formation of branches—once hidden beneath lush plumes of leaves—now stood out against the sky, clear and achingly beautiful. Sometimes, late afternoons, she'd situate herself so that she could watch the sunset through the stark branches.

While most people saw the winter trees as barren and were impatient for the first leaves, Trudi began to value trees most when they totally revealed themselves to her, when she could know every spine, every branch. People often revealed themselves like that to her—without realizing they were doing it. And she took what they gave her, held it close the way you would hold a lover. The rest—those leaves and blossoms—were gaudy and temporary. At times she wished she could shed herself down to her spine, to her bones, expose the essence of herself the way she could know the essence of those trees, know them and see them and be known. She'd come close to that with Max. And she could imagine revealing even more about herself with the child Hanna.

The longer she knew Hanna, the more she fantasized about bringing her up. She was sure that, if Hanna could express her choice, she'd want to live with her. And so she whispered to her the words that she'd only let herself think with other children.

"I know you. . . ."

"You will always remember me. . . ."

And the words that she'd never taken to another child: "I should have been your mother."

Hanna would nod as though she agreed, and sometimes she'd raise one dimpled hand toward Trudi's face and grasp whatever fistful of flesh and skin she could reach, as if to claim Trudi for herself.

Once, when a new customer asked if Hanna was her child—"She has your coloring"—Trudi was stunned, but then she kissed Hanna's forehead and said, "Yes. Thank you, yes, she's mine. Thank you."

It bothered Trudi that her father was so guarded with the child. His eyes troubled, he'd watch her when she'd bring Hanna into the kitchen or living room where he'd be reading, and once when she asked him why he minded having the child around, he said, "She is not yours, Trudi."

She stared at him. "Don't you think I know that?" But what she thought was: *She should have been.*

Still, from then on, she was careful not to kiss or hug Hanna in her father's presence and to make sure he couldn't hear any of the words that linked her to the girl. What she had with Hanna was deeper than anything she'd felt with other children, even Konrad, and she was certain it would always be there.

Her father's comment also made her more selective in her letters to Matthias. The correspondence meant a lot to her, but lately he'd teased her about not writing enough about herself. "I'm always glad to hear about Hanna," he wrote, "but what about you? What is happening in your life?"

Hanna is happening in my life. But of course she couldn't write that to him, and so her letters became shorter, summaries of what her father was doing. His doctor had told her grape sugar would be good for building his strength, but it was difficult to get since the pharmacy sold out whenever a delivery arrived. From the taxidermist she'd heard that leek-and-oxtail soup was the best remedy for weakness, but when he'd sent his wife to the library with a pot of soup, Leo had only eaten a few spoonfuls. Whenever Trudi tried to help her father, he seemed embarrassed, and she'd learned that he was most at peace when he was left to himself.

Looking at his lined face made her think how her mother had stayed young for her. While her father was aging, her mother would always be thirty-five. Once, in the bathroom of a restaurant, Trudi had seen an elderly woman studying her reflection—the carefully coiffured hair, her mask of makeup—with such panic and concentration as though it took enormous effort to keep her face together, to not let it slip. That tightness. Once she must have been beautiful. It had to be harder for a beautiful woman to age than for someone like herself, who'd never been beautiful. Everyone had something to battle—something that could either destroy you or strengthen you—and what she had battled was maybe not all that bad. At least by now she was used to her body, even if she might never get used to the word *Zwerg*. It would be easier for her to age than for this woman. Amazing—how something could actually be easier for her than for others.

It came to her that, though she still had quite a few years to go, she was on her way to becoming part of a community, that of the old women who held the real power. How comforting that she would not have to go it alone, that finally there would be a circle to enfold her readily because, as old women, they too would have come to terms with their own changes and be less unforgiving of otherness because it would have claimed them too.

All that December Trudi spent more time with Hanna because Jutta was recovering from the birth and death of her son. Joachim had died during his second week of life, and from what Trudi had heard, Jutta had rocked the dead infant in her arms, refusing to yield him to Klaus or to the doctor for hours.

When, at the funeral, Frau Weskopp, who'd worn widow's black for over six years, had tried to comfort Jutta—"Little Joachim is lucky he was christened so that he won't be in purgatory"—Jutta had turned her rage on the old woman, shouting at her to worry about her Nazi sons, who were frying in hell.

Outbursts like that against one of their own didn't make the townspeople any fonder of the dentist's young wife, who spurned their traditions and now—when the death of a son could have earned her their compassion—became only more reclusive and stopped attending church.

Though Klaus Malter continued to take Hanna to mass, this wasn't enough for Herr Pastor Beier, who felt cheated by Jutta because he'd buried her uncle, the suicide, in order to keep her in church. He felt the dentist's wife had cheated him out of her promise, and when he followed his impulse—to ride his motor scooter to her house and arrive unannounced the way she had forced her way into his study—she opened the door, wearing a black dress and over it a man's shirt with red and green paint smears along the front and sleeves as if to deny that she was a woman in mourning. She was smoking, fast, and her daughter was clinging to her leg, peering at the priest with curious eyes.

"Yes?" Jutta said. "Yes?" as if the priest's reason for being here could be stated with one word, too.

"We have missed you in church."

She stood in his way without asking him inside, her lips as pale as her face, blond hair limp on her shoulders.

"I'd be glad to hear your confession," the priest said, and she laughed, once, as if amused by the thought of confession. "I know it's terrible for both parents when a child dies," he continued, "but worse for the mother . . . like having part of her die."

"What do you know?" she accused him. "What can you possibly know?"

"Is your wife getting proper care?" the priest asked the dentist when he stopped by his office on the way back to the rectory. "She does not look well."

Klaus Malter, who had made a sizable contribution toward the replacement of the stained-glass windows above the altar, which had been shattered during the war, assured the priest that Jutta was doing as well as any woman after losing a child.

"I will pray for your wife," the priest offered.

And he did. As soon as he'd parked his scooter behind the rectory, he entered the church, where, as usual, several old women knelt in the light that fell through the modern windows in the colors he had chosen—red, white, and black. Soon, he'd have enough funds to commission wood carvings of the fourteen stations of the cross and mount them along the side walls, beneath the old windows, which some day he hoped to replace too.

Making the sign of the cross, the fat priest lowered himself to his knees in front of the altar and fastened his eyes on the Last Supper mural. The bread in Christus' hands was golden brown, as though it had just been baked. Stomach rumbling, the priest asked Christus to guide Jutta Malter back to church, to show her his mercy by forgiving her arrogance. Above him, the painted saints were feasting, and behind him, he could feel the comforting presence of the plaster saints—St. Stefan and St. Agnes and St. Petrus—and of the confessional where people left their sins for him to swallow. And he could smell fresh bread—no, flowers—though it was winter and the altar vases were empty; but centuries of church flowers had left their scents in the stone walls.

Trudi could understand why Jutta no longer went to church. At times she, too, had considered staying away, but she still liked the music, the rituals, and even the church smell that occasionally clung to people's clothes when they came into the pay-library. Besides, Hanna was at mass every Sunday morning, and though her father would hold her hand as they'd walk down the church steps, the girl would squirm away from him and run toward Trudi while he'd follow her with one of his formal greetings. Already his red beard was muted by threads of gray. "It's time to go home, Hanna," he'd remind her, or: "Say good-bye now to Fräulein Montag."

Once, when Hanna didn't look in Trudi's direction after mass, Trudi felt betrayed, though she told herself the child had simply forgotten. But it took several of Hanna's visits before she got past that hurt. She hated being so defenseless, hated how she missed the girl on days she didn't see her.

One rainy afternoon in July, while Jutta was painting, Trudi took Hanna into her mother's earth nest. "I used to play here with my mother when I was a little girl like you." She spread a towel for them to sit on.

Hanna pointed to the tiny tracks in the dust. "Tchoo-tchoo," she said. "Tchoo-tchoo train."

"Strawberry bugs," Trudi looked around. "I don't see any today. Strawberry bugs have little feet that make those tracks. And they smell like strawberries."

Hanna picked up a dry twig and scratched her own tracks into the ground. Beads of moisture glistened on the delicate strands of a huge spider web, and the musty scent of earth was comforting. If only she could stay here with Hanna. Forever. Or go far away with her, live with her in a town where no one knew them and where she could raise her as her own. Because the way she felt about her had to be how a mother felt about her child. All at once she felt angry that Max had never come back to have children with her. And yet if he had returned and married her, what would have happened to their love then? Would it have worn thin, used up and bitter, like the love in so many marriages she saw?

"Berry berry bug . . ." Hanna was singing, poking at the earth.

Trudi stroked her silky hair. Two weeks from now, Hanna's parents would take her away on a trip to Wangerooge, an island in the North Sea where they vacationed every summer. Trudi wished they'd leave Hanna with her. If Hanna were told that Trudi was her real mother, she would begin to love her like a daughter. She was only three, still young enough to forget her parents. Like, say, if they died. Both of them. If something happened to Klaus and Jutta—a train crash or some quick and fatal illness—she would bring Hanna up. She'd fix up a room for her with white lace curtains and pink—no, sun-yellow wallpaper. She'd sew dresses with ruffles for her, buy her that plush giraffe she'd seen in Mahler's department store, take her to the playground, to Alfred Meier's for *pommes frites,* read her stories at night and—

But what if Klaus Malter's relatives stepped in? Came at her with their money and power and lawyers and demanded she hand Hanna over to them? How could she make them understand that Hanna had to live with her? That none of them could possibly love her this much?

For a love like that, you deserved something in return.

She saw herself running for a train, the child in her arms though she was quite heavy, fleeing from Klaus Malter's relatives. . . . Thoughts and pictures spun through her, making her dizzy. Queasy. She scrambled up, anxious to bring Hanna back out into the light. It was raining harder than before. Inside the house she scrubbed their hands, their faces, talking fast: "Your mother will pick you up soon. Do you know what a fine artist your mother is? So beautiful . . . And your father, he's a good dentist. You're lucky, so lucky to have two parents. . . ." Afterwards she wouldn't remember most of what she'd told Hanna, only that it was a list of her parents' virtues.

Wind and rain scraped the branches of the chestnut tree against the windows of the pay-library while she waited for Jutta to appear, and when she finally arrived and the child turned her face toward Trudi for her customary good-bye kiss, she couldn't bring herself to touch her and pretended not to see.

"I'm not feeling well," she told Jutta. "Better not bring her over for a while."

"Is there anything I can do for you?" The tall woman bent and laid her cool palm across Trudi's forehead.

"It's nothing." Trudi backed away. "Nothing."

"Hanna has done something to upset you."

"Of course not."

"I'm not feeling well," she told her father when Jutta had left. "I've closed the library."

"Where are you going?" he called after her as she started for the door.

"I need some air."

"The storm is getting worse. Take a coat, at least."

But she was already out in the rain. Instantly, her hair and clothes were wet. She had no idea where she wanted to go, only that she had to get away from the place where she'd come up against her own brokenness. She should have seen that brokenness when she'd cloaked her love for Hanna with silence. There was an edge of craziness to her love—that same edge of craziness she'd seen in Ingrid when she'd spoken about God; in her own mother when it came to her escapes; in the face of Herr Heidenreich when he used to praise his Führer. And, as with all of them, that edge of craziness also presented a haven where they belonged or felt peace. As she did with this love for Hanna.

With Hanna, she was at her best.

At her worst.

And she had to stop.

Ahead of her the earth rose, and she recognized the long, even curve of the dike. She nearly slipped as she climbed up, and when she stood on top, she couldn't see the river, only the rain that slanted in a gray sheet. But she thought she could smell the river—the way she'd smelled it in her mother's hair after she'd come home from one of her flights. As she made her way down the other side of the dike, she could already feel the loss of Hanna, then the loss of Max and her mother and Ingrid and Frau Simon. For an instant there in the meadow, she thought she could see the man-who-touches-his-heart, but it was only a stunted tree. It struck her that her life was filled with ghosts: some days she thought more often of the dead than the living. She saw Frau Abramowitz standing by her window in the dark, saw the outline of her body as the sky grew lighter around her, forcing itself into a halo that enveloped her. She saw Fienchen Blomberg inside the grocery store, Eva on her wedding day, both surrounded by rims of light, and she felt terrified of all the losses that lay ahead of her, especially the loss of her father.

Blades of wet grass, icy and sharp, stung her nose and cheeks as she fell. Curling her fingers, she tried to sink them into the ground, hold

on to something solid that could ward off this soul-chilling loneliness, but all she gripped were weeds and grass. The earth beneath her
was unyielding, indifferent. If her body hadn't been in the way, the
rain would have fallen on the soil that she obstructed. Suddenly she
remembered the first blouse she'd sewn after meeting Pia: she could
feel its soft texture, the particular shade of blue, like Pia's trailer, and
was suffused with a powerful longing for that blouse; yet, at the same
moment she knew that the blouse stood for a part of her life that was
irrevocably over.

She could hear the steady fury of the Rhein above the roar of the
storm. Slowly, she stood up. Her hips were aching, her legs numb.
Still—she headed toward the river, her soggy hem swinging against
her calves. The water was an even deeper gray than the rain, but once
her eyes adapted to the various shades of gray, she could make out
rocks and bushes and tress and barges and even a swallow, a single
swallow, fluttering toward a willow tree and coming so close to the
trunk that it looked about to collide just before it veered off with shrill
cries. *A matter of timing.* It made her think of how Eva had joked
about Catholics timing their final confession five minutes before their
death.

As she lowered herself to a log, she could see how the pattern of the
water changed as it made its way past a rock that jutted from the
river. She knew the rock well: in the early floods of spring it lay submerged, hidden from your eyes though the river knew where it was
and washed across it, but by midsummer it always was exposed. Still,
the river did not stop at its base, wailing, blocking all the water coming after it. No, it continued to flow, parted, foamed, but then became whole again after it had passed the rock, leaving its impact on
the rock, just as the impact of every hour she had lived was still with
her, shaping her like the people who had fed her dreams—the earliest
of them her uncle Stefan Blau, who'd journeyed to a distant continent. All at once she felt as if she were the river, swirling in an ever-
changing design around the rock, separating and coming together
again without letting herself get snagged into scummy pools. Over
the years, she had learned more from the river than from any one person, and what she'd been taught had always come with passion—intense pain or joy. It was the nature of the river to be both turbulent
and gentle; to be abundant at times and lean at others; to be greedy
and to yield pleasure. And it would always be the nature of the river

to remember the dead who lay buried beneath its surface.

What the river was showing her now was that she could flow beyond the brokenness, redeem herself, and fuse once more. If that rock was her love for Hanna, she could let it stop her, block her—or she could acknowledge the rock and have respect for it, alter her course to move around it. She had to smile because, for a moment there, it looked as if the water were trying to crawl upstream, back across the surface of the rock in dozens of small hands, reaching against the stream, defying the current. And that was good. Over the years the rock would be transformed, just like the countless stones at the bottom of the riverbed, stones you couldn't see; they affected the flow but didn't impede its progress, its momentum, its destination. She could see how she had it in her to start out loving and become vindictive— as with Georg and Klaus and Eva, though with Eva she had ended up loving again—and how she needed to take a look at her love and make sure it was whole before she could offer it to anyone. Her love for her father was whole, but her love for Hanna was tainted. It had to heal before she could bring it to Hanna again.

If ever she could bring it to her again.

She shivered. There was something she needed to do, something she needed to give back that wasn't hers. She saw Jutta standing in another rain high above the quarry hole, smelled the sulfur of lightning, saw the unearthed roots of the birch, and recalled her apprehension that Jutta would not be all that safe in Burgdorf. She moaned. *But I never thought of myself as a threat to you.*

It was after midnight when she reached home. Though her father had left on a light for her and had tacked a note to the banister, telling her the hot-water stove in the bathroom was stoked, she didn't pause to dry or warm herself. In her drenched clothes she rushed up the stairs to her room and lifted Jutta's painting of Hanna from the wall. She didn't permit herself the comfort of gazing at it once more but carried it up the flight of steps to the sewing room, where she stored it behind the door. Tomorrow morning she would return it to Jutta and tell her it was something she should never have chosen. And if Jutta still wanted her to have one of her paintings, she would ask her to do the choosing of that gift for her.

t w e n t y - o n e

1 9 4 9 – 1 9 5 2

To stay away from Hanna—it was easier than she'd imagined be-cause when she'd see the child, even from a distance, she'd feel such a danger to herself that she wouldn't want to be near her. Of course she missed her. Taking care of her father could only fill so much time. Be-sides, he got uneasy if she fussed over him and only withdrew more into his books. It seemed he was always freezing, even on the warmest of days, and he'd wear one or two woolen vests on top of his shirt, as well as his gray cardigan. If Emil were still alive, he'd get her father to talk, engage him in their old spirited discussions.

Trudi busied herself more in the pay-library. Although the novels continued to bore her, she savored the steady flow of people who came to her without any effort of her own—quite unlike those years in school when she'd tried so hard to bring others to her. Now they couldn't stay away from her: she had a way of hooking them with ru-mors, of looking right through them with those fierce blue eyes of hers, of seeing one thing and fathoming the rest. And always, always she had new stories for them, stories that provided drama, not the melodrama of those novels in which feelings were only on full tilt—hate, love, fear, bliss—but subtle shadings of experience that would reverberate in their hearts long after they would forget the endings of the trashy books that granted them an escape from their lives.

One of her new customers was a Jewish woman who checked out three mystery novels whenever she came to the library. Though a few Jews had returned to Burgdorf, Angelika Tegern was the only Jew to settle in town without having lived here before. A tall, lovely woman with a sad mouth, she was married to an architect. When the two bought land near the river and built a splendid stucco house with a solarium, the cost of it got Anton Immers going against the Jews once again: "It's plain to see that their kind live in houses far more extravagant than honest people like us. . . ." When his daughter-in-law could no longer bear to listen to the old man and told him the Germans could never make good on what had happened to the Jews— "I'll always feel guilty even though I didn't participate"—the old butcher didn't speak to her for weeks.

The first time Frau Tegern had come into the pay-library, Trudi had been intrigued because—aside from having the name Angelika—she looked the way Trudi had described herself in her reply to Max Rudnick's ad. Though Frau Tegern kept to herself, Trudi gradually found out from her that her parents had died in KZs. When her father, a political prisoner, had been arrested in the late thirties, her mother had kept visiting him, even after the yellow star had to be worn. She'd refused to sew it on her coat, and she'd traveled freely, continuing her dangerous visits to her husband. But in 1945 she too had been deported and had died in Theresienstadt.

Once, when Angelika Tegern mentioned how the butcher made her uncomfortable, the way he watched her, Trudi assured her that Herr Immers looked at everyone with suspicion, even his old Nazi buddies.

"I'm going to tell you something about him," she said and began the first of her lessons to Angelika, letting her know whom she could trust and whom to stay away from. "Not only is he a three-months baby, but he lies."

"About what?"

"Well, essentially he's truthful—the kind of pigheaded truth, you know?—but he lies about fighting in the First World War. He wasn't fit to be a soldier, so he traded sausages for the taxidermist's uniform and had himself photographed. . . . That briefcase he always carries with him—you've seen it, right?—is supposedly for gathering information about people, but his daughter-in-law swears all he has in there are newspaper clippings of the Führer."

Trudi noticed that Frau Tegern liked to check out new books: they felt special when you cracked them open for the first time, and the pages resisted your touch—there were just the stories then, letters printed on clean paper, unencumbered by the fates of the people who would read them and whose touch would manifest itself by, say, a crease or a smudged page. Trudi began saving new deliveries for Angelika Tegern, holding them for her behind the counter before she would lend them to anyone else. She knew her customers' tastes and would recommend books of passion or crime or adventure to them, even to those who pretended not to read them, like Klara Brocker, who wore lipstick just to go to the butcher shop in the morning and claimed to borrow romances for her invalid mother, who lived with her and her illegitimate son in their cramped apartment on Barbarossa Strasse. It was said that the old woman's stroke was the result of her shock over Klara's pregnancy. Never mind that the boy who'd resulted from that pregnancy was three years old and had been thoroughly enjoyed by his grandmother prior to her illness. But now her left side was paralyzed, including half of her face, and she had to be fed with a spoon. Her mask of perpetual disapproval only confirmed that she must have suffered terribly from her daughter's indiscretion.

It struck Trudi as fitting that her customers had a choice between her stories and the published stories printed in books with gaudy paper jackets, books that were safe because they didn't implicate anyone in town. From time to time she'd remind herself to save stories about herself for Hanna—stories which, once the girl was older, she would understand. When she thought of herself with Hanna, it became easier to separate those images from much earlier ones—of herself as a child with *her* mother in the earth nest—and she'd think of the first stories she had ever told, stories that had begun with a purpose: to lure her mother into the light.

Now the purpose of her stories had changed. She spun them to discover their meaning. In the telling, she found, you reached a point where you could not go back, where—as the story changed—it transformed you, too. What mattered was to let each story flow through you. It was becoming impossible to revert to her old reasons for telling stories—to get even, to prod, or to soothe. But most people didn't know that. They were still afraid of her. They didn't understand that now she told a story for the sake of the story, taking pleasure in how each formed within her. It still would begin by feeling drawn to secrets, but she could curb the urge to tell, let it settle into something that nurtured the fragments of life which fell into her way, until a story was ready to unveil itself.

At first Hanna didn't know what it was she was missing, only that many mornings, upon waking, she'd be struck with a sudden sadness that made her want to crawl under her feather comforter and weep. Her mother would read to her, her father would let her play with his chess pieces, and she'd smile and hug them and wonder if this sadness perhaps meant what it was like to be a child. Not that it was with her all the time—no, she could go for days without it, but then it would find her again.

During her fourth year of life, her father kept raising the fence in the backyard because she roamed the neighborhood and was found inside people's houses, where she'd climb in through a window, playing with a toy, say, or a set of *Schnaps* glasses. Sometimes she coaxed Manfred Weiler, who lived in the other wing of the apartment house, to escape with her, and they'd play on the swings of the Catholic school until one of the nuns would grip their arms and lead them home.

Though the fence grew, Hanna scaled it, following a vague yearning that sent her beyond her own world. And then one humid summer day, a few months after her fifth birthday, she saw the little woman in the open market with a basket, talking to a farmer who was weighing tomatoes for her, a yellow cardigan flopping around her yellow-and-blue housedress. And all at once Hanna knew why she'd been running away. Darting toward the little woman, she slipped her fingers into the wide palm and beamed at the round face that was so much closer to hers than the faces of other grown-ups. Inside, she felt a deep blue quiet, a slow blue swirl of quiet, the same blue as the flowers on the housedress and the eyes in front of her, blue eyes that blinked while the big hand tugged to get away from her.

But Hanna was not about to let go.

"Where is your mother?"

"At home. Painting."

"Does she—"

"I climbed across the fence."

"You shouldn't do that."

"I know."

A stork flew across the roof of the bakery, and Hanna pointed toward it. They both followed its course until it landed on Potter's bar.

"When I was younger than you," said the little woman, "my mother made me leave sugar cubes on the windowsill."

"Why?"

"So the stork would bring me a sister or brother. But I ate the sugar. . . . And my brother died."

"My brother died too."

"I was at his funeral."

"But he came from my mother's belly. Not from a stork."

"At least your brother was born alive. Mine died before he was born."

"How?"

"I never got to touch him."

"What's his name?"

"Horst. It's on our gravestone."

"My brother was called Joachim. Did you see me at his funeral?"

"Yes."

"Did I cry?"

"You were too little to understand. . . . I better take you home."

"Can I visit you?"

"Those tomatoes— I have to pay for them. Let go of me."

Hanna swatted at a fly that was about to land on her sweaty arm and transferred her grip to the handle of Trudi's basket. "Now I would cry."

The blue eyes alighted on her.

Nearby, the engine of a motor scooter kicked on and grew to a clamor as the fat priest drove past the open market, his bulk teetering on the small seat. He seemed in a good mood and waved at parishioners who greeted him. In the months since his sister, Hannelore, had arrived to take his housekeeper's place, his sermons had become more uplifting. People said it hadn't been easy for him to persuade Fräulein Teschner to leave for a better job, and they said his sister was lucky to be working for him. Who else would want a spinster with crippled hands? But Trudi wouldn't let anyone say a word against

Hannelore Beier. Where once the pastor's sister would have made her uncomfortable, she now had her own code of honor toward others who were regarded as freaks.

At the next wooden stand, a farmwoman was crossing out the chalk prices on the slate signs and writing new numbers beneath. Trudi chose eight white mushrooms and a small head of cauliflower. Hanna was still holding on to the basket when they reached her mother's apartment house and wouldn't let go until her mother said that, if it was all right with Trudi, she'd bring her over to the pay-library soon.

Trudi hesitated. It had been more than two years since Hanna had been inside her house. She made herself try it out—a picture of herself and Hanna—and it no longer felt dangerous: they were sitting at her kitchen table; between them stood the satin hatbox in which her mother used to keep her paper dolls, and she was showing the girl how to fold tabs over the shoulders and hips of the dolls. Hanna laughed as she dressed them in their long paper gowns, rich shades of purples and reds and greens, and gave them matching hats and parasols.

Slowly Trudi nodded, and Hanna released the basket so abruptly that it tumbled to the ground.

"When?" the girl asked as she scooped up the vegetables. "When?"

"It's up to your mother."

Trudi felt cautious around the child who came at her with years of stored-up affection. But gradually, as she came to trust her own borders, she began to enjoy Hanna's visits. It gave her pleasure to surprise her with gifts: a coloring book and crayons; pastry with whipped cream and chocolate shavings; two green ribbons that matched her Sunday dress.

Hanna knew some of the songs that Trudi had learned as a child, and they sometimes sang them together: *"Fuchs du hast die Gans gestohlen . . ."* or *"Wie das Fähnchen auf dem Turme. . . ."* Trudi let her play with the music box that Emil Hesping had given her, and brought out photos that Herr Abramowitz had taken of her when she'd been Hanna's age. Yet those stiff prints in hues of brown, tinged with red, were all darker than she remembered it being at the time they'd been taken.

Down by the brook Trudi showed Hanna what she'd seen with her mother the day of her brother's funeral—how to look beyond the moving sheen of water and find not only the silt at the bottom of the brook, but also the sky and their very own faces mirrored in the current.

They were playing with the paper dolls the day the wooden icebox was replaced by an electric refrigerator. It stood as tall as Trudi's shoulders and made a purring sound that came on for periods at a time like the buzzing of a fly, reverberating through the house. Leo Montag, who dozed much of the day, could sleep right through it, but the first few nights Trudi was awakened by the sound, and the more she tried to ignore it, the more persistent its droning became, pulsating in her ears like water trapped in there after swimming.

At first Trudi always had something to show or give to Hanna, but she soon realized that the girl liked nothing better than to hear her stories. Far more reflective than Jutta, who burned within the moment, Hanna circled through Trudi's stories, finding links, bridging gaps with questions that drove Trudi deeper into her own memories. And as she became more of a participant in her stories, she felt a joy that came from revealing herself.

Yet, like other children who'd been born late in the war or afterwards, Hanna did not ask about the war. For these children, Trudi knew, the silence was normal: they were growing up with it. *Normal*—it was a terrible word if you thought about it. Most realized there had been a war—after all, there were still some ruins to prove that—but they'd learned early on that it was not proper to mention that war, even if, deep inside their guts, vague questions would stir. Trudi hoped that, once Hanna got older, Jutta would tell her about the war. It was unlikely that Klaus would. All she could do was encourage Hanna to ask her anything she wanted to know.

"Anything?" There was a wonder, a craving in the girl's eyes.

"Anything." They were in Trudi's kitchen, and Hanna was balancing along the platforms in front of the cabinets. "I'll answer it if I can. And if I can't or don't want to—or if you're too young to know—I'll say so."

"Are you little because your mother dropped you on your head?"

Trudi stiffened. "Who said so?"

"Rolf's mother."

"I could tell you stories about that Klara Brocker. She's the last who should say anything about me." Trudi stopped herself. She'd promised Hanna answers, not tirades. "I'm little because I was born that way. It's like being born with red hair like your father or with a crooked finger like Frau Blau. I used to think her finger was like that from dusting. . . . There's a name for people like me—*Zwerg*—not that I like the name, but that's what it's called. I know that people warn children they'll look like me if they don't brush their teeth or don't finish their liver or eat butter with a spoon or kill frogs or cross the street without looking or touch spiders or—"

"But I like it that you're little."

Trudi stared at her.

"And I want a house like yours when I'm grown-up."

"By then you'll be too tall for these platforms."

"Maybe I can stay little."

"It's nothing to wish for, child."

"And who told you about him?" Trudi said the day Hanna asked her about the man by the river.

"Herr Immers."

"The old one or his son?"

"They're both old."

Trudi laughed. "For you they would be. Just like me." The pay-library was empty, and she was letting Hanna help her return books to their shelves.

"You're not real old."

"I can still walk without a cane."

Hanna nodded, serious.

"That was a joke. About the cane . . . Tell me—what did you hear from Herr Immers?"

"He and your father got you out in time."

"In time for what?"

"To save you."

"Save me, huh? Must have been the son then . . . That man by the river is ten—no, a hundred times better than any of the Immers." She straightened her shoulders. "I could have married him."

Hanna climbed to the top of the ladder and sat there, elbows on her knees, peering down at Trudi.

"That man," Trudi said, "he was a kind man, a good man. . . ." She smelled his scent, felt the weight of his long body. How could Max be this close? This far away? "But people in this town, they can't imagine that a man like that would bother with me. No—they find it easier to believe that he must have meant me harm."

"Herr Immers said he was naked."

"Herr Immers is right. You see, the man wanted to swim and didn't have his bathing suit."

"My mother swims without a bathing suit. When she's out in the ocean. Or the river. Then she takes it off. My father says she'll lose it some day."

"He would say that."

"Did the man swim?"

"He was a good swimmer."

"Why didn't you marry him?"

"Because he didn't come back."

"Maybe he's on his way."

"Oh, Hanna." She was back to her endless days of waiting, of willing Max to come back to her. *Tell me what you saw this time, Max.* *"I'll paint it for you." "Tell me now. . . ."* The flush of yellow-orange petals spreading across white walls of cities and into the sky. "He was a painter."

"Like my mother?"

Trudi nodded.

"Do you miss him?"

All at once she was crying, crying in front of this child who slid down the ladder and wrapped her arms around her and kept saying, "You got me now."

"And I'll always have him too. You see— You see, Hanna, he had to go to another country. . . . He is a builder of cities, of houses so beautiful you can hardly imagine them. . . ." She cried as she evoked Max for Hanna, building light from memory and grief, the kind of light you find in shadowy spaces—not the pretty glimmer that passes quickly, but light that carries its own flip side of darkness, of oddness, ugliness even—like the flash of strawberry red against a woman's white fingers.

But Hanna's father was shocked by the story that his daughter brought home, and he was standing outside the pay-library the following morning when Trudi unlocked the door. With a clipped greeting, he stalked past her in his starched white jacket.

"Hanna is too young for stories like that."

Trudi closed the door and followed him to the counter. "Stories like what?"

"About that man by the river. We all know you'd never seen him before."

"Do we now?"

His eyes flicked from her and down to his hands.

She remembered how much she had wanted to touch those hands long ago. And she remembered the dress she'd worn the night she'd danced with him, the sleeveless chiffon with the Spanish bolero jacket that Frau Abramowitz had given her. She remembered walking on her toes in those absurd high heels, and she thought how much more comfortable she felt now in her flat canvas shoes and wash-softened housedress.

"And what if I had known him, Klaus Malter, what then? Would that change anything? What if I had known him for months? Or years? What if he was the kind of man who, after he kissed me, did not pretend it had never happened?"

As the dentist's face turned red, a brighter shade of red than his beard, she knew that he, too, had never forgotten that kiss, had always remembered it and felt uneasy about it, and in that moment of victory, she thought how both their lives might have been easier if they'd talked about that night. Perhaps then, rather than this victory, she could have had his friendship.

"What if this man actually loved me?" she whispered.

"I— I can't answer that."

"I'm not asking you to answer it. I want you to imagine it."

He flushed an even deeper red. "Hanna is only five. She is better off not hearing things like that."

"Hanna came to me with questions—rumors—about a man without clothes by the river, about some danger I was in. All I did was tell her enough to stop her from worrying."

"Even so—I don't want her coming here and bothering you."

"Your daughter does not bother me."

"My wife and I— It's one thing we don't agree on, Hanna coming here."

"But what about Hanna? Doesn't it count what she wants?"

He was silent.

"Think of all I haven't told her—like what really happened to her great-uncle and Eva."

"Alexander died. That's all Hanna needs to know."

"She already knows more than that— And it's not from me. She heard in the bakery that he jumped from the attic window."

"And what did you say?"

"That she heard right."

Klaus groaned.

"Your daughter says you told her Eva died from tuberculosis."

"It's something a child can understand."

"That doesn't make it true. Still—it's in your family. Right now she believes Alexander killed himself because his wife died from tuberculosis. I haven't told her otherwise. Even though I don't like it. But if she asks me questions about myself, I'll tell her the truth."

The old women thought it was a good idea when the dentist hired Klara Brocker to look after his daughter and his apartment, since his wife was too absorbed with her painting and with hoarding her grief over her son's death as though no one else had ever lost a child.

But Trudi couldn't understand how Jutta could delegate her daughter to the care of this tidy woman with her plucked eyebrows and tight permanent. Once before, Klara Brocker had found a way to get something that had been intended for someone else, and her new role in Hanna's life was harder to bear for Trudi than the trade of Ingrid's jewelry box.

Hanna, who'd lived the first five years of her life with her mother painting right next to her, and the freedom to sneak out and wander about town, resented the new housekeeper. Not only was she watched constantly and dragged to church at least once a day for prayers, but she also lost her mother, who retreated to the third floor where she painted all day. Herr Tegern had designed a studio for her in the rooms where she'd lived as girl, and from the one huge window—in the falling pattern of her uncle—Jutta could see across town.

Rolf Brocker always arrived with his mother. A chubby boy with delicately shaped ears, he fought with Hanna over her toys and told her that his father had been killed in the war. Though she knew other children whose fathers had died as soldiers, they were older than Rolf and she. Now, when she went to the pay-library, she was usually with the housekeeper and her son. But Trudi knew how to distract Klara Brocker: she'd offer to watch the children and urge her to take her time finding the right books.

Even after her mother became far too ill to read, Klara Brocker continued to get books for the old woman. She'd come into the pay-library with the two children, shake her head, and say to Trudi, "I don't know why my mother would read this trash." But there'd be a greed in her eyes as she'd touch the romance novels which, aside from French cigarettes, Gauloises, were her one extravagance.

And Trudi would play along. "Your mother . . . she might like this," she'd recommend, wondering what Klara would pretend once her mother died. Perhaps she'd stay away from the pay-library for a month, say, or even half a year, but one day, Trudi knew, she'd come in and wordlessly check out several romances.

A few days after the children started first grade, Trudi heard rumors that Sybille Immers had tripped Hanna on the playground, and that Hanna had punched Sybille's arm. When both mothers were summoned by the principal, who wanted to assign each girl three rosaries as punishment, Jutta said she would encourage her daughter to defend herself any time she was attacked. While Trudi applauded her decision, the town only saw it as one other way the dentist's wife set herself apart.

Much of the time, Leo Montag was in pain, and the new doctor in town, Frau Doktor Korten, stopped by daily to give him an injection. For a few hours, then, it would cease—that heaviness which grew from a pulse in Leo's left knee and pumped throughout his frail body—but soon it would return, press its way from the same place as if the disk of steel had contaminated his flesh and transformed it all into steel.

A few months earlier, on the coldest day of winter, the stocky young doctor had arrived from Bremen and had bought the pianist's mansion—which had stood empty since the war—with plans to turn it into a women's clinic, though people told her it was too far from the center of town. She didn't mind treating men, too, it seemed, because she'd drive wherever she was called. When she warned Leo that his ribs showed and urged him to eat more, he told her how heavy he felt. To move this burdensome body of steel took more stamina than he had, and he stayed in his bedroom, where Trudi brought him meals that he seldom finished, and where he drifted between sleep and his books that were stacked along the wall next to his bed.

Sometimes, to take the worry from his daughter's eyes, he'd let her help him down the stairs and settle him on Emil's sofa while she sat and read to him; but he was far more comfortable in his room, surrounded by Gertrud's photos. Over the decades, they had faded so much that her features were unrecognizable to anyone but himself—at most images of a ghost woman, nuances of pearly gray—yet what he saw was her black, tangled hair, the feverish pink of her face.

The night the dike broke, Leo thought he heard Gertrud laugh outside his window. The Rhein had been frozen solid all winter, and when the ice thinned, the river spilled across the bank, covering the charred remains of a shepherd's fire between the rocks, and swelling across the meadows. As in other years, the townspeople had tried to reinforce the dike with sand-filled bags and shovelfuls of earth. Yet, their river broke through the barricades, yanking trees and bushes out by their roots as if they were weeds. It flowed into streets and houses, across beds and tables. From the taxidermist's shop the flood liberated the family's stuffed dachshund and a dusty squirrel.

As torrents of rain added to the floods, the water rose. Families carried their belonging to the upper floors. Some moved in with neighbors in apartments above them. Mass was held in the chapel on the hill. From his bedroom, Leo Montag could watch the boats in the streets. He thought this flood was turning Burgdorf into more of a community than it had been since the war: suddenly, people were all fighting the same enemy, their river, an enemy that was easily defined and outside themselves. For some, the flood even became something festive: they'd point to a sparrow, to a titmouse or pigeon; they'd marvel that the sea gulls had followed the Rhein into town.

After the river had retreated, Frau Weskopp reported a grave robbery. She was hysterical when she arrived at the police station on her bicycle, but when Andreas Beil checked her family grave, it turned out that the flood—as with other graves—had simply leveled the earth above the middle coffin, leaving a shallow depression.

That same day, Trudi cooked her father a surprise dinner for his sixty-seventh birthday: a roasted chicken she'd traded for library books, new potatoes and fresh peas, a strawberry cake and wine. While preparing the meal, she managed to stop fretting about him for a while because she imagined how much he would enjoy the food. After Frau Doktor Korten stopped by to give him his injection, Trudi led her father to the table, set with candles and her mother's best linen tablecloth, which she'd ironed until you couldn't detect a single crease. His eyes shimmered as he watched the candles, but he hardly ate. When Trudi helped him back upstairs, he felt so light she thought she could have carried him, and he fell asleep while she read to him from his birthday present, a book by Bertolt Brecht that he hadn't been able to replace so far.

He died the afternoon of the following day. She knew it before she raced up to his room, knew it by looking at the branches of the chestnut tree outside the window of the library and recalling what her father had told her about uprooting that tree from its earth by the flour mill and planting it here to keep her mother home. It hadn't worked for her mother, and now—when the tree had grown taller than their house, providing shade and, come autumn, glossy chestnuts that burst from their prickly shells—it hadn't worked for her father either. He too, had gotten away, leaving his body for her to find.

Frau Weiler and other neighbor women moved into her life, her house, making burial arrangements that seemed incredibly complicated to her though, in past years, she'd helped make them for other families. Dazed, she drifted from one room to another, refusing food when it was held out to her, staring past people who stood in her path and wanted to talk to her about her father's tenderness, his thoughtfulness.

Matthias Berger arrived on the train for the funeral, and Klaus Malter asked if he could drive Trudi to the cemetery, his voice hushed as if he were afraid to wake her father. More people came to Leo Montag's burial than to anyone else's in years. The widows of Burgdorf carried flowers to his grave as if they were grieving for their own husbands, and when Trudi looked beyond her own tears, she saw immeasurable sorrow as though her father really had left behind all those widows.

At the gravesite, Herr Stosick—heavy and bald—stood behind her as if prepared to brace her should she faint. All the men from the chess club were there, even though her father hadn't attended in a long time. Ingrid's daughter, her braids in even plaits down the front of her dress, stood next to her grandfather, whose shadow would forever lie across the ceiling of Ingrid's room. If only she could say to Karin, *"I knew your mother when she was a young girl. . . ."* If only she could impart to Karin all she had loved about Ingrid. She thought of her father, who had lived with such grace, and how fortunate she was to have her memories of him. How she wished Karin could remember her mother like that. She saw herself hiding in the church the day the Americans had arrived, saw Ingrid as she bent to lay her first daughter into her arms. *"I'll be there,"* she silently promised the girl, *"I'll be there when you're old enough to ask about your mother."*

Angelika Tegern brought a bouquet of white lilies to the gravesite, and Frau Weskopp carried two clay pots with violets, one for Leo Montag, the other for Helmut Eberhardt because the midwife—who was so meticulous when it came to her house—had neglected to take care of her husband's grave ever since her daughter had become ill with polio. Now Frau Weskopp and the other widows tended the grave—not out of loyalty to Helmut, but because they couldn't let the grave of a soldier look disorderly.

The midwife was convinced her husband's spirit was punishing her with Renate's illness because she'd named the child after his mother. To combat his fury, she would invoke the older Renate. It seemed most of her prayers were directed to her, rather than to Jesus or the saints. Whenever the midwife visited her daughter in St. Lukas Hospital, she'd bring her mother-in-law's shawl and wrap her daughter in the soft folds, trusting that, at least for then, both of them were safe.

Sometimes she thought her link to the older Renate was stronger than to her own children. Out of respect for her, the midwife still lived upstairs with her children while maintaining the downstairs for Renate. And she thought it only fitting that, each summer, the inedible pears on the tree reminded her and the whole town of the day her mother-in-law had been taken away.

Leo Montag's funeral feast was held at the house of Frau Blau, who, at ninety-two, had been widowed several years and looked withered in her wheelchair. Yet, her house smelled of fresh floor wax, and everyone knew she still dusted whatever she could reach from her wheelchair.

"Your father—" Frau Blau grabbed Trudi's wrist with unsettling strength when she arrived in the Malters' car, "your father was able to love his country despite his disillusion with it. . . ." Her wrinkled chin worked, and her lips moved forward as she swallowed. "You've lost the pride in your *Vaterland,* Trudi. Never forget that we are a nation that is respected in all of Europe. . . . We are known to be industrious, loyal, intelligent, clean and orderly—" She coughed, hard.

Trudi tried to loosen herself from the old woman's grasp. "Let me bring you a glass of water." Her scalp was hurting, each single hair, as if all of her nerves ended there.

"So many good qualities, Trudi. There are a lot of good people, a lot of important people in Germany—"

"I know that, but—"

"—builders and artists and composers who are famous throughout the world. . . . Great scientists and poets, Trudi . . . You need not be ashamed of being German."

"I am burdened by being German. We all are."

"Your father—"

"My father. . . . You know what he used to tell me, Frau Blau? That as long as our country has a need for violence to settle conflict, it can happen again."

"No, no, Trudi. This whole *Unglück*—misfortune—came to the *Vaterland* through one individual, and that's very regrettable. . . . Still, it has not spoiled the entire nation."

As soon as Trudi freed herself, her hands were taken by others, while voices above her told her how wonderful her father had been. She couldn't bear to look up into those faces that made her grief public. What she wanted was to be alone in her house with her sorrow and thoughts of her father. But Frau Weiler was confiding in her that she was thinking of selling her grocery store and moving into one of the new apartments around the corner from her grandchildren; and Fritz Hansen, fresh gauze already stained with pus, was bringing her his parents' condolences and yellow-white *Käsekuchen*—cheesecake—that no one would touch. Frau Tegern was inviting her to have dinner with her and her husband—"You set the day. Any time. Just let me know. . . ."—while Matthias was whispering to her about his stolen years—"I keep postponing my vows. . . ." And then Klaus Malter, his voice filled with anguish as though he'd forgotten years of reserve, was telling her that he worried his wife, considering their age gap, would outlive him by many years, and Trudi saw him lying in his marriage bed, alone.

As the guests began to leave, she suddenly no longer wanted to be by herself and asked Matthias to walk her next door. But when he sat down at the piano and played for her, his music was a gift that had arrived too late.

• • •

In the weeks after the funeral, Trudi kept finding gifts on her doorstep, left anonymously in the spirit of the unknown benefactor: butter-soft leather slippers exactly her size; the lace collar she'd looked at in a store months ago; a blue-and-white porcelain vase like the one she'd seen in Frau Tegern's solarium; and food—complete meals arranged on plates and covered with towels.

Without her father, the house felt huge, empty, and she spent as much time away from it as possible. She no longer had her hot meal at midday but ate black bread and cheese, and wandered through town while the pay-library was closed, doing what she knew best: collecting stories. Though new bits of gossip kept her busy, people could tell that she wasn't really engaged. She'd forget she was talking in the middle of a sentence, and she'd walk away without asking the right questions. Her cheeks did not look as full as usual, and sometimes it seemed she limped.

In the evenings, which were turning lighter now, she'd walk again, until tired. Her legs ached and her lower back would lock if she sat down, but gradually her body adjusted to the walks. Still, there was no getting away from the awareness of her father's death because the women who came to the pay-library for books wanted to talk about Leo, and she'd detect the longing for him in their voices. At times she thought she still heard him moving in the kitchen or living room while she waited on customers, and she'd half expect him to open a door and stand there, leaning on his cane, wearing those layers of clothes that couldn't keep him warm enough. The day-to-day being without him was worse than his actual death. What she missed most was the certainty of being able to share the small details of your life with someone who knew you so well. Who else could possibly care what you'd thought while looking out of the window or what you'd eaten for breakfast?

When she finally brought herself to sort out her father's belongings, she began by taking down the brittle photos of her dead mother. She opened the wardrobe to take out his suits and saw herself as a small girl standing inside there, her mother's silk against her cheeks, feeling so sure her mother would return—only then she had been young enough to believe it could be possible.

As she packed her father's clothes for the poor of the church, she came across one of her mother's hatboxes with a red felt hat long out of fashion. Perhaps she could give it to Monika Buttgereit, who'd fix it into something stylish. Though Sabine Buttgereit had been dead nearly six years, the music teacher and Alfred Meier continued the kind of courtship you read about in fairy tales, the kind of courtship the priest used as an example when he counseled young couples who were eager to get engaged. Although the two went out every Saturday evening, Herr Meier wouldn't even enter Monika's apartment when he'd call for her, carrying a bouquet of flowers. She'd always be ready when he'd arrive, and he wouldn't have to wait for more than a heart-beat or two before she'd step out, shake his hand, admire the flowers, and disappear briefly to set them into a vase that she'd already filled with water. It was the same when he brought her back: he'd accompany her to the door, shake her hand, and then walk back to his car, somewhat stiff, as if—so the old women would suspect—his passion had been outweighed by the habit of romantic courtship.

When the pastor's sister sent two altar boys to the pay-library, they loaded the boxes with Leo Montag's belongings onto a wooden cart and pulled them to the rectory. All Trudi held on to were her father's books, his carved chess set, and his gray cardigan, which she kept hanging from his chair, the way he used to. At times, when she'd pass it, she'd give it a reassuring squeeze.

Late one evening, after she'd walked for hours, someone knocked on her door. It was Jutta Malter, wearing the softest angora sweater, carrying a jar of last summer's raspberries. She insisted on pouring the berries in a bowl for Trudi—with milk and a sprinkling of sugar—and she sat and watched, quietly, while Trudi ate. These berries filled something inside Trudi, nurtured her far more than the solid meals others had brought her, and though her old fear of getting ill from sugar rose briefly within her, it ceased as soon as Jutta laid one arm around her shoulders. "Hanna has missed you," she said.

That night Trudi kept waking from the same urgent dream of being at the flour mill with her father and Georg. Each time she yielded to sleep, the dream—it warned her about something she was supposed to remember, of that she was sure even while dreaming—snagged her again, and the last time it woke her, around five, she got up and stood by her window. But she couldn't separate her memories of the mill from the dream images; the harder she tried, the more elusive the dream became until, by the end of the day when she locked the pay-library, she was only left with the sense of urgency and danger she'd felt in her dream.

Instead of cooking her evening meal, she climbed on her bicycle and rode out to the mill, which had never been rebuilt. When she reached the woods that ringed the gutted building, mist rose from the swamps, and it was so quiet she thought she heard the sky breathing. Then, with a start, she realized it was her own breath.

Though the arches were shattered, she could still see the elegant sweep of the bricks as she had in her dream. Here, she and Georg Weiler had played tag, their voices spiraling above the red tile roof and the forest. She felt it again, the foreboding that had been with her that day more than three decades ago—except that now she stood surrounded by that very destruction: trees thrust their blighted crowns toward the torn roof; crumbling stairs ascended into empti-ness; a blackened beam, half burned and thinned out in places, spanned the gap between the chimney and the nearest wall. But she couldn't smell fire, only the sweet dampness of decaying wood.

A dried thistle hindered the growth of a clump of camomile, and as she pulled it out, she saw Georg and herself, laughing, gathering bou-quets of purple thistles, which they'd taken home to make thistle soup with sand and water from their brook. And her father—she saw her father's face as it had been that day and knew he'd been young like this in her dream—her father had taken a spoon and, with obvious delight, had dipped it into their soup.

And now her father was dead.

It hit her so strongly, that she crouched right where she was and brought her arms around her middle. The scent of camomile en-veloped her, and as she looked down, the tiny flowers were right in front of her, their yellow centers ringed by white petals. The closer she looked, the more she saw, and the more she forgot herself and her pain and became part of something she couldn't define as if, by get-ting closer to a smaller world, she had found a larger world. How many times had she longed for a world where she could travel free or almost free, a world where she knew she belonged? How often had she imagined living on the island of the little people? Yet, all she needed was here, already here. Pia had been right—this was where she belonged. Despite the silence of war. Because of the silence. Working with Emil Hesping and the fugitives had taught her what it was like to belong, that you could initiate it, build it, be it.

She stood up and walked over to a tree stump by the chimney. Sitting down, she leaned her back against the bricks and crumbling mortar. Her left knee felt stiff, and as she pulled her foot close and rubbed her leg, gently, from her ankle to her knee until it felt supple, she could no longer imagine herself with any kind of different body. A new body would take years to get used to. No more hanging from door frames, she promised herself, forgiving her younger self for the way she'd mistreated her body. Shards glinted among moss and weeds that sprouted from the rubble—beauty pressing through debris. Yet, the feeling of death persisted all around her, and suddenly she knew it came from her dream. *Georg*, she thought, *Georg*, and felt the danger once more, saw her father's face, young and solemn, and understood she had dreamed Georg's death. And as she strained to see further—it would come from his own hands, his death, and his wife would do nothing to stop him—he was standing there before her, *a boy who looks like a girl like a girl like a girl*, in his dainty blue smock that covered his knees, blond ringlets down to his shoulders. *"Look."* He held out a black and orange butterfly to her. *"I bet you this one can still fly. I didn't rub any dust from the wings. Look."* He tossed the butterfly into the air, watched it disappear. His face was tilted up as it used to be when he'd waited outside her window for her to come out and play, and he looked the way he had before he'd become like other boys, before that day in the barn, before he'd fought in the war, before the drinking, before the beating of his wife and children, before absolution had become a sham—while she stood there inside her body of thirty-six years, severed from him by time, reunited to him by time.

"Tell me." He caught her hand in his and pulled her up so that she stood taller than he.

"Tell you what?"

"What will happen to me."

As the sand-colored eyes probed hers, she felt herself reeling into her childhood, when she had believed everyone knew what was inside the hearts of others: she saw herself with Georg in the church tower, felt the snapping of the scissors as she cut through his curls, smelled the flowers in Frau Eberhardt's garden, heard the music drifting from Fräulein Birnsteig's mansion and the wailing of babies and boot falls; but then the music changed, and it was Matthias, playing the piano at his recital, and the boots were there, along with the dread she'd felt at the first concert.

"Tell me."

"You were my first friend—" Her voice clogged as her old love for Georg swelled within her. She took that love as solidly as if she'd touched it with both hands, extended it toward the boy. If only she could pass on to him her own tempered suffering. If only she could offer up her old wish for revenge in return for his release. What she longed for was to span those years between the boy and the man he had become, span them with the story of a friendship that had endured after she and Georg had started school, a wise and somber story with the truth to heal the wounds it uncovered. She heard the voice of her town—*"It's not good to dwell on the things that were terrible. . . ." "Nobody wants to relive those years. . . ." "We have to go forward. . . ."* More than ever, she understood the people's need to protect one another with silence. How tempting it would be to give Georg *eine heile Welt*—an intact world—and leave out anything that might hurt him. But if she did, she would perpetuate the silence that she'd fought all along.

Still—she could begin with their friendship. And what was true was that she used to have a friend named Georg, that they'd played in her mother's earth nest and walked in the All Saints' Day procession, smoked stolen chocolate cigarettes and floated boats made from leaves and birch bark, built a snowman with a carrot nose and chased sparrows and pigeons across the fields, knelt in church together and—

It was too much for her to bear, the knowledge of his death.

"Tell me."

For an instant—as sudden as it vanished—the man's bloated drinking face flickered across the boy's fine features. *No.* This was Georg, her generous friend Georg, who knew how to lure the sun from the sky and snare it inside his red-and-yellow glass marble; Georg who always invented new bets with her—how many widows or pigeons they'd count on their walk, how many baby carriages would pass by the grocery store in one hour. . . . *Luck.* For Georg, luck and miracles had been the same. He'd believed he could create his own miracle—shape a bird from earth and water, yield it to the sky.

"You were my first friend. . . ." She felt stunned by the fear of losing him, the grief of losing him. And yet, there was something exquisite in forgoing her revenge. It was not the first time that she'd turned to her storytelling to banish fear, and as Georg drew the words from her, moments of their lives came together in one swirl of a never-ending story that moved back and forth through layers of time—a story filled with magic and truth, corruption and redemption, sadness and joy, love and betrayal—connecting her to Georg as she braided in her own loves and losses, and told him about Konrad and his mother hiding in the tunnel, the unknown benefactor leaving *Lederhosen* for Georg, Klaus Malter drilling on her tooth, Ingrid taking her daughters to the bridge, Frau Doktor Rosen reading books about *Zwerge*, Max Rudnick sketching his Russian grandmother, Frau Abramowitz tearing the Hitler-Jugend office apart. . . .

It was a story that would continue beyond herself, beyond Georg. In sorting it out, she felt deep compassion for him and everyone who inhabited her story. And as what had happened began to merge with what could have happened, the texture of her story became richer, more colorful. She had Max return to Burgdorf on a barge that belonged to Georg's father, who, all along, had been traveling the river that had taken him away. She let Georg measure Seehund's head and run with him to the *Rathaus*, where a group of townspeople raised axes to the Hitler statue and chopped it into fragments. In the Braunmeiers' barn, Eva showed Georg how to hide without sneezing, while the butcher and pharmacist searched for them in vain. Opening his window wide, Eva's father wrapped himself into the coat of the Russian soldier and lay down on his bed, welcoming rain and cold and cats and other dangers. Trudi's mother stepped from the gates of the Grafenberg asylum with Sister Adelheid, their eyes clear and calm, carrying their own altar between them. To welcome their daughter, Ruth, back, Herr and Frau Abramowitz held a huge celebration at their house. . . . And throughout all, Trudi wove the assurance for Georg and herself that—once someone had been in your life—you could keep that person there despite the agony of loss, as long as you had faith that you could bring the sum of all your hours together in one shining moment.

Georg picked up a bird's nest from the ground, turned it in his fingers. This was when she'd loved him most—with the long hair and girl-clothes—before he'd changed, before she'd helped him change by cutting his hair. And yet, how could she not do it for him again if he asked? She felt the old joy of being near him, and it seemed possible that his luck would save him from the death that was waiting for him. Yet, already she knew that wasn't so. She heard their young voices in the church tower when Georg had told her he wanted to die the same age as Jesus.

"*Thirty-three is very old.*"

"*Maybe we can die together.*"

Aloud, she said: "But we're both already older than thirty-three."

The boy nodded. Though he stood absolutely still as she spoke, wind shifted his curls, his smock. She knew that the words already belonged to him though they might still change, and that the story might lead both of them to the ending she feared. And yet, just because a story was a certain way didn't mean it would always be like that: stories took their old shape with them and fused it with the new shape. She didn't understand yet how all the tangles of their lives would sort themselves out in her story, but she supposed that it would be like raking: not every bit of earth would be untangled at once. Her father had raked the earth behind the pay-library every week, and what she'd learned from him was that raking had to do with patience. But the ground of the mill's hollow rooms was rough, uneven with cracked bricks and last year's stiff weeds, gnarled roots of fallen trees, and the silver skeletons of tiny birds. . . .

She saw herself lifting her father's bamboo rake from the rack beneath the back of the pay-library, and as she pulled the bamboo teeth through the earth, she kept stepping back, drawing the rake toward herself, knowing that, gradually, all of the soil would show the smooth ribbed pattern. But until then—as in her story for Georg— there were clumps left over, and she had to pull the rake though them again and again, distributing the earth while discarding debris. It was as though every story she had ever told had brought her to this moment, to this story that would tell itself through her: it would be the best story she'd ever told, better even than the story she and Pia had woven between them that day at the circus. And as she thought of all the people who had loved her stories—her father, Hanna, Max, Eva,

Konrad, Robert, and earliest of all her mother—she felt the strength of their arms as surely as if they were pulling the rake with her through the earth. The final design wouldn't happen all at once: there would be the rearrangement of it all, a fine combing through; there would be perseverance and a reverence for the task; there would be assurance that, indeed, a design would emerge.

Georg's eyes were grave as he waited for her to continue her story. It was the brief span of evening when all things are etched lucidly into the sky, just before they yield their separateness and blur into the night. Trudi stretched herself. What she could offer Georg was far more than what had happened—a certain sequence that would lead him to the core of the story, a story that would hold an entire world. It had to do with what to tell first—though it hadn't happened first— and what to end the story with. It had to do with what to enhance and what to relinquish. And what to embrace.

———————————————— ■ ————————————————

Ursula Hegi lived the first eighteen years of her life in Germany. In addition to *Floating in My Mother's Palm,* she is the author of *Intrusions* and *Unearned Pleasures and Other Stories.* Her new novel, *Salt Dancers,* is coming out in July 1995. She is currently working on a play and on a book of interviews with German-born Americans.

Ursula Hegi is the recipient of about thirty grants and awards, including an NEA Fellowship in 1990 and five awards from the PEN Syndicated Fiction Awards. She has served on the board of the National Book Critics Circle, and she has written over a hundred reviews for *The New York Times,* the *Los Angeles Times,* and *The Washington Post.*

An associate professor of creative writing at Eastern Washington University, Ursula Hegi lives near Spokane, Washington, with her partner, Gordon.